TROUBLE

DEVON MCCORMACK

Trigger Warning: While Trouble is a steamy romance novel, character backstories include domestic violence against a minor (depicted in conversations and brief flashbacks that allude to violence, but do not describe it in graphic detail), emotional abuse, and the loss of a loved one to suicide.

****

1

JAMES

"Oh, come the fuck on," I muttered as rain slammed against my windshield.

First day. New school.

Those two things were frustrating enough in and of themselves without the added stress of inclement weather. Considering it'd been thunderstorming the night before, I should've checked the weather app on my phone before heading out, but in my rush to arrive early to get settled in and ready for classes, I'd clearly made a terrible mistake.

I'd waited for nearly ten minutes in my spot in the faculty lot before it had started to let up about as much as I assumed it would, so I fetched my laptop case and papers from the passenger seat.

The extension of the faculty lot I'd parked in was closer to the student lot, a bit of a hike from the building. Over the past few years, the school had enjoyed a major growth spurt as parents migrated to Whispersaw County to enjoy the luxury of lower taxes and reasonable real-estate prices, which meant the lot originally intended for teachers was reserved for staff with some seniority.

With my paperwork beneath my laptop case, I should have been able to make it inside relatively unscathed, but the rain began coming down harder, as if fate was eager to show me she had other plans.

Be nice to have an umbrella right about now.

There was likely one in an unpacked box—one of the many stacked up in my new living room. I needed to get it out and put it in the car when I had a chance. But it was too late for regrets, and I'd already had too many of those over the course of the summer. As Mother Nature pummeled my back with water like I was on a theme-park ride, I glanced down to see how much was collecting on the front of my shirt.

Wasn't too bad. I'd be fine once I had time to dry off.

But as soon as I looked back up, I realized my folly as my foot wedged into something—perhaps a hole in the asphalt—and I went tumbling forward. Given that I was only five foot eight, I was anticipating a short fall, but in my effort to brace myself with my elbow, the experience shifted into a roll, and then another, before a rush of water covered my back.

"Shit." The universe couldn't have conspired against me more perfectly if it'd tried.

Fuck. My. Life.

I started to my feet, noticing my paperwork floating in disarray atop the puddle I lay in. Fortunately, I still had my laptop case in my hand, above water. At least that was something. My clothes were soaked, though, something I'd have to navigate once I got myself out of this mess.

I rolled out of the puddle, crawling on my knees as I collected the papers I'd lost in my fall. As I reached for one, a hand slipped into view, grabbing it for me.

A man in a black poncho, across the puddle from me, picked up a few more. My fucking guardian angel, it seemed.

I gathered the papers with him until we managed to get them all.

"Thank you so much," I said as I took the papers from him.

"You can thank me in a minute. Let's get out of this." He put his hand on my back, and we headed the opposite direction I'd been moving in. He led me to an entrance I hadn't even been aware of, and I felt a visceral relief. The sound of the rain dulled as the door sealed shut behind us.

He pulled back the hood of his poncho. Clearly, he'd been far more prepared for this rainstorm.

His gaze pulled mine into a set of wide, bright blue eyes, the sort that seemed to peer right into my soul. With a pronounced jawline and cheekbones, he had the kind of face I would have expected to see on a men's magazine, not teaching in a town like Wyachet. Even his dark, nearly black locks of hair had me wondering if it was intention- ally styled to look somewhat messy or if he was just that goddamn pretty.

Those bright eyes studied me for a moment, like he

was trying to figure something out about me. "You must be new," he said, his words passing through full, pouty lips. He had this effortless confidence about him, which was amplified by how totally out of my element I felt.

"James," I said quickly. "I'm a new teacher—"

"Yeah, we can do the introductions in a minute. We need to take care of this first." He pointed to my shirt, which was now see-through, my nipples on full display.

"Fuck. Unless you've got a blow-dryer, I think I'm screwed."

"Come on, Big Man," he said, which I found funny, since he was clearly six foot something.

"Thank you again for your help back there," I told him as he led me down the hall.

"No problem. Anyone would have done it."

"I think people would have been more likely to point and laugh than actually get down and help me, but I appreciate it all the same."

We reached a set of restrooms, and he guided me into the women's.

"Um…"

"Trust me on this. We're both too early to be running into anyone. I promise."

I followed his lead inside as he flicked on the light, making himself at home.

"Here, give me that shirt." He waved for me like I was taking up too much of his time.

I set my laptop bag with the soaked papers on a nearby counter and stripped out of the shirt.

He mashed the button down on the side of the hand

dryer.

I was skeptical about his approach, but he seemed confident enough that I just handed him the shirt without further questions. He maneuvered it carefully, the dryer going on far longer than I figured it should have, to the point where I realized it must've been broken. And he must've known that.

The wait was awkward as I glanced around the women's restroom with my new friend, who was very diligent about his work.

He said something I couldn't hear over the sound of the dryer before he mashed the button down again, stopping the sound.

"Did you say something?" I asked him.

His gaze caught mine again, and I felt like I had to plant my feet in place to keep from getting blown back by those eyes.

"No need to have anyone calling you Mr. Nipples on your first day." As he smiled, I laughed with him.

It was true. I didn't need anything else against me right then.

"Just be thankful the school isn't up on maintenance," he went on as I took my shirt from him.

"Fuck, it has fewer wrinkles than when I left the house."

"Gonna have to watch that dirty mouth of yours when the kids get here," he warned.

"Oh fuck. Yeah. I mean, you're right."

I was making a fool of myself. But for some reason, maybe because he was one of the first people I'd met at the school and he seemed so goddamn cool, I was really working to make a good impression.

He glanced me over once more. "How about your pants? Those good?"

"I think I can manage. These are certainly less offensive than kids seeing my areolas all day long."

"Eh, they're nice areolas," he joked with a wink. "Just lucky that wasn't a very heavy shirt. Otherwise, we could have been here for a while. Trust me. I've had to do this plenty of times before for the same reason."

"Hopefully my pants will dry once I've walked around for a bit. You know, while I'm making other lesson arrangements for my classes than these soiled worksheets."

"I'm sure you'll figure out something."

"I'm sorry. I'm being rude. I still didn't catch your name."

"Kyle."

"James." I extended my hand, and he took it. Between his firm handshake and the smile he offered, I really was glad the incident happened. I'd made a new friend, something I would be sorely lacking until I managed to push myself out of my shell and meet new people.

He glanced around the restroom for a moment, his expression turning tense, before saying, "I should go. I have to help my friend Ben over in the media center."

Just like that, my excitement about having made a new friend dissolved. "Of course." I reminded myself I'd likely see him in passing, when I could discover more about my morning hero.

"See you around," he said with a nod, and was on his way.

I finished buttoning and tucking in my shirt.

My nervousness intensified, and I rechecked my shirt in my camera to ensure my nipples weren't as visible as they had been after my fall. I had some dirt on it, but I doubted it would be all that noticeable. And Mr. Dirt sounded much better than Mr. Nipples.

I headed to the teachers' lounge, made fresh copies of the worksheets I'd destroyed outside, then went about my business. My bad luck seemed to be confined to that morning, since as far as first days went, it wasn't so bad.

I'd expected to bump into my rescuer again, but the longer I went without seeing him, the shittier I felt about all the questions left unasked—who he was, what he taught, or if he was an administrator or counselor. So many assumptions I'd made, simply because I'd been too disoriented after my blunder. But I'd get those answers once I saw him again and had a chance to properly thank him for helping me out.

By fourth period, I was feeling more in my element again, offering the class my spiel as we went over the syllabus. They seemed about as entertained as they could have been for their British Lit class, but I was confident that once we got into the books, I'd have a solid chance to win them over. I always managed to do that, if only because I treated them like people, not inferiors, the way teachers always seemed to treat me in high school.

I was seated on the edge of my desk, cracking another of my little jokes, finally earning a few chuckles from the tough crowd, when the door opened. A late arrival, not unusual on the first day, but then I saw who it was.

Kyle.

I stood up quickly, my instinct being that he'd come with important news, but as I noticed his clothes, no longer cloaked behind the poncho—dark-wash jeans, white crew-neck tee, and a leather jacket matching his black Converse with black laces—I realized I'd been mistaken.

And *fuuuck.*

His gaze met mine, and that familiar warm smile he'd offered that morning returned. "Sorry I'm late." He winked as he breezed past me.

Late.

I froze in place, hardly able to process what was happening around me.

A student. Of course he was a fucking student.

How had I misread that so completely? But given his temperament outside and his goodwill, it hadn't even crossed my mind. And now that he sat down at a desk, I looked around—almost to check my sanity—and among the other kids he did look much older.

I was certain my face was blushing so much, it had to be at least the color of my shirt. Fortunately, he didn't look at me, just folded his arms.

No book, no folders, the sort of guy I figured could easily be a problem student.

As his eyes met mine once again, I swallowed, feeling much more intimidated than before he'd entered the room.

2

KYLE

I'd been sitting in my car, listening to the rain complementing my playlist as specks of water rattled against my windshield, mentally prepping myself for my final shitty year at Wyachet High. I was supposed to meet Ben to help the journalism teacher move some equipment, but he was running late. Typical Ben.

The pink shirt was impossible to miss as a man passed by my car, heading toward the building from the faculty lot. I'd thought I'd been ridiculous for grabbing Uncle Tex's big-ass poncho from the closet when I couldn't find the umbrella. But seeing this guy getting drenched assured me I'd made the right decision.

When I'd seen the stranger take that dive in the lot, I hadn't wasted a moment. He'd fallen out of view so fast, I was worried he might have been hurt. I was relieved when I'd arrived to discover he was fine, just soaked.

I'd expected him to be appreciative of my help, but it wasn't until we got into the restroom that I realized...holy shit, this guy thought I was a fucking *teach*. Could've just punched me in the nuts if he'd wanted to piss me off.

I'd assumed he must've known some kid in jeans and Converse couldn't have been a teacher, but then I remembered Tex's goddamn poncho cloaked all the obvious indicators. And he wouldn't have been the first to think I was in my twenties.

I should have corrected him. It would have taken a second, but something about the fact that he must've already felt like a fool enough as it was, made me think the best thing to do was to get the hell out of there. Odds were I'd only ever see him in passing in the halls. He'd feel a little silly for the error but move on.

But as I found an available seat, third row back, near the window, I kept wishing he would have given me his last name so I would have noticed it on my schedule and been ready for this BS situation.

I wondered if he thought I was trying to dupe him earlier. Surely, he knew that a total asshole wouldn't have bothered to help him out. But then again, when did anyone in this town ever give me the benefit of the doubt?

"Kyle, right?" he asked.

"Yeah."

"You guys are lucky," he said, addressing the class. "I had a tumble into a puddle this morning and learned just how see-through this shirt was. Was close to you guys calling me Mr. Nipples throughout the rest of the semester."

The class laughed, and we caught each other's gazes.

He wore a friendly smile.

I was shocked.

Any other teacher might have been too proud to mention it, but not James—Mr. Warner, according to the schedule. That he'd acknowledged it made it easy for me to breathe a sigh of relief, even though nothing made me cringe more than being made the center of attention during class.

He delivered a syllabus to me before moving right along with his introduction, surely having won the class over with his Mr. Nipples remark. Although, as he went on, I learned right away that he was all about a cheesy joke as he made comments about plans and projects for the semester. He was doing his best to win us over, and I would have been lying if I'd said it wasn't working on me just as easily as it had in the restroom, with his adorable dimples and those beautiful brown eyes behind a pair of glasses.

He looked like a real fucking nerd.

In the best sort of ways.

And that same charm he'd shown me earlier seemed to be working on the other kids too.

After that comment, he only looked my way occasionally, as we both seemed to silently acknowledge our initial exchange.

When the bell rang, I intentionally lingered behind so that, if he wanted a moment to discuss our encounter, we would have a little privacy.

"So," he said as I passed his desk, fully prepared to keep on walking if he hadn't said anything.

"Yes, *James*?" I teased with a wink, hoping he would take it in the playful spirit I'd intended.

"Apparently, I was making a bigger idiot of myself earlier than just falling into a puddle."

"It looked a little more like rolling into it."

His cheeks turned pink, and he lowered his head, looking up through his glasses, his beautiful brown eyes set on me. His dirty-blond hair was styled in a fresh crew cut, the slightest of cowlicks poking out at the crown of his head. The bangs were a little longer than the rest of the cut and somewhat disheveled—I couldn't tell if it was from his tumble earlier or from how he'd run his hand through his hair occasionally, a nervous tic I'd noticed while he was going over the syllabus. A thin layer of scruff accented his jawline, clearly as well cared for as the body I'd seen on him earlier. A man didn't have a bod like that without spending some hardcore time at the gym.

I couldn't help admiring the way he filled out the shirt he wore, certain several of the other students had appreciated this whole beefy nerd look he had going on. Like a dirty-blond Clark Kent. *Mmm...*

No, I didn't have an issue admiring a sexy man. Or fucking one for that matter.

"It's all good. Shit happens," I said. "I was meeting up with my boy Ben—"

"Another student, I'm guessing?"

I laughed. "Yeah, that's right. He was supposed to be helping a teacher, so I showed up to give them a hand. But looks like it worked out. Maybe the universe sent me to save the day."

"Still, I should have been a little more mindful and considered that."

"Don't worry. You aren't the first person to mistake me for a teacher. Miss Kritch did the same thing last year at a town hall event, and it was a little more...inappropriate, if you get what I mean."

He laughed, but then made a face like he knew he probably shouldn't have.

"Well, since we are now teacher and student, do you mind if I ask why you were tardy to class?"

"Oh, yeah. I was taking a cigarette break."

"What?" His entire demeanor transformed in an instant.

"Man, that was a joke. I just sort of spaced at lunch, and then I wound up being a little late. And now I'm here."

He appeared viscerally relieved.

"Sorry. Not everyone can read my sense of humor. Gets me into trouble sometimes. And you can see why."

"I really can," he said with an uneasy chuckle. "I saw a Kyle on the roll, but honestly, I was so busy that the most I thought was, *Hey, like that guy who helped me earlier.*" He shook his head, like he thought he'd been an idiot for not even considering the possibility. "Anyway, thank you again for your help, and it's nice officially meeting you, Kyle."

Despite seeming like a relatively laid-back guy, he had a nervous tension about him. I tried to decide if it was from his hectic morning, the misunderstanding, being new to the school...or something else. Of course, it was a lot to figure out for a guy I barely knew.

"Nervous for your first day?" I pried.

"Nervous? Who, me? Yeah, a little bit," he said, but I knew such an admission could only come from someone who was confident enough to cop to their insecurities. I sure as fuck didn't know many teachers like that, and I was intrigued.

"I'll get it together, though," he went on. "Worst-case scenario, I know where to find the hand dryer in the downstairs bathroom, right?"

We shared a smile, and I caught myself staring at that pretty face, admiring him until he glanced around like it was becoming awkward. Hell, it probably *was* getting awkward.

But at least I knew that, even though I wasn't particularly excited about British Lit, I would have something pretty to look at throughout fourth period.

He glanced at the clock behind him. "I don't want to make you late to fifth period." He turned back to me, avoiding my gaze. "I'll see you tomorrow, Kyle."

"See you then, Big Man."

He must've known I was teasing him about being so much shorter than me, but once again, he didn't appear bothered by the remark, only offered a pleasant smile like a cool guy, not some stuck-up asshole teach.

I headed out of Mr. Warner's classroom, smirking like an idiot.

Maybe my senior year wouldn't be so shitty after all.

3

JAMES

I mashed my thumb on the touchscreen before tucking my tumbler under the dispenser. The soft *hum* of coffee grinding in the cappuccino machine was music to my ears. I'd finished my last cup at the beginning of fourth period, and my energy was already waning.

"Better make it a double."

I glanced behind me to see Kendra, another English teacher at the school, holding her own mug, waiting patiently for her own caffeine boost. Kendra and I shared a free period, which had helped us become fast friends over the course of the first week. We finished making our coffees before finding seats in the teachers' lounge to chat with other faculty members who had some time to relax at nearby tables.

"Figured out which is your nightmare class yet?" she

asked, something that was easy enough to spot in the first few days, let alone the beginning of the second week.

"Thankfully, I've got some good kids this year. I'm surprised since I was thinking it would be trial by fire my first year at a new school, but everyone seems to be going easy on me."

"Don't worry too much," Kendra said with a wink. "Maybe they just need to warm up to you before they really start driving you over the edge."

She went on to tell me about her problem class, which I guessed was why she'd brought the subject up to begin with. But truly, I was grateful my classes had turned out to be as easy as they were. No real troublemakers, not even Kyle Forsythe, whom I'd had concerns about after our exchange. Even he'd turned in his assignments on time.

Had I not always been so concerned about the other shoe dropping, I would have allowed myself to relax and see how everything unfolded, but considering how turbulent the year before had been, I knew better than to let my guard down.

After dumping about her class, Kendra and I shifted to school and town politics and gossip, the sort of debriefing I desperately needed since I was out of the loop on all things Wyachet related.

Being in a new town was intimidating as fuck, but when it became overwhelming, I assured myself I had time to figure it all out. One day at a time, I kept reminding myself, as I had so many times before.

After the school day came to an end, I headed home.

Sheila had attempted to call during school hours, when she knew I was working, so I wasn't in any hurry to call her back. Instead, I tried to push my awareness of her to the back of my mind as I made my way through downtown Wyachet. That old life was behind me now. This was my future.

New town, new life, new me.

There was something liberating about pulling into my neighborhood. Mine. Just mine.

Wyachet had plenty of bigger neighborhoods with hundreds of homes, but I'd found a nice quiet one with just over fifty homes. It had been carved into a thick wood, offering me a little escape from what others considered a suburban paradise. As I rounded the corner, heading down the hill to my place, the last house on the left, I didn't see that familiar Audi Q8 until I passed my neighbors' overgrown Leyland cypresses.

As much as I'd been looking forward to enjoying my afternoon, in an instant, the other shoe had dropped.

What the fuck is she doing here?

The blood drained from my face, my throat dried, my hands got clammy.

I hadn't seen her in over a month, the longest we'd been apart since we married. I sighed the sort of sigh I'd let out a thousand times throughout the past five years, already feeling drained before even having an exchange with her. Memories came unbidden, despite my attempts to chase them away.

As I pulled up in the open space beside the Audi, I

turned to the driver, an AirPod visible in her ear as she chatted away with whomever she was apparently mid-conversation with. She turned to me, forcing a smile.

That face was so familiar, one I'd turned to time and time again as a confidante, a voice of reason during tough times. It evoked memories of all those moments when she was there for me, but mostly, of the knives in my back... and my heart.

Muffled, indiscernible words had me questioning who she was talking to...whoever her new man was, I was certain. Sheila wouldn't have needed more than a few days to move on from me, obviously, since she hadn't needed so much as hours away from me to find others she could pass the time with.

Maybe it was the last one I knew of: Brent. I grew to hate that name more and more with every day that passed since I found out the truth.

I snagged my laptop bag and threw the strap over my shoulder before slipping out of the driver's seat.

"He's here, so I've got to go," I heard her say from inside her SUV.

I wondered if she'd said it loudly enough to make sure I'd hear her.

But for being the one to confront me at my home when she knew I'd be off work, she sure as hell didn't seem to be in any hurry as I stood in front of the SUV, waiting for her to tell me what she was doing here. Still, she found a way of continuing her conversation, so I started toward the house, when I heard her crack the door, giving me pause.

She said goodbye once again to the person on the other end before approaching me, AirPods in both ears. My gaze shifted between them, annoyed as fuck, since I remembered a thousand times when she had similarly insulted me by being half-present throughout the course of our relationship. Just my look was enough to have her rolling her eyes before she pulled them out.

When it came to things like that, we had our familiar nonverbal exchanges that felt almost psychic because of how well we knew each other. Of course, that psychic impulse would have helped a lot more if it had been screaming, *Your wife is having another goddamn affair, dumbass!*

"Sheila, what are you doing here?" I asked in an even more exasperated tone than I'd intended.

"Well, if you keep ignoring my calls—"

"You called twice while I was at work. And it's not like my hours are that hard to figure out."

"I know you well enough to know when you're ignoring me."

It was my damned right to ignore her. "What do you want to talk about?"

"Nothing in the middle of your driveway." She looked over my home before scanning the neighborhood. "I can't believe you moved all the way to Whispersaw County. Sales tax is great, but you're not even on the good side."

Oh, she sure knew how to work me up. My cheeks burned with hot fury. "I'm not in the mood for this. Anything we need to talk about, we can discuss through email, but you don't get to show up out of the blue whenever you want to have a conversation about something."

"This is absurd. I have something important to talk to you about. It won't take long. What, you want me to go all the way home now and then shoot you an email over something that will take ten minutes?"

It was hard to fight her, always had been. There was no doubt in my mind that was why I'd had to pry myself free of her grasp.

"Whatever," I said, ashamed of myself for giving in, as I always seemed to throughout our relationship.

We headed inside, and nearly as soon as she stepped into the foyer, she remarked, "I see unpacking isn't a priority." I noticed her eyeing my neglected stack in the corner of the adjoining den—the stack I probably still needed to dig through to find my umbrella. Although, not having it with me hadn't turned out so bad at all, so I guessed it was why I wasn't in any hurry to find it.

"If this is how you're going to be, you can just leave."

"Oh, where is that fun-loving, unshakable man I met?"
You killed him.

I didn't respond to her comment, since it was evident she was trying to pick at me.

I led her into the kitchen, and she assessed the view of my backyard through the French doors on the back wall. "That's a beautiful sight. Hard to find woods like these with all the construction going on around here." I almost appreciated the compliment, until she added, "But you know all these leaves will die in the fall, and you'll have to rake them."

"I'm perfectly capable of raking a yard, or hiring someone to do it for me. What did you come over here for?"

She made herself comfortable at the dining table as I headed to the cabinet and fixed myself a drink when she said, "It's about filing."

I froze, a bottle of Maker's tilted in my hand over the glass I was tempted to fill to the brim. "You told me you filed. You stalled before begging me to let you file, and then you told me you did last week."

"Yes...I filled out the papers."

"That's not the same thing as filing them, is it? Sheila — You know what? I'm not having this fight with you. There's no fight. You didn't. So I'll do it."

"Please, James. The university insurance is a joke. Just the thought of navigating special enrollment triggers my anxiety. And I checked the COBRA site. I'd be paying six times what we pay through your work. You know money is tight for me while I'm finishing my thesis."

That damn thesis. If it wasn't her master's thesis, it was her doctorate. Her dreams had been my life for five years. As for money being tight, we had very different definitions of what that meant, considering she had a trust fund and client base to keep her in nice cars and designer clothes, but somehow couldn't cover the cost of high health insurance premiums.

I dragged out a sigh as I poured my whiskey. Then I took a much-needed sip.

She was quiet, clearly giving me a moment to digest

the news. As I turned to her, I could see her judging my afternoon cocktail.

Christ, I couldn't have anything. "Oh, I'm sorry. Is this going to be inconvenient for you? The way those messages on your phone were inconvenient for me?" I said the words through my teeth. Fuck. I hadn't meant to let that out, but the rage I felt…I couldn't help myself.

"There's something to be said about you not respecting my boundaries." She had this virtuous expression on her face, as though there wasn't a doubt in her mind that she was in the right about this.

"I'm not getting into this with you."

"After five years, you didn't think we could have a conversation—"

"You were doing stuff with this guy for a year."

"I'm just saying, I talked to my lawyer, and it would be nice if you could wait and file once I finish my program. I'll be done in a year. It'll be such a hassle. It really is just less of a headache for both of us."

"I don't see how it's much of a headache for me."

"Well, if I have all this time to work with my lawyer on the divorce, then—"

"Are you threatening me?" I asked, the words spitting right from my mouth since I was so fucking surprised by her tone.

"No. I'm just saying, we can make this a very easy process for each other, if we work *together*."

Together.

A relationship is about compromise.

A relationship isn't just about me.

I'd heard it all. Every fucking thing Sheila would say to get me to do whatever she wanted done in the moment.

"Wish you'd considered working with me on our marriage," I said.

"You were the one who stormed off, needed to get a new place, didn't want to try and make things work."

"Sheila, you have been given more chances than I ever thought I'd be willing to give another person. Than any self-respecting person should be expected to."

She quieted, as though reflecting on my comment, but I knew her well enough to know that couldn't be the case. "You can put this on me all you want, but you checked out of our relationship a long time ago."

There it was.

After all the pain, after all my heartache. After all the tears.

No remorse. No regret. Not even an apology.

Because it was my fault she went and fucked her client.

Just like it was my fault she fucked her grad professor.

Her "study partner."

Her other "study partner."

Her personal trainer.

At that point, who the fuck knew who else?

Running down the list made me ashamed of what a sucker I'd been to believe that each time had been a mistake, and even worse, somehow my fault. And the absolute worst? Part of me still believed it.

I set my glass on the counter, noticing it trembling against the marble as I released it. "Sheila, I know it might be hard and frustrating to change so much right now, but I need to file for divorce so I can move on. Don't you understand that?"

She pushed to her feet and approached. Her frustration, her annoyance had vanished, replaced with another side of Sheila I had become so familiar with in our time together—that soft face, the teary eyes. A face that had some mystical power over me.

"I know you don't believe this, but I love you."

My eyes watered as I gripped the counter. "Sheila, please."

"You don't want to hear that, but it's true. I've always loved you. Just, please. This is hard on me right now, and I'm barely hanging in..." Her voice cracked as she spoke.

Oh, how it severed through my heart.

I couldn't look at her. I knew the face she was making, and I knew once I did, it would be all over. Not just that I would cave to what she wanted, but my greatest fear, that I would fall for it and wind up back in her arms, playing out that old, familiar script once again.

"I'll file first thing at the start of next year. First thing. Then I can change over insurance. I'm just asking for this little favor."

"Fine," I said quickly, wanting this to stop. "End of this year."

I knew I'd have to face her sooner rather than later, and as I turned to her she nodded, those wide hazel eyes set on me, looking as sincere as I could imagine a person to be, but the twist of her lip, into almost a smirk, left me with that fear that some sadistic part of her was thrilled I'd submitted.

"Please just go, Sheila."

"Okay, but we will need to get together for dinner to have a conversation about dealing with everything else. You left behind so many things. I'll at least need to give you a box, maybe several."

Could she not understand why I left in such a hurry? How angry I was, how hurt?

"Okay," was all I could force out, feeling as defeated by such a short conversation as I had by the entirety of our relationship.

I led her back to the door, offering as friendly a parting as I could manage as she kept on that sad expression, and as soon as I shut the door, I collapsed against it.

Fuck me.

I downed the rest of the Maker's in my glass before pouring myself another round. Closing my eyes, I enjoyed the warm rush as it granted me the faintest relief from Sheila's visit and the reminders of the pain, lies, and manipulations. Our relationship had been little more than accusations, shame, and humiliation.

And I'd still be married to her until January. But as long as she was out of my life, that was all that mattered.

I turned and caught my reflection in the microwave, mounted beneath the cabinet on the other side of the kitchen.

I wasn't that fun-loving kid who'd first gotten together with Sheila. I was a shell of a man. Still empty on the inside, struggling to find that spark that had blown out long ago.

"We're starting a new life," I told my reflection, raising my glass to it, hoping to renew that zest I'd been feeling on my way home. Hoping that one day I could find a way to forget all those shattered pieces of myself I'd left behind.

4

KYLE

Ben moaned as I tugged on his hair, pulling tight so he'd feel it. Just the way he liked it.

"You can fuck me harder than that," he snapped, like the good, needy power-bottom he was.

His face was buried in the couch as he served his ass up to me while I had one foot on the floor and the other on the adjacent cushion.

I pounded even faster, watching my cock moving in and out of his hole, a little lube slipping out and sliding around my shaft. As much as he'd begged me to get inside him tonight, I needed a nice good tuck too. Hadn't even realized it until I was drilling away at that familiar, tight hole that opened right up for me as it always had.

He leaned back, and I released his hair and hooked my arm around his slim body, fitting it near mine as he turned and glanced over his shoulder, looking at me, all need and hunger in his eyes.

"Don't you fucking try to sneak a kiss," I said, since I'd been clear I wasn't interested in kissing if we did mess around. The fact that there were any ifs beforehand was such a fucking joke. I'd had my cock in him on just about every surface in his parents' living room (not to mention the kitchen island) since we'd gotten started.

"Come on, *Kylie*," he said, his voice a low whisper, like he was trying to be extra adorable. Considering how he'd been crying when I first arrived, I was more susceptible to caving to his desires to cheer him up. "Come on," he said again as I continued giving him my dick. "Just sneak me a little one. It'll make me shoot. It'll make me feel better."

Fucking dammit.

His face was still a little red from the tears he'd shed. It was the sort of look I couldn't deny, so I leaned forward, moving slowly, because if he wanted a kiss from me, he'd expect a little torture to get it.

He moved toward me to take what was his, but I pulled away. "Uh-uh. You know how this goes. You wait, like a good boy. Are you my good boy?" I reached my other arm around him and rested my hand against his neck. Just holding it in the way I knew he liked. We'd gotten real familiar with each other's bodies since we'd started hanging out in middle school.

As he settled, a sliver of a smile sneaking across his face, I moved closer just to torment him once again, until my top lip grazed his bottom lip. I slid the hand I had against his torso down to his shaft while sweeping my tongue across his lip. It didn't take more than a pump to get him moaning.

I chuckled as I felt warm cum shooting across the edge of my forefinger and thumb. "Give it all to me, Ben."

As he sealed his eyes shut and convulsed in my hold, I took a peek over his shoulder, watching as he sprayed the last bit of his load across the sofa cushions.

"Mmm. That's right." I continued working his prostate with my cock buried deep in him.

"You're close," he said, opening his eyes, a sort of villainous expression on his face, like he was proud he knew my body, my movements, as well as I knew his.

"Pretty close if you'll shut the hell up," I teased him.

He laughed that adorable laugh of his before the pressure in my balls swelled to the point where I couldn't handle it anymore. I cursed, shooting in the condom within him. He giggled like a fucking kid, wiggling his ass in that playful way he had of milking me. It made me laugh too.

"You dork," I told him, still coming as he grinned like having me come in him had made his night.

"You think it's cute." He winked as I slid out of him.

I disposed of the condom in the trash and returned to the couch, where Ben was now sprawled on his back, taking up most of it. I knew what he wanted, but I resisted, planting my ass at his feet, if only so he'd have to ask.

"Cuddle me," he pleaded.

"So fucking predictable."

"I'm wounded," he whimpered.

Damn, he knew every fucking way of making me surrender to him.

He rolled onto his side and scooted toward the edge of the sofa, making room for me.

"Fine." I slid in behind him and slung my arm around him. He tucked that seat that had been milking me not five minutes earlier tight against my cock.

"You're definitely a shower, not a grower," he said playfully, wiggling his ass again.

My dick perked at the maneuver. "Shut the hell up, you naughty bottom." I slapped his ass so hard the sound reverberated throughout the room.

He rolled toward me, all smiles now, a far cry from all those tears earlier.

"This isn't how spooning works," I told him.

"Whatever."

"You feeling better?"

"Yeah. I'll be fine. Doug was an asshole anyway." He wiped at his face as though searching for one of the many tears that had been on it before I'd done such a diligent job of satisfying my buddy.

"I told you he was an asshole. I just didn't know he was the   keeps-other-guys-bound-to-agreements-he-can't-follow-himself kind."

"I can't believe I didn't figure out that *Barbara* was a decoy name in his phone."

"Hey, none of that. It's not shitty that you wanted to trust someone. It makes you a good person."

"Or a sucker."

"You're good at that too, but that just makes you even better relationship material, doesn't it?"

Each laugh since his initial tear-fest assured me he'd pull through this, like he always did.

"Thanks, but it's not going to help me when I have to see *Barbara* at school."

"Just remember that Jon likely doesn't know any more than you. You guys aren't the assholes. Doug is. And what a name for one, right?"

"What would I do without you, Scowl?" he said, calling me by the nickname he and Taryn had given me.

"You'd probably still be weeping over that moron and eating a gallon of ice cream by yourself. Speaking of which, I was lured over here with the promise of a few scoops."

"I gave you plenty of cream. Not my fault you didn't eat it."

"Ooh, look at you, being all in a mood. What's new? Ice cream. Now," I ordered.

"Yes, sir." I'd never seen him move as quickly in his life as he got up and practically skipped to the fridge.

I hopped up and joined him, checking the window of his back door. "You sure none of your neighbors are going to see us?"

"If they do, maybe word will get back to Doug and he'll think I'm this amazing player." He opened the cabinet, fished out bowls, and set them on the counter with the ice cream. "Especially being with the school *bad boy.*"

"I'm not the school bad boy. That's more Wes Kenmore's thing."

"Kyle, you are so oblivious. You're all mystery and

confidence. No one, especially a bunch of high school kids, knows what the hell to do with that."

"I think we both know it has to do with a little more than that."

He lowered his gaze. We both knew damn well how I'd earned my reputation. And why it was so fucking unjust.

It wasn't just that, though. I didn't help matters by not giving a shit about school or making friends, unless they happened to be as cool and bottomy as Ben. Then again, Ben was the only guy who fit that description.

He made two bowls of Moose Tracks with extra peanuts, brownie bites, whipped cream, and a couple of squirts of chocolate-fudge syrup. We settled back on the sofa, and he sat in my lap as we ate our post-fuck dessert.

"I saw that teacher you mentioned, by the way."

"Mr. Warner?"

"You mean *James*?" he said, referring to our jokes about the incident that happened on the first day of class. "He's hot as fuck. I would let him plow the shit out of me."

"I think we both know you don't have too high standards for who you let do that."

"Big standards more than high standards," he teased. "And that bulge in his pants... Must be nice to look at in class. Don't act like you haven't noticed." He glanced at me, clearly awaiting an admission.

"What? You expecting me to deny it? I wonder if he realizes how big it looks in those khakis he wears, or if he can even do anything about it."

"I don't think there's really a way to hide that kind of dong, unless he wants to sneak it between his legs."

"Not exactly something a teacher needs to be strutting around with, on top of that pretty face." Fuck. That had spit right out of my mouth.

"So you think he's hot too?"

"I'm not blind."

"So you'd totally fuck Mr. Warner, if you could."

"Stop."

"You'd fuck Mr. Warner. Admit it."

"I would never fuck some *teach*."

"Teach? Are you suddenly going to high school in the seventies?"

"Must've picked it up from Tex, but I like it. It fits him."

"Well, I'd let him fuck me," Ben said. "No shame in that." He laughed as he took another thick glop of ice cream into his mouth.

"Oh, too big. Too big." He could hardly enunciate because of how stuffed his mouth was.

"Not even going to touch that one." And at my remark, he spit out the ice cream onto my chest. "Oh fuck!" I exclaimed as the cold stung my flesh.

OVER THE NEXT WEEK, I settled into my usual routine. I ran deliveries for a few apps, did my schoolwork to get by, and met up with Ben to cheer him up as much as I could through his grieving process.

I slid beside Taryn at the lunch table before Ben joined us. Taryn was eating a stack of mashed potatoes she'd packed in her lunch. "I can't tell if it's little Timmy yet or if I'm trying to eat for this and my next life."

Ben laughed, and I knew it was mostly because Taryn was intending to name her kid, guy or girl, Timmy.

"It's cute that you think you didn't always eat like this," I said, and Taryn busted into a laugh.

"You fucking ass. You're a terrible father."

Another inside joke.

Despite having messed around with Taryn a few times, we all knew who the father was. Still, the rest of the school had made up their minds that it was me, partly contributing to this bad-boy image I seemed to have earned. Or at least, never proven wrong.

Ben glanced around. "You guys gotta be careful joking around like that. It doesn't take much to get a rumor started around here."

"Man, I don't feel like if I start calling you a top, it's gonna dissuade anyone from that ass."

He practically howled with Taryn, making me pretty fucking proud of my tease. Although, really, I hoped he got my point too. I didn't give a shit what anyone in this dumb school thought about me.

"Besides," I added. "You're the co-host of the school news. We basically make PR at this school."

"Um...excuse me," he said, "I'm busy reporting big, important 5A topics, not run-of-the-mill gossip. Thanks for paying attention to my important updates. I'll remember you when I'm big time on CNN."

My reference led to Ben giving us the latest class news

—various self-created dramas that kept his peers and himself busy, apparently.

When I finished eating, I got out my homework for James's class and reread my responses. It was the first real assignment he'd given us on our reading of *Paradise Lost,* a poem he admitted was a bit premature this early in the semester, but he was racing through the bards and Chaucer to get us to his personal favorites—Shakespeare and the Romantics.

I would have been lying if I said I hadn't reread my answers a few times. I didn't usually try too hard with this stuff, but I'd found myself enjoying his questions.

"Is that for Mr. Warner's class?" Ben asked.

"Shut it. It's my next period. I'm proofing it." He and Taryn eyed each other, and I knew what they were thinking. "My British Lit teach is actually kinda cool, and his questions didn't feel like he just wanted to see if we'd read the chapters. I just...I don't know, liked my answers. He'll probably check it off and move on, but...whatever."

I doubted he would even care as much as I had, but I'd gotten sort of lost in my answers. Even though it was about *Paradise Lost*, it was about more than that too. And there was something nice about knowing he wouldn't ever know why.

After lunch, I headed on to fourth period.

Mr. Warner hadn't treated me any differently than any of the other kids in class since that first awkward moment we'd had. Didn't so much as look at me any differently, or notice me when I was looking at him a little too long.

I was definitely attracted to him. Ben wasn't wrong

about that, but it wasn't just his looks. Everything about his demeanor, how he bit his lip after telling a bad joke, it all had a way of unnerving me and turning me on at the same time, to the point where I had to keep adjusting in my seat as class wore on.

But he looked at me as much as he would at douchebag jock Brian Finnegan or at Mindy Martin, who sat all the way in the back, just as she did in every class I had with her. He'd call on me same as everyone else, no more, no less. I respected that.

Before class began, he drew our attention to some scribbled writing in the upper left-hand side of the whiteboard. "I don't know if anyone will be interested, but next Saturday there's an event at the local coffee-house. A poetry reading. I know it's early in the semester to be talking about extra credit, but nothing like buffering your grade ahead of time *and* supporting local artists. I'll be there, but still, even if you attend, you'll need to write a one-page double-spaced report about your experience and take a pic on your phone in case I'm left wondering whether you actually attended based on what you say."

"And you said you'll be at this event?" Valerie Briner asked, earning a few snickers because by the tone in her voice, it was obvious why she wanted to know. James looked a little flustered, his gaze shifting around the room.

Damn, could a man look like that and really be so goddamn oblivious of it? It almost made me pissed. Want to shake him like I'd wanted to shake Ben. Or really, do whatever I needed to do to show him how hot he was.

"Yes, Valerie, I will," he said, keeping his tone professional.

"His wife might be there too," Brian Finnegan noted to Valerie, clearly giving her a hard time. He was a grade-A asshole.

"Mr. Warner isn't married," Valerie said, turning to Brian, and I could imagine the foul look she was giving him. "He'd be wearing a ring."

I kept my eyes on Mr. Warner to read his expression, which was stiff. "Speculation about my personal life isn't relevant to an event I'll be attending or this class, so we'll move on now—"

"Why don't you want to say?" Brian asked. "Is it a dude?" He and his buddy Daryl looked to one another, giggling like fucking idiots.

Mr. Warner's expression stiffened further, and tension rose within me. It was one of those moments I knew could make or break James for me. He hadn't said anything blatantly homophobic since I'd been in his class. But in a town like Wyachet, you never knew when it might rear its ugly head in even the unlikeliest of people.

"Shouldn't be a problem if it were a *dude*, Mr. Finnegan," he replied, his expression unwavering.

The fuck? Again, he got into my head. For a guy who was so fumbling and had all this nervous energy about him, to throw out a comment like that with such confidence, not giving a flying fuck what Brian or any of these other assholes thought about him or spread around the school...

Who the fuck are you, James Warner?

I waited for him to say something, to take it back or clarify, but he turned the conversation back to the reading.

I didn't figure he was or had ever been married to a man, but I'd seen plenty of other teachers bend over backward to keep even the faintest rumor about them from spreading around the school.

Mr. Warner didn't give a fuck. *I knew I liked this guy.*

5

JAMES

Wednesday morning, I was sitting behind my desk, grading papers, when there was a knock on my classroom door. I turned to see Simon Hawthorn through the window. I'd pulled him aside after third period the previous day, to see if he would meet with me during my office hours, and certainly, he already knew why.

I opened the door, inviting him in. "Take a seat. We have plenty," I joked, sitting at a desk.

He took the one beside me, looking around the room like his eyes wanted to be anywhere but making eye contact with mine, which wasn't so different from the way he looked during class.

"I assume you know why I asked you to swing by. It hasn't exactly been the best start to the year." Simon hadn't turned in any of his assignments outside the ones we did in class. "Do you mind if I ask if you've even done the reading? I promise, it won't affect your grade."

He shook his head, his eyes watering.

As I'd suspected, whatever reason he had for not turning in his assignments and looking totally disengaged during class didn't have much to do with laziness. Something was going on with this guy.

"I'm sorry," he said.

"I didn't bring you in here to make you feel bad. I just want to make sure everything's okay."

"What?"

His eyes met mine for the first time, as though he didn't understand what I'd said, so I went on. "Beyond not getting your assignments in, you seem...stressed in class. Is everything okay at home...or at work? School?"

He stared at me blankly. "I've...um...had a lot going on." It seemed he hadn't wanted to divulge even that much, but clearly something was weighing on him, and I felt for him. He added, "We have a lot going on with my family. And I've been...um...I have some issues."

"What kind of issues?"

"In my head." His words were so soft, a whisper, as though he was afraid of saying them out loud. It triggered every protective impulse in me, and I could feel my fists tensing up.

"Are you all right?" I pressed, probing for more information.

"I'm doing better now. This past summer was a hard one. I didn't mean to say that to concern you. I just...I have a lot of problems with depression and anxiety, and we've been going through different...medications."

As difficult as whatever he was going through clearly was, I was relieved to hear him say that rather than something worse about his family situation.

"Tell me about it. I've had my own issues with that. Been on so many SSRIs, it'd make your head spin."

He chuckled, and I could see how my remark helped him ease up in an instant. And I knew why. I knew how lonely that journey could feel.

"Really?" he asked, taking what seemed like the first real breath of air since he'd entered my classroom.

"Yeah. Had a lot of ups and downs. I know it can get a little foggy too. Hard to concentrate and get work done. So I get it."

He smirked, the closest thing I'd seen to a smile on this guy's face since the start of the year, which I considered a win.

"It's been...rough, for sure," he said. "We're changing the prescriptions again to see if it can help me focus, but it's been harder than normal. I never used to have problems with getting things done, but recently, feels almost impossible."

"I understand that." I thought on it for a moment. "Look, how about I give you until the end of this month to get the missed assignments in, without deducting your grade. If you need more time than that, just be open with me, all right? Maybe you can get a note from your psychiatrist and I'll extend the deadline, or cut a few assignments to make it easier on you."

"Oh, you don't need to do that. I can get it all done. I'm not trying to get out of work."

"That's very honorable of you, but just know the option is there if you need it."

He breathed once again in that way that allowed me to feel his visceral relief.

"Does that all seem fair, Simon?"

"Beyond fair. Thank you, Mr. Warner."

"It's high school, not prison. You can make some mistakes here and there. If you need to ever chat about anything, feel free to swing by, during office hours or not. Life's tough sometimes, but you don't have to do it all on your own, okay?"

Tears shifted around his eyes, and he sniffled.

"You okay?"

"Yeah, this was just very thoughtful. I was sure you were going to chew me out like my Trig teacher, but..."

"Would you like me to talk to them for you?"

"You'd do that?"

"Of course."

"No, no. That's not necessary." He shook his head, as though it'd be too big an ask.

We chatted a bit more before I led him to the door.

"Just remember, I'm here if you need to chat about anything. Even life stuff." I could tell it was too soon for that based on what little he'd been willing to open up about so far, but I had a feeling he'd be back now that he knew he had an ally.

I opened the door, and as he headed out, I noticed Kyle Forsythe standing a few feet down the hall. He wasn't waiting close to the door, but by how he lingered, I wondered if he might have seen or heard some of what Simon and I had discussed. It was hard to tell based on his expression. In general, Kyle Forsythe was hard to get a read on.

"You wanted to talk," he said.

"Oh yeah. Come on in."

I invited him in, same as I had with Simon, taking a seat at the same desk and motioning toward the one beside me. "Please."

He took it. Unlike Simon, he wasn't looking around the room, but directly at me, as though trying to make sense of why I'd wanted to see him.

"Am I in trouble? You gave me an A on the assignment." He was referring to the one I'd given him back, and on which I'd noted my office hours and asked him to come see me.

"Sorry, that wasn't an order that you come see me. More an invitation."

"Oh..." He seemed puzzled by my comment.

"I was very impressed with your answers. Your writing was good, but it was also a really passionate reflection on Lucifer and Adam and Eve as God's cast-out, neglected and abused children. Why create if you're going to judge, punish, and abandon? And why would anyone have any loyalty to such a Maker? I think you missed an opportunity to tie it all back into '*Better to reign in Hell than serve in Heaven*,' but didn't seem you were as interested in quotes as meaning."

He still eyed me peculiarly. "Wait. You said you wanted

to see me so we could chat about a book we're reading in class?"

"I am an English teacher. I do enjoy talking about texts, but I was intrigued by your discussion, aside from maybe feeling a little conned by someone who's actually already finished the poem. Clearly, you had strong feelings about Michael seeming to have more sympathy for Adam and Eve's fall than the one who created them, which wasn't something you would have said if you were halfway through."

"Well...I read fast." The conceit was written all over his face.

For being a kid who rarely brought to class more than some folded sheets of paper, a pen in his pocket, and the required text, it definitely seemed more a show than he let on with his too-good-for-school attitude.

"And you liked Milton's epic poem?"

"There was a lot of *blah-blah-blah* shit I wanted to skip over, and you're not going to convince me that anything needs to be written in verse, but it was cool. I felt like I got it."

"I definitely think you did. And that *blah, blah, blah* is probably the *stuff* that makes it art."

"Doesn't mean I have to like it."

I laughed. "No, you certainly don't, Mr. Forsythe. But I have a feeling you might find the next few assignments kind of rudimentary for someone who's already finished the text and has as many thoughts about it as you have, so if you'd like to, you can feel free to write me your own thoughts about the book as a whole. I find your perspective refreshing."

"So...because I've already read it, I have to do more work?"

"Only if you want to. You can do the same assignments as the rest of the class. I would think that'd be a waste of your time, but it's totally up to you."

His brows tugged closer together. "You're a strange egg, Big Man."

"I'll take that as a compliment." I winked, and he continued eyeing me in the strangest way.

I checked the clock. Fifteen minutes until first period.

"Anyway, kids will probably be lining up outside the door soon..."

"So that's all you wanted? To tell me you liked my work and that I can write whatever I want for the next assignments?"

"Yeah, and if you keep reading ahead like that, we can do it that way for the rest of the year."

"And I'm free to go?"

"I don't imagine a guy like you needs anyone's permission to do what he wants."

He snickered, but mostly seemed as stunned by our chat as Simon had been. I knew my methods weren't exactly the norm for most teachers, but they seemed fairly common sense to me.

"You're a strange teach," he said, shaking his head as he stood from the desk and started for the door.

"I'll take that as a compliment as well," I called after

him. He headed on out, not seeming to care much about my cheeky reply.

There was something special about Kyle Forsythe, and I was eager to have an entire year to find out just how special.

6

JAMES

I sipped my black coffee as the last guy read his poem on the black platform the café had set up for the event. He trembled so much, the leather-bound notebook in his hand jerked furiously about behind the mic stand.

There were three writers in total, so what had initially been a reading of three poems had turned into six, then nine... At some point, the host even asked me and the other guy who had come with his wife if we had anything we wanted to share, which we both respectfully declined.

Fortunately, I had attended more than my share of these sorts of events, enough to be pleasantly surprised when they didn't turn out to be a disappointment like this one. It was always fairly hit or miss, but as a teacher and patron of the arts, it was my job to turn up and support local artists. And even though this time I hadn't been able to pull any of my students out, there would always be more opportunities. Although, I found Wyachet to be sorely lacking in the local arts department, especially compared to Kensington Heights, where even a small-time event like this one would have had at least six other audience members.

Regardless, I wouldn't be dissuaded. I'd find a way to make the best of it, and it was only August. Still plenty of time to discover where the heart of the arts lay in Whispersaw County.

As the event came to an end, I volunteered to help the café host stack up chairs on the tabletops before heading out. I'd had to park in a lot about a block away, since there hadn't been any available street parking. Chatting with others at the event, I learned that was because of a nearby bowling alley, which was surely a far greater attraction on a Saturday night.

Considering the rest of the shops had let out sooner than the café, the streets were fairly empty in this part of downtown. I found an alley between two buildings that seemed to act as a shortcut to where I'd parked my car. Not much light made it into the alley, but given how few people were out and that I was in downtown Wyachet, not Atlanta, I talked myself out of what might have been my usual fear, figuring I could curb the anxieties that would otherwise accompany me along through my shortcut.

As I went on my way, a wisp of wind rushed through the alley, nipping at my cheeks as I tucked my hands in my jacket pockets. For not even being September yet, nights were already getting much cooler.

Gravel scattered across the asphalt crushed beneath

my feet as I made my way through the darkness toward the shaft of orange light on the other side of the buildings. A sound behind me caught my attention, something that could have been nothing more than a squirrel. But I checked anyway for the sort of serial killer that lingered in the back of my thoughts.

A guy in a hoodie was a few yards back, his head tucked low as he walked at a fairly quick pace, though not seeming interested in me as much as getting on his own way. *Probably just going to his car*, I assured myself as he started to pass me.

I sighed, relieved, once he was a little ahead of me, but he swung back around, pulling a hand from his pocket. What bit of light made it into the alley glinted off the blade he held, stopping me in my tracks. My anxiety swelled, my thoughts spinning too quickly for me to think straight.

He shouted at me, but I couldn't even make out what he said, so I put my arms up, mimicking a response that would have at least seemed appropriate. Or at least give him no reason to fucking stab me with that blade, which, by the way, he kept poking toward me, making me think that was entirely possible.

He shouted again, and I made out the word *wallet*.

Fuck, fuck. In an instant, beads of sweat collected on my forehead.

"I'm getting it. I'm getting it," I told him, hoping he'd stop jabbing toward me with the blade so recklessly that he might cut me by accident.

I retrieved the wallet, trembling, working to calm

myself enough to make it out of this alive, but of course, in my clumsiness, I fumbled and dropped it on the ground.

"The hell? Fucking get it."

I dropped to my knees, feeling around the darkness for it, worried the guy would lose his patience and stab me while I was down. Once I felt the pleather casing, I grabbed it and made my way back to my feet, ready to surrender it to my attacker. But as soon as I looked up, he was gone like some kind of fucking ghost that had vanished into thin air.

Surely, that wasn't possible.

My brain was in survival mode, unable to piece reality together the way it normally would have. But a few more sounds captured my attention, and I turned to see him a few yards away, on his back, in the shaft of light.

Another guy was on top of him, throwing punches. Once...twice...a third time.

My attacker's hoodie was pulled back, revealing his face. He was young, maybe in his twenties, and as I got closer to the fight—really, not so much a fight as an assault by the man on his knees, going at his face like a punching bag—I saw my rescuer's face too.

No. It couldn't be.

My mind was fucking with me, as it had been after that guy had pulled the knife on me.

But another drop of his fist revealed the same face as before. It was unmistakably Kyle Forsythe.

I was so stunned, it took me a moment to realize the guy he was still hammering with punches lay limp, not fighting back. I searched around and saw the knife a few feet away, out of my attacker's grasp.

"You can stop now."

Kyle kept drilling, forcing some blood from the guy's nose and mouth.

"You can stop!" I shouted, fetching the knife.

He ceased mid-punch, looking down at his victim, surely seeing that this guy was incapable of causing him any harm. He panted, catching his breath, as I slipped the knife into my pocket.

With Kyle on top of him, it was hard not to notice that this guy couldn't have been much older than him. He was a fucking kid, spitting up blood as he muttered, "Stop...please..."

Kyle took a breath, one that seemed to give him enough time to consider his next actions. Then, to my relief, he pushed to his feet. I figured he would walk away, but he turned back around and kicked the guy in the stomach.

"Okay, he's down," I assured him once again, feeling if he persisted, I wouldn't just be calling the cops, but an ambulance too.

"Jesus fucking Christ," Kyle said, taking a breath.

The kid scrambled to his feet.

"Hey, come back here," Kyle yelled, and by the look on his face, I could tell he was about to run after him. I grabbed hold of his arm. "Hey, that's not necessary." I restrained him as the guy raced off.

Kyle's muscles were so tense. Given the chance, I

wondered what else he could have done to that kid, how far he would have taken it.

"I'm gonna call the cops. We'll give them his knife and call it a night, okay?"

He nodded, clearly still caught up in whatever adrenaline rush had seized control of him after he'd started his attack.

I went ahead and dialed 911. Kyle was zoned out, glancing around like he was waiting for the guy to show up and try something again. Apparently, two units weren't too far off, and soon we had three cops asking us about the incident.

"Sounds like we need to look for a kid with a bloodied face," Officer Howe said.

Kyle wasn't amused by that any more than he had been about any of Officer Howe's commentary.

"And where were you again when you saw this starting up?" Howe asked.

Kyle's gaze shifted. "Across the street."

Officer Howe's forehead wrinkled as he asked, "At Finley's? The bar? That's all that would have been open right about then."

Fuck.

Kyle had mentioned to them a few times already that he'd been across the street, but this was the first time since they'd begun the report that any of the officers had taken a moment to reflect on where that meant Kyle was.

"You're eighteen, and—"

The expression on Kyle's face didn't provide me with much confidence that he wasn't at the bar. "I was—"

"It was an extra-credit assignment," I interrupted. "And he was coming to the event, but I guess he was late." I was lying to cover for him, but considering they weren't supposed to be there to get Kyle into trouble, and he'd saved my ass, it was my turn to save his.

"Is that right?" Officer Howe asked him.

"Yeah," Kyle said.

"And did your parents know you were coming to this?"

"What?" Kyle seemed thrown by the question.

"If I called Pastor Travis, he'll know you were coming to this event for school?"

Pastor? Holy hell. Apparently, Kyle was more of a town celebrity than I'd realized.

"I'm eighteen. Why would you need to call my parents?"

Kyle's less-than-charismatic approach was not doing him any favors, so I said, "Officer Howe, would you like me to speak with his parents? I'd be happy to do anything to help."

Officer Howe sized me up before taking a breath. "That won't be necessary, but thank you for cooperating."

I could tell pulling out my teacher card had disarmed him.

"It's just," Howe continued, "it seems a little strange that he knew you were going to be at this place, then some guy attacks you, and he steps in."

Kyle seemed to cringe.

"Wouldn't be the first time a kid pulled a prank on a new teacher at the school. Am I right, Kyle?"

"What the—" Kyle started.

"I think if it was a prank between friends, he's going to have a very pissed-off friend later," I said.

Officer Howe seemed to appreciate my logic as he nodded. "Fair enough. But I'll say it again, if that was really some methhead looking to take a wallet—and in this town, that's likely the case—that was a dumb move. You don't throw yourself between someone and a knife. Got it?"

"Yeah." Kyle obviously wanted this whole thing to be over, and after what an ass Officer Howe had been, I more than understood why.

Fortunately, after his suspicion of Kyle tapered, he and his colleagues only asked us a few more questions until they were satisfied and moved along, promising they would contact us if they came up with a suspect matching my description.

Kyle seemed relieved when they finally drove off. "What a night," he remarked, taking a deep breath.

"I'm sorry."

"You didn't do anything wrong."

"About the way that cop acted, like you might have been involved. I know you wouldn't have done anything like that."

"You don't really know me well enough to be sure I wasn't." He took another breath. "Anyway, won't be the first time I've been accused of shit, or the last. Trust me." Between his expression and the bitterness in his tone, it was a loaded comment. I couldn't help wondering how his father being a known pastor in town played into it.

"As I told you before, and as Officer Howe said, you

really should never throw yourself in the middle of something like that."

"You gotta show fucks like that that they can't get away with hurting people."

I stood my ground. "It was dangerous."

"Are you fucking kidding me? A thank-you is all I need for what I did back there."

"That guy had a knife."

"A dumb kid with a knife doesn't scare me, Mr. Warner. Did you see the way he was holding that thing? I figured it was about to shake right out of his hand. Didn't know what he was doing."

"Well, you knew what you were doing when you were painting that gravel with his blood."

I was being a little dramatic, but not by much. I did wonder where the hell a kid like him had learned to fight like that.

"I'll have to file a report with the school too," I added. "You might have to write up something for Administration."

"Whatever."

He was over the night, and I sure as hell understood why.

"You said you Ubered?" It was something he'd mentioned while the cops were chatting with us. "Do you need a ride? It's the least I can do."

He looked me over, almost like he was trying to decide if he could trust getting a ride from me, which seemed odd at this point, after everything that had transpired.

"Sure, Mr. Warner. Let's do that."

KYLE

A s I buckled up in James's car, he asked, "Where do you live?"

"Turn on your car."

He hesitated, his expression twisting up, but he obeyed, giving me the opportunity to enter the address in the GPS on his dash.

He closed his eyes and laughed. It was nice seeing him smile after everything we'd been through that night.

"Oh, wow. Twenty minutes," he said as the address popped up. "I didn't realize you lived so far outside downtown."

"You don't know much about me."

Maybe I was being a dick for iterating the fact. I wasn't trying to be mean, but it was clear by the way he jerked back at my comment that he took it worse than I'd intended. Fuck, I was bad at being human.

"I know you have an impressive left hook," he came

back with, which broke the tension as we shared another laugh. He had this uncanny way of cutting right through the awkwardness, especially after that cop had been such an asshole.

He put the car in drive before heading out of the lot, into the street.

"*At length from us may find, who overcomes by force, hath overcome but half his foe,*'" he noted.

"Is this a pop quiz on Milton, or are you trying to make a point? Because I'm pretty confident *force* served us fine back there."

"Just an observation," he went on, "but I am curious where you learned to hit like that."

"Just a few things I've picked up in life."

Things I wasn't interested in sharing. Not with him. Not with anyone.

"As you could probably tell, I'm not much of a fighter, and really, I don't think it's necessarily an important skill to have."

"If you're gonna Mr. Rogers me for twenty minutes, I swear I will jump out of this car and fucking walk. We're not at school. As I had to remind that cop, I'm eighteen fucking years old, so you don't have to do this dumb teacher-student moment like you're about to haul me off to the principal's office to explain conflict resolutions to me."

I didn't have a problem with James, but I wasn't going to tolerate any of his teacher bullshit either. Not when I was already worked up enough from the night.

"Fair enough."

It seemed I'd effectively killed the conversation, leaving me to my own thoughts as they pulled me out of survival mode and into thinking about why the hell I'd been back there to begin with. I couldn't believe I'd even considered going to that extra-credit thing. I didn't do extra credit.

Although, I knew what had really drawn me there: Mr. Warner—James. Teach.

He continued to fascinate me.

Like when I heard him talking to Simon.

I'd known the kid since elementary school. His parents had defected from Dad's church and moved on to one of Wyachet's many cults for the über-wealthy after his brother died in a car accident. Hearing him talking about feeling messed up in the head, about his depression and anxiety...fuck, it hurt my heart.

Teach could have disregarded Simon like his other teachers and even the other kids in school, like even I had until I heard how much he was struggling. But James had talked and listened. He was different, not just than most of the teachers I knew, but most people. I wondered if he even knew what he'd done for that guy, but it seemed almost instinctual for him. Like that was just the kind of person he was, same as when he talked to me.

As James continued navigating his way to my place, I decided to break the silence, hitting one of his music station selections. A female voice played as the artist's name flashed across the screen. Made me smirk.

"Who the hell is Hailee Seinfeld?"

"It's *Hailee Steinfeld*."

I laughed at his correction. "Oh, wow. So you know who this is even? I take it you're a big pop-music guy."

"I didn't use to be, but I've needed *mindless* and *fun* recently."

His words suggested his life wasn't so mindless or fun.

That first day, it had been impossible to tell anything about him really, considering it seemed he was mostly anxious about the predicament he was in, but I could sense it in class, every day—a sort of...sorrow, maybe.

He was a bundle of questions, and I wanted answers, but he got one in first. "You mind if I ask what you were doing in town tonight?"

"Yes." The word shot out of my mouth. Quick. Forceful. Rude as hell. For actually thinking this teach was cool, I sure had a fucked-up way of showing it. But I was embarrassed that I'd been there because of him, when I should have taken up Ben on his offer for some ass.

Although, just thinking I could have been balls-deep in Ben while some stupid motherfucker had his knife in James's gut made me glad I'd made the right choice. If I hadn't gone into town, if I hadn't chickened out and ended up at Finley's, if everything hadn't gone down exactly as it had, I wouldn't have been there to help him.

What if he'd been hurt? Would have been the fucking case, I was sure. That was how life worked, wasn't it? The good people were the ones who got hurt the most.

"Sorry," I forced out nearly as harshly as my dismissive yes.

"What?"

"I'm not good at...this."

"I'm not sure what you mean."

"Talking. Everything always comes out wrong, or I say something stupid or that comes across mean or too harsh. My friend Taryn calls me Scowl when I get this look on my face. Says it reminds her of a greyhound her family had when she was little. It would sit there, wanting to rip someone's face off, but wouldn't do more than growl through its teeth. Judging by your expression, you don't disagree."

"You had a reaction to that cop that probably made him feel similarly. But it's not a bad thing."

"It's not a good thing either. Trust me." Again, my words came out more severely than I'd intended. I figured it was at least partly due to all that energy still surging through me from the night we'd had.

"Your father's a pastor?"

"Another thing I'm not interested in talking about."

I kept the memories at bay, fighting against them as I had for so fucking long. Between my reaction, the cop's comment, and that assignment I'd done in class, he must have figured there was more to that, but I wasn't going there.

"So, to answer your question about why I was downtown," I went on, since it was the only thing I was willing to talk to him about, "I was going to that dumb extra-credit thing you mentioned." I practically mumbled the words.

"Well, then at least I know I wasn't lying to a cop back there," he said, sounding relieved. "What happened? Were you late?"

"I changed my mind. Went...somewhere else."

"Can you get into a bar?"

"If I answer that, don't you feel like you might be liable for something?"

"I feel like the way you answered it might make me liable anyway." He turned from the windshield a moment to wink at me.

God, he was too nerdy to be so sexy too.

"I was surprised that cop went there, though. I never would have assumed some kid was at a bar."

"I don't have a problem getting into bars, Mr. Warner." I said Mr. Warner instead of James intentionally, to remind him we weren't friends. He was my teacher, and I was his student.

"And here I feel like I still get ID'd at the grocery store for some bottled wine."

It made me laugh, like one of his silly jokes in class might have.

"Wherever I was, let's just say, from where I was sitting, I could see that guy hanging out on that street, looking around as if waiting for trouble."

I'd been able to see James through the café window, and I'd watched him like some fucking stalker. No idea why. Maybe because I wasn't even sure what had really drawn me out tonight.

In some ways, it was like fate had pulled me to that

moment so I could be there for him. Of course, I knew that was total bull, since fate had never been there for me.

The only one who'd ever been there for me was Tex.

"So when you came out of the café and he started following you, I figured you might need backup, so I think we should both be glad it worked out as it did."

"I can't say I'm glad it 'worked out,' if that's what you want to call putting your life in danger."

"He could have hurt you. He could have stabbed you, James. These Wyachet addicts are a fucking virus. A kid like that would have done it simply because he was scared, and he wouldn't have thought twice about the fact that you're a human being."

"He could have done that to you too."

"Would have liked to see him try."

I'd considered it, but I hadn't been afraid. Not just because I knew I could take the guy, but because if he had, would it have been such a terrible thing for the world?

I knew that wasn't the way to think. Tex sure would've been worried if he knew I thought that, but it was true.

Again, James glanced over from the windshield, eyeing me peculiarly, that pretty face and his kind eyes guarded behind his glasses. His eyes returned to the road before he asked, "You ever do volunteer work?"

"The fuck?"

That came out of left field.

"We all have stuff we have to get through, and a few years back when I was going through a rough patch, I signed up for this thing called Housing 4 Hope."

"I've heard of it." It was a statewide housing project

created to help build homes for families in underserved communities.

"I was there today. I go every Saturday," he went on. "As crappy as my life can get sometimes, it's distracting. And makes me feel like even if I'm feeling bad about what's going on in my own life, at least I'm doing something to help someone else's. Not saying you need to do that, but you might be able to find something—"

"Mr. Warner, why don't you quit the free therapy session? I'm not this big mess you need to fix."

He pressed his lips together. "Sorry, I didn't mean it to come across that way."

"You might not have wanted it to come across that way, but it was what you meant by it."

"Am I speaking with Kyle or Scowl right now?" he teased, turning to me once again, and I had to chuckle.

In fact, I hated myself for laughing at it. He seemed to have this power to crack right through all my defenses, every one I'd spent a lifetime building up.

"Smartass," I muttered, waiting for him to chastise me or remark about that being inappropriate for me to call my teacher, but he grinned, as though proud of himself for earning the nickname.

"You're not like other *teaches*, Mr. Warner." Although, I wondered how much I thought that because of the kindness I'd seen him display, and how much was because he was hot as sin.

Our conversation settled, not in an uneasy way, like I'd assumed such a drive might be after the fucked-up shit that had gone down in town. When he finally made it to my neighborhood, I helped him navigate until he pulled up alongside the curb.

"I can come in and talk to your parents about where you were and what happened."

"That won't be necessary. Just go home."

"Okay. I stand by everything I said about how you should have thought of yourself more before taking action back there, but even still, I appreciate that your heart was in the right place. Thank you."

Given how annoyed he'd seemed by my jumping into action, his gratitude took me by surprise. And between that and having my eyes locked with his brown irises, I felt warmth in my cheeks.

The hell?

"No prob." I got out quickly, but before I closed the door, there was one thing I had to say, *needed* to fucking say. I popped my head back in. "Mr. Warner, you're a good guy. We don't need good guys bloodied up in dark alleys, losing them to the very assholes who should be the ones lying there, bloodied up in those dark alleys."

It was all true. Even during this short trip, all he'd been was kind and as chill as I could have hoped.

He reflected on my comment before smirking. "Very wise words, Mr. Forsythe."

"Consider that a little Kyle 101 for tonight," I teased. "End of lesson."

"That's fair. Are you sure you don't need me to come in and talk to your parents?"

I snickered, tucking my face down and shaking my head. This guy really didn't get it. "This isn't my parents' place." I winked at him. "And we'll save that for another lesson. Good night."

He started to ask something, but I closed the car door and headed into the yard, to the front door, trying to wrap my thoughts around everything that happened.

JAMES

"And he just happened to be there when this mugger attacked you?" Dr. Henry asked as she reviewed my incident report, skimming more than reading it, it seemed. I'd emailed her the night of the incident, as soon as I got home, figuring Wyachet High's principal would want to ensure we handled everything by the book. We'd agreed to meet up before school on Monday to follow up about the details. However, aside from having filed a police report, there wasn't much I could do.

"Excuse me?" I asked, caught off guard by her response, which mirrored Officer Howe's suspicions toward Kyle. "I'm sorry, Dr. Henry. Maybe I didn't say something right. He was in the area because of an event I offered as extra credit."

"Yet he didn't make it to the event, but knew when it was and where you would be." Her salt-and-pepper eyebrows pushed closer together as she seemed about as convinced as the officer from the night before.

"He beat this guy up good. I don't think he would have gotten someone to scare me just so he could hurt them."

"Kids have done stranger things. Trust me, I've been doing this a long time. It could have been a prank. Maybe even fake blood."

I knew what I'd seen: real punches pounding that mugger, and Kyle's banged-up hands. He hadn't staged that. It wasn't the Kyles of a school you had to watch for that shit. It was those football-playing goons who would work each other up into doing stupid crap like that.

Kyle hadn't done that. However, it was clear by the skeptical expression on Dr. Henry's face that she wasn't interested in being convinced of his innocence, nor did I think it was necessary to her filing this away and us all getting on with our lives.

"James, you never know with a guy like Kyle Forsythe." She shrugged, setting my incident report on the desk in front of her.

"A guy like Kyle Forsythe? I'm sorry. This might be because I'm new here, but is there something I need to know about him?"

"You'll find out sooner or later. His father is Pastor Travis Forsythe, over at the 12 Stone branch on Thompson and Main."

"The Wesleyan church?"

"That's right. Did you know there are fifteen thousand members of the 12 Stone churches in Whispersaw? That means the Forsythes are pretty much Wyachet royalty.

Pastor Travis and Leah are very involved with the community. Very generous, caring contributors to Wyachet."

The way she talked, I assumed she must be a parishioner.

"From what I've heard," she went on, "Kyle has had a lot of issues growing up. Just a bad egg."

"What does that mean?"

"Prone to violence and a pathological liar. They try to protect him from people knowing the sordid details, but they've said enough that it's evident he would get physical with both of them—Mrs. Forsythe even more so than his father, especially as he got older. The Forsythes did everything they could to get him help, but eventually he ran away from home. They think it was perhaps a combination of drugs and unresolved mental-health issues."

Considering my own interactions with Kyle, this all seemed far-fetched. Although, after seeing him serve up a beating to my mugger, not totally outside the realm of possibility. Before I had a chance to challenge anything she'd suggested, she added, "The Forsythes try to keep this all as quiet as they can."

"Yet somehow everyone knows his parents feel this way?" I asked, having my doubts.

She squinted at my suggestion. "It isn't just what they say. He has a history. Fistfights in middle school. I've had to discipline him for several altercations. Now he's gotten a girl pregnant."

"Pregnant?" Jesus, I was starting to understand why people reacted to Kyle in a way that made absolutely no sense to me.

"I'm sure you've heard about Taryn Maninski."

I shook my head, and she seemed annoyed that I wasn't fully integrated into the school rumor mill just yet.

"She's one of three pregnant girls this year, and I know kids can make up gossip about things, so take this as you will. Everyone believes Kyle is the father, and they have been in the same circles since freshman year, so it wouldn't be a huge surprise."

"That wouldn't be the worst thing imaginable. I'm sure plenty of his peers would be in the same situation if certain measures weren't taken."

"Yes, but between that and Kyle's history with his parents, his violent behavior in school, suspensions... I wouldn't jump to assuming he was being Superman last Friday night."

"Saturday."

She shrugged it off. "Even if he was doing it to help you, it was still a terrible idea for so many reasons. It's a kid venting his rage on a criminal, and putting his and your life in danger in the process."

That was more in line with my own thoughts when he'd gone after my attacker.

Still, I was surprised by how much judgment she had toward a guy who hadn't done anything to convince me that he was this bad kid she seemed to have pictured in her head. That wasn't the kid who'd helped me when I'd fallen into a puddle on my first day, who'd saved my ass when he could have left me to get knifed in an alley. He had that bad-boy look down pat, and certainly there was a reason his friend called him Scowl, but none of the things Dr. Henry had pointed out made him a delinquent.

It was something I couldn't shake from my head throughout the rest of my day. I'd seen such a different side of him than what it seemed so many others had. Even during our brief conversation in the car, it was apparent there was this friendly kid beneath that serious expression he wore most of the time around school.

That day, when he entered my classroom for fourth period, he offered a friendly smile. Something I wasn't even sure other kids would have read as that, but I knew, coming from him, it was a good sign.

As he sat in his seat, third row back, close to the window, I kept thinking about all those mysteries surrounding him.

His insistence with the cop about not calling his parents.

The violent streak I'd seen for myself.

His peculiar *Paradise Lost* responses about God's abandonment of Adam and Eve.

A possible baby on the way with one of his peers.

Who are you, Kyle Forsythe?

This wasn't a bad guy.

Guarded, yes. Abrasive, definitely. Deficient in understanding certain social cues? Apparently.

But it wasn't mischief I read in his intense expression before scanning the class. It was a guy who feared the world, who felt he had to pummel a guy to stay alive.

Our gazes met once more, surprising me.

I wondered what he would think of his weird British

Lit teacher looking at him, but a sliver of a smile slid across his face. Just as quickly, he looked out the window, as though he feared me looking into those eyes for too long.

As though, if I did, I might see too much.

9

KYLE

I collapsed onto the sofa, the sound of reporters discussing the latest on the upcoming elections droning on in the background. Tex's car had been in the driveway when I got back from making deliveries, so I figured he was around somewhere. Maybe taking a nap upstairs, which was what I was about to do on that sofa.

I searched for the remote for a few moments until I gave up my quest, surrendering to my weariness. I was done for the night.

A sound caught my attention, and I rolled my head to the side.

The creak of Tex's familiar footsteps approached, his Hello Kitty pajama bottoms coming into view—those pajamas that had the power to make me smile under pretty much any circumstance.

"I can tell you're riveted by the polls," he said, heading to the recliner.

"Are they still talking about that?"

"What do you mean still talking about? You haven't been home but five minutes." He settled into the seat, taking a deep breath, like he was happy to get off his feet.

"Has it only been five minutes? Don't know why I'm so damn tired tonight."

"How many deliveries did you have?"

"Seven. One was for this asshole girl from school who tried to chat me up."

"Oh, the horror of having those Harris looks."

I couldn't help scoffing at how he attributed my looks to his and Mom's side. "Whatever. We know I got my dad's face," I said, something I'd heard often enough growing up.

"But your mom's eyes, and don't you ever forget it."

I didn't know if that was such a great thing. The face was already enough to haunt me.

He dug into the cushions around him, retrieving the remote I hadn't been able to find. "Wanna watch some *Top Chef*?"

"You don't want to watch that other series we were working our way through? What was it? *Umbrella Academy*?"

"Ah, nah. I was gonna call it an early night."

"Now what does a retired guy have to be so tired about? I'm the one who's been shopping my ass off all night."

"You try teaching swimming to a bunch of seventysomethings who don't give a flying fuck, and then we'll talk."

Tex volunteered at the senior center, taking on odd jobs here and there. He'd retired the year before, with a nice pension from his time at the VA office. But Tex had always preferred keeping busy, so the sedentary life hadn't lasted long before he was off on his mini projects.

"Maybe I can swing by the store tomorrow, stock up on apple crullers and brownies so we can binge some of those episodes, or maybe find a couple of shit horror films?"

"Can't," Tex said.

"I thought you had a rule about not working at the center on weekends."

"Not at the center." He wore the mischievous expression he sometimes did before sneaking a piece of pie or ice cream from the freezer. "What? You don't think I just sit around here, do you? I have a date."

"A date? When did this come up?"

"It's not a big deal. I made it this afternoon."

"Not a big deal? It's a very big deal. Where did you meet this person? At the senior center?"

"No, no. It's nothing."

"This isn't nothing. Come on. Tell me where you met? SCRUFF, Grindr?"

He scoffed. "Certainly not looking for anyone on any of those apps. I was on Tinder."

"You naughty motherfucker. Here I've been thinking you're all by yourself, but you've been swiping left and right all this time behind my back."

"I just got on there."

"You didn't even ask me to look at your photos beforehand?"

"I was embarrassed even to be doing it, but one of the women in my swim class insisted, and then she took some pictures and helped me set up the profile."

"So much for a little uncle-nephew time. I was thinking I needed to spend time with you, but I guess maybe my greater concern should have been if you have condoms and if you've been on PrEP." He laughed again. I always prided myself on being able to make Tex laugh, and he pretty much did the same thing with me. Cheering up one another was almost a sport for us. "So when are you seeing this mystery man?"

"He's picking me up at ten tomorrow morning, and we're going to see a movie."

"Seems early for a date."

"We both agreed we'd rather do that than try and stay up past seven. And if I wanna get some action, then after a heavy dinner it just doesn't sound pretty."

"Just remember, if you guys end up day-drinking, you Uber back to whoever's place."

"If I have anything to drink, I'm not gonna be able to have any fun, that's for sure. But speaking of *whoever's place*, I was going to say..." He let it drag on like that so that he wouldn't have to ask, I figured.

"Shit. Are you kicking me out, *Uncey Tex*?" I asked, the way I might have as a kid.

He tucked his head low and put his hand to his chest. "You're trying to kill me here, *Kylie*. I don't know that we'll come back here, but he lives with a roommate, so I was thinking..."

"That's totally fine. It's your house. You should be able to trick out here at your leisure. I'll find something to keep me busy."

"If you can't, that's fine."

I considered my options—hitting Ben or Taryn up. Maybe we could all see a movie... But then another thought sprang to mind. "You know, my English teacher mentioned something about volunteering with Housing 4 Hope on Saturdays."

I hadn't told Tex what happened the previous weekend, knowing full well he would have freaked the hell out. He'd noticed the injuries on my hand and asked if I was okay—with that knowing look he had when I got into scuffles—but he let me have my space. He was good at that. He was one of the only people in this world who got me.

"It's probably fun." I slid my phone out of my pocket.

"I don't imagine there's a way to sign up tonight for tomorrow morning."

"Of course there is. I saw an email on their website. I'll shoot something to them to see if they need any help." I pulled up the site and clicked on the link, pulling up the email app on my phone.

"So you were on their website already? How long have you been thinking about this?" he asked.

"Since my teacher mentioned it last Saturday."

"And when did you start listening to your teachers?"

"This one's cool."

"A cool teach? I doubt it."

"I can't believe you say *teach*. What an old-timey word." Although, obviously, I'd thought it adorable enough to appropriate it for James. "He's the one I helped on the first day," I added.

Tex laughed. "Oh, that's right. Mr. Nipples."

I couldn't stifle my smile. "He's a good guy. A bit of a Goody Two-shoes, but I don't... There's something else there too." I got lost in my thoughts about him until I noticed Tex eyeing me strangely. "He's cool for a teach. That's all."

Cool for a teach. Nice for a teach. Hot for a teach.

THEY MUST HAVE BEEN desperate for people to help out that weekend because the project coordinator emailed me back within five minutes with details about the build. I was a little frustrated that I wouldn't be able to chill on the couch, binge shows, and devour a box of crullers and a pan of brownies, but not enough to keep me from going. As consolation, I picked up some crullers on the way for breakfast. Hit the fucking spot. But when I showed up at the site, I was annoyed not to see James's car in the line alongside the road, where the other volunteers were parked.

You're not doing this to see him, I reminded myself—a lie. Even though I would have been down to volunteer anyway, I had an ulterior motive. I wanted to talk to James some more, like we had in the car on the drive back to

Uncle Tex's. I didn't even know why, any more than I knew what led me to nearly going to that dumb extracurricular event.

James was a mystery to me. There was this innocent and kind quality about him. Part of me wanted him to make some asshole comment so that I could write him off like I did most people. But the more I got to know him, the more drawn to him I became, though I didn't enjoy admitting even that much to myself.

After parking my Hyundai at the end of the line of vehicles, I followed a couple of other volunteers in H4H shirts to the half-finished house. I chatted up some of the guys as we waited for instructions, and I found myself repeatedly checking the drive to see if James would show.

I hated how disappointed I became as we drew closer to call time. Then, finally, I saw something out of the corner of my eye and turned to see James jogging lightly up the road, in a dirty white tee and a pair of torn dark-wash jeans.

He nudged the bridge of his glasses as he approached the crowd collected around the captain. It took him a minute to spot me, and his head jerked side to side as he blinked a few times, as though trying to determine if he was imagining me there. Seemed like this was the last place in the world he would have expected to see me. He said hi to a couple of guys before he reached me. "I didn't mean you had to sign up for *this* project, but I'm glad you're here." A smile pushed into his dimples.

If that smile isn't enough of a reason to be here...

Where the hell did that come from? Chasing it away, I

said, "My uncle basically kicked me out of his place, and since I didn't have anything to do today, I thought what the hell."

"Ah. So that's what you meant when you said I wasn't dropping you off at your parents'."

"You're a quick study, Mr. Warner."

He shook his head, still smiling as he enjoyed my tease. "You ever decked before?"

"Decked? Like a deck?"

"Decking like roofing," he explained. "I'm the supervisor today, if you want to tag along."

"Oh, really? You didn't mention you were so high up on the H4H ladder."

"Consider it James 101, Mr. Forsythe. But speaking of heights, if that's an issue for you, you might be better off inside."

"I'm totally fine with heights," I lied, keeping my cool, especially since, if there was an option to work with him, I wanted in on that.

The team captain divided everyone up, with me on James's decking team, heading up to the roof, while other volunteers worked inside. I wasn't terrified of heights, per se, but I wasn't excited about taking a plunge off the second story of a house either. So I had some shakes and nerves I had to push through, but they seemed a small price to pay for getting to be up there.

James was as good a supervisor as he was a teacher. He made sure everyone had what they needed, took time to explain to new volunteers, like myself, anything we needed to know as we helped nail in boards across the already-constructed frame of two-by-fours. I got in the groove and eventually managed to stop shaking as I nailed in the panels with a guy named DJ. It was nice they had this thing organized well enough for even someone new like me to jump in and do it without much issue.

After a few hours, we broke for lunch. I chatted with some of the guys I'd met since I'd arrived that morning, while James worked out a few issues with the other supervisors, and then we hit the roof again. DJ, who I'd learned volunteered on the side of his usual construction gig, kept me company while we shingled. As the day grew hotter, a bunch of the guys started taking their shirts off, James included. For being a nervous sort of guy, the sort I could have seen being self-conscious about something like that, he didn't seem to give a shit as he tucked it into his pants and started hammering away at his latest obstacle, his thick triceps shifting in the process.

It reminded me of that body I'd gotten a view of, drenched in water, after he'd fallen into that puddle. His pants had hiked down, granting me a peek of his ass crack, a preview of that round ass that looked so tight in the pleated pants he wore on a regular school day.

God, to be able to slide those down his legs and push inside... I could imagine the expression on his face, how he'd moan, the way his glasses would shift up his nose as he threw his head back to call out my goddamn name...

The sunlight glistened off the sweat lining the smooth skin of his back. I caught myself licking my lips, and pretty sure it wasn't just because I needed some water. As though he'd picked up on me checking him out—or perhaps just not tending to my nailing job—I could tell out of my periphery that he was heading over to me, so I continued with my work.

"You know, the easiest way to hammer is to go for it. It'll save you time over tapping it down like that." He demonstrated with the panel of shingles I was working on. "A little trick of the trade."

"Huh. Thanks, Big Man."

"No problem. Here, I can help you with these while everyone's finishing up."

DJ had been called to help downstairs, inside the house, and some volunteers had to leave early, so I was happy to accept the help. As we worked on our knees in pads, I found my glance continually shifting to him. It became increasingly difficult to navigate my way around the roof with the ever-stiffening erection in my pants.

"Where do you work out?" I asked.

"Work out?" He eyed me peculiarly, to the point where I couldn't read it until he let out a laugh. "Kidding. I go to LA Fitness off Kennard."

"Definitely packing on some serious muscle, Teach. It's impressive."

"Weight lifting helps me de-stress."

"What do you have to be so stressed about?"

He opened his mouth and closed it, as though reconsidering sharing so much with a student. He shook his head. "My...wife and I had some issues about a year ago."

"Is that why you don't wear your wedding ring?"

He did a double take, as if surprised I'd made the connection with the day Brian had remarked about it.

"I guess the worst you can do is spread it around to the other students. My wife and I are planning to get a divorce."

"You either get a divorce or don't get one, I'd assume."

"It's a fair assumption. Wish life was always so clean and simple. But back to your question, working out was a good distraction, the best stress reliever for everything going on."

"And what was going on?"

His gaze drifted to off the roof before he answered, in so soft a voice, I was surprised I could hear it over all the guys working around us. "We grew apart."

"Sounds like BS."

"It's as much as any of my students get to hear."

We shared eye contact. I didn't like this teacher-student division that prevented me from getting to know this part of James. But I accepted that he'd shared more with me in this short amount of time than he'd shared with the rest of the class.

"Fair," I told him as I attempted to drive the nail into the shingle like he'd shown me, but missed. I cursed and did it again, more successfully. "By the way, that comment you made about the worst thing being me telling other kids at school? I wouldn't tell anyone anything you said. I'm not like that."

He seemed shocked by my remark. "I didn't mean that I thought you really would."

"I just wanted to be clear about that." There I went making things awkward again, so I tried to move on quickly. "So, you seen anyone since you and your wife split?"

He seemed about to pull his hammer back but stopped. I wondered if he was trying to decide whether the question was appropriate to answer.

"No," he finally said, shaking his head. "I've been spending most of my time healing, but I'm not much for dating either. I knew Sheila for a year before we even started seeing one another romantically. We went to UGA together, met in the library. She approached me...and approached and approached. It was nice having a friend, really. And then, well, it grew from there."

"Sounds like she already had plans for you."

"I didn't mean to make it sound like that. Just that it all seemed very natural and at a pace that was comfortable for me. Not sure what I'll do in the world now. Everyone keeps telling me I need to get on one of these apps."

"Ugh. Dating. Never even done that. I don't imagine I'd like it."

"Never dated? Really?"

"No. I'm not missing out on any fun, but that's the extent of it, if you get what I mean."

"Yeah, I don't really work like that. I like getting to know a person, finding out who they are on the inside."

"I like finding out who they are on the inside too," I teased with a wink, and he laughed.

But it wasn't a joke for me. I would have loved to feel what he was like on the inside.

"I'm gonna pretend I didn't hear that one," he said before he started hammering again.

"Hey, maybe I meant it like you did. That I like getting to know a person...fully."

He rolled his eyes as we moved on to the next shingle. "Yes, as in conversation, learning about their interests and life and hobbies..."

"Funny. That's what we're doing right now." Even the way it came out of my mouth was like I was trying to fucking flirt with him. What the hell was I thinking?

"I guess so," he said, eyeing me strangely.

We continued shingling, eventually splitting up, which wasn't as much fun, but as he worked on the other side of the roof, helping another volunteer with a section, I caught his gaze again and waved.

His brows pushed closer. "Everything okay over there, Mr. Forsythe?"

"Only nearly bashed my thumb in a few times," I joked.

I wasn't okay, though. I was annoyed as fuck. He was hot, and I had only pushed through my shakes on the roof because I wanted to spend time with him.

What little time we'd had to chat felt like...everything, the sort of everything that made my motives all too clear.

I knew damn well why I'd really gone to the café that evening. Why I was spending my weekend working on a roof with my English teacher.

My cheeks warmed as the realization became impossible to deny: I was crushing on my teach.

Fuck me.

JAMES

I was surprised Kyle returned to H4H the following week, and nearly as surprised when he showed the week after and the week after that. Unlike in school, where I never saw him with very many friends, at the builds, he naturally gravitated to a few of the other volunteers, chatting with them, eagerly catching up when he arrived. He was a friendly guy, told jokes, smiled easily, and listened intently to the others' stories.

It assured me I hadn't been wrong to assume Dr. Henry and Officer Howe were mistaken. They didn't know Kyle outside the tough exterior and his odd, at times problematic, social skills. I didn't know him either, but gradually, through what little chats we managed to share, he began opening up more and more, as did I.

We didn't discuss anything terribly consequential. Mostly it was the sort of mundane details that would have been safe to talk to anyone about—teacher, student, or volunteer. Despite initially pressing for details about my failed marriage, he must've sensed it was a touchy topic, and unlike some kids who might have picked and prodded because they knew it wasn't any of their business, he didn't persist, which helped lower my guard around him.

"Me and Taryn were gonna watch this new movie on Netflix," Kyle said as we shared a small spot on the gravel drive during our break.

He took a bite from his burger, some ketchup spilling from his sandwich onto his shirt. "Oh shit," he said, laughing. "Guess that's what I get for trying to put the whole thing in my mouth at once."

I fished some spare napkins I'd grabbed and passed them to him. "You need to soak it?"

"Nah. It's an old shirt. I'd just rather not be dripping all over the place." He dealt with the mess before heading to the nearby trash bin to discard the napkins. When he returned, he said, "Crisis averted."

"So you were talking about your date with Taryn?"

"What?" Given how shocked he looked by what I considered an innocent question, you would've thought I'd taken a swing at him. "No, we're not like that."

"Really?" I reflected on the conversations we'd had over the past few weeks, realizing that he'd never actually referred to them as dates or her as his girlfriend. I felt a little odd for making the slip. "Whatever you guys want to refer to it as," I said, recognizing my blunder.

"No, I don't have a girlfriend or a boyfriend." He seemed intent on making that clear.

"If you do or don't, it's none of my business. You mentioned the movie with Taryn, and I assumed based on some other things you've said, but obviously, I wasn't meaning to imply anything."

"Shit, I didn't mean it that way either. I would be fine to be dating Taryn, but we're not."

"I'm getting a little lost."

"I don't want you to think I was trying to distance myself from her because she's pregnant. I would be totally fine with you thinking I was the father. Hell, everyone else already does. I like Taryn a lot. I would be very proud if I were Timmy's dad—fuck, I'm really stepping in this one." He shook his head. "She and Ben are my best friends."

Again, his comment reminded me that he wasn't oblivious to what people said about him, and that it was evident the rumors were, in fact, just that.

"Can we put this on rewind and pretend this conversation played out differently?" I joked, trying to make light of the misunderstanding.

Kyle snickered before letting out a real laugh. "Sorry. I don't know why I made that so weird, Big Man. Seems more like your thing."

He was right.

"It's fine. I think some of your comments must have confused me regarding how you spend time with Taryn and Ben."

"What we do is pretty confusing, if you know what I mean," he said in a way that made me pause and really reflect on what Kyle had mentioned about Ben and Taryn.

Pretty confusing.

It was fairly clear to me what he meant, and left me wondering if he was struggling with more, but I didn't push. I didn't want to scare him off or speak too soon about something so personal.

Instead, I reflected on it some more before taking it up with Kendra the next time we had a moment together in the teachers' lounge. "Do you mind if I run something by you?"

"By all means."

"If you thought a kid in your class was struggling with their sexuality, what would you do?"

She eyed me oddly.

"I'm sorry. Not the best way to word that." It seemed I was perpetually fumbling whenever it came to Kyle Forsythe.

She continued eyeing me like I'd lost my mind.

"Okay, no need to make me feel like a freak over it."

She burst into a laugh. "I'm kidding, James. I know what you meant. Who is it?"

"Considering the subject, I'd rather not say. I feel like this student has shared a lot with me in confidence."

"That's fair."

"They've said something that leads me to believe they could be bisexual."

"It's high school. Who isn't? Sorry. Last joke. I'll be serious now."

Although, her sense of humor was part of what had helped me open up with her over the other faculty members.

"This kid said some things that make me want to let

them know it's fine if they are questioning their sexuality, and that there are resources available. At my old school, we had an LGBTQ+ program with other student peer support groups and teachers involved. Kind of lax over here, and not in a good way."

"Our school does lack a lot of the programs, compared to the Kensington Heights high school, for one."

"I just mean, it would be nice for a kid like him, if that's what he even meant."

"Oh, so it's a guy?" She took a moment, as though surveying her thoughts for a suspect.

"Kendra, please."

"No, no. I won't try to make a guess...Kline Walker..."

I eyed her curiously before she said, "I'm kidding, James...unless it's him." She winked, making me laugh again. "You know, maybe we should chat more about this sometime outside of school. Maybe over dinner?"

"It's not *that* important."

Her mouth dropped open, and her pupils wandered the room. I couldn't tell what I'd said, but it definitely hadn't been the right response. "Wow," she finally managed to get out. "I can't tell if that was a cruel rejection or if you're just that oblivious since you've been off the market for the past five years."

She'd totally thrown me with that one.

"What? Oh. *Oh.*"

"Don't. God, you can just say no, and we'll act like I didn't say anything."

"That's not why I'm acting this way. It took me by

surprise. My mind just...hasn't even been there lately. But I'd like that."

The nervous tension she'd been caught up in moments before dissolved as a smile slipped across her face. "Really?"

"As much fun as it is eating microwave pizzas every night..."

She cringed. "Don't even tell me that. How about you come over to my place this Thursday, and I'll make you pizza the old-fashioned way? That sounded like a euphemism, but I really do mean pizza."

"That would be great."

"Good. Now that I've conned you into a date, back to this student..."

"Oh, I'll figure it out," I said, more than slightly thrown by her asking me to dinner.

"If you do want to run anything by me, text or call. In the meantime..." She checked the time on her phone. "I should get over to the copier for those quizzes I need to print before class."

"Of course."

A date. I was really going on a date?

In all the times I'd been chatting with Kendra, I hadn't detected any interest, but...I'd been similarly oblivious with Sheila before we'd started seeing one another.

In general, I was fairly oblivious about these things.

◃◦▹

KENDRA and I made plans during the week before meeting at her place on Thursday evening, when she said it'd be easy for her to get a sitter for her kid. We worked together, making chicken Alfredo pizza with a gluten-free crust, enjoying the sort of conversation we might have had throughout the week. It was a nice enough night, so when it was ready, we ate at a table on her back porch.

"That student you mentioned the other day," she said after taking a sip of her iced tea, "have you discussed anything with him yet?"

"I'm not in a huge hurry, but I am seeing him this weekend. I think it could be good to break the ice."

"This weekend?"

"He does this H4H stuff with me. I mentioned it once, and he showed up. Seems to have taken to it." I took a bite of my pizza.

"You don't think he's attracted to you, do you?"

"What? Oh, no. Not at all," I spit out, my mouth still full of pizza. I took a moment to swallow. "Why would you say that?"

"Obviously, I didn't offer to make you pizza because you're nothing to look at."

My face warmed. "Well, you're very attractive too."

"James, sometimes you're like a robot. No woman wants to be called attractive. If you call me handsome next, I'm kicking you out of my house."

I laughed. "No, yeah. Of course. I...um...meant, you look..."

"You can save it for a moment where you're not trying

to redeem yourself." The grin on her face assured me I hadn't blown the date already.

Truth was, I was never the kind of guy to totally lose myself over a hot girl. Sheila was beautiful, but I was never like most guys, who could fall head over heels straight away over someone like that. As I'd told Kyle, I had to get to know a person...well, as much as I felt I had gotten to know Sheila. That was what really turned me on.

"Anyway," she went on, "has he officially come out to you?"

"Not in so many words. I was planning to wait until he volunteers something more explicit before I say anything."

"I would maybe take a brochure or a printout of a resource. Do you have anything from the program at your old school?"

"I might, actually."

"That keeps it very much a discussion with boundaries, where you're offering him something that could be of value in helping him navigate the experience. Obviously, you need to do this in private and—"

"Of course."

"But that's really wonderful that you want to help one of your kids like that."

"He's hardly a kid." I didn't know why that had pushed out of my mouth as quickly as it had, but I couldn't help it. Kyle was no *kid*.

She thought again. "Malcolm Wyle?"

"Stop!"

She enjoyed a laugh before reaching across the table, setting her hand on mine. Her touch was warm, comforting. "I'm glad you accepted my invitation."

"Me too. It's kind of amazing to be able to interact with someone like this after Sheila."

"What do you mean? You don't get together with friends or..."

"I lost a lot of friends during that relationship. Sheila was always very worried..."

"Paranoid?"

"It was just easier that way. Sorry, didn't mean to bring her up."

"It's fine. You guys were together for five years. And it sounds like there's still a lot to unpack."

Even though I knew what she meant, it made me think about all those boxes I still hadn't gotten around to unpacking.

"Yeah," I said, taking her hand in mine.

Even just touching was nice.

Really nice.

11

KYLE

W as it just me, or was James becoming even more adorable the longer I knew him?

Were his shirts tighter than usual, or was he putting on some extra muscle at the gym?

How many days had it been since he trimmed his sexy-as-fuck scruff?

I caught myself sketching his face in my notebook, not because I had any artistic talent, but because his face was becoming a bit of an obsession. Again and again, I'd draw it in the margins of the sheet I'd brought to take notes. I wanted to get the dimensions right, and when I finally got the jaw just how it needed to be, I quickly scratched it all out to keep anyone from discovering my hobby.

As soon as I'd blacked out the little cartoony face, Mr. Warner cracked a joke that earned some giggles.

He smiled like he was so pleased at the reception.

That smile... That damn smile.

It would have annoyed me more if it hadn't been so goddamn *adorable*.

I was constantly fighting both sides of the tug-of-war in my mind. One minute, the way he tucked his glasses up his nose annoyed the hell out of me; the next, it made me so hard, my dick crimped painfully in my jeans as he introduced us to the Shakespearean part of the semester.

I'd never denied myself wanting anyone—guy or girl, teacher or not. But it was different with James. I didn't feel how I typically did whenever I had the hots for a guy. It was much more than that.

Even noticing one of my classmates rolling their eyes or yawning at one of his corny jokes made me want to flip a desk over and lose my shit. I wondered if, at least in part, it had something to do with the night he'd been attacked. If some primal impulse had switched on, making me feel like his protector.

I'd tell myself I simply enjoyed his company or being friends, but that didn't account for my raging hard-on, my balls pulling close like if I made a wrong move at my desk, I might blow my load. Was I thirteen again?

What made it even worse was that, with wanting to fuck someone, I usually felt reciprocation on their end, but not with James. He didn't give me one damn reason to believe he saw me as anything more than his friendly student.

Maybe that was part of what pissed me off so much. I knew all this daydreaming in and out of class was a waste of time.

Not that it would have mattered even if he'd wanted

more from me. He was my teacher. End of discussion. But then all I wanted to discuss was how those brown eyes seemed to change ever so slightly every time we saw one another—depending on the light, or his mood, or maybe simply because I allowed myself to really take them in more and more each time we had a moment together.

The only consolation was knowing I was managing to keep my little secret. God knew, if Ben or Taryn detected my crush, they'd give me hell, especially knowing he was the reason I was busy on Saturdays now. Fuck, I was even taking on an extra delivery shift during the week to keep it that way.

I also found myself working harder on the assignments for our readings and making more thoughtful comments whenever he called on me, same as he would any of the other students in class. The best part of school had always been seeing Taryn and Ben, but now I was excited about seeing him too. I'd wake up practically bounding out of bed, which was a fucking first.

But with the excitement came the pain of never getting to have him, wanting to get him alone and chat with him like we did on those precious Saturdays, which were never enough time, especially when our conversations rarely went beyond books, movies, or TV shows.

Adding to that, it seemed I was shit at hiding it around the house. Tex seemed to take note of that one night when he remarked, "Someone's excited about another Saturday at H4H."

It was a strange thing for him to say just then, considering we were watching *Top Chef,* and I couldn't make sense of what about my getting up to fix a Hot Pocket could have made him think about that.

"I didn't say I was going to H4H tomorrow," I said too defensively, since I already knew there was no way I would miss it.

I'd started watching *Supernatural on Netflix*, based on James's recommendation. He was a big fan of paranormal series, and feeling it would give us more to chat about, I binged season one during the week, eager to discuss it with him when I saw him again.

"But you *are* going," Tex said as I opened the freezer and retrieved a packet from an open box of pepperoni-and-cheese Hot Pockets.

"You sound so certain about something that I could just as easily decide I won't do because you're being a dick about it."

"I doubt that's gonna happen. What'll she do if you don't show up?"

"How do you know it's a *she*?" I asked, grabbing a plate from the cabinet.

"I didn't. I said *she* to get a reaction and decide for myself. So who's the guy?" He practically sang the question, like it was some kind of victory for having gotten that much out of me. As I opened my mouth to give him a piece of my mind, Tex said, "I'm joking, kid. You can have all the secret high school lovers you want."

If only you knew...

I took my plate to the edge of the dividing wall between the kitchen and the living room so I could see him. "I feel like responding to that comment will give away more than I want to."

"It will. Even that gives away too much, though, so Uncey Tex'll take it."

"Ass," I muttered, both of us smiling at the exchange before I returned to fixing my snack.

Fortunately, the only thing Tex had picked up on was that I was feeling something, not *who* I was feeling it for. Aside from Taryn or Ben, he was pretty much the only one I had to worry about figuring me out. Most people couldn't read me, something I was relieved about on the build the following day, when James and I had to split up because we were short a few of our usuals. DJ was teamed with me, though, so we had a good enough time, even as I found myself listening for the sound of James's voice on the roof. I couldn't tell if I was catching it as much as I thought...or just wanting to hear it badly enough to imagine it. As the day wore on, I began fearing we might not have any time together and I'd have to wait another week for a chance to have even the most innocent of conversations with him.

It was stupid how relieved I finally was to share some time with him during the lunch break, when a bunch of the volunteers we usually hung with sat in a circle. There were seven of us in the group, men and women of varying ages from teens to sixties. Bentley—a fifty-five-year-old vet turned contractor with a penchant for tall tales—relayed a story about an epic blunder during one of his contractor gigs at a local elementary school.

Using a plastic fork, James dipped a chicken nugget in

the sweet-and-sour sauce at the bottom of the small box they came in before taking a bite. It'd been just over a month—this was the fifth day of working together like this—but I felt like I was already getting to know some of his little quirks.

As Bentley reached the end of his story, the group erupted into laughter. James got some sauce on his bottom lip, and I watched as he caught it with the back of his finger and slid it in, somehow making that totally hot. He scanned the group, like he was checking to see if anyone else had caught his fuckup, until his gaze caught mine. He closed his eyes and seemed to laugh at himself, and then our eyes met once again, briefly, before we turned our attention back to the group's suspicions of the truth of Bentley's tale.

I appreciated moments like this, where James and I weren't teacher and student. We were two guys having a laugh at a silly mishap, laughing with our peers.

Two guys, one oblivious to how the other was foolishly letting his imagination get away from him.

After we finished lunch, Bentley realized some supplies had been swapped with another build and asked for volunteers to fetch them from the other site. I promptly signed up with James, who offered to drive DJ's truck over so we could pick up the correctly measured boards and bring them over.

"This seems familiar," I remarked as I slipped into the passenger seat.

"Yeah, I prefer the reason we're in the same car this

time." He searched around. "Jesus Christ, this thing's so old, I'm surprised it's not a stick."

"I'm gonna pretend to know what that joke means."

He cringed. "*These words like daggers enter in mine ears.*'"

I had to laugh. "Dude, I'm shitting you. I know what a goddamn stick is. You aren't *that* much older than me."

He smiled, shaking his head. "I'm not the one to tease about that stuff. You could tell me gullible was on the roof of this truck, and I'd look."

It was such a self-deprecating comment, one that left me wondering about his wife, the secrets he kept about whatever had gone so wrong, what had led them to *growing apart*, as he'd put it. But I didn't push as James navigated his way out of the spot DJ had found near the lot.

As we drove to the other build site, I read directions off the Waze app on my phone.

It was the sort of moment that could have made me believe in magic—that the whole fucking universe had conspired on my behalf to put James and me together, even if just for the afternoon. Although, I knew I'd had more than a hand in it, considering I'd nearly knocked one guy over when I'd sprung forward, waving my hand to volunteer with him. Acting so nonchalant about it now was as ridiculous as it was pathetic.

While heading down the freeway, I noted the sweat he'd managed to work up, making his dark-gray tee hug his body.

"Are you?" he asked.

"What?" I must've spaced while I was checking him out. "Sorry, I was..." I didn't even know how to excuse that, but he saved me by saying, "I was asking if you were going to homecoming."

"Are you asking me to the school dance? And here I thought we were just getting to know each other." He took it in the playful spirit I'd intended it, which settled any nervousness I'd had about him potentially catching on to the sincere interest that made me play with the remark to begin with. "Dances are kind of hit or miss for me. I went to homecoming freshman year with this girl I'd asked out, and then didn't really care sophomore or junior year. But Taryn and Ben both want to go as a group this year, and I'm fine with that."

I could tell by the expression he made that he still wasn't all that clear about our dynamic.

He said, "Since we're talking about this, there is something I've been wanting to bring up with you. You don't have to say anything, but you've mentioned your friends Taryn and Ben to me a few times, and insinuated certain things..."

I tensed up. It was one thing when I was keeping the conversation on him and his own life, but I didn't share things about myself.

He continued, "Just...I hope that if you ever need to discuss anything around that, you would feel like you could talk to me about anything you might be struggling with."

Struggling with how much I want to bone my straight teacher is about it.

As I reflected on our previous discussions about Taryn and Ben, I realized I had sort of danced around it, feeling like that was best to do with a teacher. But I guessed what he was really getting at. "Are you talking about me being bi?"

He seemed taken aback by my directness. "Yes, I—"

"I'm all good with that." I had to laugh. "I thought it was pretty clear by the way I talked about my friends that that was the case. If you think I haven't been eyeing Jason's abs for the past few Saturdays, you're dead wrong."

That got him laughing again as he stopped the car at the light off the exit Waze had told us to take. "I feel so stupid. Here I was thinking you might be too uncomfortable to share it with anyone."

"Oh, I'm *very* comfortable with it, Mr. Warner."

He sighed, then chuckled. "Leave it to me to overcomplicate something." Smiling, he hoisted himself up slightly in his seat, retrieving a brochure from his back pocket and handing it to me. "That's what I was going to give you."

As the light flashed green, he pushed on the gas and kept on our path as I read the brochure title: *Staying In or Coming Out? Tough Decisions in the Life of LGBT Youth.*

I practically snorted. "This was how you were going to console me if I had a bunch of deep-seated self-hating queer shit?"

He shook his head. "It was easier at my last school because we had a whole program. I was talking to Kendra...sorry, Ms. Eiken, about—"

"About me?"

"No, no," he said quickly. "I wouldn't mention your name. I told her I was talking to a student about things that made me think that, and she thought some literature might be good. I don't know why, but it felt stupid to begin with, and now even stupider that I was concerned."

The idea of him chatting about me with other teachers didn't sit well with me, but I pushed the discomfort aside as I opened the flaps on the brochure, scanning over the text on the cheap paper stock that had cartoony graphics complementing the facts and information.

I turned back to James, who had his eyes on the road, shaking his head at himself for having thought a dumb brochure would help me with my issues.

All I could think about was that he'd done that for me. Because he was trying to help.

"It's cute, Teach," I said, unable to keep from laughing as I read over some text on the page. "Nice to know I 'have value.' I'll have to keep that in mind. You mind if I keep this, though? Just so I have something to whip out and make fun of you about later?"

"It's only fair. You can let Taryn and Ben know what an idiot your English teacher is, and—"

"You're not an idiot, Mr. Warner. And I'm appreciative you even considered me enough to talk about this. That said, you don't have to worry about me parading this around in front of class or my friends."

Mainly because the moment I got to talking about him, they would definitely pick up on what I was really feeling.

"But everything else is on the table, Mr. Nipples," I

joked, and God, that laugh. It wasn't just the resonance as it filled my ears, but the way his eyes lit up and got these little creases...

Had he always been this hot? No, this was clearly something my evil brain was doing to me. Making me think he was hotter than he was.

What the fuck? Stop it, Kyle!

As I was quickly learning, the more I fought it, the worse it got.

"So that program," I continued, "at your old school? What did they do?"

His expression, which had oscillated between embarrassment and foolishness for the past few minutes, turned serious. "Faculty and peer support for LGBTQ+ students. We tried to make safe spaces and have people the kids could talk to if they needed any help."

"That's kinda awesome. You didn't mind people thinking you're gay?"

"You shouldn't become a teacher if you can't handle students and teachers thinking untrue shit about you. And..." He hesitated a moment before pushing through. "My brother was gay."

"Brother? I didn't realize you had a brother."

As soon as I said it, the *was* in his comment sank in, and judging by that and the sadness on his face, I knew the reason why it hadn't come up.

He opened his mouth, but all I wanted to do was suck my comment back in my mouth. "No, I'm sorry. I didn't get what you meant."

"It's fine. Life's hard, but you move on. Let's just say he

wasn't lucky enough to get the support and encourage-ment he needed, so I'm happy to be there for anyone who does need that. So if you do need to talk, my door's always open."

Damn, as soon as I thought he couldn't get any more amazing, he had to go and share that shit.

His expression had transformed, and I'd spent enough time contemplating my past as I looked at my reflection in a mirror to know what pain and heartache looked like.

"Sorry about your brother. And thank you for this." I indicated the brochure before the voice from my app alerted us of an upcoming turn. "That means a lot, James. Just, um, I do have one thing…"

"What is it?" he asked as he took the turn.

"Do you mind not talking about me with other teachers?"

It'd been nagging at my thoughts since he'd mentioned chatting with Ms. Eiken. I felt bad bringing it up after he'd told me about his brother, but it was some-thing I wanted to state clearly, without question.

"I didn't say anything that would have let her know who it was. I just…I was trying to do the right thing."

"I don't doubt that, but I got enough people who talk about me at school, is all."

There was something in the way his gaze shifted, like maybe he knew that was true from things he'd heard.

How couldn't he have? Rumors abounded at Wyachet High. No one could evade them, least of all me—my own parents having used their position to run a smear campaign to keep me from ever being trusted if and when I decided to speak the truth.

My truth.

Certainly hadn't helped that I lacked my father's charisma and social skills.

Or any desire to challenge anyone's negative opinions of me.

James rolled up to the side of the road, stopped the truck, and turned to me. "I'm sorry. I won't do that again." Then he pressed his foot back on the gas and headed back en route.

Had he really stopped just to assure me of that?

I was so stunned by his reaction, his sincerity and thoughtfulness. He couldn't have known what that meant to me. He couldn't have known what *he* was coming to mean to me.

JAMES

I was glad I'd pushed myself into talking to Kyle about his bisexuality.

I couldn't help thinking that if Cody had held Kyle's attitude about who he was, he never would have taken his own life. Still, despite Kyle's openness on that one subject, it was evident he kept plenty close to his chest.

Each conversation with him was like discovering clues within the mystery that was Kyle Forsythe. Like in any good mystery, there were enough to keep me hooked. Not just for my own interest, but because mixed with all the tension and aggression—this way he had of holding himself that shouted "stay the fuck away from me"—I saw something else.

Masked vulnerability, guarded so closely.

Something I knew a thing or two about.

When I graded homework, I found myself having to

resist the urge to pull his from the stack and reading his answers first. It wasn't just because I knew him more than most of the other students, but his responses genuinely interested me. Like his rather severe thoughts about Ophelia's relationship with her father and brother, something I made sure to comment back on in the margins, while giving him an A since, as always, it was clear he had done the reading. Unlike several of his peers, whose responses either read like they had based their opinions on googled ideas of what *Hamlet* was about or were inappropriately primitive for their age.

Between the responses on his assignments and the time we spent chatting on Saturdays, it was hard not to think that in another life, he wouldn't have been my student. We would have just been buddies. Since that couldn't be, I accepted the precious fun we had on Saturdays and that warm smile he offered every day he'd walk into class. Despite constantly giving me hell about shit I rightly deserved it for, he didn't take advantage of it, the way I knew so many guys his age would have. Certainly, his classmates Brian and Daryl would have given me shit over half as much.

With each passing weekend, we spent more and more time together, goofing off or chatting about *Supernatural, which he'd gotten into after I recommended it, prompting me to cycle through a repeat viewing to be able to see where he was at in each season as he reached it.* He'd also tell me about some of the characters he'd run into while making his deliveries. Or one of his uncle's latest dates. Or homecoming stress with his friends.

We'd been working on the roof, when Maya asked us for help bringing plywood around the house to make room for a truck. It seemed Kyle and I had become her go-to guys for errands, something neither of us minded. We set a board down on the new stack, and on our trek back around the house, I pulled out my phone and responded to a text.

"Is that Kendra?" Kyle asked, a smirk on his face, though I detected something else in his expression too. Annoyance, almost. Like he'd said something and I missed it when I checked for a message, but I couldn't remember him having said anything.

"Now how could you have guessed that?"

"The past few times you've texted, I've seen her name pop up."

What I hadn't told him already about seeing her, I was certain he picked up in some of my conversations with the other guys.

"We're trying to decide if we're getting together next week," I told him. "I haven't told her anything else about our discussion." I blurted that bit out. She'd asked, and I only said he and I had talked about it, but left it at that. I wasn't about to breach his trust, especially when he had been so clear about keeping our conversation between the two of us.

"I wasn't trying to see if you'd told her anything else. Just figuring based on things you'd said that it's going well."

I shrugged, remaining cautiously aloof. "Well enough."

"Don't worry, Big Man." He headed to the next stack we had to start on. "You never push me about anything, and I'll show you the same respect. I'm glad you're getting out, though. Ben's starting to see a few guys now too. Nothing helps you after an emotional breakup like getting back out there."

I was pleased to hear that, since what he said about Ben's last serious relationship pissed me the hell off—in no small part because of how it mirrored some of the disrespect and humiliation I'd experienced at the hands of my wife.

But something else in what Kyle had said caught my attention. We approached the stack of plywood, and I went around to the far side, the way I had the past few times, replying, "I never said it was an emotional breakup."

"That I've heard so little about those five years tells me all I need to know."

"Perceptive, Mr. Forsythe."

"I should get some extra credit on that *Hamlet* test. What do you think?"

"I think you're reminding me why it's a terrible idea to volunteer with one of my students."

We enjoyed the laugh as we made our way to the stack in the back.

I didn't mean it. If I had anything to look forward to during my week, it was knowing I'd get to see him at the end of it.

"Speaking of extra credit," he said, "I notice you don't keep posting shit to the board."

"I got the hint that no one's really interested."

"You should do more."

"Will you actually come if I assign something? I don't know that I need to be flying solo every event."

"I'll come to the next one. Promise."

I didn't doubt him, but it did raise a question that had been on my mind for some time, something I hadn't pushed too hard about the night of my attempted mugging, primarily because we'd had so many other more important things to discuss.

"I have to admit I'm curious," I said as we set the sheet down on the second stack. "Why didn't you come in that first night? When you were across the street?"

He shrugged. "I don't know. I don't do extra credit."

A very suspicious non-answer, but perfectly befitting Kyle.

"There's a guest author coming to speak at the bookstore downtown next Wednesday. Talking about gender and fiction. I can put it on the board on Monday. We'll see who jumps at the chance. Who knows? Maybe people will actually start sweating their grade since midterms are coming up."

"Yeah, I figure some will be like that."

"You never really talk about grades or school. I assume you're doing as well in everyone else's classes?"

"I do just fine. It's a slick sort of way of skating by, doing the bare minimum. Tests have never been hard for me. It's the busy homework that usually cuts my grade down."

I narrowed my eyes. "A little prodigy, aren't you?"

"Shh. You're gonna kill my bad-boy image."

I embraced the laugh, but regardless of the facade he put on, I knew there was far more to him than that. "I have to say, as your teacher, I can tell by your homework you actually care about the assignments."

"You don't know. Maybe I just google stuff and put it in my answers."

I shook my head. "I don't believe that. I didn't ask you to swing by because you were plagiarizing. Besides, I can hear you when I read them."

"You don't know me," he said, and it was clearly a joke, but there was truth to it as well.

Too much truth.

"Don't worry. I won't tell anyone you're not as bad as you like to be seen."

"That's where you got it wrong, Big Man. I don't want to be seen."

He turned to me as we were about to pick up the next sheet of plywood, and again, there was too much truth in his words. I could tell by the seriousness of his expression...and something dark that always seemed to linger behind those blue eyes.

KYLE

"Sorry. Looks like a no-show," the bookstore café cashier told James, who turned back to me. "Not batting well with these events in Wyachet, am I?"

"I guess even the speakers know we're not the best town for cultural experiences. Maybe his agent gave him the scoop." I winked, hoping he wouldn't think I was genuinely disappointed about the event not taking place when the whole thing was a ruse to enjoy more time with him. "We can at least discuss *Hamlet* over caffeine. I have a few thoughts about your BS comments on my last assignment anyway."

"I'm not changing your grade over this, just so you know."

"That's fine. I'm packing in some extra-credit points to buffer it."

He shook his head, his smile widening.

I ordered a latte with whipped cream. "Oh, and two apple crullers." I turned to James. "Go ahead."

He asked for a black coffee, then reached for his wallet.

"I got it," I said, sticking my card into the chip reader before he had a chance to fight me on it.

He looked annoyed, but didn't say anything until the barista began working on our drinks. "I have cash."

"I'm not interested."

He eyed me strangely. "I think I need to set a teacher-student boundary here."

"I'm gonna pretend you offered an awkward *thank-you*, and we'll move on from there. You can hit me back next time...or whatever."

The overhead fluorescent panels reflected in his glasses as he looked me over like he didn't care for my insistence, but he didn't object further, and I was glad.

After the barista finished preparing our drink orders and bagging two crullers, James and I found chairs at a corner table. The sound of my chair scraping across the floor filled the space as I noted, "Nice place for our first date."

"Whatever." He snickered as we settled in.

"I assumed you'd take me somewhere fancy...maybe we'd have steak and wine." I hoped my joke would mask my real feelings, which were unfortunately not very far from what I was saying.

I pulled out a cruller from the brown bag and put it in my mouth as I passed him the paper bag with the other. "Go ahead. I got it for you." I took a bite out of mine and kept the remainder in my hand. I closed my eyes, savoring the taste. "I could eat apple crullers for every goddamn meal."

He reluctantly accepted the bag and took a bite out of his.

"Don't tell me you don't like crullers, Teach, because then I'm not sure we can be friends."

"It's good. I can tell by the look on your face I'm not enjoying it quite as much. You sure you don't want it?"

"Nah. If I can't get extra credit for this trip, then I'm willing to bribe you with delicious treats."

He rolled his eyes. "You'd better stop before you get the rumor wheel churning. I'm pretty sure the barista goes to Wyachet."

"Really? You recognized him?"

"Yeah. He's usually in the freshman/sophomore building, so I assume that's his grade."

"Huh. Go figure. I hardly remember faces. School's always been a blur to me. If I remember someone, I either really like them or they annoy the hell out of me."

"I think it'd be different if you enjoyed school more."

It's been different since I've known you.

"Meanwhile, it must be a nightmare, not only having to get through school, but then having to go back," I remarked. "What kind of nightmare life is that?"

"You're looking at the dream," he said, as earnestly as I could have imagined him saying anything.

"Wait? What?"

"Why do you say it like that? This is actually what I was aiming for as a kid."

"Dreams are supposed to be like...becoming a movie star or the president."

"That's ridiculous. That sounds more like people who are going to have to learn that they can fail at some dreams and then find new ones, a thousand times more satisfying than pipe dreams. Not to dissuade you, Mr. Future President."

I nearly choked on the whipped cream. "Jesus, you trying to kill me, Teach? And you don't know. I could be the next Tom Cruise. But you don't get to turn the tables on me yet. I wanna hear about this teaching dream of yours."

He pondered it for a moment. "I was always good at school. Studying was fun to me. I would even help my friends with their homework. We'd be on the phone for hours at a time. I would walk them through algebra or biology. English was my favorite subject, if that wasn't already clear, but I was the sort who studied and had to study. I couldn't just walk into a class like my brother, who would not crack a book and somehow aced every test. He was a prodigy. Just incredible. And an amazing guy on top of it."

A radiant light had sparked to life in his eyes as he'd discussed studying, but just as quickly as it had appeared, it faded with his smile, as though the reality that his brother was no longer with us had, not for the first time, crept up on him. He shook it off. "I liked helping my class-mates do better in classes, offering them studying tips and encouraging them with their tests. I guess you could say I got a lot of positive reinforcement from my peers around that. And I had some pretty amazing teachers, who inspired me. Who made it seem like it was everything to be able to be in so many people's lives, helping them like that."

"But there wasn't anything else? Any other dream?"

"I wanted to be a firefighter and an astronaut...and also a cashier at a grocery store when I was really little."

"Okay, we all wanted to do those things," I said, reflecting on my childhood dreams.

"Well, what do you want to do now?" he asked, and since he'd been so open with me, I felt it was only fair to be transparent with him.

"I just want to hang with Tex through his retirement. Make my little deliveries."

"No college?"

"Nope. Not for me. I don't know what the hell I'm gonna do long-term. Saving up my money to get my passport and take a trip to Machu Picchu after graduation. Then...stumble around and figure out how to make it all worth it."

"Machu Picchu is awfully specific. Any particular reason for that choice?"

"Just...on my bucket list." I left it at that.

I waited for him to say something more, or try to convert me the way some people had done when I'd mentioned that in the past. But he just listened, waiting for me to share more.

"This is the part where you tell me all that I'll be missing out on. Trust me, I've had that guidance-counselor session. And that I have to go to college, and I need all these specific goals to ever be somebody, yada, yada, yada."

"If I didn't have so many friends in massive amounts of student-loan debt with few career options for their given expertise in our ever-changing climate, I'd be more concerned, but I think the idea that you have to go to school to have a career is fading away as the world transforms. Hell, I would have loved to have been able to run deliveries or give Uber rides in college instead of waiting tables. Just a whole different world than the one I grew up in. And really, I admire that you can be so brazen about the future, without any set plans, without fearing uncertainty. Not that I'm saying you shouldn't go to college, if you choose."

He said that last bit quickly, as though he found himself caught between his real personal beliefs and what he should be saying as my teacher, which was a bit of a laugh. "Don't worry, James. I'm not making any life-altering decisions while having coffee with my British Lit teacher."

"Good. 'Cause I think I'm about one of the least helpful people you could be talking to about life, unless you want to discuss maybe Jane Austen's ideas about life. Oh, you roll your eyes at Austen?"

"Yeah, I'm familiar. My mom had a boxed set of her books that she never touched, but I blew through the whole lot in a few days, and I was not impressed."

"When did you do this?"

"I was like...twelve at the time."

"You were twelve and you just decided, on your own, to blast through Jane Austen?"

"Yeah, a bunch of silly stuff. Everyone ends up happy, with all this money."

"Not everyone ends up happy."

"Pretty much. It's hard to tell whether the happiness was because they happened to meet the right man or the right man happened to have plenty of money. I'm not big on happy endings anyway. That's not how life works. *Hamlet*'s more to my tastes."

"Yeah, you haven't hidden the fact that you've already made it to the end in any of your responses."

"I'm glad you brought up my assignments. As I mentioned before, I tricked you into this coffee date about my homework because I have a serious problem with that comment you made about—what was it—not using contemporary standards to judge Ophelia for kowtowing to Polonius's demands."

"That's a fair comment. I stand by that."

"You don't get to take all the comments and use them however you please. First you say classics are classics because they're relevant to things we deal with still in our lives, but then I can't judge them based on our standards."

"I stand by that statement, yes."

"I don't feel like I was just judging them based on our standards now necessarily. Romeo and Juliet were like, 'fuck what our parents want,' and that all happened in Shakespearean times, or whatever the hell."

"Don't act like you don't know that was the Elizabethan era."

"Yes, at the end of the Tudor period, if you want to get all specific like that. Is this a test?"

"No, but you can see why I'm not terribly concerned about whether you're going to make it in the world." He had this knowing expression on his face, like he could see so much more in me than I could see in myself, all from a silly argument about the last response I'd handed in about the reading.

I pressed on, "Whatever the hell time it was, it was close enough that clearly even Shakespeare thought people could tell their parents to go to hell and do what they wanted."

He smiled. "That's a fair argument."

"So you admit you were wrong?"

"I was perhaps presumptuous in assuming you hadn't considered Ophelia outside of your personal feelings about her situation, and maybe if you'd expanded upon your thoughts a little more, I would have seen that." He must've realized his answer hadn't quite satisfied me yet because he went on. "But yeah. I was wrong, Kyle. What? Why are you looking at me like that?"

"I'm trying to remember the last time I heard a teacher tell me they were wrong about something."

"Now you're being overdramatic."

"No. Obviously it's happened, but it's just...very rare."

And sobering.

"So now I get two extra points on that assignment, right?"

"You got an A just for showing you read the play. But

now maybe I'll consider docking points for being accosted about it over coffee."

"Oh, hell no."

"I'm kidding. Kidding, Kyle. I would never treat you differently than I would any of your classmates."

He said the words with such conviction, but I couldn't help thinking about how close we'd become. Even this conversation was only making me like him that much more.

"And yet, I'm not any of my classmates, am I?"

He reflected on his words. "That's not what I meant. I was saying I would never grade you unfairly. That talking and joking outside of class don't factor in."

I fucking knew that was what he'd meant. Of course it was.

It wasn't his intent that had really bothered me, though, but rather that it so clearly articulated what I was to him. I was just a kid he had a few weird encounters with at the start, who volunteered with him and came to extra-credit events.

Which I did mostly because I wanted to spend a little more time with him. And that, in turn, made me think of Ben getting hung up on guys. There I was, talking about his fucking teaching dreams, my life with Tex, caring about hearing more about his brother... And for what? No matter what we did, even sitting in the coffee shop together, we couldn't really be friends. I couldn't ever talk to him like I did with Taryn or Ben. I'd only ever be his student.

If Ben had done this with a guy, I would have told him

to ditch him. Not worth his time. Yet there I was, doing who knew fucking what with James.

"You good?" he asked, noticing I'd spaced.

"Yeah, sorry. I was thinking about the homework I need to get done tonight."

"Well, guess you're in luck that author didn't show." He checked his phone. "Yeah, it's only seven forty."

He didn't give a shit about spending more time with me, then.

God, what a fucking idiot I was.

JAMES

I t must've been quite a bit of homework he'd forgotten, considering how quickly he'd left the bookstore. Strange, since he'd made a point about how he was never the best about that. But maybe there was another class he was focusing in the way he did in mine.

Regardless of why he'd needed to leave, the chat was nice.

More than nice.

And it wasn't just about what we'd discussed. No, it was more than that. Something about Kyle seemed different to me.

Kyle Forsythe was an attractive guy—that was something I'd known since he'd helped me out of that puddle. From the moment I saw him, it was as though he'd replaced my very notion of what a magazine model looked like.

Those full lips that always pleased me most when they spread out into a smile. The stubble outlining his sharp jawline after a few days of neglecting to shave. Every muscle accentuating his body just right whenever he'd toss off his shirt during the build.

I never had an issue acknowledging a hot guy when I saw one, but it felt different with him, and not only because he was my student. I couldn't put my finger on it.

The following day, I found myself waiting for fourth period. I would catch myself eyeing his chair, imagining he would be there later. Thinking about that friendly smile he'd give me before taking his seat.

Kyle wasn't a friend, couldn't be a friend, but there was something about our relationship that I valued maybe even more than I should have. It was the sort of thing that got me out of bed in the morning, eagerly prepping for work, rather than practically dragging myself to school.

But that day, as he entered the room, he avoided my gaze and went straight to his desk. When we first met, it would have been hard for me to discern the difference between his resting face and being in a mood, but not anymore. Something was bothering him. I just knew it.

So in turn it bothered me throughout my lecture, to the point where I had to keep myself from looking at him since it was where my eyes seemed naturally drawn. Although, when I did, I noticed he wouldn't look at me.

My thoughts returned to the night before.

Had I said something wrong? Was that the real reason he'd left so quickly? Or had something else come up, with

Ben or Taryn or Tex, that had required his immediate attention?

I was impressed with myself for managing to keep moving through class as I entertained my curiosity. I considered stopping him after class, but if he was going through something, he knew he could come to me, and it wasn't my place to pry. Besides, if it was that serious, it would be easier to talk about at H4H over the weekend.

I was hoping things would return to normal on Friday, but he still wouldn't acknowledge me when he came to class, just took his seat.

Not my usual smile.

Or the glances we'd share during my lecture.

Nothing.

When Saturday came, I stood on the roof, looking out to the road, thinking at any moment he'd arrive to help out, same as usual. But he didn't come that day, and I didn't realize just how lonely a build could be without him. Between his no-show and his peculiar behavior in class after our last—what I thought had been—very pleasant discussion over coffee, I decided I needed to address it.

On Monday, as he was heading to the door with his classmates, I said, "Hey, Kyle, do you mind if I talk to you for a second?"

As he approached my desk, I couldn't read him any better than I'd been able to the week before. Evidently, something was wrong.

"Yeah, Big Man," he said, sorrow in his tone.

"Just...checking in. Obviously I don't expect you to

come to H4H on Saturdays if you're not interested anymore, but I wanted to make sure everything was all right."

"Everything's fine. I needed the delivery hours, is all."

As I nodded, his gaze caught mine for what felt like the first time since the bookstore café. I wanted to tell him I knew he was lying and that there was more to his reason for ignoring me, but something felt almost...inappropriate about it. Still, if anything was going on, I wanted to be there for him. Didn't he understand that?

You're just his teacher.

But if that were true, why did I have to keep reminding myself of the fact?

He left without giving up more than that, leaving me feeling so empty inside, dwelling on what the hell was wrong with him. And if that discussion we'd had at the bookstore café might have been our last.

No, I refused to believe that.

That it mattered so damn much to me was a problem. I knew it even as I dug through the assignments everyone had turned in at the beginning of class, desperately wanting some answers...hoping for something...

GERTRUDE'S A TERRIBLE MOTHER. *She's supposed to protect her son, but she spends all this time refusing to listen to him, not caring what he has to say. I know you're going to call bullshit and that I'm just saying this because I disagree with the premise, but I don't care.*

He should have felt that he could go to her, that he could have talked to her about what his uncle had done.

Hamlet fucks a bunch of shit up, but maybe if his parents hadn't been absolute shits, no one would have gotten hurt.

IT WENT on in this fashion.

Kyle's responses tended to be thought-provoking and insightful, but this particular assignment seemed little more than stream-of-consciousness ramblings about Hamlet's mother and uncle. His words were laced with passionate fury and righteous indignation, the entire response suspiciously short, considering the way he usually went on about the beefs he had with the texts.

Had it been any other student, I might have been able to chalk this up to being a lazy response to the play, but his deviated into...something else. And knowing some of the details of his life—about his uncle, the good man who'd taken Kyle in after his family had left him for what the rest of the town believed was his own bad behavior—made me suspect that there was far more behind his words than some pissy sentiments toward Hamlet's parental authorities.

After sixth period, I gravitated to his desk, taking a seat and rereading his response twice more. I wasn't going to be able to get it out of my damn mind.

What are you telling me, Kyle?

I had the worst feeling, which prompted me to inspect the Georgia laws on mandatory reporting: *"Child" means any person under 18 years of age.*

Technically, Kyle didn't qualify, but regardless, I was certain anyone with a brain and a bit of common sense would have told me I damn well should have treated him as I would have any other student.

I didn't have enough to go off of, but even if I had, I couldn't imagine betraying his trust like that.

There was a rattle at my door before it opened.

Kendra stepped in, smiling. "Hey there. Trolling Facebook when you should be grading papers?"

"Sort of. Mostly getting lost in my own thoughts."

She approached, settling in the desk beside Kyle's. I slid his paper between a few others. I knew she couldn't have picked up what I had from it, but I felt it was my job to protect Kyle's precious thoughts from anyone else.

They were meant for me. I just knew it. And I feared the worst.

"So...that project I'm volunteering for over at the William Handhurst library? We had a massive amount of donations, and I was wondering if you happened to be free this week, maybe Wednesday afternoon?"

"That'd be good. I'll offer that as extra credit if anyone's willing to pitch in."

"Yeah, I was hoping you'd say that. I've been asking some of the other teachers if they would do the same. They said they would, but you know how it goes."

"Hey, I can't promise I can actually get any of these kids there."

"Tell me about it. It's fine, as long as *you* can make it."

The way she said it reminded me of something that had been on my mind. We'd gotten together a few times since our first date, but they had all wound up the same. We'd spent the evening chatting, and then I'd go home. She was amazing, but...

"I've been meaning to talk to you about—"

"You don't have to say anything, James. You were very nice. If the spark isn't there, it isn't there. I'm fine with just being friends if you are." She rested her hand on the edge of Kyle's desk.

"Thank you for understanding."

"It is awfully recent between you and your ex, so if you do end up changing your mind..."

"You'll be the first to know," I assured her.

15

KYLE

I gnoring Teach was killing me.

It was the right thing to do, I kept telling myself, but if anything, it only seemed to make my fucked-up crush that much worse.

When I'd been working on one of James's homework assignments during the week, I'd been so aggravated. I wanted to talk to him about so many fucking things, but I couldn't, not to him or anyone. It all came flooding out anyway.

I'd regretted handing it in, yet I was certain if anything, it would be the end of it. He'd see my weird-ass response and disregard it, and I'd know he didn't care about me any more than any other student. It was the remedy to this fucking obsession the growing feelings for him had become.

Or was it a cry for help?

Either way, I was ready for James to let me down.

It didn't keep me from feeling on edge when I walked into his classroom the next day. I could feel his gaze on me, just as I'd been able to since last week. It seemed worse now, after having skipped H4H on Saturday, despite his reassurance the day before. He knew something was different.

Although, the fact that he was concerned made me think that at least he didn't know—couldn't know—the real reason: my stupid feelings for my teacher. Felt dumb even thinking it.

As I went to my desk, trying to keep my cool, I wondered if he'd read it, but as I peeked at him, his eyes on me in a different way than usual, I was certain he had.

He doesn't know what it means.

When class began, he rose from his chair. His biceps and triceps strained the sleeves of his shirt. His ass fit snug in his slacks.

"I wanted to let everyone know that we have an extra-credit opportunity this Wednesday at the William Hand-hurst Library."

My gaze pulled to him. It seemed like he was working to keep from looking directly at me, and as he got into his lecture, I did my best to convince myself I'd made too much of the look he'd given me before class began. But then he handed our papers back, and at the bottom of mine, I saw the note to see him after class.

Relief pulsed through me. I should have been annoyed, or bothered, or concerned about what I'd let him read, but all I wanted was to know he hadn't glossed over it, that he'd really cared. It was a fleeting relief, however, replaced with tension and the feeling of *what the fuck had I done?* Had I shared too much?

No, I told myself. I could blame it all on the play if I needed to.

And yet, even if I had shown too much of myself, this was James. And I knew he would never use any of it to hurt me. That he would keep me safe.

When the bell rang, I headed for the door, veering over to him, sliding my paper across his desk.

"Yeah?" I asked, guarded as ever, curious to see his reaction.

He stood and closed the door before approaching me and resting that sexy ass against the edge of his desk.

"That was an interesting read of Gertrude and Claudius's relationship with Hamlet."

"It was a dumb assignment. You know I read the play, so I wrote down whatever." I couldn't even look at him as I lied, and for some reason, I kept feeling like he could see right through it.

"That's all it was?"

"What else could it be?" I had to look him in the eyes this time. And I felt so fucking vulnerable, more vulnerable than I ever cared to feel.

His gaze shifted, and maybe I read too much in his hesitation before he spoke up. "Kyle, if you do want to talk to me about something, anything, I hope you know that you can."

His words were soft, almost a whisper, as though he

was letting me know how delicate he could be with the truth.

It was all right there, lingering in the back of my throat, like if I didn't tense up just right, it would flood out and I would tell him things I had promised myself to never let another person know. And I hated myself for that.

Why him?

It'd taken me long enough to talk to Taryn and Ben about my personal life, and even with them, they knew some things weren't up for discussion.

But with James, what was the point?

It was something I'd asked myself enough times to know it was pathetic how much I wanted to open my heart to him.

As we looked into each other's eyes again, I felt this flutter of hope: what if none of this was as one-sided as I feared?

No, it's all in your dumb fucking head.

He dragged out a long breath, his hand resting on his hip. "Kyle, I don't know what's going on. And I hope you're okay, whatever it is. But I would like it if you had a chance to come to the library tomorrow after school. Could use an extra pair of hands."

He had singled me out after all, treated me like I wasn't just one of the other students in his class. But no matter what I told myself, I couldn't get over this fear that, even if he did see me as more, what did it matter if we could never act on those feelings?

"I'll see if I can make time for it," I forced out, scared

that anything I said would show too much of myself. "I've been trying to pick up some extra hours for deliveries, so...we'll see." I added, "You gonna tell me my grade on the assignment?"

"It's an A for doing it."

"Well, next time you can put it on the paper instead of asking me to come up to your desk," I spit out, unable to hide the disdain in my tone.

He looked shocked by it.

"You know, like you'd do for any other student. Because that's all I am to you."

I hurried past him, toward the door, grabbing the handle.

"Kyle."

I wanted to breeze out, act too fucking cool to be giving so many fucks in his class, but I halted. I didn't even feel I had a choice—like I'd lost control of my body.

I had to muster the strength to turn back to him.

"I...uh..." He hesitated a moment before saying, "I'd really like it if you came by tomorrow to help."

There was so much confusion in his expression, but he hadn't said anything to suggest I wasn't right. It was like there was something on the tip of his tongue that he couldn't say because he was my teacher. And I fucking hated him for it.

"Whatever," I said, using what strength I could find to open the door and head the fuck out of there, wiping at my eyes quickly as I found tears collecting in them.

～

"Let's fuck," I told Ben as I entered his place.

"Okay," he said, eyes wide.

I started toward him, like I usually would have, when he put his hands between us. "Dude, no. I'm kidding. I'm not fucking you while you're clearly in a mood."

"You're the one who says I'm always in a mood."

"It's true. But something else is going on here. Normally you would just come over and fuck me, not make this big deal out of it, so why is it a big deal?"

I just felt like being balls-deep in Ben's ass would help me fuck James Warner out of my goddamn mind. Not that I was going to tell Ben that.

"I have...a lot on my mind."

"Come on in. Let's talk about it."

"I don't—"

"I meant, let's watch a movie and talk about anything but it. I know you, Kyle."

I snickered. Yes, he did. Because as much as there was a part of my body that wanted to fuck away the pain, I knew it wouldn't work. And perhaps I'd gone to Ben because I knew he wouldn't let me make that mistake.

We headed into his living room and found some cheap, barely memorable B-flick rom-com, the sort he always liked. He curled up to me, tucking his ass into my pelvis. I pretended it was more about him wanting to hold me, as he sometimes needed, but really, I needed it right then too. Needed the warmth and comfort.

Was it terrible that I was imagining it was James?

Maybe that was why I shouldn't go to the William Handhurst library on Wednesday. But I knew I would.

I'd denied myself Mr. Warner for too long already, and the fact that he'd pushed after calling out my BS assignment response, which wasn't BS at all... My destiny to go on Wednesday was now written in stone.

I just didn't know what the fuck the point to any of it was. What was I going to do, tell him how I felt? Push it on him so he'd know why this was such a shit idea? And unfair to me to get together with him, when I knew it was pointless fantasizing about tasting those slim, pink lips, running my hands through his hair, feeling that body I'd seen too many times on builds against me...

"What are you doing?" Ben asked.

"Huh?" I looked down, and he was glancing up at me.

"That move on the back of my neck. That's very... sweet. Suspiciously so."

Fuck. I'd clearly gotten carried away as I nuzzled into his neck.

"I'm not sweet. I wasn't even thinking."

"Not about me. But who were you thinking about?"

He rolled on his back, glaring at me in that playful way he had.

"Honestly, Ben?"

"I think you know I'd prefer that."

"I...can't say right now."

He rested his hand against my cheek. "I'm sorry, Kylie. You know I'm here if you need anything."

"I do. And I appreciate it, little boo. Just hold me, though."

He wrapped his arms around me, and as soothing as it

was, maybe it only made it harder, since I knew who I really wanted to be holding me right then.

And no matter how hard I tried to push the thought out of my head, it didn't do me any good.

God-fucking-dammit, you broke me, Teach.

JAMES

Following our talk after class, I was as certain as ever that I'd been right to assume something was wrong with Kyle. He was trying to reach me, to tell me something, more than what was on that page.

Even when Kendra and I were the only ones who showed up at the library on Wednesday, I was determined to get to the bottom of whatever was on Kyle's mind.

"Like you'd do for any other student. Because that's all I am to you."

He had to know that wasn't true, not even close.

In a room of half-stocked shelves, Kendra and I sat with stacks of boxes, sifting through the mess before I heard someone rapping at the front door. When Kendra went to see who it was, hope swelled within me.

It wasn't only about wanting to find out what was weighing on him. I wanted to see him and have one of our usual chats, see him smiling, be the reason for that big-ass grin I knew could stretch across his usually frowning face. That was the real Kyle Forsythe—cracking jokes and laughing—not the hard shell he showed the rest of the world.

No matter how many times I told myself not to get my hopes up, I found myself growing excited about the possibility of seeing him again, until I heard two distinct female voices, and Valerie from fourth period entered with Kendra.

I embraced my disappointment as Kendra talked us through the sorting process, pulling books from the boxes and sorting them on carts to then get on the shelves.

Valerie was all-too-eager to work near me, chatting me up. It was funny how someone else could attempt to talk to me the way Kyle or I might have, and I was so much more hesitant. Although, I guessed it had more to do with Valerie's pushiness than anything else. At one point, I glanced across the room at Kendra, who was smiling at me, that knowing look in her eyes. I rolled mine as we continued working.

"Y'all need an extra hand?"

That voice was music to my ears as I turned to see Kyle standing in the doorway, smirking.

Seemed like forever since he'd permitted me a view of a pleasant expression. And I felt like I deserved it. I missed that face. It wasn't until he'd denied me it that I realized how much I missed our friendship...no, something more...this connection we shared.

"Hey, Mr. Forsythe," I said. "Yeah. We can find plenty for you to do." I surveyed our minimal progress between the stacks of boxes and partially sorted carts. It would definitely take more than a few of these volunteer days to sort through the mess.

"Hi, it's Kyle, right? I'm Ms. Eiken. I think I forgot to lock that front door."

She likely knew his name and reputation from around school, but I worried he might believe I'd shared it in confidence, despite telling him I hadn't revealed anything about his bisexuality. But judging by his chill response, I assumed he was used to being recognized on account of his father.

Kendra headed around him as he stepped in, and Valerie turned to him. He faked a smile, which reminded me that the one he offered me usually was just mine.

All mine.

Despite knowing Valerie and Kendra's presence prevented us from the chat I desperately wanted to have with him, I was relieved he was here. At the very least, he'd reopened the door between us, the one he'd closed last week, keeping me on the other side of it.

I quickly jumped in to explain our process to Kyle so Kendra wouldn't feel the need, and then we spent a few hours sorting. Not talking too much, not even as much as we might have on a day at the build. Kyle spent most of his time working on the other side of the room from me, but just knowing we were in the same room...what that did to me... I knew I shouldn't have been so excited, but I fucking was.

Kendra had to pop out to drive her son home from baseball practice, and Valerie managed to stick it out a bit longer before she headed off as well, leaving just Kyle and me.

A rush of adrenaline coupled with a swirling sensation in my chest. Why did being alone with him again excite me so much?

I told myself I just missed our friendly chats. It hadn't been so long, yet it felt like an eternity.

He finally moved from his cart over to me. "I see you're managing to grab about as many volunteers as usual," he teased.

"Hey, Valerie came. This might be the biggest turnout I've had for extra-credit projects. I guess people in this town don't care about making As."

He chuckled before assessing my expression. "What?"

"You're laughing again. I think I deserve some kind of award."

"Shut the hell up, Big Man." He passed me a book off the cart I was working from, which I promptly put where it belonged on the shelf.

"You make me smile plenty, Mr. Warner."

"I haven't been making you smile recently."

"Have I smiled as little as that?"

"When I first met you, you didn't do it much. You were that kid who was a mix of helping out some fumbling teacher and beating the crap out of a guy in an alley."

"And now?"

"You're a strange mix of that guy I can crack up with on a roof, or talk about serious things, and the one who totally shut down on me."

His expression turned serious.

"Kyle, talk to me. No matter what you say, I know that response you wrote wasn't nothing. What's going on?"

"I could ask you the same thing."

"What?"

"Your wife, who clearly hurt you so much, whom you haven't quite divorced yet. Every time you mention her name, you get this look on your face like a dog waiting to get smacked."

Hearing him say the words, I felt ashamed, yet I wasn't surprised that's how I'd come across to him. "It's not appropriate to discuss things like that."

"Well, there's your answer."

"My answer?"

"To why I have to stop this."

"Stop what? Kyle, what are you dancing around?"

"Stop coming to builds to see you and talk to you. Because there's always going to be this line. At the end of the day, I'm your student and you're my teacher."

Again, it reminded me of the comment he'd made the other day.

"Yes, that's true." My answer only seemed to frustrate him more.

"So you just gotta treat me like any other student."

"I'm trying to do that."

His face flushed red, in a way that made me wonder if he was about to hit me.

"James, no one can be this oblivious. Do you not get it? I don't want you to treat me like any other student. I've been really getting along with you, and then there's this thing that's fucking it all up. You think it's easy to meet people who actually get you? You know how long I've lived with no one understanding me? And then you come along, and there's just barrier after barrier. All these things we have to fucking walk on eggshells around."

I could feel the hate and rage emanating from him.

"God, I hate this. It burns in my fucking chest." He took a breath, panting. "Mr. Warner, I should go."

"Kyle, wait—" He was already at the entrance to the library by this time, so out of desperation, I called out, "She cheated on me."

He froze.

It was painful to say, but I knew it was the only thing that could keep him there. To let him know he wasn't just any student to me anymore. And it wasn't that I wanted to tell just anyone what happened. I wanted to tell *him*.

"I tell everyone we grew apart," I confessed, offering that phrase I'd practiced telling myself so that when we broke the news to everyone, it would be that much easier. "It started as one guy—I thought it was a one-time thing, learned it was so much more. Then the next. And the next. The professor, the colleague, the counselor, the client. She was prolific. And I was...so forgiving. Embarrassingly forgiving."

He turned back, and I wanted to look away, feeling as humiliated as I had when it all happened, but I made myself look at him.

As he headed back to me, sympathy in his expression, I was relieved, not only because he was back, but because it felt good to finally tell someone my truth.

I snickered bitterly. "Even as I say that, I can hear the

excuses playing through my head. Every time I caught her. Every time I found out... You know, looking back, I can't even remember an apology. Just half-apologies that I considered had to be good enough to make it work. I don't think anything like that is all that tragic or can't be recovered from. I'd say the worst of it was the control. Sheila always had to have control of every situation. Now that we're not living together, I realize how much it affected me on a day-to-day basis, and put me on edge, always accusing me of the very things she was doing if I so much as hit the gym. I was walking on eggshells around her all the time. Stuff like that weighs on you a lot more than infidelity."

His face had softened, but perhaps from keeping whatever secrets he felt lingered in his mind. He was good at disguising whatever he was feeling, basically the complete opposite of my expression, which was apparently totally readable for him.

"Too much?" I asked.

"A little too close to home." He hesitated once again. "I don't know if this is even covered, but am I safe to speak freely, or do I need to worry about mandatory reporting?"

I thought about my own concerns with that, juxtaposed with how he'd reacted when I'd mentioned talking to Kendra about his sexuality.

"I double-checked, and you're kind of in a gray area since you're eighteen, but...you're safe to talk to me in confidence, even if I find out I'm in the wrong. I won't betray your trust. That isn't to say I won't push to help you."

He took a moment, likely debating whether he could trust me, then pushed through. "I know a thing or two about walking on eggshells, but I also learned that trying to avoid them doesn't keep you from getting thrown onto the stairs, or kicked in the ribs... All the stepping on those shells is only an excuse that makes it easier to justify the hurt, but it's all horrible."

I saw the truth he was trying to get across to me in that response.

"Kyle, are you safe?"

"From the abuse, but not the memories."

Seeing him standing there in such a vulnerable state was a startling contrast to the tough and defensive front he presented to the world—to me—most of the time.

He shook his head and turned the subject back to me. "She never should have made you feel like that. Controlled. No one who loves you should make you feel like that."

I wanted to push him about his own past, but it helped knowing he was safe *now*. That was what was most important. And also that he'd actually opened up to me, given me more in those words than he had since I'd first met him.

"The person you're married to should be building you up, not scaring you," he added.

A nervous chuckle escaped my lips. "I'd say I felt that way at one point, but somewhere along the line, I lost my way. Maybe my next wife will be better to me."

"She should be. She should be amazing to a guy like you." Despite the uplifting words, the way they spit forth from his mouth seemed almost threatening. He approached me, moving slowly, his jaw tense as he continued. "A person like that can really get into your head, break some shit that later you realize can't be fixed. It's like that guy in the alley. Somehow these monsters, they find someone good, they find someone who's fucking decent, and prey upon them. What kind of fucked-up world is it where shit like that happens? Where predators gravitate right to their prey?"

"I didn't mean to suggest my wife is a monster."

"I don't need you to suggest it. I don't care what you want to call Sheila, but as far as I'm concerned, she's an asshole."

As soon as he said her name, I felt like I'd revealed too much about myself, but I was more concerned about how close he was getting to me, just inches from my face. I didn't back up, if only because as much intensity as he'd worked up, I knew it wasn't directed specifically at me. That didn't keep me from believing he might haul off and punch me out of an inability to control this primal anger bubbling up within him.

He started to turn, which gave me a moment's relief, until he looked back at me, right in my eyes. "If I were your wife, I wouldn't try to control you. I wouldn't demean you or insult you, and I especially wouldn't disrespect you by running around. I would fucking worship you, because I would know what a fucking incredible human being you are, and that your love and respect are worth my fucking worshipping the ground you walk on. I would cherish you, because I know how fucking hard it is to find someone who isn't in it just for themselves, who puts others' needs above their own. So I would always put yours above mine, knowing, being absolutely certain, that you would do the same for me."

The conviction in his statement, directed at me, made it impossible not to be overwhelmed. My face flushed, my heart totally open as I thought far too much on his comment, feeling a sort of connection that perhaps I shouldn't have. I couldn't even get my mouth open to respond to all he'd just pushed on me.

Maybe we'd gone too far.

The feelings he'd roused within me were so goddamn confusing. The way I was looking at him, the thoughts that plagued me...

"Maybe we should get back to work before Kendra gets back."

"You said you wanted me to talk to you, James. This is what we need to talk about. I can't keep working with you if you need me to keep my distance, if we have to walk on eggshells with each other as we have with these other people, if I can't tell you what I'm feeling."

As soon as he said those words, I *knew* we'd gone too far.

And that intensity about him as he looked at me? It alerted me exactly to what he meant.

"Oh, Kyle. I don't think you should say any more."

"Fine. I won't say a damn thing."

He moved swiftly toward me, too quickly, and before I knew it, his lips were pressed against mine as he pushed me to the shelf behind me.

I was so stunned, it was like my brain stopped as sensation swept through me, fire in my veins, a surge of adrenaline coursing through me. I could hardly feel my limbs, let alone understand what was happening to me as thoughts scrambled. All those fears he'd ignited, about Sheila, about his past, they all shattered, and there was just this moment—the moment I clung to as I kissed him back.

Tasted his mouth.

Felt that closeness with another person.

Relief like I'd never felt before.

Relief I'd wished for in tear-stained moments, crying on the floor and in the bedroom.

The sort of relief I'd denied myself for too long as I kissed him again and again, hooking my arm around him and drawing him closer.

A distant cry in the back of my mind told me all those things that I knew damn well already, all those things I wasn't listening to as I enjoyed the sensation of his tongue sliding across mine.

Had I stopped breathing? *Fuck.* I had to pull away to catch my breath.

Kyle put his hand on the back of my neck, his breath hitting my face as I recovered from the moment, and in that instant, we fell from the heaven we'd created, colliding with the earth.

It was a painful fall. Like Milton's Satan cast from the heavens by God.

Kyle looked at my lips. I wondered if they were as wet as his.

I spit out, "I— I shouldn't have—"

"But you wanted to." He released my neck, pulling back to glance me over. His gaze narrowed, as though he'd discovered some great secret about me. And perhaps he had. Hell, I just had.

"Kyle, I—"

"Guys?"

Before either of us had a chance to say anything more, Kyle whirled around, and I saw Kendra over his shoulder. She stepped in, eyeing us peculiarly.

The real horror of what we'd done caught up with me, reminding me why it was so terrible to have caved in a moment of weakness to the desire I hadn't been able to deny myself.

"Everything okay?"

"Yeah. Everything's fine," I assured her.

Kyle turned to me, his eyes settling on my lips, then meeting my gaze. I didn't have to wonder what that look meant, and I certainly knew better than to think there was anything appropriate about it.

"Well, surprise," she said. "Apparently the sitter accidentally double-booked, so I asked one of the other baseball moms if she could watch Finn for a bit. I appreciate you guys coming to help out, but you mind if we call it a day so I can get back? I'd say I'd leave the key, but I'd feel like *something else* if I asked you to come and also to do all the work. And looks like you guys made a lot of progress while I was gone." She chuckled uneasily, clearly flustered by her predicament.

"I think heading out is a good idea," I said.

I needed to get out of there, clear my head, but how could I clear it after what just happened?

Even after closing up the library, my body was still fucking vibrating from the experience. I wondered if Kyle would try to confront me, but he went on his way. It was for the best, given what happened.

We needed to think this through. We needed to fucking contemplate the serious ramifications of our actions.

"Was everything okay back there?" Kendra asked me. "It looked like Kyle might have been trying to start a fight with you?"

"What?"

"The look on his face."

"No. We were...talking about something he's going through," I explained. Something we were both going through, apparently.

"Oh, good. That makes more sense. Just...that kid worries me."

"He's a good guy," I told her. Not because of anything that happened, but because I was fucking tired of hearing people assuming shit about him. And because I felt defensive when it came to him, now more than ever.

"You know him better than I do," Kendra said. "I'm going off rumors, but as we both know, there's always a little truth to rumors."

"Yeah, and in this case, I wonder what that bit of truth is."

She looked at me like she was curious and amused by my thoughts on him. "Maybe I should reconsider some of them anyway. He did swing by to volunteer and does that H4H stuff with you. I wouldn't have thought he cared about anyone other than himself, but people can surprise you. Anyway, thanks again for coming by to help today, and sorry for the whole running in and out. I promise it'll be easier once I can nail down a sitter who can drive and organize her calendar."

We shared a laugh before saying our goodbyes, and she headed to her car.

As I got behind the wheel of mine, I felt that energy Kyle had stirred. God, had I even been alive before that kiss? I bowed forward, caught between the passion of that moment we'd shared and the sting of knowing how wrong it was.

I recalled a forced kiss with a guy in college during a game of spin the bottle. It hadn't been like that—*nothing* like that. Nothing in my life could have matched that passion and intensity, the desire pulsing through my veins.

And it was unsettling how such satisfaction could twist into an ache, tearing through my conscience. I gasped, like I had after the kiss, taking in a refreshing breath.

Jesus Christ, I was in trouble.

KYLE

To say I was in shock would have been an understatement.

Before I went to the library, I mapped out what I'd say to James. I'd tell him how I felt and why he needed to leave me the hell alone.

That plan obviously hadn't included kissing him, but it had been so hard to see him standing there, in such pain. My impulse had proved more than I could resist.

He was supposed to push me away, not kiss me back. What was he fucking thinking? What were either of us thinking?

If Ms. Eiken had walked in a few moments sooner, I would have totally fucked up James's life.

Fuck me. Fuck me. Fuck me.

As I opened the door to the house, Tex stepped in the kitchen entryway. "Kylie, I was just making some ice cream."

Of course he was. The universe had never been fucking convenient to me, so why would he be upstairs doing Pilates when he could be seeing me like this, his expression showing the concern of one of the few people who knew me too well.

"Hey, buddy. What's wrong?"

"Tex, I just... I can't explain right now." I didn't want to dismiss him, but I needed to be alone with my thoughts. He offered a nod to assure me I wasn't betraying him by leaving him without an explanation.

I headed upstairs, burst into my room, and closed the door. It reminded me of the way I might have done it to escape...before hearing the sound of Dad's footsteps creeping down the hall...and the knock that suggested the beating wasn't over just yet.

"Leave me alone, just leave me alone," I whispered to myself.

It didn't have anything to do with James as much as the adrenaline and confusion that raced through me, and the flash of pain from my past.

I leaned against the door, battling the emotions raging through me.

I needed to shut the world out, needed James's skin back against mine.

I'd taken so much. Pushed too close, breathed him in, licked his tongue...seized every moment of pleasure, none of it denied to me. But with every minute since we'd parted, it was as if all those sensations were slipping away from me when all I wanted was to cling to them and never let go.

What fucked-up kind of world made it so the most twisted of memories haunted us forever while those most precious slipped from our grasp within the span of an hour? I practically chased it through my mind, begging for the experience not to leave me. It couldn't, not when I didn't know if I'd ever have another moment like that with James again.

But it was useless. Instead of the delicious memory, there was mostly the long list of reasons why we couldn't, all the reasons why I'd busted the hell out of there once Kendra had told us to close up.

When I'd finally convinced myself to volunteer earlier that day, I'd had every intention of telling James that I had to stop going to Saturday meetups. I couldn't fucking keep this con going, knowing I was stalking a fucking straight man.

I was all out of hope.

And then he gave me too much.

Because I could tell by the look in his eyes when I pulled away that he'd realized the same thing as me. Magical as the moment might have been, to pursue James would mean threatening everything he cared about.

THE FOLLOWING DAY, I was anxious as ever as fourth period neared, and when the bell rang at lunch, my heart sped up. Bursts of energy spiraled in my chest as my face turned warm. All those emotions I experienced when we kissed came roaring back. If this was how it felt when I hadn't even seen him again, I could only imagine how intense it would be once I faced him.

It was hardly a long walk to class, but the suspense was killing me. I was caught between time passing painfully slowly and simultaneously hurling me toward that fated moment when we'd set eyes on one another again.

This time, with a shared secret.

When we'd parted ways the day before, there'd been this fantasy in my mind where I'd solved it all before class, but that hadn't happened. I didn't have any answers, only questions, so many goddamn questions. But most importantly: had James enjoyed it as much as I had?

I entered the classroom, and saw James seated behind his desk. His gaze shot to me immediately. There they were, those brown, glistening irises, highlighted by the overhead lights. The look only lasted a moment, but all those feelings rushed back through me.

I quivered at the memory of his touch, his taste.

But just as had happened the day before, as quickly and powerfully as pleasure could overtake me, it could as easily vanish into thin air.

He rose behind the desk and began the discussion about *Hamlet*.

I knew he was doing his best not to look at me because it wasn't the same as most classes, where he would treat me like any other student.

No, I wasn't that anymore.

But as much as he tried to avoid me, he couldn't help making eye contact with me occasionally.

Through what felt like hundreds of tie adjustments and the occasional drop of his marker, James did his best to keep it together, but with every error, I felt like all my classmates' eyes would turn to me, as if through the tell of his fumbling, they'd be able to see our passionate encounter like it were projecting across my forehead. That they would see our lips mashed together, my tongue pushing into his mouth, sweeping across his. That they would be able to feel that fucking adrenaline we worked up radiating off me, making my nerves surge with that energy that now left my body aching for more. Hungering in a way I almost couldn't understand, like before I'd learned how to tend to my needs when I was twelve.

Unlike the rest of my day, where there had at least been moments when it seemed like I was flying through time, class dragged on. A fifty-minute period took up what now felt like four hours, until that familiar ring brought our gazes together. I remained in my desk as the rest of the class stepped out, except Valerie, who made sure to stop by James's desk and talk to him before making her way out. James closed the door behind her.

I pushed to my feet and tucked my notebook and text-book under my arm as I approached him.

He didn't look up this time. For a guy who couldn't keep his eyes off me during class, he was sure doing a great job of it now.

We stood in silence, for too long, considering I had to get to my next class and he'd have kids piling into his in just a few minutes.

"Mr. Warner—"

"Kyle—"

We started and stopped at the same time.

"Damn, it's even more awkward than I thought it'd be," I joked, and he laughed.

Again, as usual with us, I was relieved to lighten the mood, give him some relief. Maybe that was the issue I'd run into the day before.

"We need to talk," he said.

"Yeah, but not now, obviously."

He thought for a moment, scanning the classroom. I wasn't sure I'd ever seen him so serious about anything before. "Can you meet me here after school? If you're comfortable with that, that is."

"Isn't the issue that I'm getting a little too comfortable with you?"

"Okay, I'll see you then."

By how quickly we split and he opened the door for me, it was like suddenly we were secret agents.

Just seeing him, knowing we were going to discuss it, made the next few hours that much easier to tolerate before I was back in his classroom.

He closed the door, sealing us within another moment of privacy.

He had pit stains on his shirt, which I would've given him a hard time about had I not been standing in his classroom for a far more serious reason. And yet, all I wanted to do was fucking smell them.

We stood in front of his desk, side by side, in silence.

"Considering you overheard my chat with Simon

Hawthorn, I guess maybe right in front of the classroom isn't the best place to have this chat."

"Eh, it'll be fine. I had to put my ear against the door, and even then, wasn't that easy."

"Oh…"

"I wasn't trying to eavesdrop," I blurted out, maybe a little too defensively. "I was trying to see if you guys would be finishing up soon."

"I wasn't accusing—"

"I didn't say you were." I motioned to the other side of the classroom. "We can talk over by the window if it makes you feel better." God, I wanted us to skip this part. "Mr. Warner—"

"*Now* you keep calling me Mr. Warner?"

"Sorry. Didn't even realize I was doing that."

"Yeah. I guess I haven't been realizing some things either."

That was a fucking understatement if I'd ever heard one.

JAMES

What was I supposed to say after what we'd done the day before?

Until I felt Kyle breathing into me, tasted his wet mouth, I hadn't realized how numb I'd been. Leaving Sheila had been like washing up onto the shore, but Kyle had found me and pumped oxygen back into my lungs, giving me a jolt to help me take that first real gasp of air.

I could fucking feel my body again for what felt like the first time, in a way that left me wondering what kind of zombie I'd been before him.

It was enough to make me question ethics, morals... my very soul.

He'd snuck up on me.

Something was changing between us, and even before that kiss, I couldn't understand it. But when I saw that almost predatory expression before he came at me, I understood what I'd been feeling. And I knew it threatened to take so much from me.

As we stood in my classroom, the weight of our actions upon us, Kyle didn't rush me. He stood not far, but still too far, the soft sunlight from the window blinds glowing against him, and his distracted gaze assured me he was thinking about this as hard as I was. Where did we even begin when we were both, surely, trying to sort through what we could do about what we'd shared?

A moment that, regardless of what happened from that point forward, I refused to give up. I refused to feel ashamed of, not when it was the only sensation that made all the horrors of life feel like they'd been worth it.

"You weren't supposed to kiss me back," he finally said, his voice a low rumble.

"What?"

His jaw tensed as he shook his head. "I was trying to show you how I felt. I couldn't say it out loud, and I assumed you'd push me away and tell me you didn't feel the same, that there was no way in the world you could even imagine yourself with a man, or just me, and then I could have some peace, tell myself there was no point, and move the fuck on."

"That's a very strange plan."

"All those books you got your head into, and you've never read one where someone did a stupid thing because they had the hots for another person?"

My face warmed again. The hots for me?

Even recently, when I'd discovered Kendra was flirting with me, I'd been surprised. Of course, I'd had people crushing on me, saying they had the hots for me, but it wasn't something I had an easy time thinking about myself.

I said, "I guess that's true."

"Besides, you've known me long enough to know I'm not the most rational guy in the world, so we can stop pretending around that too."

We shared a laugh, one we both really needed as we found ourselves in this weird-ass situation together.

"I should have pushed you away sooner than I did."

His brows shifted on his forehead as he eyed me with suspicion. "Pushed me away? I hope you're not going to act like you don't remember kissing me back."

For some reason, hearing him speak the words, even as softly as they pushed from his mouth, part of me feared that someone in the hall would overhear, that the words would fly through the air, the walls, and far beyond, to the ears of someone like Sheila, who would perk up, ready to attack me for my unethical and illegal behavior.

"I'm not suggesting I didn't, Kyle. I did, more than once, and I shouldn't have encouraged it."

"Well, ya did."

He sounded angry, like it was all my fault. If he'd expected me to do the thing any teacher would have done —should have done—in that instance, he was right.

"I'm sorry if you feel I did something to violate you, or take advantage. If you need to report this..."

His forehead creased as he assessed my expression, and I could tell he thought I'd lost my damn mind. "*I* kissed *you* first, James."

"And I shouldn't have acted the way I did. That was totally inappropriate."

"'*There is nothing either good or bad but thinking makes it so.*'"

"No. Don't do that," I insisted. "There is right and wrong."

"Yes, but come on. Can we cut this teacher/student BS for a second? I'm eighteen. I can consent."

"In the state of Georgia, you are my student, so you can't, actually."

"Yeah. I googled this shit before now. So what? Would that be true in California?"

"It doesn't matter what it would be in California. We're in Georgia."

"Where the age of consent is sixteen. So you're telling me some seventy-year-old man can fuck around with a sixteen-year-old here, but I, someone who can smoke and die for my country, can't kiss my teacher who's not even a decade older than me? I'm pretty sure you and I both know bullshit when we hear it—and fitting for a state that has something on the books about alcohol before twelve thirty on Sundays, but I guess not for religious reasons because of the separation of church and state. M'kay."

"It doesn't matter what it is or why it exists. It doesn't change that what we did was wrong."

"Just because something's against the law doesn't make it immoral, and you're smart enough to know that."

"I'm smart enough to know that morality and ethics are a little more complicated than that, and I'm trying to sort that all out."

I was tired of trying to have a rational debate around this. None of it had anything to do with our feelings around what happened at the library.

"Did it feel wrong?" he pressed, moving closer, eyeing me as though he dared me to say I believed that.

"Can we not get into that?"

"It's a little late for that, James." It was like he was saying my name intentionally, because he knew it would affect me. "I'm just saying I don't give a shit about some bullshit law that's about as substantial to me as the pot laws in our backward state."

"This would be easier if you weren't so smart. If none of that matters to you, then at least keep in mind that I could lose my job. I could lose everything over this."

"You think I don't know that?" Again, his words were hostile, projected on me so intensely, I would have thought he'd kick my ass over it all, the way he did the guy in that alley. "You think I didn't spend all night fucking googling the shit out of this to figure out what the hell to do about it? You think I would ever do anything...at all...to hurt you?"

It took me a moment to realize it wasn't anger he was feeling, but hurt, as though he felt I'd thought he'd been so callous in disregarding how it would affect my life.

"I don't think that at all," I assured him, and he caught his breath, seeming surprised by how he'd worked himself up.

"I'm sorry. I'm just stressed. Like I said, I was up all night, freaking and worrying that you'd hate me for having started it. Looking up Georgia schools and laws. I went from driving myself crazy thinking you didn't feel anything more for me, to knowing the only outcome would be you pushing me away and having to deal with that. I hadn't considered the possibility that it might not go down like that, that you were even capable of wanting anything else. You said you weren't gay, and you didn't suggest you were bi too when we were talking about me."

"I'm still trying to sort through my thoughts around all that. Until we did that, I sincerely didn't believe I was. I keep going back through my life, trying to think about ever having felt that with a guy or...anyone. And there's nothing. I knew I felt something different for you. I thought, at first, it was just that I really liked spending time with you—and I admit I was getting a little too comfortable thinking of you as a friend—but then something changed, and it threw me for a loop."

"Fortunately for you, while I was scouring the net on my all-nighter, I got in deep with some Reddit boards—which, by the way, we should probably talk about how you might be demi, especially with what you've told me about how things started with your ex-wife. I mean, your wife. Goddammit."

There was plenty to complicate this.

But he took a breath, and then he looked nervous, almost timid. "So you liked it?" He must've noticed my expression because he shook his head. "Don't answer that. Going by your reaction, you obviously didn't hate it, but...I guess a part of me is relieved it wasn't all just *me*, you know?"

"Yeah."

The silence returned, neither of us seeming in any hurry to find answers to a question that didn't have a yes-or-no answer.

"Jesus Motherfucking Christ," Kyle whispered, running his hand through his hair. "This is such a mess."

Jesus Motherfucking Christ is right.

I wanted to comfort him. I was used to having to console, but how could I help when I was freaking out just as much?

"I know, with everything in me," he went on, "we can't just do whatever about this. I get that. And I hope you know I'm the last person in the world who would ever want to hurt you or stand in the way of you doing the thing you love most." He teared up. "But...I can't lose you either, James. Your friendship. The things we've shared. I don't want to stop talking to you or being around you. I can find a way to live without the rest. I'll manage, but I can't do with acting like I don't give a shit about you."

"I don't want to do that either."

He exhaled sharply, as though he'd been holding his breath. The sunlight pushing through the window blinds glistened in his eyes as he looked so worked up, he was holding back tears.

"Kyle, I'm having a hard time even understanding what happened. I knew I didn't see you as just another student. And at first, it felt like we were becoming... friends. Even that, in a way, wasn't appropriate, but that, I really needed. And enjoyed. It's hard to say when, but it transformed into something else, and now I'm in over my head."

"We're both in over our heads, Big Man."

It was the first time I'd heard him use one of my nick-names since we'd kissed, and something about it granted me a moment of relief. Maybe because it offered the false promise that things could return to the way they were before. Of course, to have never experienced that surge of passion that left everything before that moment feeling so trivial...the mere thought was torture.

He looked to the floor, his lips twisting into his cheek.

Even such a simple combination of intensity and vulnerability now appeared sexy, and I had to accept the shift that had taken place in my mind. I knew he was an attractive man when we'd met, but then it had felt like an appreciation of his aesthetic, like a work of art, a sculp-ture. But having gotten to know him, so much more of him, the shell around him seemed so trivial compared to the man I'd come to know, and yet made all the rest that much more desirable to me.

"So we agree?" he continued. "We can keep being friends, but we leave yesterday behind us and never tell anyone about it."

"I don't want you to have the burden of a secret like this on your conscience."

"Trust me, Teach, of all my secrets, this one will be the easiest to carry."

He offered a bitter smirk, and I knew he wasn't joking. It made me think about that response he'd written, and what he'd told me about his father before our kiss. That he was willing to carry it meant more than he had any way of realizing.

"Good," he added. "So we know where the line is. I'm not letting anything bad happen to you, James." That was classic Kyle Forsythe, the protective guy I'd come to know...too well, it seemed.

But even as we entered into our agreement, I knew it would be easier said than done.

I'd felt too much. My legs still vibrated at the thought of his touch, how his body had pressed up against mine, his lips sealed against my own. It was an experience that confounded me, and how could something so human and rooted in my physicality help me transcend it?

"I'm gonna head out now," he said.

No.

Yes. It was the only way this could be done.

"I think we've said all we can on this," I forced out.

"I'll see you this Saturday." That sweet smile overtook his expression so effortlessly for a guy who so rarely offered it. Although, outside of school, I'd seen it enough times to know how just a tease or a joke could grant my gaze the privilege of its return.

For a second, it was powerful enough to have me fooled into believing that life could be so simple, that we could ignore the consequences of our actions. That we could pretend to distance ourselves from it while being able to cling to those aspects that kept us close together.

He pushed around me, heading across the class to the door, taking the handle before freezing in place.

"James," he said, not turning to me. "Just one thing, and then I can be done with it." Once again, I could hear his vulnerability, like when he'd opened up to me about that response he'd written. "What did it feel like...for you?"

I was torn between honesty and withholding for the sake of what we'd have to bear moving forward. However, considering the discussion we'd just had, I felt he deserved the truth, no matter how cruel it might be for us: *Wet fire, hitting every nerve in my body, searing as it brought each one back to life. Scarred forever now that I know we could never recreate the magical moment we'd shared—that it could only ever exist as a fading memory, the cruel hands of time steadily stealing it from my grasp.*

But he didn't need to know that much.

"It was beautiful, Kyle."

Maybe that wasn't the right thing to say. Maybe the wisest thing I could have done was to deny how it had felt. But maybe, for just a moment, I wanted to enjoy the only thing I'd ever experienced that felt real.

Nervous as I was that I hadn't chosen the right words in the moment, I feared just as much that he hadn't felt the same.

"Sounds about right," he said.

And just as problematic as our words was the relief I felt in hearing them. For a fleeting instant, even my most cynical, agnostic heart knew that magic was real.

KYLE

As I slid into the driver's seat of my car, I leaned back, catching my breath like I had after the kiss. It wasn't just about his lips anymore, or the way he'd let me have my way with his mouth.

It was his admission.

I'd feared—been terrified—he'd deny he felt anything when I knew that wasn't the case, but just as bad was the fear that maybe he hadn't felt it, or not as strongly as I had. I told myself a thousand times over that there was no way, but if it had been so little to him, that would have been as bad as if he hadn't thought of me as more than another one of his students.

The kiss played on repeat in my mind, along with all the caution and apprehension I battled as I tasted him, felt him, smelled him.

Needed him.

Now that I knew he felt the same, it was like I'd been

given permission to revisit it again and again, without worry or regret.

It was all I'd be able to hold on to now that I'd have to conjure the strength to keep my distance. I could restrain my selfish desire, so long as I could remind myself in moments of temptation that everything James loved would be destroyed if we acted on anything as we had before. We risked his job, his freedom. Everything about us would vanish in a moment if anyone discovered what we had done.

If I wanted James, this was the only way I could have him. It was enough, if only because it had to be.

THE NEXT DAY was more like usual. I didn't catch any look from James that left me wondering where we stood, or anything uncomfortable that might have left me suspecting he'd changed his mind since our discussion. He would glance at me occasionally, but as he had before, with those gentle eyes and friendly smile. The simplest of looks had transformed into so much more in my head.

We weren't "back to normal." There was no going back. I would never be able to shake the memory of his lips, his taste, the way I felt he wanted me, the way I discovered I was right about all I'd experienced.

"It was beautiful."

So fucking beautiful.

Even more than the kiss, though, I treasured what we'd talked about. Him telling me about his wife and her betrayal, and me telling him about my parents. We'd shared things we hadn't with anyone else.

We didn't only have one secret, but several, and I enjoyed being the keeper of his.

A part of me felt like some switch had turned on in my brain that night in the alley, yet I was aware that what had led me to that extracurricular assignment had been more fascination with James than this overprotective impulse that just grew in intensity the more I got to know him, the more we got to know one another.

I believed Saturday would be the real test for how we would manage our agreement. And even just waking up was different. Normally I was groggy, tired from the deliveries I'd made Friday night, but I headed out, refreshed and eager. When I arrived at the site, I parked alongside the street, and as I walked past the cars, took note of James's. Then I noticed him farther down the drive, chatting with the usual gang, his gaze shifting to me as though he'd been waiting to see me as much as I'd been waiting to see him.

He didn't stifle that broad grin or that gleam in his eyes, one that had me thinking that everyone could read what the warmth in his expression really meant. Although, the obliviousness in everyone's expressions reminded me that no one could read our thoughts, despite how loud mine were screaming as I replayed that kiss for maybe the thousandth time since Wednesday.

He wore a dark-gray pullover that let me know I wouldn't be getting to see his gun show that day, but as long as he kept smiling like that, I wouldn't care. I caught up with DJ, Hanna, Bentley, and Maya before we hit the roof, working with some newbies while James did his usual thing. There was a sort of calm to it, not that sting like I'd felt before our talk. We shared the occasional looks as we did in class, and it was enough, until we found ourselves at lunch, on our own, since DJ, Maya, and Bentley had to chat with Hanna about solving an issue inside the house we were working on.

I wasn't much of a believer, but if I had been, I would have thought God, or the universe, or some sadist demon that interfered with our lives, had conspired to pull us apart from the crowd.

"Tex doing well?" James asked.

"Going on another day-date today. I think he's decided these Saturdays are his time to make the magic happen."

As James laughed, some of the remaining tension between us dissolved. It would take time, I was sure. We weren't out of the woods, not while he was coming to terms with some things about himself as well as what must have been the real worry about what we'd done affecting his life if anyone found out. Not to mention those things he'd told me about Sheila.

"I know we had a lot to discuss at once before," James said, "but now that we've gotten that out of the way, I figure there might be other things you'd want to chat about...with a friend." He was talking about what I'd shared about my parents.

"Yeah, that was all I was ready to talk about then. Maybe even more than I was ready to talk about."

"I understand. Feels like being human is having these

gaping wounds you run around hiding so no one else can pick at them. Then someone gets a glimpse, and it makes it all feel—"

"A little more bearable. Sorry, I didn't mean to interrupt."

"No, that was exactly where I was going."

We shared a look, two men who'd seen each other's open wounds—just enough to know.

"Maybe we could make a deal," I said. "I'll show you mine if you show me yours?"

His expression revealed just what a painful request it was. I didn't have any expectation of him taking me up on it, but before I had the chance to chalk it up to a joke, he said, "Deal."

We looked into one another's eyes. Obviously, it wasn't the first time we'd done that, far from it, but it felt like it was a first something. I'd gone through so much of my life wanting to be invisible, but I wanted James to see me...the real me.

We didn't say anything more about the agreement as we continued working, but I'd taken it seriously, and for some reason, judging by the way he'd said it, I knew he had too.

If I wanted to know more about James's wounds, I'd have to share mine. It wasn't something I was eager to do, but it was what had to be done if I had any chance of getting to his.

And that's what I wanted so fucking badly, it burned in my goddamn chest.

I nappropriate, that's what my relationship with Kyle was. Since we'd practically made out, there was no doubt in my mind about that. But it was even worse that, despite the potential consequences and our conversation about our actions, I didn't want it to stop there.

Any opportunity to see him excited me, including the H4H's annual Thanksgiving party. When Maya and DJ had first asked him if he'd be in attendance, he said yes, his gaze meeting mine, as though he wanted me to know in hopes that I'd be there too. I assured the group I would be attending too, and I could see his expression shift subtly to relief.

When that evening arrived, I headed through DJ and Maya's house, carrying a pecan pie and a broccoli casserole. I said some friendly *hellos* to the volunteers I recognized as I worked my way to the designated dish table. Then I searched around for Kyle, doubting he'd be there just yet. I hadn't seen his car outside, though I wondered if he might have carpooled with some of the others. I navigated into the kitchen, where I found spaces for the main dish and dessert.

"Hey," I heard behind me.

A calm moved through me, the sort that reminded me of the familiar ease I would get after I was prescribed Xanax to help me through my separation. Strange to think that Kyle was the reason for my anxiety and also the subsequent ease his presence offered.

I turned to see him in a hoodie and jeans like the ones he'd been wearing the last few Saturdays. He stood what seemed like just a little too close.

"Hey, Kyle," I said, enjoying the sensation of his name slipping past my lips.

"That your pecan pie you were telling me about?"

"Yeah, and that right there, broccoli casserole."

"I made lemon squares—or I should say, Tex helped me—and Brussels sprouts."

"I'll have to try some."

"Good, 'cause I definitely wanna taste your pie." The way he said it, slowly, his lips moving in a peculiar way, it seemed like he intended it as innuendo, but admittedly, everything that came out of his mouth now sounded like that to me. Funny how quickly things went from innocent to not-even-slightly innocent.

His gaze shifted up and down, looking over my shirt. I could tell he noticed, and I was glad, especially as he bit down on his bottom lip.

"That might be my favorite shirt, Mr. Nipples." He winked.

I snickered. "How's Taryn's kid?"

She'd had the baby the week before and had been out of school—to the delight of plenty of Wyachet High gossips, as they awaited her return. At our last build, Kyle had told me about staying with her at the hospital the night she went into labor, reminding me that he was as good a friend as I imagined him to be.

Kyle perked up. "Little guy's doing great. Thanks for asking."

"Did she end up going with Timmy?"

"Nah. And I tried to push for Kyle Jr., but she went with Matthew. Very respectable name, I thought. She's gonna have her hands full, but she's got really supportive parents, eager to help out wherever they can. Ben's already been planning the kid's wardrobe for the next three decades, so I doubt he'll ever want for new clothes."

I laughed. "I'm glad to hear that."

A loud holler came from nearby.

We turned to DJ, who embraced us with open arms. "Ah, my two best buddies!" he exclaimed, and I could tell he'd already had too much to drink. Although, I couldn't blame him when I was eager to get some wine in me.

As we got to chatting with our mutual friends, Kyle and I wound up parting ways, each of us working the room, chitchatting with everyone.

I didn't meet up with him again until the place was packed and Kyle and I were in line for food with the rest of the gang, paper plates in hand. I nearly ran into him as he stopped me at his Brussels sprouts, glaring between me and the dish as though I had better make sure to get some. I didn't hesitate, but he must have caught something in my expression as I stuffed some on my plate because he said, "You don't like Brussels sprouts, do you?"

"Not a huge fan."

"Damn. And here I was gonna impress you with the things I could do to a vegetable. Well, you didn't have to get so many, if you don't like them."

I was getting quite a few for someone who wasn't a fan, but it had more to do with who had made them than the sprouts themselves.

"No, no. I'm curious to try them," I insisted.

He eyed me peculiarly, but went on before grabbing some lemon squares. "Please tell me you don't have some anti-lemon-square thing I don't know about."

"Definitely a fan of lemon squares." And there was that smile again...

Fuck me.

We sat beside one another on the living-room sectional, and I kept noticing him eyeing me. "You're gonna keep watching me until I try your—or your and Tex's—Brussels sprouts, aren't you?"

"Fuck yeah."

"Okay, I'll give it a go, but keep in mind, I haven't had these since I was eight."

"Then maybe it'll surprise you."

I forked one into my mouth, anticipating the worst... And I could tell by Kyle's expression he'd already detected my reaction, so I allowed myself the full cringe as the potent flavor intensified on my tongue.

"That bad?" He slapped his hand against his face. "And here I figured I would impress you with my cooking."

"Maybe it's an acquired taste." I definitely meant that as innuendo.

"I'm not gonna sit here and let you acquire it when I could be having these." He stabbed his fork into one and took a bite.

"Thief!"

He closed his eyes, savoring the sprout in a way I could never imagine myself doing.

"You're not gonna eat 'em," he said with his mouth full.

"Yes, I am."

"I'm not going to let you miserably eat my amazing Brussels sprouts. Be a good Big Man and share."

I moved my plate closer to him, inviting him to continue, not just because I didn't care to eat them myself, but to enjoy the satisfied expression on his face as he dug in.

"You guys mind if I join you?" Maya asked.

"Of course not." As much as I was greedy about my time with Kyle, I knew I couldn't hoard him all to myself. If not Maya, it would have been DJ or Bentley soon enough, so I treasured the moment we shared as she pulled up an ottoman near us. It wasn't long before DJ and Bentley joined us, as I'd anticipated, along with a few other guys, and between our conversation and the wine, it was easy to relax into the experience.

I didn't see much of an issue being near Kyle as we ate our main course, but when we started on dessert, I couldn't help noticing him with a slice of my pecan pie, vanilla ice cream packed on the side, a glop of whipped cream covering both, and circles of chocolate syrup spiraled around the whole mess. I waited impatiently for his reaction, hoping for something better than mine to his Brussels sprouts.

He seemed to catch my expression before noting to Maya, "He hated my Brussels sprouts, so I'm gonna be such a dick about this even if it's good."

She laughed, and he left me lingering in suspense as he settled a spoonful near his mouth.

"I'm gonna blame all the ice cream and chocolate syrup if you don't like it."

"This is the best way to eat pecan pie," he insisted before sliding it into his mouth.

He closed his eyes, his cheek pushing out slightly, a bit of the whipped cream still on his bottom lip. He licked the opposite side as he opened his eyes and cringed. "Just disgusting," he said in what seemed to be the most facetious tone he could manage.

Maya and Bentley laughed as he grinned like he was so goddamn proud of himself for how he'd teased me. Then he took another bite, the whipped cream from the first one remaining on his lip.

"Yeah, I bet you're real proud of yourself for that."

"Whatever."

"I think I'm gonna go grab some of that myself," Maya said. "Judging by your actual expression when you tried it, it's pretty good."

"It's amazing," I noted, "and takes the skill of someone who knows how to cook the pecans just right, thank you very much."

Kyle smiled, but still didn't give me props.

Maya headed off to get dessert while DJ and Bentley got into a playful argument about a contract job they were working on together. That was my chance to tell Kyle, "While you're being so cocky, I should tell you that you have some whipped cream on your lip."

"Oh yeah?" he asked, wiping, but missing it, seemingly intentionally.

"Your bottom lip."

He wiped again, in an even more dramatic fashion, as though to emphasize he wasn't interested in actually getting it off his face.

"You know exactly where it is."

"You know where it is too, so why don't you get it for me." His gaze was all challenge and interest. He had to know how much I wanted to wipe it right off, touch his flesh and those lips that had felt so good against mine.

Had he set me up? Had it all been a ruse, his act of shoving that bite in his mouth to catch my attention? It felt like a trap, but one I didn't mind stumbling right into.

I raised my hand to his face, and he held still as I wiped my thumb across his bottom lip. I felt like our wicked intentions were so transparent. Like Bentley or DJ were moments away from commenting on it, but no one said anything. Another secret that was just ours, and why did that feel so right when it should have felt wrong, evil even?

He licked right in the spot I'd removed the cream from before winking. I turned to make sure Bentley and DJ were still too busy chatting to notice me sticking my thumb in my mouth, enjoying the flavor of the cream, but mostly knowing where it had been.

As I took a bite from his lemon bar, he seemed just as interested in my reaction.

I shook my head. "No. You started this, so I'm not going to tell you how amazing it is."

He burst into another laugh. "Just did."

Maya returned with a slice of my pie and a few extra desserts, and we continued our conversation, but throughout, I found my eyes returning to see Kyle enjoying the rest of my pecan pie, licking his lips to ensure he'd removed all the whipped cream, as though he wanted to make it clear he'd always had the power to do that from the first instance.

"You keep looking like you want some of your own pie," he said.

"Yeah, I think I might go grab some too."

"I got the last slice," Maya said.

"Well, guess it's an excuse to try something else, then."

"Here..." Kyle cut into his slice. Seemed like an innocent enough gesture before he slid his spoon around his plate, inviting me to take it. I could have used my own, but I went ahead, took his utensil, and helped myself to the bite he'd prepared for me, with plenty of whipped cream and chocolate syrup for me to enjoy.

Mmm...it was good, but I enjoyed letting his spoon rest on my tongue.

"Ew. Boys, that's so gross, sharing silverware like that," Maya remarked.

I pulled it out. "I hardly even thought about that," I lied, making eye contact with Kyle, who clearly already knew the truth. "Ah, well."

I pushed it across my tongue a little more, wanting to get what bit of him I could in me, whatever had been left over on the spoon before he'd passed it to me. Then I placed it back on the plate and handed it back to him.

The way Maya continued with the conversation we'd been having about her new job, it was evident she wasn't catching how Kyle just shoved the spoon back in his mouth, sliding it along his tongue, making eye contact with me to the point where I couldn't even look at him because it was making me blush so hard. But I could tell out of my periphery that he hadn't stopped.

There was this fear within me that Maya must've been able to catch on, that surely if his actions didn't give us away, then my reaction would, but she seemed too involved in her story about her coworkers to notice.

My cheeks remained warm, like a low rumbling fire lingered just beneath my flesh. My breathing steadied, my mind where it shouldn't have been as I thought about those wet lips...and his eyes on me, filled with that familiar determination.

So very fucking inappropriate.

21

KYLE

I wasn't sure if I was imagining things, but that spoon tasted like him, like that flavor I'd gotten to enjoy for far too brief a moment. I let the metal linger on my tongue, knowing I must've absorbed what bit of his saliva remained on the spoon. I didn't stop looking at him, and I could tell he was trying to avoid looking back, the way he would in class. But God, I could feel his desire to, as if it were pulsing through my goddamn veins.

Look at me, goddammit.

I tried to psychically speak to him, as I would sometimes in class.

He just needed to give me a peek so I could get that rush that thrilled me in a way that always left me wanting more, but even when he did that, it only made me realize he could grant me so much and then strip it from me so quickly.

That seemed cruel. And so fucking unfair.

I thought about all my attempts at getting my truth down. I'd finally mustered the strength to bring something with me, having committed to myself to hand it over to him.

But now that he was so close and I knew I could make the opportunity, it seemed foolish. He wouldn't understand. He might even judge me for the way I had my heart scattered across paper.

I didn't want to give that to anyone, but I knew it was the only chance I had at finding out the truth about him. It was a risk I was willing to take.

After we finished dessert, James and I parted ways again as we continued catching up with everyone. Whenever I had the chance, I positioned myself so I could see where he was in the room. I would need to keep my eyes on him, and just knowing he was there was enough. I'd be able to tell when the right moment was, feel it and let it guide me to sharing the unshareable.

I found that chance when he excused himself from the group he was talking with. He appeared to be heading for the bathroom, so I slipped away from the guys I was talking to before finding him in line behind several others.

"Hey, follow me," I told him.

He looked at me with a fair amount of suspicion, as he should have, but did as I told him, almost as if he knew I wouldn't have pulled him away without a good reason.

"Here," I said, guiding him to the upstairs bathroom. "Maya showed me earlier. Said it was fine for us to use." I waved him inside.

"No, you can go ahead."

"You were first in line. It's only fair."

That suspicion lingered in his expression before he stepped in, and I was right on his heels, closing the door behind us.

He whirled around.

I hadn't meant to cave to my desire, but he was so close and his lips were right there. I wasn't going to deny myself anything, and he was going to have to stop me, if that's what he wanted. I pushed him back against the wall between the toilet and the bathroom sink, keeping just enough distance, but moving my lips closer.

Why didn't he fucking push me away? Why did he make this so fucking hard?

I had to use every bit of strength in me to keep a minimal distance between us. It wasn't right for me to push when so much was at stake for him.

His lemon-scented breath filled my nose.

He licked his lips like he was wetting them so I could take them.

As my body recalled how it had felt to kiss him in the library, I knew if I went any further, it might be too late for either of us to stop.

Push me away. Tell me no.

But he didn't. *Of course he fucking didn't.* He wanted me as bad as I wanted him.

And it was cruel to do this to him.

"I'm sorry, I'm so sorry," I said quickly, pulling away, and he stood still, looking at me with surprise, but it was clear by his expression, not totally against my actions. "I just needed a moment."

"It's fine." As the words came out of his mouth, seeing that beautiful face, it was still too much...

I could do this. I could fucking control myself around him, if only because I had no other choice.

"This wasn't why I came in here, I promise."

Although, I was tempted to bail on the real reason. I could walk out, leave all of it behind me. But I reminded myself it wasn't just about exposing my wounds. It was the tool to seeing his.

And I could see that fucking loneliness written all over his face. No one was there for him, not in the way I wanted someone to be.

I bit the bullet and reached into my back pocket, retrieving the folded notebook pages, handing them to him.

He glanced at them in shock. As he started sifting through them, I said, "No. Not here, please. When you get home. Those are only for you."

His expression revealed that he didn't really know how to react to what I'd just done, that maybe he hadn't believed I'd follow through. I sure didn't believe I had.

"I was shit at getting it all down on one page," I added. "Kept tearing sheets out again and again, so I gave up and figured the truth is just as messy, but it's all in there, in some way that my mind would allow me to put it together for you."

I moved closer to him once again, testing my own discipline, my ability to control this raging storm that would have had my arms around him, my nose pressed into his face, my tongue buried in his mouth.

In another world, one not so different from our own, that's what we would have done, without consequence or regret. His body and mine, our souls battling it out through each lick and caress.

I took a breath to quiet the violent impulses within me before resting my finger against the papers I'd handed him, saying, "That's...my wound, and when you're ready, I want to see yours."

He nodded, his gaze shifting to my lips, then said, "You should probably leave the bathroom now. I actually have to go."

My laugh pulled me from that desire that had seemed so overwhelming only moments before. "Okay. I'll leave you alone...for now."

His subtle smile reassured me in the way I needed, even though I was terrified of leaving him alone with that information.

But with what strength I still had in me, I headed out, starting down the stairs, when I thought, *Fuck, I actually need to go to the bathroom too.*

22
___

JAMES

After Kyle had handed me those papers, complete with the torn edges from a spiral-bound notebook, I'd wanted to sneak away from the party to see what they said. Between everything I'd discovered so far and what I suspected, I wanted to pull back the curtain to reveal all the truths Kyle hid from the rest of the world, those things he'd given just to me.

It was a privilege that hadn't gone unnoticed.

As the party continued, my mind kept revisiting those things he'd shared with me the day of our kiss, the day I realized Kyle Forsythe had led me to see a part of myself I'd previously been unaware of.

When I finally had a chance to get away, I was practically shaking with excitement as I drove home. I wasn't sure if it was the thrill of getting to know the truth or if I was still reeling from the moment we'd shared in the restroom, when I'd had to use every ounce of strength I possessed to keep from claiming his beautiful mouth again.

But as soon as I rounded the corner at the bottom of the cul-de-sac, seeing my drive, I noticed the familiar SUV, which had the power to catapult me from excitement to frustration instantly. As I pulled alongside it, I expected to see her inside, but she wasn't.

What the...?

I checked my phone for a message.

Unread texts from Kendra and Miguel, a geometry teacher I'd become friendly with, but nothing else.

I tucked Kyle's precious secrets in my back pocket before heading along the drive, wondering if she'd really had the audacity to break into my home.

I tried the knob.

Unlocked.

I hadn't left it unlocked. Had she been so presumptuous to use the key I'd hidden outside in the same place as I used to when we'd lived together? I was on edge, not just from her intrusion, but because it interrupted the private moment I believed I would have with Kyle's thoughts.

"Honey, I'm home," Sheila announced, her voice coming from the kitchen.

I headed through the short hall to catch her at the dining table, a glass of red wine in hand.

I froze in place.

She must've read the expression of horror on my face before I spit out, "Sheila, what are you doing?"

"Relax. I wanted to chat, and you weren't here."

"Did you use the spare key I left outside?"

She seemed appalled by the suggestion, eyeing me as though I'd lost my grip on reality. "I can't believe you would accuse me of that. No, it was unlocked. You really need to be more careful. I assumed you were home. And even if I had used it, it's not like I'm a criminal."

Flashbacks of so many fights, so many times when valid accusations were met with equally dismissive expressions or irreverence toward my feelings.

Why would you look through my phone?

Why can't you believe I love you?

You don't have the right to feel that way.

Are you okay? I think you might need help, James.

Before I had a chance to collect my thoughts or make sense of her presence or what she was saying, she went on, "I brought over some of your things that you left at the house. Suits, ties, toiletries. I put the Christmas ornaments and lights together too—you know I won't bother with that. I added them to your stack. If you need help unpacking, by the way..."

I was sweating—why was I fucking sweating?

"I don't."

"You're welcome. I didn't have to do that since you just decided to leave all that when you left in such a hurry."

"I think you must be forgetting the reason *why* I left in such a hurry."

"Things happen in marriages, James. Everyone has stuff."

"We had a lot of *stuff*."

"Some of those you made into bigger deals than they were."

"Brent Wilson?"

Her face froze in that familiar expression that at one time I had such difficulty reading. It was one of her many lying faces.

She downed the rest of her wine. I wasn't sure if she needed it after my accusation or if she figured she wouldn't be able to stay very long after that.

She set the glass down on the counter behind her. "Since apparently all you want to do is fight, I guess I should go."

Fight? Me?

I wanted to shout at her that she was the one who had come into my home, uninvited, so she could remind me of all the crap I still didn't want to deal with, when the only reason I was even still married to her was so that she wouldn't be "inconvenienced." However, I bit my tongue, since any amount of time spent dwelling on that would be more time she spent sticking around.

I turned toward the door to usher her out when she said, "What's that?" As I turned back to her, she added, "Sticking out of your back pocket."

I reached back, felt the papers Kyle had handed me. "Nothing."

I'd never been a good liar, especially to her. Detecting the suspicion in her eyes, I said, "That's not really any of your business, Sheila."

"You know I hate it when you say that."

I imagine a liar like you would.

I guided her back to the front door. We exchanged stiff goodbyes before she left me to myself once again.

But I wasn't really alone.

With whatever she'd left behind with my boxes, she'd also stirred up all those goddamn memories I never seemed to be able to totally push to the back of my mind. Just when I'd been feeling so good, so alive, after seeing Kyle, and eager to read what he'd given me at DJ and Maya's.

I headed to my office, slipping the papers out of my pocket as I sat behind my desk, same as I had when I'd read some of Kyle's responses from class.

Unfolding them—he'd divided them in four places, like he might have done if he was the kind of student to pass a note to a friend at school—it was like opening a book, ready to experience this whole other reality, fearing what I might find.

Scribbles and a tear across the top sheet from where he'd clearly either thrown it away or attempted to before deciding to give it to me.

I went to the next and then another before something more than incoherent scribblings were on the page, and soon, between the scratched-out phrases and the repeats, I was starting to catch on to the truth.

I don't know why this has to be so hard. It should be easy, take up a few paragraphs.

I keep thinking I need to go back and connect it to Claudius and Gertrude, and then maybe you'll think I'm clever. But then I figure this needs to be straightforward, from my heart, but I don't want to do that either. It hurts too much when I try to write it down. My hand freezes up. It's like the muscles stop working, can't remember how to write.

I've tried typing it a few times, thinking that might help. That doesn't seem personal enough, though. But then I have to look at my crap handwriting.

I chuckled, a tear escaping the corner of my eye.

I could just imagine Kyle being annoyed by his chicken scratch, but even as I enjoyed the lightness of that comment, it pained me to know what he was going through to get this out, and I was also moved that he had gone through the effort to share it with me.

I assessed some more of the jumbled writing, unable to make it out on the badly damaged page—Kyle had scribbled the text to the point where it had torn through the paper.

I flipped to the next sheet.

I was eleven the first time I remember my father kicking me.

My eyes watered. It was one thing when he'd mentioned abuse before, but another to have the image in my mind of a child, so innocent and harmless, being assaulted like that by an adult...by his father, for Christ's sake. I could see Kyle's face, all that strength and power, the man so quick to a fight, and it made sense, but so many couldn't see that vulnerable part of him that had been so hurt.

I didn't want to read on. I wasn't eager to see the horror he'd endured, but I didn't have a choice. If he'd gone through so much at eleven, surely even earlier, then I could get through reading it.

I had dropped a plate after rinsing it off in the sink, as I was about to put it in the dishwasher. Dad had already been in a mood, and he lost it and dragged me into the hall, throwing me against the wall.

Mom was right there, sitting at the kitchen table, eyes downturned. I think I imagined she'd come and help me, but she just let it happen. Like, as he kicked me, everything was totally normal. A part of me thought that was just the way it was, but of course, I knew better, even then. I must've because otherwise I would have mentioned it to my friends, or members of the church, or teachers, but I kept it to myself, even though no one told me I needed to. Mom and Dad never had to tell me not to say anything. They must've known I wouldn't by the fact that I never told anyone anything about the things he'd do to Mom. That was just how it was around our house, I'm sure from even before I could remember. I know now that it wasn't right or healthy, but back then, it was a kid's idea of a normal home. I just assumed everyone else's families looked like that. Sure, I'd heard about domestic violence, but I guess in my head, it involved throwing punches or hits. The idea of Dad dragging Mom across the floor by the hair or shoving her face against the edge of the kitchen table would have never really crossed my mind...until I saw it happen.

So many pieces of Kyle started fitting together as his story unfolded.

Innocent, confused, scared.

The only solace I found in reading his words was knowing he wasn't living with that monster anymore, that he was safe with his uncle.

Again, his wording became incoherent, jumbled scribbles, so I turned to the next page.

I know it's not real, but some spots still feel tender, like they've never really healed all the way. Something else that's never healed. I don't know that it can or should. I just know that it would be nice if the injuries had just been on my body.

That was the end of that before I turned to the final piece, a printout sheet of paper.

A hospital bill for $5,200, itemized out for his insurance—a forearm fracture.

Oh, Kyle.

My poor, beautiful Kyle.

I put the sheets to my face as I inhaled, smelling him on them, tears flowing down my cheeks.

I looked a little too quickly back at the address on the bill, some impulse in me wanting to hunt that bastard down and destroy him.

How could he have done that to a kid?

How could he have done that to his family?

And then just as bad, to have turned this town against an innocent boy to keep his own crimes from ever being discovered?

As my heart broke for the kid I knew was in Kyle, I also felt tension because I knew there was no turning back.

KYLE

A thousand times I regretted having given those sheets to James.

I'd wanted to tell him, but I wasn't sure that was the best way.

I should have collected those thoughts together and found a better way to articulate them. He was an English teacher, so surely he was judging the jumbled mess that was even more of a mess than an assignment I might have done for his class.

He wouldn't be like that, I kept reminding myself.

But allowing myself to be so vulnerable had made me suspicious. He would judge me...think I was exaggerating...or even worse, that I made it all up.

Please believe me.

It had been impossible to convey so much in just a few pages, but even a hundred or a thousand couldn't have covered every painful memory, every time my heart ached more than my body. Every time I was made to believe it was my fault, or that this was the way the world worked.

I chased those thoughts away.

I would have plenty of time to think on them when I saw James again. In the meantime, I would be appreciative I had Tex, who'd taught me what it really meant to be loved and respected...to be protected.

When I entered James's classroom for fourth period, he was jotting some notes down on the board about the Romantic era.

I hoped—wished—for a moment that he hadn't read the pages I'd given him. That he'd gotten busy, or lost them. I didn't really want that, but it was a fantasy I could cling to for the sake of the kid in me, whom I was trying to protect not just from James, but the world.

He glanced over his shoulder, to the door, as if he'd had some psychic impulse that had alerted him I'd arrived, but I figured he might have just been glancing over his shoulder from time to time, knowing I would be there soon enough, and we'd have to have a moment to discuss what I'd offered up to him.

The expression on his face was softer than usual, and I detected enough in it to know he'd read it. Because of course he had.

I didn't want his pity, but at the same time, what kind of person would he have been if he'd read that and not felt some?

I did my best to offer the sort of smile I might have on a regular day, but that was nearly impossible. I could barely fake a smirk in his direction.

Since before I'd gotten to class, I'd assumed the lecture might be as awkward as so many of our exchanges had been, but there was something about knowing what bits I had managed to get out and into his head. Even when he glanced at me, I could feel all his support, his kindness, and some intangible quality I couldn't put my finger on.

After the bell, when I stopped by his desk, we gazed into each other's eyes.

"I can't imagine you want to discuss this here," he said.

"Not really, no."

Once again, we were reminded of our limitations under these conditions.

But I didn't want to be at school when we talked about everything I'd shared.

"How about Wednesday?" he asked. "We'll probably be just as packed full of volunteers for the library as usual."

"Wednesday would be good. Maybe you could give me a ride there and back?"

He thought on it for a moment, as though deciding if that would be appropriate.

"Even Coach Williams had to give me rides back when I was playing football."

As he chuckled, he must've seen how much he was overthinking us, but I didn't blame him. There was so much to overthink. "Yes, of course."

Surely it complicated matters that we both knew what we were doing was wrong, but to the rest of the school, we were just teacher and student. Hell, he was the married teacher who had acted so straight, I hadn't suspected he could have even been capable of being attracted to me, let alone what we were doing.

In truth, the time between having handed James those pages at the party and when we talked about them was helpful in giving me a chance to wrap my thoughts around it all, to brace myself for an encounter I hadn't allowed myself to have, not even with myself.

"Kyle... I told you, I won't tell anyone these things you've shared, but you really should at least talk to the guidance counselor."

"Oh, which one? Mrs. Grames or Miss Chewer? I can talk to them. They'll recognize me from Saturday services when I was a kid. If not them, maybe a local therapist like Dr. Kramer or Mr. Spears? Funny, I know them through Dad too."

I saw the moment of realization in his expression, when he understood exactly why this had been so hard for me. "I get what you mean."

"Welcome to Wyachet, Teach."

His gaze shifted around the room. "I'm sorry you've had to carry this, Kyle. But I didn't say that because I planned to share anything you gave me in confidence. There are other ways you can get help. You don't have to do this on your own."

"I'm starting to realize I *can't* do it on my own," I confessed, enjoying even just the relief that he knew...that someone fucking knew.

The world felt different to me.

A secret revealed lifted a veil of fog in my mind, as

though making the world around me, particularly James, appear sharper than ever.

Even though it was just a crack of the door that I'd opened for him to see, God, what it had done for me. I was relieved when Wednesday afternoon came and we were finally walking down the hall together, to his car.

Despite what I would have to discuss, I enjoyed walking alongside him like that, knowing there was so much more between us than anyone else could have figured. When we reached his car, I slid into the passenger seat, recalling the last time I'd been in there. Feeling as though I'd taken it for granted and wanting to memorize that new-car smell...and just a hint of that familiar scent of his cologne tickling at my nose.

Turning to one another, again, something felt different, if only because of my vulnerability now that he knew the worst.

I turned up his music on the drive over, and we chatted about nothing of consequence. He asked about Tex, before the conversation shifted back to his class.

As we headed into the library parking lot, I noticed Ms. Eiken's car was parked outside. Even working with her, there was a surreal calm to the experience. Like with the rest of the week, I didn't feel a need to race to the moment where we discussed my pain, but certainly there were moments when I feared it was because I never really wanted to get there. Because I wanted to pretend for a little longer that I could have told him that and it wouldn't have changed anything.

Yet even by the subtle looks we exchanged as we

shelved books, I knew nothing could ever be the same again. When Ms. Eiken headed out to pick up her kid from baseball practice, we waited to hear the front door click shut before turning to one another.

The moment I knew would come had finally arrived.

"It's funny," I said. "I thought there was enough time between handing you those notes and now for me to be ready for this conversation, but..."

"Kyle..."

My eyes watered. "It's not so bad. I got Tex now." But even as I said the words, a tear escaped my eye and traveled down my cheek. I scrambled to wipe it from my face.

"You've never talked to anyone about this?"

I stiffened my jaw and shook my head. "Nah, I'm good. I'm fine. I survived it. Doing just fine now."

There was suspicion in his expression, which I was quick to call out. "You don't get to decide how I deal with shit."

"That wasn't what I was doing. I'm worried about you."

"I know. Just...being so open with someone makes me feel so on edge."

So weak.

"Can I ask about the hospital bill?"

I quieted.

James was always so fucking perceptive. He got me in a way that kept catching me off-balance. Of course I expected him to ask, but I could have seen anyone else, even after seeing that, just assuming it went hand in hand with the shit I'd told him.

"Can I not answer?" I half joked, wanting to back out.

But I'd gone too far already. There was no point in hiding anything else. "Even with things the way they were, I was always a little rebellious. Feels like it's something in my DNA. Just didn't take crap, even from him, which I paid for more often than not. And don't think I didn't imagine getting help, but I don't... I guess I knew, no matter what I said, it wouldn't be only his word against mine, but Mom's too. It's so strange, the conversations we never had, all the things I assumed...but assumed correctly.

"Usually I just went off...in my mind. In sixth grade, when we were learning about South America, my sixth-grade teacher, Ms. Neal, used to tell us stories about going to Peru. Sounded like such an adventure. And it gave me a place to go in my mind, to escape the pain...far away, in another country where he couldn't hurt me. Don't get me wrong. Sometimes it was a book or a movie, Narnia or Wonderland, but something about Machu Picchu being real made it feel like maybe one day I could get there, and be safe."

What a dumb fucking thing to tell him. I felt so exposed and vulnerable. I hated myself for sharing, but it felt too damn good to stop.

"It was my thirteenth birthday," I forced out, "and we kept birthdays within the family. I didn't have many friends anyway, so it wasn't a big deal. I still don't know what it was...if he was bothered because the night was all about me...or if he was pissed about something else, but I guess I was annoyed, and I said something in a tone he didn't care for, and he lost it. Next thing I knew, I was on the floor, and then I was up and on the floor again.

"I think it was the first time I tried to fight back. Learned my lesson. And I remember lying there on the floor, and Mom telling me over and over that we were gonna say I fell down the stairs. We'd never talked about it before, she'd never asked me to lie about any of it before, so it was like suddenly, I knew she'd seen all that, knew it was wrong enough to need to lie about it, and she'd just let it happen."

I couldn't look James in the eyes.

"And when the nurses and doctors talked to me, I kept telling that same lie...looking at her, seeing how fucking relieved she was that I hadn't told the fucking truth. How's that not supposed to fuck a kid up?"

I had to take a moment to wipe my face as the tears released, far beyond my control.

"Shit. Haven't even told Tex about that." My voice cracked.

I needed to shut the hell up until I could regain control of my emotions, but it didn't seem like that would be happening anytime soon.

Before I had a chance to lift my head, I felt something across my back and realized it was his arm. He drew me into his chest, holding me close. His firm hug felt soothing for a moment, made me feel so safe, that I just fell the fuck apart.

His face traveled near my hair, to beside my cheek as he whispered against my ear, "I'm so sorry you had to go through that. But you know you can still go to the police."

I would've laughed if it hadn't been so painful. I pulled away from him. "Oh, my sweet, naive James. I did. Just a few months later, once I'd healed, I'd worked up the courage to go to the station. I think he broke the bone and my loyalty at the same time, because after that I was done watching him shove her around. I went to the cops—a lot of higher-ups are in good with the biggest megachurch in Whispersaw County. *'That one may smile and smile and be a villain.'"*

Fucking Hamlet was sure as fuck right about that.

"So there was an investigation," I went on, "into the fact that I was a fucking liar, I suppose... Why do you think Dad had to do a number on my reputation? His crazy, bad-boy kid."

"Oh my God, Kyle." He pulled me back into his hold, and God, it felt so good, it made me hate myself.

I gritted my teeth as I took a breath.

Get it together, Kyle.

I pushed away again. "I don't do this. I'm good. I'm fine. It made me tougher."

"It did, but you don't always have to be tough, Kyle."

"Whatever," I said, avoiding eye contact. Clearly, I was just strong enough to throw all my defenses back up.

I finally looked at him, and I could see he didn't know how to help me. How could he? No one could make it better. No one could make this ache in my heart vanish. Not even my Big Man.

"I guess it was an awfully emotional trick."

"A trick?" he asked.

"Yeah. Because now you have to share yours with me."

"Fair is fair," he said.

I could still tell he wanted to be there more for me than he could.

"Thank you," I told him.

"What for? I'm not able to do anything for you."

"It does more just telling someone than keeping that all to myself."

"I'm glad I could be the one you trusted with it."

Trust. Interesting word. I didn't trust many people, but I trusted him. Maybe I was foolish to trust him, but I did.

"Kyle, I—"

A clicking sound came.

Fuck.

Our time together had gone too fast.

As Kendra popped in, I faced away and grabbed some books. I didn't want her to see me looking like a mess.

"Good news. The sitter could get Finn, so I think we'll be able to knock out a lot of this in no time."

Although, I didn't want to move too fast, since I knew once this was gone, one of the few opportunities I had to see James would vanish with it.

JAMES

As I thumbed through an old photo album of me and my family, my eyes fixed on a picture of my little brother and his classic broad smile and bright eyes. The happiest kid in the world, at eight, holding up a catfish, eagerly displaying it for the camera, with me, rather oblivious that a picture was being taken, at his side.

I swept my thumb across the image of his face. Those full cheeks, speckled with freckles.

I needed the picture to really remember what his face looked like back then.

I was only ten at the time, so it made sense that the distant memory would feel elusive, but even more than that, they had nearly become inaccessible, as though my mind sought to tuck these into the darkest corners of my memory to protect me from the pain.

But without pain, there was no Cody.

Even memories from high school, from our late-night trips to the Shake Shack, I had to chase them through my mind to keep them from escaping me. It made me regret all those tear-streaked nights when I'd pushed those memories away to deny myself the agony, the pain that felt so potent, it could only lead to my end...

When Saturday came, Kyle and I worked together inside the house since we had too many decking supervisors arrive that day. We conversed and joked as usual, but the way we interacted made it evident things would never be the same between us after what he'd told me about that hospital bill.

Kyle didn't make any remarks or jokes that made me feel like he needed to know my wound in any hurry, but I would need to tell him, not only to reciprocate, but to have a chance at the sort of catharsis I watched him experience as he opened up to me.

I took my time crafting my response. There could be no shortcut when it came to allowing myself to be as vulnerable with Kyle as he had allowed himself to be with me.

The following week arrived, and Kyle and I exchanged one of those soulful glances I found we could without anyone realizing what we were doing.

"So now that we're beginning our descent into *Frankenstein*, who wants to start off, maybe by giving me their feelings about the first few chapters?"

I searched for hands.

I knew from my chat with Kyle on Saturday that he'd

finished the novel already, and was about as much of a fan as I figured most of the other guys in class would be.

No one volunteered right away, so I said, "Any thoughts...?"

Still no one, leading me to fear that perhaps not many of them had made it through the chapters I'd assigned.

"Brian?" I asked, picking someone at random.

I felt bad that I had when I saw the doe-eyed expression on his face as he glanced at me from his desk.

I hadn't meant to put him on the spot. His responses in class and in assignments led me to believe he typically made time for the readings, even if they weren't the sort of in-depth analyses I'd come to expect from Kyle. It was, however, the minimum required from someone trying to get by in their high school English class.

Brian hemmed and hawed for a moment before I said, "Who is Victor Frankenstein telling the story to?"

He sighed. "The reader...?"

Admittedly, I was a little unnerved. In a world where these kids could so easily look up synopses online and cheat their way through our entire semester together, he did not even have the respect to use CliffsNotes as kids my age would have done when we were in high school.

"Brian, in the future, you can just tell me you didn't do the reading. I'll have to dock your participation grade for the day, but it's not the end of the world. That said, if you want to do well in my class, particularly when we get to tests, I suggest you crack open the book at some point."

"Yeah, of course, Mr. Warner. Just been busy with practice."

I detected a few eye rolls around the room, and I couldn't let it slide. "I'm sure your peers have equally busy lives, yet they manage to make time for their assignments."

"Of course, Mr. Warner." He gave me that ever-obedient expression, the sort I was sure he gave his parents when they told him to behave before he went out and boozed the night away with his friends.

I moved on to Valerie, who, to my relief, offered a competent enough response to get our discussion going. As I turned to jot down a few character names and themes on the board, I heard Brian mutter, "What a fucking asshole."

I froze mid-word.

It was that perfect volume he'd said it at, enough that everyone in class heard, a test to see if I would pretend not to hear him or if I would challenge him, make him deal with the repercussions of his actions. Expecting the denial and the insistence that he hadn't said such a thing, creating an investigation out of the classroom, it was the sort of thing a kid like him banked on me avoiding, which was why I had to turn and deal with it.

As soon as I did, I noticed a desk topple over.

A figure dashed across the classroom, at a pace that startled me and earned gasps around the room. I hardly had time to react before Brian shifted in his seat. Kyle grabbed him by his shirt collar and yanked him from his desk, kicking it aside as he moved through the row of seats beside his, and pushed him up against the wall. I jumped into action as quickly as I could, moving over to them as Kyle got in Brian's face.

"I think you should show Teach a little respect," Kyle said.

"Fuck are you talking about? Get off me, dude." Brian pushed, but Kyle firmed his hold, keeping Brian pinned against the wall. "I think you owe him a fucking apology."

"Mr. Forsythe, this is unnecessary," I said. "Please let go of Mr. Finnegan. He's already in trouble, and this is only getting both of you detention."

"I don't give a shit about detention," Kyle said. "He needs to apologize."

Despite Kyle's temperament—and he seemed ready to punch someone's lights out—I stepped up to him to spare Brian, hoping Kyle didn't lose it and turn his aggression on me. "Mr. Forsythe, this is not how we manage this. Please let him go."

As Kyle turned to me, I could see something had been triggered. I hadn't seen him look like that, totally out of himself, since the night he'd helped me in that alley in town.

But as if seeing me for the first time, he took a breath. Something changed in his expression as he seemed to understand that what seized him wasn't all him. And now that I knew the source of his pain, I understood that he was in the grips of something far more powerful than anything Brian could have understood.

He stepped back, taking a breath.

"The fuck?" Brian asked.

I could tell by Brian's reaction it wasn't going to be

enough to give them warnings. If I didn't take this to the administrators, my job would be on the line if his prissy parents called and tried to hold me or Kyle accountable for what had just taken place.

Of course, when I took them to the principal, Brian acted as though he'd been decked, so we had to manage all the red tape. Brian, of course, was given a warning for his attitude during class, while Kyle would face detention, something that even as Dr. Henry gave it, she didn't seem fazed by—it all clearly encouraged her very wrong assumptions about him.

When I finally managed to get Kyle on his own in the guidance counselor's office, he sat on the sofa, looking about as put out as he and Brian had seemed when Dr. Henry was lecturing them. I struggled to think of how to even start the conversation, especially knowing all that I knew now.

"Kyle, is everything okay?" was all I could think to say.

He was still so tense and stiff, as if waiting for me to chastise him like I might have Brian, but my question seemed to catch him off guard, and he looked up to me with surprise.

I sat down beside him, not wanting him to feel like I was trying to look down on him during any of this.

"I…"

He didn't go any further with his thought, so I figured I'd help him out. "I think I have a better understanding of what happened in that alley and why you always look like you're ready to kick someone's ass, but what happened in class… Nothing justifies lashing out at him like that."

"I wouldn't have done that to you," he insisted. "I was just trying to scare him."

It wasn't lost on me that he was more concerned about how that would have affected me than Brian.

"Really? Because it looked like you weren't able to control much back there."

"I...lost it for a minute, yes, but by the time I got to him, I knew what the right thing to do was...or wasn't."

"What made you feel you needed to react like that?"

"He was being a dick to you."

"People are like that to me all the time. They've been that way for years."

"You don't deserve that. Just like you didn't deserve it from Sheila."

He looked into my eyes as he said that, and I didn't know why I hadn't thought of it like that before. I remembered telling him about the ways she hurt me or put me down, and then the way he would always get so on edge, looking like he wanted to start a fight.

He turned away from me, his eyes watering. "I don't like seeing the people I care about get hurt."

"I get that, Kyle. I really do, but some kid mouthing off to me in class isn't the same as me getting mugged in an alley or..."

"...or watching your mom get her head banged up against a cabinet."

Clearly, he already knew where the instinct had come from, and it broke my heart knowing that Brian's asshole remark had done a number on him, dredged up those cruel memories. I wanted to wrap my arms around him and let him know everything was going to be all right. I wanted to protect that little boy who'd been wronged too many times.

"I really am sorry," Kyle said.

"You don't need to apologize. That's not why I'm talking to you. I worry about you."

"You don't have to be concerned about me. As you can see, I'm a fighter."

"It's not the fight on the outside that worries me."

He looked me in the eyes once again. "Yeah, that worries me too sometimes."

"I don't want to sound like I'm playing teacher here, but we can find you help outside Wyachet if that's what we need to do."

He nodded. "I know that's what I need, but I'm not sure I'm ready for that, James."

"I get that, and I'm here for anything you need, or if you want to talk more about any aspect of it."

He seemed nervous, and I thought about how I'd worded everything, hoping I hadn't concerned him.

"But I would like you to get comfortable enough that you can seek something more. The things you're dealing with, they're too much for anyone to carry without help."

"I know. Just...I think there's still this part of me that remembers Mom asking me to lie, and I know it sounds fucked up, but it's like I'm betraying my family by telling people."

"Your family betrayed you. Not the other way around."

"Easier said than believed," he remarked, a bitter smirk on his face.

"I don't blame you there."

"Either way, I guess I can enjoy a little detention time. Maybe I can get some time to finish a final essay for a certain English teacher."

I laughed. "I'm not too concerned about that."

"This isn't going to change anything, though, is it?" He must've sensed I wasn't sure what he meant, because he added, "You're still going to follow through with our deal?"

"Of course, Kyle. This has nothing to do with that. I wish it hadn't happened, but I would never betray your trust like that."

His shoulders relaxed, and he took a breath, as though he'd been holding it.

"There's going to be an event next Thursday at the bookstore. I'll be adding it to the board for extra credit. I was thinking I might be able to get it to you then. Figured it would be better than our usual spots."

He smiled. "I'd like that."

I allowed myself to fantasize it was a sort of date for us, still wondering how we'd gone from the connection we'd initially discovered to...whatever we were now.

25

KYLE

I changed into my third shirt for the night, a blue polo that fit my arms and chest pretty good. I wouldn't be pretending I didn't want James checking me out in it. Imagining his eyes on me, drinking me in, was enough to make my cheeks flush.

I studied myself in the mirror, obsessing over my look nearly as much as Ben had obsessed about it before the homecoming dance. This must've been what it felt like to go on a date.

Virgin dater.

I laughed at the thought, but then quickly reminded myself it wasn't a date. It couldn't be a date between James and me, even if that's what we both wanted. But even as I tried to push that thought out of my mind, it didn't change this secret hope. I forced myself to accept the reality of our situation as excitement was replaced with disappointment, and urged myself to finish my quest for the "perfect shirt." Once I found something that satisfied my ego, I fixed my hair in a hurry, still wet from the shower I'd taken after running deliveries, before heading downtown to the bookstore.

James was already seated upstairs in the café, near a window. What remained of the setting sun cast a soft orange glow across the crown of his head, making his hair glisten in a range of orange hues. He was reading a handful of papers, making marks across what I assumed were assignments from the day before. His gaze shifted and found me, and his lips curled into that familiar smile.

Considering our week had begun with me totally losing my shit, it was a refreshing reminder that the bond that had formed between us wasn't that easily destroyed.

I wasn't proud I'd snapped. I could feel Brian's words grating on my ears before they'd even escaped his stupid goddamn mouth. I didn't know what they'd be, but I knew his voice and all the snarky expressions he could make from having been through enough grades with him to already have a predisposed hatred toward his arrogant ass. I'd grabbed the edges of my desk, hoping I'd be able to restrain myself, but as soon as he spoke the insult, it was like an out-of-body experience, and I was on my feet, rushing across the classroom. By the expression on Brian's face, the terror in his eyes, it was how I imagined he might've looked if I'd transformed into a werewolf before his very eyes.

When James got in between us and I calmed down, that's when it really hit me what happened. I didn't like that side of me—who it made me feel like. It frustrated me that even just seeing James brought up such a bad memory, spoiled the moment, but at least James had a better idea of where all that intense hatred came from.

As I neared him, he pushed to his feet and offered a familiar warm hug. When I pulled away, I removed my jacket and draped it over the back of the chair across from his.

"Did I get an A yet?" I teased him.

"I'm working on third period's assignments."

"You mean you don't pull mine out first to see what an insightful analysis I had of Shelley's blah, blah, blah about trees and shit?"

"I wouldn't admit it if I did." By the clever little smile on his face and the gleam in his eyes, I knew I was right.

He glanced me over. "I like that shirt. I don't think I've seen you wear it to school."

"Oh, thanks. Yeah, not usually my kind of thing, but when we were out, Ben insisted. Said it made me look really studious."

"It's sharp, for sure. I enjoy it when you change things up."

I happened to look around and noticed Brittany and Valerie from fourth period heading our way.

Fuck my life.

As I looked to James, who had them in his sights too, it was evident we were both disappointed that what we'd hoped would be another private moment had been spoiled. Perhaps we needed a reality check, though.

"Hey, Mr. Warner," Valerie said as she neared. "I'm surprised to see you here, Kyle."

"He's come to a few of these," James said.

"Don't rat me out and ruin my rep," I said, which got Brittany and Valerie laughing, far more than I deserved for the joke.

"I'm genuinely surprised you guys came," he added. "I assumed no one was even paying attention to the extra credit anymore."

"We only have three weeks until the final," Brittany said, "and I didn't exactly kill my midterm, so..."

"And she didn't kill her midterm, so that's why I'm here too," Valerie joked.

James and I enjoyed a laugh before I heard, "Hey, ladies."

As they turned, between them, I noticed Daryl and Brian coming our way.

Seriously?

I didn't have to turn to James to know he was eyeing me, wondering how I was going to respond.

Brittany and Val greeted them as I muttered to James, "Oh, this is gonna be fun."

"You good?"

"Slightly annoyed, but I'll be fine."

I'd have to be, since I was going to be seeing him from this day through the rest of the year. Plus, as long as he didn't talk any more shit about James, we didn't need to have any beef.

Brian eyed me uneasily as they got closer.

"Hey, man," I said, trying to break the ice.

"Hey." He reached his hand out for a truce. "We cool?"

I took his hand, and we tapped shoulders. "Yeah, man.

We're cool. Even though I've gotta do some time over you."

He snickered, but I felt the tension dissolve, and it reminded me that I hadn't needed to put on such a show, that he was relatively harmless. With that out of the way, we all found seats. The lecturer arrived and began discussing his novel about the depression era. I'd half expected the other guys to be a bunch of assholes, especially considering the speaker wasn't the most entertaining, but they were well mannered and listened intently.

James and I sat next to one another. At first I kept my distance, but as my leg grazed his, I realized what an opportunity we really had and pushed it closer, nonchalantly, as though my leg just happened to push against his like that. I wondered if he would pull away, but he kept his in place.

As the lecturer went on, I kept pushing my leg a little closer...and then I felt him shift his leg closer to mine too.

I suppressed a sigh of relief as I looked to my classmates to make sure they hadn't caught on. I knew they couldn't any more than they could read my interest during class. Each day, this aura of feelings for James grew bigger and bigger, to the point where now I was sure even the lecturer was enveloped in it.

By the end of the event, I wasn't sure I'd be able to come up with a paper about the lecture, since I'd been so caught up in how much warmth we'd managed to generate with our legs wedged together as they were. After applauding the speaker, we all stood, James and I exchanging a look as we grabbed our jackets. It confirmed he knew exactly what we'd done.

Like so much of what we did these days, it wasn't right, but that couldn't rob me of how it felt.

James thanked the other guys for coming, and we headed out to the parking lot.

A drizzle was coming down, which made everyone dash off to their cars. James hadn't mentioned anything about our agreement, so I left same as they had. I figured maybe we'd have to save it for another night. But as I was on my way back to my car, I heard his voice behind me, calling my name. I whirled around so fast, I had to work to keep myself from doing a spin.

James jogged to catch up with me.

Something about the way the streetlight caught his smooth face reminded me of how his skin had looked in the orange glow of the setting sun. It seemed as though each time I looked at his face, I unearthed some deeper layer of beauty than the last. Not just because he was hot, which was something I'd known from the beginning. Only...every little piece of him I had discovered had led me to the sort of beauty that permeated beyond flesh.

He reached into his jacket pocket and retrieved a box wrapped in brown paper. He eyed it for a moment, seeming to struggle with the thought of handing over his secrets, his darkness. That feeling was familiar to me, considering what it had taken me to hand him mine.

He finally pushed it toward me, and I took it, being as cautious with the package as I would be with his delicate heart.

Droplets collected on the paper.

As I felt his hold let up, I said, "Thank you," then quickly tucked it into my jacket pocket to protect it from the rain.

"We'll have to find time to talk about it, maybe this weekend."

"For sure."

"Guess I should go."

I wanted to hug him again, but we were caught in this gray area, struggling with what was and wasn't appropriate, lying to ourselves, it seemed, as we acted like we hadn't crossed far too many lines already.

He headed to his car, and I went to mine, turning on my overhead light and looking at the packaging of the box he'd given me as the rain started to come down harder against the windshield.

Here it was, what I'd been waiting for.

Eagerness mixed with tension as I tore through the paper and pulled the lid off the box inside, revealing a small stack of pictures.

The first was of a boy—had to have been four or five years old—smiling for what appeared to be some sort of professional photo. He had the brightest smile. *His brother*, was my first thought as I turned the picture over to see the name Cody written in cursive.

The next picture, an old 3x4, was Cody with another kid, unmistakably little James, who looked like he might have been in middle school. And after that, another had what I could only assume was James's parents. I reflected on how little he'd mentioned them, almost as if he'd never had any parents.

They looked like such a happy family, his mother with long blonde hair, similar enough to James's that it was likely the side he got it from. Although, he had his father's face—that nose and jawline.

I flipped to the next one, another picture of his brother in a letterman jacket, much longer hair than in the last picture, still smiling brightly. It was a gorgeous smile. He had this magic about him, and I wondered if that was something I imagined because of what James had told me about him.

I was surprised by the next item—not a picture, but a brochure, torn and wrinkled up. Some summer camp, looked like, with images of kids horseback riding and swinging rope into a creek. As I opened the brochure, I scrutinized it...realizing what it was.

We aren't defined by labels like gay, lesbian, bisexual, or transgender.

We are God's children.

Here at Light and Love, we will help remind you that God's love really is enough and that you can live by the teachings of Christ. Build your foundations on a rock!

Rhetoric like that went on and on, mixed with promises of activities and friends, and apparently so much of Christ's love that you wouldn't need anyone else.

I knew what this was. It wasn't my idea of Christianity or a fun summer camp.

It was a conversion camp.

And suddenly, so many of the things James had

mentioned about his brother—and even his initial concern about my sexuality—made sense.

"Oh fuck," I muttered, turning and seeing a photocopied page from a journal. I read a passage, noting those parts that stood out most.

I miss home.

I miss my brother.

I'm so scared.

Tears filled my eyes, making it hard to read.

I turned to the last page, a newspaper clipping about a kid jumping from his dorm at Georgia Tech.

Oh, my fucking heart.

James...so many things made sense now that I'd seen all that.

His guilt about his brother's death, his distant relationship with his parents...

Goddammit.

Fuck next week.

JAMES

After I returned home, I went into the kitchen and poured myself a glass of whiskey. I opened the French doors to the porch, taking a look at the rain coming down, before going back inside.

Life always had a way of throwing a curveball. Just when I wanted a night with Kyle all to myself, of course his classmates would show up. I should have been happy that some of my students had actually taken me up on the extra credit, but I missed our alone time in a way I knew I shouldn't have. And I'd hoped I would have the opportunity to be present when he saw the contents of the box I'd arranged for him.

But it seemed that wasn't our fate.

I savored a sip of whiskey, thinking about another life...a world that didn't exist...where Kyle and I were friends, without this obstacle standing between us. Where

I could sit with him and discuss it comfortably, openly, without fear of repercussions.

I went into my office, set my laptop bag alongside my desk, and enjoyed another drink.

There was a knock at the door.

I told myself I was imagining it. I'd wanted Kyle so much, I'd obviously planted the idea in my head, but I left my office, going to the front door and opening it.

No one.

Yes, just in my head.

An unsettling feeling stirred within me as I thought of Sheila accusing me of imagining things. I hadn't *imagined* anything. All those things I'd accused her of had been true, but it didn't change the fact that I still felt as if reality was slipping away from me, that odd mix of being totally destabilized and full of fury, at Sheila, at myself.

As I closed the door, contemplating the sound I believed I'd heard, I grew agitated that I hadn't gotten my wish.

Then the knock came again. It hadn't been coming from the front door.

"The fuck?" I muttered.

I thought maybe I was mistaking a squirrel or raccoon for a knock, but it sounded so deliberate.

Heading into the kitchen, I saw him through the French door, drenched from the rain—Kyle Forsythe. His face had that familiar scowl I'd seen far too many times during class, the one that made me feel like he didn't give a shit and that he was mentally undressing me all at once.

Was it so evil of me that I was glad he was here?

But how the hell did he know where I lived?

He lifted his hand, offering a friendly wave and the faintest of smiles that set me at ease right away. I dashed to the door, noticing I'd left it unlocked. I cracked it open. "What are you doing here?"

"Do you mind if I come in first? I'm getting a little wet."

Don't fucking let him in, a part of my brain warned me.

I knew once I did that, it was over for me, but with him standing there as though he'd fallen into a swimming pool, it was impossible for me to deny him.

"Guess it's my turn to help you out of the rain," I joked. "Come on in."

I hated myself for saying it, particularly because I wanted him inside my house.

All to myself.

"Your shoes," I told him, noticing they were covered in mud.

"Yeah...there's a park behind your house. I left the car there and came through the woods."

"You walked from there?"

"I didn't think it'd be great if your neighbors saw me pulling into your driveway. You're welcome."

He had a point, but it didn't make me feel better about him trudging through the rain and mud.

As I closed the door behind him, he said, "Don't act so happy to see me."

I avoided looking him directly in the eyes, mostly because I figured I knew why he was here...what he'd seen...what he now knew.

I was still wondering how the hell this could be happening. He didn't know where I lived. No, I had to be dreaming this. I had to get away and think for a second. Fortunately, I had an easy way out. "I'll grab you a towel."

I went into the laundry room and fetched a towel from the dryer. As I turned, he was coming in. His damp long-sleeved shirt clung to his body, curving with every muscle, making it nearly effortless to imagine what he looked like under it. He ran his fingers through the damp locks of hair that clung to his forehead, pushing them over his brow.

"On second thought," I said as I continued looking him over, "while we're in here, let's get some dry clothes."

"Am I making it difficult for you to think right now?" he asked with a sly wink.

"Kyle, how did you know where I lived?"

His brows tugged closer together. "Really? I programmed my uncle's address into your GPS, meaning..."

"You saw mine."

He tapped his forefinger against his head. "Delivery guy. I'm a pro with Wyachet addresses."

It was a relief to know it wasn't anything creepy, yet I wondered if I would have been so upset if it had been.

"Always full of surprises," I noted.

"You like it when I surprise you."

Of course I fucking did.

I grabbed some clothes from the dryer and handed them to him before walking back into the kitchen, closing the door behind me, accepting that now I really was going to have to deal with the consequences of what I'd entrusted to him back at the bookstore.

Moisture collected on my forehead. I knew it wasn't from the rain outside. I was sweating as I considered the consequences of someone finding out that Kyle was in my home—and why he was in my home. The fact that he had to leave his car at the park behind my home served as a reminder that we both knew there were consequences for our actions. I went into my office—yes, that was the most appropriate place to talk to him once he'd dried off.

Or perhaps I was just looking forward to being behind my desk, to have that barrier between us. To protect us both from my desire.

Sitting in my swivel chair, I thumbed through some papers I had left to grade, sweating even more, to the point where I wondered if I had the goddamn heater on too high. I started to get up to check, when he walked through my office doorway, wearing the pair of pants I'd offered him, wiping the tee across his forehead.

I couldn't help noticing he still glowed with patches of water scattered across his beautiful, smooth flesh. It was the sort of moment that made me vividly aware that, even though I hadn't felt this kind of intense desire for a man before, I certainly did in that moment.

"I promise it wasn't raining that hard when I was leaving the car. It was a downpour just at the end there."

"You should probably put that shirt on," I warned him.

"Maybe if you didn't look at me like that, I would."

I took a moment to enjoy the view, saliva collecting in my mouth, and he stepped right in front of my desk, a smug expression on his face as he studied me, as he seemed to know what he was doing to me. A brief stand-off, before he smiled and found his way into the holes of the shirt, my eyes enjoying what I knew was going to be a short-lived preview of his V lines, navel, and happy trail before the curtain closed. *For the best*, I reminded myself, since obviously, restraint wasn't something I was very good at when it came to Kyle Forsythe. And judging by that expression on his face, he damn well knew it.

As we looked into one another's eyes, I thought about all the things that had gone unsaid. He hadn't even mentioned the very reason I was certain he was there.

"You can take a seat, if you'd like," I told him, motioning across the desk to the available chair.

He winced as he looked between me and the chair, as though he knew I sought to keep some physical boundary between us, but he acquiesced.

Despite his shower in the rain, I could still smell a hint of pine from his deodorant.

Slouching in the chair, he rested his hands on its arms and sighed, and we sat in silence for a while.

I could have lived in the quiet with him, the peace of us getting a moment alone with one another, in the safety of my home, which felt like it was in another realm, distant from the world we'd just come from, from the memories I knew would be brought up far too soon. He reached into his back pocket and retrieved a slip of paper.

The conversion-camp brochure that had been in the box.

Seeing it assured me of what I already knew—that

he'd seen the contents of the box. That he already knew too much about my past.

"I guess I know why you don't talk about your parents much," he said, and my face tensed up, my chin quivering.

"Yeah..." I took the brochure, and as I opened it, a picture of my brother in high school slid out.

"You guys were close?"

"I thought we were close enough that he would have told me what this summer camp was really about. Seems I had a lot of assumptions about my family, and I didn't really figure things out until after he passed, when I discovered how cruel parents could be to their own children. Mine didn't even mention the camp after he killed himself. I found out when I was going through his belongings. And then to find out that he'd confided in them, trusted them, only for them to make him promise to keep it from the one member of our family who would have been there for him, who could have protected him from that fate... I just..."

A tear escaped my eye, one that surprised me how quickly it had fallen, yet it was amazing how just a conversation could transport me back in time, into each fucked-up memory.

"To think they were trying to 'protect' me from the truth when we should have been protecting him."

"James, you didn't know."

"But why didn't I know?"

"He didn't tell you."

Kyle was only trying to help, but it couldn't change the truth.

"He shouldn't have needed to tell me. He was my brother. There were so many times when I could tell he was struggling, going through something, I just didn't know what. I would ask, and he would say that work or school was hard. I was never really very interested in guys or girls, so I didn't think much like everyone else. It wasn't even on my radar, but I wish I'd mentioned that if he was gay, or bi, or anything, I would have loved him just the same. I thought we had the kind of relationship where he felt he could come to me and— Jesus. Fuck me."

A flood of emotions overwhelmed me. I spent so much of my life keeping these memories at bay, but now I was letting them flow from my mouth, and it brought up even more pain than I'd anticipated.

I felt a hand on my shoulder and turned swiftly to see Kyle beside me.

Fuck no.

I could tell by the look in his eyes that he just wanted to be there for me while I was in pain, but he was so close, and I was so fucking weak.

"I just wonder how I didn't ask the right questions, or if I wasn't really listening. I remember sometimes he would give me this look, like there was something he needed to tell me. And I should have pressed, or figured something was wrong, but I was so fucking selfish that I never..."

"There was no way you could have known what he was thinking back then. You only know now because you've seen the letters and journal entries. He wouldn't have wanted you to put this on yourself like this."

His sympathy, his kindness, his hand against my shoulder...it was all too much for me.

"Kyle, I know you mean well, but can you please not touch me right now?"

His eyes widened as he pulled his hand away, looking stunned, hurt by my request. His gaze wandered the room, as though he was having a hard time understanding what he'd done wrong. "I'm...I... What did I..."

"Kyle, I didn't mean that it wasn't thoughtful or that I didn't want your support. It's just...complicated."

His expression tensed up. "No, you're making it complicated. There's nothing complicated about what we're doing right now. Or that I want to be here for you. Or that I want... God, I can't even say what I want because I'm worried you're going to freak the moment I spit the words out."

I tucked the brochure and picture on the bookshelf behind me as I rose to my feet. This was a conversation that needed to be had eye to eye, man to man.

"Whether we like it or not, you're my student," I said, not just for his sake, but my own. Reminding myself why the hell even the conversation we'd just shared was a mistake.

No, not a mistake, but wrong.

"This isn't appropriate." I regretted saying the words, but it was the truth, and I had to admit that, to myself, to Kyle.

"Fuck what's appropriate. Is that why you brought us into your office, put this desk between us? You tell me about your brother, and you think I'm not going to want to console you?"

"I'm sorry, I—"

"I don't need you to be sorry. I need you to be honest with yourself. You think I like this any more than you do? You think you're the only one who's struggling with what's happening between us? You think I woke up one day, thought I'd get the hots for some rule-following, pushover nerd who isn't fucking man enough to say what he really wants in this world?"

Damn, that one hurt, but it was true.

"It isn't fair or right that you put this wall up," he continued, "but then open these doors just enough to show me these beautiful things inside you that I don't even think you see sometimes. But then, just when I think they're going to open even more, they snap back shut, *every time.*"

"I was just trying to be there for you, see why you were so hurt, and I thought..."

"Don't lie to me or yourself. You wanted to get inside me as much as I wanted to get inside you. And everything we've been doing has been to pretend we can skirt a line we've already crossed."

He wasn't wrong about anything, something that was impossible for me to deny as he stood before me in my office, me feeling as vulnerable as ever beside him, wanting him as much as I ever had.

"I'm sorry. I—"

"Jesus Christ, James. I don't want you to be fucking sorry. I want you to stop being a coward. I want you to stop pretending and be honest with yourself about what I'm doing here right now."

I couldn't listen anymore.

We had crossed the line, but we had to go back.

"I think it's best if you go."

He moved toward me, the intensity of his expression fucking frightening me as he cornered me against the wall.

"If you want me to stop pursuing you, say it." A bead of spit shot out of his mouth, landing on my face as he said the words through his teeth. It only intensified my already overpowering desire. "Tell me you mean it, that you don't have to turn and adjust your pants in class because of me. That you don't jizz thinking about how good I might feel, how if fucking is anything like kissing, your nerves might never stop buzzing, stinging with life...real life...the kind that's the only thing that makes living in this fucked-up world worth it. Tell me you don't spend every day fantasizing about where we could finally make this happen. Tell me that you want me to stop. I want to hear you lie to me and yourself, out loud, and then I'll be fucking gone. I'll never bother you again."

I noticed him trembling with rage. If his words hadn't expressed his pure desire for me, I might've believed he was about to sucker punch me.

"I-I..." I stammered as I attempted to force the words I needed to say out of my mouth.

But all that desire radiating off him, mixed with anger and fury, was so confusing. I knew he meant what he said, and that if I could just tell him to leave me alone, he would, so why couldn't I force myself to do what was right?

I already knew the answer.

He snickered, not like he was laughing at me, but like he was relieved. He moved even closer, until his lips nearly grazed mine. "You can't do it, can you?"

I wanted to lurch forward and take a kiss.

Tears welled in my eyes, and I knew they had nothing to do with what we'd discussed before and everything to do with this war I was waging on every impulse trying to seize control of my will.

He scanned my face, taking a breath, like he was fucking breathing me in.

"I don't know that I can take much more," I confessed.

"You have to be the one to take this next step, James. I can't make you. But when you do, I will make you come like no one's ever made you come before. Just think about having every inch of me to your greedy self...but fair play, that means my mouth can go wherever on your body, that I can shoot my load wherever the fuck I want, because my body will be all yours and yours will be all mine."

I ground my teeth, if only to distract myself from how hard I was as I clung to what I could manage of my restraint. Which was becoming next to impossible.

His confidence diminished as he seemed surprised at how I'd managed to continue to resist. His expression, all hunger and desire, shifted in an instant as he assessed mine. He looked horrified, as though he'd had some striking realization.

"Oh shit. I really have been a fucking idiot, haven't I?"

He took a breath. "I won't torture you with this anymore, James."

All that bravado, all that confidence he strutted, had vanished, and I saw this real side to him, this part that was so much more than the flirting that had certainly been hot as hell, but didn't allow me to remember that vulnerable quality to his personality.

"I'll leave you alone now."

A tear shifted in his eye, and I could sense his hurt, the rejection he felt. His gaze fell to the floor, and he started to turn.

It felt as though he'd given me so much life and then stripped me of it in an instant.

All those things that had held me back, the logic and reason I felt I'd clung to for as long as I could manage, I pushed to the back of my mind as I moved quickly, taking Kyle's arm and pulling him back to me. No matter how many noes cried out in my head, I pushed my lips against his.

The tears that had already been crawling forward pushed out even more as I stole what I felt I'd been denied too long. Guilt and shame mixed with passion and pleasure, until skepticism and doubt were overtaken entirely.

I wouldn't have believed I could have needed his body more until I'd had a taste that let me know I wouldn't be able to chase away my desire so easily again.

Along with the fears that had prevented me from making this moment happen sooner, my awareness of my surroundings evaporated. It was just me and Kyle, our lips and limbs, as I stumbled backward until I felt my wrists at my sides as he pinned me against the wall.

My mouth welcomed his tongue as he pressed his body against mine. We kissed as though we were racing against time to keep it from stealing another second from us.

"*Kyle,*" I murmured, wanting to hear his name on my lips once again.

"It's just you and me," he whispered. "Let's leave the world behind, just for a moment. Don't we deserve to feel alive? Don't we deserve the pleasure to make up for all the pain?"

He clearly didn't need an answer, since he kept kissing me. Taking what was his. What I was realizing had been his for longer than I had been able to admit to myself.

KYLE

W e were wolves, James and I, all hands and teeth, clawing at each other's clothes. He was savage, roughly pulling off the shirt I'd just put on, then working my fly.

I hadn't meant to lose it in his office, to confront him about what we both needed to accept at that point, but it had been too much for me. And by the way his tongue teased mine, the same was true for him.

What had started as lust had evolved into so much more, and even though I would have respected his space had he let me leave, I was sure I would have hated him for the rest of my life—it would have been the only way for me to bear the pain of his rejection.

He'd had every reason to let me leave, but he hadn't.
Thank God.

He shoved my pants down my legs with my briefs, and I shuffled them down my legs as I helped him unbutton his shirt. He started to undo his fly, but a burst of inspiration overcame me and I stooped down, hooking my arms around his legs, hoisting him into the air, and setting him down carefully on the desk. I pulled off his shoes as he pushed his pants down his legs. By the time he'd gotten to his ankles, I ripped the pants right off him and discarded them in the pile with my clothes.

We could only be away from each other's mouths for so long, though, and each time they came back together, our jaws and teeth would clash for a moment as we worked back into our rhythm.

Seeing James seated in just the open shirt reminded me of everything he hid behind all those nice button-downs and khakis on a typical school day. Every curve, every hint of hair that had slipped out of the open button just under his collar, had given way to fantasy after fantasy, erection after erection through fourth period, and now I had him.

"You've been very naughty, withholding all this from me," I told him, making him laugh as we kissed once again. His legs tucked close on either side of my hips. The heat radiating off his face warmed my cheeks as I tugged him even closer, my cock resting on his pelvis, nestled in his trim pubes. I licked my palm before gripping his cock, stroking while we made out.

Water hurried down my cheeks. I assumed it came from my damp hair before realizing it was coming from James. I pulled back, noticing the tears flooding from his eyes. I put my hand to his face, wiping away a tear with my thumb.

"Hey, you okay?"

He opened his mouth and seemed to choke on his words.

"Whatever it is you want to say, you can tell me. You're safe with me, James. If this is too much, if you want me to stop, if I pushed too hard, I may fucking hate it, but talk to me."

"No, these are good tears. I didn't realize I could feel like this. I had a moment when we kissed before, but this...it's like everything bad in my life, and that searing pain that sometimes cripples me, is all gone. Fucking *gone.*"

I relaxed, my forehead against his, enjoying the pure relief his words offered.

"That must sound crazy," he added.

"No. I've had chemistry with many, but when I touch you, it's different. There's this ache all through my body. Tension in my chest, stiffness in my jaw. Sometimes I ball my hands into fists like I'm white-knuckling a steering wheel. I spend so much time trying to do things to make that pain go away...and then I touched you, and we shared that kiss, and in a moment, something I spent my life trying to make go away, it was all gone, and I was free, really fucking free."

James leaned back, studying my face, his eyes narrowed. "You're too young to feel that kind of pain."

"Pain doesn't have an age limit."

"I didn't mean it that way. Just doesn't seem right or fair."

"None of it is right or fair. The world makes all these

goddamn rules we have to blindly obey. And it feels like every rule is just to keep us from having a moment where we can think clearly, a moment where we can fucking *breathe* without the weight of the universe crushing us, fucking suffocating us."

I closed my eyes, pulling close to him once again, breathing him in. As I felt his flesh against me, that healing sensation being near him brought me, I ran my nose along his cheek to his ear, whispering, "No more fighting, James. We felt all the pain, endured it as much as we could bear. Isn't it time to feel something else?"

"Yes," he said, a word he couldn't have known how much I'd wanted to hear from him.

"Say it again," I whispered, and as he did, I kissed his neck beneath his ear. He whispered it again and again, as though he could intuit that was what I needed in that moment, and what it was doing to me. Yes, he wanted this as much as I did. Yes, he would surrender to me, as I'd been wanting him to for far too long. Yes, we could finally explore one another freely, physically, as we had done emotionally since the day I'd first seen him coming from the faculty parking lot.

Yes, yes, yes.

"I've never done this before," he said.

"Don't worry. This is the last time you'll ever have to say that."

JAMES

Despite the ease Kyle brought me, I was tense too.

It was difficult to pinpoint exactly *why* when there were so many good reasons to be on edge.

What we did was unethical, and criminal. Perhaps it was even immoral, and I was fooling myself into believing it wasn't. After all, I was still technically married to Sheila.

I'd barreled right through all those mental barricades, torn through the lists of *shouldn'ts* and *couldn'ts*. What remained was a more primal fear, of this thing I'd never experienced before—being with another man. Here was a kid who'd been fucking around with guys since who knew how long, while for me, Sheila was my first and only.

Kyle caught his breath before kissing me again so frenzied, like it bothered him to have been so far from my lips for even a brief amount of time. I lapped up everything he offered as we made out.

When his lips left mine once again, it was agony, but he quickly made up for it as he kissed my chin, down my neck. My body was caught in a fever as my flesh prickled with sensation, as though every part of me was begging Kyle's mouth to make its way there.

As I lay back, he moved to my chest, kissing and licking before he reached my nipple, which he whirled his tongue around. Rolling my head against the desktop, moaning at the sensation as he flicked my nipple with his tongue, making my cock even harder as he gripped it and stroked me. He made his way down my body, taking his time with each bit of flesh until he reached my navel. His tongue traveled right over it before his face slipped through my pubes.

My dick was painfully hard in his grip as his lips drew closer and closer, and then he swept that tongue across the head. A bead of precum dropped onto my abs, which Kyle didn't waste time licking up before slipping the head of my cock into his mouth.

I gasped again, reaching down and resting my hand on the back of his head. He built up to taking me fully so quickly, like he was hungry to have it all in his mouth, and I heard the *pop* as he dropped it from his mouth and took a breath, keeping it in his hand, stroking me some more, keeping me excited, before putting it back in his mouth, taking more care as he seemed satisfied with knowing he could get it all to the back of his throat.

I climbed higher and higher.

I was surprised by how fucking crazy he could drive me with his mouth, and just when I thought it couldn't get any better, he let my dick fall once again and buried his face in my balls. Lick after lick, he made his way down, and I pulled my legs back, offering up my ass as he wedged my cheeks apart with his face and licked along the crack until I felt that sensation against my hole.

"Oh fuck," I groaned, and then felt him slip his free hand toward it.

Kyle's confident movements stilled what nervousness remained.

He licked a finger before navigating it within me, then pulled it out and added another, leaning back and looking at me, a sly smirk spreading across his face.

"How does that feel?" he asked. And it was good enough until he pushed just a little farther back and hit—

"*Oh...*"

Another bead of precum spit out of my shaft and dropped down to my abs.

As I looked up to him, he was gazing down at me, smiling, seeming so pleased with how he was able to affect me.

He massaged gently, and I noticed my feet trembling from how much energy buzzed through me.

Licking me, shifting his fingers within me while stroking my cock, it was sensory overload. I felt my body flushing with waves of heat and sensation.

Releasing my cock, which twitched against my body as it hit, he licked up the middle of the shaft, then swirled his tongue around the head. Noticing the precum that had dropped on my abs, he quickly licked it up before slipping my cock back into his mouth.

"Do you like that, James?" he asked a moment later, looking down at me, a bit of precum lingering on his bottom lip before he licked it, reminding me of that day when he'd encouraged me to get the whipped cream off.

He stood, his cock seeming disproportionately large even for a man his size, but perhaps it was because I was so fucking intimidated by it. He put his cock against mine, stroking them together in his grip, then leaned down and pressed our foreheads together.

We panted as I rested my hand on his neck, enjoying the closeness I had been truly longing for all this time.

The way the heat rushed to my face and my body spasmed, I knew where I was heading. "Kyle…"

"Give it to me, James. I'll come with you. Come on."

He leaned back. Our gazes locked, and it was too much for me. I shot, and as I did, I felt the cum on my chest. As I glanced down, I realized it wasn't mine, but his that was shooting up across me.

He slid his thumb through his mess and raised it to my mouth, stuck his thumb in, and I licked it right up, moaning as he leaned down and mashed our mouths together.

As we came crashing down from the experience we'd caved to, the guilt, the fears, the worries all returned in an instant. So I kept kissing him, each one dulling my awareness of the reminders of the world we really lived in.

Along with my fears of the natural consequences, I had this horrible feeling in my gut that Kyle would leave me there, covered in our cum, soiled in our sins, and head off, having gotten all he'd really wanted. I thought he might grab his clothes and leave, but he lay on top of me, keeping close, his nose pressed against my cheek, his breath still hitting my skin, making it tingle.

Sweat and cum glued us together as he ran his nose up to meet mine and kissed me some more. I relaxed into his lips, cupping his face in my hands, enjoying the sensation of threading my fingers through the short sides of his hair. I slid my hands down his neck, around his shoulders, down to his sides, feeling his back muscles.

I only wanted a little longer to pretend this was all there was in the world.

Every sweep of his tongue made it that much easier to imagine. It was strange how we could share the same act over and over, and yet it felt different every time. There was something gentler, even more passionate in his movements, unlike the excitement, the rush we'd experienced as we scrambled out of our clothes, forced our bodies together again and again. There was such calm, as though each of us just wanted to stay in this sacred space and appreciate the beauty of all we shared.

He pulled back and gazed into my eyes, a softness in his expression unlike any I'd seen in it before. It was a rare vulnerability for the man who so rarely showed any.

He chuckled, and it caught me by surprise. "What is it?"

"Just a crazy turn of events to my day, is all. Why did you ask it like that? Why do you look so concerned now?"

"I thought I might have done something stupid or ridiculous. I was nervous that I wouldn't know what to do."

"Everything we just did is the opposite of stupid or ridiculous. Definitely far better than anything I imagined it would be. And trust me, Mr. Warner, I had very high expectations." He leaned closer as he said those words before granting me another kiss.

"Can you just call me James now?" I asked between kisses.

He purred. "But it's so much more sexy to call you Mr. Warner, isn't it?" He wasn't wrong. In fact, something about the more problematic aspect of our relationship was enticing, but only when I divorced it from the very real issues it could present in my life.

"Sorry. I'll call you James if that's what you'd rather. No need to make this more uncomfortable than it already is."

"I'm very comfortable right now."

"I think it might be more comfortable if I get you to a bed instead of having to lie on this desk."

"Yeah, could be more comfortable."

He grinned. "You have to be a good boy and help me clean up this mess first."

I wasn't sure what he meant until he moved down and licked up some of the cum on my chest, but he didn't make it quick or stop. He pulled it into his mouth and continued licking and sucking, then moved to the bit above my navel, doing the same with it. He lapped some off the head of my dick before licking his way up my body, over the ridges of my abs.

A few soft kisses traced across my jaw, his lips nearing mine. I opened my mouth as he gave me the taste of us before his lips slammed down and we shared it, licking and sweeping tongues together, each of us swallowing what we could of ourselves. A droplet slipped out through a crack in our kiss, and we both fought to get to it first, chuckling at our greediness.

"You need to learn to share," he said, which made me laugh too.

He hooked his arms under mine. "Wrap your legs around me, James."

I obeyed, and he hoisted me into the air, carrying me toward the door.

"Fuck," he said as he stumbled and hit my back against the doorframe.

"*Ow,*" I cried out.

"Shit. That was supposed to be all swoony and romantic."

I unleashed a howl of laughter, something that felt new, like I'd never done that before him. And the way he cringed, as if he felt like such an idiot, was so disarming, I couldn't resist another kiss. We were playful, silly.

He pulled away from the kiss and glanced down the hall. "Okay. Let's try this again. Which way is the bedroom?"

I navigated him to the master bedroom, and he set me on the bed, stealing some more kisses. Our taste lingered on our tongues, and I didn't know why that gave me such a rush.

Maybe because it was evidence of that experience we'd shared in my office.

It was real, and it was ours.

I rolled on top of him and kissed down his body, reaching his cock, which I licked, lapping up the remaining cum. This was the first time I'd ever tasted another man's cum, and I was hooked. I was addicted to everything about being with a man.

Not just any man—Kyle.

I kissed my way up him, enjoying each and every muscle before our lips met again. There was a quiet to our kissing as it evolved, as we were no longer just lust and hunger. There was a sensuality to it we could relax into.

He nuzzled his face against my cheek, taking a whiff, like he just wanted to smell me. "Why did you make me wait to enjoy this? Why were you so cruel?"

"You know that's not what I was—"

"It doesn't change how it felt, and now that I've had a taste, you know you can't take this away from me, James. You don't get to show me all that and then strip me of it. Tell me you know that."

"I don't think I can resist you anymore if I try." My voice quaked as I said it, and Kyle pulled away, assessing my expression.

"You don't sound happy about that."

"There's a part of me that wishes I were stronger, that I could fight this, for the right reasons, and then there's this other part that can't fathom how this can't be right."

He leaned in again, running his tongue along my bottom lip before whispering against my face, "I'm not going to let anything happen to you, James. This will be our secret."

"I don't doubt it. It's just something I wish we didn't

have to keep secret. I'm not ashamed of anything about you, Kyle. You are...*incredible.*"

He pulled back, his brows tugging closer. "Aren't you complimentary after a little messing around."

"Not a compliment. Just a fact."

His expression sobered.

"This is going to be complicated," I warned.

"I know."

"We might both wind up regretting it."

"I don't believe that."

Neither did I, even though I was certain I should. But some part of my mind had switched off to permit me to enjoy this with him, and I welcomed it. Because I never felt like this before, and I couldn't imagine what life could be for if not for a moment like the one we'd just shared.

"Now shut up and kiss me before you get lost in that head of yours," he said, and mashed his lips against mine.

And it was easy to obey his order and lose myself in him once again.

29

KYLE

We slipped under the covers and made out, such an innocent act compared to everything we'd done in his office. We rolled together until he lay across me as we nipped at each other's lips, allowing those primal impulses to carry us through the experience.

He kissed down my body, guiding me onto my side before his lips stroked across my hip. He lingered, kissing and licking, his thumbs and fingers massaging my back and stomach. Sliding down farther to my ass, his mouth traveled along the curve before taking small bites into my flesh, like he was trying to get as much of me into his mouth as he could. I closed my eyes, enjoying the sensation as I found myself getting hard once again.

Licking my lips, I enjoyed what remained of us on my tongue as his hands cupped my ass, his face sliding between my cheeks before he kissed just under my balls.

It was a brief kiss, but as soon as he finished, he went back, licking and taking a deep breath as he teased my nuts into his mouth.

"You like that?" I asked.

He leaned away, and I rolled onto my back so he could see me, fully erect, right in his face.

He was flustered, and appeared surprised I'd called out his interest.

"You ever done that before? What the fuck am I saying? Of course you haven't."

"You have to know I've never done that before." He smirked, but his cheeks reddened as though he was embarrassed for how I'd addressed his inexperience.

"It's not a bad thing to want to see what it's like. Take your time. There's no hurry."

He glanced down at my erection.

"Pro tip: it's real similar to yours."

He laughed again.

Just like every other time we spent together, there was something so gratifying about being the one to help him lighten up.

"Put it in your mouth." It was an order, maybe more than he needed, but I wanted to encourage him along. He leaned down, rubbed his nose against the shaft, same as I'd done to him when I was working him up. His tongue came next, licking down to my balls and then up to the head. He hesitated, and I remained silent, curious if he would follow through.

As his breath hit the head, still sensitive from coming before, my dick perked up a little more in anticipation. He licked once more before sliding it into his mouth. His tongue explored as he moved with a bit too much caution. He didn't have any experience with a cock in his mouth, but he kept going at it, assuring me it wasn't a great challenge.

He gripped my hips as he pulled me even farther into his mouth, and I had to keep from rocking my pelvis since all I wanted was to get him to take as much of me as he could manage. I needn't have worried. When he choked a bit, he pulled back, chuckling before turning up to me.

"A little too ambitious," I teased.

"Maybe just a little."

Now his face was bright red.

"You don't have anything to be embarrassed about."

"I have a lot to be embarrassed about, actually." He was being self-deprecating, reminding me of how he'd call himself out on something in the middle of class.

"Not here. Not tonight. All that needs to get out of your beautiful head."

"You're saying that just to make me blush more."

"I'm saying that because you have a beautiful head, red or otherwise."

His expression didn't seem like an appropriate response to a compliment, but like I'd fucking slapped him.

I sat up, and he leaned back, his gaze shifting about uneasily, surprisingly so considering everything we'd done up to that point. Resting my hand against his cheek, I ran my thumb across his smooth scruff.

I'd imagined moments like this so many times, but

reality hadn't allowed us to break through and just be fucking human, to enjoy something so simple.

I grabbed his glasses and pulled them off.

"What are you doing?"

"Just want to see your eyes like this, without anything in our way."

He tried to turn again, but with my hand still against his cheek, I held it in place. "Don't leave me hanging, Teach. Look into my eyes."

He obeyed. "I don't get what you're up to."

"I'm gonna teach you how to take a compliment, beautiful."

He turned the opposite direction, but I pressed my hand with his glasses in it on that side, tugging him back. I would have let up if he'd fought me, but he submitted to my will, allowing me to look in his eyes, his cheeks burning against my fingers.

I forced a kiss. Again, he didn't deny me.

"I'm sorry you have such a difficult time hearing the truth," I whispered, barely pulling our lips apart.

"Not really the truth, since beauty is subjective."

"It's *my* truth."

He chuckled.

"Still impressed with how clever I am?"

"I continue to be impressed by everything about you, Kyle."

He nibbled at my lip. It should have felt like an odd interruption, and it might have been stranger had it not felt so right and perfect, like everything else we'd done. He slipped away for a moment before his lips returned to my neck, and he bit softly again, then nuzzled against my skin.

He traveled down to my chest, reaching my left nipple. He licked it, then hovered, his breath fanning against it.

We were both so vulnerable as he freely explored my body and I was the subject of his undivided attention.

I set his glasses down beside us while taking the back of his head in my other hand and reeling him close to my body, savoring how warm he was as he covered my flesh in saliva and breath.

It was so cruel that he could only offer so much at any time because I wanted to bathe in every part of him.

He moved back down to my cock, taking it into his mouth once more. I relaxed into the sensations, lying back as he explored, taking his time before he released my wet dick, which bounced against my abs, making him laugh.

"How are you this hard already?"

"I bet I can go again."

"Really?"

"You're just as hard," I observed.

"But I couldn't come."

"Try my dick out a little more, and I'll show you how quick my refractory period is."

He took me up on my offer as I tucked my hands behind my head, enjoying the way Teach sucked a dick. I wouldn't have said that to him, since I figured it might weird him out, but fuck it was a hot thought.

What had begun as a slow experiment turned frenzied quickly. Once he got the hang of it, he sure didn't play around. His movements sped up. Clearly, he could tell by how I jerked about that I was getting close again.

"James..."

He moved even faster, like he knew exactly what that meant, and I warned him, "I'm about to..." But I wasn't able to reach down fast enough before I shot. "Fuck, fuck, fuck," I said as he took my cock to the back of his throat, swallowing me right up.

My thoughts scattered, my eyes rolling back as I enjoyed the sensations moving through me, leaving me falling as my nerves relaxed from the experience.

James hadn't given up on my cock, though, and the sensitivity I wanted to bear became too much for me.

"Ah, okay. I can't."

He pulled off quickly, having caught on to my discomfort. He kissed up my happy trail, burying his face in my navel for a moment before continuing upward and giving me a warm, wet kiss.

Each kiss felt more intense than the last, and I grew terrified that I might wake and discover it had all been a cruel dream.

JAMES

Amazing as it had felt to cave to Kyle, I couldn't quiet the screaming in the back of my mind— all the voices of so many throughout my life, in some distant place in my mind, judging me for my actions. *Monster*, they would have said.

Why wasn't that enough to stop me from kissing him? Why wasn't it enough to convince me that what I did was evil? Somehow, the self-judgment and scorn only made me cling that much tighter to Kyle, to refute every argument against this with the demonstration of what his touch had the power to do to me.

We kissed until my lips chapped, then just held one another in bed.

I rubbed my nose against his.

The night had ended so differently than I'd expected, especially once I'd seen his classmates turn up for the event. At first, I'd believed they'd spoiled everything, but now I thanked them because had they not shown up, he might not have ever needed to come to my home.

He might never have pressed me about my feelings.

I might never have been weak enough to fuck up so colossally, my guilt and shame eclipsed by my need for pleasure.

Eventually, Kyle glanced behind him, and I could tell he was eyeing the clock on my nightstand.

In a moment, the magical world we had visited together—that had permitted us an escape—shattered. We would never be able to recapture that same moment, not in the way we had, so I treasured it as much as I could before Kyle said, "So..." His voice dragged out, deeper than usual before he cleared his throat and looked at me. "Four a.m. Should...be getting back. I'll take a shower first, I think."

I seized his wrist gently, wishing I could keep him there.

He rested his free hand on top of my grip, rubbing soothingly. "You can come with me." There wasn't a trace of humor in his tone, and I could tell by his expression that he could sense how serious I was about keeping him near.

"Yes, I think I will," I said, trying to calm myself. "It's just...four a.m. came far too soon."

"It had to come at some point." I detected the disappointment in his tone, as the collision of realities started to fill my mind, terrorize it.

"Just one more kiss without any of that," I said, moving

close and resting my forehead on his. "One more where we pretend it's just us and none of the rest matters."

"We already had that kiss. We can't ever get it back, but I can give you a reminder."

His words were true, and his kiss enough to do exactly as he'd said.

As we pulled away, he took my hand. "Come on. Doesn't a nice, warm shower sound good after all that?"

It did, but there was another part of me that never wanted to shower any of him off me. I wanted every bit of remaining sweat, saliva, and cum to stay imprinted on me.

But we slipped into the shower.

"Figure I can't borrow your clothes for today," he said, stepping under the running water. "Otherwise I'd stay."

The water trailed down, traveling along the curves of his body.

He noticed me watching and said, "Mind handing me some soap?"

I grabbed the bodywash from the corner nook and started to hand it to him.

"That's not how I want you to hand it to me."

He had a mischievous look in his eyes. I laughed, collecting some in my palms and lathering it between my fingers. As I approached him, he stood tall, letting his arms hang at his sides. I began rubbing him down, enjoying his form the way I had all night.

He squinted at me. "So how well can you see me without your glasses?"

"You're a young, sexy blonde from my class, right?"

He burst into a laugh. "You are such a dork...and I do love me a dork."

I gripped his cock, getting him hard again, and moved close, taking another kiss. I wasn't done, not anywhere close, which was what had upset me so much about the interference of Time.

"I'm nearsighted," I replied to his initial question. "I can see you, but I'd have an issue seeing our reflections. It would be a little blurry."

"So basically, you're saying that the closer I get, the better you see me." He did just that until he was so close, his eyes turned into four.

I laughed, but he hardly gave me a chance to get much out before his lips slammed against mine.

After we finished showering, we rinsed off, goofing around, pretending for as long as we could that we could keep this going. We dried off and returned to the bedroom, where I practically pounced on top of him, throwing him back against the bed and enjoying another of what would soon become our last kisses here.

As I pulled away, his expression suggested he was reaching the same bittersweet conclusion.

"Would have been nice if we'd done this tonight instead of a Thursday. Then we'd have all weekend."

I opened my mouth to make the suggestion, but he must've intuited what I was going to say because he blurted out, "Don't. I'd rather not end the night with empty promises."

It wouldn't have been a lie that I wanted to spend the weekend with him, but I could see why he would be worried. It was easy to let our imaginations run free when it was just the two of us, lost in our beautiful dream world. In reality, both of us had to decide what to do next. Just as I could lose my mind the moment the fantasy ended, he could do the same. Better to head on our ways and see what happened from then on.

I was careful with what I said next. "Maybe then I'll just say...we'll discuss the possibility of tonight later, but if we do agree on another night, then we'll have to talk about what the hell we're doing too."

He smiled, seeming pleased to know I was considering not just what we'd done, but what we were about to enter into...if we really could even do that much.

"Yeah, that sounds like a better plan anyway. I'll feel better if we've both had time to think on this before we talk about it."

"Are you going to sneak back through the woods?"

"Yeah, but it's okay. I might have to get used to it."

It all sounded wonderful, but I knew reality would set in the moment he left, and when he finally did, I could feel myself waking from the dream. Whatever spell we'd cast on one another lifted. It wasn't just the conflicting thoughts warring within my mind, but the weariness in my body, which no amount of coffee could remedy. Although, a few cups, along with the surge of excitement Kyle had given me, would be enough to get me through the day.

A stack of papers to grade would have normally been an amazing distraction, but I found it hard to convince myself to do that when I didn't want anything to pull me out of this night.

Or the future.

Practicalities came to mind. Too many reasons why we never should have crossed that line stacked one on top of the other: I'd breached an ethical boundary. I'd risked everything in my life. I'd committed a crime.

Why hadn't any of it been enough to keep me from taking things too far, and why wasn't any of it enough to make me stop?

KYLE

My heart pounding in my chest, I replayed the night in my head all the way back to Tex's to get a fresh set of clothes, then headed to school.

Until the night before, I believed I had quite an imagination, one that had kept James and me fucking in my mind all through the semester. But no amount of daydreaming could have prepared me for how it was going to feel to see myself all over him. After such an intense night, I figured I would have been groggy, but a lingering spark kept me going through the day.

Each class turned out to be the same as every other day—the predictable lectures, homework checks, pop quizzes—and I would close my eyes at times to keep those precious memories close to me.

Every caress, every stroke, every breath.

Despite how eager I was to see his face again, unlike

other days, I didn't mind the lag. I needed the time to reflect on those moments without an expression or stray gesture leading me to question any of it.

When I finally stepped into his classroom, I noticed him, the cowlick at the crown of his head more severe than usual. Under the glow of fluorescent lights, everything looked exactly as it might have had nothing happened the night before, but when his gaze shifted to me, I knew that wasn't true.

Such a simple look transformed all the usual to the very unusual that we were caught up in.

I took my seat, sliding my textbook and notebook across the desktop as I enjoyed my view of my teach, doing what he did best, what he loved most.

We'd see each other again that night, I was sure.

And despite not wanting a false promise, I was determined to spend the weekend with him. I struggled with the fantasy, because if he did end up seeing this dream as the nightmare it could become for his life, I would have to find a way to come to terms with that. It wouldn't make me hate him less for denying me all I wanted, but how could I pretend not to understand?

At the bell, when everyone left class, I lingered behind, the way I might have any other day, and we exchanged the subtlest of looks before I left.

Oh, the secrets behind those beautiful eyes.

The terrible things we did.

The magical moments we shared.

When school came to an end, I headed home, waiting for a text as I lied to myself and acted like I was fine even without hearing from him. But as soon as I'd showered off, he'd already messaged: *Too soon to ask about tonight?*

I had to laugh. He wasn't slick or smooth in his approach, but that was part of what made him so damn adorable.

I'll be over in an hour if that works.

I deleted *if that works*, since if he didn't want me over, he'd bring it up himself.

A smiley face popped up in reply.

Texting with James.

Finally.

Fina-fucking-ly.

So many fina-fucking-lies.

I told Tex I was heading out, without mentioning why, knowing he would assume I was running deliveries. Then I went over to James's, cutting through the woods from the park, as I had done the night before. His house was positioned perfectly, so I remained out of sight all the way to his back door, which I rapped on softly as excitement pulsed through me.

I could hardly remember him opening the door before my lips were pressed against his. I shoved him back against the adjacent kitchen counter.

No time was wasted as we wrestled our way to the bedroom, fighting together against the clothes that threatened to keep our bodies apart for too long. Soon he was on top of me, rubbing his cock against mine, as we'd done on the desk the night before. With his weight pressed against me, I had to remember to breathe as we kissed with an intensity that let me know the chemistry was as potent the second time. He kissed down my body, his mouth feeling its way around my flesh, learning every part of me. He took my dick into his mouth, enjoying it for a moment before he lay back, and I played with his cock and ass, fingering him like I'd done before.

Like so much of our relationship, there was a fresh innocence in the way we probed each other's bodies, moving at a pace just right for us.

I had my fingers in his ass, my mouth around his cock, when he came, calling out my name. I sucked his cum right up as he petted my head. Then I leaned up and jerked off so that my cum sprayed over him, droplets scattering across his torso, drenching the tiny hairs. He slid his fingers through some before taking them to his mouth and lapping me up, tasting me like he might have a delicious dessert.

"*Oh,*" he moaned as he ran his tongue around his fingers with as much care as he had my body.

I collapsed beside him, resting my hand in what remained of my cum on him, then wiped it across his torso and chest. I wanted to cover his body, to claim it for myself, to let anyone who came after me know I was there.

Our mouths weren't apart for long before he rolled on top of me, getting my own mess across me too.

I wasn't close to being done with him, but it was a beautiful start.

As we settled after that first encounter, we held one another. It felt like no time had passed since the night before. It all threaded together seamlessly.

The only thing that shook me from my enchanted state was the rumble of his stomach.

He laughed, looking to his belly. "Guess I should have eaten before you came over."

"Ah, is that why the poor baby was having to eat my filthy cum?"

"I don't think that was really the reason, but now that you mention it..." He swiped across a wet spot on my abs and pulled it back into his mouth, looking wickedly pleased with himself for the inspiration.

"You evil little thing you."

He smiled brightly, and I couldn't resist taking another kiss.

"Then what are we making for dinner, James?"

JAMES

"Some beef, steaks that are probably about to go bad, chicken," I called back to him as I surveyed our options in the fridge. Kyle came up behind me, so I headed off any potential criticism. "Please don't judge the mess."

"I like your messes." He kissed my cheek, snatched my ass, my pajama bottoms a cruel barrier between us.

"You know what I mean."

"I'm not your douchebag wife, so I don't care. You should see the mess Tex and I keep the fridge in. At least your fruit looks fresh. Speaking of, mind if I have one of these Honeycrisps?"

"Of course." I grabbed an apple from the shelf and handed it to him.

"Thank you. You sure were trying to make me work up an appetite in there," he said as he walked to the sink and rinsed off the apple.

As he chomped into it, I asked, "How do you feel about fajitas—chicken and steak?"

"Ooh, my little chef. That sounds delicious."

He made himself comfortable on the kitchen table, in just black briefs, his taut abs creasing along the lines in his impressively defined six-pack. While still chewing, he took another bite of his apple.

"Jesus, how hungry were you? I wasn't trying to starve you."

"Pretty damn hungry. I forgot to pack a lunch this morning. It's all right. Ben gave me some of his pudding, but I didn't eat much because...I guess you could say I kind of got some good news last night." He displayed a cheeky grin before taking another bite.

I enjoyed the sensation his words stirred in my chest as I reflected on that special night. But unlike the night before, the pleasure we'd shared that afternoon came with a tinge of guilt, since I knew every moment I delayed confronting reality was another moment of lying to myself. Although, I feared that honesty might do little more than chase away everything we'd enjoyed.

I closed the fridge and approached him, took another quick kiss, hoping it would drown out my worries. It helped, but I knew I would have to get used to the pain.

Something Sheila had made me damn good at surviving.

"Don't worry, James," he whispered, as if intuiting everything I felt.

"I'm trying." I nuzzled my face into his cheek before pulling away.

"Here. Maybe some of my apple will cheer you up, Teach."

I cringed at his use of the nickname, especially after all we'd done. But I knew he was trying to cheer me up with the playful symbolism.

He turned the apple to where he'd already taken a bite, and I accepted it, savoring the refreshing taste before swallowing. Kyle watched like it was a show, and I struggled to pull my gaze from those deep blue eyes that had a hypnotic effect on me, in a different way than they usually did.

Now I was their willing prisoner.

"Teach, this apple's only gonna last me so long. We gotta get started on these fajitas, or we'll be ordering out. And I'm not doing a delivery run for us."

I laughed as he hopped off the table and made himself at home, opening my fridge. "Let's see what we've got to work with…"

I admired his ass in his briefs as he pulled out peppers.

"Got any tomatoes?"

"A can of diced in the pantry."

He shook his head. "Guess it'll have to do. And tortillas?"

"I have some in the fridge—"

"That's not gonna work for me." He set the peppers on the counter and returned to the pantry to inspect the contents. "I can work with this," he mumbled, grabbing the flour and vegetable oil to add to our collected ingredients.

I manned the meat while he made fresh tortillas. It reminded me of the sort of teamwork we'd come to know through our volunteer work together.

The pan sizzled as he spread some of the dough he'd prepared inside it. He'd thrown on a tee to keep from getting burned by any stray pops of oil. As he kept busy with his task, I pan-fried chicken on a skillet beside him. Our primary goal seemed to be evading the truth as we embraced the sound of the cracking juices on our skillets until we had our meal ready and were sitting adjacent to each other at my table.

"Try the tortilla by itself first," he said. "I want you to marvel at my skills."

I laughed, shaking my head as he rested his foot against mine, rubbing gently as I cut one and bit into it.

Damn, of course he could make a tortilla.

He eyed me as though waiting for the compliment he was sure would follow. "I don't see why I have to say anything. You already know they're good."

"Maybe you could do wonders for my self-esteem if you copped to it."

"Since when did you start running low on self-esteem?"

"Since you tasted my tortilla and didn't lose your fucking mind."

As he always managed to do, he got me laughing.

"Fine," he said, annoyed. "I'm going to take these away and get you some from the fridge."

He took my plate like he was going to snatch it from me, but I seized it and confessed. "No, no. These might very easily be the best tortillas I've ever had. You are some kind of tortilla god. Is that what you want to hear?"

He smirked but then frowned. "Now I'm a little disappointed I haven't been called a god in other areas yet."

"Trust me, Kyle, you're a god in any area I've seen...and felt."

"And I can't wait to show you the god I am in even more areas." He winked, taking another bite of his fajita, grabbing the tortilla with his hand and shoving it right into his mouth as I cut a slice of mine. He had a thick chunk of meat in his mouth when he said, "So..."

By the tone of his voice and the awkwardness in how he dragged it out, I didn't have to be psychic to know what he meant. And for some reason, I didn't feel like he was about to spit out a joke like he usually would have.

I just threw it out there: "Is this the part where we have that awkward conversation where we figure out what the hell we're going to do about this?"

It took him a minute to finish chewing and swallowing. "Yeah, that's the one."

"Well, we would have gotten there sooner or later." As we sat there, facing off against the fears that had been mounting since the night before, I decided it was best to be honest. "I keep running through all the reasons why this is a terrible idea. I see the consequences, and I see the worst like it's a premonition."

I teared up as I spoke the words because of how it all haunted me in the moment. It was strange how we could go from having such a good time to everything bubbling up at once, to the point where it was fucking over-whelming.

He pushed out of his seat and approached me, putting his arm around my shoulder. "I know, James. I see it too."

"I don't want to ruin my life," I spat out, turning my gaze to him. I could see the fear in his eyes, but I was quick to help soothe it with the truth: "But I don't want to lose this either."

He pulled me into his chest, and tears rushed from my eyes.

"It wasn't supposed to be like this," I muttered.

"I know, James," he iterated.

If only I'd never fallen that first day. If only I'd never assigned extra credit...or been nearly mugged. If only I'd never mentioned H4H to him. But no matter how many times I told myself I would have been better off never having had those experiences, what the hell was the point to a life where I never knew Kyle Forsythe?

"Trust me," he went on, "this was the last place I ever thought any of this would lead. But you don't have to figure it out by yourself." He kissed my forehead. Closing my eyes, I enjoyed the sensation of sweet relief as it moved through me.

He moved down, kissing my right eye, then my left.

I took a breath and pulled back, looking into his sincere gaze.

It startled me how familiar that side of him had become to me, snuck up on me. At the beginning of the semester, I had grown accustomed to his scowl, his almost sinister-looking face. All those hard edges he kept around him to guard himself from the world, but there was this softer side of him, a side I felt he reserved for so few, and I was lucky enough to be one of those few.

"We'll sort this out," he whispered. "But just know, if anything you're considering involves me keeping my hands off you, that's not going to work for me."

"I could lose my job. My reputation. My dream. Go to prison." Even as I said the words, though, I knew I'd already accepted that before we'd touched. And I'd crossed that line anyway. "I've always been so good at playing by the rules, and I finally have too good a reason not to."

"We just have to be careful. I'll never come up to the house. I'll sneak in like I have been. Nothing has to change outside of that."

"Everything's going to change, Kyle."

"Everything's *already* changed." He kissed me again.

He was right.

Because before Kyle, there was only pain and hurt. And after him...it was like I'd just learned how to really breathe for the first time.

In a dark world of so much despair, I found a speck of light. Even if it dimmed or faded...or was cut off, to know it had existed for any stretch of time was better than the alternative.

33

KYLE

We'd taken that leap of faith into the unknown.

We were the only ones who could know what was right for us. Fuck the world and its oppressive rules and laws that demanded too much of our hearts.

Naturally, with our arrangement came secrets, which were hardest to keep from the people closest to me—Tex, Ben, and Taryn. No one could know where I was spending most of my time since James and I had admitted the truth: that what we had, what we felt, what we shared was too much to fight against anymore.

What had begun as some inexplicable connection had turned emotional and then become wildly physical. We spent sleepless nights desperately grasping at the time we made together, our fears of what we did reminding us to never take a moment for granted.

Each kiss was a wish...a hope...a fear, so I cherished every fucking one.

He kept a key for me beneath a lawn ornament in the yard—a concrete frog that had been left by his house's previous owners.

Weeks felt like months before winter break began, and I was looking forward to spending as much of it as I could with him.

I locked the French doors behind me before walking through his home, enjoying how familiar it was starting to feel to me. I followed the short hall to the foyer, peered out the window, and saw his car in the driveway. Heading up to the bedroom, it wasn't long before I detected the sound of running water in the master shower. I stripped down, eagerness mounting now that I could enjoy this fully—the exams were behind us, and we had two weeks without the stress and worry of having to see each other during class, doing our best not to be totally enamored with one another through one of his lectures, which now had a way of making me painfully hard.

I slipped around the corner, and he turned and jerked back, eyeing me through the glass pane between us. "Oh shit. You surprised me." He grinned, assessing my body.

Behind the bright smile, I could see the worry, the dread, and I joined him, offering kisses as fast as I could to remind him why they were worth everything.

I'll protect you, James. I won't let anything happen to you. Ever.

It was my vow to both of us.

His lips found their way down my body, moving with

the water rushing over me. He stroked my cock before getting it in his mouth.

"Fuckin' A, you know how I get at the end of the day —" It was too late. I shot inside his mouth, releasing all that tension I normally would have done in the privacy of my bedroom. "Fuck me," I said as he lapped up my cum.

He pushed to his feet, his grin expanding.

"You know damn well what you did," I said, glaring at him.

"It's hot, and it makes you blush, which is refreshing, seeing how it isn't me for a change."

"Yeah, well, next semester I'll be ready for this and make sure to jerk off in my car before I get over here."

"You wouldn't do that."

"What makes you say that?"

"Because you know how much I enjoy making you come quickly...and because it doesn't keep me from being able to make you come more."

His arms folded around me as he backed me up against the tiled wall, our bodies fitting together as perfectly as always, his cock sliding against my pelvis as mine slid against his smooth, wet pubes. He kissed away from my mouth, to my neck.

"Is now a bad time to criticize your essay exam questions?"

James laughed near my ear before biting at the lobe. "You little shit."

I did my best not to make too many jokes about our situation, but they made the difficult parts more bearable.

He sucked and nipped at my ear before kissing his way down my body.

I was learning his favorite path—traveling between my pecs, to my navel, where he'd offer a quick lick before returning up along my right side, his lips back on mine as though the trip away had been too long. It made me think of my own paths as I navigated my way around his body, working to explore and determine my tongue's favorite routes.

I slid my hand between his stomach and cock as he stroked against my belly. "Come on," I told him between kisses. He pushed up close, as though against his will, driven by sheer need to get to the end. I could tell he was getting close, so I reached around and tucked my fingers between his cheeks, massaging his hole, and it was like a trigger as I felt the warm rush against me.

We gasped together as he continued shooting across me.

We licked and panted. Some of the movements we made didn't make any sense to my logical mind and left me wondering what he must've thought, but it was a judgment I let go with all the rest as we let ourselves submit to the instincts that had us tugging and pulling at one another, close never seeming close enough.

I liked to think it was becoming habit how quickly we wound up in the bedroom with me having little memory of when I'd dried off or had done anything other than rolled around with him.

He bit at my jaw, teasing me before doing it once

again. He started to kiss, then stopped, before lunging forward...and stopping.

"You're cruel," I told him, and he laughed, his eyes lighting up.

Had I ever been as happy as I was in that moment?

Had James?

Even with reality nagging at our consciences, it was a small price to pay for the kiss that came next to grant me what he'd left me hungering for.

Torture, pure, delicious, spectacular torture in Mr. Warner's bed.

When I came the next time, I didn't make James pull away. His face traveled right to my balls, which he licked in a frenzy as I shot across my abs again. I was surprised by how much I came, considering it was such a short time since I'd blown my first load.

He started to lick it before I said, "No, no. Come on me."

He got on his knees, obeying my command, knowing I wanted him to shoot over my load. His hips jerked as he finished up, and I wiped my hand across it, moving it in a circular motion, wanting it all over me, both of us, pooled together. James rested his hand on my belly, helping me massage it over my skin.

We managed to get it all across my torso.

He glanced me over before leaning down and licking at the edge of my abs, between my navel and hip. I relaxed into the feeling as he traced the ridges of my abdomen. I put my hands out to my sides, wanting him to enjoy it in whatever way pleased him most.

He licked and sucked his way around me, taking his time, and I closed my eyes, reveling in his tongue's exploration of my flesh. It became clear as he retraced the path he'd taken up to my chest that he was going back over every centimeter to make sure to get it all.

My face heated up as he reached my navel, his tongue swirling around it, then within the rim, like he was trying to clean me off. He kissed it and then continued on his path.

The experience was a reminder that we could finally take our time with each other's bodies. We didn't have to race through each moment like it would get away from us if we didn't.

When he reached my right pec, he licked under it before kissing and taking my nipple between his teeth, gently teasing. Then he moved up to my mouth and claimed it with just as much enthusiasm. I grabbed the back of his head, pulling him close as I embraced that familiar taste. He pressed his body against mine, warming the cool sensation of the air against the saliva he'd left across me.

We kissed until it was too exhausting to keep going, until we just had our lips close, breathing into each other's mouths, gazing into each other's eyes.

We didn't speak, but it was the loudest, most beautiful silence, complemented by every breath, every slight shift on the bed, every time our lips touched.

"Mr. Warner..."

"Yes, Mr. Forsythe?"

I laughed—no, giggled—before he kissed me again.

As soon as he freed my lips, I went on, "I think this is my favorite extra-credit assignment."

"You dirty boy. If I thought you needed to improve your grade, I'd be worried about you using me for an A."

"Pretty sure there needs to be a plus after that A."

"I haven't graded the finals yet, so I don't know."

"Oh, naughty teach. You need to get those grades in for our report cards."

"If someone doesn't spend the break distracting me, I'll be able to do that."

"If I'm not distracting you, then I'm not doing my job."

As I smiled, he said, "You'll need a break eventually, and I figured I'd get those in tonight."

"I think you underestimate my stamina."

"That just makes me more determined to test it."

We did just that through the afternoon, and as the evening approached, I agreed to make dinner while he finished keying in the grades to the system. He was finished with grades around the same time as I was finishing up with dinner, plating the food.

"It sure does smell damn good," he said.

"Don't come over here. Sit down and let me finish playing wifey."

He obeyed, and I prepped our plates before heading over and setting them down in our usual spots, privately enjoying that we'd crafted a routine since we'd begun seeing each other regularly.

"Ooh, meatballs."

"It's ground-chicken meatballs. Better for you. With some spaghetti. Oh, let me get the parmesan."

"I don't think I have any."

"Pfft. I got some while I was on my route the other day. I'm no amateur." I fetched it from the fridge and handed it to him. "So what are our Christmas plans?" I pressed.

"Besides the obvious?"

"I noticed you don't have a tree up or anything. We'll have to fix that."

"I was figuring I would skip that part."

"Fuck no. You need to get a tree. This year more than ever. What the fuck else are we gonna make time for if not to decorate a little, watch some stupid Christmas movies on Netflix, enjoy some songs. What did your family use to do for Christmas when you were growing up?"

"My parents were very religious, so we did all the things you'd expect. The big production of it, and me and my brother would feel so guilty because we couldn't get to sleep and we were told if we didn't go to sleep, Santa wouldn't come."

"Mom would go all out for Christmas too. You know, looking back, things like that still confuse me. Because she did do everything she could. She adored me, but her love was always contingent on my playing by their rules. But it was nice. We talked about going to Atlanta and the Botanical Gardens. Mom would always want to go there, and she'd show me the lights, but Dad would always be in a mood, ya know?"

"I'm sorry. You shouldn't have been treated that way."

"We all should have been treated better by a lot of people, but that's not really how life works, is it?"

I wondered if the expression he made had to do with

his brother, or Sheila, or some combination of so many things in his life, still many I'd yet to discover about him.

"I guess I'll have to at least buy some extra lights for this tree too, then," James went on.

"You don't have lights?"

"I'll have to check the lights in my boxes of crap, make sure they still work, but I like the idea of a Christmas in my new home."

"I'm glad to be here for your new beginning."

"I can toast to that."

We raised our glasses and clinked them together.

Because this was just our fucking beginning...

JAMES

Criminal. *Villain. Monster. Those were* words that came to mind when I thought about what Kyle and I did.

But if I was a monster, so be it. I wasn't going to stop, that much was obvious.

We weren't hurting anyone. Just appreciating the time we shared with each other. But no amount of rationalizing could subdue the fear of discovery. As long as we explored our secret affair, each time he arrived at my place, each chat, each kiss, every moment we spent at H4H was another chance to get caught. The moment when Kyle's reputation would be further tarnished as my life would go up in flames.

And yet these risks couldn't keep us apart.

As I pulled alongside DJ's house, excitement stirred within me. It surprised me since I'd spent most of the past few days annoyed by the message exchange I'd had with Sheila earlier in the week.

Mom's in the hospital again, she'd texted, and kept texting.

Another few weeks, a month at most.

Please.

Please, I need your help on this, James.

I wasn't glad her mother was in the hospital with another hip injury, but it seemed more of a convenient excuse than a dire issue that prevented her from moving forward with the divorce.

After all, life had taught me there would always be something...

Her excuse hadn't bothered me as much as the fact that I'd caved once again, but I wasn't going to let that ruin my holiday. Not now that I had someone to look forward to spending my time with. Despite seeing Kyle nearly every day since the break had begun, I didn't know how it could ever be enough.

There was so much left to learn about each other's bodies. Messy as we could be with our cum, what we did still felt so innocent. What amounted to little more than humping, jerking off, and making out...oh God, the making out. It reminded me of those early days of learning my own body in the privacy of my bedroom, questioning, imagining, stroking.

He never pushed me too far, too soon. The pace was... so perfectly us.

When I headed inside, I noticed Kyle chatting up some of our mutual builder friends. In a red Santa cap that matched his thermal, he laughed at something as I neared the group, collected between the decorated tree and the fireplace.

Kyle had a way of looking hot even in the ridiculous Santa cap.

He turned, catching me in his sights, his smile expanding, eyes lighting up just a tad more. It was a good thing I'd had time to adjust to being around him—through class, volunteering, and extra credit—time to adjust to being with him around other people, seeing that I could be practically screaming with excitement on the inside as the world went on, unaware. Surreal how even the most powerful sensations that left me vibrating with eagerness would go totally undetected by anyone around us.

Had I been a man of faith, I might have believed the universe protected us, shielded our feelings because it must've known that what we felt was something sacred. A secret worth hiding from the prying eyes of an unsympathetic world.

I greeted my buddies, sneaking closer to Kyle gradually. I hadn't even meant to, yet found myself beside him. Some subconscious desire must've been leading me there all along. We stood side by side, arms occasionally touching, as if by accident, but something I could always tell when I looked into his eyes was never an accident.

There were moments where I pretended everyone knew—that we were out and just like every other couple present.

DJ and Maya.

Bentley and Hanna.

DJ had just finished talking about a fundraising team he was organizing for some of the guys at the Wyachet homeless shelter, when Maya mentioned wanting to get together and go see the Christmas lights.

It was the opportunity I'd been waiting for. "Would you guys be interested in heading downtown to see the winter lights at the Botanical Gardens?"

I, of course, had an ulterior motive. Since Kyle and I had discussed past Christmases and broken promises, I had been planning to find a way to get a group together. We couldn't do something like that on our own without possibly being discovered, or perhaps someone becoming suspicious, but with our mutual friends, it would be a way to be together in public without a chance of being found out.

"That would be wonderful," Maya said. "We'll have to check what night would be good. It'd be nice to actually do something this year. Usually we go to the downtown lights, but it's not exactly spectacular." She chuckled. "We'll have dinner beforehand too."

Dinner too? Yes, that's perfect. Just perfect.

I couldn't look at Kyle until we detoured back to casual conversations. When I finally caught his gaze, he winced slightly, just enough to show me he thought I was up to no good.

And was I ever.

～

"SLY MOTHERFUCKER," Kyle said as soon as I entered the house. Not for the first time, he'd beaten me there. Still in his Santa cap, he attacked me against the front door, lips forcing up against mine. With every kiss, I could feel his appreciation for convincing the others to go on an outing with us, to give us a special moment in public. Taking his arms, I pulled him closer as his tongue slid across mine, a reward for my sneaky plot. Our lips smacked before parting.

"That was a little too sweet," he said. "Maybe annoyingly so."

"Annoyingly sweet? Is that what I am?"

"Sometimes. But you're lucky I like annoyingly sweet."

He pushed against me, and I started to step back, not realizing his heel was behind mine, making me stumble backward. His arms were right there to brace me, but I pulled him back until we were lying against the stairs.

"Fuck," I said, my hip taking the brunt of the fall.

"What the hell?"

And then I couldn't stop laughing.

"Yeah, ever the annoyingly sweet klutz." He laughed with me before kissing me again.

We were still smiling and giggling, but only for a few moments, since as we continued working up some heat, the mood shifted to deadly serious as we both became filled with that familiar determination. We tugged at one another's clothes as we made out. The stairs were perhaps the most uncomfortable place for us to be doing this, but it was something I could distract myself from as I worked to tear Kyle out of his clothes. He undid my fly, and we pulled my pants down.

He growled. "I want to be inside you, James."

"I want it too," I said, even though my body was trembling.

The more we'd done, the more curious I'd become about having him like that. Up until then, it hadn't even come up, as if he was giving me time to adjust to how new this all was. It wasn't something I thought I would ever want...until I knew the feeling of Kyle's body against mine. And now I knew I could trust him with all of me.

"Would you prefer a condom?" he asked me. "I just got tested at my doc's last week."

"I've been tested too. Had to because of..." I didn't want to even say her name, not when we were having such a good time.

"I just want to make sure you feel safe."

"I feel safe with you, Kyle."

He snickered. "Sorry. I'm not laughing at you. I just... I'm glad you said that, because the thought of having my cum inside you drives me crazy."

Why did that excite me so much too?

Why did it seem like his cum pushing up within me was as close as I needed him to be?

"Do we need lube or something?" I asked, genuinely oblivious to what I needed to make this happen.

He nibbled at my earlobe before whispering, "I can make this work. We'll just take it real slow, and let me know if you need any, and we can stop."

I wasn't sure what to think about that, but I knew I

trusted him, that he wouldn't do anything that would hurt me. I lay across the steps, and he crawled down, spread my legs, kissed my inner thighs, so fucking softly, a warmth pulsed right through my entire body, landing in my cheeks.

I grabbed the bannister slats on either side of me to support myself as Kyle ran gentle kisses along the inside of my legs. I offered my ass up to him as he reached his destination, his tongue sliding around it before he kissed it the way he might have kissed my lips. It was the sort of kiss that sent quivers through me, making my legs shake noticeably. My face flushed, and I knew it was because I was embarrassed at how effortlessly he was able to affect me.

Warm, wet kisses set me at ease before I felt the tip of his finger pushing within me. It didn't take him much time to work his way in. I closed my eyes, allowing myself to fully experience the pleasure of mounting pressure, my body opening right up for him, welcoming Kyle to take what was already his.

What he must've known was all his.

Another finger.

And then a third.

"Kyle, just give me your cock, please," I begged. I could feel it in my bones that I was ready. At one time, his fingers had felt so good, but now they felt like a cruel tease, an obstacle to what I found myself desperate for.

I peeked as he licked my hole once more before glancing up at me, this fierce expression in his eyes, that animal in him that just wanted to fuck. Had I not known him better, I would have been frightened by the intensity in that expression, but with it, I could also feel that protectiveness, the same sort that had been there for me on that night in the dark alley.

It wasn't going to be easy to take him, I was sure, but he would protect me through the experience.

The pressure mounted, but he didn't push in. It was like he was getting me used to the feeling of the head of his dick against my hole. He leaned down and kissed me, resting his hand against my face and stroking through my scruff as he parted from me long enough to lick his other hand a few more times, guiding it back to his cock and then to my hole.

"Is this going to be enough?" I asked.

"Only one way to find out. Just tell me if it hurts."

"That won't be a problem," I said with a nervous chuckle.

He offered a few more spits and licks to his palm, lubing his cock and my ass. I trusted his expertise over my expectations and assumptions.

"Relax, relax," he whispered, kissing my temple.

Taking deep breaths, I did the best I could, which was made easier by him taking his time, the pressure building as I felt his cock pushing in.

His lips and tongue lingered at the corner of my mouth as I moaned.

He permitted me a moment to relax, with my hands clinging to the slats, his body pinned against mine.

Steadily, the pressure climbed, my body shivering in

anticipation, but it was just the right speed, Kyle paying close attention to my comfort or when I would tense up.

Farther and farther still, he navigated within me, his lips traveling behind my ear before he nipped at the lobe.

The discomfort of the stairs against my back was easily made up for by the pleasure Kyle roused within me and the hot fire my face felt as he grazed his teeth down my neck, biting softly before offering a lick.

He leaned back and gauged his work. "My cock looks so beautiful in your hole. How does it feel?"

"Still adjusting, I think."

"Is it too much?"

"No, no. Just not used to this sensation."

He stroked his hand against my ass, helping me ease up even more.

"Better?"

I nodded, and he smiled, as though knowing that it felt good for me meant the world to him.

"How is it on your dick, though?"

"Tight virgin ass? Really? Pretty fucking amazing."

A swirl of energy radiated in my chest as his cock dug farther within me until I felt that stimulation I did when he'd put his fingers deep inside me.

"Yeah, right there," I told him, and felt his hips press up against my ass, assuring me he was all the way in.

And it felt even more amazing than I'd imagined.

"*Fuck.*" My eyes rolled back. "*Fuck, fuck, fuck.*"

He snickered. "I like seeing you needing my dick inside you."

I couldn't deny it.

I wasn't sure what to expect before, but I never could have anticipated it until I had Kyle's cock buried in me.

He studied my face as he moved slightly, and the way his dick shifted across my prostate had my leg twitching, my foot slapping softly against the bannister. He stroked his hand along my thigh as his thrusts became more pronounced, more dramatic, as my ass allowed. A bead of precum spilled from the head of my cock onto my belly.

"How's that?"

He leaned back down, his lips returning to mine, so I had to fight back just to tell him, "Perfect. Just right. Amazing."

"The *perfect* was enough," he told me with a grin, hooking his arms under mine and thrusting much harder.

Now that Kyle had moved around some inside me, I was more confident that I could handle that cock, and my hunger for more overwhelmed me. "Oh God... Fuck me. Fuck me, Kyle."

He picked up the pace, his breath rushing out with every bit of energy he exerted as he fucked me. My back would regret this, but considering how good it felt to have Kyle finally lodged within me, my future self would have to fucking deal with it. Nothing else mattered as long as we were as close as we could be to each other.

He nibbled at my bottom lip as he continued drilling my hole, and I could hardly manage the range of sensations moving through me, stimulating me on so many levels.

He leaned back again, locking my legs in the crook of

his arms before thrusting, his six-pack flexing, his arms fully pushed out as he dominated me.

"Give it to me, James," he said, his eyes on my dick. "Come on."

He must've been able to tell by how much I was precoming that I was close, without even touching myself. It wasn't an experience I was used to. But I felt my climax pulsing higher and higher, to the point where I had to roll my head back as I clung to the bannister slats.

"Come in me. I want you to come in me first, please." My voice was all need, hunger, and desire.

Somehow we'd managed to devolve into the most animalistic parts of ourselves and transcend our very humanity all at once.

It hurt how badly I needed to shoot, but I didn't rush it since I could tell by the way Kyle's cock was hitting my prostate that it wouldn't be long, and I wanted his cum inside me first...fuck, I didn't even know why I needed it inside me so badly.

Between all the sensations—the steps, Kyle's cock, the pulsing pain in my shaft as my body worked me close to release—my vision of Kyle collided with every stray moment when I'd wanted him just like that, when I felt like my dream had finally come to life.

"Come in me," I begged him once again, feeling torn between reality and the fantasy world where Kyle and I were free to enjoy one another without shame.

His face twisted up in that beautiful way I'd become accustomed to, his hips slapping against my ass, a clapping sound echoing through the foyer, mixing with the sound of his guttural cry.

He collapsed forward, gasping, before his lips pushed against mine, but only for a moment, since I had to pull away as a jolt of excitement shot through me.

"*Ah,*" I called out as my cock throbbed.

Kyle continued shifting within me, and my cum seemed to shoot out in the same rhythm, each rub of Kyle's cock against my prostate guiding it from me.

The fire in my soul settled, leaving me panting, kissing and licking Kyle's lips as my body assured me, incredible as the experience had felt, I would definitely be feeling it in my back tomorrow.

KYLE

After James had asked the group about the Botanical Gardens' winter exhibit, I could hardly think straight. No matter how many times I saw James's thoughtfulness, it always shocked me. Even though no one could have understood his motive, and he'd done his best to keep from looking at me at the party, the moment our gazes met for the first time since he'd mentioned it, I hoped he could feel how goddamn grateful I was. Not only because of some exhibit, but because it reminded me that this man I'd come to appreciate was everything I'd imagined and so much more.

While I couldn't demonstrate how appreciative I was at the party, I was eager to express it as soon as we made it back to his place.

Like so much of what we'd done since we'd met, it was wild and unexpected. Our feral nature overtook us, and despite the effort it required to make it work on his stairway, it was a fuck that was more than worth the coordination.

What it felt like to be inside him, to feel him and see the pleasure in his expression as he shot all over himself... Knowing I'd be able to recall that experience for the rest of my life gave me so much fucking pleasure. I replayed it again and again as I lay in bed beside James, feeling as satisfied as ever.

I rolled toward him. He gazed at the ceiling through his glasses, his hands resting on his chest.

Noticing a red spot on his elbow, I stroked it with my thumb. "You okay?"

He inspected it. "A little carpet burn." There was this dreamy expression on his face as he assessed the damage.

"Should have been a little more careful, I guess."

"I think that was the perfect amount of careful." He rolled toward me, kissed my cheek, the rim of his glasses tapping my skin.

"So you enjoyed your first time?"

He smiled, glowing. "I can't believe I never did that before. I knew there was a prostate. I certainly heard about it. I understood that it probably felt good, but it's not exactly where my mind went to when I was married."

"Not even experimenting a little? Come on. You had to be at least a little curious about what was going on back there. I've never bottomed, but I've played with myself enough to know what's up there."

"It's not something that's typical of straight relationships, maybe."

I glared at him. "Come on. There's a reason pegging's a thing."

"Pegging?"

"When a woman wears a strap-on. Seriously, how am I the more experienced one in this?"

He laughed before his expression turned serious. "Not too difficult, really. I haven't...done as much as I figured a guy in a five-year relationship might have. We were very sexual in the beginning—crazy, wild, which was wonderful—but it was a very brief period of time. Then, when the affairs started, I had a difficult time even getting hard, and she would make comments... And even if I could, there was constant criticism during. The sort of things that burrowed into my brain. I sometimes wonder if that's how she meant it or if that was just how I took it. It became almost a terrifying prospect. Usually I couldn't even satisfy her, which led to me retreating into myself, thinking maybe that was why she needed the other guys."

"Don't talk like that. If there was an issue, she could have talked to you. What she did wasn't an answer to anything."

He nodded, but the way he did it, I could tell he wasn't convinced.

It certainly wasn't the sort of thing we could resolve in a quick conversation.

I did my best not to be disrespectful, given she was his ex—not ex, his wife. His whatever the hell he wanted to call her. Regardless, I didn't trust my own feelings toward Sheila, since I could have just been jealous she'd once had his heart, but I also didn't imagine a guy like James would have said things like that about a decent human being, someone who hadn't torn his heart apart with such reckless abandon.

Such a loyal man. He deserved better, and I wanted to be his better.

"Anyway, it was nice to feel again...to really feel again," he went on, and his smile returned.

"I can kiss to that," I said before taking one, and then another. "Mmm. I think we're going to have a very merry Christmas."

IT WAS HARDLY TORTURE BEING CONFINED to James's place, spending our days ordering meals in or fixing them in his kitchen. It would be a short break from school, but not from studying, since I kept myself busy, learning every part of him, his tastes, his interests, in the bedroom and outside of it.

We arranged to meet DJ, Maya, Bentley, and Hanna out for dinner and then the lights.

Sitting next to him at the dinner table made it feel like the sort of date I wanted it to be. We kept our legs pressed together, the way we had at the extracurricular event the night my classmates showed up.

"Kyle, you don't want any wine—" Maya said before pressing her lips together. "Oh. I always forget you're still in high school." She sipped her red wine before turning to James. "He must look older than most of the other kids, right?"

"He does look older than them, yes," James acknowledged, and DJ piped up, "I have a bit of a game with the newbies where I ask them to guess. Usually it's twenty-two."

"Right?" Maya said. "No offense, James, but you look more like a student than Kyle."

"Aw, Teach can't help that he's got that baby face," I said.

"Do you have good classes?" Maya asked him. "Or do they give you hell?"

"They don't give him hell when I'm around," I joked.

"What do you mean?"

"Oh no. We have to go there, don't we?" James said, and we shared the story of my beef with Brian. Everyone enjoyed it, and James finished the tale with, "But this guy's managed to behave himself since."

"You must go a little easier on Kyle, though," DJ said. "I mean, you're basically friends now."

I knew he was basing that on the interactions he'd seen on Saturdays, but if only he knew...

"I don't really have to go easy on him. He's a good student. In my class, at least."

"A good student? That's so funny," Maya said.

"Why?" James prodded.

Her face turned serious. "Oh, nothing. Kyle surely knows because of how he grew up in the church, he was... a big deal in Wyachet. And I guess..." She was struggling like she was afraid of saying the wrong thing. She took another sip of wine, as though wanting to buy herself time to think. "Small-town talk is weird like that. You hear these stories about someone, but you don't really know people until you know them."

James's jaw tensed. He must've known what she was referring to, the sorts of things she would have heard from my asshole father pitting as many people in his congregation as he could against me.

"I don't know why you'd believe any of the nutjobs in this town," Bentley said. "Either they're methheads or cult members."

"And which are you?" Maya asked.

"The small minority of normal people."

"If you're normal, I think I'll be joining one of the cults," Hanna mused, but while everyone was enjoying Hanna's tease, I caught a glimpse of James, noticing his serious expression.

It was nice that the awkwardness of Maya's comment had passed, but really, James couldn't have known...this had been my life for a long time. I'd been lucky enough to find people like this crew, who were kind, who didn't dismiss me based on the things they'd heard.

I was lucky to have my friends and Tex.

And him.

When we finished dinner, we walked over to the Botanical Gardens, just a few blocks from the restaurant. The walkway through the entry was decorated with giant bright-white snowflake ornaments, the trees lining the path covered in white lights. They had a variety of themed areas. My favorite was an *Alice in Wonderland* winter exhibit, with giant ornamental red-and-white roses, the red roses covered in fake snow. James and I kept to the back of the group, permitting us moments where we could graze the backs of our hands against one another's.

Close, but never close enough.

I just had to remind myself it wouldn't be that way when the night was over.

We took photos and bought hot chocolate at a nearby stand. When we finished up, we headed back to our cars. I'd known my destination before we'd even started the night. Back to the park in the woods behind James's home. As I followed that familiar path, I received a ¡text from him: ***Running an errand, so may be a minute.***

An errand?

It was all well and good. Gave me time to shower off and get ready for a movie before fun and then bed.

I turned on *Supernatural* and watched an episode. I must've dozed off, because the next thing I heard was the familiar *hum* of his car as he pulled into the drive. I waited not so patiently...and waited, and waited. If I wasn't so paranoid about getting caught, I would have raced to the door and seen what he was up to, but finally, the sound of the door opening came, and I heard a bit of a commotion followed by, "A little help."

I hopped to my feet and practically sprinted to him when I saw him pushing a tree about a foot taller than him through the doorway and closing the door behind him.

I could have melted into the floor.

"I figured since you offered to help me decorate for Christmas, I wasn't going to let you get out of helping me."

He knew damn well what he was doing, being too cute

for words, his cheeks reddened, some pine needles stuck in his messy bangs.

"I'll dig through the boxes for the stand, if you want to grab that adorable Santa cap."

"I'll find it. But I might lose some other clothes while I'm doing it."

He beamed.

Moments like this made it all feel totally normal.

It wasn't us versus the world. It was just James and me and these feelings that expanded with every moment more that James welcomed me into his beautiful world.

I streamed some Christmas tunes on my phone while we got to work decorating the tree with the ornaments his wife had brought over. We got a little carried away between impromptu dances to favorite songs and a few innocent kisses before we had the tree covered in multi-colored bulbs and James's assortment of ornaments.

"So you think star or angel this year?" He stood at the box, holding the two.

"Star, for sure."

"But my angel's so cute."

"No, you're fucking cute," I said before kissing him. "And I think your corny is rubbing off on me."

"Can we not get into rubbing off until we finish?"

It made me think of the way he told cheesy jokes during class.

I snickered.

We didn't jump right into bed, though.

We streamed a film we found on Netflix—*The Spirit of Christmas*—on his downstairs TV. He lay against my chest, the way we were beginning to when we watched TV together. I ran my hand through his hair, without inhibition, feeling the right to do it.

"Tex recommended this?" James asked.

"Hey, he recommended it as a goofy movie, which it is. Don't defame my main man."

He rolled over in my lap and faced me.

"I wouldn't do Tex the dishonor."

James smiled, and I leaned down and took another kiss.

"So as far as presents go..." I said.

"I think I know what I want, but I'm kinda scared to mention it." His expression was serious, especially for the night we had.

"Tell me."

His gaze shifted. I could sense his hesitation, but I had a feeling I knew where he was going with this.

"I'll start seeing someone after the break," I said, my words a promise.

There was relief in his expression, tears shifting in his eyes. "It's clear there's so much in there still...and I really want you to be able to work through it in a healthy environment. There are plenty of resources in Atlanta... Are you mad I brought it up?"

"Not at you. At myself for not having done this sooner."

"Don't beat yourself up over this. Some people go much longer without getting help. I just...even in the best of times, I can see it in your eyes, lingering. And if I could tear through those chains for you, I would."

"I know you would."

He'd more than revealed the sort of man he was in the time I'd known him.

"But...uh...if you get that as your present, then I'm gonna need something too," I confessed. It took me a minute to push the words out of my mouth. "Help me get help. Help me find someone, and give me the strength to get my body through the door."

His hand was on my face in a moment as a tear escaped my eye. "Of course, Kyle. I'm here now. I'm not going anywhere."

I leaned into his touch, turning and kissing his palm.

KYLE

Taryn settled into a chair next to me, taking a breath as she let her shopping bags hit the floor. Ben and I had accompanied her to the mall for a Sunday outing.

Since James and I had become a regular thing, Sundays had usually been reserved just for us, but after a few weeks of using that greedily only for each other, we agreed we could spare a day with friends. So while I hung with Taryn and Ben, James was out at a movie with some teacher friends from school.

Ben pulled out containers from the paper bag, inspecting each before passing them to us.

God, I couldn't even look at General Tso without thinking about James.

As we settled in, Taryn swallowed some of her pad thai before saying, "It's been a while, but Ben proved once again that you just don't have what it takes to be full-blown gay."

"Full-blown gay?" I asked.

"Yeah. I only befriended you guys so you could help me with my wardrobe. You're so useless in that department."

"That's not entirely honest about why you befriended me," I said, glaring at her.

"Okay, that dick didn't hurt in that department."

"Didn't hurt at all?"

"Please. I'm not one of your boy toys. I know how to fake all that." She winked, assuring me of what I'd already known about the times we'd messed around. "Okay, I won't perpetuate any more stereotypes. I'll let Ben take care of that."

"Happy to do it," he practically sang.

"And I love the pink bangs," she said, noting the subtle pink streak he'd dyed into them.

"Really? Kyle hasn't said anything, so I figured..."

"Please. It's fucking hot as hell. The whole football team is gonna be trying to get in that ass."

He blushed at the deserved compliment. He'd seen several guys since Doug, and I could tell his confidence had returned since the beginning of the year, when he'd been so wrecked over a moron who hadn't realized what an awesome guy he'd had all along.

"Well, thank you both," Ben added. "I was gonna do this for when we go to prom...you know, since someone and her baby are the reason we missed our first big dance of the year."

Taryn shook her head. "I told you we're pretending I don't have a kid for this outing."

"Like we're pretending Kyle doesn't have a secret lover?"

I neither confirmed nor denied Ben's accusation. Even though they'd also been busy themselves, they must've known by the fact that I hadn't pushed them to hang out that I was up to no good on my own.

"Baby, secret lovers..." Taryn said, "Ben bottoming for the Orman twins."

"The hell is this about?" I asked.

"See what happens when you don't keep up with friends?" Ben asked with a knowing smile.

Taryn opened a packet of orange sauce and sprinkled it over her rice. "I'm also noticing you're not diving into your food, which makes me think you're gonna save it for later so you can share a meal with someone, making it more than just a hookup. You're not the first to play that game, mister."

"What's with the interrogation?"

"It's not an interrogation, since we don't expect any answers. But, Scowl, we're your friends, and you can imagine all the talk we've been having behind your back about how mysterious you've been recently."

"Mysterious? Me?"

They laughed together as Taryn opened another packet of orange sauce.

"Yeah, like why you couldn't hang last Thursday," Ben noted before popping a piece of shrimp tempura in his mouth.

"As a matter of fact, I had a therapy appointment that day."

"Really?" Taryn asked, her eyes wide.

"Just a virtual thing, but yeah. I liked it."

I thought the shrimp was about to drop from Ben's mouth as they both looked at me, stunned, like they believed the last thing in the world I would have considered was therapy. Had I never met James, they would have been right. The woman James had found for me was friendly and listened. We hadn't gotten into details on any of the shit I'd told James, but I was warming up to her. I'd get there, but it wasn't going to happen in so few sessions.

"Anyway," I said. "Moving along."

"To your secret lover?" Taryn asked.

"Secrets, secrets, Kyle Forsythe..." Ben said, grabbing another shrimp, studying my face as though all the answers would be right there.

"You guys...if I could tell you..."

"No, I'm sorry. Didn't mean to pry," Ben said. "Listen, Scowl. We've known you long enough to know that secrets are part of being friends with you."

"Yes," Taryn added. "And the only thing we want you to know is that, whenever you are ready to talk to us, about *anything*, we're here."

Ben reached his hand across the table, waving for me to take it. I offered my hand before giving my other to Taryn.

"God, this is gay," I noted.

"We've taken that word back, and that means this is super awesome," Ben teased.

"Good, since that's how I meant it."

We enjoyed the moment, and there was relief in having actually chatted about what they had been sort of dancing around. Even though we couldn't talk about the secret I had, at least I didn't feel like I was keeping it from them.

As our mall outing came to an end, I did as Taryn suggested, keeping my General Tso leftovers in my container since I wanted to make dinner with James. When I headed out of the mall, on the way to my car, I called him. Judging by the time, his movie should have been over.

"Hey, sexy," he answered.

I'd come to accept that all his greetings would make him sound like he was still in high school too.

"How was the movie?"

"Would have been better with you, but it was good. On my way home now. Need me to pick up anything?"

"Did you guys eat?"

"No, saved that for you."

I had assumed he might not have, but that he'd been thinking along the same lines made an eagerness swell in my chest.

"Good. Then grab some veggies and chicken. I say we make stir-fry. Correction: I'll show you how to make stir-fry properly because if you get me frozen veggies, I might have to be done with you."

"Really? Is that all it would take?"

"It would take a lot to make up for that."

"Could be fun to try and make up for it, then."

I was grinning like a fucking idiot, and I loved it.

"Listen, Big Man. I'll text you a list, and then I'll see you at the house, okay?"

"See you soon, Kyle."

I hung up, and as I tucked my cell back in my pocket, I thought, *here we fucking go...*

JAMES

I'd never expected falling to feel so much like flying.

Years with my wife had dragged on while days with Kyle Forsythe soared by. As quickly as time passed, I felt more on top of my workload than ever before. My energy—my soul—had returned. I was fucking alive in a way I'd never felt before. I didn't know what I'd been doing before Kyle, but it couldn't have been called living.

Lounging on my side in bed, I counted his breaths, waiting for him to wake. It was becoming a habit, and from time to time, I caught myself doing it.

His mouth cracked open, his chest rose and fell, his bangs flat against his head from when he'd been sleeping on his stomach. He stirred, as though he could psychically feel my gaze prodding him.

Another perfect start to our Sunday, a day I'd come to cherish, since those were just ours—no school or volunteering or set plans. The best of them were spent in the bedroom, our legs weaved together, with only Chinese dishes wedged between us. Sometimes we'd have *Supernatural* or *Buffy* or *Charmed* on as we entertained one another with soft touches, warm kisses, sweet expressions.

Kyle finally shifted, his bangs sliding over his forehead, his eyes flitting open. I pretended to have just caught him, but the smile on his face made me believe I'd been made.

"You have a sneaky expression on your face," he said, wincing.

"Do I? I feel like I'm pretty innocent right now."

"You're far from innocent after last night."

"Never felt so good to be so guilty."

It reminded me of the way he'd tossed me around the bed, all the positions we'd explored—surprising me with how much was left to explore, even after all we'd done since those first experiences together.

I leaned into him, taking a kiss. His hand cupped my neck, holding me in place as he seized the moment the way we had so many others. He moaned before pulling his lips back, but kept his forehead pressed against mine. "So...what are we gonna get up to today, then, my naughty teach?"

I didn't have issues with him calling me that anymore. In fact, addressing the more problematic element of our circumstance made me feel like we weren't hiding from the truth, not with each other.

"I checked the weather, and it looks like it's getting in the seventies. Maybe we could go to our spot."

Kyle had shown me a place behind my home, farther back in the woods, in a secluded area—a clearing where we could enjoy the outdoors together. It was open enough that we would be able to detect anyone who might be coming our way, but isolated enough to make it feel like it was only ours, an alternate world we could slip away into, where we would remain undiscovered. We'd begun exploring it at night to ensure we wouldn't be caught, but had gradually built up confidence to go there for picnics during the day. I kept waiting for us to be found out, or at least for a scare, but just as in so many other areas of our lives, it was as though the universe had shielded us from view, protected the wicked deeds we did from the judgment and scrutiny of a world that wouldn't have understood us.

"That sounds nice," he said. "We can make sandwiches beforehand. Grab the blanket. Then come back and find something to watch over..." I waited for him to tell me what he wanted for dinner, but he asked, "What do *you* want?"

"I was going to wait and see what you said and then act like I wanted the same thing."

"Tell me what you want, and I'll let you know if you were about to be a liar."

I inspected his face. "Hmm...we've had Chinese the past few Sundays, the extra-pepperoni pizza throws me sometimes, and I know you're a burger guy when we change things up...so I'll go with the burger, two double, no cheese, with mayo and pickle."

His forehead creased as he cringed, making a buzzer

sound. "I can't believe you said *Chinese*. We've had *Asian fusion*. And I could eat that every day. You're the one who gets tired of shit like that."

"Fuck me," I said.

"Consider it done."

He moved quickly, nibbling at my neck before pushing me onto my back. He straddled my waist, his dick sliding over mine as he pinned me beneath him, looking awfully cocky.

"What are you laughing at, nerd?" he asked like some kind of schoolyard bully.

"You have this expression on your face like you won something, when I clearly was more than willing to be overtaken."

"Maybe you're just confused about what I know I've won."

My cheeks warmed. Like with so many things with Kyle, it was a sensation I'd had to adjust to.

He must've detected my swelling pride because he eyed me suspiciously. "Here I am being sweet, and it's making me think how pissed I am that I didn't stop by the store to grab some fucking crullers for breakfast."

In the time I'd known him, I'd learned he wasn't kidding about loving an apple cruller. Even a dozen didn't last very long around him.

"I can head to the store and get some."

"No. Looks like Teach's healthy granola it is. One day this metabolism is gonna catch up to me, so I'd better start training now."

"Or enjoying the way things snap back right now," I assured him.

"Speaking of snapping back..." He licked his fingers and reached under my leg, around to my hole.

I felt so exposed as he probed me like some kind of sex toy, but nothing felt as good as being objectified by Kyle.

"Yup. Just right," he joked before taking another kiss.

We messed around a little more before showering off.

His stomach was growling on his way into the kitchen as he strutted in a pair of my pajama bottoms, his hair still damp, when he froze in the kitchen entryway.

I blushed again as he turned to me, eyeing me with a cross look, thwarted by his smile. "You sneaky moth-erfucker."

I stood a little taller as I passed him, heading to the fridge, doing my best to act nonchalantly. The crullers I'd slipped out onto the table before joining him in bed said it all, so I didn't have to.

He shook his head as he approached the table and snatched one. "Whatever," he said, taking a bite. "Still didn't know I want *Asian fusion* later. Don't act like you know me." He winked, giving me every bit of props despite his words.

It was the most innocent of moments, and those were the most life-giving for me. When we'd first submitted to our impulses, I'd worried being stuck in my home wouldn't be enough space for our relationship to flourish, that Kyle would feel trapped or become agitated by our limitations, but it only helped us explore what we were really searching for, something within one another.

Through new extra-credit assignments and group get-togethers with DJ, Maya, Bentley, and Hanna, we had incognito dates. We knew what they were, but having our secret, that was just ours, made them that much more special. And the turbulent fucks we'd share after almost made the restrictions that much more worth it.

We were thieves, stealing every opportunity, every moment that we could from the universe, greedily storing up everything so we could share it with one another.

After breakfast and watching a couple of our shows, we found ourselves on my blanket in the woods, on a picnic, enjoying the early return of warm weather on a lovely March afternoon.

March.

That much closer to the end of the school year, when what Kyle and I shared, though scandalous, would fall outside the bounds of the law.

Kyle's voice came from beside me. "What are you thinking about?"

Stretched out, my hands behind my head, I enjoyed the warmth of the sun against my face, lost in my thoughts while Kyle continued eating his cheese-and-pepperoni sub that we'd prepared and packed before leaving my house. His eyes were narrowed, I figured in part because of the position of the sun.

"I was thinking how quickly this year has gone by since..."

"You found out how good I taste?"

"You were so sweet this morning. Where did Dirty Kyle come from?"

"'I'll be as dirty as I please, and I like to be dirty, and I will be dirty!'"

"You did not just go full Emily Brontë on me."

"If you hadn't thought of Brontë, I'd worry you weren't doing the reading, Mr. Warner."

I laughed, rolling onto my side and propping myself up on my elbow. "Were you quizzing me just then?"

"An easy quiz. It's been a month since we finished it. I think I wrote some of my best responses on that one."

"I remember them," I said, because since we'd started spending time together, little excited me as much as reading about Kyle's notions of love, lust, desire, particularly as they always seemed directed at me.

"That's why I brought it up." He took another bite of his sub. "Maybe we can pretend we're not in the woods, but the moors. I could be your Heathcliff, Cathy."

"I think we should probably be Hareton and Cathy."

"Where's the fun in that? You don't like wild, feral desire, James?"

"Toxic, painful desire is more like it."

"Speaking of which, have you heard from..."

He was generous in not saying her name. She'd made an art out of delaying the divorce.

"No. I like it that way. I'm assuming she's too busy with her new guy and helping her mom."

"I still think that's a bullshit reason not to go ahead and file."

Guilt rose within me. "I know the reason I didn't step up again was because I wanted to enjoy what we were beginning and ignore all the rest. To pretend there isn't a problem. I'm too good at that. Maybe that's why Sheila and I made it as long as we did."

My thoughts traveled too easily back through the hurt and the pain, to one particular night. I shook my head. "You know, after I confronted her about the final affair, I checked into a nearby hotel. Just needed to get out of that house, needed to get her out of my mind for some time. Even after all that happened, I was still considering going back. Sounds pathetic to me now, but I thought I could help her. That I could change, and she would be good to me.

"She came to visit me, and I remember her holding me as I relived all this pain, and I told her that I was struggling to figure out if she was a woman who made mistakes or a monster. And she didn't say anything to that. Just kept holding me. Just silent. I remember thinking, I could never imagine someone I loved saying that to me, and not being horrified to know I caused them so much pain. I tried to make excuses, but then realized excuses for her were what had gotten me in so deep. I'm not saying she is a monster, but the fact that she wasn't more rattled by that, it still haunts me...makes me question all the years together."

By now, Kyle was gently stroking the back of my hand with his thumb, as though wanting me to know he was there for me, to listen to my pain and heartache. "She really did a number on my Big Man."

"Yeah, she did. She had a hard past. Her dad was toxic and abusive, something I had to remind myself of every time she did something that felt cruel to me. I think I confused the explanation for an excuse, used her own pain to right so many wrongs."

"Just because bad things happened to her didn't give her the right to do bad things to you."

I knew he was right, but this surge of energy pushed through me, and I caught myself. "Funny, I was about to tell you that we shouldn't have been talking about her like that. My instinct is still to protect her. Yet I don't ever recall a time that she protected me. And then I wonder if maybe I'm misremembering it all, painting it all black because of my pain, and I get lost..."

"No more of that," Kyle said, the anger in his tone cutting through the air like a knife. "She did you wrong. She's still doing you wrong. But a part of me understands why she still wants to be in your life, because if I were your wife, I wouldn't let you go easily." His gaze fixed on mine, and he looked as determined as ever. "I would fight to show you I was worthy, to show you what it means to be respected and appreciated. I would never let you forget you're special. That you deserve to be worshipped."

It reminded me of that day when he'd talked as if he could be my wife. It wasn't just the peculiar scenario he presented that caught my attention, but how full of conviction he was about what he said. It caught me off guard.

"Why did you look away from me when I said that?" Kyle asked.

"Did I? I hadn't noticed." A lie, and he glared at me to let me know he knew me too well for that. "You sound so serious when you talk like that, angry even. I don't understand how you could say things like that and sound so hateful."

"I hate what she did to you, and I hate what the world is doing to us. We are like Catherine and Heathcliff. Don't we feel pain too? Don't you feel that sting, that burn of what we're doing? The fear and worry, but then knowing none of it fucking matters because everything else is so worth it?"

"Yes, but *you* aren't the thing causing any of that pain. You're the remedy, which is the way it should be."

He gulped, smirking.

But his words were reminiscent of his responses for class, and made me reflect on his comments about pain now.

"It's painful for me too," I said, "but you'll tell me when it's too painful, right?"

His gaze drifted, and I knew it was there, just as it was for me. How could it not be?

"I'm sorry, Kyle. I wasn't trying to spoil the afternoon."

"No. I like that you asked. It's one thing with my friends and Tex...even not telling the therapist. It's okay dealing with one secret, but now I have this other, and secrets are hard, aren't they?"

After our talk over winter break, I managed to get him to see a virtual therapist about his issues with his father, and once he'd become comfortable, he'd been willing to head into Atlanta a few days each month to talk with someone who wouldn't be associated with his old church. I could tell it was helping.

Yet even with that, there were some things he had to keep to himself, and I was the reason for that.

"But that's not the hardest part for me, James. It's so much worse that it keeps getting stronger and stronger, and I'm terrified that it will always be like this. Or that it will have to stop at some point. That's what hurts."

"Why would it have to stop?"

"Come on. I'm young, not dumb. There's only one way we can keep this going past all this, and I've been good at pretending because it's been a whirlwind and everything, but I know you have too much to lose that, even if we did want something more, we'd always have to be quiet about it."

It was something I'd thought about, and it was clear this wasn't his first time thinking about it either.

"I guess in getting carried away and working to keep our secrets, we've been so focused on seizing the day that we didn't really consider the future as much as we should have."

"I'm not trying to pressure you into anything," he said. "You mentioned pain, and I was telling you where it was. I'm sorry. I shouldn't have."

He was so uncomfortable, on edge, as though fearful I was about to spoil everything in a moment.

"Forget I said it," he added.

"No."

He turned to me, wide-eyed. I could see the terror in his expression. I hadn't realized until that moment just how scared he was. How scared *I* was.

"After the school year ends, just through the summer, and then we do whatever the hell we please."

"James, you're out of your mind. They'll talk."

"I don't give a shit about talk. They can talk all they want, but they won't know. You're nineteen in August, and once you're not my student anymore, no one can touch us. Unless...that's not what you want."

He set his sandwich down behind him and slid toward me, his gaze piercing mine, his jaw tense. "I've been the talk of this town for plenty of years. About time I give them something worth talking about."

He kissed me, without shame or inhibitions, like he might have kissed me in my bedroom, something neither of us usually allowed outside. But we shared the unguarded moment. Reveled in it.

A sound caught our attention, startling us, and we turned together, only to notice a rabbit a few yards away, near a shrub that shook, I assumed from when the rabbit had moved past it.

We laughed together, our faces red, our expressions knowing. It reminded us of the cruel reality we lived in.

"I'm sorry," I said.

"It's the rabbit's fault." He smiled. "And it was perfect. Six months more, and this town will know what trouble really looks like. I don't give a shit about any of it as long as I have you."

"Okay, maybe more Heathcliff and Cathy than I was thinking," I joked.

"Damn right. Kiss me, Cathy."

I obeyed.

Again, I expected it to be quick, but he didn't let me go easily, and as we continued, I allowed myself to relax into it. To cherish the experience the way we both deserved to be able to. The way one day we would, without fear of consequences greater than chatter around Wyachet.

38

KYLE

James and I made the best of the time we shared, and as fate carried us to the end of the school year, with each passing day, I knew we had so much more to look forward to.

I stood at the floor-length mirror, assessing my rented tux.

Excited as I was about spending prom with my friends, it would be impossible for me to deny wishing it were James I got to go on a date with. I was learning that life didn't necessarily make things easy, but I didn't need easy—I could have endured everything I had and more, so long as I could have him.

A knock at the door caught my attention.

"Come on in, Uncey Tex."

The doorknob rattled before he stepped in. "Hot damn," he said as he approached. "Looking as good as ever." He flashed those familiar whites as he settled beside me.

"Thank you."

His forehead wrinkled. "Just an adjustment needed here." He seized my tie and removed it, making me laugh. "Here I thought I was preparing you for the world, but I can't even get you to tie your tie properly."

"I thought I did good."

"It was all right, but you can do better."

I shook my head at his slight as he made the knot on himself before handing it off to me and pulling it tight at my collar. He inspected his work in the reflection. "Now *there's* a handsome man. Oh, look. You're in there too." He winked, and I laughed again.

"Handsomeness courtesy of Men's Warehouse and those Harris looks," I joked.

"Nah. I meant whatever has you smiling big as ever. It's made the spring that much more worth it."

Even though I knew he was right, I protested, "I've always smiled."

"Not the smile you have now. I know you too well for that, Kyle. I've even seen the smiles with the hurt and pain behind them, but this is different. This is... He's something magical, isn't he?"

"I'm bi, doesn't have to be a he."

"No, it doesn't. But I am psychic, so I know these things."

I shook my head. "You don't know shit."

"Might be a giveaway that the cologne you wear home

after you sneak off isn't something I'd take a lady to wear, but I could be wrong."

"Fuckin' A."

He laughed so hard before adding, "Busted."

"You clever fuck."

"Come on. For a second you thought we had some mystical mind-meld from all this time we've spent together. You can hide a lot of things, but it's those little details that give a man away. But even without the cologne, I knew there was someone special—disappearing all these weekends, smiling brighter than I ever thought you were even capable of. God, what it gives me to see you like that again."

"Again?"

"That's the little kid I remember. When you were carefree and saw all the beauty in the world. Only a monster could have wanted to take that smile away from you, but perhaps that's how it's easy for me to know it's a monster, because all you wanted were the simple things in this world. Didn't need much to have everything. And we still don't, do we?"

"I definitely have plenty. More than I ever thought I deserved."

What had an asshole like me ever done to deserve guys like Tex, Taryn, Ben...James...in my life?

"You're a sweet kid, Kyle. Trust me, anyone who gets to have you in their life is the lucky one."

He offered me a hug, that familiar warmth that could only have come from the sort of hug Tex gave.

I wished I could tell him all about James. It killed me

to keep something so important from him, but I reminded myself it wouldn't be much longer.

We were so fucking close. In less than a month I would graduate, and as we'd planned, we'd have only the summer to go through before leaving behind all our fears. After that, things wouldn't be the same, and one day they would all be talking about James Warner and Kyle Forsythe of Wyachet, Georgia.

Speculating about the school year when we first met...

The summer after...

And how it all came to be when we began our public life together.

They'd wonder when it began, and some of our trusted friends would know, but only James and I would ever know our truth.

Uncle Tex finished helping me get ready before demanding plenty of pictures, if not for my future, for his own. Then I headed over to Taryn's, where Ben was already waiting. We went out to dinner and then to the hotel hosting the event. En route, I passed the alley where I'd rescued James from that asshole scum...before James rescued me from myself.

It was strange to think about the angry kid who'd saved him, and now the kid who'd finally worked up the strength to talk to his therapist about his father and so many years of pain.

As soon as we entered the ballroom, I noticed the lights spread around the room, made to look like a starlit sky. It reminded me of the nights when James and I slipped away to our private hideaway.

We greeted some of Taryn's and Ben's friends while I searched the room for James. I caught him chatting near the punch fountain with Kendra and a few other faculty members. His gaze shifted around the room, and I knew as soon as our eyes met that he'd been looking for me too.

We shared knowing grins for a bittersweet moment where we both seemed to know the truth—that moment was all we could have tonight.

I took a breath, refocusing on my friends, who were on their way to the dance floor. I forced myself to enjoy the moment, keep myself from spending the whole dance pining over a man I'd not only seen plenty throughout the year, but who I'd get to enjoy plenty of moments with after. Tonight needed to be about Taryn, Ben, and our last school dance together.

I managed to succeed in having a good time, not just with Taryn and Ben, but with our classmates, many of whom I'd spent several years seeing around but never really chatting with. The way we laughed and busted silly moves let me know what a night like tonight was all about.

As soon as we started slowing down, despite the pop remixes the DJ had been playing, the beat faded into a much slower song. The lights dimmed to a dark-blue shade as white specks of light traveled around the ballroom, looking like stars shifting along the wall. All of time seemed to move with the music as I searched for James, who stood at the edge of the dance floor. God, he couldn't have looked more beautiful in his suit, the lights traveling over him, sparkling off his glasses.

Ms. Eiken approached him, I was certain for a dance, as Taryn said, "Come on."

"What about—" I looked for Ben, noticing him already coupled off with one of the guys I recognized from around the halls, always wearing his football jersey.

Go get him, kid.

I took Taryn's hands.

She had this magical glow about her, looking radiant as ever, but even though I was with the most beautiful woman in the room, I couldn't keep from looking over her shoulder when I was facing James's direction.

There were brief instances where we'd catch each other's gazes at just the right moment. It felt so cruel for us to be so far away on what, as James had noted, was supposed to be a special night. There we were, in the same room, during a magical moment, but one we couldn't share because of our circumstances.

Taryn looked over her shoulder. "Where are you off to?"

"Huh?" I asked, trying to play it off unsuccessfully.

"Everything okay? You seem awfully...distracted tonight."

Fuck, I was.

As much as James had wanted me to have a good time, this was just...torture.

I felt bad even thinking that, since I'd never want him to feel responsible for my not having a good time. I wanted him there, yet having him so close and so far away all at once was excruciating.

"I'm a little distracted, but I'm having fun."

She eyed me suspiciously. "So mysterious these days, Scowl. But Ben and I are going to get to the bottom of it, and then you'll really be in trouble."

I laughed again. "That sounds about right."

When I looked up, I noticed Kendra and James dancing right by us.

"You kids having fun?" he asked, winking at me, acting about as teacher-y as a teach could.

It felt like I was smiling for the first time since the song had started. "Yeah. You guys?"

"Best night ever," James joked as he continued along, brushing his shoulder against mine.

It was so subtle, but at least it was fucking something.

No...*everything*.

When the song came to an end, James and Kendra settled near the punch fountain. Taryn, Ben, and I got to dancing with our classmates until I noticed Kendra chatting with some other chaperones.

I made a beeline for James while he was in the middle of drinking some punch. "Is it spiked yet?"

"No, but I keep going for it all the same, hoping for the best."

I laughed as I poured myself some.

"Did you enjoy the slow dance?" he asked.

"Not the same when it's not the special one you're thinking of."

"Tonight's supposed to be—"

"Special, I know. Got it." I sidled up next to him, putting my free hand in my pocket and taking a sip from my cup.

"Well, if you're not out too late partying, maybe we can have our own dance."

I imagined sharing a dance with him in the kitchen... or the living room...maybe the office where we'd shared that first intense exchange. Dancing would lead to more, I was sure.

"Guess I won't be going out partying, then," I said.

"No. You need to. Just text me before you get back."

I didn't say more, since I didn't want him trying to talk me into staying out, when all I wanted was to be in him. We only spent a few minutes near each other, getting the closest thing I could to a fix before I returned to Taryn and Ben. Having had that moment and anticipating a private one with him was enough to let me cut loose and enjoy myself, sharing those brief looks with him throughout the night.

And once the lights came up, my buddies started making arrangements with some of the others, and I agreed to head to a house party with them. James was going to have to help clean up and stack chairs, anyway. Also, it was going to be easier to slip away from a party once Taryn was chatting away with her buddies and Ben snuck off with Malcolm. And when my opportunity came, I slipped out without much fuss and drove to James's place, giving him a text warning as he'd requested, hoping he'd still be in his sexy suit when I got to the house.

I'd swapped out of my rental tux, folding and putting it in my duffel bag before switching to my street clothes for my trek through the woods. As I did, I checked my phone.

A message from James: **Meet me at our spot.**

The hell?

Tired as I was feeling from a night of dancing and fun with friends, a rush of excitement pushed through me, granting me a second wind. I headed through the woods, following the trail I showed James when I first led him out to our special place. I noticed a light in the distance, which I used as my guide to the clearing.

James was sitting on an upside-down Rubbermaid box, fidgeting on his phone.

I didn't say anything. I wanted to drink him in without worrying about being caught like I had been at prom. As I neared, he must've heard me because he looked up quickly.

The orange glow from the lantern on the ground just a few feet from him reflected in his glasses as a smile spread across his face—the sort of look he got when I'd show up at his place, like I was the answer to every problem he'd ever had.

He still wore his suit, and as he moved, I noticed something in his other hand. As he put it in front of him, the light caught the rose he held.

"Motherfucker," I muttered as we met each other halfway. "You're such a dork."

"You told me you love a dork."

I kissed him, grabbing his waist and tugging him close. "Damn right I do."

I hadn't intended to kiss him as long as I did, but having been forced to be apart from him all evening, I had to make up for every moment that had been robbed from us.

"Wait, wait," I said, pulling away.

I set the duffel bag on the ground and unzipped it.

I undressed and swapped out my clothes while he watched, not talking, clearly enjoying the show before helping me with a few bits, until we were snickering at the ridiculousness of it all—being in the middle of the woods, in our nice clothes.

I was checking my suit when he asked, "You good?"

"Yeah, why?" I turned to see James. His iPhone was lit up in his hand as a tune filled the air.

It only took me a moment to realize it was the song that had been on in the ballroom, the one I'd wanted to dance with him to. He set the phone on the plastic container he'd been sitting on, and approached me. "Mr. Forsythe, I think you owe me a dance."

I giggled, yes, fucking giggled like a dumbass kid, and I didn't even care, because with the moonlight in his eyes and that cocky smile across his face, he had me under his spell.

He moved close, running the single rose along my jaw, to my chin, his expression turning serious. Keeping it at the base of my chin, he took a kiss before pulling away and weaving the stem in the buttonhole of my lapel. Then he took my hands.

"Who's going to lead?" I asked.

"Are you kidding? Did you see the moves I was working on Kendra? Watch and learn."

He took charge, guiding me through the dance.

"Oh fuck. *Duh.*" He stopped, went to the lantern, and turned it off. "Now it's perfect."

Perfect? Although there was plenty of moonlight to cast light across both of us, I couldn't understand the expression on his face.

"Look up," he told me, and I obeyed, seeing the starlit sky.

"Now it really is just like prom."

"Only better," I noted. "Since it's real."

Fuck, was that a tear in my eye?

He took my hands once again, moving to the music.

Being so close to him, with the moonlight and stars captured in his eyes, I felt as though I was transported into them.

"Why are you crying?" he whispered.

"I'm not crying," I said, so sure of myself until he kissed my cheek and I felt the warmth of what had clearly been a falling tear.

"Fuck me."

"We can get to that later," he teased, which made me laugh again. "Is everything okay?"

He stopped our dance, and I said, "Yeah, yeah, let's just keep going."

He obeyed, but my tears kept coming. He still looked so worried about me, and I was starting to become a little concerned by how much emotion overtook me.

"Kyle?" he asked, his voice the faintest of whispers.

"I just...didn't know I could feel this happy."

His smile returned, and I noticed his watery eyes,

which made me feel a little less self-conscious about mine.

"Neither did I."

I reveled in the power of this intense emotion moving through me, so much vulnerability and fear colliding with a surprising amount of strength. It wasn't like anything I'd ever felt before.

"I love you, James," pushed effortlessly from my lips.

"I love you too, Kyle."

His words felt like they pulsed right through my very being.

I'd thought meeting James had brought me to life, but really, it was like nothing until that moment had truly been real. Like this was all that was worth living for, and I hadn't truly known, couldn't have known, until I'd experienced it for myself.

He reeled me in effortlessly, our lips locking as we embraced that perfect moment.

Savoring it, in the back of my mind knowing it wouldn't last forever, but appreciating that what was a brief moment seemed to stretch on and on in my mind, like my consciousness was trying to fill infinity with a single emotion.

"I want you, James." I tugged at his shirt. "Get out of this."

"Just to be clear, we're not getting your rental dirty," he said, pulling away. "Here, take it off."

I handed him my blazer before kicking my shoes off and removing my pants, which I passed to him as I removed the shirt. He carried them over together, draping them across the box he'd brought out there.

I slipped off my socks, tucking them in my shoes at my side.

My trunk boxers clung tight to my thighs as I shivered with a gust of wind. "Ooh, cooler night than I was expecting," I said, feeling my nipples.

"Don't worry. I'll keep you warm." James approached me, looking over my moonlit body. I forced my arms away from my torso, wanting him to be able to take me all in.

He couldn't have realized, but just the way he was looking at me made me hot, kept me warm as he'd claimed he would.

But he didn't jump me like he sometimes would when I was undressed before him.

"God, you're a beautiful man, Kyle."

He moved in and kissed my neck, a soft, careful kiss. I shivered as he kissed down to my chest, his hands resting against my hips.

"I don't know how exactly we're planning to make this work."

"Just gotta get creative." He pulled back and started unbuttoning his shirt.

I watched as he removed it and laid it across the ground. "You're gonna ruin that," I warned.

"Could stand to lose a few button-downs."

He kicked off his shoes and removed his pants with his briefs. My eyes went right to his hard cock.

He was so fucking hard.

And were my eyes deceiving me, or was he bigger than usual?

Whatever the reason, I couldn't deny myself another moment. I got down on my knees on his shirt and gripped his thighs, guiding him to me, his cock sliding right into my mouth. I felt my tongue along the base of his shaft, following every familiar groove to the tip, then taking it deep once again.

James rested his hands on the back of my head, his moan letting me know I was doing it the way he liked. I took him in and out before teasing my tongue against the tip, feeling his precum leaking onto my tongue before sucking it up.

James started moving back, then got down on his knees before me. A kiss, followed by so many others, his tongue sliding into my mouth like he needed a taste of himself.

One hand caressed to my back while the other gripped my ass. Since we'd started messing around, our progression to him bottoming evolved so naturally, I hadn't really been interested in doing anything else with him. But tonight something within me had shifted, making me hunger for him in this new way. And somehow I knew he felt it too.

"James...I want..."

"I know what you want," he said against my lips as he firmed his hold on my ass.

We parted long enough for me to lie against his shirt. He navigated between my legs, kneeling over me, one hand planted against the ground as he offered tender kisses, which traveled from my mouth, down my body, past my navel. It was as though he'd never lacked the experience he claimed to when we first began messing around, he pulled my boxers right off, and in no time, his mouth was around my dick.

I lifted my legs, tilting my ass for his use. He kissed and licked around it. But then he stopped and leaned back.

I inspected his expression, and I could see his concern. "What's wrong?"

"I'm scared I won't be able to satisfy you like this. I told you, Sheila never—"

"Shh. Just give it a try, Big Man. Whatever happens, you're safe with me...safe inside me."

He smiled, but I could see so much tension and anxiety on his face, as though what we did had transported him back to those far less exhilarating encounters.

It made me hate that he'd been made to feel so inadequate, when he'd never shown me anything that would have led me to believe he could ever be anything other than considerate and generous.

"It's my first time doing this too, so we're in it together. I got you, Teach."

His expression shifted. He looked determined as he spit in his palm and rubbed it across his shaft, again and again, before pushing it against me. As I'd anticipated, he was careful, and oh-so-considerate. Every centimeter was a gift, every inch a blessing. I felt so safe with him, so cared for as I lay on his shirt, that my body opened up effortlessly for my Big Man.

I thought I was over the biggest hurdle when I felt the tension. "Ah...ah..." He retreated slightly, and I said, "No, stay there. Stay in."

"Deep breaths," he told me.

"The voice of experience."

I took a moment, letting my body relax after the sensation of that pressure, then nodded for him to go again. He obeyed, watching me as carefully as before, nudging his way inside me until I felt the rush of my prostate, reminding me of the times I'd explored it on my own in private.

"Fuck, fuck."

"You good?" he asked.

"I'm fucking amazing," I assured him, sliding my arms back and tucking my hands behind my head.

He beamed, leaning down, his arms hooking under mine as he kissed me, keeping his cock still in me, before he began his work again. My muscles shifted and spasmed, moving in their own dance of excitement with every nerve he stimulated with his movements.

As he pulled back, I gauged his expression again. All the worry and nervousness I'd seen on it before had dissolved, and I saw his confidence, his strength. Yes, this was the man I'd come to know. "Show me, James. Show me how much you love me. And I'll show you."

He rested his hand against my cheek before burying his tongue in my mouth and his cock deep within. I gasped as the sensation overwhelmed me with excitement.

Despite all the dancing we'd done that night, this was our best, our own DJ playing fast and then slow as we celebrated beneath the stars everything we'd discovered about one another. James was relentless in his exploration, guiding me in every position he could think of, as though trying to make up for lost time...or perhaps to rediscover this dominating side of himself that had me submitting entirely to his power.

I was all his to probe and explore.

He got lost in me, and then I got lost in him.

It was impossible to keep track of how many times we swapped off...hell, at some points, which limbs were mine and which were his. I just knew the pressure, the warmth, and all his affection.

I lay on him, my back to his chest, his hand around my cock. He was buried inside me once again, hitting my prostate just right until it became impossible for me to manage the escalating pressure.

"James," I whispered, turning to him, our lips meeting as he continued thrusting. "You have to let go, or I'm going to..."

"Do it. I'm about to..."

I relaxed into it, and I wondered if it was just my imagination or if I really felt him swell within me as my own climax tore through me, my cum shooting across my abdomen.

His body continued jerking the way it did sometimes after he shot. I milked his dick with my ass, feeling like a fucking pro from what I'd learned in the time we'd shared in our special place, on this special night.

Despite all my previous experience, this would always be James's.

Just his.

Like I'd been saving it for him all my life.

My prostate was so sensitive when his cock continued sliding against it, but I didn't care. I didn't want him out of me. I took it and continued kissing him, his hand massaging my abs, spreading my cum over me.

"Was that okay?" James asked.

Noticing his cocky grin, I said, "You know damn well that was perfect."

He leaned in and bit gently at my bottom lip. As he released it, I whispered, "I love you."

"I love you too."

I licked up his lips, his breath slamming against my tongue, our noses grazing one another.

Knowing how cruel life could be and how easily we could be robbed of this kind of beauty, I savored the moment as I'd never savored a moment before, fearing that one day I might mistake it for a dream.

39

JAMES

Kyle's head rose and fell with each breath I took as he lay against my chest. With an arm around him, my hand at his waist, I kept him as close to me as I could manage. Between the prom and then our dance in the woods, he must've been exhausted from the night. Yet I could tell by how he breathed against me that he was still awake, even before he began offering the subtlest of kisses just beneath my right pec, tickling me. I exhaled with a snicker.

"Oh, is this a ticklish spot?" he asked, licking in the same place with deliberately light licks that got me laughing.

"You are a demon."

"Yeah? Let's see if your dick agrees." He pulled the sheets down, revealing my cock, hard again, leaking with precum. "Uh-oh. Did I do that?" He licked in the same place as before, and my dick twitched. "Oh, yup. That's my bad."

I laughed some more before he began kissing down my body, to my shaft. He slid his tongue across the spot where the precum was collecting on my abdomen before taking the head of my dick into his mouth.

Slow, controlled movements, much like how he'd worked my body when we'd gotten back. Once he'd properly wet my dick, he kissed back up my body, shifting in bed so he could reach my lips again.

Then he surprised me by moving up and kissing my nose before licking it like he had my pec. Moving back, he gazed into my eyes the way he had an hour earlier.

"I love you, James."

I still heard those words, saw his face lit up with moonlight, his gaze leaving me without any doubt about his feelings for me.

Then again when we'd made love.

"I figured you'd be asleep by now," I whispered.

"After a fuck like that? No. That's the kind that keeps a guy up all night."

I set my hand against his face, running my thumb across his cheek.

He closed his eyes and leaned into my touch before turning his face, taking my thumb into his mouth, and sucking it gently, as he'd done with my cock. He started to release it before taking a soft bite, then turned back to me, letting it fall from his mouth.

"Three weeks until we can do this every day," I told him. "I want to have it all, exactly like this."

"I don't think I can rent a tux for every night this summer."

I could tell he was being playful, but I went on, "Not the dance, or even the woods, or what we shared when we got back here. This, right here. Just you and me, my cum on your tongue, your saliva on my thumb. Lost in your eyes."

"Don't go all postcoital romantic on me."

My head rolled back as I laughed. "*Postcoital romantic?* Is that what I'm being?"

"Yeah, and it might be more adorable than I can handle."

"This is the kind of shit that makes the idea of waiting all summer to be with you the way I want to practically impossible."

"I'll be over here every day, James."

"That's not what I mean. I don't want to creep around like this. Like we have something to be ashamed of. I'm not ashamed of anything about us."

"I could never be ashamed of this," he said.

As I scrambled for solutions, one idea that had sprung to mind in moments where I allowed myself similar fantasies pushed to the forefront. "What if we go away together? Take a trip somewhere far away, for a month, maybe two, and then when we come back, we toss off all the bullshit and just be who the fuck we are."

His expression turned serious. He glanced down at my chest, ran his thumb against my side. "People will definitely talk."

"But they won't be able to touch us then. They can

imagine all they want about this time, but no one will ever know, not if we don't tell them."

"That would never happen." There was something dark, almost sinister in his tone, as though he would have been willing to do terrible things to keep our secret.

"Then it's settled? We ditch this town for a bit. Get away and come back and be exactly what we are. And Wyachet can go fuck itself."

"I don't know that I've ever heard you so confident before."

I wasn't sure I ever was more confident about anything as much as I was about us.

He added, "Where would we go? London, Barcelona, Lisbon—"

"Peru." I didn't have to go through a list. I knew what my Kyle needed.

His eyes shifted quickly with his smile, letting me know I was fucking right.

"So guess you'll have to get started on your passport sooner than you thought," I told him.

"You're being real romantic tonight, Mr. Warner."

Feeling I'd earned it, I leaned in and took another kiss.

"So we'll go to Peru for a few weeks, and then when we get back, we'll have our life together. No more hiding behind closed doors. No more close-but-not-close-enough moments in public."

My knuckles rested against his face, and he moved his head side to side, like he just wanted to feel the rub against his cheek.

"You can't even imagine what a spectacle I'm going to

make about us when we're finally free," he said. "I'm gonna snatch your ass in the grocery store. Kiss your cheek at the gas-station pump. Hold your hand close when we head into a movie theatre. I'm going to PDA you so hard, you'll have to fight to keep my hands off you in public."

"I think we've decided you're too strong for me to fight."

His eyes watered before his gaze downturned sharply, his mood seeming to transform in an instant.

"Kyle…"

"Just don't pull the rug out from under me. Don't talk up this big dream and leave me hanging. Or if you change your mind, just fucking tell me. I don't want to be the stupid kid who held on to a hope that was never really there."

"Hey." I slid my hand down his face, pushed his chin up. He looked at me once again. "There's no turning back now, not for me. So if anyone's backing out, it's gotta be you."

"That won't be happening."

"Then it looks like we're stuck together, whether we like it or not."

He moved close, lingering near for a moment, his breath pushing against my face. He didn't make a move for a kiss just yet, even though it would have been easy for him to do in that position. We just breathed each other in.

I gripped the back of his neck as we moved a little closer, our noses against each other's faces as we breathed in each other's souls.

I SAT IN THE RESTAURANT, scanning the menu to narrow my choices down between pasta or pizza.

I'd anticipated she would be late, so there was no harm in taking my time to settle on something for dinner until she arrived.

I checked my phone to see a text from Kyle: *Tell Sheila I said hi. :)*

I was surprised by how much it made me smile, especially when I was so annoyed to be out in town when I could have been at my place, watching an episode of one of our shows—currently *Buffy* and *Charmed*—with him.

But to get me through the meal, I kept reminding myself we could get to that later. And what I planned to discuss with Sheila benefited Kyle and me long-term.

As was her way, she managed to show up late, finding plenty of opportunities to offend me before turning on the charm for our young male waiter, batting her eyes and faking a few laughs. Once she had finished making me feel like I was interfering with their own date, he headed on to fetch our drink orders.

She glanced around the place...our old restaurant.

"Don't you miss this?" she asked, and she must have sensed my uneasiness because she reached across the table. "Oh, James. I'm joking. I can still do that, right?"

I decided I needed to just blurt this out before the waiter came back or I ran out of courage. "Sheila, I want to go ahead and get started on the divorce paperwork."

"What?" Her reaction, a double take and rapid blinking, made it seem as though I'd asked her if she could give me ten grand.

I'd been feeling this way even before prom, but after what Kyle and I had discussed, I became more convinced that this was one of the remaining things holding me back. Until this part of my life was finished, I couldn't feel confident in moving on with Kyle and the life I wanted us to have with each other.

"It's time, Sheila."

"I thought we were going to wait until January."

"We already passed one January."

"I'm sorry, but I just lost the man I thought I was going to spend the rest of my life with. Mom's finally getting around on her own. I just need one more semester without another thing on my plate."

I could see the tears percolating. Fuck my life, why did they still hold so much power over me?

"Sheila, I'm happy to fill out the COBRA paperwork for you, but there's no more reason for the delay. This isn't about your doctorate or health insurance or your mom being sick, and we both know it."

The moisture in her eyes dissolved surprisingly quickly as her expression shifted. She scanned my face, like she was trying to make sense of something, yet I knew her well enough to know what for.

"James, if it's because you are with someone else, you can just say that."

"I shouldn't need to give you a reason."

It was an answer I expected she wouldn't be satisfied with, and I was right.

The tears returned, and she grabbed a napkin off the table. As though she'd asked the universe for an audience, the waiter arrived, giving her the opportunity to make a bit of a scene as she seemed to struggle to keep herself together, asking for another minute to look over the menu.

So fucking dramatic.

She didn't even wait for the waiter to be out of earshot before she went on, "If that's what you want, I can go ahead and get started on filing the paperwork."

"No, I'll do it."

"Let me talk it over with my attorney, get a few things squared away, and then I'll file. Just promise me you won't file."

I sighed.

It was fucked up how close I kept getting to what I wanted without ever actually getting there. But any progress was progress, and at the least, I could put down some rules to make sure this happened by the time I wanted it done.

"Okay, but it has to be done in three weeks, or I'm filing." Then I could really be free after Kyle's graduation, when we made our getaway.

"Three weeks is very specific. I hope you're not planning on remarrying in a month."

She wasn't just teasing; she was testing.

"I don't have to respond to that, Sheila."

Her eyes widened for a moment before she recomposed herself. "If that was what you were planning, it would be within your rights. I'll take care of it. Thank you for letting me be the one to do it."

For someone who had so many tears ready for me moments before, I was suspicious of this calm, certain attitude. I'd played games with her before, but at the very least, I had put my foot down this time, and I was finally ready to follow through for a change.

40

KYLE

As wonderful as it was spending the bulk of my free time with James, we both did what we could to maintain the other relationships in our lives, which meant days and nights away from one another so we could spend time with friends, and in my case, Tex. Since he'd discovered Tinder and I'd discovered James, we'd had a tricky time coordinating our schedules. But when he expressed interest in the Whispersaw County Fair, I knew we had to make time, especially as summer neared.

Yes, summer. Soon the school year would come to an end, and James and I would be off on our Peruvian adventure. After James and I had decided upon the plan, we'd gone ahead and booked the trip and filled out applications for passports. Soon, we'd be far away from Wyachet and free to be with one another without fear or shame.

Until then, I would have to cherish the secret I still kept close. The secret I guarded, even from Tex, whom I trusted with my life.

As Tex and I hit up our usual suspects at the fair— bumper cars, the haunted mansion, roller coasters—I found myself enjoying the good time the way we did most years. It was a beautiful reminder of what it was like when it was just Tex and me, looking out for each other. He was shit at winning prizes, but I entertained him through the sinkhole that the darts and water-gun races became, winning him a stuffed bear at the gun range.

"I feel like a princess tonight," he said, the large plush blue bear tucked under his arm. He was being cheeky, but I could tell by his smile he was having a good time. "Need to get out and do more. Starting to get a headache."

"You need us to stop and grab something?"

"Nah. I got some Tylenol in my pocket, and this princess already has a lot of water in her bladder, so..."

"Ew, gross, Tex."

"Here, take my new boyfriend while I'm taking care of business."

I took the bear as he headed off to the nearby facilities. It was packed, so I assumed I had a little free time. As much as I'd tried to convince myself to leave James to the movie night he'd arranged with some of his teacher friends, when I saw there was still an hour until his film started, I couldn't resist calling.

The phone rang...and rang...and rang.

He was likely mid-dinner with his buddies, surely

assuming that the man who was head over heels for him could have gotten by without him for a few hours.

That's totally fine.

Even though I was spending the night at Tex's, I'd see Teach tomorrow, which wasn't a big deal.

But the pause in the ring, followed by his soft, "Hey there," soothed me in a way that I knew I'd been lying to myself about being fine if he hadn't picked up.

The fun rush I'd enjoyed from spending time with Tex transformed into a calm that moved right through me. Like suddenly I knew all was right in the world.

"Just a second...trying to get outside," he said as I anxiously eyed the restroom.

"Wish you could be here," I said once I saw the coast was clear.

"I wish that too, but look at how social we're being! How's Tex?"

"Same as when we talked this morning. It's good. I'm getting to catch up on his active dating life. God, I didn't realize he'd become some kind of Tinder slut."

James laughed that sort of laugh that was a reward in and of itself. "Seems like you've both been getting plenty of action."

"You'd think we'd have done enough that I wouldn't be sitting here craving it at the fair."

"Absence makes the heart grow fonder."

"Really? I was thinking it just pisses me the hell off."

I wasn't sure if the sound I heard on the other end was him grinning, but I could have sworn I knew exactly what his face looked like in that moment.

"We can make up for it with a *Buffy season six marathon* tomorrow night. How's that?"

"I expect a little more than *Buffy.*"

"Oh, you know you'll get some ass."

"Hey, it's not just that part you've got me craving anymore," I assured him, biting down on my bottom lip, imagining how good it felt and the expression on his face when he came.

"Here I'm trying to be good with my fellow teachers," he said, "and you're making dirty jokes."

"Nothing funny about that dick."

He gave me that laugh again, but just as soon, I noticed Tex heading out of the restroom.

"Hey, Tex is coming back, so..."

"Oh, go ahead. I'll see you soon. I love you."

"I love you too."

I didn't even try to soften my voice as Tex neared. It was something I told James whenever I had the chance. Now that I knew what the fuck love was, I wasn't taking it for granted.

As I hung up, I couldn't help thinking that it was shitty that, in another world where what we did wasn't an issue, James would have been with Tex and me at the fair, and we would have been holding hands, and sharing cotton candy, and I would have won him his own stuffed bear, or watched him try to win one...or hell, maybe like so many other times in our relationship, he'd surprise me and win something.

Patience. We were nearing the finish line, and once we got there, we would have the whole world.

"Was that him?" Tex asked as he stepped up to me, a knowing grin on his face.

"Who?"

He shook his head. "Don't tell me I'm gonna find out about this guy when I'm walking you down the aisle. I don't know that that's the best time."

"Don't be ridiculous, Tex. I'd tell you at least so you can get a decent suit."

As I handed him his bear, he said, "Well, now that you're all grown up, making plans to go to South America, you're gonna be ditching this old man sooner rather than later."

"Tex, that would never happen," I said, serious as ever.

His expression relaxed. "Oh, I was just kidding, buddy."

"You were kind of kidding."

His gaze shifted. "It did scare me when you mentioned it. All these secrets, and then this mysterious trip."

"I don't like keeping things from you."

"Kylie, I know that. I haven't pressed because I didn't want to put that on you when I can tell, whatever it is, it's making you the happiest kid alive and also one of the most stressed. I'd just like you to be able to keep the happy and lose the rest."

"We're getting there. Very soon."

He smirked, but I could see the concern in his expression. How could he not have been when he didn't have a clue what the truth really was?

"I'm sure you have your reasons, but just know, whatever they are, I'm here for you when you're ready."

"I know that. Would never doubt it."

He put his arm around me and kissed my forehead, reminding me of the way he used to when I was a kid.

We enjoyed a few more rides before heading to the ice-cream stand, as we had always done, not only at the fair, but during our secret ice-cream runs, when he would promise my dad that he definitely wouldn't be getting me any ice cream, even though he most definitely would.

At a nearby stand, when it was finally our turn in line, Tex told the woman behind the counter, "Two scoops of the strawberry for me..." He eyed me for a moment. "Should I take a guess at what you want, or have you changed that much?"

"Some things never change."

He cracked a smile, turning back to the cashier. "And a vanilla, two scoops, with fudge and Ree—Ree—"

It sounded like he might have gotten something caught in his throat, or just forgotten how to say Reese's cups.

"Cat got your tongue?" I asked before he turned and I noticed his stiff, disoriented expression.

More than what was happening, though, I had this foreboding feeling in the pit of my gut.

Something was very wrong.

Panic coursed through me as he reached out to me, terror in his eyes.

"Tex?"

He was all shivers as he collapsed to the ground, with me doing my best to brace his fall.

Holy fuck, holy fuck.

"Tex? Tex?"

I wasn't thinking clearly, or quickly enough, but as people gathered around, I was just glad that I was pulling out my phone, dialing 911.

41

JAMES

I'd abandoned Kendra and my other fellow faculty friends at the restaurant, rushing to the Wyachet Hospital. Every light along the way, every stop sign, even the hospital parking garage, agitated the hell out of me.

Tex was hurt, and that meant Kyle would be hurting too.

I hurried to the reception desk of the floor Kyle had texted me to meet him at.

"I'm here for Tex Harris," I told the receptionist, who pointed me in the right direction. I found the waiting area, a room with about a dozen chairs and a large table in one corner. Kyle sat, hands covering his face before he lowered them, revealing how red it was and tear-streaked. When his gaze set on mine, he pushed to his feet and hurried over.

There was no one else in the room, so I didn't have to

stop him as he threw his arms around me, not that I would have been able to muster the courage even if there had been.

He pushed me back against the door, putting all his weight against me as he sobbed into my shoulder.

"Fuck," he muttered.

There was so much pain in the word. I could feel his desperation about the man he cared for with every part of his being.

"He was totally fine. We were having fun, getting fucking ice cream, cracking jokes...and I was making fun of him for stuttering...God, I made fun of him..."

"Hey, no, no." I pulled away and looked into his eyes. Tears pushed free, sliding down his beautiful face. "You didn't do anything wrong. You didn't give him a stroke. You didn't know what was going on, and neither did he. Okay?" They suspected a stroke, but were still running tests.

The tears continued as he nodded, even though I could tell he still wasn't convinced of his own innocence.

"Come here. I've got you."

But just as he started to get close again, I heard something behind me and turned to see a nurse in the doorway.

Goddammit.

It was like the whole fucking universe was conspiring against us.

Kyle pulled back and turned away from me, batting his hands at his eyes.

"Oh, hello. Are you family too?"

"No, he's not. He's...my teacher." Kyle said the words so bitterly. I knew he didn't mean them as anything against me, but because he was as bothered as I was by the obstacle that prevented us from sharing this moment the way we needed to.

"What's up with my uncle?" he asked.

"He's been stabilized, and he's about to be transferred to ICU. We'll let you know as soon as we have results from labs and testing. In the meantime, you have some friends here to see you."

Taryn and Ben stepped in behind her, rushing to Kyle's side. They comforted him, pulling him into a nearby chair as we all sat there, doing our best to be there for him. To make him feel less alone through the fear and uncertainty that lay ahead.

Once the conversation had petered out, we were all on our phones, Kyle and I texting each other.

Kind of wish we'd had more time alone, Kyle messaged.

No, you don't. Your friends are here. You need them right now.

I do, but...IDK

He knew, and I did too. I also knew that no amount of kisses or caresses could soothe what he was going through.

As I pulled up the news, a call from Sheila popped up. I declined the call, feeling more than justified to ignore it under the circumstances.

Hours passed before the nurse finally led us to the unit where Tex was. She said she could permit the four of us, but after, they'd have to limit visitors.

Tex's face was as white as his hair, and he'd been hooked up to a ventilator via an endotracheal tube, with electrodes placed across his head, and two IVs attached nearby. He looked peaceful enough as he slept.

Taryn and Ben stuck around as we waited for more information. I noticed a few looks my way from both of them. They surely wondered why I was there, or so concerned.

Maybe I was overthinking it, but I texted Kyle: *You sure you want me to stick around with your friends here?*

I don't give a fuck. They won't care. Don't leave me.

I won't.

If he needed me to be there, I would be, for as long as he needed me to.

The doctor finally arrived to tell us the prognosis based on the results of the CT scan: a hemorrhagic stroke. As she described what this meant, I could tell Kyle was overwhelmed. How could he not be? The doctor dumped enough information to leave us all confused and googling like crazy, with a couple thousand more questions for when we saw him next, so basically a typical hospital experience.

For all that was happening, Kyle was doing amazing, but looked tired as fuck. It was a heartbreaking reminder that even having answers didn't shake the worries or fears of the unknown.

As midnight rolled around, my stomach growled, but it wasn't my own hunger that concerned me. "If you guys want, I can bring you something to eat," I told them.

Taryn looked up from her textbook, stopping what

calculus she'd been working in the notebook on one side of the page. "Um..."

"You guys need to get home," Kyle said. "I appreciate your coming, but it's a school night. I'll text you if anything comes up."

They hemmed and hawed about it some before caving to his wish.

"In that case, Kyle, can I get you something?" I asked him, but he shook his head. "Hey, you've gotta eat."

"I had some mini-Oreos earlier."

"You have to eat more than mini-Oreos."

He snickered. "Maybe some Chips Ahoy!, then?"

"You're not any good to Tex if you aren't taking care of yourself," Taryn told him.

Kyle seemed to be considering her remark, so I said, "How about some *Asian fusion* from the place down the street?"

He grinned. "That sounds good too."

We shared the closest thing to a smile I'd seen from him since Tex had wound up in there. Understandably so.

I said my goodbyes to Taryn and Ben, and as soon as I was out the door, my phone buzzed. Sheila again. She couldn't have had worse timing. But it was unusual for her to call like this, so I answered, "Hey, Sheila. I'm kind of busy. Can I—"

"What are you busy doing?"

Her question was as invasive as it might have been if we were together.

"I'm at the hospital," I said, wishing I could have

sucked the words back into my mouth. "I can't talk right now."

"I need to talk to you about something."

"It's not a good time, Sheila."

"I just think—"

"I'll call you when I get a moment, okay? Goodbye." I didn't give her a chance to get another word in. I knew where that would lead, and I was too fucking exhausted to deal with it.

As I stood in line at the Asian fusion restaurant, I called Kendra to follow up with her about my emergency, apologizing again for bailing before the movie.

I could only imagine what Kyle was thinking, what he was worrying about as he feared losing the only decent parent he'd ever known. I saw a younger Kyle, desperately needing to be loved, the way any child deserved, only to have his own blood and most of his hometown turn their backs on him. Too young to know that sort of betrayal and loneliness.

And now to fear that he might lose the man who had been there through it all.

I hoped he knew he wasn't alone now. That no matter what happened, he'd still have Taryn and Ben...and me.

When I returned, I found Kyle in the ICU waiting room, a man and a woman sitting beside him. I tensed up. They seemed old enough to be his parents, but by the expression on his face, it was hard to tell.

Kyle turned and saw me as I neared.

"Aunt Cheri, Uncle Mel, this is James."

I noticed he didn't qualify it. Didn't call me his teacher or friend, or try to justify why I'd be there.

I shook their hands.

"Hi, James," Cheri said. "It's wonderful meeting you."

"If I'd known you guys were coming, I would have offered to bring something back."

"We're fine," Mel said. "We had a bit of a drive, but ate before we came in."

I handed Kyle the bag with General Tso and garlic chicken with crab rangoon—his favorites. I had to admit, I was disappointed that his aunt and uncle had arrived before I had a chance to be alone with him, but I was glad to see that at least other members of his family had shown up to support him.

"I'm gonna go to the restroom real quick, but I'll be right back," I let him know before slipping out.

I stopped by the nearby facilities to use the urinal, and after washing my hands, turned toward the door, when it swung open. I saw those bright blue eyes coming at me quickly and felt his arms hook around me before he spun me around and shoved me back against the door.

It was disorienting, and he kissed my chin instead of my lips, as though on accident from the frenzy he was in to take what was his. And when our lips met...Jesus, it was like everything I had been wanting, selfishly and for him, was finally there and real.

We tugged at each other's bodies. We hadn't wrestled like that since those early days of exploration, when it was like we were trying to fuck so the experience wouldn't escape our grasps. When we felt so hungry and needy and desperate.

And he needed me.

"I'm here," I whispered to him. "I'm here."

I felt his tears against my face as I continued whispering the words between kisses, wanting him to know he wasn't on his own right now.

I would never let him be on his own again.

42

KYLE

I couldn't stand to be away from him any longer.

It had been hard enough when Taryn and Ben had been in the room, when I could tell they were noticing him sticking around.

They knew.

Fuck, there was no way I could have hid it then, but I didn't give a shit, and I knew fucking well enough they didn't either.

Befitting of my friends, they didn't ask questions, giving me the space I needed.

We were so fucking close...too close to fuck it up now.

But when he'd headed to the restroom, it was too much for me not to take advantage of an opportunity I could seize. Tasting his lips made me want to rip off his clothes so that he'd help take away this searing pain within me, the fear that I might lose the man who'd been there for me in the darkest of times, who'd saved me and given me a reason to believe that life could be better.

With each frenzied, reckless kiss, James helped me forget.

A push from James, followed by the sound of the swinging door, made me jump back and whirl around to the sink behind me, as though while I'd been allowing myself to follow my desire, my subconscious had been prepping me for a possible escape.

As I rinsed off my hands, another guy entered the restroom and headed into a stall.

James and I turned to each other, sharing a smile before he led the way out.

I was right behind him, and some selfish impulse made me take his hand and tug him back, pushing him against the adjoining wall and kissing him once more, quickly, knowing I had to be cautious, before pulling back and looking into those affectionate brown eyes that had given me so much relief night after night since December.

But even knowing he would be there for me through this didn't take away the pain. Just gave me enough comfort to keep powering through.

I stayed with James in the waiting area until Cheri and Mel returned to swap out with us, since the nurse had pressed for us to limit the number of visitors.

I wanted to race back and see Tex, but nearly as soon as they'd settled in their chairs, Ms. Eiken walked in, carrying a brown bag in her arms, a warm smile on her face.

"Hey, I thought I'd swing by. I hope that's all right."

"Of course," I said, surprised she'd bothered.

"I brought a Bundt cake I picked up at Kroger. My mom always said you can never have too many Bundt cakes, though the amount I take home after parties tends to suggest otherwise."

"I think we can definitely make use of that," Mel said.

"You must be Kyle's parents."

"I'm his aunt," Cheri said. "Tex's sister. This is Mel, my husband."

"Oh, sorry. I just assumed."

She glanced at me, like she was awaiting some explanation, but I didn't offer one. And I was glad that Cheri and Mel didn't either.

I noticed James, seated in the chair propped against the adjacent wall, eyeing me uneasily. He must've known that as devastated as I was about Tex's state, the situation opened another deep wound, the one that never healed. Although, since I'd started seeing a therapist, I'd learned more could be repaired than I'd once believed.

Ms. Eiken introduced herself to my aunt and uncle, then set the paper bag on the table, pulled out plastic utensils and small plates, and cut us slices of cake. I saved mine for after I finished the Asian fusion James had brought me. I recalled my tension about Kendra when James would first talk to me about her, and as she chatted with my aunt, relaxing her through this tough time, I had to face the truth: this was a good woman. It made sense she'd gravitated to a guy like James.

There was something else that lingered in the air, but it didn't come up until Ms. Eiken left.

"You think I should try calling her again?" Cheri asked. She didn't have to qualify who as she looked at me, as disheartened as I'd ever seen her. As innocent as she was in it all, a part of me hated that she'd suggested it again.

Because it reminded me of the hurt.

The rejection.

Not just of me, but of Tex, this man who'd never been anything but good to our family—good enough to take in the kid they refused to raise.

"I'll do it." I gritted my teeth and pushed to my feet.

I could see the concern in her expression, Mel's and James's too. I didn't want to make a goddamn production of it, so I headed out of the waiting area.

I'd texted her when it happened. Cheri had made a few attempts to call, leaving messages that went unreturned.

I didn't want to be around my family or James when I called, but I didn't think she'd answer, so I went ahead and did it right outside the door.

Waiting.

And waiting.

Of course she's not going to pick up.

I hated myself, because no matter how many times I iterated that thought or a similar one, it didn't keep me from wishing, hoping to hear her voice again.

It was that final moment of silence after the last ring, just before the voice mail—a familiar sound to me by then —that said everything.

And the tears fell.

Of course she didn't. What did you think was going to happen, you fucking idiot?

I positioned myself toward the wall to keep anyone passing by from seeing my tears, but James stepped out of the waiting area.

Something about him seeing me, knowing what I was about to do when I left, made me lose it. I threw an arm around him, crying against his chest.

Fuck me.

I heard James chatting with someone nearby, I figured a nurse or PA. I would have tried to pull myself together, but I was lost in a sea of grief. He guided me down the hall, and I wasn't really sure what was happening until I noticed we were in an empty patient room. I appreciated that he'd managed to spare me from total humiliation.

"It's okay, Kyle. I'm here."

I just spit it out, because I couldn't keep it all to myself, not anymore. "She didn't pick up. I knew she wouldn't."

He rested his hand on the back of my head, the way he had done so many times, but not even that touch could save me from the despair.

"I fucking hate her so much...but she's my mother."

"I'm so sorry, Kyle."

"No matter what happens, no matter how much I tell myself I didn't do anything wrong, there's this part of me that keeps screaming, *Why...why did you fucking abandon me? Why did you let him tear us apart?* I know she thinks I betrayed her by leaving, but she betrayed me too." Like all the other things I'd attempted to tell myself, one thought always remained, and I couldn't help but spit it out. "What did I do wrong?"

"You didn't do anything wrong."

His words fell on deaf ears.

I struggled to look at him, hoping his face might help me feel better. "Some days I think I could have done it. I could have taken it. I could have done it to stay with her, to protect her. I could have stayed until he fucking killed me. But then I think that might have been my only other way out. What did I *do*?"

"Nothing. Absolutely nothing. Kyle, your parents have issues. They're trapped in their own dark world, and you're lucky to have gotten out. I don't ever want to hear you say that you'd rather have stayed, because what would that have meant for Tex? Or Taryn? Or Ben? Or me? You didn't deserve that. You deserve people who can love you in a healthy way."

It wasn't the sort of thing I could just believe in a moment, but I could see the conviction in his expression as he spoke, and I couldn't deny that, had I stayed, I would have missed what had truly become the best part of my life.

"Seems easier for you to say than for me to believe," I admitted.

"Well, fortunately, I have plenty of time to convince you."

The strength in his voice as he spoke the words and the way he held me didn't leave much room for me to doubt that, at the very least.

EVENTUALLY, we said screw the two-at-a-time rule, and I snuck James in with Cheri and Mel.

If they wanted me to pick who would stay, they'd have to put up a stink about it, because I couldn't do this without James. But no one bothered us, and as the hours passed without change, Cheri and Mel eventually went to a hotel nearby, leaving just James and me. At some point I fell asleep in my chair, and when I woke, it was light out again.

"Fuck," I muttered, then saw the box of doughnuts near me with a coffee and a passed-out James in the opposite chair. As much as I'd bawled on him the night before, I could have cried just seeing him, sticking by my side, having gotten me doughnuts.

I opened the box to see the goddamn crullers. I was too emotional for this kind of sweetness. Although, I was starving too, so I devoured them as quickly as I could shove them down my throat before I heard him stir.

He turned to me, smiling at my mouth being stuffed.

"Don't say a goddamn thing," I warned him, hardly able to say the words with how much cruller I had shoved in.

He raised his hands before him in surrender. "Not touching this one, for sure."

"You didn't go to work?"

"This is what subs are for." He winked, and I glanced around, ensuring we were alone before I said, "I love you, James."

"I love you too."

And fuck anyone who didn't get it. Fuck anyone who tried to stand in our goddamn way.

We spent the remainder of the day at the hospital.

James was good enough to bring my books from school, more than willing to bring me anything I needed. But just him being there was beyond enough.

Taryn and Ben came by after school for a few hours, Mel and Cheri as well, and we played a few card games and Catch Phrase before things wound down.

Another day without Uncle Tex regaining consciousness.

Another day reminded that my mother didn't give a shit about her own blood.

Another day I feared our time at the fair might have been my last to spend with my uncle.

Sometime later, I said, "Go home, James. You have to work tomorrow."

"I haven't taken off any time this year. It's fine. Come over here."

He didn't have to ask twice. I went to him, and he patted his lap. I checked the nearby curtain before settling in on his leg, his arms naturally folding around me, our foreheads pressing against one another's.

I let the tears fall as he pushed soft kisses against my lips. It took me a moment to find the strength to return them.

I did my best to keep aware of the curtained-off entrance, to make sure we remained alone, a reminder that we couldn't truly let go and abandon ourselves to this moment.

There would be time for that later, I told myself, yet after what happened with Tex, I couldn't help but reflect on how precious each moment was, how I had to take advantage of it with my all.

"Guess we'll have to save that trip for another time."

He caressed his hand across my scruff. "It's fine. We have all the time in the world now."

"I don't know that I've ever been this scared for him my whole damn life, James."

"I believe it. It's okay to be scared."

And I knew I could be scared with him, that he would protect me and keep me safe while I was weak.

"I love you, James."

"I love you more."

A sound caught my attention, and my eyes shifted to the curtain. I leaped off James, not really thinking it through, and tripped on the leg of an adjacent chair. I went tumbling back, catching myself in an awkward position, my hand firmly grasping the arm of one of the chairs we'd dragged in to accommodate everyone in our crew. Once I realized I was safe, I glanced around for the source of the sound, and saw Tex watching me, a broad grin on his face, the sort that let me know he'd seen far too much. His eyes lit up in that familiar way he had when he smiled.

"Looks like we've been caught," I noted, pushing back to my feet, unable to make my stumble look cool in any way.

I didn't waste time, rushing to find the nurse, who returned to do a neuro assessment and tend to him.

When she left, Tex eyed me. The nurse said it would take a few more days before they removed the endotracheal tube, but he didn't have to speak for me to know what he was thinking. "How long have you been awake while we were talking, Uncey Tex?"

He gave me his best wink, and I shook my head.

"Who says Wyachet doesn't have its scandals? But if you say anything, we're gonna have them run a couple of MRIs on you until they can figure out why you're seeing things."

He glanced between James and me, and I could feel the warmth of his love and appreciation.

I could feel his approval.

I took his hand. "You little fuck," I told him. "You scared the hell out of me."

His expression sobered as he gripped firmly. I teared up as I put my arm around him and kissed his face.

Turning, I saw James at the foot of the bed, watching us. He didn't look worried that Tex had discovered our secret, surely because he knew enough about him from me to know he would keep us safe.

For the first time in days, I finally breathed a sigh of relief.

43

JAMES

After everything he'd been through, the last thing he should have been thinking about was having to sneak through the woods on a rainy night. I turned to my Kyle, his head tucked against my shoulder, seemingly getting his first bit of rest since Tex had wound up in the hospital.

That our situation had made the past week so fucking complicated only pissed me off that much more.

We didn't deserve that. He didn't deserve that.

I hated the fucking world we lived in.

It wasn't right or fair. I was his, and he was mine. Nothing else should have mattered or weighed on my conscience. Perhaps that was why I'd so recklessly defied our rules as I parked in my driveway.

"Hey, sexy," I said, and he stirred, searching around, surely thinking, just as I was, that someone was watching us that very moment, ready to catch us in our crime.

"James..."

"No. Not tonight. Not after everything you've been through."

I took his hand, and he gripped gently. I could feel his appreciation.

It was unlikely we'd get caught, but it was riskier than anything we'd allowed ourselves to do before, a reminder of all those nightmares that could become my reality. However, to have him walk into my home the way he should have been able to was worth it.

"No one's going to notice," I told him. "And even if they did, I'm tired of being afraid."

"Me too."

We got out of the car and went inside.

No fuss. No rush. But still, with that fear I didn't imagine would flee right away once what we did was fine in the eyes of the law. I figured, hell, if any of my neighbors did make a big deal out of it, there were plenty of excuses we could make, considering all that happened this past week. But as much as I kept telling myself we'd be fine, it didn't erase that sting in my gut, like my sloppiness would spoil everything.

As soon as I closed the front door behind us, my arm was around his waist as I guided him into the living room. We sat together on the sofa, holding one another the way I'd wanted to hold him at the hospital so many fucking times.

He trembled against me. I could tell by the sniffling and heavy breathing that he was crying. After everything that happened, he deserved a good cry.

"James," he said, his voice as weak as I'd ever heard it.

"Hey, beautiful." I pulled back and looked at his tear-streaked face—not the face of a guy nicknamed Scowl at all. "Talk to me."

"It's all hitting me at once, I guess. Mom and Dad not giving a shit, but preaching about love and acceptance to their congregation. And seeing Tex in that state, so *pale*, and thinking I could lose one of the most important men in my life." His forehead creased as tears pushed from the corners of his eyes and trailed down his face.

I couldn't help but notice and appreciate how effortlessly he'd said the *men* in his life...knowing I was included in that. And what an honor it was to be a man in Kyle Forsythe's life.

"You need to eat." Despite everyone else getting second helpings of some Olive Garden before we left, I'd noticed Kyle just fork at his to pretend he was joining us. "Mini-Oreos and Chips Ahoy! don't count as a meal."

"I knew I should have eaten some Cup O Noodles to set you at ease." His joke made me laugh as a smile crept across his face.

It was the moment of release we both needed. I put my hand on his cheek and wiped away a tear.

"Sorry. I'll stop now," he said.

"You don't need to stop. I like wiping them away for you."

As another tear fell, I leaned forward and kissed it.

"You might be busy tonight, then."

"Worse ways to spend a night," I told him, kissing under his other eye.

"That wasn't even a tear."

"Better safe than sorry."

He seemed to stifle a grin.

"Why are you fighting that beautiful smile?" I asked. "I think I deserve it with how adorable I'm being."

He let loose and allowed it to expand across his face. "I hate it when you get to me like that."

"Clearly, you like it."

I wasn't sure he could smile much bigger than that, and then he did, and it warmed my heart as he leaned into me and took another kiss. My lips were at his disposal for as long as he needed them to chase away the pain.

"You know what I think we need?" I said. "Some fajitas."

He sniffled again. "Fajitas would be nice."

"Well, you sit here and binge-watch *Buffy* while I do the heavy lifting, okay? No worries about school. You're not going tomorrow. Got it?"

"Yes, sir."

I turned on the TV and again noticed him struggling against his smile. I could tell by the appreciative expression on his face that I was doing the right things, the things he needed in that moment.

But really I knew, more than anything, he needed someone to be there when all the people who were supposed to be there for him were either hurt or had already abandoned him.

He kissed me, not a playful or quick kiss, but deep and meaningful. We pulled close to one another, and I felt the tears escaping his eyes once again.

I'm here. I'm here for you, I thought, hoping to convey it with every nip, every swipe of my tongue in his mouth.

When we finally pulled away from the kiss, we hugged.

Tex would be back home soon, and Kyle and I would be back to normal...with just a couple of weeks to graduation. We wouldn't be able to leave for the summer as we'd planned, but that wasn't changing what we would do after graduation.

People could say what they wanted, assume what they wanted, but I would never be ashamed of the man I loved or what I'd done. No one could ever convince me what we felt was wrong.

We held each other for a few more minutes before I headed into the kitchen to defrost some meat. I checked in on Kyle occasionally. He watched the show, his head resting on a pillow against the arm of my sofa.

Then, on one of my trips to the fridge for veggies, the sound of the doorbell filled my place. I froze as our gazes met.

I checked the time: 11:22 p.m. Who the fuck could have been at my door so late? And why? The first thought I had was that someone had seen us when we came in, but it seemed so far-fetched.

I went to the door and checked through the side window, my mouth falling open as I saw who it was.

"Sheila," I said as I opened the door. "What are you doing here?" My words dragged out as I stared at her, stunned that she would be at my place at all, let alone so late.

"Do you mind if I come in?"

"It's not really a good time for me."

"I need to talk to you. It's important."

I glanced around. This was a horrible idea. And the worst time for her to make a surprise visit, but I could tell by her expression she was deadly serious about something. "Give me a second."

I closed the door and headed back to the living room. Kyle was already up and off the couch.

"What is she doing here?" he whispered.

"I don't know. She wants to come in. It seems important."

"Just—"

"Smells like you're cooking. Making dinner so late?" Her voice echoed through my home.

Fuck my life. I should have locked the door.

Kyle jumped to the love seat against the dividing wall between the living room and kitchen so she wouldn't be able to spot him.

I heard her coming down the entry hall and bolted out of the living room, back into the kitchen. That guilt and shame I'd believed I'd shaken when Kyle and I arrived at the house that evening seemed to flee my awareness as I felt us coming close to being caught in the act by one of the worst possible people.

She stepped into the kitchen, her heels clicking against the tiled floor. I hadn't noticed at the door, but she was dressier than usual, as though she'd just come from somewhere. In Jimmy Choos and a Gucci jacket, she set her Prada bag on the kitchen table.

"I said I'd be a minute," I told her through my teeth. "You could have waited outside."

"I've been waiting for you for a while."

It was a strange remark. That wasn't really possible since I hadn't seen her SUV outside, but I thought maybe she was referring to the message she'd left earlier in the week.

"I was at the hospital, and—"

"With Kyle Forsythe. Yes, I know."

I froze in place, my muscles stiff as my thoughts scrambled. Why the fuck did Sheila know any of this?

"May I sit down?" she asked, motioning to a chair at the table.

I couldn't even reply before she helped herself.

"Oh, James... Would you tell me if you were in trouble?"

She looked at me, and I had to remind myself there was no way she could have known what Kyle and I had been doing. No way at all.

And yet, how could she even have known about Kyle?

"What have you done, James?"

The way she said it, tilting her head, disappointment in her tone, it left little room for skepticism.

My thoughts threw me back through the past. What had I done? Where had I fucked up? Why the hell would Sheila know any of this shit?

She reached into her purse and pulled out her cell.

"Sheila, what is going on?"

"I got a little paranoid after you told me you wanted

the divorce this last time. You wouldn't tell me who you were seeing, so I came over one night and—"

"*What?*"

She pulled up an image, taken through the blinds of one of the windowpanes at the front door—my lips on Kyle's. To my fucking horror, she ran through a series of images.

"I expected you left me for another woman."

"I was very clear about why I wanted to *finally* file."

She was the one cheating on me. She was the one who was always cheating on me. There was no way she believed I'd left for someone else. This was bullshit.

"It was so out of the blue."

"It's over a year that I've wanted this."

"We'd worked through so many other things. You can understand why it would have played on my mind."

None of it was out of the blue. Her remarks about Kyle, about the past... I was so fucking confused.

"So you came to my home to spy on me?" I asked, the only question I could spit out as I tried to sort through it all.

"Yes. And apparently I had every reason to. As you can see, I have pictures of this student of yours, Kyle Forsythe, coming and going."

"How did you even find out who he is?"

"It doesn't matter." Her countenance was stiff, as though she was working to prevent even the subtlest of twists in her expression from revealing how she'd discovered his name and that he was my student. I suspected she must've followed him, or perhaps hired a private investigator. At that point, I wouldn't have put anything past her.

I thought about the clothes we were wearing in the last picture displayed on her phone. I recognized the polo I wore because I had agonized about what I'd wear that afternoon at the restaurant when I talked to her about filing. She had been over that night, had this information for all this time before telling me.

Like she'd been waiting for the right time. The worst fucking time.

"I obviously have these backed up to the cloud, and I don't think you need to see any more."

Backed up? There were more?

"I don't want you to think I'm trying to make you feel worse than you must already feel."

I did feel bad, but not for any of the reasons she was suggesting. She didn't know us. She didn't know anything about us, yet she knew too much.

She tilted her head, her eyes watering. "James, what have you done to yourself? To your career? To your life?"

"It's not any of your business what I do with my life now. He'll be nineteen in two months—"

"We both know that doesn't mean very much in the eyes of the law." For someone who had seemed so reasonable up to that point, I could now hear vindictiveness in her tone, letting me know she wasn't there to help me, her poor, misguided husband.

"James, this is not you. This is wrong. Vile. Immoral. You know this. The man I married would have never done anything so disgusting."

"The man you married couldn't have done a lot of things," I said all too bitterly as I looked at her phone. "What are you doing over here, showing me this?"

"I came to help my husband, who's clearly in trouble. I'm worried about you. You're sick in the head. Can't you see it? Surely, you must see that what you're doing to this kid is wrong." She said it with such conviction, like someone morally repulsed by something she knew nothing about.

"What the fuck do you know about what we're doing?" Kyle asked, stepping in from the living room.

Fuck. As if this wasn't already a shitshow.

She sighed again, resting her hand against her head. "Oh, James. I came over because I don't know what to do. I believe—no, I know—you're a good man, but something's happened, and I think you need to turn yourself in to the police."

"Like hell he's gonna do that," Kyle said, his face bright red. He didn't show any signs of the grief I'd seen earlier. He was all rage and defensiveness. If anything, I was going to have to keep him from attacking her.

"Kyle, please." There was enough going on in my head without him throwing himself into the mix. I turned to her. "The police? Sheila, what are you going on about?"

"I don't want to force your hand. I'll give you until tomorrow night, and then I'll do it myself."

"Why would you do that to me? You know that would ruin my entire life."

"You fucking asshole," Kyle spat out.

She pushed to her feet, ignoring him as she asked me,

"You think I want to do this? The last thing I would ever want to do is hurt you. To think of you suffering in prison over something so foolish. I wish I could help you, but clearly you've gone and ruined everything in your life. I hate that I have to even be involved."

Have to be involved?

No, this was wrong. There was never a need for her fucking stalking me. Or taking photos. Never a need for a threat.

Everything she was saying was bullshit, and I could see in her fucking eyes something sinister, something like all those times when I'd been weeping as she told me I was paranoid or making things up...before falling into her trap once more.

"I know it's a lot to process, so I'm going to leave it here, and if you need to chat, if you need someone to help turn you in, I can be there. I can help you do the right thing."

It was all bullshit. What the fuck did Sheila know about doing the right thing?

But I was caught off guard, my emotions stretched to the max as tears rushed from my eyes the way they had from Kyle's earlier.

"Sheila—"

"Shh, baby." She approached me, shaking her head. "Not now. Just think on it."

Without acknowledging Kyle, she put her cell in her bag before heading through the hall and out the door. As I heard it close behind her, tears continued pushing from my eyes, and my body was lost to a fit of trembles.

It was my turn to be the mess Kyle had been before.

I grabbed my chest as I collapsed to my knees.

Dozens of nights entered my mind as she had left me similarly crippled with anxiety. It burned in my chest like fire.

Why would she do this? played over and over in my head, along with the horrifying realization of what she'd done and said.

44

KYLE

James sobbed on his knees.

His pain renewed the strength I had struggled to find over the past few days. Stooping down, I put my arms around him, checking the hall to make sure that bastard was gone.

"She's not fucking this up for us, James. No one is."

"How did it take me so long?" he asked, his words taking me by surprise, especially after what she'd threatened.

"What?"

Turning to me, with his glasses fogged up from his tears, he said, "How did it take me so long to see through it all? Her facade? The deception?"

"You did see through it. That's why you left."

He shook his head. "Not to this extent. I knew something was horribly wrong, but what she just did... I never realized what she was capable of."

I didn't know how, when everything he'd told me made perfect sense as she stood in the kitchen, doe-eyed and acting so surprised at the shit she'd clearly put together to torment him, to make him feel like he was about to lose everything.

"I've been so *stupid*." He buried his face in my shoulder. "I kept thinking we couldn't communicate, or that she didn't understand my pain, but...she's not a good person."

"She's evil."

"Five years she made me feel like I deserved it. Like I was so lost...or like there was something wrong with me."

I couldn't help reflecting on all the things he'd shared with me about their relationship and her affairs. Her demeaning him in the bedroom. Her cruelty toward him.

All those things she'd told him back then, she'd done the same even in that brief conversation earlier tonight as she tried to make him feel so ashamed and guilty for something she knew nothing about.

And of all the people to judge us, she sure as fuck didn't have the goddamn right.

"We'll figure this out, James. I promise you."

I didn't know how the fuck we were gonna pull it off, but that didn't matter. I knew I was all in with James. Through whatever the fuck crap anyone, Sheila included, threw our way.

"What kind of pictures does she have? I'll say I came over here and did this to you. I'll say I assaulted you. I'll say whatever the fuck I have to so I can protect you."

"No. That won't be necessary." Again, I was taken aback, but this time by the certainty in his voice.

As he pulled away, taking a breath, I saw determination in the way he narrowed his gaze behind his glasses, which were starting to clear up. The confidence in his expression set me at ease, but I didn't allow myself to get too comfortable. The worst we had feared was here, and I wouldn't be satisfied until James was safe again.

He looked me directly in the eyes. "I know what I have to do."

"You can't turn yourself in. I won't let you do that."

"I won't have to."

There wasn't a hint of doubt in his tone, and given what Sheila had revealed and how he'd fallen apart right before me, I wasn't sure why.

"What do you mean?"

"I see what I couldn't see before. I know Sheila better than anyone. She's not going to the police. She's had these images for long enough that, if that's what she wanted to do, she would have done that. She wants what she's always wanted from me—to control me. That's all any of this has been about."

"We can't let her get away with that."

"She's not getting away with anything this time."

It was clear he had a plan, which he was keeping to himself.

"Kyle, all I'm going to say for now is that we're not going anywhere or changing a damn thing. I'm not running anymore. I'll see her tomorrow and make sure this ends."

Given the intensity of his words, I couldn't help asking, "You're not going to do anything...to hurt..."

"Jesus, no, Kyle. I'll explain it all, I promise. Not right now. Just know that you and I will be together. And Sheila won't be sharing this information with anyone once I'm finished talking to her."

He rested his hand on the back of my neck and pressed his forehead against mine. "No one's taking you away from me."

And even in the face of so much evidence to the contrary, I knew he meant it.

45

JAMES

I was still rattled from Sheila's visit the night before.

It wasn't just that Kyle and I had been caught in the act of what we had hidden from so many, but that she was one of the worst people who could have discovered our truth. On top of everything else that happened the past few days, it had nearly been too much for me to handle.

Until I saw the light at the end of a long, dark tunnel.

Sheila hadn't just happened to swing by because she thought I was running around with another woman. She'd been struggling with keeping me under her control after the separation, trying to keep me from filing for divorce, and then, for the first time, I'd asserted with confidence that I would move forward without her. When she found something she could use to get me back within her grasp again, she was eager to use it against me.

She didn't even present it as blackmail...yet. She

would go to the police, or I would go to the police, she'd said, but I had a feeling her story would change during this discussion with her.

Only it wouldn't be like the other times, because I wasn't under her spell anymore.

Driving through the old neighborhood, I thought about all those Homeowners' Association meetings and barbecues that felt like they took place a lifetime ago. Back in my life before Kyle.

As I came up to the two-story home Sheila and I had shared for four of those years together, where she had held me her psychological prisoner, a calm moved through me. It was a peculiar feeling, since I'd never felt so at peace around this house. It was a source of stress, grief, anxiety. I'd kept telling myself we were in a normal relationship, lying to myself nearly as much as Sheila had lied to me, until I couldn't keep lying anymore.

I parked alongside her SUV, noticing the brown and grays in the neglected flower garden between the garage and the front porch. I took the steps to the porch and knocked.

Can I come over and talk to you? I'd texted earlier, which was followed by a series of reply messages that had seemed so innocent and helpful.

Of course. Please.

I've been thinking about this all night.

I don't want anything bad to happen to you.

I quaintly reflected on Lady Macbeth's words: "*...look like the innocent flower, but be the serpent under't.*"

I was about to knock a second time when the door

opened, and there she was, her hair straightened, dressed in designer clothes as she had been the night before, as though she wanted to look her best when she fucked me over.

"Thank you for coming over," she said, wrapping her arms around me.

It was a warm, deceptive hug. I could sense the act she had prepared for me—me groveling on my knees while she acted oh-so-fucking-innocent. I wondered if she'd encourage me to come back to her...for what reason, I couldn't imagine.

Why had she ever wanted me around when all I did was cry in despair?

I had my answer now.

"Come on in," she said, sounding exasperated. It was as though she'd scripted a performance. The benevolent wife coming to her husband's side in his time of need. A reminder that all the other times had been equally scripted.

She guided me into her kitchen, and as I entered the space, the same decor around as before, I had to admit to some nostalgia for my previous cell.

A part of me questioned everything I'd been so sure of before I crossed that threshold. What if I was wrong? What if she wasn't bluffing, and I was so fucking out of my mind that I lost my ability to discern right from wrong?

I shook that fear away. It was easy enough to do when I recalled all the lies and confusion that had directly clashed with all the evidence against her. And the very act that had led me to her place.

No, there was nothing left to question.

I'd seen it all flash through my mind, clearer than ever before, as I'd been on my knees with Kyle trying to help me pull myself together.

After she offered me a seat at the kitchen table, she said, "It was a crazy night, and we both said some things we didn't mean. I'll make us something to drink."

She fetched a bottle of rosé from the fridge—a clever and undoubtedly intentional wine selection since it had been our drink of choice on anniversaries and birthdays. I didn't rush the conversation. I didn't see a reason to, when everything would be out in the open soon enough.

She finished pouring, offered me a glass, and sat in the chair adjacent to mine, setting the bottle beside us, as though she thought we would enjoy a long day of drinking together after we talked. The way she went about it all—so planned, it seemed—made me rethink so many of our fights in the past. How many times had she cleverly coordinated our fights to keep me right where she'd wanted me?

"How are you feeling?" She reached across the table and put her hand on my arm.

I pulled away instinctively, and she flinched, clearly surprised by how quickly I'd retreated from her touch.

"James, what's wrong?"

"You came to my home and took pictures of me, and you want to know what's wrong?"

"It wasn't right. I knew that even when I was doing it, but people do crazy things when they're trying to hold on to things they love. I thought I would see something that night, but I certainly wasn't expecting to see him. I'm not the bad guy here, despite what you may think about my actions."

Her words implied who the real bad guy was, and it made me consider that talk we'd had in the hotel room before I'd finally found the strength to leave.

"I was hard on you last night," she continued. "There were a lot of emotions coming up... You have to know, I was shocked to discover what you were doing with...one of *your students*."

Even the way she said it, it was clear she was trying to dig into my conscience.

But it was also a reminder that she went beyond taking pictures since that day, to finding out who he was, and I even had my suspicions on why she'd brought it to me when she had.

"You wandered on your own, and look what happened," she added. "I don't think you're a bad person, James. I love you. I'm the only one who knows and understands you. He confused you, made you lose yourself."

So funny how she was accusing him of the very things she'd done to me.

"What did you think would happen?" I asked her. "By showing me those pictures?"

"I want you to get better, and yesterday I thought that meant going to the police, but I can't stop thinking how awful that would be. And I don't know... The prison system we have isn't set up to help people. I can help you deal with this. It's my practice. Maybe we could find a way for you to come back, and we can sort this out together. I still love you. I can get rid of these pictures. I can destroy them, make it all disappear. I'd do that to protect you."

"To protect me? But I would have to come back?"

"Have to? James, didn't we have a great life together? Weren't we happy?"

As much as I wanted to keep myself together, I felt the tears coming on. "No, Sheila. I wasn't happy. I was miserable. Some days I didn't want to keep on going."

"And I just know that's part of what led to all this. You have these issues you need to work through, and we're trying."

"Even the worst days without you have been better than the best days with you."

It was as though she hadn't even heard me. "Clearly you aren't making good choices. Can't you see that? Can't you see you're slipping from yourself?"

"No, Sheila," I spit the words out louder than I'd intended, bashing my fist on the table in a way that had her eyeing my fist with concern. "You're not doing this anymore. You're not convincing me that I'm bad or evil or misguided or confused."

"What are you talking about?"

"I'm talking about what really happened in this house for four years. I'm talking about the confusion and gaslighting and cruelty. Time and again, you fucking around with one person after the next. I'm confused why you even want me here still, but I actually got an answer to *that question...*"

She eyed me peculiarly.

"Do you remember that night in the hotel room? I told

you I was trying to figure out something about you?"

She almost seemed to be listening for the first time, but couldn't come up with a response.

"Sheila, I don't think you're a woman who just makes mistakes anymore."

Her expression stiffened. Her eyes were cold, unreadable. It was as though she was working out a plan for how to deal with me now that I'd pulled back the mask and seen the real woman beneath it.

"I'm not a monster," she said.

"I think that's something we'll have to agree to disagree about."

She stared at me, plotting her next move, I imagined. There was something darkly gratifying about knowing she couldn't so effortlessly get out of this one, not now that she didn't have me questioning my every thought.

"I think the reason I always lost is because I was always fighting fair," I said, "but you weren't, were you? Lie after lie, manipulation after deception, you found a way to keep me from ever being able to fight you back. It's my turn now."

"Your turn? James, what is coming over you? This is worse than I thought."

"I have video of you with Brent Wilson." I threw it out there. It was time.

She was quiet for several moments.

"Do you remember Brent Wilson?" I prompted, and her face remained stiff, like she wasn't willing to give away anything more than that.

She wasn't the kind to show her hand. No, she was

never as foolish as I had been.

"I don't need a reply," I added. "I have the video all the same. I've had to familiarize myself with Georgia code Title 16, Chapter 6, for obvious reasons, so in case you aren't aware, it is illegal since you were counseling him at the time of the recording. I imagine if that makes its way public, you'll have your own issues, if not legally, then at least damaging to your career, this PhD program you're finishing up."

She continued staring at me like she didn't even know me.

And maybe she didn't. Maybe because the James she had been with had died at the hand of all her fucked-up games.

"There's no such video."

Denial. No surprise there.

"I never told you how I found out the truth," I admitted. "I was too ashamed of what I saw, which is why I blamed the texts under that fake name. You didn't need to know I'd seen you getting hammered by a client."

"You went through my phone to find video of me?" she asked, acting horrified by the thought.

"No, Sheila. Remember when you kept trying to upload lecture files to my laptop? I guess you hadn't fixed the settings right because it synced up all your media content to my Mac. And there they were. Plenty of videos."

"And you kept them?" Her tone suggested she was looking for some way to make me the bad guy in this. The perv who jerked off to images of his wife having an affair.

"I kept them because I didn't have the strength to go back to the files and acknowledge they even existed. I hoped one day I would, but now I have copies, Sheila. And I don't give a fuck what you do to me as long as you go down with me."

"Who is this? Who have you become?" She sounded afraid, like she was the victim.

"I don't know what I've become, but I like it a lot more than that pathetic guy who wept at his computer, thinking it was all him, that he was the one who was broken, messed up, fucked up. But it was *you* all along."

"I made a mistake, but—"

"You never made any mistakes, Sheila. Just like you didn't come to me last night because you wanted to let me know you were going to the police. You never were lost. You never were uncertain. But now you are."

The tears built in her eyes. "Why would you say these things, like I'm this unfeeling, uncaring person? Who calls their wife a monster?"

"Who stays with a man who tells her he can't decide if she's a person who makes mistakes or a monster?"

"You need help, James."

"You're right. I really do. But in the meantime, keep in mind what I have on you."

"Don't be like this."

Oh, the big dramatic tears. They fell down her face so effortlessly, taking me back to so many times when she'd done this to convince me to stay. Even then I could see why it had been such a compelling performance.

"Oh, Sheila. I've missed your lying face so much." I pushed to my feet.

"James, wait..." She followed me to the door. "Stay a minute and talk. Sit down. I don't want to leave things like this. We can work something out."

"No need to work anything out," I said as I reached the door. Grabbing the handle, I turned back to her. "By the way, you won't be able to use that app to keep track of where I am anymore. I should have turned it off a long time ago, but I never connected the dots, that that was how you had this almost psychic timing every time I got home. Clearly I underestimated you, but you also underestimated me."

When we'd first used it, she'd said it was for her own safety, so I'd know where she was if anything ever happened. I'd hardly thought about it all this time, but I'd checked it after her visit, realizing she'd used something to track my location, to find out where I was, and when I returned home that night.

Her eyes were wide, the tears having dried all-too-quickly. She was stunned that, unlike all the other times, I finally knew what I was dealing with.

A master con.

I turned the knob and opened the door. As I started out, I felt her tug on my wrist. I turned back to her. She didn't move, didn't speak. I wasn't sure she knew what she could say now that the jig was up.

"Let go of me, Sheila."

She took a breath. "I'm sorry. I didn't realize how hard I'd grabbed you."

"I wasn't talking about my arm. Goodbye."

She released me, and for the first time in any fight we'd ever had, she was frozen.

That must have gone about as contrary to what she'd been expecting as possible.

There was this feeling within me that maybe I was wrong, that maybe she would take it to the police anyway, if she was genuinely concerned about doing the right thing, but a brief reflection on our relationship was all I needed to remind myself that wasn't going to happen.

Because she had never been innocent, or kind, or even decent. I wasn't blinded any longer by excuses and disorienting arguments and crocodile tears. For the first time in my life, I could reflect back on my time with Sheila with clarity.

When I returned home, Kyle popped in the kitchen entryway, a dish rag and small plate in hand, like he'd been so eager to see me and find out how it went that he'd forgotten what he was in the middle of.

I hurried to him, and he didn't deny me the kiss I needed after what I'd just been through.

All my strength returned as he gave me the only encouragement I needed. I pushed him back to the counter. In my carelessness, he dropped the plate, but I took his body in my arms, holding him right there as it shattered on the floor.

Fuck the plate. Fuck Sheila. Fuck the world. Fuck everything that had made me feel so goddamn terrible about who I was and what I wanted.

I let myself simply enjoy the moment with Kyle.

We were right.

"Jesus Christ," he said when I finally pulled away. "I was expecting you to come home in a mood, or worried."

"Nope. This is the first time in a long time that I've really felt free."

"So...she's not going to the police?"

"Doubtful."

He eyed me suspiciously. "What did my sneaky teach do to make that happen?"

I snickered. "Considering some of the other schemes she's been up to, I'd prefer to check the house for mics before getting into it."

"But it's something wicked," he said, his eyes narrowing.

"Very wicked. Looking to fuck you with this evil dick of mine tonight."

He rolled his head back, letting out that familiar, care-free laugh that made me feel like everything was really going to be all right. "Your evil dick. Ooh, I'm not sure I can handle all that."

"As long as you're willing to try, we should be fine."

"I think I can do more than try."

We kissed again before he said, "But to be clear, how sure are you we don't have to worry about Sheila?"

"Maybe ninety-eight percent sure, but pretty damn sure. Let's just say we were married long enough for both of us to know some shit about each other, and I know what she's not willing to risk."

If I was wrong, then maybe she would take it to the police. And if she did, I wouldn't have anything on her. It was all a bluff. I'd deleted those videos off my laptop, couldn't stand to look at them. If she was a moral and decent person, she would do what she claimed was the right thing and turn me in, regardless of what it meant for her own career. But the Sheila I had come to know wasn't any of those things, and I was certain she would imagine I was as cruel and vindictive and manipulative as she was... and be too scared to chance it.

"So what are we having for dinner tonight?" I asked, tugging him close.

"I was gonna try to persuade you to grab some Taco Bell with me on the way to see Tex."

I shook my head. "Nope. That's not gonna work for my evil dick tonight."

"I can probably compromise with KFC."

We shared another laugh before I rubbed my nose against his.

"You are so giddy," he said. "This is the James I prefer."

"I know it's been a rough week, but things are gonna change for you and me."

"Yeah, I think they are."

"No more being afraid," I whispered to him, and his face turned serious. "No regrets. No fear. Just you and me. You got that?"

He nodded. "Yeah, I got it, Teach."

I took another kiss as a reward for my renewed sense of freedom.

I could feel it in my soul that this moment, right there in the kitchen with Kyle, was the beginning of my life.

EPILOGUE

KYLE

I folded another shirt before setting it on a stack I'd made on the bed, beside my open suitcase.

It was strange to think that soon this bed would be my old bed, joining so many old beds from my past. There were those from my childhood, back in the home I'd survived. Then there was the one Tex had for me when I visited him occasionally, and the one he'd purchased after he took me in during my teens, once I finally had enough and escaped the only family I'd ever believed I could have. The sets of sheets had changed over the years, but even these were reminiscent of the ones I'd cried into with the vain hope that by some miracle, Mom would come back to me...and somehow Dad would be better.

It disturbed me that I ever needed to have this image of a dad who never could have imagined hitting his child.

A man who could love me without the pain.

But that hope had been little more than a pipe dream.

Now I was moving on to another bed, and just like with those first beds, there was no goodbye. This particular one had been there for nights of working in private on my homework, or jerking off, joking and gossiping with Ben and Taryn, chats with my uncle, and holding James close the nights we spent there while caring for Tex. It had been my companion for every heartache, every feeling of loneliness and despair that reminded me of this journey I was on, my own quest in life.

I smiled at the thought of James seeing it as my very own *Odyssey*.

I folded another shirt, glancing into the floor-length mirror on the inside of my closet the way I might have on mornings when I'd woken up and checked myself more than usual, because I wanted to impress *him*. At the time, I wouldn't have copped to it, but I knew it was true.

I'd spent so many days wanting to impress Teach.

It was painful to want someone as much as I wanted him, but now I knew it was so much worse to fear losing something that had turned into so much more.

A rap on my door made me brush my hand across a warm tear I felt slipping from my eye.

I turned to see Tex, his knuckles against the open door.

"Sneaking into my house?" he joked. "I need to change the locks, I guess."

"I figured you might be napping. Didn't want to disturb you."

He approached, eyeing my suitcase and the stacks of clothes.

"Obviously, I was going to wake you up before I headed out." Something about his somber expression made me blurt that out, since he didn't exactly seem thrilled at the thought of me leaving.

It'd been a month and a half since he was discharged from the hospital. Still working through physical therapy, he was doing well on his own, without the noticeable issues walking he'd had initially. James and I had practically moved in to Tex's at first, watching him during the ensuing recovery until gradually we'd become more comfortable with allowing him his space.

"It's strange not having you around," Tex said. "Like you've already moved out."

"Gonna need to be more moved out once we get back. Don't want to use your house as my storage facility."

"Do me a favor and leave some things around. If you don't, I'll have to accept that most of the mess was me."

"Most of the mess was always you."

"But you don't have to make me aware of it. I'm too old to manage things like that."

We shared a laugh.

"What are you gonna be doing while we're gone?"

"Mope."

A fucking lie. "Are you pretending Perry McGraw isn't going to be over here all the time? The reason you aren't coming to dinner tonight?"

He had this guilty gleam in his eyes, the sort that told me everything. He'd met Perry on Tinder during the free time his recovery had granted him, and gradually, the more time Perry spent over there, the more comfortable James and I had gotten with spending our time at James's house once again.

"I think someone's crushing on this guy."

"Maybe a little. Not as whipped as you, though." He winked.

"I don't know that it would be very healthy for anyone to be as whipped as me," I confessed.

"I'm good now. You guys can get away for a weekend," he assured me, surely working to soothe the lingering uneasiness making me worry even when I'd spend nights over at James's.

It was for the best. I had to get used to allowing Tex to be on his own again, but that didn't make it any easier.

"Come on, Kylie. I'm the one who's supposed to be worried about how you're going to go off and fuck up your life as you try to sort it all out."

He put his arm around me and planted a familiar kiss on my forehead. I fell into his hug, throwing my arms around him and pulling him close. I didn't take any of these hugs for granted. I wouldn't allow myself to ever do that again.

"Just make sure to come back," he whispered.

"You know I'll be right back. You're not finished getting better. James and I will be over here plenty—"

"For now, but eventually you won't be anymore. We both know it. You're growing up now, finding your own way in the world."

"I don't want to leave." I was clearly more worked up

than I realized, because I had to strain to get the words out as tears filled my eyes.

"But you don't want to stay either, Kylie. It's not how life works. And this bed will always be here if you need it. Well, unless Perry and I decide to have kids. If we start now, they'll be able to take care of me in my nineties. Don't tell him just yet, though."

I laughed through a sniffle.

"I'll be the one taking care of you in your nineties, so don't you dare let anything happen to you in the meantime, okay?"

"If things work out right, something should be happening to me before it happens to you. We had an amazing time, and now you gotta get on to new adventures."

"I love you."

"I love you too, kid. Don't forget you always have your phone, and it'll be all right."

It was something I'd had to remind myself of far too many times.

We held each other, both of us seeming to realize that this moment didn't have much to do with James and our weekend camping trip. This was the beginning of a shift in our lives, an inevitable future that would lead us further from one another.

Once we finished hugging, he helped me pack. We chatted about the usual—shows and our men. He caught me up on what gossip he'd managed to get into with the guys from the retirement center. Things were getting back to a sort of normal, but not the same.

There was no turning back to the way things were before, and I never would have wanted that, since it would have meant I'd never have met the special man who changed my world.

The man I was on my way to see after finally leaving Tex's.

We had a dinner date with friends at his place. It would be similar to those dinners we'd shared when it was just the two of us in his kitchen.

I texted to see if he needed anything, but he was already at the store, so I swung by unannounced to see if I could catch him before he checked out. I discovered my nerd in the fruits & vegetables section, collecting Brussels sprouts into a plastic bag. As I approached, he turned, with that almost psychic instinct, as though he could sense my very presence. The corners of his lips tugged into a smile, and I hooked my arm around him, kissing his cheek, the scruff of his beard soft against my lips.

I noticed a woman by the melons, glaring at us. Samantha Brewer or Braun—a parishioner of my father's church—one of the many who had likely been scandalized when news about James Warner and his former student had penetrated town gossip.

Surely, we had assured everyone of what they already knew.

That I was just a bad kid.

Trouble.

We were the town's most infamous couple, but as was Wyachet's way, it was all just talk and rumors. James hadn't experienced any inquiry from the school. After all, what could they do now that I wasn't his student anymore? For all they knew, nothing happened until after school. For all they knew, we were just student and teacher those two semesters at Wyachet High. And the only one who could have sought to destroy us clearly had no intention of doing that, something I understood once James had revealed to me how he'd managed to keep Sheila from talking.

I grabbed James's cheeks and turned him toward me so he'd kiss me on the mouth. We shamelessly displayed our feelings in front of at least one scandalized 12 Stone member.

"Is there someone we're trying to piss off?" he whispered as I pulled away.

"Mr. Warner, you know me too well."

His cheeks turned red as I winked at Samantha What's-Her-Face.

No, I wasn't going to feel ashamed of us ever again.

JAMES

WE FINISHED our shopping run for dinner and headed back to my place.

Kyle caught me up about the latest between Tex and his new boyfriend, Perry. I'd been nervous about suggesting the camping trip, but Tex's eagerness about Kyle getting out had assured me I'd made the right call. It was time for us to start giving Tex his space again.

He didn't need Kyle, not the way he had right after he

got out of the hospital, and he was ready to get back to his own life and let Kyle get back to his.

When we returned to my place, we got right to work, in that natural rhythm we'd developed, working together on dinner while also noting anything we might have still needed to pack before we left for Lake Harwell in the morning. We didn't have much time before our guests began arriving, though.

Ben and his boyfriend—or as Kyle called him, his "summer fling" Malcolm—arrived with Taryn. They worked together to situate Matthew in a high chair before the doorbell rang, and Kyle answered it, returning with Kendra. They laughed together as she came in with a homemade Bundt cake.

"I'm really glad you were able to make it," he said, taking the cake from her and setting it on the counter.

As she turned her smile on me, it reminded me that I was wrong to have ever thought any of the real friends I'd made in Wyachet would have doubted my feelings for Kyle. In fact, none of our friends had made a fuss. No one asked the inappropriate questions I'd run through my mind before we began parading around town shamelessly after graduation.

I was surprised, and yet not. I couldn't imagine anyone seeing us together missing that magic I felt whenever I looked into his eyes or felt his electric touch. They must have known it was special.

Or...perhaps broaching the subject was more awkward than I imagined.

We added a few leafs to my new dining-room table.

We'd need a lot more space to accommodate everyone, since I'd also invited the build crew. By the time everyone arrived, we were seated arm to arm, barely managing to fit everyone in.

I sat right at Kyle's side, our legs pressed up against one another's, just as they had been at the bookstore café that special night. He caught up with Ben and Taryn about their college plans before DJ managed to get a minute with Kyle.

"How are you liking it over at the Safe Support Network?" DJ asked him.

At the encouragement of Kyle's therapist, whom he'd made so much progress with, he'd taken up some hours over the summer to volunteer at the domestic-violence center in downtown Wyachet.

"I'm really enjoying it," Kyle told DJ. "I'm trying to steal as many hours as I can manage now that Tex is feeling better."

"Just make sure you keep Saturdays free," Maya piped up.

"Of course! I wouldn't miss a Saturday."

"Wait, wait," Taryn said, pulling her attention away from Matthew, whose face was practically covered in mashed carrots. "Don't we need to be toasting James's divorce getting finalized last week?"

Kyle turned to me, unable to hold back a grin. I was sure I must have been smiling ten times as wide.

The pain, the hurt, the trauma. It had all finally come to an end.

Kyle and I shared a private knowledge of just what

that had all meant to me, not only that I had filed, but that I'd taken my life and my mind back for good.

Until it had truly happened, I hadn't realized how much it'd been weighing on me, how much Sheila and those horrible memories haunted my life.

"I don't like the idea of drinking to the end of something," Kendra chimed in. "I say we drink to the beginning. To James and Kyle."

Her gaze was right on me, that friendly expression, revealing her kindness, the sort that reminded me that, in spite of all the bad from my and Kyle's pasts, there were good people in the world too. The world could be so cruel and take so much, but it could also be kind and giving.

"I think that's definitely worth drinking to," I said as we struggled to clink glasses because of how many people we had shoved at the table.

It was a night of introductions, laughter, and stories, the perfect evening before our next adventure together.

But it was best once we'd cleaned it all up and it was just Kyle and me once again, in the bedroom. Rough and tender kisses mixed with panting and orders as Kyle lay beneath me, my cock inside him.

He tugged at the small of my back, urging me deeper.

I pressed my hand against his face, my thumb in his mouth, which he bit and sucked on, his face flushing red.

"James, I'm about to come..."

I glanced down to see the spectacle as he shot across his abs. I pushed my body close to him, just to get some on my torso before pulling my hand from his mouth, sweeping a bit up, and tasting as much as I could gather.

Fucking my man harder, I looked him in the eyes.

"Kiss me," he begged.

I pulled my hand from my mouth and took his mouth, his tongue sliding across my tongue like he wanted to enjoy a taste of himself too. I bit gently on his bottom lip, tugging as each thrust took me to the end, before I felt myself shooting within him.

It was a transcendent experience. In my release, I felt totally free.

His arms hooked around me, his legs locking mine in place as we came down from the high together.

"Mmm...I love having my cum inside you," I said, biting at his cheek.

"You fucking dork." He laughed. "Besides, it's mine now that it's in me."

He ran his hand through my hair, messing it up even more than it must've already been from our fuck.

I found myself getting lost in those bright blue eyes, sparkling as much as ever.

Kyle Forsythe.

The man I'd guarded and unlocked so many secrets with.

Somehow, we'd really fucking made it.

Behind that smile, though, there was something else too, and I wanted to be inside it just as much as I wanted to stay inside his body.

"What are you thinking?" I asked.

"About us. About how far we've come. About how free we really are."

"Funny, I was just thinking the same thing."

We kissed again, firming it together until we pulled away just far enough to breathe one another in. Once we managed to force ourselves apart, we cleaned off before returning to the bedroom, lounging side by side, my hand on his side.

But again, he still had this distant look...

"You're thinking about more than us," I insisted.

He eyed me, as though surprised I knew him so well.

"Tell me. I want to know. Please."

He hesitated, but then smirked, as if realizing how silly he was being for keeping any secrets from me...the keeper of my Kyle's secrets...at times the reason for them.

"I...um..." he began. "You remember me talking to DJ about the Safe Support Network downtown? I know I've been like, fuck college, but I think I might want to go to school...maybe become a counselor."

"Really?"

Since he'd begun opening up more in therapy, I could tell he was starting to change, become more relaxed and at peace. I knew it was the spark that got him interested in volunteering, but I hadn't expected this.

"I kind of didn't want to say anything," he added, "considering your experience with..."

"Oh, fuck her. I'm a free man now."

"Like hell you're free," he snapped playfully.

I rolled onto my back, and rolled my head for a good laugh.

Kyle didn't miss the opportunity to straddle my waist, grabbing my wrists and pulling them to the sides of my head, pinning me in place.

"If I were your wife," he said, looking serious as ever, "I would promise to be loyal, honest, and faithful. I would build us a cage and give you the key...so I could be trapped in our love for the rest of my life...forever and ever."

His words were almost vows, a wink toward where we both knew we were heading.

"I can live with this sort of bondage," I said as we shared another of so many smiles. He kissed me again, but there was something I wasn't letting go of. "I know you're trying to gloss over it, but I think you'd be a great counselor, Kyle. Maybe as good of one as you'll be my wife. And I think it's amazing that you want to take your experience and help others."

"Well, whoa, it's an idea still, but something I keep thinking about."

Yet somehow, I felt it was more than that. "I think it's beautiful."

"You're beautiful, Mr. Nipples," he said, taking a gentle bite at my pec.

I snickered, but I still wasn't going to let him get away with shifting the conversation. "Whatever you decide, Kyle, you know I'm here for you."

"I've just been thinking a lot more about where my life's heading, now that my friends are going off to college. And I don't know... I'm kind of lost, I guess. But I don't mind it."

"It's a big transition. I can see you've been giving it a lot of thought. How could you not? You can act all tough and like you're too good for the world, but...I've never been worried about you, Kyle Forsythe. There's something special ahead for you."

It wasn't something I doubted. My Kyle would find his way, and I would be proud to witness it all as it unfolded.

He released one of my wrists and ran his finger along the crease in the middle of my palm.

I could see the worry in his expression. There were a lot of unknowns ahead of us. There would be laughter, tears, anger, pain... Life would show us everything awful, but it would show us everything good as well. As long as I had him close to me, that was all that mattered.

"You've got time to figure it out," I assured him, "just like we have time for Machu Picchu next summer."

His grin perked back up. We hadn't talked much about those plans since we'd had to cancel after Tex had his stroke. It had been too much to consider, but I'd known even when we'd made our camping plans that we'd get there eventually. And now it felt like it was time to look forward to that special journey I wanted to take with him.

"If you're ready by then," I added.

"We can play it by ear. We're pretty good at that." He snickered. "It's so funny."

"What?"

"That morning we met, I was thinking senior year at Wyachet was going to be so shitty. It was a hell of a year, all right. But definitely not a shitty one." He ran the backs of his knuckles along the scruff on my face.

"No, not such a shitty year at all..."

THE END

Keep up with new releases via Devon McCormack's newsletter:

http://eepurl.com/cqEUjT

And make sure to check out Devon's FB group:

Devon's Reading Room

OTHER BESTSELLERS YOU MIGHT ENJOY...

ALSO BY DEVON MCCORMACK

Romance

Standalone Titles

Pretty Things

#ROYAL

#BURN

Forever and Ever

Still Your Guy

Filthy Little Secret

Romance Co-Authored with Riley Hart

The Metropolis Series

Faking It (Metropolis Series, #1)

Working It (Metropolis Series, #2)

Owning It (Metropolis Series, #3)

Trying It (Metropolis Series, #4)

~

Weight of the World

Up for the Challenge

Beautiful Chaos

The Clipped Saga

Clipped (Clipped Saga, #1)

ABOUT THE AUTHOR

A good ole Southern boy, Devon McCormack grew up in the Georgia suburbs with his two younger brothers and an older sister. At a very young age, he spun tales the old-fashioned way, lying to anyone and everyone he encountered. He claimed he was an orphan. He claimed to be a king from another planet. He claimed to have supernatural powers. He has since harnessed this penchant for tall tales by crafting worlds and characters that allow him to live out whatever fantasy he chooses. Devon is an out and proud gay man living in Atlanta, Georgia.

facebook.com/groups/devonsreadingroom
twitter.com/devon_mccormack
instagram.com/devonmccormack

Piece
By
Piece

Susan Tuttle

Published by: WriterWithin Publications

Copyright © 2015 Susan Tuttle

A WriterWithin Publication

ISBN: 1941465102
ISBN-13: 978-1-941465-10-3

WRITER
WITHIN

DEDICATION

This volume is dedicated to the real brave men and women who put their lives on the line daily in their efforts to make our streets and cities safer places to live. Without all of you, we would devolve into chaos. You are the true heroes of our lives.

Piece By Piece

Susan Tuttle

CONTENTS

ACKNOWLEDGMENTS

No book is possible without the help of so many people, especially the South County Critique Group of SLO NightWriters (Dennis Eamon Young, Ginger Lasher, Judythe Guarnera, David Georgi, Evelyn Cole, Anna Unkovich and Claire Gordon), all of whom kept me honest in my writing. To my wonderful beta reader, BJ Butka—thanks for catching so many typos and errata when I thought I had them all out.

To Mark, my coffee buddy, who listens to all my bitching and moaning—what would I do without you?

And of course, a million thanks go to my computer guru, Debra Davis Hinkle, an amazing writer in her own right, without whom I could not do any of the computer work a book needs. To say nothing of my blog and website.

And bunches of hugs and kisses to my amazing cover—and interior artwork—designer, Aaron Kondziela, who is busily working off the orange juice he drank while growing up. I have truly been gifted with the bestest son in the whole universe!

CHAPTER ONE
October 14, 1987
Harrisburg, Pa.

The phone's scream shattered the silence and sent Ogden Wilkes' pulse racing. He hated the anemic electronic beeps that passed for telephone bells nowadays, though his pounding heart wouldn't have minded one now, at ten after four in the morning.

He reached out and snared the receiver before he opened his eyes, not wanting his wife to wake, though he knew Judy couldn't sleep through even one shrill ring. It was a game they played. He grabbed the receiver as quickly as he could so she could sleep on, and she lay with her back to him, eyes wide and heart thudding, he was sure, pretending she had not heard.

It allowed him to leave the house with a minimum of fuss. And it allowed her to roll over and mumble at him, questions that did not touch on the reasons for the untimely calls. He knew the only way Judy could accept the dangerous work he did in daylight was not to acknowledge why her husband was called out of bed at night. Ogden Wilkes respected that, which was why he played the game.

"Yes, what is it?" he said now in a low tone, though he already knew. Only the murder of someone big or the wounding of one of his men would drag the precinct Captain out of his warm bed. He inched himself up against the padded headboard, trying not to shake the mattress. Musuko, who slept on the floor under the partially open window, sat up, head cocked, ears aquiver, front paws restless on the soft carpeting.

"Traynor here, Captain. I'm with Snelling in an alley near the river, between Fourth and Lexington. I think you'd better get down here."

Through the static from the squad car mic, Wilkes could hear a jumbled commotion in the background.

"Who is it?" He threw back the covers, swung his feet to the floor.

"Cliff Davisson."

"Channel Three's reporter?" Wilkes glanced at his wife's stiff back. "Who found him?"

"A couple on their way home from a bar. She needed to puke, they cut down the alley."

"You first on scene?"

Traynor paused. Wilkes ground his teeth. Then Traynor gave a sharp sigh.

"Almost. Abernathy caught the squeal on patrol, beat me by maybe five minutes."

"We need to contain this, Bill," Wilkes growled. "You know that."

"Yes. I'm on it, sir."

"OK. Ten minutes. No one goes near him until I get there, including the lab boys."

"Yes, sir."

Wilkes rubbed his eyes. It took ever-greater will power to motivate his forty-seven-year-old body to start a day at four a.m. But there was no help for it. The popular TV reporter's murder would spread ripples of shock and righteous indignation throughout the entire community. If Wilkes were not to be buried in the fallout, he'd have to supervise every step of this investigation personally.

He rose, took up the clothes laid out on the chair beside the bed and went into the bathroom to dress. Glancing in the mirror, he rasped a hand over the dark stubble on his chin and decided not to shave. It would enhance his image of dedication to be caught in disarray by news hounds' flashbulbs—hot from his bed and indifferent to his own grooming in the face of tragedy. He growled with annoyed exasperation that he knew would only grow as the hours and days passed. This one would be a ball-breaker, front-page news all the way.

Judy turned over and stretched her arms over her head when he reentered the bedroom.

"What is it, Ogden?"

"It's nothing, go back to sleep." He crossed to the bed and kissed her cheek. She didn't open her eyes. "Just a little trouble down at the station. Don't worry about breakfast, I'll pick up something downtown."

"Um-hmmm," she mumbled, turning back onto her side. The streetlight shining in through the window silvered her pale hair. Her lashes cast long shadow-streaks down her plump cheek like narrow slashes of blood. "Just be careful, honey."

"Aren't I always?" he replied with a tender smile. He wondered how many men married for twenty-six years still lusted for their wives the way he did for his. "Sweet dreams," he whispered, kissing the soft, rounded flesh of her bare shoulder.

Judy didn't answer. That, too, was part of the game: she pretended to have fallen back to sleep and he feigned belief. She would, he knew, share her worries for his safety and sorrow about the tragedy over the next few days when they were alone together, but she would not burden him with them now, when he most needed to be clear-headed and alert. It was her way of supporting him, of giving him the freedom he needed to do his job well. He adored her for it.

Musuko padded behind him, bushy tail curled up over his back. At the front door Wilkes bent to stroke the short, rough reddish-brown back with a firm hand.

"No, boy," he said. "Just me, this time."

The heavy-set dog cocked his head. The pointed ears twitched. Wilkes could barely make out the dog's features, but the white blaze on his chest and his front paws gleamed in the darkness.

"Sit, Musuko. You stay and guard the girls."

The dog sat, obedient as always, the quivering of the powerful, stocky body attesting to his desire to accompany his master. Wilkes shut the door and strode to his six-year-old, dark gray Chrysler LeBaron. He would have liked to bring Musuko as he often did when called out late at night or early in the morning. But he knew that this time the commotion, especially since the media would probably get wind of this before Davisson's body could be removed, might upset the Japanese Akita's normally calm disposition. Not even Wilkes wanted to tangle with Musuko when the dog got riled.

Wilkes drove fast, ignoring stop signs and signal lights. He passed few cars on the streets. He kept to side roads, winding through the sleepy upper middle class area of the city where he lived, into the deteriorating poorer section. Fourth and Lexington was the center of a narrow no-man's-land six blocks wide and four miles long. It was a mixture of shops, warehouses, and single family homes a century or more old that separated the wealthy upper class from the reality of life on the firing line of drugs, crime and poverty. The area teetered on the fence, as it had for some years now. Neither rich nor poor nor middle-class, it defied designation, thumbed its nose at statistics. Tumbledown rat-traps interspersed with houses freshly painted. Vacant storefronts hobnobbed with successful, growing enterprises. Deserted warehouses stood beside converted loft apartments. Anything could come out of the Fourth and Lexington district, a big part of his precinct, and it often did.

The scene wasn't hard to find. Five blocks up from the river half a dozen police cars with lights flashing stood canted out into Fourth Street, blocking the alley entranceway. The meat wagon and a lab van blocked the Lexington Avenue access. Two patrol cars and one unmarked detective's vehicle flanked the crime scene in the alley itself. Wilkes studied the scene and found he couldn't fault the way this had been handled so far. No one, except the police and two civilians Wilkes assumed were the ones who had found the body, was anywhere near the corpse. Even the lab boys and a scowling medical examiner stood at a respectful distance. A few curious residents, awakened by the commotion and clutching sweaters over nightclothes, peered around police barricades and patrolmen. But his men had been busy. When and if the press did arrive—which would be soon, Wilkes was sure—there were enough barriers to ensure an uncompromised beginning to the investigation.

The body lay in a small cul-de-sac on the left, halfway down the one-way alley. A niche about ten feet deep had been sculpted into the surrounding brick building, a vacant pottery factory, creating somewhat of a courtyard effect. The original purpose of the niche was anybody's guess. Now the dark, secluded area, hemmed on three sides by windowless brick walls and faced by boarded windows in the storage warehouse across the alley, made a perfect meeting place for transactions of the unsavory sort. This was not the first body to be found here, and Ogden Wilkes knew it wouldn't be the last.

He parked, then edged around the unmarked whose headlights floodlit the crime scene. The car's owner, tall, beefy, lead homicide detective Bill Traynor, turned to intercept Wilkes as he approached the body. A uniformed patrolman stood nearby, just within earshot. Traynor's trainee, Andy Snelling, stood a few feet further away, hands and jaw clenched as he watched the grisly scene.

"Any problems, Bill? Wilkes asked.

Traynor opened his mouth, then closed it without speaking. Wilkes' eyes narrowed. After a beat, Traynor's chin dipped once as though to reassure his Captain. Wilkes allowed himself to relax slightly.

"All's secure, sir," Traynor said, his hazel-green eyes glancing at the patrolmen guarding the Fourth Street entrance. "No one's been near him since I called you."

Wilkes nodded, then grimaced at the sound of tires screeching outside the alley. Slamming doors and shouting voices heralded the arrival of local news reporters.

"Goddamn, I knew it wouldn't last," he growled. "As if this isn't going to be difficult enough, now we have those fucking idiots to contend with. Well, we knew going in what it would be like, didn't we?"

He glanced at the detective. Traynor's lips twitched. Again his chin dipped in an abbreviated nod of agreement.

"The boys well-briefed?" Wilkes asked.

"Yes, sir." Traynor's eyes held a trace of amusement though his expression remained stern. "They'd keep the President out if you ordered it."

"I doubt it will come to that." Wilkes' chuckle held no mirth. "Davisson was big, but only in a pond this size." He stepped closer to where the body lay and turned to Snelling, his eyes narrowed on the young detective's face. "What's it look like to you?"

"Drugs, most likely, sir." Snelling swallowed obvious nervousness and took a deep breath. "Or organized crime. I'd say it was a pro job, all the way."

Wilkes grunted, pulled on latex gloves, and crouched beside the body, which lay on its side in the niche's rear corner closest to Fourth Street. The feisty, tenacious investigative reporter had taken quite a beating. Savage cuts marred his photogenic face. Blood matted his waving blond hair and stained the front of his white Italian silk shirt. His hands were bound behind his back, his blue eyes open, glassy and staring, the deep, resonant voice silenced forever. Snelling's high-pitched nasal tone showered down on Wilkes.

"Judging by the state of the body, sir, I'd say it took Davisson a long, hard time to die. That slug must have felt pretty good by the time they got around to it."

Wilkes nodded and rose.

"It certainly looks like someone with a grudge made damn sure Davisson got the message before driving the point home with a bullet."

Wilkes waved Bob Lesky closer. The M.E. waddled toward Wilkes.

"What would you say, Bob?" Wilkes gestured with his chin at the blood-ringed hole in Davisson's left temple. "A thirty-eight?"

"How the hell would I know?" Lesky's acerbic tone and sour expression confirmed his disagreeable disposition. "You think I have x-ray vision? When I go in, I'll know. I'll have it plated in silver and mounted like a trophy for your desk if you want. I'm not paid to make guesses. And I don't get out of bed at four a.m. so I can watch you prance around in the dark doing my job. You want to play games, fine." He turned away. "I'm going home. Wake me when it's over."

"Five more minutes, Bob, that's all. We can't afford a mistake on this one."

"What 'we'?" Lesky snarled as Wilkes again crouched beside Davisson. "Quit lumping me in with the rest of you clowns."

Wilkes chuckled absently as his gloved hands folded back the grimy, blood-encrusted suit coat. His fingers quested into pockets. He found keys, a wallet, three pieces of chewing gum and a white handkerchief with CDG monogrammed in blue in one corner. A silver Cross pen still peeked above the hem of the blood-stained shirt pocket. But there was no notebook, not one scrap of paper, not even a book of matches on which to write. Wilkes stood up and nodded at Lesky.

"He's all yours once the photog's done. ASAP, and don't leave one inch of him unexamined. I want to know everything that's happened to him since he was born."

"Oh, sure," Lesky wheezed as Wilkes turned away. "I won't bother to cut him, I'll just use a crystal ball, or better yet, my time machine." He pursed his thick lips and stood rocking on heels and toes while the lab men shot rolls of film.

Wilkes walked to the back wall of the niche and crouched where a pale tan epauletted raincoat, Davisson's 'trademark' in weather both sunny and foul, had been tossed. With careful fingers he examined it. Not a scrap of paper lurked in its deep pockets. The harsh light from the unmarked police car's headlamps made him squint when he looked up at his two detectives—Traynor, broad and muscular, with a prize fighter's face and his Italian mother's coloring; Snelling, red-haired and thin, with facial features more suited to a horse than a human. Good cops, both of them.

"Nothing," he said. "Not even his pocket recorder."

"Strange, that," Traynor said, his eyes skewing to Snelling and back to Wilkes. "For a reporter."

"Yeah. Isn't it?"

Wilkes rose and looked over to where television and newspaper reporters surged against police barricades. Television cameramen had added their lights to those of the detective's car. Telephoto lenses captured every movement. Boom mikes thrust forward like horizontal antennae. Wilkes knew he had to be careful about what he said, what was captured on film.

"This has to be connected with whatever Davisson was working on. Why else would they take all his notes, and the recorder? He had to have been onto something really big. Drugs or organized crime, you're probably right, Snelling." He looked at the detective and gestured at the crime scene techs. "I want every inch of this alley gone over. Tell them to print every goddamned brick if they have to. I want something to go on, fast."

"Sir," Snelling said, and marched down the alley to the knot of men scouring the cobbles where Davisson lay.

"I think we're going to need it, sir." Traynor's gravelly voice echoed slightly in the narrow space, his eyes scanning the press mob a short distance away. "One of their own has been killed. If those news hounds don't get acceptable answers, and get them fast, this is going to turn ugly."

"Shit!" Wilkes exclaimed as the thought hit him. Was it already too late? Reporters were nothing if not quick and clever. "Get someone over to the T.V. station, fast. Seal up his office. All we need is one of them getting to his files before we do. And his house, he must have kept some things there, too."

"It's already taken care of, sir." Traynor's flat voice rang in the enclosed space as Snelling returned to stand by his side. "Joe Sillitto's sitting on Davisson's office, checking through his paperwork. Won't nobody get inside 'til you OK it. And I sent patrolman Bates over to the house. Figured it wouldn't hurt to have a little protection already in place."

Wilkes' head turned in the dim light. He looked at Bill Traynor. The detective's eyes, still hooded and secretive, stared back. Wilkes nodded.

"Good thinking," he said and turned away to the bustling crime scene. Lab men worked on the ground around where Davisson had been found. Bob Lesky's assistants had already bagged the body and were lifting it into the coroner's van. Patrolman Abernathy stood beside his black-and-white talking with the young couple who had made the gruesome discovery. The woman sat sideways in the back seat, her feet out on the pavement, one hand clasped in her companion's. Abernathy's pen moved across his notebook. Anxious and angry camera crews and reporters milled at the Fourth Street barricade. Television cameras pointed in their direction. Wilkes had no doubt the mike booms could pick up his every word.

"Okay, Bill," he said, his quiet voice sounding almost menacing. "You and Snelling go help debrief the civilians. I'll run the press gauntlet. Then we'll move on this thing and we won't stop until we get the ones who did it. We'll start with Davisson's current stuff and work backwards if need be. I suppose it could be someone he nailed in the past." He turned and looked at the place where Cliff Davisson had died. "But I doubt it. It's someone current, and someone big. And we're going to nail him. We're going to nail him but good."

CHAPTER TWO
December 18, 1987
Harrisburg, Pa.

Wendy Wilson sat relaxing at the kitchen table. With the kids finally off to school and Jeff at work, she had a few minutes of peace to enjoy her breakfast of fried eggs, toast and coffee before plunging into her pre-Christmas routine. The morning paper lay spread beside her plate. 'Trail Cold in Davisson Murder— Police Stymied,' the headline read. 'Lack of Clues Hinder Two Month Old Investigation.'

Wendy shook her head and pressed her lips into a thin line. She hated the thought that whoever had killed the reporter might get away with it. She had enjoyed him on the news, often teased her red-headed

Jeff about Davisson's classic blond, blue-eyed handsomeness. But though he'd looked like a mindless beach bum, Cliff Davisson had been an efficient and effective investigator. He'd uncovered more than one illicit operation in Harrisburg, resulting in arrests and embarrassment for a number of so-called 'upstanding' citizens. The papers and networks had been especially hard on the police's inability to bring his murderer to justice.

The phone rang. With a sigh Wendy rose and lifted the receiver off its hook, sure it was Mrs. Quinlan about January's mid-winter festival for the church. Why couldn't she ever learn to say no?

"Hello?"

"Listen, Wendy, let me—"

"Vic? Is that really you?" Wendy's heart had leapt when she'd heard that husky voice on the tother end and she couldn't help but interrupt. "You guys are finally home? How was the trip? You could have at least sent a postcard, you know."

"Under the circumstances, I didn't think that was appropriate. Let me talk to her, Wendy. It's important."

The cold, distant tone in his voice bewildered her. Wendy's mouth dropped open.

"Talk to who?"

An exasperated sigh echoed through the line.

"My *wife*, Wendy. Who the hell else would I mean?"

Wendy gritted her teeth at his imperious tone even as the words sent a surge of alarm through her. Vic Remsen could be such a bastard at times. It was no wonder Carole's marriage traveled a more than rocky road.

"What are you talking about, Vic?"

"Goddamn it, Wendy, I've had enough of this nonsense. I've got to talk to her. She hasn't looked at the mail since I left and that puts her in deep shit. She missed the court date and never even called a lawyer. Put her on the line—now!"

"But... But she's not here. She told me she was going to Italy with you, Vic. She had her passport and everything. I thought she was with you." Wendy paused, took a deep breath to dispel the panic that had begun to fray the edges of her words, then realized this was probably another example of Vic's twisted sense of humor. "This isn't funny, Vic. Really. Put Carole on the phone, let me talk to her." She closed her eyes, listening beyond Vic's raspy breathing. She heard nothing in the background, no hint of her sister's presence.

"You're as stupid as she is, Wendy. Why the hell would I be calling you to talk to Carole if she was here?" The sneer in Vic's tone shattered Wendy's complacency and she caught her breath. "She said she'd go stay with you, slammed out of here not ten minutes before I left. It doesn't look like she even bothered to come back. What'd she do, buy herself a whole new wardrobe, using *my* credit cards?"

"Vic, s-stop it." The fear that had built while Vic Remsen spoke shook Wendy's voice. "Y-you're scaring me. Carole has to be with you. Where else would she be?"

"That's just what I want to know. That bitch. I should have figured she'd pull something like this to get back at me. When I get my hands on her..."

A voice murmured in the background. A woman's voice, low and breathy. Not Carole's. Vic's palm blotted out his reply. Wendy fisted a hand in her hair and stared out the kitchen window at the denuded trees and bushes ringing her back yard. A wood sled bloomed like blood against snow-dusted grass. Swings dangling from a frame painted blue and purple wavered slightly in the cold December breeze. Her home. None of it looked real to her.

Wendy began to shiver. This couldn't be happening, it just couldn't.

"Who is that, Vic? Answer me! I know someone's there, I can hear her. Is *she* why you don't know where your own wife is?" A sob pushed up, cut her words short. Wendy put her hand on the wall to steady herself. "My God, what have you done to my sister?" she whispered.

"Me? I haven't done a goddamned thing! And neither has she, the bitch. I told her to get her stuff out of here before I got back, but she didn't bother to—"

Wendy slammed the phone onto its hook, silencing Vic Remsen's vitriol. The edges of her vision lightened. A faint buzzing sounded in her head. She could barely breathe. She stood a moment, hands pressed flat on the wood-grain counter, until the dizziness and nausea passed. When she straightened up she felt empty, completely drained. Not a thought or emotion remained within her.

Wendy picked up her purse, turned off the coffee maker and left her house, locking the door behind her, barely aware of her movements. She saw nothing on the three-mile drive to Carole's apartment, remembered not one inch of the journey, though she braked for red lights and stop signs and signaled for turns just as she always had. An eternity passed in the fifteen minutes it took to traverse the distance, a barren eternity overflowing with desperation and fear. She rapped on the apartment door, knuckles insistent against the wood, gaze fastened on the name tag perched in the brass slot on the mailbox: *Vic and Carole Remsen*. She wished she had a gun and had brought it with her.

Vic merely stared at her when he opened the door, his face belligerent, his large, soft body blocking the entryway. Wendy said nothing. She gazed at his chest, at a pearl button that jumped with his every annoyed breath. For once, she was totally unaffected by the aura of menace he exuded, the huge muscles and small, inhuman eyes that had so unnerved her in the past. After two awkward, silent minutes, her sister's husband snorted.

"Christ! You're worse than Carole. What the hell do you want?"

Still Wendy remained silent, not trusting herself to utter a word to this man who had let his wife run off into the night, and then left the country for two months. She let her eyes, when at last she raised them to his, speak her contempt. Vic blinked and stepped back from the door.

Wendy moved when he did. She pushed past him and came to a stop in the center of Carole's neat blue and gray living room. Except it wasn't neat now. Suitcases and tote bags, magazines, coats, half-empty water bottles, the debris of international travel littered the room. A tall peroxided woman stood barefoot near the kitchen archway, wrapped in Vic's burgundy panne robe.

"Uh, this is Melanie." The discomfort in Vic's voice echoed in his stance. He moved closer to Wendy, stopping just beyond her sight line. "She stayed here last night, we got in really late. She's, uh—"

"Your whore?" Wendy turned her head, let her eyes bore into his.

"You fucking bitch! What gives you the right—"

"The fact that you're still my sister's husband! *You're* the adulterer here, Vic, not Carole."

Vic snarled and stepped closer to Wendy, his hand clenching into a fist. Wendy thought of the bruises she'd seen on Carole's arms. Her chin rose in defiance. Vic's arm pulled back, his muscles bunching. The blond he'd called Melanie gasped and reached out a pleading hand to which neither Wendy nor Vic paid any attention.

"Vic, don't, please," Melanie pleaded in a wispy voice. "Just ignore it. She's too upset to know what she's saying. Don't make it worse."

"I know exactly what I'm saying." Wendy's eyes never left Vic's.

Vic slowly dropped his fist. He flexed his fingers as if to threaten further violence. His lips lifted into a sneer. Wendy refused to back down.

"Get out of here," he growled.

"Not without Carole."

She turned on her heel and stalked down the short hall to the bedroom, shouldering past Vic's blonde floozy. The sight of the bed, sheets and blankets twisted awry, the imprint of two bodies still on mattress and pillows, struck her like a fist. She paused in the doorway, pain gnawing at her. *That bastard,* she thought, *bringing his strumpet to this room, slobbering*

*over her in his marriage bed—and all the while not knowing,
or even caring, where his wife was, if she was safe.*

Oh, God, please make this only a dream, she prayed
as her feet took her unwilling body to the closet. Her
hand reached out to open the door. Vic and Melanie
both watched as she went through it all carefully—
closet, dresser, nightstand, vanity drawers in the
bathroom. Nothing seemed missing. Carole's clothes,
her jewelry, shoes, makeup, medicine—God, even her
hairbrush and her toothbrush were still there.

In a carved soapstone box on the dresser Wendy
found the parking ticket for her sister's car. The date/
time stamp told her Carole had left it in a downtown
long-term parking lot at ten-fifteen a.m. on October
13th, just ten hours before her flight. Carole had said
she didn't want to worry about it parked on the street
in front of the apartment for two months, gathering
tickets, or impose on someone to keep moving it for the
alternate-side parking regulations. She had left it, and
not redeemed it. Wherever Carole was, she had not
driven herself there.

How the hell could Vic have seen all this and not
known something was wrong? And why hadn't he
called to check on Carole when he'd arrived in Italy?
How could he have simply dismissed the woman he'd
lived with for over seven years, not cared what was
happening to her? Two months. Carole had been
missing for two months and nobody knew, nobody
was even looking for her. How could the police find
her now, after all this time? They couldn't even find
that reporter's killers and they'd been on that from the
start, had all kinds of clues. Here, there weren't any

clues. If they couldn't find Davisson's killers, how would they ever find Carole?

Clutching the parking ticket tight in shaking fingers, Wendy walked out into the living room where Vic and his harlot now sat side by side on the couch. They were holding hands. Wendy thought she'd be sick all over her sister's thick gray carpeting.

"Something's happened to her. Have you called the police?" she asked, already knowing he hadn't.

Vic looked at Melanie then back at her. For the first time, a glimmer of concern shone in his dark slanted eyes. He shook his head.

Wendy nodded, turned away and picked up the phone that sat on a table near the couch. She would call the police first, then her husband, Jeff. She thought it ironic that Jeff was a shift foreman in the same shoe factory where Vic was a design engineer, that they had introduced Carole to Vic. Good old Vic, a design engineer, for shoes of all things. And a cruel, abusive, womanizing husband who let his wife disappear without saying a word.

"I didn't know she was missing, Wendy. Honest. I thought she was with you, that's where she said she'd be. I didn't know."

Wendy looked up. Vic stood near her now, twisting his thick fingers in the soft flannel of his shirt. Worry finally frowned across his broad face. Moisture sheened his blinking eyes. The blond slipped into the bedroom, closed the door behind her. Wendy caught a glimpse of the movement from the corner of her eye and her mouth twisted. A lot of good discretion would do now. Wendy blinked back tears.

"And you didn't care much either, Vic, did you?" He opened his mouth, but Wendy stopped his words with a quick shake of her head. "It doesn't matter, Vic, not now, anyway. It's Carole who's important. You just pray she's still alive."

Hands trembling, she dialed 9-1-1. While she spoke, she stared at a portrait of Carole and Vic taken three years before, a picture of Carole from happier times. Light glinted red in her long dark hair. Only a trace of shadow lay across her long-lashed, big gray eyes.

"My sister is missing," she said to the clipped, impersonal voice that answered on the fourth ring. "She's been gone for two months. I don't know what to do." Her voice broke. Her eyes overflowed, sent a river down her face. "Please. Please, help me find her."

CHAPTER THREE
June 3, 1990
Buffalo, New York

She stood alone in a field in the middle of the city park. Sun poured like hot molasses onto her head. A fine film of sweat misted her pale face, stuck her long dark bangs to her forehead. The turgid air felt like a weight crushing her ribcage. A jogger, panting in the heat, lifted a hand in greeting then ran past her on the path. She remained motionless, staring at the bridge.

Her heart pounded. She'd thought, when she'd started out, that this was the day, the milestone in which she'd begin to reclaim her life. Or a life, at the least. After all, she'd already survived the terrifying bridge behind her. And she had four days of memories to bolster her. But now another bridge stood before her, barring her way, threatening to destroy all she'd worked so hard to gain.

She studied the graceful arches of pale stone that spanned the shallow creek while her body shuddered and her legs threatened to collapse beneath her. What kind of place was this, that bridges sprouted everywhere you turned? How was she supposed to keep looking, searching, if she was blocked at every step? The sweat on her brow thickened. It ran down her face like tears, stung into her eyes. She blinked and shook her head.

You can do this, she told herself. The broad lawn on which she stood undulated down to a small man-made lake on the edge of the park. On the far side of the water, a copper roof slowly greened atop a two-story, arch-windowed, stone building. Tiny figures moved like ants up and down the steps to the lake and the grassy hills near the quaint building. Children's laughter echoed faintly across the lake and tapped at her eardrums. Parks, she knew, were good places to search. Unexpected memories could lie around every bend—not that she'd ever found any. And parks were easy to hide in when necessary.

Besides, if she gave up, if she went back, she'd just have the first bridge to contend with again. And she'd found no answers back there on the street. Her only hope was to move forward. *You* can *do this*, she told herself once more, and forced her feet to move. Not until the path began to rise did she realize that she would have to cross this bridge, not walk beneath it. She wasn't sure which thought scared her more.

She paused at the top of the path, one foot poised to step out onto the bridge. Two men and three young boys dangled fishing poles over the side of the bridge where the lake flowed into a narrow, meandering creek. Bikers whizzed across the span with careless abandon. Cars threaded around pedestrians, heading for the expressway entrance off to her right. Parents towing children and lovers holding hands strolled the bridge's sidewalks, unaware of the menacing danger poised coil-taut in the glittering gray stone. She wished she could be like them. Just once, to move, to speak, to live without fear dictating her every breath. Just once.

A massive, imposing building perched atop a gentle rise to her left beyond the bridge. Sculpted from glittering white stone, it boasted a colonnaded portico and an ancient copper roof. A long series of curved, shallow stone steps lead up to elegant glass doors set into the stone. She fixed her gaze on the stone lions that reclined on pedestals at the base of the steps, clenched her teeth and marched down the bridge. She paid no attention to the stone beneath her feet, the carved railings or the people. She just kept moving until suddenly she found herself standing before the lions.

Her breath gusted out in surprise. She hadn't been aware of leaving the bridge behind. She could feel the smile curve her lips as her second victory of the day filled her with warmth. She looked up. A large banner spread across the building's facade above the doors at the top of the steps, but she couldn't decipher the words printed on it. Groups of people sat on the sloping lawn at the side of the steps, in folding summer chairs or on blankets, laughing, talking, some sharing picnic foods and drinks from wicker baskets. Men and women dressed in elegant black began congregating on the wide expanse of the top landing, carrying musical instruments to waiting chairs. Her smile died. Something was about to happen and she wasn't sure she would be allowed to stay. She turned away, unwilling to risk a confrontation.

She walked across the street to where shallow arced concrete steps led down to a wide paved walkway. It curved around the end of the oval lake, giving way to soft grass a hundred feet beyond the green-roofed concession building she'd seen from the other side of the lake. There were people everywhere but, though she'd come here for the people, she suddenly felt exposed. Fear again took hold and shattered the fragile illusion of triumph and safety that had filled her. She angled down the street, away from the building. A sudden resonance of music behind her pushed her up over the curb, across the grass, and onto a path that wound its way through a small field of low bushes just beginning to leaf.

She could see prickers on the dark, almost-bare branches, thorns thick at the base and tapering to wicked-looking points. She wondered what the bushes were, if they would eventually bear flowers. She loved flowers, their enticing aromas, their delicate beauty. The sometimes vibrant, sometimes ethereal colors captivated her. If these bushes did flower, how long would it take? Would she still be here, able to savor their loveliness? She doubted it. She couldn't afford to stay anywhere very long.

The mouth-watering aroma of roasting meat captured her attention and she looked over at the concession stand to her left. People stood in lines, or wandered away with hands laden with food and drink. She dug in the pocket of her jeans, pulled out a small wad of bills and a few coins. A little over seven dollars. Her shoulders drooped. Hunger gnawed at her stomach but she couldn't afford to assuage it this day. What she had would have to last until she could find work of some kind, at a place where questions wouldn't be asked since she had no answers to give. If such a place existed. Slaking her thirst would have to do. She walked back to the concession stand, bought a small soft drink, and tucked the remaining six dollars back into her pocket.

She continued searching the park and ended in the southwest corner two hours later. Her quest was hopeless. There was nothing here for her. The whole park might as well be empty, as empty as this part of it appeared to be. Her feet dragged with weariness, leaving faint grooves in the dirt path. Hunger made her head swim. Heat and exhaustion pulled at her eyelids, misting her eyes so she could not see clearly. Sweat stuck her clothes to her body, ran down her face and stung into her eyes. Trees thickened, blocking out sounds of merriment that echoed in the open spaces she'd left behind her. It was hard to breathe. Not a leaf stirred on the trees, not a cloud marred the sun-bleached blue of the sky. Shadows slanted long across the ground now, but the heat and humidity had not lifted despite the lowering of the sun. She kept her head bent, moving slowly along a path, any path, she no longer cared. Someone passed her. She didn't bother to look up.

A cheering yell and sharp clapping burst close in front of her. Startled, she raised her head, blinked her eyes to clear them. Ahead to her left stood a small clearing filled with people. Some, mostly women and children, sat on rickety make-shift bleachers set at one long edge of the cleared field, beside the path on which she walked. The rest, all men, stood at various places out in the clearing, most with a huge padded glove on one hand, a few others barehanded but looking poised for sudden flight. One man, far to her right, held a fat stick over his shoulder. The ghost of a memory flitted through her mind, but it vanished when she reached for it, leaving no trace of itself behind.

Hoping the memory would return even though she knew it wouldn't, she moved closer until she stood up against the back of the wooden plank seats, staring at the men through the open spaces. They yelled to each other, laughed, made faces. The one in the middle threw something and the man with the stick swung at it. He connected with a sharp crack. She raised her head, trying to keep the small white object in sight. It arced up as it sped down the field and she turned her head to follow it, all the while aware that the men closer in had moved for some reason, racing to stand in new places. Someone far out caught the object in the big glove he wore. An agonized groan sounded from the other men when he held it up with a wide grin, and she realized that it was a ball he held. Intrigued, she stayed to watch longer, wishing she didn't feel so alone and empty.

She moved away from the wooden seats about ten minutes later, when the men stopped and the people watching gathered up bags and baskets and prepared to leave. She, too, would have to leave soon if she was to get back to her sleeping place before dark. Despite her double triumph, she knew she could never face those two bridges without daylight surrounding her.

Still, the thought of the bridges caught at her feet, kept her leaning against a large tree on the other side of the path. She waited until most of the people across from her were gone, then pushed away from the rough bark and began to follow them.

Her heart stopped dead in shock. He came along the path toward her, from the direction in which the others had disappeared. Stray motes of sunlight glinted on the badge pinned to the dark blue uniform. *I can't let him see me!* she thought, but it was already too late. He looked right at her, his dark gaze boring into her eyes. She couldn't move, couldn't breathe. What she most feared was about to come true. Then he smiled, nodded at her, wiped the sweat from his face and turned toward the four men who remained in the field.

"Hey, Reed, how'd it go?" the cop called as he tucked the handkerchief back into a pocket.

"You have to ask?" came the answer. Laughter tumbled close beneath the deep voice's injured tone.

"Lost again, huh? Don't you guys ever win?"

Trembling, she sidled behind the wide bole of the tree behind her, losing awareness of the men's voices in her own frantic need to draw air into her lungs. She stood leaning against the rough bark, eyes closed, and pressed a hand to her lips to silence her raspy breaths. Her ears strained to hear if the ominous footsteps drew closer. Had he seen her move behind the tree? How much longer before he would come after her?

It seemed forever, an eternity and a half, before the laughing banter ended and she heard soft footfalls, the steps muted by the pine needles that cushioned the path. She held her breath. The cop's feet hesitated just opposite the tree, moved on three more steps and paused again, then continued on down the path. She sidled around the tree, keeping it between herself and her enemy, careful not to make a noise or betray her presence in any way. After a moment she peered around the tree to see a broad dark blue back vanishing around a turn in the path. She waited a few moments longer, terrified that he would return. But the path remained empty. She had escaped.

The close call weakened her knees. She could barely stand upright, even clinging to the tree. She needed to sit down before she fell, so she wobbled over to the tier of wooden planks and sank onto the lowest one. Despite the heat, chills racked her as shock spread its reaction through her body. She propped her right foot up on the plank and wrapped her arms around her bent leg, seeking warmth. She closed her eyes, wishing she knew why the police terrified her so and hoping her strength would soon return. She still had those damned bridges to face.

The plank bobbled beneath her. Startled, she opened her eyes to find one of the men sitting not three feet away. His hazel eyes sparkled at her beneath an unruly shock of light brown hair. He was slightly overweight with well-developed biceps, his tee-shirt and shorts still showing signs of heavy sweat. He grinned at her, further rounding an already round face. An open cooler sat on the dusty ground between his feet.

"Hi, how's it going?" he asked, his voice the same deep rumble that had answered the policeman.

She blinked into his face. Who was he? What did he want with her? Had the cop told him to find her? What was she supposed to do now?

CHAPTER FOUR
June 3, 1990
Buffalo, New York

She blinked into his face. Alarm flashed in her lovely gray eyes, so swiftly gone he wasn't sure he'd seen it. Ken Reed felt his smile fade into an enquiring frown. She looked away, a slight shudder shaking her body, and dropped her foot down to the grass.

"Hi," she answered, her soft voice trembling. Ken decided she must be painfully shy. Not that that explained her curious reaction to Pat O'Connor, who'd merely been on his regularly scheduled swing through the park. Shy was one thing, sidling around tree trunks to avoid cops quite another. He wondered if perhaps she was in trouble of some sort. Maybe he could help, if he could get her talking.

"I saw you watching the game a while ago. What'd you think?"

She merely shrugged in reply, placed her palms on the wooden plank, one on each side of her, and gripped the edge. He chuckled, thinking she was attempting to be diplomatic. She looked older than Ken had first thought, maybe somewhere in her early to mid thirties, close to his own age. A woman, not a girl. That might make things a little easier. Maybe.

"Yeah, we stunk, as usual," he admitted with a rueful grin. "Lost twenty-three to nine. I don't know why I keep torturing myself like this." He reached down into the open cooler and extracted a can of root beer. "It's supposed to be good exercise for the body, but losing almost every week sure isn't beneficial to the soul, I can tell you that." He popped open the top of the can and held it out toward her. "Want one? I've got plenty."

She turned and looked at him, her eyes wide as though surprised by the offer. She looked at the frosted can in his hand and Ken saw intense longing, quickly stifled, flash across her face. Then she shook her head and glanced at him again, giving him a small smile before she turned to stare out across the empty field.

"No. Thanks."

"You sure? You look thirsty." And hungry. God, but she was thin.

She didn't look at him, she merely shook her head again. Ken sighed and took a long draft of the icy beverage. He was striking out again, and for what, the hundredth time just today? Why couldn't he be better with women than he was at playing ball?

"Come on, Ken! Let's get going before the light fades!"

The shout seemed to startle the woman and she jumped. They both looked at the men who stood at home plate, about fifty feet from where they sat, and for a moment Ken caught a stranger's-eye-view of his three friends. Jason McGuire, short and freckled, red hair aflame in the late-day sunshine, stood tossing a ball in the air and catching it with the mitt he wore, his face twisted in the intense concentration with which he attacked all of life. Teddy Harper, husky body bent at the waist, baseball cap obscuring riotous black hair, knocked his bat on the ground, raising small puffs of dust, a man obviously used to amusing himself. Dave Atwood, tall and lean with blond hair bleached almost white even this early in the season, stood rocking on his heels, hands jammed into the back pockets of his jeans, the studied casualness not quite masking his keen awareness of his surroundings nor the humor that sparked in his eyes. Man, he loved those guys. He smiled at the woman, shook his head and waved in response.

"Those idiots. They think if we practice we'll actually win more games. Though God knows why. We've been practicing for two years and our best is four wins for a whole season. When we lose by only a ten-point spread, we consider it a near-win." He sighed. "Sometimes I wish I'd never heard of baseball."

"Baseball," she murmured, her eyes taking on a glazed, faraway look as she surveyed the all-but-deserted field.

Ken frowned, wondering if she was all right. He opened his mouth to ask.

"Damn it, Reed!" the redhead yelled again, before he could speak.

"Oh, hold your horses, Jason. I'm coming!" Ken shouted back.

He stood up and looked down at the girl, noting the clean lines of her narrow face, her small straight nose, a lower lip that was slightly overfull and pouty. The sun painted red highlights in her long hair, and though her collar and wrist bones showed, her breasts retained an appealing fullness that strained against the low scoop neck of her red top. Though she was more girl-next-door than truly pretty, Ken liked her looks, liked the way she hunched her shoulders and twisted the toe of a ragged sneaker in the grass. He liked the way she looked up and gave him her tiny, shy smile.

"Listen, I'd better go pretend to get better at this stupid game before they bean me with the ball. I'll make it quick, ok? And help yourself, take anything you want. I brought too much, as usual. Like I really need it, right?"

He patted his over-ample stomach and winked at her, drawing another half-smile. Turning, he trotted back to the men who awaited him so impatiently.

"Criminie!" Dave exclaimed, running a large hand through his pale hair. "What were you doing over there, getting married?"

"Blow it out your ear, Dave. Let's get this exercise in futility over with." Ken bent and picked up his glove. "I'll catch for you, Teddy, OK?"

"Just be sure to keep your eye on the ball, Ken, and not the girl," Jason McGuire advised, turning for the pitcher's mound.

"Yeah? You just try getting the ball in over the plate for once, Jase."

"Up yours, Ken," Jason shot back, settling the bat on his shoulder.

Laughing, the men took their positions, Dave Atwood heading for a spot where the infield joined the outfield, just in case, as he put it, Teddy Harper actually hit the ball. The woman sat where she was for so long that Ken's hopes rose, though it didn't look like she was watching. Maybe she liked him, too, but didn't want to seem obvious about it. Maybe she really would still be there when they'd finished this nonsense. It wouldn't be much longer. Already the light had faded enough to make distances indistinct, and a hint of night chill rode on the slight breeze that kicked up and began cooling off the day's sweltering temperature. He waved to her a few times, even saluted her with the bat when he was up, and though she didn't wave back he thought he could see her smile as she ducked her head. But she rose before they had finished, while he was catching for Dave, and with a sinking heart he watched her move to the near end of the bleachers and start to walk slowly away.

Teddy Harper, on the mound, threw a 'curve' ball that missed even Ken's long-armed reach by a mile. With a shout, Dave slammed the bat into the dirt. Ken saw the woman stop and pause beside the bleachers to look back at them.

"Damn it, Teddy! You call that relief pitching?"

"Sure it is," Jason yelled from the field. "It's a relief when he *stops* pitching!"

"Fuck you guys," Teddy snapped, snatching his cap from his head and wiping the sweat on his face with it. "I'm the best we've got and you know it!"

"Let's face it, gentlemen," Ken puffed, trotting over to pick up the ball. "We're simply too old for this kind of thing. We should be rocking on our porches with beer in hand, not making asses of ourselves in a public park."

"Look who speaks of age," Dave crowed. "The baby of the bunch."

"Only by six months, *Grandpa,*" Ken replied, tossing the ball to Dave and retrieving his bat from the ground. "I've had it. I'm going to see if I can rescue what's left of my Sunday."

He shouldered the bat and started for the woman, who bit her lip and stepped back a pace at the sight of him approaching. She looked off down the path, but she didn't walk away. Ken's grin widened, but before he had taken five steps two teenage boys raced full tilt out of the trees to his left, heading for the path and the open park beyond. The first passed perilously close to Ken and the girl, swerving at the last moment. But though the second missed Ken, it seemed either he didn't see the woman or he headed straight for her on purpose. He smacked into her with stunning force, smashing his shoulder against hers and shoving her sideways. He stumbled momentarily, but did not stop running or even look back.

Propelled by the force of the collision the woman staggered off balance, her arms rising as though to protect her face. The boy's shove slammed her against the edge of the bleachers. Ken saw the sharp jar ripple through her body. Her legs buckled and she fell forward onto the hard, sun-baked dirt that ringed the wooden seats. The sound her head made as it thumped on the hard ground echoed loud in the early evening stillness, almost as loud as the sound of Ken's heart thudding in his chest.

He dropped the bat and raced to her side, as did his friends. Being closest he got to her first. He dropped to his knees in the dirt beside her, his hands hovering mere inches above her body.

She lay half on her back, her right shoulder canted up against the bleachers, knees bent and twisted to the left. Her right hand draped gracefully across her ribcage. The left lay palm up on the ground beside her head. Her neck was bent, her head turned toward her left shoulder. She wasn't moving. Her face looked deathly pale.

"Oh, shit, shit, is she dead?" Teddy asked in a croak.

"Don't even say it, Harper," Dave breathed as Ken reach out to touch the woman's shoulder. "You'd better not move her, Ken. We should get an ambulance."

"I think you're right, she's—"

The woman moaned, cutting off Ken's words. Her eyes fluttered open, her right hand lifting shakily to her head.

"Hey, lie still, that was a nasty fall. We're going to call for an ambulance."

"What?" she asked, her voice breathless. Her eyes blinked rapidly, as though she was having trouble focusing on Ken's face. "No. No, don't. Please, I'm all right."

"I think we should, just to be safe. You hit your head pretty hard, you know, you were out about thirty seconds."

She closed her eyes. "It doesn't matter, there's nothing wrong. I don't need an ambulance. Please, just leave me alone."

Tears rode in her voice. She sounded close to hysteria. Ken sighed, sat back on his heels, and looked his consternation up at his three friends.

"Why don't I go get some ice?" Jason McGuire suggested. "It'll give her time to calm down and start thinking rationally again, and since she's awake and talking it's probably not life threatening."

"Good idea. Get some water, too," Ken added, thinking of the cans of root beer sitting in his cooler. He doubted that carbonated, overly-sweetened soda pop would mix well with a head injury.

"I still think we should call an ambulance," Dave insisted as Jason, with Teddy in tow, headed for the concession stand on the other side of the park.

"We'll see." Ken shrugged.

"No, we won't," the woman said, drawing their attention back to her. "I don't need one. I'm perfectly fine. Really."

Lifting her head, she rolled to her left, trying to sit up. Suddenly, she gasped. Her eyes scrinched shut and the pale color that had begun infusing her face drained away. She subsided against the bleachers with a shaky, pained sigh.

"You see? You are *not* fine." Ken slid his hand gently beneath her shoulders and laid her flat on the ground. "Now, just do as I say and lie still, you hear me?"

"All right," she agreed, her eyes closed, her breath panting in short gasps. But her voice was firm, a thread of steel in the soft tones. "But no ambulance. I'm just a little dizzy, that's all. It'll go away in a minute."

Ken looked at Dave and shook his head. Damn, but she was stubborn, not at all sweet and shy like she'd seemed earlier. Could a clock on the head actually change someone's personality, or had he been wrong about her in the first place?

"Those damn stupid kids." Dave looked down the path where the two boys had disappeared. "What the hell did they think they were doing? He ran right into her, didn't even try to swerve."

"The dumb punk." Ken rose, his eyes glittering anger. "He never even looked back, didn't care if he'd hurt someone. I'd sure like to get my hands on him."

"So would I."

They stood silent a few minutes until Jason and Teddy loped into view. Each carried a soft drink cup. Jason also clutched a wad of paper napkins. When they reached the end of the bleachers where the girl lay, Jason nestled four ice cubes from his cup in the center of the smoothed-out napkins and twisted the ends together, handing the improvised icepack to Ken with a small flourish. Teddy removed the wrapping from a straw and popped the straw into his cup. Then he set the water on a plank within Ken's reach.

"Thanks, guys," Ken said, wondering what he'd do without friends like these. He'd known them for years, ever since high school. No matter what happened, he knew he could always count on them for advice, support, or a swift kick in the ass when he needed one.

Holding the icepack in his left hand, he knelt again and brushed the woman's long dark bangs back from her forehead. Not wanting to hurt her, he kept his fingers gentle. Still, she caught her breath at the soft touch and her eyes fluttered open to stare straight into his face before closing once more. Ken frowned, both at the fear and panic he saw in the gray depths, and at the discolored swelling on her left temple that already spread a red patch out across her forehead and down to her cheekbone.

"Here," he said, laying the pseudo-icepack on the injury. "Hold this on the bump for a while. It'll help the swelling."

She gasped when the icepack touched her head. Her body tensed, but her right hand lifted to hold it in place. Jason motioned to Teddy and they moved away to gather up the equipment still left on the field. Slowly, the cold ice appeared to ease the pain. The woman relaxed. Her breathing deepened, and she looked almost as though she slept. Ken glanced up at Dave, then gently touched her shoulder.

"I'll be right back. Don't move."

"I won't." She shook her head a tiny bit in confirmation. "Not fast, anyway."

Ken chuckled softly and touched her shoulder again, then the two men walked over to home plate, where Jason and Teddy had piled all the gear, jackets, sweatshirts and coolers included.

"Listen, you two go on," Ken said. "There's no sense in all four of us staying here."

"Are you sure?" Teddy asked.

"Yeah. What more can you do, anyway? She's adamant about no ambulance, says she's just a little dizzy. I guess that's to be expected, the way she hit the ground. Dave and I will stay, make sure she's on her feet and okay before we leave."

"I still think we should have called an ambulance. Head injuries are nothing to fool around with," Jason said.

"You're right," Dave agreed, "but she doesn't want one. Wouldn't we look like idiots if we called one anyway and she refused to let them treat her?"

"Once she's calmer, maybe we can talk her into going to the emergency room, just to be on the safe side," Ken suggested. "If not, we can always insist on driving her home. That's about the best we can do." He shrugged, feeling helpless and frustrated.

"Well, if you're sure," Teddy said, his tone doubtful.

"Go on. I'll call you tomorrow and let you know how it turns out."

Teddy and Jason nodded, picked up their things, and headed slowly away to where their cars were parked on the adjacent side street. Ken took his sweatshirt from the top of the cooler and looked over to where the woman lay with the icepack clasped to her head.

"I'd better get back to her before she decides to run the Boston Marathon or something." He cocked a brow at Dave, who laughed softly in response.

"Why don't I take all this out to the car?" Dave suggested. "Maybe by the time I'm done, she'll be ready to go."

Ken nodded. "Good idea."

Dave bent to the task at hand and Ken walked over to squat beside the woman. Her eyes were open again, one leg stretched out straight, her right knee bent so her foot rested flat on the ground.

"How're you doing?" he asked, crouching next to her.

"I'm all right. It doesn't hurt as much, now. Will you help me sit up?"

"If you're sure you should."

She nodded, a faint smile curving her lips. Ken slid his hands around her shoulders and lifted her up, turning her so she could lean against the side of the bleachers. She still held the icepack to her head. Beads of water ran down the inside of her arm. Ken smiled at her, and picked up the second cup Jason had brought.

"Here, drink some of this, maybe it'll help."

She put the disintegrating icepack in her left hand, which lay in her lap, and took the cup from him. Goose bumps raised up on her arms. Ken saw her shiver as she sipped the water. The chill in the air had deepened and Ken was sure the cold liquid and the icepack only made it worse. He was glad he'd kept the sweatshirt with him.

"How do you feel?" he asked, taking the cup and soggy, disintegrating napkins from her still-shaky hands.

"Not bad, just a little dizzy. I'm sure it'll go away soon."

"My name's Ken. Ken Reed. What's yours?"

Her smile faded. She bent her head, the fingers of her right hand toying with those on her left. When she looked up again, she shivered.

"I'm cold."

"I don't doubt it. Here, put this on."

He shook out the sweatshirt and helped her slide it on over her raised arms. He heard her catch her breath. Her eyes looked clouded when at last the warm fabric dropped over her head but she smiled at him, her shoulders hunched gratefully beneath the sweatshirt. Ken smiled back.

"That feels good. Thank you."

"Dave's just taking our stuff out to the car. When he gets back you can try standing up, OK? Then we'll drive you home."

"No. No, you don't have to do that. I-I don't need a ride."

Ken frowned, hearing a note of panic in her voice.

"Are you all right?"

She looked at him. For a moment her big gray eyes seemed lost and empty. Ken felt a shock go through him. Then she looked down at her lap and nodded.

"Yes, of course I am. You don't have to stay with me."

Ken sighed and looked down the path, wondering what was keeping Dave. He really didn't want to deal with this all alone.

"Listen," he finally said, looking back at the woman, "we talked it over and we all feel the same way. You really should be checked out."

"Checked out? What do you mean?" She frowned at him, alarm clear in her face, her rapid breathing.

"At the emergency room. You got hit pretty hard, you were out a good thirty seconds. You could have a concussion, even a skull fracture. You need to have a doctor look you over."

She started shaking her head before he'd even finished speaking. "No, I'm fine, really. I don't need a doctor."

"It won't take long. There's a hospital just down the street."

"I won't go to a hospital. I-I can't. I-I'm not from around here."

"That doesn't matter, your insurance will pay for it." She shook her head, making a small, negative sound deep in her throat. "Don't you have any insurance?"

She opened her mouth to speak, but caught back the words. Her eyes lifted to his momentarily. She looked like a small child caught doing something wrong. When she looked down again she bit her lip and shook her head.

"No," she said, her voice shaky and tear-filled.

"Don't worry about it. I'll pay for it, anything, just so I know you're all right."

"I *am*. I won't go to a hospital! I won't!"

She tried to stand, using her hands to push herself up off the ground. Her breath caught in her throat, her face scrunched up in agony, and she huddled back against the bleachers, her body shuddering. Quickly, Ken put his hands on her shoulders to steady her.

"You see? You're in no condition to go anywhere," he chided. Still, in pain as she was, she shook her head. "Damn it! All right, at least let us drive you to wherever you're staying. I just hope it's with friends who can talk some sense into you."

"No, I-I don't need a ride. I can walk." Her voice sounded weak; it shook badly. There was no conviction in her voice.

"You can't walk, you can't even stand up!" Ken argued. Movement caught his eye. He looked up and sighed with relief. "Good, here's Dave. Come on, I'll help you up."

He closed his fingers around her left arm, midway to the elbow. She bit back a cry of pain, the agonized sound gurgling in her throat. She folded sideways into his arms and sat huddled in his embrace, shuddering, trying to catch her breath. Gingerly, he pushed back the left sleeve of the sweatshirt.

Her arm was swollen from wrist to elbow. A darkening bruise spread out on the skin, a long reddish oval in the center of the swelling. It seemed to grow even as he looked at it.

"My God," he breathed, aghast. "It must have happened when you hit the bleachers. Can you move your fingers?"

"A little." Her fingers moved a fraction of an inch, as if to prove her words. But she winced, and her body tensed as though pain surged with the movement.

"I'll bet it's broken," Dave said. "We'd better get you to the hospital right away."

She looked like she wanted to fight them on this. Then she stilled, and Ken could almost feel her draw away from them emotionally. Dave helped Ken lift her to her feet. They steered her gently along the path to the edge of the park, their strong arms around her waist keeping her trembling legs from buckling. Ken thought she must have finally understood the seriousness of her injury, for she went with them willingly enough.

"Who are you staying with?" Ken asked as they walked along. "We ought to let them know what's happened."

"I... No, there isn't anyone. I'm alone."

"Where are you from, then? We'll call your family."

She didn't answer. Frowning, Ken looked down at the girl in his arms. She was taller than he'd thought, he estimated now about five-foot-seven or eight. It had been her thinness and delicate, child-like air that had made him think her small. They reached the side road where Dave's car sat waiting. Ken stopped, holding the woman tight, while Dave went ahead to open the car doors.

"Are you going to answer me? Where are you from?"

Annoyance at her silence made his tone harsher than he'd meant. Ken felt her cringe in his embrace. She looked up at him, studied his face in the light from the streetlamp, and then nodded to herself as though she'd come to a decision.

"I don't know," she said, her voice almost a whisper.

"What is that supposed to mean? You don't know?"

"I-I can't remember." She looked up at him, pain and confusion and a watchful stillness in her eyes. "I'm scared."

"It's probably from hitting your head," Ken said, giving her what he hoped was an encouraging grin. "I'm sure it won't last long."

"No, you don't understand," she said, tears sparkling on her lashes. Dave moved closer, frowning.

She studied him a moment, then took a deep, steadying breath.

"It'll be all right," Ken said. "Really."

She shook her head. "No, it won't be. At the hospital, they'll ask questions I can't answer. And then they won't let me go, I know they won't."

"What do you mean? What questions?"

She hesitated, looking at both Ken and Dave before answering. "My name," she said.

"What about your name?" Dave asked.

"I don't know it. I haven't for a very long time. I don't remember anything about myself, or where I'm from." She looked up at the first stars glimmering in the darkening sky, then studied the two men as though gauging their reaction to her words. "There's nothing. I'm completely blank inside. I have no memories of myself at all."

CHAPTER FIVE
June 3, 1990
Buffalo, New York

They stood outside the car after they had buckled her into the seatbelt, arguing as the last light faded around them. About her, she knew, angry voices pitched low, gestures sharp and quick with intense meaning. The tall one, Dave something, she couldn't remember what, kept glancing at her, his eyes almost hostile in their icy blueness. She sat still, trying not to stare at them while they decided her fate. She tried to think of a plan of escape if they refused to help her, but her pounding head and throbbing arm kept coherent thought far away.

She'd had no choice but to tell them. She had known, once the extent of her injury became apparent, that they would not let her walk away. Even she had to admit she needed medical care. But would these men understand her desperation and fear and give her the help she needed instead of the help they thought she should get? She didn't think it was possible to make anyone else understand what she herself couldn't. That was why she needed an alternate plan, a way to escape the net in which she was certain to be snared. She'd be able to figure it out, if only she didn't hurt so much. Gritting her teeth, she closed her eyes and concentrated on not moaning aloud.

The car doors opened and the men climbed into the car, Ken in the back with her and Dave behind the wheel. Ken put a warm, comforting hand on her shoulder.

"We worked it out," he told her. "Trust me. We won't say anything about the amnesia, I promise."

Trust him; as if she had any choice. Dave started the engine and drove away, displeasure scowling from his handsome, sharp-featured face. It was obvious which side of the argument he'd been on. She wondered if he was unhappy enough to renege on his agreement to keep quiet about her.

It didn't take long to reach the hospital. They drove a few blocks on quiet streets divided by wide treed malls, passed huge houses whose windows gave teasing glimpses of sumptuous interiors, curved around two traffic circles and they were there. A matter of minutes, only. Ken told the emergency room nurse that she was his cousin, Julie Martin, from somewhere in Michigan. The fact that she was between jobs explained why she had no insurance. He gave his own address for the place she was staying, and himself as the party responsible for paying the bill.

It took hours in the hospital, a few minutes of testing here and there separated by elongated periods of waiting alone in a small curtained cubicle. It was a torturous ordeal. All she wanted was to disappear, to crawl into a safe hole somewhere and hide. She was terrified, certain that they would discover her deception and keep her, turn her over to the police. But even more afraid any movement would prompt questions she could not answer, she lay still and in silence did whatever they told her to do.

In the end they did let her go, pushing her in a wheelchair out to the reception room where Ken and Dave sat bleary-eyed and yawning. Even after all the questions, the poking and prying, blood tests, X-rays, shots and the cast they'd put on her arm, she still wasn't sure if it was really broken or not. The doctor, using words longer than she was tall, basically said she had suffered a hairline crack in the ulna, whatever that was. Did a crack constitute a true break? She didn't know, and she was too busy being good and trying to remember the little Ken had made up about her to ask.

Julie. She'd thought about the name Ken had chosen while she waited. It was funny, but she had never thought to give herself a name, not in all this time. At least she didn't remember doing so, although she must have in order to get by. She simply couldn't remember. She lay behind the curtain, her eyes heavy with pain and weariness, and savored the rhythm of the word, the feel of identity the small sound imparted. It wasn't who she was, she knew—Julie—there was nothing at all familiar about it. But maybe it was who she could be. She smiled, glad that she would be able to take something this wonderful away with her. She had memories now that stretched back more than four days and showed no sign of vanishing. Had the accident happened earlier, she most likely wouldn't have remembered the name for very long, or the feeling of security it imparted. She hoped she could hold onto this memory, this name, for a long time.

It was after one a.m. when they arrived home. Ken's home, that was. She didn't even try telling him to take her to where she'd been sleeping. She knew, without asking, that he wouldn't. He lived alone, he told her during the almost-silent drive, in a small, two-story house on a three-block-long street called Radcliffe Road, barely three miles from the park. In the quiet darkness she saw a three-foot-wide raised median strip bisecting the two halves of the narrow street and little else at that late hour. The old-fashioned street lamps hoarded their light close, and only two houses evinced a faint hit of a glow in shaded upper windows. Ken's house was on the west side of the street, the second in from the corner of the first cross street, Deveraux.

No lights showed in the windows of his dark brown house for, Ken said as he helped her out of the car, when Dave picked him up for the game, he'd expected to be home before sunset. Leaving his blond-haired friend to lug in his gear, Ken led Julie to the second floor and showed her where the bathroom was.

"I should apologize for the mess," he said. She said nothing, merely stared without really seeing the towels strewn everywhere, the capless toothpaste tube on the counter, crossword puzzle books littering the floor, a sink that needed cleaning, the raised toilet seat. "Housework isn't my strong suit, I guess. Just close your eyes for tonight, and I'll get to work in here tomorrow."

"Please, Ken," she said, trying not to stumble as he led her to the spare bedroom, "I shouldn't bother you like this. I don't have to stay here—"

"Yes, you do," he interrupted, clearing the junk off the bed as he spoke. "The doctor said you need to rest for a few days. You do have a cast on your arm and a mild concussion, not to mention a purple forehead and probably a raging headache. I think a bed is the best place for you. A bed, in a house. My house. Here." He rummaged in the bureau and handed her the top to a pair of pajamas that looked brand new. "This should be adequate, it's not too chilly at night anymore, and the sleeve should be wide enough for the cast. There's a blanket on the bed already. Do you think you'll need another one?"

"No. I'll be fine," she said, almost whispered. For some reason, she couldn't seem to get more volume out of her voice. "Thank you."

Ken smiled at her, a smile she hadn't the energy to return, and closed the door behind him.

She stood a moment wondering what to do. She didn't really feel capable of doing anything. Ken was right, her head did hurt, and her arm, too, despite the painkillers they'd given her. The room swayed gently, as though the house sat on water and not dry land. Nausea built slowly in the pit of her stomach. With unsteady steps, she backed up until her legs touched the bed. With her last ounce of strength she sank down to wait for her head to clear.

After what seemed hours, a faint tap sounded on the door.

"Can I come in? I brought you some towels and stuff." She looked up to see Ken crack the door open a few inches and peek in.

But she couldn't answer, could barely even hear him. The whole world seemed very far away. She huddled into herself, shivering although she wasn't really cold, and pressed a trembling hand to her lips. She couldn't get her eyes to focus when she looked up at him.

"Hey, you OK?" Quickly, Ken set the towels on the bureau and moved to her side.

"I'm so dizzy," she whispered, her sluggish tongue tripping on the words. What was happening to her? "I'm afraid to move."

Smiling, Ken took the pajama top from her lap and laid a hand on her cheek. "That's the meds kicking in, the doc said they were pretty strong. Let me help you into bed."

Her heart lurched in fear. She shook her head, but could not stop his hands when he slid the sweatshirt over her head, carefully easing it off her left arm. The tight red knit top beneath wasn't quite so easy. It took some doing, but finally he managed to pull the snug garment free of both her body and the bulky cast. He said something about his own clothes, but the words held no meaning for her. She was so groggy she was barely aware of his actions until he removed her bra and his gaze roved over her bare shoulders and breasts.

No, please! she pleaded, tried to plead. But no words passed her lips. Her body shuddered. Her arms were so heavy, she couldn't move them to push him away. She was helpless, completely at his mercy. And though it wasn't the first, or, she was sure, even the last time she would feel like that, she knew she would never get used to it. She would always hate feeling helpless, despise being used. Ken dropped his hands to her jeans and undid the snap. She gasped. Terror rippled through her. Ken picked up the pajama top and opened the buttons.

"It's OK, Julie," he said, tipping her head up with a gentle hand on her cheek. "I'm not going to hurt you."

It was true. He really wouldn't hurt her. She could read it clear in his beautiful hazel eyes. Her fear slowly evaporated and she nodded her understanding. She tried to smile back at him, but her lips, like her arms, remained motionless, too heavy to move. Ken slid the brown and blue striped cotton fabric up her arms and buttoned it securely. It felt good, soft and warm, and the width of the sleeve easily accommodated the cast. It had no collar. The vee neckline fell low enough to reveal most of her cleavage. Kneeling, Ken pulled off her sneakers. She wasn't wearing socks, didn't even own any.

"OK, let's get you in bed."

He had to help her stand up, and even then she stumbled off-balance. He held onto her with one hand while he folded back the covers, then he sat her down on the cool sheets, swung her legs onto the bed and eased her down onto the pillows. Keeping the pajama top modestly covering her—it reached midway down her thighs—he unzipped the jeans and pulled them off her legs. His large hands tucked both blanket and bedspread snug around her still-shivering body, close under her chin. He smiled at her again and she felt a funny little tingle in her breast at the way his eyes crinkled, the dimples that deepened in his cheeks.

"Don't worry about a thing, you just get a good night's sleep. If you need anything, call me. I won't be far away. We'll talk more in the morning, OK, Julie?"

She wanted to answer, tried to speak. But her eyes blurred, and in blinking them clear again she forgot what she wanted to say. A frown crossed her brow as she fought to bring the words back. Ken sighed and shook his head.

"Sorry. I guess I've been thinking about you as Julie ever since I told the doctor that was your name. Do you mind?"

"No," she mumbled, struggling against drug-induced lethargy. She was almost out. "I like it."

"Good. Then, Julie it is. I'll see you in the morning."

She nodded, her eyes closing despite her desire to stay awake. She wanted to keep watching Ken, to hold his image in her mind while she slept. But her injuries defeated her. The strong painkillers whirled her far away even before her thoughts were formed. She didn't feel Ken gently kiss her cheek before he left the room.

* * *

Dave was halfway through a beer when Ken at last descended the steps. He held an unopened can out to Ken as he spoke.

"Is everything all right up there?"

"Thanks." Ken took the can, popped the top and took a large gulp. "Ah, I needed that. Yep, she's fine, fast asleep already." He dropped into a chair opposite the couch where Dave sat.

"I don't think we did the right thing," Dave said after a moment's silence. "We should have told the doctors about the amnesia."

"Maybe." Ken shrugged.

"Maybe? She needs help, Ken. *Professional* help. Doctors, psychiatrists, police, not a schoolteacher and a computer programmer. What the hell do we know about amnesia?"

Again, Ken merely shrugged, shaking his head. He didn't say anything.

"You know, Ken, someone's got to be looking for her. How would you feel if it was your sister or your wife who was missing?"

"I know." Ken sighed and rubbed his face with his hands. "I know, I know. But we promised her we wouldn't say anything."

"*You* promised her. I went along with you under protest, remember?" Dave finished his beer. "What's really weird is she acts like she doesn't want to find out who she is. I wonder what she's so afraid of?"

"I wonder what happened to make her lose her memory. What causes amnesia, anyway? Some kind of traumatic shock, isn't it?"

"Yeah, I think so. Or a sharp blow to the head. The doctor said her skull had been fractured once, just behind where she hit it today. Maybe that had something to do with it. Or maybe not. How the hell are we supposed to know, Ken? What kind of help can we give her?"

"I don't know. The kind she needs, I guess."

Dave snorted. "She needs doctors, Ken. That's what she needs."

"No doubt. But maybe she also needs a place to be safe, and someone she can trust. I know, I know." He raised a hand to stop Dave's interruption. "You're right, I'm not an expert, I don't know anything about amnesia. But I do know about trust. I know how to be a friend. And I think that's what she needs more than anything else, at least for the moment. Someone to trust. A friend."

"You could be wrong, Ken." Dave set his empty beer can on the coffee table, rose and walked toward the door. "You could make it worse, you know. You could even end up hurting her more. Just keep that in mind, will you?"

"Yeah." Ken nodded, his eyes dark with seriousness. "And you remember what you agreed to, Dave. She's in *my* house. She's *my* responsibility. It's up to me to make the decision on what to do. Don't go breaking your promise."

Dave's blue eyes stared into Ken's face for a long moment before his lips lifted into an ironic smile. "What the hell are you talking about, breaking promises? What, you think you've got the corner on friendship?"

Ken chuckled. "Thanks, Dave. I'll call you tomorrow, let you know how she is. And, Dave!" The tall blond man paused halfway down the porch steps. "Next week, try not to hit so many foul balls, will you?"

"Fuck you," came the soft reply.

Ken waved as Dave pulled out of the drive, and waited until his tail lights had disappeared in the dark night before closing and locking the door. He carried the empty beer cans into the kitchen, then put out the lights and climbed to the second floor. He checked on Julie both before and after he took a quick shower. She had barely moved since he'd gone down to Dave. She slept soundly, twisted half onto her right side, totally unaware of his presence in the room. A bar of light slanting in the partially open blinds cast spider-shadows from her lashes onto her cheek. He touched her gently, her face, her neck, her hair, and found her body warmed by the covers he'd tucked around her. He had the strangest urge to climb in the bed with her and hold her safe all night.

Reluctantly, he went back to his own room and slid between the chill sheets. Though it was almost two-thirty it took him more than fifteen minutes to fall asleep. All he could see was the look on Julie's face when she'd seen the policeman in the park. He couldn't stop thinking about the way she'd sidled around that tree and the way her body had trembled, her steps wavery and uncertain when she'd stumbled to the bleachers. He thought about the fear in her eyes and her voice when she begged him to help her, to keep her secret from the doctors at the hospital. He'd been right when he'd thought she was in trouble. She most certainly was. He only hoped he wasn't getting himself in trouble by trying to help her.

CHAPTER SIX
June 4-17, 1990
Buffalo, New York

The room was cool when she woke, filled with clear light slanting between gaps in the blinds. She lay still, luxuriating in the unaccustomed comfort of a warm bed, until memories of the accident and the hospital flooded her mind. Heart thudding, she sat up. Too quickly. Pain stabbed into her eyes and pounded at her skull like sharp, hard knuckles. Forgetting the cast she raised both hands to her head, evoking answering pain in her injured arm.

She sat still then, hunched over on the bed. When at last the agony faded to twin dull aches, she raised her head and looked around the room she had barely seen the night before. It was small, the walls papered in a pale blue stripe. A mismatched double bed, six-drawer chest, nightstand and diminutive armchair filled it completely, even without Ken's leftovers piled on the floor. A clock stood on the nightstand, its hands proclaiming the time as ten fifty-three. On the foot of the bed lay a man's green cotton summer robe. Like the pajamas, it also looked unused.

Ken must have put the robe there while she slept. She wrapped it around her and slowly slid from the bed, hoping her legs would hold true. They did, but she was shakier than she wanted to admit and the room still undulated around her, though quite not as giddily as it had the night before. Her clothes were nowhere in sight. After a successful struggle to tie the robe's sash with one hand, she crossed the room and opened the closet door. Men's clothes, mostly heavy woolens and flannel shirts, winter coats and jackets. Julie took a last frowning look around the room then opened the door to the hall and inched her way down the steps.

They led her into the southwest corner of the living room. The sparse furnishings—a green and beige patterned couch, two upholstered armchairs in coordinating solid colors and a few tables and lamps—lent the room more dimension than it owned. Plush carpeting in a deep emerald green lay underfoot. A glass-screened fireplace stood in the center of the northern wall. Hammered brass tools gleamed dully in the bright daylight. Unlike the upper floor, this room was neat, almost Spartan. It was also deserted. Julie stood clinging to the newel post until the pounding in her head had eased. When it did, she heard sounds of movement from beyond the narrow archway to her left.

Holding the neck of the robe closed with a nervous right hand, she walked slowly through the arch, past stairs leading down to a side door, and shuffled into what proved to be the kitchen. A cheerful yellow print brightened the walls. Kelly green and white tiles covered the floor. Ken sat at an oval oak table, writing on papers spread out before him and sipping coffee.

"Hi," Julie said, hunching her uneasiness into her shoulders and biting her lip.

Ken looked up, his thin lips lifting into a wide smile. "Hi." He put down his pen and rose. "I see you found me. You were exhausted, weren't you? Here, sit down, I'll get you some coffee." He pulled out the oak Captain's chair opposite him, sat her in it, and set a steaming mug in front of her. "There's milk and sugar on the table, help yourself. Are toast and eggs OK for breakfast? I don't have much in the cereal department, I'm afraid."

"Please, don't bother. I'm not really hungry. Coffee's fine."

"Only for a start. Don't argue with me," he cautioned, shaking a finger at her when she opened her mouth to protest, "you haven't a prayer. When I was head of the debating team at school, we never lost. I think scrambled would be best, easier on the stomach than fried." He set a skillet on the stove, added butter and lit the burner. "How do you feel?" he asked, taking eggs from the refrigerator.

"Not too bad. Really," she insisted, smiling at his skeptical look. "I am still a little dizzy but my head doesn't hurt much, or my arm. Honest." Without thinking she shook her head to emphasize her words. Pain flared again, red hot whorls of agony shooting like arrows into her skull. She winced, bending her head into her right hand. "Not unless I try to move, that is."

Ken stepped to her side and gently tipped her head up. Brushing back her bangs he inspected the injury. She knew what he was seeing, she'd seen it herself in the bathroom mirror. A left temple badly swollen, with skin bruised deep purple from her hairline to below her cheekbone. Ken nodded, his lips pursed.

"I can see why. You look like you went ten rounds with Sugar Ray."

Julie gave him an uncertain smile, wondering what he meant. Who was Sugar Ray? Ken turned back to the counter, put bread in the toaster, and picked up an egg. "The doctor gave me a prescription for pain. I'll go get it filled after you eat."

She watched him crack the eggs into a bowl and whip them smooth, knowing it would do no good to protest either the food or the medication. And if she wanted to be honest, she had to admit she could use something. Her head was controllable if she stayed still, but the ache in her arm was becoming sharper with every passing minute. The aroma of the food cooking made her mouth water, and she realized she hadn't eaten at all the day before. She was starving. Then she remembered the bedroom upstairs.

"Ken, where are my clothes? I couldn't find them."

"In the dryer. They looked a bit worse for the wear, so I threw them in with my stuff. Oh, and your money's up on the bureau. Six bucks and a little change." He glanced over at her. "Is that all you have?"

"Yeah," Julie said, hoping he wouldn't pursue it. She blinked in relief when he merely nodded and turned back to the stove. She sipped her coffee while he finished the eggs and buttered two pieces of toast. He set the plate in front of her. Then he sat back in his seat, frowning, fingering the papers as he watched her eat. She had to force herself to go slow, not gulp the food down like a pig, right in front of him. There was more on the plate than she usually ate in a whole day. It tasted like heaven.

"Julie," he said, breaking the elongated silence, "if you don't remember who you are or where you live, what have you been doing? Where would you have gone last night, if this hadn't happened? Six bucks wouldn't go very far toward a room anywhere."

"I manage." She shrugged, hoping to put him off. She didn't want to talk about that, not now. "You can sleep most anywhere when the weather's warm." Looking to change the subject, she took another bite of the eggs and glanced at the papers littering his side of the table. "Are you a writer?"

"Me?" Ken laughed. "Far from it. I'm a high school English teacher. These," he gestured at the papers, "are the essays I assigned as part of my students' final grades. From the look of them so far, if any one rates more than a C, I'll drop dead from shock." A faint buzzer rang. Ken stood up, stretched his arms over his head. "That's the dryer, our stuff is ready. Be back in a jiff."

Relieved not to be watched anymore, Julie couldn't help herself. She wolfed down the rest of the eggs and toast while Ken was in the basement. Still, it wasn't easy despite her raging hunger. Her stomach wasn't used to so much at one time. But she finished it all, knowing from just the past four days how long it could be between meals. *How wonderful*, she thought, staring at the empty plate, *to be able to eat like this all the time*. She was contemplating moving, trying to figure out how to do so without making her head pound again, when Ken appeared in the basement doorway, a half-filled laundry basket in his arms.

"Done? Don't worry about the plate, just leave it. Come on, I'll tuck you in. You can take your pick, down here on the couch or up in your bed."

"What?" Julie couldn't believe her ears. "I just got up."

"You have a concussion. The doctor said you had to rest, that too much moving around could be dangerous. So, you're going to rest. Now, take your pick, or I'll choose for you."

His hazel eyes twinkled and his lips smiled, but Julie heard the thread of steel that ran beneath the bantering tone. Her options were limited to those he allowed, period. She sighed and rose, wincing as the pain in her head awoke once more.

"I'll go upstairs." That, she knew, was where her clothes would be.

Ken stared at her a moment, his lips pursed. Then he nodded and turned to lead the way.

As she pulled herself up one stair at a time, trying to ignore the throbbing in her head, her mind raced. She could dress once he came back down to his papers, and if she was quiet enough she might get out of the house without his knowing. Or better still, when he went for the prescription. She could be long gone before he got back. It wasn't that she didn't want to stay, she did, but she knew what would happen if she didn't leave. She had fragmented memories of twice before trusting someone to help her, trusting their promise to hold to her conditions. Both times it ended in intensifying questions, anger, and insistence on doctors and police when she could not give valid reasons for her fear.

But she didn't have reasons, she only had fear, overwhelming, all-consuming fear that kept her from remaining anywhere too long. She was surrounded by danger, unknown and unknowable, and all the more lethal because of that. It was better to remain a stranger to herself and stay alive, than to ask for help, and die.

Ken helped her into bed, telling her to stay there. He didn't want her taking the stairs again. When dinner was ready, he'd bring it up to her. She nodded agreement, hoping her deception didn't show in her eyes, and relaxed in relief when he smiled and left the room, pulling the door almost shut behind him. Just a few more minutes, and she could begin to dress.

But he didn't go downstairs. Julie could hear him moving around on the second floor. Hangers clanged together, drawers opened and closed. Water ran in the bathroom. He hummed while he worked, his voice a deep baritone that moved facilely among the notes and was pleasant to listen to, though Julie barely noticed. Her frustration deepened as the minutes ticked away and Ken showed no signs of going back down to his papers. And sometime while she waited, with teeth clenched and heart thudding, Julie fell asleep.

Pain woke her at two-thirty, burning pain deep in her arm. Startled at the time that had passed, she tried to get up despite the way the room whirled around her. She stumbled and fell to her knees, knocking against the nightstand. The clock hit the floor with a loud crash. Ken came running and lifted her back into the bed, giving her two of the pills the doctor had ordered —he'd filled the prescription while she slept. He sat with her until the pills took effect, taking away both the pain and her consciousness. Unshed tears glittered on her lashes as once again she fell asleep.

Ken brought dinner up at six, carrying a tray with two plates piled high with thin slices of roast beef, fluffy mashed potatoes, baby carrots and Chinese pea pods.

"I hope it's ok that I didn't make gravy," he said, shoveling books off the occasional table beside the armchair and pushing the table close to the bed. "I thought it might be too rich for you. I doubled up on the veggies instead. More vitamins, which is way healthier."

He pulled the small armchair up to the table, sat down and picked up his fork. He put it down again a few minutes later and frowned as he watched her push the food around on her plate.

"What's wrong, Julie? You're not eating."

She glanced up at him, then looked back down at her food. What could she say? How could she explain what she herself did not understand?

"Please, Julie, I want to help. But I can't if you don't tell me what's wrong."

There was no help for it. She was out of options, at the mercy of Ken's vigilance and the potency of the medicine. She still felt weak and queasy from the fall and knew she couldn't leave town until she'd retrieved her possessions. She had no choice. She decided to trust Ken a little further. At this point, what else could she do?

"I left my things in a backpack," she said, fastening on the least of her problems, "outside, in the place where I've been sleeping," she told him, studying his face as she spoke. "It's hidden, but... if I leave it much longer I'm afraid it won't be there anymore. Someone will find it. There's not much in it, but it's all I have. I don't want to lose it."

"You won't. If you're up to it, we'll go get the backpack once we finish eating."

He gave her a reassuring smile, and with an answering smile of her own Julie bent to her meal. In less than ten minutes, her plate was empty.

"That was really good, Ken. Thank you. Can we go, now? I do feel much better." And she really did.

Ken nodded, rose and set the empty plates with the tray on the dresser. Then he fetched her clothes from his room. He had left the red knit top behind, substituting a bright blue safari-style shirt of his that slipped on easily over the cast. This time Julie felt only a little unease while Ken helped to zip, button and snap the clothes onto her body.

She knew little of the city's layout, and had no idea where the place she'd been sleeping was in relation to Ken's house. He took her back to Delaware Park. From there she directed him around the picturesque 'S' curves north on Delaware Avenue until they neared Linden. Leaving the blue Tempo on Knox Avenue, one short block south of Linden, they walked to the corner of Delaware where a Valvoline Instant Oil Change outlet stood.

"It's up there," she said, pointing to a steep, grass-lined slope behind the oil change building. It led up to the abandoned bed of the railroad tracks that had once spanned Delaware Avenue.

"You've got to be kidding!" Ken exclaimed, his jaw agape.

Julie shook her head, slowly so as not to start up the pounding again, though it hurt much less after a full day of rest.

"Julie, you've got a concussion. You can't climb up there. Tell me where it is and I'll go get it."

"You'd never find it," she said, wondering if she herself would recognize the place. "I have to show you. I'll be all right," she insisted when Ken shook his head. "Please."

Ken sighed and closed his eyes, then led her across the paved lot, displeasure apparent in the down-turned corners of his mouth, the hard glint in his eyes, the stiff slope of his shoulders.

"This is not a good idea," he muttered, helping Julie up the grass-slick incline to the tracks. "You shouldn't be doing this."

Julie didn't say anything, afraid that any sound from her would change Ken's mind.

She immediately felt the effects of the climb. Her head swam, and her feet stumbled on the uneven ground. She did her best not to reveal her difficulties to Ken though she wasn't sure how successful she was, since he kept a steadying hand around her waist once they crested the rise and progressed along the flat hilltop. The bushes dotting the scarp, sparse at first, grew ever thicker the further away from Delaware they went. Trash glinted in the slanting rays of the sun. Discarded beer cans, broken bottles, decaying food wrappers and filthy unidentifiable debris littered the weed-studded, gravel-strewn slopes. Backyards on both sides of the raised track bed were cordoned off, many of the barriers tall, solid cyclone-type fences.

"Do you have any idea how dangerous this place is, especially in the dark? How long have you been sleeping up here?" Ken asked, his face screwed up in distaste. Incredulity rang in his voice.

"Only a few days, I think. Three or four? I'm not sure, I still have trouble making sense of time." He looked at her, obviously puzzled by the remark, but Julie stopped and pointed to their right before he could comment. "Here, I'm pretty sure this is the place. Down near the fence. I'd sleep in the bushes there, up against the wood, so no one could see me." A world of emotion seethed in her emotionless voice. "It should still be down there, in the bushes." She sighed. "Unless someone already took it."

"I'll look. You stay here, understand? Right here."

Julie agreed, knowing she could not manage that steep slope. Ken slid down on his heels into the bushes. In only a few moments he located the dirty, threadbare canvas backpack she'd hidden, the kind that kids used for schoolbooks. He held it high and Julie almost cried, she'd been so sure it would be gone, vanished into thin air like her life, her identity. Ken climbed back up to her and held it out. She clutched it to her chest, barely aware of the slow walk back to Delaware Avenue in the warm sunshined silence. Once in the car Julie sat mute, the backpack on the floor between her feet. She didn't have the courage to open it until they were halfway home, she was so afraid it might be empty.

It wasn't empty, though the contents were meager enough. A pair of stained shorts. A ragged, long-sleeved blouse. A torn pale blue windbreaker. A pair of raveling panties. A deodorant bottle and a well-worn toothbrush. An almost-empty tube of lipstick. A half-toothless comb. A blue hair ribbon. And at the very bottom a somewhat ostentatious bracelet of large square black stones held in ornate silver frames. She draped the bracelet across the cast, fingering the intricate settings, the cool smoothness of the onyx.

"This is the first thing I can remember," she murmured, looking over at him. Ken braked for a red light and turned to study the expensive-looking piece of jewelry. "I was lying in a field with tall plants all around me. This was on my wrist. I don't know where I got it, or how. And I don't remember anything else for a long time. But I do remember the field, and this."

"It's pretty."

Julie nodded. She sighed and dropped the bracelet into the pack with her other things. She would have to leave, she knew. As soon as her strength had returned, the first time Ken relaxed his vigilance, she'd have to go. It wasn't safe to linger anywhere. Neither for her, or the person she stayed with. And yet, she wanted to stay. Ken asked no questions, demanded no promises from her. He simply wrapped her in a snug cocoon and let her be who she was, whoever that might be. It wasn't that she actually felt safe—she didn't think she would ever feel safe again—but she could tell the feeling of safety was there, waiting in the background. It would be better to leave before it had a chance to grow. If only he weren't so nice, so caring…

She leaned back and closed her eyes, letting exhaustion overtake her. She was almost asleep by the time they pulled into the driveway.

* * *

She slept most of the time for the rest of the first week. Ken considered it a positive side effect of both the medication and the concussion, since he couldn't stay home to care for her. There were final exams to prepare and barely-graduating seniors to nurse into cap and gown, tasks made no easier by the worry he felt that Julie would not be there when he arrived home. But the week slowly passed and Julie seemed content to stay where she was, snug and quiet in his small brown house, almost as if she was hiding from the world outside. That was fine with Ken. The longer she stayed, the more he wanted to keep her to himself.

He isolated himself with Julie like a child with a coveted new toy, putting off friends who called and refusing invitations. He also kept her away from Dave and his questions by telling his friend that she was less strong than she really was. He skipped the weekly ball game on Sunday, leaving a mystified Dave to explain the unusual absence. He plunged his whole self into Julie. The look of her, the feel of her, the sound of her voice, the wry humor that emerged at unexpected moments consumed his every moment. He never once wondered at his odd behavior. If he thought at all, it was of her. Julie, the tall, thin, long-haired mystery woman whom he had found, and named. In a strange way he felt almost as though he had invented her.

Father's Day fell on the seventeenth. Since all but four of the group—the four who had witnessed Julie's accident—had children, they bowed to convention, cancelled the ball game, and spent the day with their families. Ken called his father in Florida, listening in silence while his mother scolded him for ignoring them for over two weeks. He held Julie's hand while he talked, kissed her fingers while he listened, but he didn't say anything about her to his parents.

After all, what could he say? Remember those stray dogs I was always bringing home when I was a kid? Well, now it's a stray girl. Haven't the faintest idea who she is or where she's from, and neither does she, but she'll be staying with me for a while. Until she takes off again. And though he was tempted to say something like that just to see what reaction he'd get, one look at the sad longing mixed with fear on Julie's face drove the urge out of his head. He said nothing, kept the call short, and took Julie for a ride.

They went to Erie Basin Marina, situated where Buffalo's downtown snuggled up against the lakeshore. They wandered along the docks, peered at picturesque sailboats and munched hot dogs from the snack shack. Families crowded the beautiful waterfront park, enjoying togetherness in the festive sunshine. Crisp white sails dotted the lake beyond. Julie's face took on a wistful air as she scanned the people, searching, Ken knew, for some sign of familiarity that she obviously didn't find. Eventually her shoulders drooped, and Ken could feel the desolate emptiness in her eyes darken the brilliant skies above him. In an effort to lighten the mood, he pulled Julie over to watch the colorful clowns who had come out to entertain the picnickers.

It seemed to work. Julie's smile widened, became more spontaneous. Her gray eyes sparkled. Ken even heard her laugh once or twice. The tallest clown, sporting a wild shock of yellow hair, a bulbous blue nose and a bright red grinning mouth, must have spotted Julie's bruised face, now a ghastly shade of purpley greenish yellow, and the cast on her arm. He— at least Ken thought it was a man beneath all that makeup—somersaulted his way over to where they were standing, produced a square of bright yellow paper from his gigantic shoe and proceeded to deftly fold it into a crane, which he presented to Julie with a flourish.

Her eyes shone with pleasure when at last the entertainers bowed their farewells, and disappeared. But it didn't last. Her joy faded quickly, to be replaced by a bittersweet melancholy which enveloped her as she looked from the paper bird to the live gulls soaring overhead, the glittering sail-dotted water and the chattering families all around them.

"I like it here," she said, her voice full of regret. "I don't want to leave."

"We'll come back."

"No, I mean... here, this city."

"Then don't leave." Ken stroked her cheek with gentle fingers.

She looked up into his face, a world of doubt, pain and fear in her dark eyes. She shook her head.

"I have to. I don't ever stay anywhere. I can't."

"Why?"

"I don't know." Her eyes grew misty, vague. Ken could barely hear her quiet murmur. "I just have to keep moving. There's something... I don't know what, or why. I just know I can't stay anywhere. It's not safe."

"You can stay with me, Julie." Ken folded his arms around her, laid his cheek on her sun-kissed hair. "Forever, if you want. You'll be safe with me. I promise, Julie. I'll keep you safe."

She looked up into his eyes, a grave, thoughtful expression on her face. He watched the battle rage inside her, her desire to remain with him warring with her fear of the consequences—not to her, but to him. He knew what she would say before she shook her head, knew what the sacrifice would cost her.

"I can't stay. I don't want to hurt you," she whispered.

"Don't worry about me, Julie." Ken caressed her cheek, ran his thumb over her lips. "I'll be fine. And so will you. I'll keep us both safe."

Gently, Ken touched his lips to hers, pledging himself to her, a woman who, for all he knew, could already be married. Could have children somewhere, waiting for her. He didn't care. He was falling in love with her, incredible as it seemed, with a woman who had no past, no name, no identity than that which he had given her. Why or how he did not know, did not care. He knew only that Julie was the first thing he thought of in the morning, the last thing he thought of at night. He saw her in his dreams, both sleeping and awake. He, who had never let any woman get close to him, who was terrified of love and abhorred the idea of marriage, now gave himself body and soul to a total enigma. Julie. And it didn't frighten him in the least.

Smiling, he linked her arm in his.

"Come on, let's go home. I've got some steaks in the freezer and charcoal in the garage. We'll have a feast together, just you and me. The first of many."

Julie smiled and looked down at the yellow bird she held. They walked slowly away from the water, each savoring the peace they had found that day. It was a peace as fragile as the delicate paper figure Julie cluthced in her hand, and as easily shredded as soft clouds in the wind. But they didn't know. They didn't even guess. They were wrapped in themselves and the promise that had begun to flower between them. With hearts light and happy they drove back to North Buffalo, ignorant of a fate that soon would tantalize them with the truth, piece by terrifying piece.

CHAPTER SEVEN
June 18, 1990
Harrisburg, Pennsylvania

He almost missed it. Lyndsay and Melissa were quarreling again, pulling Ogden Wilkes' attention away from the morning paper. He had little enough time to read as it was. He didn't need to be distracted by his two oldest daughters arguing about bridesmaids' dresses and wedding flowers.

"Enough!" he roared, slamming a fist on the table. Dishes jumped. Silverware clinked together. The syrup bottle tipped over. His wife, Judy, wide blue eyes casting a quick warning glance at the girls on each side of her, reached out and set the bottle upright before the sticky liquid could pool on the tablecloth.

Wilkes clenched his teeth, his eyes flashing. He glared first at Lyndsay, blond and blue-eyed like her mother and soon to be a married woman, then at Melissa, his fiery, auburn-haired nineteen-year-old. The cautious remorse on their faces cooled his anger somewhat. He closed his eyes and sighed, grateful that Lisa, who with her dark hair and eyes resembled him most, was still asleep. For some reason, though he loved all his girls passionately, he found it hardest to be stern with his sixteen-year-old 'baby'.

"If you two would not mind," he said, enunciating with pointed precision, "I would appreciate having breakfast in peace. I get little enough of it at the office. If you must begin World War Three, please do so after I have left."

"Sorry, Dad," Lyndsay mumbled, having the grace to look uncomfortable beneath his icy gaze. She finished her orange juice and stood up.

Melissa, expression still truculent, glanced at her watch.

"I have to leave, anyway, or I'll be late for class. We can finish this at lunch, Lyndsay. The Beer Keg, at twelve-fifteen?"

Lyndsay nodded, her lips tight. "You don't *have* to be my maid of honor, Missy," she said, rising. "If it's too much *trouble* for you, I'm sure *Lisa* wouldn't mind the privilege."

"Some privilege," Melissa muttered, kissing her father's cheek. "You'd have to win the lottery to afford it!"

"Fat lot of help it would be if you won it," Lyndsay shot back as Melissa stalked toward the hallway. "You'd be too cheap to spend any of it!"

"Girls," Judy warned, giving her oldest a quick smile and a reassuring pat on the hand. "Go on now, Lyndsay. We'll work it out."

Wilkes turned in his seat to watch them leave, feeling again the funny tightness in his chest he often felt nowadays when confronted with his children's adult independence. It would certainly seem odd not to have Lyndsay in the house once September twenty-second had passed. After all, she'd been around for twenty-four years. And soon, all three would be gone. Only he and Judy would be left. It would be like starting over again. All alone. He shook his head, he slipped a piece of bacon to Musuko and turned back to his wife.

"Do weddings have to be so damned traumatic?" he asked. "I thought they were supposed to be for celebrating."

"They are. They're for celebrating the fact that all the preparations are finally over. And if you think this is bad, wait until we start compiling the guest list."

Wilkes rolled his eyes and looked down at the page from which he'd been so rudely interrupted. But he couldn't concentrate. He kept thinking about Lyndsay, wondering how in hell she could be old enough to get married. Wasn't it only yesterday they'd brought her home from the hospital? God, how old did that make him? He sighed again, his gaze fixed unseeing on a montage of pictures of Father's Day celebrations from Harrisburg and across the nation. *I might as well just go to work,* he thought, his hand lifting the paper, beginning to fold it. He didn't really have to leave for fifteen minutes or more, but since his promotion to Assistant Police Commissioner was only four months old, it didn't hurt to appear early now and then. Especially since he had his eyes on the Commissioner's job, and the Mayor's, and beyond perhaps to the governorship of Pennsylvania.

Suddenly, one picture came clear. Wilkes froze, unable to breathe. His heart thudded in his chest. Musuko, beside him, cocked his head; pointed ears pricked forward and his body quivered. Wilkes stared in disbelief, his lips parting in a silent gasp. It wasn't, it couldn't be. But it was. Blurred as the newsprint images were, he was positive. As positive as he was that Lyndsay was being married in three months. How long he stared he didn't know. The shock was so complete, so isolating, he lost track of time. Finally, an eon later, his mind began working again.

With an angry movement he crushed the paper in his hand. His chair scraped across the linoleum and almost tipped over as he surged to his feet.

"Ogden? What's wrong?"

He ignored his wife, who stared at him with bewildered questions in her eyes, and stalked into the den. Musuko padded quickly after him, gaining the room just before his master slammed the door shut. Crossing to the desk, Wilkes lifted the phone and jabbed savagely at the buttons.

"It's me," he snapped, when after three rings it was answered. "I want you both up at the cabin in half an hour. Don't give me any excuses!" he exclaimed, cutting off the deep voice on the other end. "You've got thirty minutes, both of you. Be there."

He slammed down the phone and stood with dark eyes gleaming, thinking hard. Musuko, who sat nearby, front paws restless on the beige carpeting, whined deep in his throat. The sound penetrated Wilkes' thick fog of concentration. He bent and stroked the dog, soothing the tautness he felt beneath the thick coat.

"It's OK, boy. I know how to handle this. Let's go for a ride, okay?"

The dog bounded to his feet, trotting bright-eyed to the front door. Judy met her husband in the hallway.

"What is it, Ogden? Is something wrong? You haven't finished eating."

"Of course nothing's wrong. Don't look so worried, Judy." He gave her an absent smile and laid a gentle hand on her cheek. "I just forgot a meeting, that's all. I'll see you tonight." He turned away and strode quickly to the door. "Come, Musuko. Heel," he ordered, pulling the door open and hurriedly descending the steps, leaving Judy speechless behind him. He had never before taken the dog with him to a police meeting. He still carried the morning paper crushed in his hand. And it was the first time in twenty-seven years that he hadn't kissed his wife good-by.

CHAPTER EIGHT
June 18-19, 1990
Buffalo, New York

A moonless night, the air ink-thick around her. She was running. Running for her life, crashing through a dense, dark forest. Suffocated by terror, she could barely breathe. Needle-studded branches scratched at her arms, her face. They snagged in her clothing, slowing her progress. Their whispered laughter pointed at her, marked her passage. Close behind, footsteps pounded in pursuit, drawing near, nearer.

"Get her! Damn it, get her!"

The shout echoed like thunder, crashed onto her head with stunning force. She gasped, twisting beneath the onslaught. Whimpers of fear bubbled out of her mouth. Suddenly, the earth vanished from under her feet. She dropped like a stone, her terrified scream overpowering the voice's menacing echo.

The footsteps drew closer, pursued her into the void. Then abruptly they ceased, and hard hands closed on her body. Engulfed in horror she struck out, desperately seeking freedom.

"Julie! Wake up, Julie! It's me, Ken!" He ducked away from her flailing arms, sighing with relief when he managed to pin them to her sides. One blow from that hard cast might very well crack his skull. "Come on, honey, wake up. You're dreaming. Do you hear me, Julie? It's just a dream."

His words finally seemed to penetrate. Slowly, she calmed. Her eyes blinked. She began to focus, looking at him with a measure of recognition.

"Oh, God!" she cried, still gasping for air. Tears spilled from her eyes, streaked down her cheeks. Her shuddering body shook the bed frame.

"It's all right, Julie, it was just a dream." Ken pulled her closer into his embrace. "You're all right, now."

"It was so real." Tears and his chest muffled her voice. "He was chasing me. I tried to get away, but the trees were too close, they kept pulling at me. Then there was no ground, and I fell, but he still came after me, he grabbed me— "

"That wasn't the dream, it was me, Julie. I was trying to wake you up, to stop your screaming." He reached over to the nightstand and pulled a blue Kleenex from the box. Gently, he dabbed at the tears on her face. "That was one hell of a nightmare, wasn't it? Are you okay, now?"

"I think so," Julie replied, nodding slightly. "But how could it be just a dream, Ken? It was so real."

"Of course it was. That's why they call them nightmares. Don't let it spook you, Julie. Everyone has dreams of being chased at one time or another. I had a tiger chasing me, once. I woke up just as it caught me. I think that's why I don't like cats."

Julie gave him a shaky smile, and an even shakier laugh. Her eyes still looked frightened, but at least the tears had stopped and she wasn't trembling quite as violently.

"I don't remember ever dreaming before," she said, laying her head on his shoulder. "I hope I never do again. It's awful."

"Not always." Ken smiled, remembering the dream of her he'd been caught in, the one her screams had interrupted. "Sometimes they can be quite... satisfying. Do you want anything? Some hot milk, or maybe a glass of wine?"

Julie shook her head. "No. I'm all right. What time is it?"

"Too late to still be awake, and much too early to get up. Go back to sleep, now."

Ken kissed her cheek and laid her back on the pillows. Faint light filtered through the half-open window, misting her face with shadows. Her eyes gleamed in the dimness.

"Don't leave me, Ken." She clutched at his hand. "Please. I'm afraid."

Ken sighed, knowing he could not walk away from her. But he also knew he would lie awake beside her, fighting to keep from kissing her, from touching her. It would be a long day in school tomorrow, after an even longer night.

"Move over," he said, lifting the covers.

She snuggled up against his warm body, her head nestled on his shoulder. Her bare legs slid against his, sending shivers through him. He could feel her heart, racing still from the fright she'd had. He lay quiet, trying to ignore the feel of her breasts pressed against his side, her breath warm on his chest. He knew that if she looked up at him he would kiss her. Kiss her and not stop, not until they both reached the heights of ecstasy. But she did not look up at him. She fell asleep quickly, relaxing into the strong arm curled around her body. The heavy weight of the cast on her left arm pressed across his ribcage. Ken concentrated on the hard reality of her injury until at last sleep overcame him, too.

She was still asleep when he left in the morning. He waded through the day with head pounding and eyes bleary, thankful that he merely had final exams to monitor. He didn't think he would have been capable of actual teaching and found it more than difficult just to stay alert to surreptitious attempts at cheating. The unnatural silence in the classrooms, punctuated by the scritch of pencils on paper, drove him crazy. He was more than grateful when the day was finally over. All he wanted was to go home, have dinner, and go to bed.

He found Julie in the kitchen. She must have heard the car pull in. An unopened cold beer waited for him on the table. Julie stood at the counter struggling to slice a block of cheese with one hand.

"Hi, honey. That looks good. Give me a minute, will you? I'll be right down to help you."

He kissed her, then went up the stairs to change into lighter clothes and wash the day's sweat and chalk dust from his face and hands. When he returned to the kitchen, his beer still sat on the table, sweating cold droplets of water down the outside of the can. Julie had managed to slice a few pieces of cheese. They sat on a plate beside the beer, nestled together with a handful of Ritz crackers.

Julie stood at the counter, leaning against the white Formica, looking cool in the beige shorts Ken had bought her on Saturday. Over them she wore a short-sleeved green shirt of his. It looked much better on her than it ever had on him, dropping low enough to almost hide the shorts. Though she smiled, she looked tired. Her face was drawn, and dark circles rimmed her eyes.

"Did you do the laundry? You didn't have to, you know," he said when she nodded. "You need to rest."

"I like helping you. And I don't want to be a burden."

"You're not. You never could be." Ken grabbed the beer, opened it and took a gulp. "Ahhh, that's good. Want one?"

"Sure." She gestured at the table with the knife she still held. "Not bad, huh? Maybe I should try for a job as a cheese slicer. I could specialize in uneven slices."

Ken sampled a piece of cheese after taking another beer from the refrigerator, opening it and giving it to Julie. She was right, it was uneven. It resembled an axe head, thick on one end, tapering to a razor thin edge. He shoved it into his mouth. "Well," he said, his words muffled by the food, "you could always nail the cheese to the board first. That would keep it from moving around so much."

"That wouldn't work. I'd still need two hands. One to hold the nail, and one to pound it in." Laughing, she moved to the table and sat.

"Here." Ken handed her a cookbook, opened to the page he wanted. "Read that to me. I'm so tired my eyes keep crossing."

"We could order a pizza delivered."

"Nah. This will be faster, and better for us."

He pulled the wok down from the cupboard and set it on the stove. Opening the refrigerator, he turned to see Julie watching him with wary eyes.

"What is it, hon? That dream still bothering you?"

"A little," she said, a slight tremble in her voice. "I just—" She looked down at the cookbook and back up at him. "Which one?"

"Didn't I tell you?" She shook her head and he grunted. "God, I really am out of it, aren't I? The shrimp stir-fry. It's quick, only takes about ten minutes. Anything longer and I'd fall asleep before it's done."

"Sounds great," a deep voice said from the back door. "Got enough for me, too?"

"Dave."

Ken suppressed a wince and felt his body tense. He wondered if Dave had heard the lack of warmth in his tone. He stared at the tall, blond man a moment, almost hating the sight of him. He knew what Dave had come for, answers that neither Ken nor Julie had. *Go away,* he thought. Then he blinked. *For crying out loud, what's wrong with me? This is my best friend.* He shook his head and smiled, waving Dave into the kitchen.

"Got enough to feed an army, which is barely enough, the way you eat," he said, taking a can from the fridge. "But we'll make do. Here, have a beer and take a load off."

"Don't mind if I do. Thanks." Dave took the offered beer and sat opposite Julie. "You've been a bit of a stranger lately. What's up?" His lips smiled, but there was a shadow of hurt in his eyes and his voice.

"Oh, same old stuff." Ken shrugged, his hand on the still-open refrigerator door. "Busy time of the year, exams and all. You know."

"Sure." Dave took a long swallow of the cold brew, then looked at Julie. "How about you? How are you doing? Anything come back to you?"

Julie, looking uncomfortable under Dave's piercing gaze, shook her head and dropped her gaze to the book. Ken clenched his teeth and took a deep breath.

"The food is starting to wilt, already. What do I need from in here, Julie?" he asked, hoping to turn the conversation to the task at hand.

Julie didn't respond immediately. She kept her head bent over the book, her index finger tracing the printed words. Ken watched her, frowning. It was obvious she was struggling with something.

"Uh, shrimp... bay-bee car... car..." She gave a pained sounding sigh and closed the book. "I can't read it, Ken. I'm sorry. The words just... don't make sense to me. I don't know why. Maybe it's because of the amnesia. Or maybe I was just a lousy student who never learned to read." She shrugged her shoulders. "I don't remember."

"You can't read?" Dave asked, his voice skeptical. "Are you kidding?"

"Leave her alone, Dave."

"No, it's time for some answers. Julie, how long have you been like this?"

"I don't know. A long time, I think." She looked up, but didn't quite meet his eyes.

"What does that mean?"

"That's enough, Dave!"

"No, it's not. We agreed, Ken. We'd wait one week. Well, it's been two, so it's time to ask some questions." Dave turned back to Julie. "Come on, Julie, what do you mean?"

"I told you about the bracelet," she said, looking at Ken. He nodded and she turned back to Dave. "It's the first thing I can remember, waking up in a field with a bracelet on my arm. Then the next thing I remember I was somewhere else, but I don't know how I got there. And I had different clothes on, but I don't know how I got them, or where they came from." She frowned. Her teeth caught at her lower lip. "It was like that for a long time. I'd be somewhere, but I couldn't remember how I'd gotten there. Or I could remember another place, vaguely, remember being somewhere else, but not leaving it. Or I'd remember leaving somewhere, but I'd have no idea where the new place was, or how I got there." She paused and gave him an apologetic shrug. "I lost whole weeks, at first. Sometimes even more. That doesn't happen as much now, but I do still sometimes lose... days. Here and there."

"Is that what you meant when you said you still have trouble with time?" Ken asked, intrigued despite his annoyance with Dave.

Julie nodded, then laughed, a quiet laugh at her own shortcomings. "I was so confused at first. I wasn't even sure what the *words* meant—day, week, hour, minute. And for a while, it seemed that every time I'd figure it all out, I'd forget everything again and have to start all over. But not any more. I do still lose time, but at least now I remember what it is."

"I don't get this, Julie," Dave said, his voice puzzled. "It's crazy. It sounds like you've just been wandering aimlessly around ever since you woke up in that field. Why? Haven't you ever tried to find out who you are? Haven't you ever tried to get help?"

Julie seemed to shrink in upon herself. She held herself very still, panic and anger chasing across her face. She stared at Dave, then looked at Ken, the pain of betrayal clear in her wide-eyes.

"You said this wouldn't happen!" she cried. "You promised!"

Ken stepped forward, reaching for Julie, but Dave spoke before he could reassure her.

"We do want to help you, Julie, really, but we're not professionals. You know that. There's nothing we can do to help you remember. You need doctors for that, medical experts."

"Come on, Dave. Leave it alone." Ken moved to Julie and knelt, draping his arm around her shoulders as though to protect her. Dave ran a hand through his hair and shook his head.

"I don't understand, Julie. Why won't you get the help you need? Why won't you see a doctor? Are you keeping something from us? Don't you want to know who you are? Don't you want your life back?"

"No," Julie whispered, shaking her head. "No!"

"Why not? There's nothing to be afraid of. We won't desert you, I promise. We'll all go together to the police. They— "

"Oh no. No." Julie covered her face with her hand. "Not the police. No, I can't. Please."

"Damn it, Dave. Cut it out!"

Ken glared at Dave who, after a moment, sat back with a sigh. He shook his head and turned to look through the screen on the back door. Gently, Ken reached out and cupped Julie's cheek in his palm, turning her eyes to his.

"It's all right, honey. There won't be any police, I promise. Just tell me why, Julie? What are you so terrified of?"

"I don't know," she whispered, her voice breathless with panic. "Oh, God, I don't know. But I am. I'm so scared of them it hurts. But I don't want to know why. It isn't safe to know. It isn't safe."

It isn't safe. Ken looked up to find Dave's puzzled eyes studying him. Ken, equally mystified, shook his head and lifted his shoulders, the echoes of Julie's nightmare reverberating in his mind.

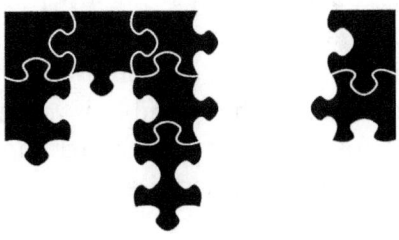

CHAPTER NINE
June 19-27, 1990
Buffalo, New York

Dave showed up every night that week, ignoring with good cheer Ken's not-so-subtle annoyance. Ken wanted to keep Julie all to himself, and like a spoiled child he resented that Dave's intrusion reminded him of unanswered questions, impossible promises, and adult responsibilities. Twice Dave brought dinner with him—foot-long Sahlen's hot dogs, potato salad and beer on Tuesday, shish-ka-bobs, wine and ice cream on Friday. After they'd eaten, the men fell into their old routine, playing chess, arguing politics and watching television until ten or later, their strained conversation attempting to approximate the ease and familiarity it used to have. Dave did not bring up Julie's amnesia, talk about doctors, or ask questions about her past. Not out loud. But his blue eyes bored into her, silently pressuring her until she trembled more and more openly. She excused herself earlier each night, pleading fatigue, and sat alone in her silent, shadow-shrouded room.

Dave's presence only exacerbated Ken's concern for Julie. She stopped eating, quickly losing what little weight she had managed to gain. She got little sleep though she denied it, and Ken knew Dave's accusing eyes and the terrifying nightmare were to blame. The dream returned every night, sometimes more than once, exactly the same in every detail. By Thursday she stopped screaming, though somehow Ken, lying wakeful in his own bed, could feel when she woke gasping, her heart pounding. When he asked her about it, she told him the dream had stopped. But her fear-haunted face and dark-rimmed eyes gainsaid her words and confirmed a truth Ken already knew.

Drumming rain and lightning flashes woke Ken at three Sunday morning. He rose to shut the upper floor windows and found Julie huddled in a chair near her bedroom window. Moisture glistened on her cheeks, glinting in slivers of the backyard security light that seeped through the blinds. Quickly, Ken crossed to her and knelt at her side.

"What is it, Julie? What's wrong?" She didn't answer, merely shook her head. "It's the dream, isn't it? Don't lie to me, Julie."

She nodded, forcing words through her tears. "It won't go away. I tried to stay awake tonight, I didn't even go to bed. I stayed here, sitting up, but I was so tired my eyes kept closing. And then he was chasing me—"

"Hush, now, it's all over. I'm here, Julie. I won't leave you alone."

He led her to the bed and settled himself beside her, his arms strong and warm around her shivering body. Her head lay on his shoulder. Her hair smelled like fresh apples. His whole body tingled. He felt invincible, omnipotent. Dave be damned, they didn't need doctors. Ken was the only one who could truly protect Julie. As long as they were together, nothing could harm either one of them. He would never let her go. Never. Then Julie's mumbled, sleepy words burst his illusory bubble.

"I'm scared, Ken. I don't think it's a dream. I think it really happened. I don't think it's a dream at all."

Ken didn't—couldn't—answer. He lay holding her, staring into the rain-soaked night, his heart thumping. He, too, was afraid. Afraid that she was right, and that soon he would lose her. When he fell asleep, the fear accompanied him into the darkness.

Ken was able to spend every day with Julie now that school had ended. His constant presence seemed to calm her, ease the tension that kept her poised as if for flight. After that Sunday night, she slowly relaxed and began to eat once again. She slept better, too, wrapped in his arms every night. The nightmare faded and did not return, perhaps because of his presence. But Ken's nights were not easy. Aching for her as he did, still he restrained himself, made no move to make love to her. He didn't know how she would react if he tried. She seemed to have accepted him as a protector, someone she could trust, yet she held him still at arm's length, treated him more like a little-known relative than a possible lover. He was afraid of scaring her off.

The following Wednesday, in the early evening, they gathered on the front porch to enjoy the cooling breeze. Dave, having been absent on a business trip for three days, had arrived a few minutes earlier. He sat on the porch rail, swinging his legs, watching Julie who stood nearby gazing out at the kids playing in the small, triangular park that divided the two halves of the street, a wistful look on her face. Ken had just poured them each a glass of white wine. Vegetables and dip sat on a low table nearby. Suddenly, Julie's face drained of color. She swayed and leaned against a thick white pillar. Her hand shook, spilling the wine.

"Julie, what is it? What's wrong?"

She shook her head and blinked frowning eyes as though to clear them of something. Ken quickly took the glass from her hand, set it with his beside the dip, and pulled her over to the cushioned glider.

"What's happening to me?" she cried softly. "Ken? Where are you?"

"Honey, I'm right here," he said, caressing her cheek. His hand tightened on her arm. "What's the matter?"

Julie shuddered, gasping for breath. Her eyes, wide and almost fully dilated though the late day sun shone brightly, stayed locked on the park a hundred feet up the street. Abruptly, she froze. She sat unmoving for an endless minute, completely oblivious to Ken's comforting hands, his worried face. Then she turned her eyes to him, an expression of total bewilderment in the gray depths, and shook her head.

A single tear trickled down her cheek. Quickly, Ken gathered her into his warm embrace.

"Honey, what is it? What's going on? You look like you've just seen a ghost."

She didn't answer. After a moment, Ken kissed the top of her head and tilted her face until their eyes met.

"Tell me, Julie. Now. What happened?"

She sat up and pushed away from him, wiping her face with a trembling hand.

"I don't know. I was looking at the kids and the trees, and suddenly they weren't there anymore."

"What do you mean, they weren't there?" Dave asked, his tone quiet and thoughtful. Ken stifled an unreasonable urge to tell Dave to butt out.

Shivering, Julie swallowed hard. She didn't answer Dave. Ken watched her face, noting the telltale signs of shock—dilated pupils, the ashen pallor of her skin, rapid shallow breathing. He wanted to cover her, keep her warm, but to do so he would have to go into the house for a sweater or an afghan and he didn't want to leave her alone even for a few moments. He took her hand in both of his and tried by sheer will power to send his own body heat into her.

"Julie?" He kept his voice soft, coaxing. "What do you mean?"

"They disappeared," she whispered. "There was a brick wall, all I could see was a brick wall. No park, no trees, no people. Just a brick wall." She looked up at him, her chin quivering. "Am I going crazy, Ken?"

"Don't be silly. Of course you're not." He rose and picked up the abandoned wine glasses, stopping to top off Julie's on the way back to the glider. He ignored

Dave, who shook his head before turning to look out at the park. "Here, drink this. It'll warm you up."

He waited until she took a sip, then sat again beside her. Squinting, he, too, looked over to where children still ran and laughed in the post-dinnertime sunshine, pondering her words. The chill that filled him was one no sweater or wine could banish. When he spoke, he tried to keep his tone light, and unworried.

"Huh. A brick wall. That's an interesting vision. Why a brick wall, of all things? Tell me about it, Julie." He turned back to her. "What did it look like?"

"Bricks," she answered, her voice curt, annoyed. Ken cocked a brow at her, one side of his mouth lifted. She sighed and looked down into the pale yellow wine. "Sorry. They weren't red bricks, they were light colored. Tan. And not new. They were old and dirty. And there were red splotches on some of them. I don't know why, but that really frightened me. I looked at those splotches and I couldn't breathe. I just couldn't breathe."

"What was the ground like? Could you tell where the wall was?" Dave asked, and Ken felt grateful he'd kept his tone as casual as Ken's own had been.

"No." She shook her head slowly, frowning. "I couldn't see the ground, just the wall. I don't know where it was. And it was dark. There wasn't any sun, I think it was night, a dark night. But I could see the wall, it was very clear. There was a light of some kind on it, but it wasn't the sun." She took another sip of the wine. The glass rattled against her teeth. She didn't look at either one of them. "Then it was gone, and the park was back."

Ken studied her in the silence that fell, trying to visualize what she had seen. He looked over at the park once again, analyzing the scene. Perhaps something there had triggered Julie's vision. But there were only the same trees and grass, the same few scattered benches the city had put in a few years earlier, the same roughhousing kids that were always to be seen. Nothing different, nothing unusual, nothing that Julie hadn't seen a dozen times already. Her soft, hesitant voice recalled him to the porch.

"Ken? What do you think it was? What happened to me?"

He buried his own fearful speculations and smiled at her, cupping her cheek in his palm. He could feel Dave's eyes, knew what he was about to say, and spoke quickly to forestall Dave's words.

"Don't look so worried," he said. "It's not that big a deal. It was kind of like a waking nightmare, I guess you could call it." Dave snorted, and Ken shot him a warning frown. "You probably saw that wall somewhere around here lately, and for some reason the memory surfaced when you looked out at the park. Maybe there were kids playing nearby when you first saw it and that's what brought it up, the kids over there. Let's just forget it, Julie." He rose and held out a hand, pulled her to her feet. "We don't want to borrow trouble."

She looked from him to Dave and back again, her gray eyes solemn. Ken could tell that she knew his thoughts, and feared what he was keeping from her. Then she sighed and nodded, her lips smiling though her eyes didn't. She moved into his arms, snuggling close, her head resting on his shoulder.

"What would I ever do without you?" she whispered, lifting her face to his.

"You'll never know," he answered, kissing her. "I don't intend to ever let you get far enough away from me to find out."

Dave merely watched them, and said nothing.

CHAPTER TEN
June 27, 1990
Buffalo, New York

When they walked over to the park after they ate, Dave elected to stay behind to read the paper. Ken was glad to get away from Dave, for his presence kept shadows lingering in Julie's eyes and disquieting suspicions nagging at him. And guilt. This was the first time a woman had threatened the deep friendship they shared. She had unknowingly driven a wedge between them, and the worst of it was that, despite his feelings of guilt, Ken didn't really care. He only cared about Julie.

A mere half-dozen kids remained in the park, teens who languidly tossed a football back a forth. The younger ones were already inside for baths and bed. Strolling hand-in-hand like school-age lovers beneath the cool leafy canopy, Ken and Julie were the only adults around. The mellowing light had lost its sharp edge, the breeze stilling in this pre-dusk hour. The only sound beside the hushed voices of the kids and the faint whine of traffic a block away was the furious buzz of late-foraging bees returning to their hives.

They walked up to the apex of the triangle and sat together on the green-plank-and-wrought-iron bench that overlooked the spreading vee of the park. Ken folded his arm around Julie's shoulders and smiled down at the plaintive expression on her face as she watched the ball players end their game and one-by-one head for home. He had seen that expression so often on her face, it was hard to think of her without it. It had almost become a permanent part of her. *And she's a permanent part of me now, no matter what,* he thought, his gaze tracing the glints of red picked out in her hair by the last rays of the setting sun. He refused to think further, pushed the image of the brick wall out of his mind. If it meant what he feared it did, he might soon lose his precious Julie. And that he would not consider. Not until he had no choice.

After a few minutes she sighed and turned her face to him.

"I love you, Julie," he whispered, his heart thudding at the way her smile grew. "Come on, I want to show you something."

They walked halfway down the western edge of the triangle to a large maple tree that towered almost fifty feet in the air. Its huge, craggy trunk split into a dozen substantial arms, the first a good ten feet from the ground. Ken laid a reverent palm on the wide, scarred bole.

"This is my tree," he told Julie. "I used to climb it when I was only eight years old. I'd take a running start, jump up and grab the first crotch, and just keep on going." He tilted his head and looked up into the still leaves that blocked the sky. Ghosts of his youth flitted among the branches. "Once, I climbed up over thirty feet. It was great, I could see everything from up there. I felt invincible, king of the world. Nothing could touch me." He laughed and shook his head. "Until I tried to come down. Man, did I feel small then. And scared. All that brave invincibility evaporated like that." He snapped his fingers. "But I did it. I backed all the way down for what seemed hours, feeling blindly for toeholds, terrified to look down, sure I was going to break my neck. I didn't even get a scratch. I swore I'd never go up this thing again, but the next day here I was, raring to go. I took a flying leap, missed the first branch, fell about four feet and broke my arm. Life sure is funny, sometimes."

"I know," Julie agreed. "Do you still climb it?"

"Are you crazy? I haven't been that dumb since I turned twelve. That's when I discovered girls and realized it was a whole lot more fun down here on the ground, where they are. I still love this tree, though. It taught me a lot about life, and myself."

A metallic jingle sounded behind them. Ken turned to see Russ Peterson, who lived on the east side of the street near the top of the triangle, walking his Irish setter. Peterson often exercised the energetic animal in the park once the kids had left. He bent now and unsnapped the leash from the dog's collar.

"Hi, Russ. How's it going?" Ken asked, holding out a hand. Peterson took it in a firm grip.

"Not bad, Ken. Not bad. Beauty and I are just out admiring the weather."

"This is Julie, Russ. She's been—"

Julie's panicked gasp cut Ken's words short. Startled, he turned to see her pressed tight against the tree, her eyes widening while the dog's nose vacuumed her body. As Ken watched, she flattened herself even more, looking as though she was trying to disappear into the wood itself.

"Get it away from me. Get it away," she cried.

"Oh, don't mind Beauty, Julie. She just wants to meet you," Ken said, moving to her side. "She won't hurt you, she's really friendly. She loves people."

As if to underline his words, Beauty turned her head and licked Julie's hand. Julie screamed, a strangled sound jammed in her throat. Her face drained of color. She began to hyperventilate.

"It's going to kill me!" she gasped, turning her head from the dog who now jumped up and put its paws on the tree trunk beside her. "Oh, God, it's going to kill me. Get it away. Please, don't let it kill me!"

Quickly, Russ Peterson snapped the leash back onto Beauty's collar and pulled the dog down. Julie's knees buckled. Ken caught her, his strong arms holding her on her feet.

"It's okay, honey, the dog can't hurt you. She's on a leash, now. It's okay."

Julie shook her head and buried her face in his chest. Ken could feel her nails dig into his back through the fabric of his knit polo shirt.

"Good heavens, I'm sorry, Ken," Peterson said. "I've never seen anyone so terrified of dogs. If I'd known, I'd have kept Beauty on the lead. I didn't mean to upset her like this."

Ken looked at Peterson, his brows pulled into a frown. "It's my fault, Russ. Julie hasn't been very well this last week, I probably shouldn't have let her come out. I think I'd better take her back to the house."

He turned away, half-carrying Julie away from the tree, and the dog.

"Let me know how she is," Russ called after them. "I'm really sorry, Ken."

Julie had stopped trembling by the time they reached the house. Dave, who had watched the incident from the porch, met them on the sidewalk and followed them into the house. Ken took Julie into the living room and sat her in the green lounge chair that had been his Dad's. Then he went into the kitchen. When he returned moments later with a glass of water, Julie still sat where he had left her, statue-still, her face blank, expressionless. Dave shook his head, his shoulders lifting in a shrug. Ken frowned and moved slowly closer.

"Julie?" She didn't answer, didn't move. "Julie, are you okay? I brought you some water, I thought it might help."

Her head tilted to the side, her brows drawing together as the sound of his voice penetrated her fog. She looked up, her gaze snagging on the glass he held. She studied it a moment before her hand reached out and took the glass from him. Once again she began to tremble. Drops of water slopped from the glass and darkened her shirt and jeans. Ken told her to drink and obediently she took a sip, then lowered the glass to her lap. His heart thudding, Ken crouched on the floor beside her.

"Julie," he said, but she shook her head, stopping his words.

"I don't know." She kept her eyes on the shimmying water in the glass.

"I figured you'd say that."

Dave's words sliced through the still air. Julie looked up at him, her eyes flashing rebellion and fear. Anger burst in Ken's chest.

"For God's sake, Dave, shut up!" he growled. "Stay out of this!"

Dave stared at him, the muscles in his jaw working. Finally he shook his head, muttered an incoherent curse, and dropped down onto the couch. Ken turned back to Julie, who sat coil-taut in the chair, her stare shifting between the two men. Smiling, he picked up a lock of her hair and twined it around his finger.

"It's okay, Julie. I can understand being afraid of dogs, lots of people are." He chose his words with care, kept his voice low and gentle. He didn't want to spook her more than she already was. "And I can understand thinking one might bite you, especially if it was growling or snarling, or even barking. But Beauty wasn't. She was licking your hand and wagging her tail. Why did you think she was going to kill you?"

"I don't know. I just did."

"But, kill you? Isn't that a little extreme?"

Julie merely shrugged and looked back into the water glass. Dave moved restlessly on the couch. Ken sighed and tried again.

"Did a dog attack you once, is that why you're so afraid of them?"

"I don't know, Ken. I don't remember anything." Her voice rose. "I just know they're going to hurt me, that they want to kill me. I don't know why, but I do. I just do!"

"It's all right, Julie, Beauty's gone, now. Calm down, okay?"

Julie bowed her head. Ken caressed her dark hair with tender fingers.

"Think back, Julie," Dave suggested. "There must be something about a dog. Try," he urged when she shook her head. "Think. What went through your mind when you saw that dog out there? What made you think it was vicious? There's a reason, Julie, you know there is. What is it? What happened when you saw that dog?"

Dave's words seemed to terrify Julie. Her head snapped up. She stared at Dave, her eyes wide and dilated, but Ken didn't think she saw Dave. He was sure she was seeing Beauty again. She drew breath in desperate, gulping gasps, her head moved from side to side as if to deny what she saw, or felt. Suddenly, she twisted in the chair, sobbing aloud. The water glass tipped. Cold liquid flooded into her lap, splashed onto the chair arm and her cast. Ken took the glass from her fingers, set it on the rug beside the chair and gathered her into his arms. He could feel the chill of her wet clothes against his own.

"I'm sorry, I'm sorry." She was crying so hard Ken could barely make out her words. "I can't tell you what you want to know. They want to kill me, but I don't know why, I don't. I'm sorry, I'm so sorry."

"It's all right, Julie, I'm here. Don't cry, sweetheart. It's all right now. You don't have to remember, Julie, not until you're ready. Not as long as you're with me. You're safe here. You don't have to remember."

He pulled her to her feet and clasped her tight until the tears slowed. She looked up at him, her face red and swollen. She stiffened her spine and swallowed.

"Do you want me to leave?"

"No, of course not. Never. Why would you think that?"

The look in her eyes answered for her, a reminiscence of the ghosts of unexplainable nightmares, visions and fears. She glanced quickly at Dave, then buried her face in his chest. She shivered, and he tightened his clasp.

"Come on, you need dry clothes. And some rest wouldn't hurt, either. It's been a tough day, hasn't it?" He raised her face. His smile earned a tiny answering one from her, though tears still beaded on her lashes.

Hoping Dave would be gone when he returned, Ken led her up the stairs. Leaving the light in her room dark he stripped off her wet shirt and jeans, trying to ignore her waif-like eyes and his own quickening heartbeat while he toweled her slim body dry. When he slid the striped pajama top up her arms, onto her shoulders, she reached out and touched his hair, lacing her fingers into the thick waving strands. Ken's fingers froze on the buttons. His head lifted and he felt a shock go through him as their eyes met. Time stood still. His awareness of her presence expanded until it filled the universe. Only the two of them existed.

Julie's lips parted. Her fingers tightened in his hair, drew his head closer. He kissed her, softly at first, his passion rising as their bodies pressed against each other. He could feel her breasts, the heat emanating from her torso. Slowly, he laid her back onto the bed, stretching himself out half on top of her. The pajama top gaped wide. Ken's strong, warm hand found her breast, and his body thrilled to the touch. Julie breath hissed in and she arched her back. Her lips opened to his. Their breath mingled. A soft moan sound deep in Julie's throat. Her fingers tightened, clutching him against her. Soft luminescence from the hall spilled in to halo their entwined forms in the early darkness.

Suddenly, behind his closed eyes Ken saw a vision of Julie, his Julie, standing with another man, a faceless man whose arm circled Julie's shoulders in a gesture of possession. Two equally anonymous children played at their feet. He gasped, pulled his lips from hers and gazed into her shadowed face. The vision remained, superimposed over her features, fading slowly into a bitter memory. Julie raised her head, her lips seeking his. Ken shook his head and pushed himself up, away from her. She lifted her hand, her fingers barely brushing the bare skin on his arm. Her touch burned, making Ken shiver.

"Ken?"

He heard a world of fear in the single whispered word. Fear, uncertainty and pain. Ken gritted his teeth and shook his head, keeping his face turned away from her.

"I'm sorry, Julie. I can't."

She didn't say anything. Her hand fell away from his arm though he knew her eyes stayed locked on his back. Ken could feel them, big and round and full of anguish that slammed at him in undulating waves. Clenching his hands he rose, walked over to the open doorway and leaned on the wall. He could just about look at her from there. Her face was buried in such deep shadow he could pretend that her eyes weren't staring at him, that her lips weren't waiting for his kiss, that he didn't want her so badly the craving was almost unbearable. A bar of light fell across her chest but she made no move to pull the pajama top over her bare breasts. She made no move at all. Fighting a maelstrom of emotions, he tried to sigh away enough emotion so he could speak.

"I'm sorry, Julie," he said at last. "It's not that I don't want you. I do. So much that it hurts. I've never felt like this about anyone before. It's just that—damn it, Julie! It just hit me, out of nowhere. Really hit me. You have a whole other life out there somewhere. You could be married. You could have children waiting for their mommy to come home. How can I make love to you, when I see these little kids..."

He broke off, unable to find words for what was in his heart. Julie lay still, unmoving, and Ken wondered if she was even listening. Slowly, he felt all emotion drain away. He was glad the wall was there to hold him up.

"Please don't misunderstand me. I love you, Julie. And I want you desperately. I don't want you to go away, not ever. And I don't really want you to find out who you are, because then I probably will lose you. It's just that all of a sudden... that other life of yours seemed so real. I just need some time to deal with it, okay?"

She didn't answer. Ken could detect no movement in the shadowed room. Sighing deeply, aching to take her into his arms and never let her go, he turned away and slowly descended the stairs. He listened as he moved, but there was nothing to hear. Julie made no sound, didn't try to call him back.

Dave was waiting in the living room, standing before the empty fireplace. He turned when Ken reached the bottom of the stairs.

"We need to talk, Ken. She's starting to remember things, you know that, don't you?"

"No, I don't," Ken snapped, denying his own fearful conclusions. "I'm not one of your God-almighty experts, remember?"

Dave nodded, slowly. "And neither am I. But we both know what's happening. So, what are we going to do about it?"

"We? There is no we. There's just me. I'm going to take care of her. Me. By myself. Without your meddling interference. I know what she needs, and it's not any damned doctors."

Dave crossed his arms, leaned against the mantel and studied Ken a moment. "You know, I did some research on this. Amnesia."

"Yeah? You an expert now?" Ken winced at the bitterness in his tone, but Dave didn't seem to hear it. Or he chose to ignore it.

"Not hardly. But I know a lot more now than I did."

"So?" Ken perched on the arm of a chair, curious about what Dave had discovered despite his protests to the contrary.

"From what I read, most amnesia isn't total, and it doesn't last long, either. People lose bits and pieces but get them back fairly quickly, either all at once, or a little at a time. If anything is lost permanently, it's usually only the events right before whatever happened, like, say, a car accident. All the literature says total amnesia is very rare. And it's rarely permanent."

"Are you accusing Julie of lying?" Ken's hands clenched knuckle-white. Rage built in his chest. "Is that what this is about? You think she's faking?"

"Actually, no. I don't." His expression thoughtful, Dave looked up the stairs as though he could see the room where Julie slept. "What I think we're dealing with here is what's called traumatic amnesia, which, if I remember right, can be either retrograde—the inability to recall events before the injury—or anterograde, which affects recent and short term memory. It can also be a combination of both."

"From what Julie told us, that makes sense." Ken nodded, intrigued despite his annoyance. "She remembers nothing before waking up in that field, and can't remember much between then and now. So, a combination."

"Traumatic amnesia is caused by a severe head injury. You remember the hospital said she'd once fractured her skull near where she hit it when she fell?" Again, Ken nodded. "It must have been a pretty bad injury to cause amnesia this severe. She's lucky to have survived it."

Pain seared Ken's heart. He shook his head. "Poor Julie," he whispered, wishing he could take all her suffering away.

"And now she's starting to remember." Dave sighed and looked at Ken who blinked, startled at the sorrow he saw in his friend's eyes. "She may remember it all, eventually. Or she may remember just a small fraction. Traumatic amnesia, unfortunately, can be permanent. But however much she remembers, it's going to be hard on her. Emotionally. I don't think we're equipped to help her. I wish we could. I wish—" He broke off and shook his head.

"No. You're wrong. I *can* help her, Dave. I know I can."

"Yeah, well." Dave shrugged. "Maybe. But are you sure you've got your priorities straight, Ken? Are you sure it's Julie you're most concerned with?"

"What the fuck is that supposed to mean?"

"It means she's not Mark, Ken. You can't change the past by reliving it now. Julie needs what *she* needs, not what *you* want her to need." He picked up his jacket and moved to the front door. "Think about it, Ken. Do everyone a favor and really think about it. I'll be around if you want to talk."

He was gone before Ken could say another word, the door shutting with a soft thud as he left the house.

Ken did think, long and hard. Taking a beer from the refrigerator he sat out on the front porch steps, his gaze on the shadowed park. But he didn't see the dark silhouettes of trees. He saw, instead, his brother lying in a flower-banked coffin, dead by his own hand. He felt again the grinding guilt, heard Mark's voice on the phone asking if they could get together, have dinner and talk. Ken had been eighteen, full of himself, too busy with his own life to bother with someone else's. He'd put Mark off, saying maybe next week. Only next week hadn't come, not for Mark. Two days later, alone in his car, he'd swallowed cyanide.

Would Mark be dead if Ken had gone that night, if they'd had dinner and talked? That was the crux of the issue, the foundation for the guilt on which his adult life had been built. Could he have stopped it had he been there, and listened? And was he, as Dave had implied, substituting Julie for Mark? Was he trying to salve his conscience, atone for the past, through her? He didn't think so, but how could he tell for sure? Her needs were so much the same as Mark's had been. Someone to trust, to listen, to help make sense of the world. How in hell was he supposed to separate the two?

But he did know one thing. Julie had somehow opened the door he'd locked tight the day Mark had died. He had closed off his fragile, vulnerable self and vowed he'd never again let anyone get that close to him, or mean so much to him. He would never love anyone so deeply that their leaving could damage him so irreparably. He'd pulled back from everyone, family and friends alike. He hadn't even felt lonely, and as much as he'd wanted a woman in his life, he had been content to merely coast along. It felt comfortable, safe. He would have coasted happily forever. But now that Julie had become a part of him, the very thought of losing her terrified him. It filled him with such atavistic fear that he could barely breathe. He would rather lose his arms, his legs, his eyes, than lose Julie. What, then, would he do when she left?

Because he knew that she would go. One day, sooner or later, she would remember fully, or the past would somehow catch up to her and reach out to claim her for its own. She would return to the life that once had been, leaving him cut adrift and alone. He wished he could go back, or lock himself away again, but it was too late. He was filled with Julie and haunted by the unknown past that stood between them. He thought again of Mark, of what he had learned from him of death. Then he replayed it all in his mind, wondering at last what it could teach him of life.

It was after midnight when he rose and went inside, locking the doors securely after himself. Then he lifted the phone. Dave answered on the first ring.

"You're partly right," Ken said. "It did start out because of Mark. But it changed somewhere along the way, Dave. I don't know quite when or how, but it's not about me anymore. It's about her. Who she is. What she needs. And for now, at least, I know I can give her what she needs—a safe place, somewhere she can live without looking over her shoulder. Or fighting for survival."

"Okay."

"She is starting to remember, you're right about that, too. But she's not ready to face it, not yet. When she is, I'll help her all I can."

"And if you can't?"

"I'll find someone who can."

"And when she leaves, Ken? When she goes back to her family? What then?"

"Then I'll be a better person. I'll feel like shit, but I'll be whole for the first time in years."

"Good." Dave fell silent. Ken could almost see him nodding his head. Then Dave spoke again. "Good. You need help, just ask. I'll do whatever I can."

"Thanks, Dave. For being my friend. And for kicking my ass."

"Back atcha, man," Dave said, and hung up.

Ken climbed to the second floor and walked down the hall to check on Julie. His heart stopped, abruptly, when he looked into the room, the world spinning out from under his feet. Her bed was empty! He died a million times before he shifted his eyes and discovered her in the wicker chair near the back window. She was sound asleep, tears long dried upon her cheeks. Bars of light from the half-open blinds striped her face. The pajama top was not buttoned but she had shed her jeans. Her bare legs gleamed softly in the darkness. In her right hand she clutched her one treasure, the onyx and silver bracelet from her backpack.

Ken moved close and stood watching her a long time, his hand cupped beneath her cheek, not quite touching her. He could feel the warmth of her breath on his palm. Finally, he bent and picked her up, nestling her slight weight in his strong arms. The bracelet slipped through her fingers and thudded softly on the carpet. He carried her to the bed and laid her down, buttoning the pajama top before snuggling the blanket around her. She sighed, burrowing deeper into the softness, but did not wake. Ken could see the almost-faded bruise on her forehead in the reflected light from the hallway.

He had found all that he needed out there on the porch. Smiling, he pushed Julie's hair back from her face and said a silent prayer of thanks to Mark. The present was all anyone ever had, and if together they made the most of their present, then each day could last a lifetime. Bending, he brushed Julie's lips with his. She smiled, and sighed.

"I love you, Julie," he whispered. "From now on, that's all that matters."

A few minutes later, ready for bed, Ken slid beneath the covers beside Julie. He fell asleep with the feel of her in his arms and the echo of her contented sigh in his heart. He, too, smiled in his sleep, unaware of how little happiness their lifetime together would hold, and how very soon it would end.

CHAPTER ELEVEN
June 30, 1990
Buffalo, New York

Bernard Maximilian Keel stood statue-still. He listened, saying nothing, the black receiver pressed against his ear. Not a sound escaped into the hot, midday air as he stared through the phone booth's Plexiglas. People walked to and fro. Traffic passed a few feet from where he stood. But though he took in every detail, including his own reflection in the glass, he knew that to those passing by he did not seem to be looking at anything. Even to himself his eyes appeared fixed and glazed. Not a flicker of body movement betrayed his interest in the world around him or his concentration on the store across the street. When he spoke, his menacing voice just above a whisper, his lips barely moved. They were the only part of him that did.

"You doubt my word?"

The question sent waves of menace rippling through the wires. Keel almost smiled at the fear gibbering beneath the words of denial that echoed in his ear.

"No, no, of course not. It's just that you hadn't much to go on, only that one picture and it wasn't very good. He wants you to be quite sure."

"I am." Keel gave his respondent a few moments to contemplate the finality of his tone before continuing. "She's living with the man in the picture, his name is Kenneth Martin Reed, Jr. He won't cause any trouble, he's just a teacher. And it will be no loss if he gets in the way."

Keel pitched his tone to promise that Reed would get in the way. The high-pitched voice on the other end protested any unnecessary action, but Keel didn't bother to listen. The dress shop door across the street opened and Keel's quarry emerged into the overcast light of day. He turned his head a fraction, studied her from the corner of his eye. Reed-the-teacher accompanied her, carrying a large bag in his right hand. His left he slid around the woman's waist, square fingers disappearing beneath the sling that supported her cast. They crossed the street and walked past the phone booth, intent on each other. They didn't see him. Keel swept his gaze up her body, letting his eyes linger on her face just long enough to send shivers through her. When her smile faded and she frowned, he dropped his head to stare at the small metal shelf that jutted beneath the long oblong box of the telephone. If they looked around, and he was sure they would, Keel knew all they'd see of him was the top of his dark-haired head. Accordingly, they would dismiss him. Idiots.

"She calls herself Julie, now," he said, interrupting the flow of annoying words from the other end. "Not as a disguise, she claims to have lost her memory. I shall have to return it to her. There is nothing more frustrating than to die at someone else's hands without knowing the reason. Don't you agree?"

"Listen, you're not to take any chances. Just get rid of her. That's what you're being paid to do."

"Are you telling me how to do my work? *You?*" His malignant tone effectively silenced the other voice. Keel took a deep breath and let it out on a twelve-count, easing the anger that banded his chest, the tension that tightened the muscles of his jaw. Thirty feet up the street his target disappeared into a compact car. Keel spoke on as he watched the car pull out into traffic and cruise past the phone booth. "This is our final contact. It will be done within the week. Leave the money as instructed by six p.m. today. No later. You will receive newspaper notices of her demise, as proof of fulfillment."

"Oh, no. We didn't agree to any advance payment. You don't get the money until the job is done —to our satisfaction."

"Did I say I would take the money before-time?" Keel sent the anger that tensed his body thrumming through the wires straight to his listener's ear. "You knew my working methods before you hired me. We have a contract. You agreed to my conditions. You will

leave the money, *today*, in the place that I selected. I will confirm it is there, and that it is clean, before I fulfill my end of the contract. I will not take it until I have fully earned it." He paused and closed his eyes, seeing in the sudden darkness an image of the Julie-woman's smiling, little-girl face. "I am an honorable man," he added as his mind planned the means of her dispatch. "I have never yet broken my word. I suggest you do not break yours."

He set the receiver gently on the hook, unmindful of the shrill, panicky voice issuing from the ear-piece. Amateurs. He hated dealing with amateurs, especially imbeciles who thought they were smart. Let them get mixed up in something sordid, let them once eliminate a threat and out of sheer, dumb luck not get caught, and they thought that made them professionals. Some professionals. They always left loose ends to be tied, ribbons of evidence that led straight to their own doors. Not until then did they hire a true professional, like Keel, to wipe away their mess. Always after-the-fact, never when they should, at the start, so there'd be no mess to begin with. And they always questioned his methods, the secrecy, the payment plan, the means of dispatch, the timing. Did those assholes think he wanted to be caught doing their dirty work?

He shook his head, a movement almost imperceptible to the naked eye, then left the telephone booth and ambled down Delaware Avenue. When he reached the corner he turned right and strolled completely around the block. He needed time to clear his head, to rid himself of the anger he felt before he continued with his plan. Anger was dangerous, it could make him careless. The money would be there, he knew. When the mysterious 'Mr. Z.' sent a veiled threat, the recipients always acceded to his wishes. Indeed, they had little choice. If they didn't follow his instructions perfectly, they would find themselves part of the 'mess' he so efficiently cleaned up. And they knew it. Keel had built a flawless reputation on solid, ruthless fact. He never took any chances, never left any clues. All arrangements were made long-distance. His clients never knew his name or saw his face. Modern technology had indubitably made the free-lance elimination business both easier and much safer to conduct.

By the time he reached his Audi his temper had calmed and his mind settled snug around the task at hand. He would take a few more days to observe the woman—and the man, that asshole teacher—to absorb their habits and their schedule. Then he would check the money, finish the job, pick up his payment and leave quickly, as usual. He thought about what his nameless contact had said as he guided the car through the summer-crowded streets. The idiot was right about unnecessary chances. To toy with this quarry would be a self-indulgent whim. It would serve no real purpose. Keel decided he would not bother to restore her memory. This time, he would kill from a distance. As much as he regretted it, the Julie-woman would die without ever knowing the reason.

CHAPTER TWELVE
July 3, 1990
Buffalo, New York

Hands lifted her even before the echoes of her fall stopped. Then sudden stillness, the blackness flash-lit, scalding her eyes. Fleeting seconds full of walls looming close above her, a shadow-form she barely glimpsed before the light vanished. Imprisoned in a space that would not let her move, she heard the snick of a door closing, heard its faint echo in the inky darkness of the night. And she knew. She was in a car, in the back on the floor, pulled upright now and pinned in place by the seat in front of her and the hands, the legs, pressing from behind. A man. She knew, somehow, it was a man.

Knees jammed tight against her shoulders. Heat radiated from the insides of his thighs. The car swayed. Soft thuds reverberated from behind in the night. She tried to turn, seeking the source of the sound. Without a word the man touched her face and she froze, her heart pounding like a steam hammer in her chest. She felt his silent laugh, felt it thrum through his body and vibrate into hers. It felt more evil than the darkness surrounding her.

She moaned and tried to bend her head. He stopped her, wrapped her face, her eyes, with a wad of cloth he knotted tight. Startled, she raised her hands. He imprisoned them in his own, his hot flesh enveloping her icy bones, and leaned close to breathe in her ear. She shuddered at the contact. Her lungs would not work.

"Leave it be," he whispered, pushing her hands down to the rough-carpeted floor. Silence fell. They sat still, his body entrapping hers for endless minutes. His nearness burned, sent ripples of dread deep into the core of her being. A sudden noise echoed behind them. Footsteps crunched near and her heart leapt with foolish hope. The man stroked her hair and a scream jammed in her throat, reverberated unheard through her body. The car rocked again. Its engine broke the silence like glass, and they began to move.

"Now the fun begins."

She barely heard the whispered words, caught her breath in wondering if he had actually said them. He gave her little time for thought. His strong hand fisted in her hair, arched her head back into his lap. A hard mouth crushed down on hers, scraping her lips against her teeth, drawing blood. He licked it away, let his hands drop lower to play among the buttons on her sweater. The car picked up speed, the curving road now smooth before them, his hands picking up speed to match. She shook her head, tried to cry out. He grabbed her face and squeezed. Pain raked across her life. Red flashes kaleidoscoped into her darkness, stinging embers that ate away at her flesh. She pressed against him, shrinking from the agony, clawed hands questing for freedom. Again his eerie laugh. His hand closed around her breast.

Gasping, Julie sat bolt upright, her eyes wide in the dimness of the room. *Oh, no, not again, please!* Shuddering, she pressed a hand hard against her mouth to keep herself from screaming. It seemed she woke up screaming almost every night now. But she hadn't been asleep very long this time. The clock beside the bed glowed green, its digital numbers showing 11:52. Julie had to squint to see the glow, dimmer than usual and fading fast even as she looked at it. Or did cloth still cover her eyes? Was that why she couldn't see? She wasn't sure, not until she lifted a hand to touch her face and found no blindfold.

Had it been only a dream, as Ken said the other had been? But it seemed so real. Horribly, frighteningly real. She could still feel the hand pawing at her body, the hot breath misting in her ear. Her stomach rebelled at the strong metallic iron taste on her tongue. She wiped a shaking hand over her lips and stared with mouth agape at fingers that came away clean. Where was the blood? It had to be there, she could taste it! If it had been only a dream, why could she still taste blood?

It had happened, she knew it had, long ago in the buried mists of a past shut away from her. Or perhaps it was happening now, this very minute. Perhaps this life, the bed in which she sat, was the true mirage. Again her vision clouded, otherworld darkness reaching out to drag her back into a nightmare existence. Choking on panic, she looked around a room that wavered, began fading from view. Ripples of darkness undulated through the air, clinging mists of deadly mirage that wrapped breathless tentacles around her. Oh, God, which was real, the room or the darkness? Ken, or the man in the car? Which vision should she believe? What should she hold onto?

"No, please," she pleaded, her voice a tiny whisper that even her ears could barely hear. But it was sound enough. The faint vibration of her own voice shredded the dark vapors. The room reappeared, substantial and solid. The vision of the car, the feel of the man's hands, collapsed, leaving her rapid heartbeat the only sound in the night. Pain stabbed a counterpoint at her, lanced deep into her eyes, her arm. Gasping, Julie pushed herself from the bed and stumbled across the floor. For long minutes she clung to the dresser, the silky nightgown Ken had bought falling in soft folds from her shivering body. At long last the cold penetrated, and her mind began to work again.

What was wrong, why did she hurt like this? The pain in her head solidified, centering above her left ear. Her arm felt like it was on fire. She groped her way down the hall toward the bathroom, guided by light spilling from the open door. As she drew closer the brightness sent sharp stabs through her eyes and down into her stomach. She knew she could go no closer, even through she desperately needed the pills the doctor had given her for pain. The light was too bright, she was no match for it. She would simply have to do without the medication.

Gritting her teeth against waves of nausea, she turned into the darkness of the stairwell. She clung to the banister as she stumbled down the steps, then made her way into the living room and sank onto the softness of the green lounge chair. Light from street lamps, diffused by the overhang of the front porch, radiated through the windows to limn shapeless mounds of furniture with ghostly life. The air felt misty, the silence deep and impenetrable. Julie sat amidst the wraiths, oblivious to the eerie atmosphere. She huddled unmoving in the chair with her knees pulled up. Low moans escaped her lips though she tried to contain them. She closed her eyes and clutched at the silk she wore as she rode out the malicious attack. Gradually, so slowly that at first she was not aware of the change, the pain began to abate. By the time a low scraping step sounded on the stair, she was able to lift her head and open her eyes.

"Julie?" Ken's soft, worried voice hammered at her skull, making her wince. "What are you doing down here? What's wrong?"

She couldn't answer, as much because of the pain that still held her in its thrall as because she had no idea what to say. Everything was wrong. Her whole life made no sense. Ken crouched beside her and looked into her dilated eyes.

"Are you in pain? Is that what woke you up?"

It was easier to nod agreement than to tell him of the new dream. Ken rose and she closed her eyes, bending her throbbing head into her hands.

"I'll be right back, honey. Don't move."

She would have laughed had the pain not been so bad. She could barely breathe, how could she possibly move? It was the last thing in the world she wanted to do.

He brought her two pain pills and stayed with her after she'd forced them down, kneeling beside her and gently rubbing her back. It hurt at first to have him touch her, but she didn't tell him to stop. His presence eased the fearful loneliness she felt and took away her desire to cry. Once the pills began to take effect and the pain faded into a memory, Ken's hands filled her with a delicious sense of belonging, something she couldn't remember ever feeling before.

"Better now?" he asked. Smiling, she nodded. "Come on over here, it's more comfortable."

He led her to the couch. She lay with her head in his lap, looking up into his shadow-hidden eyes. Ken smiled, and twined a lock of her hair around his fingers.

"How did you know I was down here?" she asked. "I thought you were asleep."

"Not really. I guess I was worried about you, about having the cast removed after just four weeks." He traced his fingers lightly on the elastic bandage wrapped around her newly-liberated arm. "I didn't hear you get up, but I heard you on the stairs and you didn't sound too steady. When you didn't come back up, I decided to investigate."

"I'm glad you did."

"I guess the doctor was right when he said your arm might hurt for a while, wasn't he? It's a good thing I wasn't sound asleep."

Julie knew by the question in Ken's tone that he suspected more than just an aching arm. He had seen the way the agony had beat at her, seen her holding her head. She sighed, knowing she owed him an explanation.

"It wasn't just my arm, Ken," she said at last. "It was my head, too. It felt like it was exploding. I was really afraid I might die."

His arms slid around her, pulled her close to his chest. She could feel his heart pulsing, a slow, ponderous beat that reverberated through her, making her feel sheltered and safe. Before she could think about it, she found herself telling him about the latest dream, the eerie reality it possessed, the way it clung to her even after she woke. By the time she finished her lids were drooping, and the strong medicine had started to slur her words. Ken smiled, his expression bittersweet in the misty shadows as he pushed her hair back from her face. He leaned down and kissed her temple, his lips gentle on the still-tender site of her injury. Then he placed his lips on hers, and spoke.

"I love you, Julie. Whatever these dreams are, whatever they mean, I'll always love you. We'll face it together, you and I. You won't ever be alone again. I love you."

His lips pressed down. Julie tried to respond. Her heart began to jump. A warmth kindled deep in her body. But the painkillers had too strong a hold. She slipped away from Ken even as her lips opened to his. She heard his quiet laugh, felt his hands caress her face, felt him lift her in his arms. She snuggled her head into his shoulder and folded her left arm around his neck, but by the time he carried her to the stairs she was fast asleep. She dreamed not of claustrophobic cars and eerie, malicious men, but of Ken's lips, his caressing hands, his mellow voice saying, 'I love you.' She woke completely contented the next day, for the first time in her too-short memory.

CHAPTER THIRTEEN
July 4, 1990
Ceredo, West Virginia

Michael Cortaid handed his sister a gin and tonic and watched her walk down to where Twelvepole Creek flowed past his three acres. Willows drooped graceful branches into the sun-sparkled water. White clouds floated overhead in a sea of pale blue. The breeze, which earlier had sent flowers dancing, now collapsed in upon itself, leaving the hot, humid countryside encased in a waiting silence. It would rain soon, Michael knew, catching a glimpse of the darkening horizon. No fireworks. Too bad for the kids. He hoped they would have time to finish their picnic before the sky started to weep.

He freshened up his wife's drink, and his brother-in-law's, and made sure his mother's soda glass was full before mixing a dry Manhattan for himself and following his sister to the river. He found her leaning against a willow, looking back to where the children gamboled around their grandmother's wheelchair.

"I was really glad you and Jeff could come, Wendy," he said, smiling at the delight Mary Cortaid took in her seven grandchildren. "Mom's been so lonesome for your brood ever since she moved down here with us. It's sure nice to be all together again, isn't it?"

"Except we're not, are we?" Wendy replied, her gaze dropping to the sweating glass she held. "We're not all together."

"Come on, don't spoil the holiday, Wendy."

"It's already spoiled," she murmured. Michael made an impatient sound deep in his throat and Wendy shot him an angry glare. "What do you want me to do, Michael? Forget Carole ever existed? Pretend she's not still somewhere out there, hurt maybe, needing us? Pretend she's dead and buried?"

"Come on, Wendy, that's not what I meant—"

"That's what *he* did, if you remember," she interrupted. "Vic, her 'devoted husband.'" She turned back to the sluggish river. Tears trembled in her eyes. "He forgot she existed even before he left, that bastard. Vic never loved Carole, he was just using her, puffing up his damned ego at her expense. I think she was beginning to see that. She really was. It sure didn't take him long to file for divorce once she disappeared, did it?"

"This is old stuff, Wendy," Michael said quietly. He didn't look at his sister, couldn't bear to see her anguished face. He needed all his strength just to hold on to his own emotions. "It all happened long ago. Can't you let it rest, at least for today?"

"No, I can't. She isn't dead, Michael. How do I bury someone who isn't dead? How do you do it?"

"That's not fair, Wendy. It's not fair, and it's not nice."

Wendy sighed, closing her eyes and pressing a shaking hand to her lips. When she looked at him, Michael saw the apology standing stark in her eyes, and he nodded his acceptance of her silent regret. Wendy took a long, slow sip of her icy drink.

"I can't stop thinking about her, Michael. I keep wondering what happened to her, why she left like that. Or if someone took her."

"The police found no evidence of abduction," he reminded her.

"The *police*," Michael winced at the bitterness of her tone, "found no evidence of *anything*. I don't think they even tried very hard to find her. They barely spent any time looking, they were too busy worrying about who killed that stupid reporter, not that they ever found that out, either. They're all idiots."

"There wasn't a whole lot to find, Wendy, not after two months. If Carole left on her own, she certainly didn't want to be found. And if someone took her, well..." He shrugged, then decided not to leave the words unsaid. Too much was being left unsaid lately. "She could be dead, you know. In fact, she probably is. Why else wouldn't we have heard from her in more than two-and-a-half years? Someone grabbed her off the street that night, killed her, then buried her somewhere in the mountains outside of town. That's wild country up there. Her body will probably never be found. And we'll never know for sure."

"No." Wendy's whisper was a wail of anguish. "No, it's not true. She's not dead. I don't believe that, I won't!"

Michael cleared his throat. "I don't want to, either, but it's the most likely explanation. I hate to think of the way she must have suffered and I pray it was over quick. But at least I can live with that, Wendy, awful as it is. I can handle a few hours of Carole being hurt, raped maybe, then killed. At least that way I'd know it was over." He took a sip of his drink and shook his head. "But if she's not dead, if someone took her and she's still alive, then that means he still has her. He's still hurting her. It means her life is a nightmare, every single day, a nightmare that doesn't end. And that I can't live with. It hurts too much."

Wendy didn't speak. Tears dripped down her cheeks. In the far distance, thunder warned of soggy weather to come though overhead the late-day sun still shone bright. Behind them the children ran, holding sparklers aloft, their young, innocent voices laughing as if to negate the harsh reality that held their parents in thrall. After a few moments, Wendy wiped her face and looked back at where the rest of the family began to gather around the picnic table. Her husband, Jeff, stood at the smoking grill, mitted hands waving barbecue implements as he directed the youthful traffic. Michael's wife, Sharon, pushed her mother-in-law's chair over the bumpy lawn to the table.

"It's just so hard," Wendy said. "I can't talk to anyone about it, they all think I should be over it by now. But I still see her, Michael. On the street, in the stores, even in church. It's never her, just someone who looks a tiny bit like her. I can't tell you how many strangers I've stopped, what a fool I've made of myself." She finished her drink and looked up at him. "You'll probably think I'm crazy, I know I do, but sometimes I even get in the car and drive around, looking for her. It's as if she's calling to me, pleading for help. I can almost hear her voice..." She gave him a sad smile. "I don't sleep well most nights, even after all this time. I guess it's beginning to show, huh?"

"A little," Michael agreed, laying a hand on her cheek. "But you're not alone, Wendy. I do it too, look for her at times. Especially since we moved out here to Ceredo. I keep thinking maybe she found her way to West Virginia. She wouldn't know where I'm living now, she'd think I was still in Huntington. Maybe she's wandering around trying to find me. It's stupid. My head knows better, but sometimes I can't help it. I don't want her to be dead, and I don't want her to be alone. I want her to come home."

Wendy slipped her arm around Michael's waist and gave him a squeeze. "Thanks, Michael. I needed to hear that. Jeff's been really supportive and he tries to understand how I feel, but there's a limit and I think he's reached it. He says it's time for us to get on with our lives. Our kids need us, and we need each other. We can't center everything around a missing sister forever. And I agree. It's just that every time I try to put it aside, it feels too much like I'm abandoning Carole. I can't stand the guilt."

"I know. But Jeff's right. You can't spend each day waiting for the phone to ring, or for Carole to knock on the door. You have to accept that she's gone—for now, at least," he added, raising a hand to stop her protest. "Maybe someday she'll come back, but today you've got children and a husband who are here, and who need you, too. If that's not enough, then maybe you ought to re-think your priorities."

"Hey, you two! Dinner's ready!" Jeff shouted, his hands holding a plate piled high with grilled chicken. "Dawdle at your own risk!"

"Dibs on the drumsticks!" Michael called, waving. He turned to Wendy, who stood with her head bowed. He knew the last thing she wanted to do was join in the family festivities. "Listen, Sis, I'm ordering you to put Carole aside for the rest of your visit. As big brother and head of the family I'm entitled to a few orders," he said, winking at her, though a thread of steel ran beneath the light tone he used. He knew from her startled expression he sounded exactly like their father, who had died more than fifteen years before. "Since the stroke, Mom doesn't handle strong emotions very well. She already feels helpless, about herself and about Carole. How do you suppose the way you're acting makes her feel? She needs to avoid any unnecessary stress, so from now on I want you to be happy and cheerful, even if it kills you. Understand?'

"Maybe I should just go home," Wendy said, her expression truculent.

"Don't be ridiculous." He took her arm and began guiding her across the broad lawn to the picnic table. "I just don't want what time Mom has left to be filled with nothing but pain and worry over Carole and us.

After what she's been through, she deserves whatever little happiness we can give her. She puts on a hell of a front for us, you know. Carole might be our sister, but she's her daughter, her child. Imagine how she feels not knowing. How would you feel if it was Lisa who was missing? Have you really any right to make it worse for Mom?"

Wendy stopped, her eyes wide on her brother's face. "I never thought about it that way. Mercy, I've really been selfish, haven't I? Okay," she said with a tight smile. "You win. It's put aside. And when I get home, I'll try to make it stay there. It is time to start thinking about what I still have, instead of what I've lost."

"That's my Little Sis. Now, let's go eat before I die of starvation. Hey, that chicken looks wonderful, Jeff. Gimme those drumsticks," he said, sitting opposite Wendy at the long, redwood table. Mary Cortaid rapped on the wooden surface.

"Grace," she declared. Children and adults alike quieted, heads bowed over folded hands. Mary's frail slightly-blurred voice wavered clear in the silence.

"Lord, for Thy goodness and bounty, we thank Thee. For Thy blessings upon this table, we thank Thee." She paused a moment. Michael looked up at his mother and clenched his jaw when he saw the pain etched clear on her aged face. "Be with my Carole this day, Lord," Mary continued in a whisper. "Give her strength. Keep her safe in Your arms. And bring her home to us, please. One way or another, bring her home to us. Amen."

For a few moments, only the children spoke or ate.

CHAPTER FOURTEEN
July 4, 1990
Buffalo, New York

Bernard Maximilian Keel stood in the background and watched as streams of people, wending their way to LaSalle Park, spilled over the sidewalks and into the streets. The glorious weather, hot and sunny with a brisk breeze that made the humidity bearable, had drawn huge crowds to the waterfront festival. Cars clogged the narrow streets for blocks around as drivers searched for overlooked parking spaces. Police patrolled the park and stood in the main intersections, keeping open those lanes of traffic that led to the Peace Bridge that crossed the Niagara River to Ontario, Canada. A joyful atmosphere reigned despite, or perhaps because of, the surging crowds. Music from the Park's band shell rode the wind, caressing late-comers with celebratory welcome. The tragic crash of a stunt plane had marred the opening celebration four days earlier, but the final day of the Buffalo-Fort Erie Friendship Festival promised a perfect conclusion with carefree fun, great music, delicious food and breathtaking fireworks.

Don't trust promises, Keel thought.

He edged away from the excitement's focus toward a long, ornate brick building half-screened by trees. The isolated four-story structure, closed for the holiday, paralleled the waterfront some fifty feet from the rear boundary of the park. Keeping a watchful eye on both celebrating crowd and patrolling cops, Keel forced open a small side door and let himself into the vacant edifice. His black clothing melded him into the dark interior. He carried a small duffel bag in his hand. Once inside with the door secured, he waited a few moments to let his eyes adjust to the abrupt dimness, then moved on silent feet that took him up a stretch of stairwell to the top-most floor. He noted the placement of alternate escape routes as he moved, should such become necessary.

He chose his window with care, based on the layout of the park from which he'd just come. He knew exactly where they were, the Julie-woman and Reed-the-teacher, he'd earlier stood not ten feet from them. They sat on a blanket near the band shell in the middle of the park, sharing cold fried chicken, cheese, white wine and kisses. They had eyes for no one but themselves. Reed's blond friend sat on an adjacent blanket with a somewhat chubby red-haired woman, but though they spoke back and forth with Reed and the Julie-woman they did not move from their places.

That is fine, Keel thought, adjusting the binoculars he'd taken from the duffel, searching for his quarry. *As long as they stay where they are, they won't get hurt.* Not that he cared. He was prepared to take out whoever he needed in order to kill the woman. The people in the park below had no reality for him. They were merely targets, that was all.

He found the Julie-woman on his second sweep. He could see her perfectly and there were no obstructions in the way. A clear field of fire. He kept his gaze on her a long time, watching her smile, noting how her hair danced in the breeze, her almost-perfect profile when she turned her head, the way her slender hand lifted the plastic glass to her lips. He could almost taste the hunger with which she kissed the teacher, and read the private messages contained in their looks. *She will die happy, the Julie-woman.* Regret filled Keel at the thought, sharp as a knife-blade. Lips pressed tight, he bent to the task of assembling his weapon.

The sun sank into Lake Erie with slow deliberation, as though reluctant to leave the festivities. Its arc painted the gathering clouds with bands of vivid color. Moment by moment the hues softened into pinks, orchids and yellows pale as ash-blond hair. Misty teal green accents sparked at the edges. The sky overhead darkened early thanks to the thickening clouds, a deep purple-gray that crept closer to the pastels on the horizon until at last it overtook and smothered them. An almost-full moon played hide and seek in the east. Saucy stars winked through rents in the clouds, their twinkling echoed by lights on the

Canadian shore across the water and the running lights of boats anchored in the canal that flowed between the park and the lake. Scattered skyrockets arced into the dark sky all over the city, accompanied by sharp bangs, whistles and pops as kids shot off contraband fireworks, a mere prelude to the well-planned, official show to come.

Keel hefted the powerful rifle and peered through the infrared scope attached to the top. In less than ten seconds he focused on the Julie-woman. The still-brisk wind whipped her hair around her face as she huddled in Reed's arms. Keel could barely see her. In the scope the two figures looked like one large, elongated target. Keel's lips lifted in a pleased grin. If she didn't move away from the teacher, and he hoped she wouldn't, he'd be obliged to shoot Reed, too. During the fireworks display, under cover of the noise and excitement, they would die. Both of them. He slowed his breathing and gained control his quickening heartbeat, then laid the rifle down and cut a neat round hole in the windowpane.

Faint strains from the Buffalo Philharmonic Orchestra in the band shell wafted to Keel's ears on the wind. A breeze caressed his face. The darkness deepened, solidified. The fireworks' scheduled ten o'clock starting time came and went. Still the wind blew, showing no sign of abating. Keel's heart began to thud, and he once again lifted the rifle, sighted in on his target. He'd have to be ready to shoot if they cancelled the show, before the crowd moved and obscured the woman.

The wind died momentarily, then began again, this time from a slightly altered direction. Keel could no longer feel it on his face, nor was the sound of the music as clear as before. He glanced at his watch: ten-twelve. A loudspeaker blared, excited words he could not decipher at that distance. He raised his gaze to the window once more and watched the first of the show's rockets explode overhead.

He indulged himself for a few minutes, watching the spectacular pyrotechnic display that danced in the sky in time with glorious strains of music played by the Philharmonic. The fireworks burst red, green, white and orange, sparkling silver and glittering gold, whistling up to mushroom out into sparkling cascades that arced across the darkness like swift-opening blossoms, or hung shimmering for endless seconds like hovering angel lights. Bright flashes and sharp cracks interspersed between staccato pops and deep booms.

Pale smoke drifted to the southeast, away from the gathered crowd. It reminded him of his childhood, before life's grim realities had set him on his true path. That last innocent summer before his father had murdered his mother and the police had killed his father, and sent Keel and his sister into the hell of the foster system. *And good times were had by all*, he thought.

Keel pulled his attention from the majestic celebration and once again sighted in on his target. The Julie-woman still sat wrapped in Reed-the-teacher's arms. Keel saw Reed turn to his friend and gesture to the right. Then he bent over the Julie-woman. When he straightened up, he leaned away from her, gathering up the things from the picnic basket they'd brought. Keel frowned, watching the man's movements, and with a shock it hit him. Reed was packing up. They were leaving. In a few moments the target would no longer be in range. Keel growled and swung the rifle back to his main target. *Good-bye, Julie,* he thought, centering the scope's crosshairs on the back of her head.

The night lit up in blood-red blossoms as Keel squeezed the trigger: once, twice, four times in rapid succession. The exploding fireworks buried the sound of the shots.

CHAPTER FIFTEEN
July 4, 1990
Buffalo, New York Waterfront

Julie could feel excitement build in the crowd around her as the sun sank into the cool blue of Lake Erie. Soon, if the wind cooperated, the fireworks display would begin. She tipped her head up to watch the sun's rays brush the sky overhead with glorious hues. The heavens darkened, brilliant tones paling into misty ghosts of color. At the extreme edge of her vision, dark clouds inched toward the rainbow blush. The brisk wind slowed somewhat as though to watch nature's perfect artistry unfold. Soft strains of classical music echoed on the air.

And then her view was blocked by Ken's head. His mouth pressed down on hers, his tongue probing gently between her parted lips. Julie shuddered at the contact and raised her hand to caress his cheek. She could taste wine and cheese on his breath.

"I love you," he whispered, his lips still touching hers. The movement tickled, and she laughed. She kissed him back, then pulled away to look into his eyes.

"How does that feel?" she asked, her heart beating double-time. She didn't think he'd understand the question or the confusion that prompted it, but she wanted to know, had to know. "How do you know what you feel is love?"

Ken stared at her a moment, his face merging slowly into the deepening gloom. A skyrocket went off somewhere nearby, startling Julie with its whistle and bang. She jumped, her gaze jerking to the surrounding dimness, but all she could see was the press of the crowd. When she turned back to Ken, he was smiling at her. A mocking smile? She didn't know, it was too dark now to tell.

"It feels," he replied, reaching over to refill her wine glass, "like being reborn. Everything seems brand new. Colors are brighter, sounds are crisper, things taste sweeter. You're ten feet tall. The whole of creation belongs just to you. Soft is softer, the sun feels warmer, the moon glistens with stardust. That's what love is, how it feels."

"You're teasing me," she accused, taking the wine glass from Ken's hand. Tingles tickled her breast when their fingers met. She felt on the verge of tears, but didn't know why.

"No, I'm not. That's really how it feels to be in love with you. As though my life is just starting."

"Hey, you two." The deep voice rolled out of the darkness at them. "We've got some shrimp over here. Want some?"

Reluctant to look away from Ken even though she could barely make him out in the gathering night, Julie turned to look at Dave Atwood who sat on a blanket spread to their left. His date, a bubbly redhead named Bonnie Greenman, smiled at her.

"We sure do," Ken said, reaching across Julie to take the plate that Dave held out. In return, he passed Dave a plate from their blanket. "Here, have some of this gooey French cheese. It's great with these little wafer things."

"Spoken like a true gourmet," Dave said. Julie could just make out his grin. "Thanks."

"Here, Julie, the first one's yours."

Julie turned back to Ken. He had dipped a shrimp in cocktail sauce and held it up for her. She smiled and opened her mouth. Ken popped the morsel in and licked his fingers. Savoring the mingled flavors of sweet shrimp and hot, spicy sauce, Julie chewed while she watched Ken select a shrimp for himself. His words echoed on in her mind. She frowned, pondering their meaning, trying to fit them into the sense of her life.

"You look confused," Ken said, feeding her another shrimp. "Wasn't my answer lyrical enough for you?"

"It's not that," she said around the food, pushing her wind-whipped hair out of her face.

She could tell from his bantering tone that he hadn't taken her question seriously. She didn't blame him. How could someone not know what love is? Her mind worked on while they finished the shrimp, searching for words that would help him understand. She had never thought about love before, not in connection with herself. Love belonged to other people, other places and other lives. In the world through which she moved, love had no place. Survival came first and there was room for little else. Not until this man had brought her into his world, had held her and kissed her, given her a space in which she felt safe did the idea of love take on some semblance of possibility. If only she knew what it really was.

Ken pushed the empty paper plate into the trash bag they'd brought and put his arm around her shoulder. With gentle fingers he traced the outline of her cheek.

"You're serious, aren't you?" he asked. "You really want to know what love is."

Julie looked at him, barely able to see him though his face hovered inches from hers. She nodded, feeling again an irrational urge to cry. But why? She wasn't sad or lonely. Far from it. Nor did she hurt. So why should she want to cry?

"OK, let's see if I can make sense on the subject." Another rocket exploded not far away, and Julie cringed at the noise. Ken tightened his arm, pulling her closer. "I don't know if I can describe love in the abstract, what it means for everybody. All I know is what it means for me."

He sat still a moment, his gaze on the dark sky where encroaching clouds blotted out the stars. Then he turned his head and kissed her, a long, slow kiss that sent her pulse racing. She strained toward him, pressing closer, aching to feel his body against hers. When at last he lifted his head, she could barely breathe.

"Do you feel it?" he asked, his voice a whisper that breathed in her ear. "The way your heart beats and your breath stops? The ache deep inside for more, the need to touch and be touched? The desire to merge into one being? That's love's feeling, Julie. It's a small, exquisite, indescribable part of love, the part you usually notice first."

He moved his hands, clasped her wind-blushed cheeks in gentle fingers. His thumbs traced the outline of her parted lips.

"But for me there's more to love. Much, much more. It goes far beyond feeling and lasts long after the feeling loses intensity. That's the part that's based on choice. You see, for me that's what love is, Julie. A choice, one that's freely made.

"It can be a scary thing, love. It opens you up, makes you vulnerable. Your whole life gets turned upside down, because when you make that choice, your priorities change completely. You start thinking 'we', instead of 'I.' Almost like there isn't an 'I' anymore. Every decision is based on how it will affect the two of you, even if what you're doing only involves you alone. That's because it doesn't, really. It can't. You're no longer you alone, anymore. You're part of a pair."

He fed her a slice of cheese, and she watched him lick his fingers before he continued. "For me, love means commitment, Julie. For life. It's a pledge to stay and work even harder when things go wrong, when the road gets rough. It's easy to stay when everything's great. But when there's trouble, love based on feeling alone will fall apart because it isn't complete. There has to be a conscious choice to belong to one person above all others, forever, or it doesn't really mean anything. A commitment to one life lived in unity."

Ken paused and looked deep into Julie's eyes. She could feel herself being drawn into him, into his very soul. Strangely, it didn't frighten her in the least. She heard Dave's voice, heard him say something, but the words held no meaning for her. Ken did not answer his friend, or look up at him. He seemed as oblivious to everything and everyone else as she was.

"It's a big world, Julie. I've met lots of people, known lots of women. I've had love feelings before, but I've never made the choice, not until now. Not until you came along and opened me wide up. You're my choice, Julie, and I'll love you forever."

He leaned forward and kissed her again, then pulled her close. Julie's arms folded around him, holding him tight. She buried her face in his shoulder.

"Does that answer your question?" he asked in an almost inaudible whisper.

"Yes," she answered, her muffled voice sounding breathless. "Oh, yes!"

Above them, the first of the fireworks display exploded in a glittering shower.

"Hey, kid alert. This is a G-rated show. Cut the lovey-dovey stuff, you two," Dave said, laughing. "Besides, you're missing all the fun."

Embarrassment swept over Julie as she suddenly remembered Dave and Bonnie's presence on the blanket beside them. She could feel heat flush her face and was grateful for the darkness that covered it. She turned in Ken's arms and looked up to where silver sparkles twinkled as they arced across the sky, trailing faint graceful plumes of smoke behind. They winked out fast, leaving the crowed poised in hushed expectation. The wind carried the smoke to the southeast, clearing the sky overhead for more of the spectacle.

On and on it went, glorious bursts of orange, green, red and silver, dancing in time to the Philharmonic's music. Awed, Julie stared upward with mouth agape, Ken's wondrous words still ringing in her ears. It seemed at first as though the celebration was just for her, a private extravaganza that echoed the joy she felt. But slowly the joy faded, replaced by a growing sense of unease. The noise of the explosions dug at her, left gaping holes through which the relentless wind blew. The showering sparks took on a hard edge, sharp enough to cut. Scarcely able to breathe, Julie pressed close against Ken, seeking refuge in his arms.

With a loud boom, a huge rocket burst into a gigantic ball of blood-red, a glittering chrysanthemum of fire. The sparks fanned out in a circular pattern and trailed down toward the people below, tracking red-tinged tails across the dark void overhead. And, superimposed over the sky, Julie saw the brick wall again. The red sparkles turned into blood, crimson snakes slithering down the cracked, time-aged bricks. Horror flooded her. She stiffened in Ken's arms and pressed her hands against her mouth to hold back the screams that welled from deep within. Eyes wide, she stared transfixed at the evil scene.

"Julie, what is it?" Ken's arm tightened on her shoulders. "What's wrong?"

"The wall," she managed to choke out. "Oh, no, I see blood. Blood!"

"Julie? What blood?"

"Oh, no. No!"

Before her terrified eyes a figure appeared, thrown against the wall with stunning force by someone or something out of her range of vision. Blond hair gleamed in the harsh light. Blood streamed from his nose and chin, streaked across the bricks where he hit them. He slid slowly down the wall, out of view. Another rocket exploded, sending more dribbles of blood cascading down the uneven brick surface.

"No, no," Julie whispered, pleaded. "Help him, please, someone help him!"

"Help who, Julie?" Ken's voice was frantic but Julie barely heard him, hardly felt his hands on her arms. "What's happening? What are you seeing?"

Again the man slammed against the wall. A deep gash now traversed his forehead. Blood spilled down into his eyes; droplets sprayed over the bricks. He could not raise his hands to defend himself. They were bound tight behind his back. His dark suit coat had torn down one arm. Dirt and blood smeared his white shirt. He stood a moment against the wall, his lips lifted in a mocking sneer, before his legs buckled and dropped him out of sight. The vision vanished. Only bursting cascades of colorful sparkles remained in the heavens.

Julie gasped for breath and covered her face with her hands, barely aware of Ken's presence beside her. Once more the thunderous explosions gouged at her, making her cringe. Ken hugged her tight and kissed her hair. She could not make herself look up as she listened to Ken's voice speaking around the on-going fireworks. She had no awareness of their meaning.

"Dave! Julie's sick. I'm going to take her home."

Ken's arms let go of her and she shuddered. She heard the rustle of papers, the creak of the picnic basket being opened.

"Don't bother with that. Leave it," Dave said. He sounded worried. "We'll pack it up and be right along. Go on, get her home."

Loud, sharp cracks sounded almost directly above them. Half a dozen brilliant flashes lit the night sky. They pierced through Julie's closed eyes. She screamed and grabbed for Ken. He lost his balance and fell sideways, pulling her down onto the blanket beside him. She lay shuddering, her fingers digging into his shoulders. Ken slid his arms around her, enveloping her in his warm, strong embrace.

"It's okay, Julie. It's okay," he soothed. "They're only fireworks, honey, they can't hurt you. It's okay."

She clung to him a moment longer before she opened her eyes. It took all her courage. She didn't know which she would see, Ken or the blood-smeared brick wall. To her relief, it was Ken.

"I'm sorry, Ken," she said, but he shook his head and laid a hand on her cheek, stopping her words.

"It doesn't matter, Julie. As long as you're okay, nothing else matters." A scream sounded somewhere in front of them, and Ken chuckled. "See? You're not the only one who's scared."

Julie gave him a tremulous smile, but a woman's hysterical voice turned it into a frown.

"Oh, my God! Charlie! Nadine! Help us, please! Charlie!"

Ken raised up on his elbows, turning his head to look at the area in front of their blanket. Julie peered over his shoulder. She could discern little in the darkness but humped shapes lying on the ground and darker shapes moving toward the woman's voice. The screams went on and people all around them began stirring and rising from their places, drawn by curiosity. In a moment, they were surrounded by a small crowd straining to see the cause of the disturbance. Feet trod on their blanket. Fireworks bloomed overhead to the throbbing beat of the Philharmonic.

"Come on, let's move before we get trampled," Ken said.

He sat up and quickly shoved the rest of the food into the basket. He helped Julie to her feet, pulled the blanket off the ground and wadded it beneath the basket's wooden handles. By the time he was finished, Dave and Bonnie stood packed up and ready to leave, also.

"You guys can stay," Ken said. "We don't want to spoil your time."

"Nah, we've seen enough," Dave said. "Besides, someone's hurt over there, probably a heart attack or something. We'll only be in the way if we stay here. We'd rather go with you and make sure Julie's all right."

"Thanks, Dave. Can you see all right now?" Ken asked, looking at Julie.

She nodded. Ken took her arm and steered her through the growing press of curious people to the street half a block away, trailed closely by Dave and Bonnie. Overhead, sparkling multi-colored blooms still spread out across the cloud-lined, music-filled sky.

"What happened back there, honey?" Ken asked when at last he seated her in the car and started the engine. He steered the car carefully down the close-packed streets. "What was all that about blood?"

Julie didn't want to talk about the vision. Too much had happened, it was all tumbling crazily in her head. She needed to think, needed time to make sense of what she had seen and what Ken had said. There were meanings there she could not quite grasp, realities just beyond her reach. But she could feel Ken's eyes on her as they waited for a signal light to change, and she knew she had to say something. She sighed and turned her head to look out the side window at the dark street.

"The red splotches I saw before on the bricks, they were blood," she told him. "I could see it clear this time, dripping down the wall."

"I see. And who needed the help?"

The car began to move, blurring the houses they passed. Julie could still hear the booming explosions far behind them.

"I don't know. A man. He had blond hair, and he was covered with blood. It was his blood on the wall."

"Julie," Ken began, but she shook her head.

"I don't want to talk about it, Ken. Not now. Please."

Again she felt his gaze, felt its probing curiosity. She was afraid he would push, certain that if he did she would lose control. She tossed in a sea of fear and confusion, clinging desperately to silence to hold her afloat. She feared she would drown if he took it away from her.

At last she heard him sigh.

"All right, Julie. We'll let it go, for tonight. But just for tonight, okay? I want to hear the whole story tomorrow."

"Yes," she agreed, numbness descending upon her like a smothering blanket. "Tomorrow."

Neither of them spoke for the rest of the drive home.

She went upstairs when they arrived home, leaving Ken to unpack the picnic hamper. But she didn't go into the room they now shared. She went to her old room, the spare bedroom. She needed solitude, space in which to breathe, to think. Darkness hugged her tight as she stood motionless in the unlit room with the door closed. She heard Dave and Bonnie arrive, but she didn't go down. She shed her clothes with slow deliberation, slipped on a nightgown, and lay beneath the sweet-smelling sheet. Down pillows cradled her head. She had never felt so alone before, not even when she had awakened in the field with no memory of who she was, where she was, or where she was from. But this was a good aloneness, comforting and soothing to her aching spirit. Dark shadows buoyed her as she floated to the accompaniment of the murmuring voices below. They were, she was sure, talking about her.

But she didn't worry about them. Their presence was insubstantial, meaningless in the welter of emotions that roiled inside her. She let the voices drift away and thought of what she had seen in the dark, cloud-covered sky. She examined every inch of it, gradually adding to her thoughts the dreadful nightmares that would not let her go and the fear that held her in thrall. She pulled them apart, spread the pieces out before her, shifted them around. A pattern began to emerge, glimmering in her dark prison, a pattern more terrifying than the uncertainty with which she'd been living.

She thought, too, of Ken. His face, his hands, his kisses, his definition of love. The refuge she had found in his home, and his arms. For long hours she thought, her eyes wide in the inky gloom, her heart tattooing in her chest. She went over and over it until at last it all made sense. A terrible, unbelievable, frightening sense, but sense nonetheless. It all fell into horrific place, piece by tiny piece.

CHAPTER SIXTEEN
July 5, 1990
Buffalo, New York

"Good lord, look at this," Ken said, unfolding the newspaper the carrier had left on the porch as he sank down beside her on the wicker couch.

"What?"

Julie knew her fear showed in her voice. She had spent the day mostly alone, keeping to her room to avoid talking about the night before. She knew it would have to come out soon, that it was past time already, yet she cringed inwardly at the very thought. It was a bridge that had to be crossed and she hated bridges, even if they were only symbolic.

"Here, this." Ken held up the paper and pointed to a large picture that spanned four column-widths on the front page. "Three people were shot last night at LaSalle Park during the fireworks display. It was a family, parents and two kids," he scanned the rows of print, "a boy of ten and a thirteen-year-old girl. They were sitting near the band shell in the north end of the park—" He broke off and looked up at her, his eyes wide. "That's right where we were. That's what all the screaming was about. We thought it was a heart attack or something, remember?"

Julie nodded but Ken didn't see. He had bent back to the paper and the gruesome story it held.

"Why would anyone do something like that?" she asked. "It's horrible."

"No one seems to know. There's some speculation it might be drug-related, and in the dark the shooter hit the wrong target." Ken folded the paper to an inside page. "Or maybe it was just some crazy lunatic who gets his kicks shooting into innocent crowds. They're not even sure where the shots came from." He sighed. "God, what a tragedy. The girl died almost instantly, it says, and the father is in critical condition with two bullets in his back. The mother was hit, too, in the side. She's in pretty rough shape. The boy didn't get a scratch." He set the paper aside and sat a moment, his gaze somewhere far away. "Man, that's scary. We were so close, right behind them. It could have been us. Or Dave and Bonnie. It's unbelievable something like that could happen. Go to a Fourth of July fireworks celebration and get shot to death. Damn. Nothing's safe, anymore."

Julie looked at Ken, studied his face in the soft evening sunlight. The clouds and cool breeze of the morning, which had actually felt cold after the oppressive heat of the day before, had vanished, leaving warmth and sunshine behind. The light picked out traces of gray in his brown hair, emphasized the lines radiating out from the corners of his eyes, revealed faint stubble covering his cheeks and chin. She could see the pulse beating in his neck, count the breaths that lifted his chest. Soft hair covered arms tanned golden from hours of playing ball in the sun.

She hated herself for what she had to do, for the pain she would cause each of them. But it would be nothing compared to what not speaking would do. She took a deep breath, then reached over and took his strong, square hand in hers. Ken turned to her and gave her a smile. His eyes still looked far away.

"Come into the house with me," she said softly, almost hoping he wouldn't hear. "There's something I need to tell you."

His smile faded. A slight frown creased his brow. She saw questions crowd his eyes. But he didn't speak. He sat very still a moment, his eyes locked on hers. Then he nodded. The time had come for his questions to be answered, and she knew he didn't want to hear the explanations any more than she wanted to speak them. Still, without another word, they rose together and went into the living room.

It seemed dark, after the brightness outside. Ken sat in the green lounge chair, his face half-hidden by shadow. Julie knelt on the floor in front of him, knowing her face, too, could be only half-seen. But it didn't matter. Words were enough. They didn't need to see each other, it would only make it harder to speak. The darkness wouldn't cover her words, they would ring clear no matter how softly she spoke.

"Julie," Ken said, but she shook her head, silencing him.

"Please, Ken, listen to me. Don't speak, just listen. Please."

He looked at her a long time, his lips compressed into a thin line. White tension spots flared at the corners. Finally, he nodded and sat back with a sigh. His gaze never left her face.

"I-I know I need help, Ken," she said, her voice faltering at first as she groped for words to express what filled her heart. "I've known that for a long time, ever since I woke up in that field. But I've been so afraid, terrified of some monstrous unknown that's been hovering over me like a dark cloud. It's kept me running, moving from place to place, not knowing why and scared to death to find out. That's why I never got any help. I was too afraid of it."

"I know."

He reached out and took her hand in his, imprisoned her icy fingers in warmth and safety. Julie wished she could simply crawl into his arms and stay there, forever. But life, she knew, would not let her. Other hands now tapped her shoulder, beckoned her on, and she could no longer resist the pull. She spoke on.

"But I can't run anymore. I can't hide forever. As much as I want to, I can't. The decision isn't mine to make anymore."

"Julie—"

"Please, Ken. Just listen. I've spent hours and hours thinking about it, trying to make sense of what's been happening." She looked down at their joined hands. Her voice shook. "And I have. I know what it means now, and what I have to do about it.

"I'm starting to remember things." She looked up at him again, into his shadowed eyes. "I think you know that, too. What's happening is not just dreams, or visions, they're memories, things that really happened. I don't know how jumbled or distorted they are, but I do know they're real. They happened." She closed her eyes, then opened them and took a deep breath. "And I'm afraid they mean I'm not a very nice person."

"Julie—"

"No, let me finish, Ken. Please."

She paused a moment and licked her lips. Ken sat stiff, leaning toward her. This was harder than she'd thought it would be, much harder. It was difficult to breath, and she could no longer look into Ken's eyes. Her hands and her voice both trembled. She wished it were over. She wished she'd never begun. She hated herself, who she was and who she'd been.

"You know that I saw the wall again last night," she said finally, and Ken nodded. "With blood dripping down it. A man's blood. A man with blond hair. He'd been beaten, was being beaten as I watched. It was horrible, seeing him slam into the bricks with his face all cut open. He couldn't fight back, his hands were tied behind him." She closed her eyes and bit her lower lip, gathering courage for her next words. When she opened her eyes she looked straight into Ken's and spoke in a rush. "I knew him, Ken. I don't remember how, or why, or even who he is, but when I saw his face I knew it. It was familiar, like seeing a photograph of someone I knew a long, long time ago. I knew that I knew him, and I think I had something to do with him being beaten like that. I don't know why but I think he was killed. And I was there. I was part of it."

"That's not true, Julie. God, how can you even say it?"

"Because it's true, Ken. It has to be. It's the only answer that makes any sense."

"No, it doesn't. It's ridiculous. I know you, Julie, you couldn't do something like that. I don't believe you could ever be involved with something so awful."

"No, I don't think I could," she agreed, pulling her hands from his. She stared into the distance, seeing not the kitchen archway but misty echoes of the life she'd lost. "Not the person I am now, at least. But I'm not talking about Julie, Ken." She looked back at him, her heart twisting at the anguish in his face. "Julie hasn't existed very long. She only came into being because of you. I was someone else before that, someone I can't remember, someone who hurt people, maybe even killed them. Listen to me!" she pleaded when Ken stubbornly shook his head. "I've gone over and over it. It's true, it has to be. Why else would I be so terrified of the police—unless they were looking for me for something I did? Something terrible, like helping to kill that man."

"I don't believe it," Ken whispered. "I won't."

"I don't want to, either, but I have no choice now. The memories are there, they're real, and they're getting clearer. I can't just ignore them. They won't let me."

Silence fell. Julie's words echoed into stillness, shimmered in the space between them. Ken sat very still, his head lowered. Julie died a little inside with every second that passed. She could see tears trembling on his lashes when at last he looked up. *How strange*, she thought. Just last night, when life felt safe and warm and wonderful, she had to fight to keep from crying. And today, when her whole beautiful world was falling apart, it was Ken who shed the tears, not she. She felt empty inside, barren and desiccated. She didn't think she'd ever cry again.

"What do you want to do?" Ken finally asked. His low, quiet voice reverberated in the dim stillness.

"I want to go away with you."

Ken's head lifted, his mouth agape, eyes wide. It was, obviously, the last thing he'd expected her to say. Julie smiled, grabbed his hands and tugged them, sliding him off the chair and onto the floor beside her.

"Just for a week. In a place where no one else goes, where we can be alone, just you and me. Somewhere we can spend a lifetime together. A week's worth of lifetime." She kissed him, her lips gentle on his. "I love you, Ken. I realized that last night, when you told me what love really is. I didn't understand what I was feeling, what was happening inside me. It scared me. But you made me see it so clear. I love you. You're my choice. *Julie's* choice," she clarified. "But Julie's dying, Ken. She's starting to slip away. The one I was before is coming back. Once she does, Julie won't exist anymore. Oh, maybe I can hold onto pieces of Julie, I don't know. I hope so. I think she'd help make the real me a better person. I just wish I could have more than mere pieces."

She sighed. "I know it's asking a lot, you've given me so much already, more than I ever knew existed. But while I still can, I want to be just Julie. The Julie you made, the Julie you created with your love. Just for a week, that's all. A week no one can take away from me when Julie's gone, no matter what happens."

She pulled her hands from his and turned away, wrapping her arms around her body. Her heart folded up, shriveled in horror at the risk she had taken. Even her breath stilled, lay inert within her lungs. She could barely hear her own voice speak the words she'd practiced, alone in her room through the long dark night.

"Then, when the week's over I'll go to the police and let them do what they have to do. I'll start paying for whatever it is I've done."

Ken didn't say anything. He remained silent for so long that Julie was sure she'd lost him. He didn't love her now that he knew what she really was. He couldn't separate what she'd been from who she was now. It had been stupid to expect that anyone could. She was on the verge of rising when she felt him stir at her side.

"Wait here," was all he said, laying a warm hand on her shoulder.

She turned her head, watched him cross to the stairs and disappear into the shadows at the top. Wait? For what? Had he left her, abandoned her to the darkness? She sat on the dark green carpeting, surrounded by an icy vacuum that blocked all sound, all sensation of movement, feeling isolated and infinitesimally small.

And then he re-appeared, descending the stair with slow steps. Had he come to free her, or to tighten the bondage? She rose, her heart quaking, unable to form words with her lips. He stopped at the bottom of the stairs and looked at her, locked his eyes on hers, probed deep into her soul with his gaze. The universe separated them, a frozen void she dared not cross. Eons crawled by in the few seconds before he opened his mouth to pronounce her doom.

"It's all set. I called Jason McGuire, his family has a small cabin down at Bear Lake, near the Pennsylvania border. Very primitive. No phone, no running water, no electricity. It's deep woods country, very few people around. Nearest neighbor is more than a quarter mile away. His brother's there now, but he's coming back on Saturday. Jason will drop the keys off on Sunday. The cabin will be vacant until the fifth of August, so we can stretch our one week to almost three." He smiled, flooding the frigid room with warmth. "Three weeks of lifetime, Julie. Just for us."

The bonds snapped. The dam burst. Joy welled like water in the arid desert of her being and rivered down her cheeks. In three strides Ken crossed the endless wasteland between them and gathered her into his arms. He kissed away her tears until her lips got in the way. Julie moaned and swayed against him, reveling in the heat of his body, the aura of strength that rolled from him in waves. His hands caressed her, sending shivers through her body as they ran up and down her arms. The kiss deepened, roughened. Hunger consumed them both. Ken's fingers deftly opened the buttons on her blouse.

He broke the kiss and Julie found herself gasping for breath. Her whole body tingled, cried out for more. She strained toward him, but Ken's hands held her away until her eyes finally focused on his. He cupped her cheeks in his palms and brushed her lips with his.

"Marry me, Julie," he whispered. "My sweet Julie. Here. Now, tonight. I'll call Dave and Bonnie, they can be our witnesses. Be mine, forever."

Marry him! Her heart leapt and she feared it might burst. He had understood! She hadn't lost anything, she had gained more than she had ever dreamed possible. She knew, they both knew, that forever meant only the next few weeks, that the marriage would have no legal validity. But it would be their forever, a time of endless peace and happiness nothing could ever destroy. It would sustain them in the dark times ahead, when Julie vanished and they walked their separate paths alone. Julie knew that, whatever horrors awaited her in the future, she could face them with courage and dignity, because once she had been capable of, and worthy of, God's greatest gift. Love.

"Yes," she sighed, barely able to see his beloved face through her tears. "Oh, yes. I'll marry you. Julie will marry you. We'll be together, forever."

CHAPTER SEVENTEEN
July 6, 1990
Buffalo, New York

Keel waited. Two days and nights he waited, until the small blue car finally drove away with both of them in it and the street was momentarily deserted. He walked quickly up the uneven concrete drive and paused next to the side door. No alarm system. His dark eyes gleamed with satisfaction. He turned his head and scanned the nearby houses, saw nothing, nobody. It felt as though the neighborhood approved, and cleared a path for him.

Swift strides took him into the small, narrow back yard where he inspected the rear of the house. Wide windows on the left offered a clear view of a sparsely furnished dining room and the living room beyond. On the right near the drive, three steps led up to a four-foot-wide rear porch. There a door opened into a tiny mud-room built off the kitchen. The doored portal between the rooms gaped wide. Keel could see cupboards, a stove, and the corner of a wood table through the opening. The lock on the porch door was ancient, easy to spring. It was the inner door that could have caused him problems, had it been shut, for that door sported both a new deadbolt lock and a sturdy slide bolt on the kitchen side of the frame. But unsuspecting, trusting hands had left that door open, just for him. In less than fifteen seconds, Bernard Maximilian Keel stood motionless in Ken Reed's kitchen.

For long moments Keel did not move. His dark gaze traveled around the cheerful yellow and green room as he methodically reviewed each step of his plan, searching for a flaw. He knew he would have to move fast, he had no idea how long his quarry would be gone, and he did not want haste to cause him to miss something, or lead to failure. The fiasco two days earlier still rankled, eating at him like acid through wood. The bitch would pay for moving, for sending his shots awry, for escaping into the darkness and the milling crowd. He'd felt like an amateur, no better than those who had hired him. His lip lifted in a sneer as he thought again of breaking down the weapon, descending the darkened steps and walking swiftly through the warren of streets, reveling in his triumph, unaware that the wail of police and ambulance sirens mocked him at every step. Not until he read the papers the next day did he discover his bullets had not reached their target. *I will be revenged,* he promised himself, pulling on a pair of thin, skin-tight gloves. *This time she will beg for death long before I bestow it.*

He walked with single-minded purpose through the ground floor, noting its appointments. He didn't touch anything. Then he ascended to the upper level. In the front bedroom, the place where they slept, he pulled a soft down pillow from its case. Into the dark blue make-shift bag he thrust the items of value he encountered as he systematically ransacked the room. Reed's jewelry. An antique pocket watch. The change from a tiny sterling silver bowl atop the dresser, along with the bowl. Two small ornate silver picture frames that stood on the night stand. He dumped out drawers, pulled clothes from the closet, tore apart the bedding, smashed cologne bottles against the wall, wishing they were Reed-the-teacher's face. When he was finished, it looked as though a hurricane had erupted in the room.

He left the bathroom a shambles, dropping prescription drugs into the bag and shattering everything else in the medicine cabinet. He used his knife on the shower curtain and drapes, just for the seer pleasure of it. The unfinished storage room received the same treatment—boxes opened, the contents scattered across the rafters. Christmas ornaments smashed, pages torn out of books. Aware of the time that passed, still he lingered longest in the back bedroom, fingering the Julie-woman's clothes, absorbing the feel and the smell of her. That room, too, he tore apart, smashing her perfume bottle and powder box, emptying the dresser drawers onto the floor, tossing her money and a black onyx bracelet into the bag. But her bed he left alone, for now. He'd need the bed when she returned.

He repeated his performance downstairs, trashing knick-knacks, ashtrays, vases, even lamps. Reed's sterling silver flatware and half a dozen plates and serving bowls went into the now-bulging bag. He slashed the seats of the dining room chairs just for fun, and smashed the contents of the kitchen cupboards onto the green and white tile floor. Then he set the bag near the front door and checked his watch. Forty-five minutes. Not bad, considering all he'd had to do. He moved away from the front door and positioned himself in the deep shadows cast by the half-open living room draperies. He could not be seen from outside the house, though he could clearly see the front steps and the street beyond.

Was everything in order? He took his equipment out of his pockets and checked each one. He didn't carry much; a thin garrote, a length of thick, strong cloth for a gag, his wide-bladed knife and a 9 mm Ruger. The fifteen-shot semi-automatic was merely a precautionary measure, for emergency use only. It did not figure in the plans Keel had for the Julie-woman. The knife, the garrote and his hands were all he'd need.

He went over what he'd done so far, made sure he'd forgotten nothing. Then, with his gaze sweeping the street outside, he settled himself to wait. When she came would she be alone, or would Reed-the-teacher be with her? He'd like the opportunity to end that bastard's life. Teachers had made his life miserable for years. It would give Keel great pleasure to watch the man die. It was why he'd brought the gun. But even if Reed didn't return with her, Keel knew he'd still get him. Whatever he did to the Julie-woman would hurt the teacher. Her death could very well destroy Reed. Keel's thin lips moved into an eerie semblance of a smile.

He looked again at his watch. An hour and fifteen minutes, now, since they'd left. His heart began to thud in anticipation. She might return at any moment, though it could still be hours before she walked into his trap. He didn't care. Either way, he was ready.

CHAPTER EIGHTEEN
July 6, 1990
Buffalo, New York

"Are you sure you don't want to come with me?" Ken asked, spooning rich fudge sauce into his mouth. "It'll only take an hour or so."

"What would I do there?"

"I don't know, read a book or something." He reached over and wiped a smear of ice cream and caramel sauce from Julie's cheek.

"Oh, right. On what level, first grade?"

"Well..." Ken said with a shrug, his lips lifting into a sheepish grin. Julie laughed.

"I can just see me, surrounded by a group of high school English teachers. Me, the reading whiz of the century. Can you imagine what that would do to your reputation? They'd probably fire you." She sighed, shook her head, and spoke around a mouthful of ice cream sundae. "Obviously, whatever happened in the past, English class was not high on my priority list. I want no part of it. You go to your department meeting. *I'll* go home and start getting ready for the deep woods. There aren't any books there." She looked up at him, gave him a mock wide-eyed innocent look. "Are there?"

Ken leaned across the red-stained wood and kissed her lips. "I love you, wife," he whispered. "Wife. My God, how I love the sound of that!" Smiling, Julie spooned more ice cream into her mouth.

The stand was crowded that Friday afternoon. A horde of kids and their drooping mothers stood in two long lines, the adults at least waiting patiently to obtain fleeting relief from the high temperatures. Heavy pre-weekend traffic on Kenmore added to the sweltering heat that half-melted the ice cream almost before customers turned away from the service windows. The few picnic tables set outside in the relentless sun were all occupied, and cars continuously turned into the dark, baking parking lot as others pulled out onto the street.

The humidity had been climbing all day. Now, the slightest movement filmed one's skin with sweat. Only children seemed unaffected by the enervating heat. They chattered and romped while waiting for their cold, sweet treats. Julie eyed them with envy, wishing she, too, was young and carefree and had her whole life ahead of her instead of only three weeks. She wanted to go back and do it all over. Or better still, go back and be Julie from the very first moment of life.

Ken spoke but Julie, lost in reverie, did not hear. When he laid his hand on hers the touch startled her, brought her back from a bittersweet distance. She looked into his eyes and read sorrow there, peeking from behind his smile. He'd guessed her thoughts, she knew, and she could see it pained him that he couldn't make her dreams come true. Feeling guilty for being so transparent, for hurting him yet again, she looked down into the sticky goo left in the bottom of her plastic bowl.

"Sorry," she whispered.

"See that nursery over there?" He pointed over his shoulder across Kenmore Avenue. Julie looked and nodded. "There used to be a field there, when I was just a kid. Before they built the gas station that became a body shop that became a nursery." He stopped and frowned. "Shit. Either things are changing awfully fast around here, or I'm getting old."

Julie laughed, because she knew that was what he wanted. "Maybe it's both."

"Bite your tongue," he said with a mock scowl. "I refuse to admit I'm aging. Anyway, someone in one of those houses there on Montrose dug up part of that field one year and planted corn. In the middle of the city. I watched it grow all summer, it was fantastic. It grew at least ten feet high—or maybe it just seemed that tall because I was so short. I was only eight or nine at the time. Anyway," he gave her a huge grin, "one night Frank Palmeri and I picked every damn ear. Left nothing but the stalks. Told our folks some farmer gave it to us because he couldn't sell it. I don't know if they believed us or not, but Mom cooked it for dinner the next day. I had one ear and could barely eat half of it, I felt so guilty, and I was sick all night with a stomachache from the little I did manage to get down. Couldn't eat corn for years after that."

He turned and looked over to where blacktop and large bins of topsoil, crushed stone, rolled sod and wood chips now stood where once corn had grown tall and proud.

"I wonder if whoever planted it knew who stole it. All that work, and they didn't get a single ear. They never planted it again, but if they had I sure as hell wouldn't have taken any. Though I did," he added, turning to her with eyes twinkling, "clean out someone else's bean patch the next summer."

"You're awful!" Julie exclaimed, not sure if she should believe his tale or not.

"Yep," Ken admitted with a cheerful grin. He glanced at his watch. "And I'm also going to be late if I don't get going. You want a ride home?"

"No, it's only two blocks. I'll walk. You go on."

"Two long blocks, so be careful. I won't be long. See you soon."

He handed her a set of house keys and kissed her good-bye. She watched him walk to the car, and waved when he pulled out onto University and turned left on Kenmore Avenue. When she looked away, her gaze caught on the neat, colorful grounds of the nursery, and she wondered what it must be like to remember being young, to know what had happened to you, the things you had seen and said and did. To know what made you who you were. But she wasn't sure she wanted to remember her connections to the past. Given what she'd already discovered about her real self, she doubted her memories were the kind she'd enjoy reminiscing over.

Rising, she gathered their empty bowls and used napkins and deposited them in a trash barrel as she walked away from the Dairy Queen. The heat radiated from the scorching sidewalk through the soles of her shoes as she walked. She loved the shoes because Ken had bought them for her, flat sandals made from woven strips of leather in multicolor pastels. The thin, hard leather soles squeaked faintly with each step she took. They were city shoes, of course. She probably wouldn't have much opportunity to wear them in the woods. And when she returned?

She took a deep breath and pushed the thought away. She didn't want to think of what would happen then, it would ruin the pleasure of the next three weeks. And she needed those weeks. It was the only way she could survive the future. She wouldn't let anything spoil them, or make them less than perfect.

She concentrated on her surroundings during the rest of the walk home, consciously cataloging every tree, bush, flower and bird, the people she passed, the cats and dogs sleeping on porches, the cars on the road. She wanted to be able to remember every moment, every song the birds sang, every horn that honked, every voice that spoke, the feel of the sun on her head and her arms. Life was so good, so full of vitality. She thanked God that she had this special time in which to fully experience and appreciate it. And especially that she would remember it.

She approached the house thinking about dinner. After those huge sundaes, it would have to be late or they wouldn't be able to eat it. Something light, maybe a salad or fish. It was not until she had climbed the front steps that she saw Ken's baseball bat lying on the wicker couch with his glove and ball.

He'd said he would put them away when he came in after the game. He'd played all morning with the neighborhood kids in the park while she'd watched from the porch, memorizing the way he moved and the sound of his voice. But she'd gone in before him and hadn't checked the porch again before they'd left for the Dairy Queen. Ken was lucky the things were still there.

Laughing softly, she cradled the mitt-wrapped ball in the crook of her left arm, and clutched the bat in her left hand. She jiggled the keys around with her free hand until at last she managed to slide the right one in the door lock. A quick twist and the lock snapped open. The door swung wide, letting the sharp afternoon light slant into the living room. Julie pulled the key from the slot and stepped into the house.

Someone grabbed her from behind. A hard arm caught her around the chest, pinning her left arm to her side. The baseball glove dropped near her feet. The ball bounced twice on the thick carpeting and rolled away into the alcove behind the door. The bat flew from her hand. Its grip end struck the floor. It tumbled once and came to a stop halfway to the stairs. The house keys hit the wall adjacent to the door, which slammed shut with a resounding crash.

Cruel fingers clamped onto her face, over her mouth, keeping her scream jammed into her throat. Her captor moved, forcing her further into the room, toward the stairs. She struggled, her heart pounding, kicking out with her feet as she was borne across the carpeting. She felt her shoes hit shin bones, but the hard arm and hurting fingers did not loosen. She clawed at the gloved hand covering her mouth to no avail, finally in sheer desperation reaching up behind her to where she could hear stertorous breathing. Over and over she struck, her fist pounding on his head, fingers yanking at his hair, until at last her nails raked down his face. He groaned, the sound a roaring growl in her ear, and let her go.

She stumbled forward and almost fell. Before she could get her feet steady beneath her he grabbed her right arm and swung her around. She glimpsed a narrow face, black hair and glowing dark eyes. Blood welled in the gouges down one cheek. A gloved hand smacked across her face, knocking her sideways. She stumbled again, but the cruel fingers on her arm kept her from falling. Then he hit her again, a savage backhand blow on her right cheekbone that yanked her from his grip and dropped her onto the carpeting.

Stunned, Julie lay gasping for breath, fighting to remain conscious. She had to move, to get away! Something hard lay under her, digging into her shoulder and she squirmed away from it. The hands seized her again, dragged her on her back across the rug. Julie kicked wildly, seeking escape. Her foot hit something solid. The man grunted and his fingers loosened. Julie rolled onto her side, pulling away from his hands. She clawed at the rug as she tried to put distance between them.

She couldn't. She had barely gained her hands and knees when he hit her again, knocking her flat. Then he turned her over, one hand holding her down.

He gripped a dark-handled knife in his other hand. He jabbed at her with the razor-sharp blade, his eyes narrowed and lips curled in a sneer.

"No! No, don't!" Julie pleaded, raising her hands to fend off the attack.

The blade tip sliced down her arm. Blood oozed across her skin, dripped onto the pale pink blouse she wore. He followed its track with the knife, slashing at her clothes, leaving neat slits in the fabric, slits that filled with dark red blood. Julie screamed, consumed with panic. Pain from the cuts gouged deep into the pit of her stomach. She twisted in his unyielding grip and hit at him with her fists but they made no impression, did nothing to stop the knife blade. She tried to grab his hand, to deflect the knife from her body. Her hands grew red from cuts on her palms. Her body convulsed and writhed until at last she broke free of his grasp. She rolled to the side, kicking out at him, forcing him to raise his hands to his face in defense.

Her arm hit something hard. It rolled slightly on the floor. Ken's bat. Julie closed her fingers around it as her attacker once again pulled her close. He yanked her onto her back and she swung the bat in an arc. It smashed it into his right shoulder. He swayed sideways. His left arm buckled and the knife dropped from his hand. Again Julie swung the bat, hitting him in the head this time. He dropped to the floor, his pained groan echoing in the entryway. Sobbing, Julie pushed away from him and crawled to the stairs.

On her hands and knees, still clutching the bat though she was unaware of it, she clawed her way up: three, four, five steps. A hand grabbed her leg and yanked her back down. The knife blade struck again, slicing into her calf, her thigh. She screamed and raised the bat, brought it down with all her strength, smashing at the knife and the hand that held the knife. Again and again she struck, at his head, his shoulders, his arms, until he lay in an unmoving heap at the bottom of the stairs.

Unable to move, the breath frozen in her lungs, Julie stared at the man, at the dark hair and clothing, at the carpeted stair runner spotted now with blood. She sat motionless on the steps, clutching the bat like a life buoy, her body shuddering with terror and pain. She felt numb, as though she had no real substance. She couldn't think, couldn't speak, couldn't look away from the crumpled form below. Long minutes ticked by, minutes of silence deepened by twittering birdsong and children's carefree voices outside the house.

And then he moved, a pained, groping, shifting of his head, his hand. The motion released her. Julie's scream drowned his low moan. She whirled and, choking on terror, half-stumbled, half-crawled up the steps into the hall. The bat dropped from her fingers to lay like a barrier across the top of the staircase.

She had to hide, couldn't let him get to her again. He would kill her, she knew he would. But where? Oh, God, where? She plunged into her old bedroom in the back and tripped over the clothing scattered on the floor, then scrambled across the room on her hands and knees, searching for refuge. There was nothing, no place to hide. At last she pulled the comforter off the bed and backed into the corner between the ransacked bureau and the wall. She gathered the thick fabric around her, pulled it over her like a shroud, and pressed her hands to her mouth to keep the fear from tumbling out. She sat in dark silence, wide-eyed, blood puddling beneath her, listening for sounds of her pursuer.

CHAPTER NINETEEN
July 6, 1990
Buffalo, New York

Ken pulled in the drive and sat still a moment, listening to the engine ping as it slowly cooled. It had been one hell of a meeting, designed not to make their teaching jobs any easier, but to raise tempers and blood pressures with new regulations and increased paperwork. His head had begun pounding not ten minutes into the session, and frustration still beat a painful tattoo inside his skull. Jeez Louise, didn't he have enough going on in his life without having to put up with more bureaucratic nonsense?

Sighing, he leaned back and let his mind wander among more pleasant topics, like Julie and the trip to Bear Lake, until at last the throbbing abated and he felt more like himself again. He hoped Julie didn't have dinner ready, he was still stuffed from that sundae. Not the best thing to eat at three o'clock in the afternoon, but what the hell? Somehow, ice cream always tasted better to him if he ate it when he shouldn't.

He stretched, sliding his hands along the felt-padded ceiling of the car, and flexed his shoulders to work out the tension that had settled there when Andy Klauk had passed out his wad of forms. Ken got out of the car and patted the trunk that held the unwelcome papers, and would until late August. He had no intention of even looking at them until he had no choice. The hell with state rules. This was supposed to be a vacation, not an excuse to do more work. He ran up the porch steps to the front door, mentally giving bureaucrats everywhere the finger.

Not until he opened the screen door did he see it. The inner door stood ajar, its pale beige paint smeared with rusty-red stains. What the hell? A premonitory shiver ran down Ken's spine. Julie would never have left the door open, not when she was alone in the house. He looked again at the splotches on the door and his heart skipped a beat. They looked like blood, dried blood. He began to tremble. Holding his breath, he cautiously pushed the stained door wide.

"Julie?"

Silence. Gritting his teeth, Ken stepped into the house.

The place was a shambles. Shocked, he stared at the debris that littered the living room, the slashed chairs overturned in the dining room archway, the bulging pillowcase on the floor near his feet. Straight ahead past the staircase, broken dishes glittered on the kitchen floor. He had to look twice, shaking his head and blinking hard, to assure himself he was not hallucinating.

"My God," he whispered, moving further away from the door.

His foot hit something. He looked down and saw one of Julie's shoes. It lay pale and helpless on the deep green carpet, its soft colors dribbled with dark red spots. Blood. Slowly, Ken stooped and picked it up. Horror overwhelmed him as his fingers closed around the stiff leather. Julie! Dear Lord, where was Julie?

"Julie! Julie!" he yelled, tearing through the downstairs rooms. All he found was destruction, and an open rear door.

He was close to tears by the time he started up the staircase. Fear hammered at him as his feet slowed on the steps. There were smears of blood on the banister railing, and on the wall to his right. Dark spots on the treads, leading up. What would he find on the second floor?

He saw the bat first, lying at the head of the steps. It was stained with blood at both ends. He stared at it for endless moments, wondering who had used it. Whose blood was on it? Julie's? His heart pounding, he stepped over the bat and looked down the hall.

"Julie? Julie, where are you?" He wondered if she could hear him. His voice was so low, so shaky, he could hardly hear it himself. But Ken couldn't force any more volume into it. "Julie? Answer me!"

Silence. Deep and impenetrable. Ken couldn't even hear noises from the world outside. Fear had blocked them completely.

He started with their room, horrified at the complete destruction he encountered. But Julie wasn't there, or in the bathroom or the storage room. His body had gone numb when at last he reached the back bedroom. A sense of doom gripped him tight. His fingers, clenched into fists since he'd picked up her shoe, would no longer open. His legs felt like wooden lumps. He knew what he would see.

He forced himself forward, into the room. He stood staring at the empty bed for what seemed forever before it penetrated that there was no lifeless, bloody body on it, no beaten, raped Julie anywhere on the floor. His breath sighed out with a rush, then caught in a pained gasp. If Julie wasn't in the house, where was she? Where?

He turned to leave, to find a phone to call the police, and saw her. She was on the floor, jammed in the corner beside the dresser, huddled into the bed's comforter. Her hands and face were bloody and her eyes were closed, but her body moved, shuddering uncontrollably. She was alive. Ken almost cried.

"Julie!" he whispered, his heart twisting with both rage and relief. Why had he let her come home alone? Why hadn't he been with her?

He crossed to her and knelt down, almost afraid to touch her. The right side of her face was swollen and bruised. There was blood in her hair, on her cheek. Gently, he put his hand on hers.

"Honey?"

She screamed.

Over and over she screamed, punching at him with bleeding fists. She twisted away from his hands, trying to burrow into the solid walls. Frantic himself, Ken tried to hold her before she hurt herself more, or hurt him, shouting at her to break through the hysteria.

"Julie! Stop, Julie, it's me! It's Ken! Julie, stop!"

Finally, he caught her hands and held them tight. She looked at him, her wide eyes wild, her breath huge gasps that tore at her lungs. Then she blinked and her eyes focused, actually saw him. She stared at him, her mouth gaping wide, as though she expected him to vanish at any moment.

Almost inaudible at first, slowly growing louder, a pained mewling sound issued from her throat. Tears welled up in her dry, shocked eyes and she folded into his arms, sobbing. Ken pulled her close and rocked her, his cheek resting on the top of her head.

"It's okay, Julie, I'm here, now. You're safe, honey. It's okay," he murmured over and over, keeping his arms tight around her until at last her tears slowed and she lay shivering in his grasp.

He didn't know what to do. He was sure he shouldn't move her, but he needed a phone and the closest one was in their room. He had to call an ambulance, and the police. But unless he moved Julie he would have to leave her here, alone, and that he wasn't about to do, not for a moment. Not even if Julie would let him, which he doubted, judging by the tightness with which she clutched him.

"Can you stand up, Julie?" he asked finally.

"I think so," she said. Her voice was so low he could barely hear it.

He pulled the coverlet away from her, wincing at the blood that stained her clothes. She was covered from head to foot. He helped her stand but her legs buckled beneath her when she tried to take a step. He swung her up into his arms and carried her into his room, laying her on the slashed mattress and covering her quaking body with a blanket he found on the floor.

It took a few minutes to find the phone in all the mess. The base lay in front of the nightstand beneath a pile of his shirts. The receiver was wedged between the nightstand and the wall. Amazingly, the cord was still attached and plugged into the outlet, though there was no dial tone. He set the receiver on the cradle and sat beside Julie, smoothing the matted hair away from her face. She was still shivering violently. Spots of blood slowly bloomed on the blanket covering her.

"How many were there, Julie?"

"Just one," she whispered. Her voice shook as badly as her body. "H-he grabbed me when I-I came in the door."

"I'm sorry, Julie," Ken said, his fingers tracing the darkening bruises on her face. Then tears rose to clog his throat, and he had to swallow hard before he could speak again. "I'm so, so sorry. It's all my fault. I shouldn't have let you come home alone. I should have been with you. I'm so sorry."

Julie shook her head and reached for his hand, folding it inside her bloody palms. She held it tight, as though to draw strength from his touch. Her eyes closed. Ken watched her a moment, shocked by the pallor of her face. Then he bent and kissed her forehead, and picked up the receiver once more.

This time there was a dial tone. Quickly, he punched 9-1-1 with his left index finger. After three rings, a woman's voice answered.

"Nine-one-one. Do you have an emergency?"

"Yes, I need an ambulance. My house was broken into and my wife was attacked. She's covered with blood, I don't know how badly she's hurt." Julie's fingers loosened on his and slid away. Ken laid his hand on her cheek, tried to rouse her, but she didn't respond. "Julie? Julie? Oh, God, she's not answering me!" he yelled into the phone. "I can't wake her up. Please, hurry. She needs help right now!"

CHAPTER TWENTY
July 7, 1990
Batavia, New York

With painstaking slowness, he inched his hand across the mattress. The dim lighting barely allowed him to make out the room with the one eye that wasn't covered with gauze. His entire body hurt, agonizing pain that ground into him without letup. All he wanted was to float away into darkness. But he refused to give in to it, refused to relinquish his consciousness. As long as he had that, he knew he was still alive. And as long as he remained alive, she would never escape. If it took the rest of his life, he would track her down and take her apart, inch by tiny inch. She would suffer horribly, excruciatingly, for endless eons. And then she would die.

Soft beeps sounded nearby, pieces of machinery that catalogued and analyzed his bodily functions. He concentrated on the sounds, counting them over and over, while his hand moved closer to its goal. It was the only part of him that could move, his left hand. That and his head, which he could turn to the left only a few inches before pain made the motion unbearable. But it was enough, all he needed to lift the receiver, focus on the telephone, and punch the proper buttons. He knew that because he'd done it four times already since they'd brought him to this room. They didn't know that, of course. He continued to let them believe he couldn't move, couldn't hear or talk, was beyond the pain. It was easier that way. They didn't befuddle him with narcotic drugs, and it eliminated annoying questions he wouldn't have answered anyway.

The phone hadn't answered either, those other times, but that hadn't bothered him. He hadn't expected anyone to be there, on the other end. After all, they weren't expecting a telephone call from him, they were expecting obituary notices in the mail. But he'd not be mailing anything, not for a while, not if what the doctors said was true. And judging by the pain he felt, the fragmented state of his awareness, he was more seriously injured than he'd ever been in his life. And by a slip of a girl, that little bitch. She had bested him. Him. Bernard Maximilian Keel.

Grunting in disgust, he turned his head to watch his hand move, the hand that should have snapped the Julie-woman's neck like a stick the moment she stepped through the door. But he'd decided to play with her first, tease her with his knife in retaliation for her escape in the park. And she escaped yet again, played him for a fool. Anger rose in his breast, hot and seething. The machine's beeps sped up, kept pace with his raging heart. From the corner of his eye, Keel saw a glowing green line quaver unsteadily. It would bring the nurses running, he knew from experience. With supreme effort he calmed himself, brought the line and the beeps back to their steady, un-alarming rate. He forced thoughts of the treacherous Julie-woman out of his mind and concentrated once more on moving his hand, reaching the phone, punching buttons.

"Yes?" The voice, curt and tense, answered on the fourth ring.

Keel wasn't prepared. It took him endless seconds to fill his lungs, open his mouth, force vocal cords to work. He was afraid his party would hang up.

"It's me," he said, the words issuing in a pained croak. The voice on the other end pounced before he could continue.

"What? Who?"

"Listen to me. There's been an...accident. There will be... a delay in fulfilling the contract."

"What do you mean, a delay? You promised quick action, that's why we hired you. We can't afford a delay!"

"It is not... of my choosing," Keel growled. A red-hot poker began to stab in his skull. "In a month —"

"A month? Are you crazy? We can't wait that long. There's too much at stake here. If you can't deliver sooner, we'll make other arrangements."

"With who? There is no one else who can do my work, and you know it!" Accelerating beeps echoed in the dimness. The green line spiked rapidly up and down. A red light began flashing on the machine, but Keel was too angry to pay attention. "We have a contract. You must honor it. You cannot hire someone else. I will not allow it!"

"I can and I will. Consider yourself fired."

The phone went dead in Keel's hand.

"No!" Keel choked on his rage. "She is mine! *Mine! I* will eliminate her!"

Agony burst in his head. His skull felt like it was shattering into pieces. The receiver slipped from his fingers and bounced off the mattress to clatter onto the floor. His left hand rose, clawed at his neck. He couldn't breathe, pain had closed his throat completely. His body arched on the bed as he fought for life, for breath. Alarm buzzers brought nurses running and frenzied calls for emergency crash carts.

The pain increased, consumed him until he had no body other than pain, no existence other than agony. It was like being transported back to childhood, where first his father and then his foster parents would beat him senseless and he was powerless to stop them. But he wasn't powerless, not anymore. No one had ever touched him again, not after he'd turned on that last one and then run away. He held the power, now.

So where was it? Where was his control? Why would the pain, the agony, not stop? Strangled choking sounds issued from his throat. A hole opened in the red-hot torture. Black and fathomless, it promised surcease, escape, oblivion. Eaten alive, he reached for the darkness, drew it protectively around him. The pain eased. His awareness drained away. The room came into focus for a split second, clear and sharp. And he knew he had failed, finally and for the last time. Then he faded into the darkness, leaving his uncovered eye sightless and staring.

* * *

Peter Mindari, the resident on night-call, rubbed sleep from his dark eyes as he raced down the corridor to join the senior staff doctor, Wilbert Michaelson. They worked over the patient for more than half an hour, but it was no use. No life signs registered on the monitors. Dr. Michaelson, his shoulders bowed with sorrow and weariness, signaled to Dr. Mindari to pull the pristine white sheet over the dead man's bandaged head. He himself closed the curtain around the bed.

"You did everything you could, Doctor," night nurse Amy Daniels said as they walked back to the nurses' station to enter the death on the chart. "With the amount of head injury he sustained, he was lucky he survived as long as he did."

Though she spoke to Dr. Michaelson, she glanced at Peter Mindari who walked beside them. Amy Daniels had been on Batavia Hospital's trauma floor for ten years. She'd seen her share of death. But it was new for Mindari. She knew he would take it hard. He was still young enough, and idealistic enough, to expect miracles.

"I suppose so," Michaelson said, "but it was for that very reason I hoped he would make it. He was certainly a fighter." He picked up the patient's chart, jotted notes on the procedures used, and noted the time of death. "The autopsy will confirm, but I'm sure what they'll find is a brain embolism. It was almost to be expected, the way his skull was fractured. Does anyone know who he is, yet?"

"I don't think so. The police are working on it. You know," she took the chart from Michaelson and slid it back into the rack, "I've seen a lot of accident victims over the years, but I've never seen one with injuries like these. I heard them talking when they brought him in. The car hit the guardrail on the left, but most of his injuries were to his right side, his back and the back of his head. His right hand was a mess, it looked almost like it had been crushed. If you ask me, I'd say he was beaten with a club of some kind, not injured in a car crash."

"Well, it's not our problem anymore. You'd better notify the police, let them know he's dead." Sighing, Michaelson walked away toward the doctor's lounge.

"I will. Good night, Doctor." Amy looked at Peter Mindari, who had stood quietly listening. "It's barely midnight. Are you going back to sleep?"

"No, I think maybe I'll take a walk down to the chapel. I don't know why, but somehow I get the feeling our nameless patient could use a few prayers."

He walked slowly away, and Amy Daniels smiled at his broad back. The trauma unit was tough on residents, a harsh education in reality. Some of them didn't make it. But Peter Mindari would, she was sure. Someday, he'd be one hell of a doctor.

CHAPTER TWENTY-ONE
July 12, 1990
Bear Lake, New York

"Are you sure you're all right, honey?" Ken asked.

Julie smiled from her reclining position in the stern of the boat. She didn't open her eyes. "I'm fine, Ken. A little sore still, that's all."

"I can't believe I let you talk me into this. The last place you should be in your condition is in a primitive cabin in the woods halfway to nowhere!"

"It didn't take much talking that I recall. Three or four words, at most."

"You took advantage of me. I was distraught."

Julie laughed. When she opened her eyes and started to sit up, Ken dropped the oars and reached for her.

"Let me help you."

"Don't be ridiculous. I'm perfectly capable of sitting up."

"You were half dead just six days ago! The way you were cut up—"

"Minor cuts, Ken. The doctor didn't even bandage most of them."

"What about the one on your thigh? He had to stitch up that one."

"Eleven stitches. Big deal. It doesn't make me an invalid, Ken, or half-dead. Quit worrying, will you? I've survived worse, believe me."

Ken reached out and laid a gentle hand against her bruised cheek.

"I can't help it," he said softly. "When I saw you like that, covered with blood... It was the worst thing that's ever happened to me. I was so afraid I was going to lose you."

Julie turned her face, kissed his palm. "You won't. Not for a few weeks, at least."

They looked at each other, lost in painful thought. The boat drifted slowly on the mirror-surface of the small lake, caressed by golden sunshine. Birdsong echoed in the stillness. Pine trees scented the air with pitch, made even more pungent by heat and humidity. They were all alone, the only two people in sight. It was their own private paradise. After a moment, Ken grinned.

"You've got one hell of a shiner. Does your eye still hurt?"

"No. Not anymore," she said softly, then smiled in return. "But everything else does."

Ken turned and scanned the shore. Far in the distance he could just make out their rickety dock. "We'd better head back before we get lost." He bent to the oars, straining to make the boat move in the direction he wanted. "Damn! I thought this was supposed to be a vacation. I haven't worked this hard in years."

Julie laughed and leaned back again, closing her eyes. Comforted by the warm sun above, she let her thoughts drift back to the days following the attack.

Her injuries were more painful than serious, but shock combined with loss of blood prompted her doctors to deny the police immediate access to her. She'd refused to remain in the hospital overnight, terrified to be out of Ken's sight and his protective arms. Bandaged, her thigh stitched, dosed with pain-killers and sedatives, they sent her home just after midnight, where she fell asleep in her own bed with Ken's hand tight in hers.

She had awakened and just finished breakfast in bed the next morning when two detectives arrived. She'd been terrified to see them, sure they would recognize her and take her away. But Ken had reassured her, promising they only wanted to talk about the attack. They had no reason to suspect she was anything other than Ken's wife, who had come home alone and surprised a burglar. Still reluctant, she had finally agreed to the interview and had gone downstairs to meet them.

They both were big men, one dark haired and olive complected, with strong, handsome features and large hands and feet. He wore a cream-colored summer suit, and already looked too warm for the day though it was barely mid-morning. He introduced himself as Ed Maher. The other man, called Steve Olkowski, had fair skin burnt red by the sun and sandy hair threaded with gray. Though tall like his partner he looked smaller, his body lean and narrow, his hands small and delicate, his face a thin oblong with high cheekbones and a jutting nose. His dress was more appropriate for the heat, tan slacks and a light green polo shirt.

Though completely different in looks and build, they were alike in one way. Both wore an unmistakable air of authority. They were men used to getting their own way. Julie felt herself shrink beneath their alert gaze. She couldn't stop her hands from trembling, and kept her eyes averted. She found it impossible to look either of them in the eye.

Ken kept an arm around her as she made her way across the living room. The detectives apologized for disturbing her, but she barely heard their words. Ken placed her on the couch and sat beside her, offering the detectives the chairs opposite them. Jason McGuire, who had dropped in half an hour earlier to drop off the cabin keys and still looked shell-shocked by what he'd found, sat beside Ken on the couch. Julie took Ken's hand in hers and held it as tight as she could with her bandaged hands while the policemen took her through the events of the day before, step by painful step. When asked what her assailant looked like, there was little Julie could say.

"I don't know, it happened so fast. I barely saw him before he hit me." She raised her hand to her right cheek but didn't touch the distended bruise. Her eye was swollen half-shut. "I remember dark hair and dark eyes. I don't think he was very big or tall, but he was strong. Very strong."

"What about his voice?" Maher, the dark-haired detective, asked. "Do you remember anything distinctive about his voice?"

Julie shook her head, her wide gray eyes focused back in time. Ken's hand tightened on hers. "He didn't say anything. He just hit me, then pulled the knife."

"His hands," Steve Olkowski put in. "Was there anything unusual about his hands, or his arms? Scars, marks, tattoos?"

Again, Julie shook her head. "He had gloves on. I didn't see his hands. Or his arms."

"And when he pulled the knife, you hit him with the baseball bat?" It was the dark-haired one again, Ed Maher.

"I'd brought it in with me, Ken had left it out on the porch. He kept jabbing at me, cutting me—it was right there on the floor, I didn't even know I'd picked it up until after I hit him and he fell over. I tried to get away but he came after me, to the stairs. I hit him again, over and over, until he didn't move anymore."

She could barely breathe. Her body shuddered. The memories suffocated her, sucked her back into a vortex of terror. Ken put his arm around her and held her close.

"That's enough, please," he said, shaking his head at the two detectives.

"We're almost done, Mr. Reed," Ed Maher said. "Mrs. Reed, I know how hard it is for you to go over this, but it's necessary." Julie nodded, but she didn't look at the men. She remained huddled in Ken's arms. Ed Maher spoke on. "Is that when you went upstairs, Mrs. Reed? After he stopped moving?"

"No. I sat there, looking at him, I didn't know what to do. I couldn't think, couldn't make myself move. Then he moved and I panicked. I ran upstairs and tried to hide, I just wanted to hide. The next thing I remember is Ken holding me."

There hadn't been much more after that. They'd returned again on Sunday afternoon to see if she had remembered anything more, but she hadn't. It was then that Ken told them they would be leaving for Bear Lake on Wednesday for a delayed honeymoon. Ken had been reluctant at first to consider going at all, but Julie had pleaded. It was all planned, Jason had given them the keys, how could they let a burglary spoil it? Ken's stare had lingered on her half-closed eye, the gauze on her hands, the scabbing cuts on her arms and abdomen, the stitches in her thigh.

"Please, Ken. I have the rest of my life to get over these cuts, but we only have the next three weeks together. I don't want lose any of that time, not even one day. It has to last me the rest of my life."

And he agreed, though he'd insisted she take two days to rest at home. And so they had left on Wednesday instead of on Monday, to find a two-story rustic cabin beside a still lake, a wood-burning stove on which to cook, a spider-ridden outhouse, an old-fashioned well and a rickety thirty-foot dock with an ancient wooden rowboat beached on shore. No neighbors anywhere in sight. It was absolutely perfect. Julie never wanted to leave.

The boat bumped the dock, startling her. She'd daydreamed the entire way back. Ken tied the bow to a piling and helped her up onto the dock. They walked together down the length of the old wooden planks with their arms wrapped around each other. The cabin sat fifty feet from the shore. It had one large room downstairs and three small bedrooms up under the eaves, with a wide, open porch facing the lake. When they reached the front door, Ken stopped and turned to Julie.

"What?" she asked.

"I want to carry you over the threshold," he said, swinging her into his arms. She laughed.

"You're crazy. You've already done that twice. Are you going to carry me every time we go in?"

"Yep."

He pulled open the screen door and stepped into the dim interior. Julie knew that whenever she entered a room from now on, it would be with the feel of Ken's arms around her, carrying her. His bride. Even if it was a prison cell she entered.

"I love you," she whispered. Ken kissed her, then laughed.

"Remember the look on Jason's face when those cops called you 'Mrs. Reed'? God, I thought he'd explode."

"You have to give him credit, he hid the shock very well. I don't think he quite liked it, though, when you explained it to him after they left."

"Jason's just jealous, because you're mine and not his."

"No, he's not. I don't think he likes me, Ken. Or maybe it's just the whole situation," she added when Ken started to protest. "And now that he knows... He won't tell anyone, will he? He won't take our time away from us?"

"Of course he won't. We can trust Jason. I wouldn't have told him if I wasn't sure we could."

Ken set her down, but kept his arms tight around her. He laid his cheek against hers, her left cheek, the one without the bruise. Julie curled her arms beneath his and clutched his shoulders with stiff, sore fingers.

"I love the feel of you," Ken whispered in her ear. "I love your weight in my arms, the smell of your hair, the taste of your lips. I love the way you laugh, and the way you look at me when you think I'm not looking. I'm glad we're here, Julie. You're right. This is our forever, yours and mine. I can't believe how much I love you!"

He kissed her again and swung her once more into his arms. Julie laced her fingers into his hair as he carried her up the stairs to the bedroom. She hoped the dreams would not return again tonight. She wanted just one undisturbed night in Ken's arms to remember. Three weeks of love, and one undisturbed night. An endless forever, that, though she didn't know it, would end in just over a week.

CHAPTER TWENTY-TWO
July 14, 1990
Harrisburg, Pennsylvania

"Isn't this rather sudden?" Judy Wilkes asked, watching her husband pack a duffle bag.

"In my line of work, I can't always plan ahead. You know that, Judy."

"Yes, but ..."

"But what?" he snapped, his voice rising. "Just because I'm behind a desk most of the time doesn't mean my job is easy. I deal with scum all day, Judy. Scum! Don't you think I have the right to relax, to go off on my own, to get away from robbers and arsonists and murderers for a few days?"

"Don't shout at me, Ogden. Please."

"I'm not shouting!" he yelled, yanking the zipper closed. He picked up the bag then stomped out of the bedroom and down the stairs.

Judy followed him and sighed, unsure why she was so uneasy about her husband's sudden vacation. It wasn't just that he had never before gone away without her and the girls, not since the day they'd married. Or that with the wedding just two months off there was so much to do here at home, so many decisions to be made. She really didn't resent that he wanted, or needed, to be alone for a few days. She didn't think she was as petty as that.

No, it was more because he was not going off on his own. He was going with Bill Traynor and Joe Sillitto, who were not her favorite people. Especially Joe, who reminded her of a snake. He had a lean, compact body and two of the cruelest blue eyes she had ever seen. They sent shudders through her whenever he looked at her. In her opinion, he belonged in late-night gangster movies, not on the police force.

And Bill Traynor wasn't much better. He was too watchful and intense. His golden-brown eyes saw everything, analyzed and categorized it, and filed it away for future reference. She always felt like a lab specimen around him. But at least he looked like a cop, broad and solid and authoritative, and not like a snake. And he knew how to smile and laugh. Joe Sillitto only knew how to smirk.

Wilkes was in his study by the time Judy descended the stairs. He had closed the door, but the fitful breeze blowing through the hall had pushed it ajar. She put her hand on the wood to open it further, to apologize for her moodiness, but stopped when she saw what he was doing.

He stood behind the desk, a gun in his hand. It was big, hefty-looking, the thick barrel at least eight inches long. Another, smaller and trimmer, lay on the blotter pad. Two boxes of ammunition sat nearby, one open. As she watched, Wilkes pulled out the magazine of the gun he held and began loading it, his slim fingers flexing with neat, precise movements. Judy could hear the sharp clicks of the bullets sliding home. Musuko, beside his master as usual, uttered his high-pitched 'hurry up' whine. His front paws danced on the soft carpeting.

"In a few minutes, boy," Wilkes said, snapping the clip in its channel and chambering a round, "we'll be on our way. I said from the start this was something we'd have to handle ourselves, didn't I? And we will, you and I." He picked up the smaller gun, pulled out its magazine, and opened the second box of ammunition. "No more screw-ups. We'll put an end to this once and for all."

He began loading the second gun. Judy's breath caught in her throat. Dark shudders rippled down her spine, and she knew she was right to feel afraid. She didn't know why, didn't want to know why, but she was sure that somehow this trip would be a turning point in their lives.

Wilkes found her in the living room a few minutes later. Though she tried, she couldn't keep from looking at the duffel bag, which now held the two loaded handguns and probably the boxes of ammunition as well. *Strange things to take on a fishing trip,* she thought. *What is he going to do, shoot the fish if they don't cooperate and bite the hook?* She almost asked him, almost opened her mouth to speak the words, but a horn sounded outside and broke the tension.

"Well, that's Joe," Wilkes said. "I'd better get out there. Are you going to give me a kiss good-bye, or are you too angry that it's men only?"

He smiled at her, his I'm-sorry-I'm-such-a-bad-boy grin, and she had to laugh. Despite her fears and misgivings she could not resist the impish expression on his face. She never could. Rising, she gave him a kiss and hug, holding him tight for a moment. His arms slid around her, the strong, comfortable arms that had kept her safe all these years, the arms she so trusted. She wished he would never let her go.

"Stay home," she whispered. "Please."

"It's only for a few days, Judy. A week at most. What's the matter?" He loosened his arms, held her away from him. "Are you afraid to be alone in the house?"

"No." Judy looked away, not wanting her eyes to betray what she'd seen. She tried to laugh but only half-succeeded. "Don't be silly. I just—Ogden, why fishing? You haven't been fishing in years and you never liked it the few times you did go. You don't even have any equipment."

"Joe says I can rent whatever I need when we get there." He shrugged. "But I may not bother. This is really just an excuse to get away and relax for a few days. I took a couple of books from the study, the ones Lyndsay gave me for Father's Day. I haven't found time to read them yet. I'll probably spend more time with them than drowning worms on the lake with Joe and Bill."

The horn tooted again and Wilkes picked up his duffel. Judy went with him down the front walk. Musuko, tail curled high over his back, pranced down the bricks to the waiting car. Joe Sillitto, sitting behind the wheel, turned his head to watch their good-bye.

"It'll probably take us two or three days to get there. And there's no phone in the cabin," Wilkes said. "I left the number of the general store on the dresser. If you need to, you can leave a message there. With no electricity, we'll have to go into town every couple of days for food and I can pick up messages then. Take care of yourself, sweetheart, and the girls. I'll be back by the twenty-first at the latest."

He kissed her, then strode to the car and opened the back door. Musuko leapt in with an excited bark. Wilkes tossed his duffel after the dog, then climbed in himself.

"I love you, Judy," he called out the open window.

"Have fun, Ogden," Judy said, shaking her head and forcing a smile. "Don't eat too much fish. Good morning, Joe. Drive carefully, will you?"

"Oh, I will. I always do."

Joe smirked at her, his blue eyes narrowed. Judy had the uncanny feeling he could see through her clothing. She crossed her arms over her breasts. After a moment, Joe shifted his gaze to the rear-view mirror.

"Got everything, sir?"

"I believe so." Wilkes laid a hand on his duffel. "Everything but Bill."

"Right."

The car pulled away and Judy waved, her forced smile dying as she lost sight of her husband's face. She stood watching until the car turned out of sight, her heartbeat slow and ponderous. Something was wrong, she knew it was. Ogden had been acting strange all summer, tense, testy and introspective. There had been secretive phone calls and mysterious meetings to which he'd taken Musuko. And now this so-called last-minute 'fishing trip.' It wasn't right.

He wouldn't socialize with his men, not this way. It wasn't appropriate for an assistant police commissioner, and Ogden was, if nothing else, always appropriate. Something was going on. Something dangerous. He'd lied to her. Or rather, as he would say, he'd spared her the unnecessary details. She knew what it had to be. He was involved in an undercover operation, something really big. It would have to be, to take him out from behind his desk. Or maybe not. Maybe he just missed the danger and excitement of the streets.

It would be just like him, she thought, turning and walking back into the house, *to jump at an assignment like this rather than send one of his men to do it*. He really wasn't much of a desk man, her warrior policeman husband. She closed and locked the front door, then walked into his study. The desk was locked, she couldn't open the bottom drawer. It was from there, she knew, he had taken the guns. She wondered if there were any more in there. After a moment she turned and looked at the bookshelves. There were no spaces. Not one book was missing. The volumes Lyndsay had given him still sat there on the shelf.

A dead calm filled her, spread like a blanket over her body and soul. She felt as though she was encased in a vacuum, a soundless void nothing could penetrate. There was no panic, no unraveling of her nerves. She wasn't even afraid. She wouldn't lie awake at night wondering if he was all right, worrying about the risks he took. No, this time she knew. She was certain. He would not come home to her. He had dared the odds one time too many. She would never see Ogden Wilkes alive again.

CHAPTER TWENTY-THREE
July 15, 1990
Bear Lake, New York

Blood. Bright and fresh, it stained the pale bricks, shone like liquid fire in the harsh, flattening light. Darkness haloed the scene, an ebony aura of evil that isolated the players from life, from sanity. The light did not waver.

Someone grunted, a pained, agonized groan that echoed on and on, ricocheting from the darkness. A battered form rebounded from the bricks, fell from sight. More blood smeared the wall. She watched it crawl slowly down the rough surface, beaded runlets channeling along the minuscule chasms pocking the clay. Shadowy shapes blocked her view, two misty cardboard figures that bent and hauled the first upright once again, held him in the light.

Unlike them, he was solid, three-dimensional. He knelt in brilliant color: torn dark gray suit coat; dirty, blood-spattered white shirt; matted blond hair; anguished blue eyes. Eyes that squinted against the light, half-blinded by the uncompromising brilliance and the blood seeping down his face. Eyes that looked to his left, their expression echoed in the disdain that lifted his thin lips into a sneer.

Light glinted on shiny metal as a gun rose slowly into view, clasped tight in a rock-steady hand, a hand small and neat. It pointed directly at the man's head. She could see every detail of the gun: the silver barrel only three inches long; a small triangular sight that caught the gleaming brilliance and sent it careening into the darkness; the tiny fluted cylinder with brass-encased bullets peeking from narrow chambers. It was hard, that gun. Hard and cold and deadly, the carved wooden grips pressing with pinpoints of pressure into her flesh. She could feel the hardness, feel the cold permeate her bones, feel infinitesimal pricks against her palm. It was her *hand?* She *was holding the gun? Oh, no! Oh, please, please, no!*

The man's eyes shifted and he looked at the open end of the gun's barrel held mere inches from his face. Fear flashed in his blue eyes but he visibly swallowed the terror and straightened his spine, turning his head to his right. His eyes met hers across the gun-measured space and she gasped, the sound absorbed by the sponge-dark night. The gun did not waver. The man's eyes widened, twin blue pools set in a bloody ground. He moved his head in a gesture of negation, took a breath—his last—and opened his mouth.

To scream? To plead for mercy? She did not know, would never know. Her heart lurched, her hand tightened.

Her fingers curled, squeezed against the cold, hard ache of the metal. The gun fired, point-blank into his head. A flash in the darkness, ricocheting away from the flat, brilliant light. The bullet drilled a small hole through the man's left eyebrow. Blood, bone and brains sprayed the bricks. He jerked sideways, almost lifted from his knees before he fell. His eyes, still open when he hit the cobbled ground, stared glassy and unseeing at her feet. Her feet. Her numb, unable to move feet, pinned by his gaze, by the sticky redness snaking slowly across the cobbles. He would never again close them, those intense, accusing blue eyes. They would stare at her forever. A small puff of smoke wafted from the barrel of the tiny gun.

Panic engulfed her. Her hand moved, released the gun. It fell away out of sight and she turned, seeking the darkness, desperate for its annihilating touch. Ebony blackness reached out, caressed her face, her body. Behind her, misty shadows moved, merged into the inky web and cast sticky tendrils in her direction. Voices growled. Sharp clicks pinged on the cobbles. The darkness bent closer, began to smother her. She couldn't move, couldn't breathe. Frantic, she battered her fists against the all-too-solid, imprisoning night. Pain bit at her, stabbed through her legs, up into her body like red-hot daggers. She screamed, and the darkness exploded.

Her eyes flew open and she sat bolt upright, sweat streaming from her body. The images of the dream danced in the darkness, tormenting her. Ken rolled over, pushed up to an elbow.

"Julie? What is it? What's wrong?"

He reached out for her but she pushed his hand away.

"No!" she gasped. "Don't touch me. Oh, God. Don't touch me!"

She shoved the covers aside and slid from the bed, stumbling on the rough-hewn floor. Groping through darkness seeming as solid as that in her dream, she made her way out of the bedroom and down the stairs. Behind her, she heard the bedsprings creak as Ken got up to follow her.

She fled toward the cabin's front door as though he were the dream pursuing her. Darkness threatened to smother her. She could not clear the horrible images of death from her head. She stumbled into night-shrouded furniture, cracking her shins and falling twice, seeking the freedom of the outdoors. Something fell onto its side with a tinkling crash. Ken's voice called her name. A light flared behind her, but she didn't—couldn't—stop. She wrenched open the door and ran across the porch onto the pine needle-strewn path beneath the trees.

A half-moon rode just above the treetops. Light glimmered down from a sky crowded with stars. A gentle breeze slowly shredded the clinging mists of terror, leaving behind a desolate emptiness that ached unbearably. Julie walked on trembling legs down to the dock and stood staring at the calm, moon-sheened water. She willed her mind blank, refused to acknowledge anything, not the dream-memory, the sound of Ken's feet on the dock behind her, water slapping gently against the moored boat whose oarlocks gleamed in the moonlight, nor the soughing of wind in the trees. If she could stand still long enough, not think for the rest of her life, she would be safe. The past could not touch her, nor the future destroy her. If only she could stay still, and not think.

"Julie?" Ken's fingers touched her, butterfly-soft on her shoulder. "Honey, what's happened?"

His voice broke the silence. His hand shattered the stillness. The past and the future engulfed her. Keening in agony, Julie wrapped her arms around her body and sank down on the wooden planks. Ken sat and pulled her into his arms, holding her close while she sobbed. There were no other sounds on the lake, and no other light save the one Ken had lit in the living room.

At last the tears dried. Julie lay in Ken's arms, but derived no comfort from his nearness. She deserved no comfort. Her mind was no longer blank. The scenes from her scattered memories played over and over, though they no longer had the power to hurt her. She knew the worst, now. She was a murderess. She had no right to any future at all, not even the few weeks left with Ken.

"Another dream?" Ken asked, smoothing her damp hair away from her face.

Julie nodded, then took a deep breath and pushed away from him. His face was wreathed in shadows, as was hers, no doubt. She could make out his eyes, see the curve of his cheek, but that was all. She wondered idly how much of her he could see.

"I killed him," she said, her voice barely audible.

"What?"

"I shot him. I looked right at him, looked right in his eyes, and then I shot him. In the head. Like he didn't matter, like he was nothing. An animal, or a target. I just looked at him and shot him."

"The one who was getting beaten? The blond man?"

Julie nodded, not caring if Ken could see or not. Pain twisted in her heart and she gasped, folding double. Ken caught her, held her shoulders.

"I don't want to go back to being her," she whispered. She looked up, wishing now that she could see his face, read his expression. "I don't want to be somebody like that."

"You're not. You won't ever be. I don't care what you think you remember, Julie. That's not what you are. The memories are wrong, they're all jumbled up. You never killed anyone." He shook her slightly. "Do you hear me? You never did!"

"I wish I could believe that."

"You can. I do."

Julie shook her head and looked out over the lake. The breeze stirred tiny ripples here and there, fracturing the reflection of the night sky. Pines swayed in an arrhythmic dance at the water's edge. Julie shivered in the damp air as she slid to the side of the dock and wrapped her arms around a piling, letting her feet dangle in the cool water. Her toes made soft splashing sounds.

"I love it here. It's so beautiful. So peaceful."

"Then why don't we stay?" Ken asked, moving beside her. "We don't have to go back, Julie. You don't have to go to the police. I could get a job in Alma, or York Corners. It doesn't matter what, we wouldn't need much. Maybe we could even get a place here on the lake. We'd be together, you and I, and you could forget those damn dreams, just ignore them. They don't matter, not out here."

"Yes, they do."

"No, they don't. Not if we don't let them. Damn it, Julie, who'd know?"

"You would. And so would I. I don't want to live a lie, Ken. How long do you think all this would last if it was built on a lie?" Julie looked at him, then swept her gaze across the lake. "I killed a man, Ken. What would stop me from doing it again, from maybe killing you?"

"I'll take my chances. I'd rather die at your hands than live without you." Julie shook her head again. Ken leaned over and kissed her lips. She could feel his passion and desire. "Just think about it, Julie. Think about what we'll lose if we go back. The dreams are wrong, you know they are. And even if they're not, you're not that woman anymore. No matter how much you remember. You're Julie, now. Is it really fair to destroy her life because of what someone else did?"

"It's not that simple, Ken."

"Yes, it is. If you want it to be, it is. It's up to you, Julie. Think about it. It doesn't have to be difficult. We don't have to lose everything. You have a right to live. And I have the right to love you. Come back to bed, sweetheart."

"Not yet. You go. I need to be alone, just for a while," she said, forestalling his protest. "Please, Ken. I'll be in soon, I promise."

He stared at her a long moment, then rose and walked down the dock to shore, his barely-clad body glimmering in the starlight. He didn't look back. Julie watched until he disappeared into the cabin, his words echoing in her head. She wanted to believe him, wished she could believe him. But he hadn't seen the dream-memories, hadn't experienced the visions. He hadn't felt the cold steel of a gun in his hand, seen the bullet pierce a man's skull. Maybe he'd feel differently if he had.

Or maybe not. He was right, she was no longer that other woman. Perhaps she'd never really be her again, not entirely, not even if the memories returned in full. For Julie was real. She was as much a part of her now as that other woman. And Julie had as much right to live as the other one had the duty to pay for her crime. But it wasn't simple, Ken was wrong about that. No matter what she decided, it would be unfair. If she went back, Julie would suffer for something she didn't do. And if she stayed, the nameless one would get away with murder. Either way, she would lose. And so would Ken, whether he was willing to admit it or not.

The moon had disappeared when at last she rose and followed Ken. Her head ached, her thoughts more jumbled and confused than they'd ever been. She didn't know how to decide, couldn't tell anymore what was right and what was wrong. She hurt from thinking about it.

He'd left the oil lamp burning for her. She blew it out and slowly mounted the steps, unsure of what to say to Ken. But he was asleep, his face bathed in moonlight, one hand flung out across her pillow as though reaching for her. Smiling, she curled down onto the mattress and snuggled into his arms. They folded around her, though Ken did not wake. Julie lay with her head on his chest, listening to the beat of his heart. As she slipped into sleep, she decided at last that she would not think about her dilemma. She would live through these last two weeks one day at a time, savoring each moment. She knew, somehow, that the decision would make itself when the time was right. Until then, she had Ken's love to keep her warm, and safe.

CHAPTER TWENTY-FOUR
July 16-17, 1990
Bear Lake, New York

Ken hung up the phone, his face creased into a frown. Though he'd kept the door propped open, it was hot in the small glass-encased booth. Sweat beaded on his brow, snaked slowly down his cheeks, ringed his shirt beneath his armpits. With a sigh he slid the quarter from the return slot and stepped out into the open air.

"What's the matter?" Julie asked. She stood nearby on the sidewalk clutching a bag of groceries. Another bag sat at her feet.

"There's still no answer." Ken bent and picked up the bag. The cool that radiated from its sides reminded him that they had to stop for ice on the way back to the cabin. "I don't like it, he should be home by now."

"Maybe he was held up at work," Julie suggested, following Ken to the car. "Or he's out with Bonnie."

"Maybe. That's probably it." He opened the trunk, set the bags inside. "But he wasn't at work yesterday and he wasn't at home, either. He knew I'd be calling on Sunday, I set it up before we left. I can't believe he'd just forget. Dave's not the type to forget things like that." He opened his door, slid onto the seat, and reached across to open Julie's door.

"He could have been at our house when you called yesterday," she said, getting in and shutting the door. "It was early, and you always feed the goldfish first thing. Maybe he thinks he should, too."

"No, I tried our place when there was no answer at his. He wasn't there, either."

Ken twisted the key and fired the engine, the frown still worrying at his brow.

"We could stay in town longer. You could call again in an hour or so."

Ken hesitated, then thought of how much he'd spent on perishables that were rapidly warming in the heat. He looked at Julie and smiled.

"No, that's silly. Dave's a big boy, I'm sure he can handle watering a few plants and feeding a tank of goldfish without my mother-henning him. Besides, if something is wrong, I really don't want to know about it. I'm on my honeymoon, remember?"

He gave her a grin and drove to the convenience store for a block of ice.

Once they left Alma, it took almost fifteen minutes on the two-lane back road to reach the turn-off at the northern end of Beaver Lake. Close-packed trees hemmed both sides of the hairpin road, the land dropping sharply away from the pavement on Julie's side of the car. After they turned, it was another fifteen minutes of slow bouncing down the rutted unpaved track that circled the southern side of the lake before they came to the narrow twisting lane that led to their cabin. On the way, Ken pointed out the turn for the cabin nearest them.

"Of course it's a lot closer to just go straight through the woods. It's only about half a mile that way. The road's at least three times longer. Hal Denby down at the gas station told me a fellow named Morgan owns it. A bit of a loner, Denby said, folks don't often see him. They don't even know if he's there year-round or not. He's not exactly the friendly type, though he's not overtly unfriendly, either. Just doesn't like people very much. Sounds like an interesting character."

"Not to me."

"I don't know, he's probably just old and lonely. I think we should walk over and say hello."

"You go. I'll stay home and make dinner," Julie said, clinging to the window frame of the rocking car. "If I don't burn the cabin down, that is."

Ken laughed. "That wood stove does take some getting used to, doesn't it?" The right side of the car plunged down and rebounded with a loud thunk. Ken winced, firming his grip on the jerking wheel. "Damn, I always forget that one's there. Oh, well, it means our turn-off is just ahead. If we decide to stay here, I'll need to trade this poor thing in for a four-wheel-drive truck."

He turned right into a lane even narrower and more filled with holes than the perimeter road. The half-mile crawl down the lane seemed to last forever, the jouncing of the car making conversation almost impossible. Both Ken and Julie breathed a sigh of relief when at last they reached the clearing where the cabin stood.

"At times like this I could wish for electricity. If we had a fridge instead of an icebox we wouldn't have to go to town so often. I'm sure the car would appreciate that. Come on." Ken handed Julie a grocery bag then hefted the ice block along with the second bag while she shut the trunk. "Let's go see if we can actually cook our diner instead of burning it to death."

Once again Ken misjudged in building the fire, so they used skewers to roast hot dogs in the flames shooting out of the top of the stove and ate sitting on a blanket spread on the rough plank floor. It was dim beneath the thick canopy of trees even though it was only eight o'clock. Little light spilled through the cabin's narrow windows. Ken lit an oil lamp, which shed a soft glow over their picnic. After they ate, they walked out to the end of the dock to watch the light disappear from the sky.

It was quiet now, though the past weekend had brought a dozen or more city people out to their cabins, mostly on the other side of the long, narrow lake. Saturday and Sunday had rung with shouts and laughter. Boats buzzed on the water, towing skiers and inner tubes. Ken and Julie sat on the dock watching the activity, enjoying the fun the other families were having, though Ken was secretly anxious for them to leave. He much preferred the quiet that had reigned when they'd first arrived. He didn't want anything to remind him of the world that waited not far away. All too soon it would tear him and Julie apart.

Sunday night brought a return of peaceful silence, heralding the quiet week to come. Once more a feeling of complete privacy enveloped them as families headed back for nearby cities. Now, on Monday night, it seemed they were the only two people left on the face of the earth. Ken folded his arm around Julie's shoulders and watched the evening stillness settle on the water's surface. Daylight faded from the sky, replaced by glittering diamonds shimmering in the velvety blackness of space. They looked close enough to touch. He wished he could reach out and take one down for Julie to wear on her finger, or in her hair.

What is happening with Dave? Why hasn't he been home? The thought arrowed through Ken's mind before he was aware of it, shattering the illusion of peace. Frowning, he turned his head and squinted down the lake, trying to pierce the deepening darkness. He knew he was being ridiculous, worrying about a thirty-five-year-old man who lifted weights and jogged five miles a day. But that didn't stop the little worm of unease from burrowing into the space he'd reserved solely for himself and Julie. *He should have been home, damn it*, he told himself. *Dave should have been home.*

"Ken?" Julie touched his cheek and he turned his eyes back to her. "You're still upset about Dave, aren't you? Do you really think something's wrong?"

"No, of course not," he lied, forcing a smile. But he did think something was wrong, for absolutely no reason other than a phone that didn't answer. It was stupid, insane. Dave was simply out with Bonnie, or with one of the two hundred other women he dated. That was all.

"We could go home and see," Julie said. "We don't have to stay here. As long as we're together, I don't really care where it is."

"You're amazing," Ken said. He kissed her. She would give up these last days of privacy and freedom, just to ease his mind about a friend? She was unbelievable. More than ever, Ken was convinced her memories were wrong. There was no way Julie could have so much as slapped someone, much less shot a man in the head.

He tightened his arms around her and looked up into the night stars.

"We're not going anywhere, Mrs. Reed. In fact, we're never going back. We're staying here. Forever."

"You said that was up to me."

"I changed my mind. We'll be like old man Morgan. We'll hide away and only let people catch fleeting glimpses of us. We'll become a local legend—the Reclusive Reeds. They'll tell ghost stories about us in the dead of night around campfires, scare little kids into obedience with threats of our presence. We'll go naked, and live off roots and wild berries. We'll hide in the cabin all day and only come out after dark, to moonbathe and swim in the lake."

"You're crazy," Julie said, laughing. Ken shifted his hold on her and she gasped. "Ken, no. Don't. Don't you dare!"

She hit the water with a splash, her words gurgling into silence as her head disappeared beneath the surface. In a second Ken was beside her, his laughter echoing from the tall pines. Julie came back up, wiped the water from her face, and lunged for Ken, pushing his head under. He came up sputtering and reached for her.

They wrestled and splashed for long, laughter-filled minutes, until at last Ken took her in his arms and kissed her wet lips, his strong kicks keeping them afloat. Julie twined her arms around him and laid her cheek against his.

"I'll get you for this," she whispered. "You won't be safe anywhere for the rest of your life."

"Promises, promises," Ken taunted, clamping his lips on hers and letting their clasped bodies sink below the surface. When they rose again, Julie's eyes looked glazed in the faint moonlight.

"Let's go in," she said. "I need to punish you."

"That sounds like fun," Ken said. "I can't wait."

They swam to the ladder attached to the end of the dock and climbed up out of the lake, clothes dripping and sneakers squishing with every step. Halfway down the dock, Julie wrung out her hair, twined her arm around Ken's waist and laughed.

"Look at what you've done to me, you horrible fiend. You'll have to pay for this, you know. You won't get any sleep. I'll make you pay all night long."

"I certainly hope so," Ken said.

He kissed her, long and deep, then swung her into his arms, carried her down the dock and up the porch steps, and bore her across the threshold of their honeymoon cabin.

He found her outside in the morning, on a fallen log placed like a bench about a hundred feet from shore. She sipped coffee from the mug she held, watching the birds that skimmed over the lake. Though just after six-thirty, it was already hot. The air dripped with humidity. Hazy clouds covered the blue dome overhead, seeming almost to hug the tops of the surrounding trees. It would be a day, Ken knew, for lazing along in the boat, barely moving, or submerging their bodies in the cool, wet water. If it didn't rain. He poured coffee for himself and went out to join her.

"You're up early," he said. She turned to him and smiled, but she didn't speak. "How about a reading lesson after we eat?"

Julie shrugged. "There doesn't seem to be much point, does there? I'm not improving any."

"You've got to give it time, honey. You don't learn something that complex overnight."

"I know, but it makes me feel stupid, looking at lines that make sense to everyone but me. You'd think losing my memory would have been enough, wouldn't you? I don't see why I had to lose the ability to read, too."

"The amnesia might not have anything to do with your reading problem. People who have amnesia don't usually forget the rote kind of things they learned, like talking or reading, riding a bike or driving a car. It's the remembrance of events and people that get erased, not often-repeated, mechanical stuff."

"How do you know?"

"I read it somewhere," he said with a grin. Julie groaned and shook her head. "It could be a physiological problem—like a form of dyslexia." *Or brain damage*, he thought, remembering she had once fractured her skull. "With work, I'm sure you can overcome it, Julie."

She shook her head, then kissed him and rose. "But I don't feel like working. I'd rather play hooky—with the teacher."

"I think that could be arranged," Ken said.

He came up behind her and folded his arms around her. She leaned against him and he buried his face in her hair, holding her tight and wishing he would never have to let her go. Suddenly, she stiffened. The mug dropped onto the needle-strewn ground, starring the dirt coffee-dark. Julie gasped, a tiny cry of protest issuing from her lips.

"What is it, honey? What's happening?"

She didn't seem to hear his words, nor was she aware of his hands on her arms. She stared out at the lake, her eyes wide. Whatever she was seeing, Ken knew it wasn't their dock, or Beaver Lake.

"No, please!" she whimpered, twisting in his grasp.

"Julie, what is it? What are you seeing?"

She screamed, a strangled sound deep in her throat. Her face drained of color. She began hyperventilating, shaking her head from side to side though her eyes remained fixed on an image only she could see. She struggled in Ken's grasp, trying to break free.

"Julie! Stop! Listen to me!"

Ken swung her around to face him, his hands hard on her arms. He shook her, desperately trying to force awareness back into her eyes. She stared at him, her eyes wide, pupils dilated, body rigid with shock.

Then a shudder rippled through her and she collapsed against him.

Swiftly, he picked her up, carried her onto the porch and set her on the wicker lounge. Her eyes were closed, her skin ashen. He sat beside her and gently pushed her hair away from her face.

"Another vision?" he asked. She nodded without opening her eyes. "What was it, Julie? What did you see this time?"

She frowned and turned her head away, curling her body onto its side as if for protection. Away from him. When she spoke, he could barely hear her.

"It was a bridge, I saw a bridge with trees close around it. It was narrow and dark, all stone. And water below, deep water, and rocks. Bushes. There was just the bridge, no one was on it, not then, but I knew they'd come back. They'd come back and kill me. I had to get away!"

"Who would come back, Julie?"

"I don't know. I don't know, but they wanted to kill me. They wanted me to die on that bridge."

She raised her hands, pressed shaking fingers to her temples.

"What's wrong?" Ken asked. "Does your head hurt?" Groaning, Julie nodded. "Hang on, I'll get your pills and some water."

"No. Don't leave me, please."

She grabbed his hand, sandwiched it between hers and hung onto him as though her life depended on it. She still lay with her back to him. Ken could only see the curve of her cheek. But he could feel her heartbeat with the hand she clutched at her breast. It pounded rapidly, echoing her ragged breaths. Gently, he ran strands of her dark hair through the fingers of his free hand, wishing there was more he could do for her.

"It's OK, Julie. I'm not going anywhere. I'll be right here with you, always. I'll keep you safe," he said, wondering how he could keep his promise when they returned to the real world. "I'll keep you safe, forever."

Gradually she quieted, and in a few minutes let Ken bring her water and two pain pills. When at last she fell asleep, Ken moved a chair close to her and sat with his hand on her shoulder, his mind sorting through the strange dreams and fears, phobias and visions that haunted the woman he loved. Bridges and brick walls, dogs, guns and eerie moonlight rides in the back of dark cars. They all fit together somehow, he was sure, though the pattern was still beyond his ability to make sense of. He only hoped that when the meaning did become apparent, it wasn't what Julie believed. That she had, in cold blooded, murdered a blond-haired man one night by firing a bullet into his head.

They went out on the lake in the afternoon. The boat drifted beneath the hazy heavens. Julie trailed her fingers in the cool, still water, seeming entranced by the misty reflections of the trees that ringed the lake. They caught glimpses of other cabins sheltering deep in the shadows under the pines, and the bottoms of boats pulled up on the shore. But only twice, far on the northwestern end of the long, narrow finger of water, did they see other people, tiny figures that moved in a world far removed from theirs. They didn't go close enough to shout a greeting, or even wave.

On the way back, Ken anchored in the middle of the lake and they swam for a while, gliding through the refreshing water like nymphs. With all but their heads submerged, the heat and humidity seemed much less daunting, though when they climbed back into the boat the relief didn't last very long. They shared iced tea and watermelon slices while all around them birds sang and wheeled through the misty clouds. Fish jumped not a hundred feet from where they sat, sending gentle ripples out across the water's surface. The shadows that had lingered in Julie's eyes slowly began to fade away. When at last Ken took the oars and pulled for their dock, her laughter sounded easy, her smile joyous and natural. Once again he had succeeded in pushing back the inexorable tide of reality that soon would overwhelm them.

Julie disappeared upstairs when they got back to the cabin, leaving Ken to attempt lighting the wood stove for dinner. Half an hour later he realized she was still gone. He found her in their room, sitting half-dressed on the bed, staring at the rustic pine dresser. The shadows were back in her eyes.

"Someone's been in here," she said. She didn't look at him.

"What do you mean? No one's been here, there's no one around for miles."

"Everything's been moved. Someone went through our stuff."

Ken moved to her side, wrapped his arms around her. "Honey, you're imagining it. We're all alone out here."

She shook her head. "No, everything's been moved. Just a little, as though someone was trying to make it look like they hadn't been here. I'm not imagining it. That pillow," she pointed to the rocker, "was against the other arm. And I always keep my hairbrush on the right side of the comb, not the left." She moved the brush back to its usual position, then held up her onyx bracelet. The silver frames around the gemstones glinted softly in the lamplight. "And this. I found it in the drawer on top of my sweater. But I had buried it under my shorts, Ken. I know because it was caught on my bathing suit. I distinctly remember unhooking it and sliding it under the shorts so it wouldn't get caught again."

"You probably think you did because that's what you meant to do. Instead, you were worried about tearing a hole in your suit, and once the bracelet was free you dropped it on your sweater and inspected the suit and then forgot to stash it safely away from bathing suits and sweaters and other snaggy stuff." He leaned forward, kissed her nose. "Things like that happen all the time, Julie. It just means you had a lot on your mind, not that someone was poking through your things."

"You're wrong, Ken," she said as he pulled her to her feet and buttoned up her blouse. "Someone was in here."

"Well, if so, there's only one person it could have been. Old man Morgan. He's probably been curious about us, so he took advantage of our absence to sneak a peek. I told you we should have gone over to say hello."

"That's crazy. He doesn't like people, you said so. Why would he care anything about us?"

"Are you kidding? We're a local legend, remember? The Reclusive Reeds. How could he resist?"

Julie laughed and dropped the bracelet on the dresser. Suddenly, she frowned and sniffed the air.

"Did you leave something on the stove?"

"Oh, jeez Louise! Dinner!" Ken exclaimed.

Forgetting Julie's concerns, they raced down the stairs to rescue the remains of their meal.

CHAPTER TWENTY-FIVE
July 19, 1990
Bear Lake, New York

Ken decided to go into Alma late Wednesday afternoon for three reasons. He needed to replace the ice block that was almost gone, their fresh food supply had dwindled, and he wanted to contact Dave, find out where he'd been over the weekend. Julie elected to stay behind, swearing to conquer the wood stove or turn raw vegetarian. She walked to the edge of the clearing and waved as he bounced down the narrow trail toward the perimeter road. Trees grew close around the lane. She lost sight of him quickly, though she could hear the squeaks and groans of the car negotiating the rutted surface for long minutes. Not until the echoes of his passage had died away did she wish she had gone with him.

Shivering despite the sweltering heat, she walked back to the cabin, suddenly unnerved by the pervading silence. Ken wouldn't be gone long, maybe two hours. He'd be back well before dark, by seven o'clock at the very latest. It was ridiculous to feel scared just because she was alone. She'd been alone often enough in the past and hadn't felt this frightened. It didn't make any sense. She was the one who had wanted privacy and seclusion. Why should it disconcert her now?

She knew why, but she didn't want to admit it, didn't want to think about it. That would give it too much substance, make it real. But she knew it was true. No matter what Ken believed, someone had been in the cabin yesterday afternoon. Someone had pawed through their belongings, though nothing had been taken that she could tell. It was frightening enough in itself, knowing someone had made himself free among their things. But it was the sneakiness that disturbed her most, the attempt to conceal an invading presence by returning everything to almost exactly the same places they'd been in.

What had he been looking for? He? Yes. She knew, somehow, it had been a man.

She paused on the top of the porch steps, her arms wound around the pole that supported the roof, and looked around the clearing then out across the lake. There was nothing to see. The small breeze had died, leaving the trees still, as though turned to stone. Even the rustlings of animals in the underbrush, background noise she had finally grown used to, were absent. She was alone in the silent woods, the only other visible living things the birds that skimmed the surface of the water, feeding on bugs. Their rowboat sat motionless at the end of its mooring rope. Julie could see the oars lying on the dock where Ken had left them. Fish broke the surface of the lake just on the edge of her vision. Nothing else moved, or breathed, not that she could see.

Yet she had the distinct feeling that something, or someone, was watching her, intent on her every movement. Her heart began a slow tattoo in her chest, and her breath shuddered in her lungs.

She whirled and plunged through the open cabin door, slamming and locking it behind her. She stood on trembling legs in the center of the main room, surrounded by murky gloom, until at last she forced herself to laugh. This was ridiculous, insane. There was nothing out there except trees and the lake. She was being paranoid, and for absolutely no reason. She hated to think what Ken would say if he could see her like this. Still, she couldn't get her hands to stop shaking. She lit two oil lamps to banish most of the crouching shadows, then took one of Ken's books and tucked her legs beneath her on the couch.

She spent close to an hour puzzling through the book, finding familiar words here and there, words Ken had taught her to recognize. But she had little success in sounding out words she did not know, and the meanings of the sentences totally eluded her. Finally, she laid the book aside, sighing with frustration. A book on the environment and its problems might hold her interest, but a Jane and Dick reader was more her speed. She'd have to give up trying to read, at least until Ken returned.

She looked at the wood stove, sitting smugly in the corner. She had promised Ken she'd have a fire going, at just the right temperature to cook the pork chops he was buying. But she wasn't sure she could face that recalcitrant old appliance, not after her abortive attempt at reading. *Maybe,* she thought, slipping into her sneakers, *a walk will inspire me.* There had to be a few pioneer ghosts still lingering somewhere in the woods from whom she could coax the secret of cooking on a wood stove.

She locked the cabin door, something she hadn't done since they arrived, and set off up the slight rise behind the building. Her earlier uneasiness had almost completely vanished. The air remained hot and humid though daylight had dimmed as the sun dropped toward the horizon. Another difficult night for sleeping. The woods were silent, deep and green, the pines bare of branches up to five feet from the ground. Maples and birch peeked from between the conical firs, heat-wilted leaves hanging dispirited in the early evening dusk.

How incredible it must have been for the pioneers, Julie thought. *They were the ones who cut the roads and cleared the land. Everywhere they went it was forest, close-packed dense trees like these. How did they know which way to go? How many times did they get lost, trying to find that one small clearing they'd made?*

She looked around and saw nothing but trees crowding close. She would have no idea where the cabin lay had the ground not sloped to her right. She decided to go back before the land leveled out and she ended up wandering like a lost pioneer.

A branch snapped somewhere behind her. Julie spun. She saw nothing but trees. Once again the feeling of being watched descended, sending a shudder down her spine. *It's just my imagination,* she told herself, edging sideways down the slope, her gaze searching the green shadows. *Or maybe a raccoon. Ignore it. It'll go away.*

Leaves rustled off to her right. Julie froze, unable to breathe, then she turned and skidded down the needle-covered slope. She ran into a tree and scraped her arm on the rough bark. Blood welled from elbow to wrist. Tears stung into her eyes and she stopped to brush them away. Another branch snapped, close behind her. She yelped in fear and raced on, her heart pounding fiercely.

Twice she fell, tearing a hole in the knee of her slacks. Leaves and bark bits peppered her hair. A low-hanging branch slapped her face, scratching her cheek. The rustling sounds and snapping of twigs pursued her, moving closer and closer, circling around her until she lost all sense of direction. She ran blindly, upslope and down, seeking escape. At last, driven by the unseen hunter, she stumbled out of the trees into the far side of the clearing where the cabin stood.

She almost fell, her knees were so weakened with relief at the sight of refuge so close at hand. She raced across the open space and onto the porch, but the door would not open to her frantic hands. She whirled and looked around the clearing, her back pressed against the door. There was nothing there, no figure either human or animal stalking the edges of the trees or crossing the clearing to pounce on her. Not until she turned back to the door did she remember the keys in her pocket.

Her breath hitched; what if she'd lost them? She probed deep and in a moment her trembling fingers pulled them from inside the pocket. It took her three tries before she could insert the right one into the lock. She turned the key and twisted the knob together. The door swung wide like a welcoming arm. She fell into the cabin's main room, managing only at the last second to keep her feet beneath her. She slammed the door shut and rammed the slide bolt home before she stood fully upright.

She stared at the door, panting for breath, then slowly backed into the center of the large, square room. Her gaze flicked to the narrow windows, one to the far right of the door, the other on the left wall at the bottom of the staircase. Heavy canvas curtains masked the glass. Even with the lamps lit, she didn't think anyone could see her. She thought about closing the shutters. But to do so she would have to move the curtains aside and open the windows, and that would leave her too vulnerable to whatever was out there.

What was it that had chased her so relentlessly through the woods? It sounded like a big animal—perhaps a bear? One more frightened of her than she was of it? Or was it a man, the one who'd gone through their things? She listened intently, but could hear no sound outside the cabin. Had it—he—gone away? Was she safe now? Or had she simply imagined it, the rustling of underbrush and snapping of twigs that kept her running madly through the trees? What if she had gotten lost out there, hadn't found her way back to the cabin? The way the sounds had circled around her—

Startled, she caught her breath. The noises had had a pattern, a purpose. They had herded her, forced her through the trees behind the cabin and around to the east, opposite the place from where she'd started. The noises had kept her running, toyed with her, terrified her, then almost pushed her into the clearing. Whatever it was that was out there, it was definitely human. And it was after her.

How long had it been? Surely Ken would be back soon. She lifted her hand, but her wrist was bare. She had lost her watch somewhere in the trees. The only other clock was the travel alarm in their bedroom. But there were no lights up there, and no curtains on the windows. She'd have to take a lamp with her, and whoever was out there would know where she was. She'd just have to hope it was close to seven, pray that Ken would come back soon.

Something scraped on the ground outside. A loud thud sounded on the porch. Julie jumped and clasped her hands to her mouth to stifle her cry. More thuds echoed, softer than the first. Then sharp scrapes, like booted feet sliding on the wood plank flooring. Julie sank to her knees behind the upholstered pine armchair and peered over the top at the door. Silence fell. She waited. One minute, two, three. Then two loud thumps on the door, a fist pounding on the wood, demanding entry. Julie bit her lip, closed her eyes and stayed behind the chair.

There was nothing more. No thuds or thumps, no scrapes, no sound of footfalls on the ground outside. Centuries passed in the five agonizing minutes that

Julie crouched listening. The lamps in the room shone brighter as the light outside slowly faded. Crickets resumed their chirruping serenade in the reeds at the water's edge. An eerie bird cry ululated in the stillness. Finally, Julie could take no more. She rose and sidled to the window on the left wall.

Carefully, so slowly that she seemed almost not to move, she pulled the edge of the heavy fabric away from the frame. Though the shadows were long in the dusky twilight, she could still see the area around the cabin clearly. There was nothing there, no sign that anything had ever been there. Pulling the curtain out further, she craned her neck and looked as far as she could, from the clearing in back of the cabin to the edge of the lake in front. All was quiet.

She dropped the curtain and, breathing heavily, moved to the front window. Through it she could see the entire shoreline in front of the cabin, and most of the porch—except for the end near the door. All seemed deserted, the cloud-laden sky fading from red to gray to ebony as she watched. Trees swayed as the evening breeze rose. Stars began to wink on above the lake. Crickets chanted their mating song, undisturbed by her fear. Surely, if anyone was out there, it would still their voices.

Tiptoeing, she went to the door and laid her ear against the wood. She could hear nothing but silence. After a few minutes she straightened up and looked at the slide bolt, heavy wrought iron that ensured her safety. She put her hand on the tiny knob and froze. If someone was out there, waiting, she would be playing right into his hands by opening the door. It was getting dark, long past seven by now. Ken should be back at any second—no, he should already be back, should have been back for a while. Where was he? Had the man abandoned her only to find Ken, an easy target on the lane in his slow-moving car? He could be hurt, dying. She had to help him.

She didn't stop to think, just threw back the bolt and flung open the door. And screamed.

CHAPTER TWENTY-SIX
July 19, 1990
Alma, New York

Ken pulled the receiver from his ear and stared at it. Faint ringing echoed from the earpiece. He'd already let it ring thirty times. He counted ten more before he finally overcame his reluctance and hung up the receiver. This was the fourth time he'd called since he'd arrived in town, both Dave's place and his. No answer, anywhere.

He was torn by the feelings pulling at him. He was done shopping, he should be back at the cabin already. The block of ice was slowly turning into a lake in his trunk. Julie would be worried, and after the attack in Buffalo he hated to leave her alone for long. But he couldn't stand not knowing why Dave wasn't home.

He dismissed the groceries wilting in the car while he stood thinking, more and more alarmed with each passing minute. Something was seriously wrong, he was sure of it. Dave was as trustworthy as a man could get. When he said he'd do something for you, he did it, come hell or high water. Ken's brow creased into a deep frown as he picked up a quarter and slid it into the slot once again. He punched in a number then followed the quarter with the rest of his coins as the operator dictated.

"Hello?" The voice was familiar, high-pitched and breathless. A woman.

"Hello, Mrs. McGuire, this is Ken. Ken Reed. How are you?"

"Oh, I'm fine, Kenny. Are you home?"

"No, no, I'm still away. Is Jason there? I need to talk to him."

"No, he's at the hospital. He goes every night after work."

"The hospital? Why?" A shiver ran down Ken's spine. For just a moment, he didn't want to know the answer.

"Oh, that's right, you wouldn't know, would you? It happened after you left." Mrs. McGuire clicked her tongue. Ken could picture her, shaking her head, lips pursed. His heart began to thud. "It's Dave, he's been hurt real bad. He's in a coma, has been since that night."

"Since what night, Mrs. McGuire? What happened, a car accident?" Ken's hands were suddenly sweaty. He had trouble holding the receiver.

"Oh, don't we wish it was. At least that a person can understand. No, someone beat him, Ken. Broke into his apartment, Jason doesn't think anything was even taken. They just beat him terrible, left him for dead. It was Sunday night, after the baseball game. He was so happy that night, Jason said, because they'd won. They joked about it, you being gone and all. Then he went home and—"

Mrs. McGuire's voice choked off. Ken knew she was wiping tears from her eyes. He and Dave had been as much a fixture at Jason's house as Jason had been at theirs. To Mrs. McGuire, he and Dave were like family.

"Jason, he goes to the hospital every night, talks to Dave, tries to wake him up. The doctors are still hopeful, but the more time that goes by the less chance they say he has. I don't—"

"Please, Mrs. McGuire, I'm at a pay phone, I don't have much time," Ken interrupted, his own voice clouded with unshed tears. "Do they know who did it, or why?"

"No, Jason says there doesn't seem to be a reason, Ken. Dave just—"

"Your three minutes are up. If you wish to continue, please deposit three dollars more."

"Damn, I don't have any more change. Tell Jason we'll be home tomorrow, Mrs. McGuire. Tell him—"

The phone went dead in his hand.

Cursing, he slammed the receiver onto the hook and left the booth. Anger gripped his chest like a vise. He couldn't understand it. Who would do something like that to Dave? And why? It was even more senseless than what had happened to Julie. At least that was semi-understandable. She walked in on a robbery and the guy panicked. If Julie hadn't hit him, hadn't hurt him like she did, he'd have killed her and walked off with their valuables. Ken could still see it, the bulging pillowcase set ready by the front door, behind which the guy had waited for Julie.

He stopped suddenly, his hand on the car door. Chills traversed his spine, ominous ripples that took his breath away. Had it really been just a thief, or was it someone out to get Julie? Had he succeeded in killing her, would he actually have taken the bag or left it to enhance the set-up of an interrupted crime? Was it just a random break-in by someone who panicked, or was it someone from that mysteriously sinister past of hers?

Ken frowned as he pictured the house. Blood on the door, the floor, the walls. The case from his own pillow loaded with his silver and jewelry. The wanton destruction everywhere—chairs slashed, dishes shattered, clothes shredded. Thieves didn't do that. They rifled through drawers, emptied out chests, overturned boxes and went through pockets. They didn't take time to break dishes or slice through upholstery and clothing just for the hell of it. Not unless they were trying to create a picture, a picture no one would question. A crazy thief who had panicked, and killed a woman by mistake.

Only he hadn't. Julie was still alive. Alive and out of town, her whereabouts known to only two other people. Jason McGuire and Dave Atwood. Ken's eyes widened. His breath froze in his lungs. It couldn't be, it was impossible. He was crazy to even think it. He had nothing to go on, no proof at all—except Julie's frightening half-memories of blood and guns and murder, and the attack on Dave a scant week after the attack on Julie.

He slid into the car, shut the door and fired the engine, moving on autopilot as his mind churned on. He had to be wrong, it was simply a coincidence. But what were the odds that two of the people closest to him would be attacked within a week of each other? It wasn't coincidence. Someone wanted Julie dead for some unknown reason, a reason connected with who she had been in that other life. He had tried, and failed. And when he came back for a second try, he'd found not Julie and Ken, but Dave, feeding fish and watering plants. Dave, tending the house while the master was away. Dave, who knew where Julie was. Who'd had the knowledge beaten out of him on Sunday night.

"Julie!" he shouted.

She was alone at the cabin. He'd left her alone for that bastard to find. Frantic, he pulled out of the lot, tires squealing on the hot pavement. He drove like a madman, totally unaware of anyone else on the road, running stop signs and the single light in the center of town. He pushed the car for all it was worth. Dark trees flashed past the windows. The tires skidded on the curving road. Only two cars passed him once he left the town behind. The closer he got to the perimeter turn-off, the fewer lights showed along the route, until darkness was his only companion.

The car lurched and fishtailed when he turned onto the perimeter road. The force of the jouncing almost yanked the steering wheel from his hands. The grocery bag bounced off the seat beside him and spilled onto the passenger-side floor. He ignored it, letting the damned groceries fend for themselves. He didn't slow down until the car bottomed out twice, the last time with a jarring thud that left ominous rattles echoing from the underside of the chassis and bounced his head off the roof, sending pain stabbing down into his jaw. He drove a bit more carefully then, one foot on the brake, trying in the dark to steer around the worst of the rutted holes as they appeared in his headlights. He feared that the car would break down before he got to the cabin, and Julie.

Oh, please, don't let me be too late, he prayed, glancing at the path that led to old man Morgan's place. He thought he caught a glimmer of light far away through the trees. He wondered if perhaps he should stop, ask for Morgan's help. He might have a shotgun or a rifle Ken could use. But he couldn't stop, couldn't take the time. Julie might need him now, and there was no guarantee Morgan was there, or that he'd help if he were.

A night mist had risen from the lake and flowed out over the land. It swirled now in his headlights, obscuring the rutted road. Ken slowed even more and rolled down the window, trying to see through the white vapor. The front passenger wheel hit a bump, then dropped abruptly into a hole. The bumper thunked into the hard-packed dirt. The undercarriage of the car shrieked as it scraped over loose rocks and stones. The steering wheel jerked out of Ken's hands, sending the car in an arc toward the trees. Swearing aloud he lunged and grabbed for the wheel, and the night exploded around him.

There was no noise, no sound of a blast, only a quick flash of fire somewhere off to his left and an eruption of pain that seared him like fire. It hit his shoulder and spread like a plague across his back, up his neck, down his spine. It consumed him entirely. He couldn't scream, couldn't breathe, couldn't move. His muscles contracted and his foot pushed down on the accelerator as he fought to remain conscious. The car lurched forward following the right-hand cant of the front wheels. Propelled by the power surging through the fast-revving engine, the vehicle bounded up over the foot-high row of boulders that lined the edge of the road and tore down the slanting slope beyond. Ten feet into the forest it crashed head-on into a thirty-year-old pine. The front end folded like an accordion. Ken's body smashed through the windshield. He bounced off the tree and crumpled into a heap a few feet from the car. He lay unconscious in a widening pool of blood as the agonized sound of torn metal slowly faded into silence. In a few moments, only the pinging from the twisted, dying motor and the light from one crazily canted headlight cutting into the mist was all that was left to mark the place where Ken lay.

CHAPTER TWENTY-SEVEN
July 19, 1990, 8:45 p.m.
Bear Lake, New York

It swung at the end of a rope, the opening of the door setting in motion a macabre death-dance in the deepening dusk. The huge raccoon, now a mass of matted fur and oozing blood, hung heavy with the eerie flat emptiness of death. The gore-slimed torso dripped dark blood onto the wooden planks of the porch floor. The ominous tap-tap-tapping echoed Julie's horrified breaths. Glassy eyes reflected the soft lamplight behind her with a lifeless glare of their own.

The blood-slick rope from which it dangled wound around a partially-severed neck, canting the small, masked head at a painfully oblique angle.

Predatory teeth glinted in the gaping mouth as the body shifted in the light. Julie's horrified stare followed the movement and snagged on the piece of blood-bespattered paper impaled on a dagger-sharp fang. Three words slashed in red blood across the pale surface, promising death and destruction. She had no trouble reading those words. They almost screamed at her.

You're next, "Julie"

She took a jerky step back from the gruesome thing hanging in the open doorway. She had to get out, get away from the cabin, lose herself in the dark night before whoever had done this came back. But the grotesque messenger caught at her, stopped her feet. She could not tear her gaze from the mutilated animal and the words of doom it carried. Suddenly, the room tilted. The animal's body wavered, faded, the matted fur blending into the hard outlines of pale, blood-splattered bricks.

"No!" Julie cried, shaking her head, holding out her hands to fend off the vision. The bricks wavered, became solid and then faded again, leaving tracks of glistening blood on the dark of the night and the walls around her. A fey breeze gusted. The obscene message shivered, lifted from its enamel perch and fluttered to the surface of the shallow blood lake below. Julie spun, seeking escape in the nether reaches of the cabin. And stopped dead, a scream strangling in her throat.

He stood not six feet behind her, watching with a bemused expression on his broad, hook-nosed face.

Muscles bulged on his crossed arms, straining at the fabric of his black t-shirt. A huge pistol protruded from the dark leather shoulder holster wound around his torso. Frozen, Julie stared at him, at the huge bulk of the body blocking her escape, the alert poise of a stance set ready for her merest flicker of movement toward freedom. The deep brown eyes held no recognition of her as a person, a human being. She was merely an object to him, that was all. She could read it clear in his eyes. He was the hunter and she the prey. The chase had been fun, but now it was over. He had her in his trap.

His lips, thick and hard, rose into a smile. Julie gasped at the cruelty in it.

"You're next, 'Julie'," he whispered.

Screaming, Julie whirled and ran for the stairs.

She didn't even get close. He was on her in a moment, huge hands closing on her shoulders, yanking her around. He spun her into the center of the room and dropped her to the floor with two forceful blows from his open hand. She lay shuddering, face throbbing, ears ringing, barely aware when he knelt beside her, turned her on her back and pulled her arms up. Something coarse scraped across her wrists. She blinked her eyes clear to see him jerking a rope tight on her flesh.

"No! No, don't! Let me go!" she screamed, twisting beneath him, fighting strong hands whose hold she could not hope to break.

"Shut up," he said, his voice calm, dead-sounding. It lacked any emotion at all.

He hit her again, rocking her head on the hard floor. Tears stung behind her closed lids. She could taste blood in her mouth. He yanked her hands up again. A sudden pressure on her stomach wrenched open her eyes.

He knelt on her, one hard knee pressed into her diaphragm, driving the air from her body. Sharp stabs of pain radiated in all directions. Hot red flashes lit the darkness that descended over her vision. She couldn't breathe, couldn't speak, didn't exist past an agony that tore her in two. She shook her head, her eyes pleading for release. Her captor smiled his inhuman smile, over-tightened the knots on the rope, and drove his knee deeper into her middle before rising to his feet.

Gasping for breath, Julie curled onto her side, her knees drawn to her chest. Pain gouged deep in her stomach. Her hands throbbed. Blood trapped by the constricting rope beat a frantic tempo beneath her skin. She knew he stood mere inches from her, she could feel his presence, the heat that radiated from his legs. Her mind groped for ways to escape as she fought for breath even though she knew it was hopeless.

A black-sneakered foot nudged her ungently.

"Get up."

The calm order, full of icy death, shuddered fear down Julie's spine. She pulled her legs in more, tried to force her body to move, to roll up onto her hands and knees. Pain exploded through her torso and, gasping, she sank back onto the floor. Again his foot swung, a swift kick low on her back. Nausea rose over the pain. She groaned and forgot the aching stabs in her stomach.

"Get up!"

Like a whip the words slashed across her, promised more anguish to come. Still fighting for breath, she nodded and forced her arms beneath her, pushed until at last only her forearms, knees and toes made contact with the floor. But try as she might, she could not move further. Her body refused to stand.

He reached down and hauled her to her feet. She stumbled in his grasp, her head reeling, her legs buckling beneath her. He held her tight, one iron-hard arm around her waist, one broad, long-fingered hand cradling her cheek and chin, pulling her head snug against his chest. His thumb rubbed gently, almost sensually, along her lips, as though to absorb the moist heat from her sobbing breaths. Slowly the pain assaulting her faded. Her feet steadied beneath her, the dizziness vanished. She blinked open her eyes as he slid his hand from her face to embrace her shoulders and placed his lips beside her ear.

"So, we meet again, Carole." The whisper and his hot breath made her shudder.

"I'm n-not C-Carole," she stammered. "M-my name is Julie."

He laughed, a deep sound of pure mockery. There was no laughter in his voice.

"Don't be stupid. You won't get away this time, sweetheart. You were just lucky before, you know that, don't you?"

He paused and she nodded, wondering who he was. Carole. Was that really her name?

"But now your luck has run out. We're going to finish what we started, and you're going to be a good little girl, aren't you? No more trouble, right?"

Again he paused, his hands tightening in warning when she remained silent. Quickly, Julie nodded.

"Now, let's take a little walk, sweetheart. Out to the dock."

He pushed her forward. Julie twisted in his hands, panic overwhelming her as he forced her closer and closer to the blood-drenched carcass. She barely felt the pain of his grip, the way his fingers dug into her arms. She fought with all her strength, her shoes skidding on the rough wood floor, to no avail. She could not break his hold, or twist away from the grotesque horror that slowly came nearer. Almost before she could draw breath, he shoved her against the sticky, matted fur, his hands keeping hers from rising to protect her face. The rope shivered, moved. The body swung out and then back. It collided with her face in a rolling motion that seemed to envelop her head. It was still warm. Horrified, Julie screamed, the sound half-absorbed by the oozing, mangled flesh and fur that kissed her face.

He laughed again, a low rumble of evil that held her imprisoned against the ruined animal body for a few seconds that seemed an eternity. Then he shoved her across the porch and down the steps, where she sprawled on the pine needle and stone littered dirt.

"Come on, sweetheart, move it," he growled, kicking at her bound arms. "I haven't got all night to waste on this." He kicked at her again. "Get up, you little bitch!"

Julie forced herself to her feet and wiped her face with the backs of her hands. When she stumbled, he reached out and captured her hands in his, twisting them in his tight grip. Julie bit back a cry of pain. Swiftly, he jerked on her hands, pulling her close.

"I said, come on!"

She shook her head, wrenching at her hands, hoping the slick blood would loosen his hold. It didn't. He growled, turned and began towing her behind him.

"No!" she cried, digging her heels into the soft dirt. He turned back to her and lifted a massive fist.

"Are you causing trouble?"

His tone cut into her and her breath froze. His eyes glittered like glowing embers in the light spilling from the open cabin door. Terrified, Julie tore her stare from his and with a shock realized it was fully dark. Ken! Her eyes widened. He could be back any minute, he would save her!

Again she twisted in her captor's unyielding grip, looking to her far left where the lane emerged from its leafy tunnel into the clearing. *Where is he? Please, please let him come.*

"What are you looking for, sweetheart? Your boyfriend? You think he'll come to save you?" Mocking laughter engulfed her, forced her stare back to the man who held her. "Well, he won't. My partner's waiting up on the road to take care of him. He's an excellent shot. Your precious Ken won't have a chance."

"You can't! No!" Julie screamed. It wasn't true, couldn't be true. No, oh no, what had she done to Ken?

"In fact," he grinned at her, "I'd say he's probably dead by now. Long dead."

She screamed again, a long, high wail of pure torment.

"Shut up!"

The man's hand lifted, cracked against her face. He hit her again, a backhand blow that crumpled her into the dirt. Julie lay still, her arms raised to protect her head, rocking with the despair that filled her. Her face felt like it was on fire.

"That's better," her captor said after a few moments. He hauled her to her feet and shoved her ahead of him, toward the dock.

Dead. Ken was dead. All the fight went out of her, she felt it pour out like water down a wide-open drain. Her heart folded up and she no longer cared whether she lived or died. Not that what she wanted mattered. Such decisions were out of her hands. A fatalistic calm descended over her as she wondered how long it would take, how long this man would make her suffer before releasing her into death.

She staggered forward down the dock, guided by the hard fingers poking at her. Halfway to the end, a few feet from the boat, she tripped, landing on her hands and knees with a jarring thud that knocked her breath away. But when she started to rise, her tormentor slammed a hard hand on her shoulder, shoving her back down to her knees on the rough, splintery wood.

"Stay there, just like that," he ordered. "Don't move, or I'll blow your fucking face off."

He walked on past her toward the stern of the boat and stumbled over a length of rope laid neatly along the side of the dock. Cursing, he kicked at it, sending it arcing along the wooden planks. Blinded by tears, Julie watched him turn to face her. He stood less than fifteen feet from where she knelt, casually leaning on a tall piling. With slow, deliberate movements calculated to torment her, he shook out and lit a cigarette then looked beyond where she knelt at the clearing behind her.

"Why are you doing this?" Julie whispered.

He glanced at her, then went back to studying the clearing. "Because you know too much."

"But I don't know anything." Julie shook her head, wishing she could make him understand. "I don't even know who you are."

He shrugged and drew in on the cigarette. Its faint glow cast his heavy features with an evil red shadow.

"Oh, yeah, I heard about the amnesia. You don't think that's gonna save you, do you, 'Julie'? Besides, I bet if you try real hard, it'll all come back."

Julie looked at him, tilting her head to meet his eyes. There was no mercy there, no point in pleading. He was looking forward to watching her die. He stuck the cigarette between his lips and, ignoring the pistol beneath his armpit, he pulled a revolver from his belt and with slow, deliberate movements dropped a bullet into each chamber. Snapping the cylinder shut with a sharp crack, he looked up and smiled at her.

"What are you going to do to me?" Her voice trembled less than her body, but not by much.

His smile broadened. "What do you think?"

He cocked the gun and pointed at her. Julie flinched and cowered back, but she couldn't force herself to look away from the deadly weapon. The man laughed, then he put his thumb on the hammer and carefully lowered it down. He took another drag and tapped the gun against his thigh as once again he studied the clearing. A moment later, he grinned, cocked the pistol and again aimed at Julie. Again, he lowered the hammer without firing, twisting his hand to look at his watch.

Julie, pushed beyond endurance, straightened up on her knees and almost spit her fear and anger at him.

"Go ahead, do it. Get it over with. What are you waiting for?"

The man frowned into the darkness and shook his head. "He should be here by now," he murmured, more to himself than in answer to Julie. "What the hell is taking him so long? Don't you move," he growled as Julie looked back over her shoulder at the cabin.

Ken isn't dead. If he were, the partner would already be here. The thought arrowed through her mind, a bright spark lighting the impenetrable darkness, and her heart lurched. She almost gasped aloud as the will to survive, to find Ken and live, surged back into her being.

"Damn, I can't wait much longer." The man turned and glared at her, as though it was her fault the plan's timetable had derailed. "He should be here for this."

"For what?" Julie whispered, looking at the rope around her wrists, wondering how she could loosen them, get them off.

"For finishing what we started." He flicked the cigarette butt into the water and his voice hardened. "Well, time's up. It's on me, now. And because you've been such a bitch, we'll do it the hard way. Real hard."

Julie looked up at him, startled at the growling menace in his tone. Her world tilted. Trees rose up behind him where water had been moments before. The dock had vanished, replaced by the hard stones of a bridge, the bridge she had envisioned just yesterday. He leaned not on a piling but a waist-high parapet. A car stood by his side, its trunk gaping wide. Cinder blocks were piled at his feet and he held not a gun in his hands, but a thick rope.

"Oh!" she gasped, scrunching her eyes shut and shaking her head. "No!"

"It's only right, sweetheart." His voice came to her out of a far distance, wrapped sinuous tentacles around her and squeezed tight, tighter. "You have to pay for all the trouble you've caused us, and there is a certain rightness in having you here like this. Sorta brings it all full-circle, wouldn't you say?"

Once again he cocked the gun and used his thumb to lower the hammer. The ratcheting sound shattered her vision. It collapsed around her like falling snow and she blinked up at him again. And knew where she'd seen him before.

In her dream, the one about the car. He was the driver. It had been his face she'd glimpsed when he'd stopped and gotten out into the darkness. He was the one who had driven her to the place where she should have died. The bridge, a stone bridge that spanned deep, dark water. She looked down between the planks and saw water rippling below. Full-circle, he'd said. He meant to bury her beneath these waves. She was staring into her grave.

"I wonder if they'll ever find you?" he mused, scratching his chin with the gun's barrel. "Or figure out who you really are if they do? What do you think, 'Julie'?" He reached in his pocket, pulled out a small cylinder that he screwed onto the gun's barrel. "Just stay nice and still, now. You wouldn't want to spoil my aim, would you?"

Panic washed over her like flood of molten metal. He was going to shoot her, kill her right here, right now. She twisted to her right and threw herself flat on the dock. A bullet pinged mere inches from her shoulder and ricocheted off into the night.

"Don't make this difficult, Carole," the man growled. He stepped forward a pace. "You're the one who'll suffer for it, not me."

She felt rope beneath her hands. Could she use it? Julie looked along its length. It was the piece the man had kicked across the dock, a strand that led to the neat coil lying close to him. He cocked the gun again and took another step. His foot came down on the rope coil and he staggered, momentarily losing his balance. Julie's instincts took over, a desperate play for freedom, for life. She grabbed the rope and yanked with all her strength. The coil shifted and unwound from beneath his foot, throwing him completely off-balance. His arms pin-wheeled. The gun flew from his hand and vanished into the lake with a sharp plunk.

"Damn you fucking bitch!" the man roared, smacking down on one knee. "I'm gonna hurt you so bad!"

Julie rose to her knees and reached for one of the oars Ken had left lying on the dock. Her grip determined and panic-tight despite her bound hands, she swung it with all her strength. The broad blade hit him square on the shoulder just as he lurched back to his feet, knocking him sideways. He staggered a few steps and toppled off the dock with a shrill scream. A dull thud resounded in the darkness.

The force of the contact threw Julie back and spun the oar from her hands. She smacked onto the far edge of the dock, the shock sending a jolt up her spine. She gasped in pain, then rolled off the edge and dropped like a stone into the dark rippling water of Bear Lake.

CHAPTER TWENTY-EIGHT
July 19, 1990, 9:35 p.m.
Bear Lake, New York

Julie struggled in the deep, dark water as her bound hands and waterlogged sneakers dragged her down. Wanting only to get to Ken, she refused to give up. She kicked as hard as she could, trying to cup her palms as she slashed at the cold darkness. Her lungs ached, screaming to breathe. At last her head broke the surface. She gulped air. Wind-riffled waves splashed into her face. Water sloshed down her throat and choked her. She coughed, forgetting to kick, and immediately sank again. Propelled by panic she twisted in the water, her arms lashing out. *No, please, don't let me drown,* she prayed. *Don't let me die like this.*

Her hands smacked into something hard then slid across a slimy surface. Instinctively she pulled back, only to sink deeper. More water slid down her throat. In sheer desperation she reached out again, grabbed the soft, slippery coating, and pulled her head up out of the water. Gagging, she clung with clawed fingers, wrapped her legs around the gelatinous-feeling slickness. Not until her heart had slowed and she could breathe freely again did she open her eyes and lift her head to look around.

She was below the dock, clutching a piling across from where the boat lay moored. There were no sounds other than her ragged breathing and the chirruping of crickets and frogs. No sound of footsteps paced above her. No evil, whispering voice dug at her with promises of pain and death. No soft pops from a silenced gun, no bullets tracking through the water, seeking her body. She looked up, squinted at the dark spaces between the weathered boards eight feet above her, but saw no sign of the man who had tried to kill her.

Where was he? Why couldn't she see him, hear him? Could he see her there in the water? Was he waiting for her to move, waiting with gun drawn, ready to fire? Closing her eyes, Julie leaned her forehead against the damp, splintery piling, biting her lips to keep from screaming. She couldn't stay here, it was too close to where she'd fallen in. It wasn't safe. And the water-aged wood was too slimy, she couldn't hold on. Already she had slipped down a few inches.

Restless water lapped at her cheeks and chin. Nor could she swim away from the dock, not with her hands tied. If the man wasn't up there sitting motionless, waiting for her to give herself away, then he must have gone to find the partner he'd talked about. They'd be back soon, and against two of them she'd have no chance, no chance at all.

Once again she lifted her head and peered up at the dock's underside. She held her breath and listened close, but there was nothing to see or hear. He was either being more than careful, grinning as he waited in the darkness, or he had gone for help. If she was going to make a break for it, she had to do it now. She couldn't afford to wait. At last she decided, not that she had much choice. She was completely helpless in the water. She had to get out of the lake and onto dry land. There, with trees and darkness to hide her, she might find a way to get to Ken and escape.

She looked around, searching for a solution, and glimpsed the boat half-hidden by the pilings. For a moment her heart leapt. The boat could take her across the lake. But her hope quickly died as she realized that even if she could climb into it, she couldn't use the boat's oars. She needed two separate hands for that. But she could use the boat for a shield while she worked her way to the ladder at the end of the dock. Then maybe he wouldn't see her—if he was still up there, and if she didn't make any noise.

Arms stretched in front of her, Julie pushed off from the piling and let herself float slowly to the other side of the dock, where the boat softly bumped the pilings. She used her feet to propel her, slow kicks beneath the lake's surface. Water splashed into her face, blinding her, but she kept her eyes open, blinking hard to keep the blurred boat in sight. It seemed to take hours, though in reality less than twenty seconds passed before she raised her hands and clamped desperate fingers on the bow of the boat.

She hung in the water, her head almost submerged, her body still, gaze fastened on the dock above her. She saw only stillness, wisps of thick mist swirling in the dark night air, and faint glints of stars poking through tiny rents in the ominous gray cloud cover. Crickets and frogs sang on uninterrupted. Leaves rustled in the stiffening breeze. Tied bow and stern, the fifteen-foot rowboat bobbed a stationary course parallel to the dock, riding the undulating waves with an almost-human stoical acceptance. After a few moments Julie slowly began edging her way along the outer rim of the boat, her progress hampered by the tight rope around her wrists.

Fearing to see her doom grinning down at her, she didn't look up again. She kept her head down and stared at the boat's side. The white-painted planks showed signs of age and weather. The protective paint bubbled in spots, exposing the wood beneath to wind, water and rot. Feeling her way with hands only, she tried to time her movements to the boat's bobbing, grateful for the breeze that concealed the way the boat swayed beneath her weight. Inch by agonizing inch, she left the bow behind.

Her hands bumped against something. The oarlock? It must be, though it felt strange, not at all like metal. And it was oddly warm. Startled, Julie raised her head. Her heart lurched and surged into her throat. She bit back a scream, turned her head away and screwed her eyes shut. But the fearful image stayed with her, burned into the darkness.

It was him, the man from her dream, the man who had tried to shoot her. His face, those burning dark eyes, hovered mere inches from her. Terrified, frozen by fear, she waited for him to laugh in triumph and grab at her, waited for his huge hands to push her down, hold her under the water until she drowned. But nothing happened. No one touched her. No one spoke. Finally she opened her eyes and turned to look at him once again, and saw what shock and fear had caused her to miss.

He lay spread-eagled across the width of the boat like a broken marionette, his face turned to the side. His right arm dangled in the water. One long leg stuck out to jar against a piling whenever the boat rocked. He was very still. And very, very dead.

His head rested on the edge to which Julie clung, just where the oarlock should be. The dark eyes were open, mouth agape in a silent scream. Beneath his left temple a wavering ebony line flowed over the wooden edge and glistened down the boat's white side as it snaked into the water. It widened as she stared, stark blood black in the dark night. Gagging, Julie backed away, pulling her gaze from the gruesome sight to stare into the bow of the boat.

He must have fallen when she hit him with the oar and dropped off the dock just as she had. Only he hadn't landed in water. The boat had been waiting below, the same boat in which he had planned to take her body out into the center of the lake. Weighting her, no doubt, with the heavy anchor still glistening in the bow. She looked at the thick rope tied to the anchor, a rope no longer attached to the boat. It had been cut and lay ready to be looped around her waist. Or her neck. We'll do it the hard way, he had said. The soft words reverberated in her head. Realization burst over her. He hadn't been going to kill her, only make her wish she were dead. He would have played with her, hurt her, teasing her with life until she sobbed and pleaded before he let the heavy anchor carry her to the bottom of the lake. At last Julie understood the full evil she'd seen in his eyes. She would still have been alive when the water closed over her head, awake and aware of the full horror of her death.

But he was the one who wasn't alive, not anymore. When he fell he smashed down onto the boat, driving the oarlock into his skull. Had he died instantly? Shuddering, Julie closed her eyes and hoped he hadn't, hating herself for the satisfaction that possibility gave her. Her hands tightened on the hard wood and silently she thanked the boat for its unwitting help. This small lumbering vessel, slated to be her funeral bier, had become instead her salvation.

A moment later, spurred by the thought of the unknown partner of whom her would-be executioner had spoken, she forced herself to move on past the still, lifeless body to the ladder at the end of the dock. The climb was almost impossible the way her hands were tied. She fell back into the water twice, but she persevered, laboriously pulling herself up the rusting iron rungs until finally she reached the safety of the thick wooden planks above.

She knelt motionless on the hard surface and scanned the clearing in front of the cabin for signs of movement, straining to hear any sounds that did not belong in the night-time forest. Nothing seemed out of place. Trees swayed in the breeze that now sent shivers through her. Night birds called, answered only by frogs and crickets. Fingers of mist swirled in the changeful wind. They retreated up into the trees, leaving the way to the cabin clear and open. Warm light spilled from the open door. The dangling wind-prodded raccoon carcass threw a wavering shadow down the steps. Nothing moved in the cabin's bright depths. There was no flicker of movement anywhere.

Julie took a deep breath, cast one last glance down at the boat's gory burden and then rose. She stayed low, sneakers squelching with her every step, as she raced down the dock, across the clearing and up the porch steps. But she could not force herself to push past the dead animal's remains. She stood staring at the carcass, the slime-slick feel of blood soaked fur and muscle still vivid in her mind. She couldn't bear it to touch her again. She edged carefully around the eerily swaying body, her own body vulnerable in the bright light, until at last she gained the interior of the cabin.

She stood pressed against the wall beside the door, her eyes and ears alert. Had she walked back into a trap? Her attacker might be lying dead in the rowboat, but his partner wasn't. Was he somewhere here in the cabin, waiting to capture her?

She studied the room, starting on the right with the steps to the upper floor. Beneath them was a doorless closet, a shallow rectangle filled with hooks and shelves for storage. Beyond, stretching halfway along the rear wall, stood the partition for the kitchenette, again doorless. Within the long, narrow alcove hung rough cupboards for dishes and canned goods, a waterless sink, and counters for preparing food. The cooking was done in the main room, on the old wood stove that stood in the left rear corner. The only two windows, covered with rust-colored curtains, were both shut and locked.

Silence stretched, grating at her nerves. Nothing moved except her eyes. She looked again at the inky shadows at the top of the stairs and knew she couldn't bring herself to go up there. Her only safety, fleeting though it might be, lay within these walls. She would simply have to trust that he was not in here with her.

She pushed away from the wall and shut the front door, ramming home the thick iron slide bolt. She began to shudder as again she thought of the body in the boat. Had she really done that, killed a man? By accident, yes, but the man was dead, and by her hand. And beneath the horror she'd been glad. What kind of person did that make her? She lifted her hands to stare at them, a killer's hands, but the tight rope on her wrists caught her up short. *Don't think about it*, she told herself, *not yet*. She couldn't afford to fall apart. That man's partner was still somewhere out there. She had to get the rope off her wrists. She had to turn off the betraying lights, and she needed something to fight with. And she had to find Ken. Somehow, she had to find Ken.

She stumbled across the room to the kitchenette, hesitating only a moment before forcing her feet to carry her into the shadow-shrouded space. Little light spilled in from the main room. Her eyes, blinded by the brightness without, felt almost useless. She groped her way to the counter then, hampered by her bound hands, fumbled in dark drawers, searching for a knife.

A butcher knife, one with a long, wide, sharp blade. She cut her fingers twice, the lancing pain making her gasp, before she found what she looked for. With bloody fingers she lifted the sturdy knife from the drawer, raised her head, and dropped the blade as shock flooded through her.

An ebony rectangle gaped at her, its ink-black slash jarring in the clinging dimness of the kitchenette. Abruptly a vision rose before her now-dark-adjusted eyes. A huge, hard man grinning with the promise of pain and death standing in the center of the main room, his evil eyes locked on hers. Standing behind her, watching and waiting, in a room whose front door had been securely bolted, whose windows were locked. She'd never even wondered how he'd gotten in. Why hadn't she thought of the back door? Why wasn't it locked?

Was it too late? Was the other one standing close, concealed in impenetrable shadows, watching her every movement? Heart thudding, Julie sidled to the narrow opening and peered into the darkness beyond. She could see nothing except eerie patches of ground fog winding among trees that stood thirty feet directly in front of her. It was as if someone had hung thick black curtains to each side. The partner could be standing within inches of her and she'd never know it, not until he touched her, grabbed at her. Slowly, wincing at the faint creak of the ancient hinges, she eased the door closed and slid the bolt across the frame.

At least she knew now where the other one had come from. Shivering, she relocated the knife, pushed the drawer shut, and carried her treasure into the main room where two kerosene lamps dispelled the darkness. She stood a moment to still her heart and slow her breathing, then moved to the lamp on the table near the stairs and blew it out, plunging half the room into gloomy shadow. Her heart began pounding again. As she walked across the room to the lamp that stood on a table beside the couch, she caught sight of the wood stove. Her feet paused and she looked back at the kitchen opening.

Of course. The woodshed. She hadn't thought of the back door because it opened onto the woodshed. She hadn't really considered it a back door because they'd never used it to go in and out of the cabin, only to bring in wood. Grateful for the guidance that had led her to the kitchen area and the forgotten opening, she put out the lamp, closed her eyes, and sank onto the couch.

After her eyes adjusted all they could to darkness that appeared solid, Julie carefully set the knife between her knees, cutting edge face up. The wet fabric of her torn slacks helped to hold the blade steady. It slipped only a little. She scraped the constricting rope along the sharp edge, working with great care in the darkness. Anxiety hammered at her, pushing her to hurry, but she forced herself to ignore her fears. She was more afraid to cut her hands or her wrists on the razor-sharp blade, for she knew she would need her hands again before this night was over. Her attacker had turned and knotted the rope four times around her flesh, but gradually the strands binding her wrists began to fray. The tension eased, and she could feel blood begin to flow more freely into her almost-numb fingers. At last the rope parted, fell away. Julie sighed with relief and gently pressed her palms over the raw skin on her wrists Then she flexed her tingling fingers.

"I know you're in there, you fucking bitch!"

The sudden high-pitched shout drove through the walls. Alarm surged through her. Her eyes flew wide. Her heart stuttered in terror. The knife clattered to the floor at her feet.

"I'll get you, bitch! You'll pay for what you've done! You hear me? You'll pay!"

The partner! Frantic, Julie bent and scrabbled for the knife. A loud crack sounded outside. Something smashed through the side window and shattered the lamp beside her. Four more small explosions resounded, echoed by dull thuds along the front wall and in the front door. Julie screamed, rolled from the couch to the floor and closed her fingers over the knife's handle. Another shot. The front window shattered and a bullet slammed into the back of the couch. Julie crab-crawled across the floor, toward the kitchen.

He kept shouting about what he'd to to her. His shots shredded holes in the canvas curtains and tore chunks from the front door. Bullets zinged past her and ricocheted around the room. Julie threw herself flat and pulled herself along the rough planks. The knife thumped on the hard wood. At last she gained the relative safety of the kitchenette partition and lay curled on the floor, her hands covering her head, her body tensing as bullets smashed against the walls around her, her own panicked breaths unable to drown out the malicious evil of the man's screeching voice.

CHAPTER TWENTY-NINE
JULY 19, 1990; 9:45 pm
Bear Lake Perimeter Road, New York

He could see nothing at first, feel nothing but unrelenting, burning pain. He thought, at first, that pain was all there was, all he was. But slowly, an outer world intruded. Chirruping and rustlings sounded far above him. He smelled hot, burnt metal and cool, dank loam. He could feel labored breath in his lungs and throat. Air rushed fitfully across his body, a sensation both soothing and agonizing.

That meant he had a body, or parts of one at least. He lay in his cocoon of agony and took stock. He couldn't feel his left arm or shoulder. His back burned. He could move his feet and legs, though hot lava needles punctured his back when he tried to shift position. But the worst of the agony centered around his head and neck.

He couldn't open his lids. They seemed to be glued shut. He raised his right hand and began exploring with shaking fingers, ignoring the pain that erupted when he touched his forehead, his nose, his cheek. He used his fingers to free his eyelids.

Darkness at first. Then inky shadows resolved out of the void, moving spots of darkness against a swirling background of pale colors fading into velvety black. The shadows danced to eerie, restless soughing as they bowed and scraped across the misty floor overhead. He watched perplexed, entranced, glimpsing quick sparks of pinpoint light at odd intervals. His eyes widened when at last recognition dawned.

Stars. The sky. He was staring at a cloud-dotted night-time sky laced with silhouettes of wind-tossed trees. And beneath him? His right hand moved again, groped along the ground, found fallen leaves, pine needles, damp earth, trembling ferns. Where in God's name was he? What had happened to him?

A sudden surge of urgency rose within him, froze the breath in his burning throat. His heart began to flutter and he thought it might burst. He had to move, had to get out of here. He had to—do what? Go where? Confused by the sense of impending doom that clamped around him, he frowned and rolled his head on the uneven soil, squinting into the darkness. What was it he couldn't remember? What pricked out the sweat on his body? What was so important that—

Then he saw it, the car, crushed against the tree beside him. He stared at it, willing it to speak, to tell him what he needed to know. Silence answered. There was no sign of a driver, no other person in sight. He blinked hard, focusing on the shattered windshield. Wisps of memory teased at the back of his mind. Slowly, he tried to reconstruct the events that had brought him to this place and time.

An accident, obviously. He'd been walking along the road and been hit by a car. This car? Then where was the driver? Had he simply walked off into the night and left his victim to die alone? No. He knew, somehow, that wasn't right.

The mysterious sense of urgency built to an unbearable level. Doors deep in his mind swung ajar. Memories flitted past his consciousness. He grabbed at them and caught fragments. A drifting boat and laughter. A ringing telephone that didn't answer. Pork chops, flames shooting out of an old black stove. Driving fast, too fast. Skidding around turns, slamming into potholes, desperate to get back, to reach a cabin— what cabin, where?—to warn her, to help her, to save her.

Julie!

Alarm flooded Ken like burning flames. In a rush he remembered it all. The conversation with Jason's mother. Dave lying near death in the hospital. Julie's fear that someone had been in the cabin yesterday. The pain that had exploded through him just before the car had crashed. Someone had been waiting for him in the dark, waiting to prevent him from getting to Julie. And what? Shot him as he drove along? It had to be. Ken couldn't remember hearing a shot, but what else would explain the searing agony he'd felt in his shoulder and back before the crash? Someone had fired through his open window just as the wheel wrenched out of his grip and pulled him askew in the seat. The bullet had struck not his head but his shoulder and sent the car careening into the trees.

Then why hadn't his attacker finished the job, made sure he was dead? Ken looked at the car again, at the shattered windshield, and understood. He'd already felt the state his face was in, it was obvious he'd been thrown through it on impact. In the dark he must have looked quite dead when the gunman stood over him, ready to shoot again if need be. But obviously the man had been in a hurry. He had another target on which to spend his bullets. Why waste one on a bloody wreck such as Ken? Ken could almost picture him, malignant, filled with blood-lust, stalking away from what he believed was a dead, or soon-to-be-dead, body, heading for the cabin. Heading for Julie.

He had to save her. Ken rolled onto his side, his agonized groan stilling nearby crickets, and dragged himself to the remains of his car. He pulled himself to his feet by clinging to the twisted metal, and took stock. He could barely keep his feet under him. He had to lean on the smashed machine to keep from falling. His blurred eyes refused to focus. His head whirled, throbbing with an intensity that frightened him. His left arm was completely useless. It hung from a shoulder he couldn't feel, like a thick lump of clay. Nausea gnawed at his stomach, making him gag.

But he stood his ground, every atom of his being centered on thoughts of Julie. He would not give in to the agony, or to the darkness that threatened at the edges of his vision. Julie needed him, there was no one else. He was all she had standing between herself and death. He had to find her, rescue her. There was nothing else he could do. He refused to even consider that he was already much too late.

He blinked at the road then stared ahead to his left. If he cut straight through the trees, he'd hit the lane that led to the cabin about halfway down its length. What he would do when he got there, weaponless, almost too weak and dizzy to move, with only one arm that worked and consciousness that kept fading out, he didn't know. He didn't care. All he wanted was to get there. The rest would take care of itself.

He gritted his teeth, let go of the car and lurched forward, stumbling to the tree around which it was wrapped. He clung to the rough bark for a few moments, fighting to stay awake and aware. When at last he could see the next tree ahead of him, he set off once more, staggering on from tree to tree. Sweat foamed on his trembling body. Dark blood spotted the ground where he stepped. But he could feel his eyes burning bright in the bloody mess of his broken face, a mirror of his fierce determination to save Julie from the madman who stalked her in the dark night forest.

CHAPTER THIRTY
July 19, 1990; 10:20 p.m.
Bear Lake, New York

The attack stopped. Silence fell, deafening in its ominous stillness. Not even crickets spoke. Julie uncurled and sat up, straining to detect any movement.

Where was he? What was he doing? She held her breath and listened, but could hear nothing. Had he given up and gone away? Was she safe now? She rose and sidled to the opening in the partition wall, taking care not to make any noise.

She stood behind the partition wall and peered out around the shattered main room. Faint light wavered through the shredded curtains. She could just make out the outlines of the furniture. Broken glass and spilled oil gleamed softly on the plank flooring. A gusting breeze poked through the gaping holes shot in the windows, lifting their tattered canvas coverings in undulating ripples. It was the only movement she could detect.

An eerie whisper sighed on the wind.

"Juuuulieeeeee!"

Julie swung out of the opening and pressed her back against the partition wall, clutching the knife tight in shaking fingers. *He's still out there! What am I going to do?*

"Juuliee. Juuuulieeeee."

The wind buffeted the disembodied words, making them waver: loud, then soft. Close, closer, then far away. She couldn't tell where they were coming from, the front of the cabin, or the side. Icy shivers shuddered down her spine. Her knees weakened and she pressed harder against the wall to keep from sliding to the floor.

"I'm coming for you, doll-baby. There's no escape, not anywhere. Not for you. You belong to me, Julie-girl, and I'm going to kill you. You're going to die, bitch. Die!"

A huge crash echoed in the darkness. Julie spun in the open doorway, clinging to the wall for support, her eyes wide on the main room. Something big, a large rock or a heavy log, thudded onto the floor and bounced twice before thunking to a stop. The tinkle of falling glass reverberated from the side window.

"Come out, Julie-girl, come out and play with me," the weird, sing-song voice called. "Don't make me come in and get you. Come on out, doll-baby. Let's play *dead!*"

At the last word another missile shot through the side window, tearing away a large strip of canvas. Julie knew it was only a matter of time before the man outside climbed through the opening himself. When he did, he'd tear the place apart. She would be trapped. There was no way she could get up the stairs. The side window sat at their bottom, she'd have to pass within a few feet of where he stood. He couldn't help but see her. And there was nowhere either up there or down here to hide. There was nothing she could do to keep him from finding her.

"Julie!" he screamed. "I want you! Now!"

Something large slammed into the side of the cabin. The walls shook and Julie screamed, clapping her hand over her mouth to muffle the sound. The curtain on the side window moved, pushed inward by something long and slender. His arm? His leg? Was it him, coming for her? Terrified, she backed away from the partition opening and bumped against the kitchen counter. Startled, she spun around. Her heart gave a huge thump. Blinking, she looked around in the darkness and saw the outline of a door.

The rear door. She'd forgotten it again. She could go out the back while he climbed in at the front. By the time he discovered the cabin was empty, she would be gone, vanished into the trees. She moved to the door, her heart hammering, the carving knife still clutched in her right hand, and drew back the bolt with her left hand. *Please, don't let him hear me,* she prayed, slowly pushing on the door, wincing at the faint squeak of the rusty hinges. She opened it only enough to slip through into the woodshed. Casting a last look behind her into the ink-shadowed kitchen, she took a deep breath and sidled through the opening into the deeper ebony shadows beyond the doorway. Then she eased the door shut again, hoping he would not discover her deception for long, long minutes.

She stood with her eyes closed, breathing heavily, trying to control the shudders that rippled through her. Her body screamed for rest, for an end to the tension, but she had to ignore it. She couldn't afford to waste time, she had to keep moving. A moment later she opened her eyes and examined her surroundings.

The cabin at her back formed the rear wall of the shed. The side walls stretched out about ten feet, lined ground to sloping roof with eighteen-inch lengths of wood. There was no fourth wall. Straight in front of her, on the other side of twenty feet of clearing, stood the dark forested slope that rose behind the cabin.

The eerie, taunting voice had stopped. So had the thuds of rock and wood hitting the cabin walls. Silence vibrated around her. Had he heard her open the back door? Was he even now edging silently toward the woodshed? Julie inched to the opening, feeling her way with her feet, terrified she would fall or make some noise that would betray her presence. She held her breath as she peered out at the darkness, half-expecting to see his face grinning at her. She didn't. Nothing moved except ghostly fingers of mist winding around ebony trunks. The only sound was the rustle of leaves high in the treetops.

Where was he? Inside already? Or still standing at the side window, listening for any movement she might make? She looked back into the black depths of the shed, but could hear no sound of her pursuer searching through the cabin. Were the walls thick enough to shield the noise? If he was in there, then at any moment he could discover the open rear door. If he found it while she was still in the woodshed, she would never be able to escape him. She had to move. Now.

She turned back to the clearing, dark and still beneath the cloud-filled sky. She had no idea what to do, which way to go. But she had to choose quickly. Time was running out. She needed help, she couldn't fight him alone, but what choices did she have? The lake was almost deserted. She and Ken were the only ones on this side, and Ken was lying somewhere out in the dark forest, dead or injured. There was no one but her, no one—

Suddenly, she remembered Ken pointing out the lane leading to a cabin owned by the recluse named Morgan. Would he be there? If he was, surely he would help her. What was it Ken had said? The cabin was barely half a mile away measured in a straight line. Going by the road would take three times as long. She couldn't risk the road. It was too open, and the longer it took to reach Morgan's place, the more chance the killer would have to catch her. Plus, the lane leading to the perimeter road was visible from the cabin's side window. If he were in the cabin, he would be able to see her all the way across the clearing and partway up the lane. Going straight up the slope behind the cabin and through the trees wouldn't be much more help. No windows overlooked this part of the clearing, but she would still end up on the perimeter road, the long way around. And what would stop her from getting lost like she had earlier, even before it had gotten dark? She could easily find herself running in circles, only to end up back here, in the killer's hands.

No, the only thing she could do was follow the lake straight to Morgan's clearing. It was the fastest route, and if she kept the lake in sight, she shouldn't get lost. She cast one last look around the darkness both inside and outside the shed, then stepped from the ink-black shadows and edged around the woodshed to the cabin wall. Staying close to the rough wood, she sidled to the corner and peered down the length of the east wall. There were no windows on this side. She would be safe from the view of anyone within the cabin until she reached the front corner. Then, if she angled off sharply to her right, she could cross the clearing and be hidden by the trees near the water before being seen from the front window. Not that she had any choice. It was the only plan that had the remotest chance for success.

Taking a deep breath and firming her grip on the eight-inch-long blade, she rounded the corner and stepped slowly along the side of the cabin. Trees shook in the restless breeze, covering the sound of her footsteps, her ragged breathing and hammering heart. But the rustling also concealed any noise her pursuer might make. It was impossible for her to tell where he was. She stopped twice and pressed her ear against the rough bark of the log wall, but could hear no sign of his presence in the cabin through the thick wood. Tension frayed her nerves as she neared the corner. She licked her lips and swallowed hard, trying to push away the terror that ate at her courage and weakened her knees.

A scant ten feet from the corner she halted and stood still, her breath held, listening hard one last time. Wind-rippled silence caressed her ears. She scanned the dark, deserted clearing and lakefront, skipping quickly over the rowboat and its grisly cargo. She saw nothing out of place, no hint of movement. Quickly, before she could think about it and change her mind, she turned for the line of dark trees twenty feet away.

One step, two, three—and suddenly he lunged at her out of the darkness from where he must have been waiting, pressed against the front wall of the cabin. He reached out, grabbed her shoulder, jerked her around and raised a gun, its long, thick barrel gleaming faintly beneath the cloud-studded sky. Julie screamed and slashed at him with the knife. The blade struck the gun, skidded over the metal and bit into flesh, jarring on bone as Julie twisted it, intent on inflicting as much damage as she could. He cried out, a moaning growl that reverberated in his throat. The gun fell from his fingers. His left hand loosened on her shoulder.

Julie jerked back a step and struck at him again. The sharp blade sliced across his face, opening a deep gash from the bridge of his nose to his jaw. Howling, he crumpled to the ground, hands clutching his face. Blood ran free between his fingers. Julie whirled and raced for the trees.

"Damn you!" he roared, his voice pelting after her like stinging darts. "You're dead, you fucking bitch! You hear me? You're dead!"

Propelled by panic, Julie ran headlong through thick underbrush and thicker shadows. Branches whipped across her face and her body. Tears stung into her eyes, blinding her. She tried to keep the lake in sight, but darkness and terror completely confused her. Within moments she had no idea where she was, or in what direction she was headed. She ran on, uncaring now where she was going, wanting only to put distance between herself and the man with the gun.

He pursued relentlessly, barely slowed by the savage injuries she had inflicted. Crashing sounds close behind and his malicious, roaring voice kept her racing on. Her feet stumbled on the uneven ground. More than once she came close to tripping. Bony branches reached out to catch at her clothing, slowing her down. The darkness was so thick in places she could have cut it with the knife she clutched. Finally, she ran full-tilt into a tree and sagged to her knees, stunned, fighting to her feet moments later as his words again hammered at her ears.

"I'm going to hurt you, bitch! I'll cut you to ribbons! You won't even look human when I'm finished with you!"

He was in front of her now, to the right. How had he gotten ahead of her? Was she going in circles? She looked around at the close-crowding trees, her eyes wide in the inky night. The lake. She had to find the lake, and Mr. Morgan's cabin. She could see no sign of water in the darkness, but the land sloped gently to her left. Praying that was the way, Julie spun and ran down the incline, her feet skidding on the carpet of slick pine needles. She had little control over her direction or her headlong speed. She couldn't see what was in front of her.

Her left shoulder smacked against a tree trunk. The force of the blow sent her staggering in a spin to her right. In seconds she found herself on the ground, half-buried in a thick, prickly bush. There was no time to move. She could hear her pursuer, close on her heels. The underbrush rustled and crackled as he drew nearer and nearer. Julie cowered lower, biting her lips as thorns scratched her arms, holding the knife ready. The man burst out of the darkness not ten feet from where she was hidden. Julie closed her eyes and held her breath, terrified he would see her. But he didn't pause. He ran on past the bush in which she crouched and disappeared into the darkness. The crashing rush of his progress grew fainter and almost vanished.

Julie counted to ten, then rose and looked around. Off to her right the dark tree shadows seemed to thin out. She caught a faint gleam of water. The lake. The gunman had run to the left, away from the water. If she was quiet and careful, she still might make it to Morgan's place in one piece. Surely together they could defeat one man even if he had a gun.

She stepped out from the center of the bush. Sharp thorns clutched at her, twined in her shirt, her slacks, holding her fast. She twisted and pulled. The thorns dug deep and she couldn't prevent a moan of pain from escaping. The thorns held fast, refusing to let their captive go. The bush rustled as Julie fought their grasp, slashing with the knife. Her slacks abruptly tore loose. The ripping of the cloth echoed on the dark night air.

Rustling sounded yards away, out of sight in the trees but drawing nearer. The evil, triumphant voice assaulted her ears.

"I've got you now! It's all over, bitch!"

Panic engulfed her, a gigantic wave of heat and terror that wrung a despairing cry from her lips. Julie surged forward, slashing with the knife at the last clinging branch that kept her moored to the bush. Abruptly her shirt parted, the ragged section fluttering like a wind-whipped flag as the thorny branch sprang back into place. Julie staggered, almost falling before she regained her balance and began running again, toward the faint gleam of water. She could hear him behind her, each step bringing him nearer. Pain stabbed her lungs with each gasping breath. She could feel her pace begin to slow.

A hundred yards past the bush the trees thinned. Almost staggering now, Julie ran into the open. In the distance she glimpsed a cabin perched close to the shore. Forty feet of clearing knee-deep in wild grass and clover separated her from sanctuary. Warm light glimmered from its windows. An SUV stood parked on the far side of the structure where the access lane opened into the cleared space. Julie's heart lurched at the sight, but she had no breath to spare to scream for the help of the man inside the building. She ran toward the cabin, forcing her body beyond its endurance.

Fingers touched her, grabbed at the back of her shirt. The hard yank knocked Julie off-balance, then abruptly released. Her feet stumbled in the thick grass. She fell headlong and slammed onto the ground. Her body skidded five feet before stopping. Her lungs deflated and refused to refill. White sparks lit the darkness as pain rose to claim her. The knife bounced out of her fingers and disappeared into the long grass.

Move! Get up! her mind screamed to her shocked body. Barely able to breathe, Julie clawed to her hands and knees and began crawling through the grass. A hand slammed onto her back, knocking her flat. Strong fingers grabbed her, dragged her back to where the killer knelt.

"I told you, bitch," he panted, turning her over, smashing a hard palm against her face. "I told you I'd get you. And I did. Do you remember me, bitch? Huh? Do you remember good old Joe, and all the fun we were gonna have?"

Julie screamed, struggling in his grasp, punching him and clawing with her nails. He hit her again, two vicious blows that knocked her breath away. Sobbing, Julie covered her face with her hands. He knelt astride her, settling his weight on her abdomen. Thin lips lifted into a parody of a smile in his blood-streaked face.

"This won't be quick, doll-baby," he whispered, "I promise you that. We're gonna play games, just like we would have before. Oh, the things I'm gonna do to you. You're gonna die for hours, bitch. Hours."

He slapped her hands away from her face and settled his strong fingers around her throat. He began to squeeze. Julie's eyes widened in horror. She whipped her head from side to side, clawed at his hands and arms, pushed her heels against the ground, trying to unseat him. It didn't help. He was too heavy, too strong. Inexorably the pressure increased. Blood drummed in her head, her face. Her eyes started to throb. They felt swollen in their sockets. Arrows of pain lanced deep into her head. Bone and cartilage crackled beneath his hands. Sharp agony stabbed through her throat, exploded at the back of her neck. It radiated down into her breastbone, and up into her jaw. Tears filled her eyes. Red flashes sparked at the edges of her vision. Frantic for air she reached up, clawing at her attacker's face. Joe reared back and laughed, a rough, mocking sound that drowned her desperate wheezing.

"Don't panic, doll-baby. I've done this before. I know just when to stop. I won't let you die yet. Not for a long, long time."

Her face throbbed. She thought her forehead and eyes would burst. Julie could feel her strength fade, as rapidly as though drained by a siphon. Her arms collapsed, thudded onto the ground beside her head. Her lids closed.

"That's a good girl," Joe crooned.

His fingers loosened. The throbbing ceased, air rushed down her throat, into her starved lungs. He leaned down and kissed her, his tongue questing in her gaping mouth, blocking the air Julie needed. When he sat up, he began unbuttoning her shirt.

Julie gasped, fresh panic flooding her. She hit at him, smashing her fists into his arms, his chest. She raised her legs, tried to jab her knees into his back. Joe chuckled and shifted his position, pinning her legs to the ground.

"You always were a fighter, weren't you?" He closed his hands on her neck once again. "That's good. It'll make you last longer."

He squeezed harder this time, faster. Julie felt herself fading quickly. Her lungs screamed for breath. Pain flowed from her neck like sunbeams streaming through clouds. Blood thundered in her face, beating for release. It roared in her ears, refusing to be denied, but she could not loosen Joe's unrelenting, iron-hard fingers. He sat atop her, his lips sneering, his pale eyes locked on hers, completely unheeding of the nails she raked down his arms.

The pressure increased. A dark mist covered her eyes. Joe's narrow, savage face, his pale hair glinting in the dark, wavered out of focus. Her eyes rolled up in her head and her hands fell from his arms. She couldn't fight him anymore, she hadn't the strength. The tiny trickle of air he allowed to squeeze past his fingers was not enough. In moments she would lose consciousness and he would do whatever he wanted to her. Julie prayed for death. She could see its dark form menacing close, held at arm's length by Joe's sadistic pleasure. For how long? Hours, like he promised?

A screaming protest reverberated through her body. Her legs began to vibrate, her feet drumming on the hard earth. Her arms flopped like fish out of water as her muscles spasmed, her hands clutching at the long grass. The fingers of her left hand closed on something hard. Julie gripped it tight, for no reason other than to hold onto awareness, to remain conscious as long as possible. A split second later she realized what she held, and with her last ounce of strength she moved her arm, raised her hand and plunged the broad, eight-inch blade deep into Joe's stomach, beneath his ribs.

His fingers clenched with a jerk as molten-hot pain lanced through his body. The pressure completely blocked her windpipe. Pain echoed through Julie and the knife twisted deeper as her body shuddered.

Darkness covered her vision. She concentrated her every effort on staying awake, keeping her grip on the knife. Joe sagged. His eyes lost focus. Her body rippled and the blade moved again, severed vital organs, slashed up into his lungs. Hot blood flooded over Julie's hand, down her arm, spread out across her body. Then the remorseless hands loosened and fell to either side of her neck. Joe folded down, his head thunking onto the ground beside hers, his every movement tearing more soft tissue and flesh.

"You... fucking... bitch!" he whispered.

His body vibrated then tensed before collapsing on her like a dead weight. A grotesque wheezing rattle sounded in Julie's ear, but she was too busy trying to breathe to absorb its meaning.

She lay gasping, her burning swollen throat barely able to carry air into her starved lungs. The body atop her crushed down on her, preventing her lungs from expanding. The handle of the knife, sandwiched between them and still clutched in her hand, dug into her stomach, sending stabs of agony up into her ribs. She forced her right arm to move, raised her hand to clutch at the man's shoulder. Gathering all the feeble strength she had left, she pushed at the lifeless body, using her right foot to twist her own body to the left. The man who had nearly strangled her rolled onto the ground beside her, open eyes gaping at the swirling clouds above, knife still protruding from his abdomen. Shuddering, Julie peeled her blood-slick fingers from the handle and backed away on her hands and knees.

She crawled across the clearing, still gasping for breath, her head throbbing and her neck on fire. Her left hand and forearm looked darker than the dark night, black with the blood she had shed, gored with the life she had ended. Two lives, two men, dead by her hand. The horror of it rose up suddenly and engulfed her, folded her down into the grass. Her stomach roiled. She gagged and retched, spilling the contents of her stomach onto the earth. Tears streamed from her eyes. Her body shook so hard she feared she would never be able to move again.

At last the nausea abated. The retching stopped. Julie pulled a handful of grass and wiped her mouth with shuddering hands. She tried to get to her feet but her legs collapsed, refused to hold her. After a few moments, resisting the urge to look back at the body stretched out behind her, she crawled toward the cabin near the lake. Light still shone from its windows. The station wagon still sat mute near the lane. A lean, dark figure stood in the open doorway, motionless, arms crossed, staring in her direction. Mr. Morgan? Julie raised her head, tried to call out for help. Only a hoarse croak emerged, punctuated by hot pain that forced her to bow her head again. When she looked up once more, the figure had disappeared. The cabin door was shut.

Why hadn't he come out to help her? He had to have seen what had happened, or at least seen her crawling through the grass. How could he have gone back inside and shut the door? What kind of man was he, if he wouldn't try to help?

She almost stopped, almost turned away. But where else could she go? Morgan was the only other week-day resident on this side of the lake. She had nowhere else to turn. He was here, and he had a car.

He could help her find Ken, she couldn't rest until she had found him. Then Morgan could take them to the police in Alma. Or York Corners. It didn't matter, wherever he wanted, as long as he helped her. And he would help her, she would find a way to make him.

She thought of the knife, buried still in Joe's body. She almost wished she had pulled it out and brought it with her. She gagged at the thought and again saw the blond man from her vision, the bullet hole in his head. Three men now she had killed. *Don't think about it, don't*, she told herself as she crawled on, forcing her abused body to move faster. She had to hurry, Ken's life might depend on it. At last she found herself at the cabin, staring up at six enormous-looking steps.

I can't do it! Tears rose up to blind her. She tried calling out again, but though her voice was louder now, she knew the hoarse croak would not carry through the thick log walls. The thought of Ken pushed her on. She placed her hands on the steps and pulled herself up with dogged determination. When at last she reached the door, she hit it with all the strength she could muster, her palm flat on the smooth wood.

Nothing happened. The door didn't open. Sobbing, she grabbed the doorknob and dragged herself to her feet. Leaning on the door she hit it again, over and over, forcing volume out of her torn, bruised throat.

"Please, help me!" she called, wincing at the pain the words caused. "Open the door. I need help, Mr. Morgan. Open the door, please. Help me!"

She heard a slide bolt ratchet. The doorknob turned. The door slowly swung open. Julie clung to the doorframe and looked at the lean, compact man who stood studying her with curious dark eyes. He stood not much taller than she and was dressed in tan slacks and a dark brown polo shirt. He didn't look much like a backwoods hermit to her. He was neat, clean-shaven, and his short dark hair, silvering at his temples, was meticulously combed. High cheekbones winged to either side of a tomahawk nose, the hollows of his cheeks emphasized by the gleam of the lamplight in the room behind him. He stood still, made no move toward her. He didn't speak.

"Please, Mr. Morgan," Julie gasped. "Please, help me!"

The room tilted. A white mist rose to cover her vision. The dark-haired man began to vanish into the foggy swirls. Julie's knees buckled. Her body started to slide down the doorframe. Quickly, Morgan reached out and caught her as she fell. She lay limp in his arms, barely aware when he shoved the door closed and locked the night out of, and the two of them into, the cabin.

CHAPTER THIRTY-ONE
July 19, 1990; 11:05 p.m.
Bear Lake, New York

Morgan handed her a glass of water laced with whiskey.

"Here, drink this. Then tell me what happened."

"Thank you," Julie croaked.

She sipped slowly at the pale gold liquid. It burned her throat and she winced as she forced herself to swallow. She held the glass with both hands but her shaking fingers could not keep it still. Dark splotches dripped onto her slacks, mingling with the dirt and blood. But the alcohol did help. Her trembling began to ease and a soothing warmth spread slowly throughout her body. The pain in her throat ebbed into a dull, pulsating ache. She finished half of what he had given her, then looked up at her reluctant rescuer.

"Two men," she said. It came out as a grating rasp. She stopped, tried to swallow what felt like gravel, and began again. "Two men tried to kill me. The first one, he had me on the dock, he was going to drown me. I hit him with an oar, and he fell—" A vision of dark dead eyes and slick blood snaking down to where water met wood rose to choke her words. Julie shuddered and pressed quaking fingers to her lips.

"In the lake?" The soft question held tightly-reined emotion, but Julie was too caught in fearful memories to be surprised at the quiet, menacing quality of the tone. She shook her head.

"No. He... fell into the boat, hit the oarlock with his head." She shuddered again, and took another sip of the watered whiskey.

"So, you killed him. Interesting. And that one out there?"

"He—he chased me through the woods. I had a knife, from the kitchen. He tried to strangle me, I couldn't breathe. The knife was there, in the grass. I–I picked it up, and—" She looked down at her hand and arm still streaked with dried blood and gagged. "There was blood everywhere. He just lay down on top of me and died..."

She looked up at Morgan, who leaned against the empty fireplace, his dark eyes thoughtful. Slim, neat fingers toyed with a coin, turned it over and over, hypnotically. He didn't seem at all affected by the horror of her story.

"You saw him catch me, didn't you? Why didn't you help me? He almost killed me. Why didn't you help?"

"Do you know those men?" he asked in return, ignoring her question. He lifted the coin, rubbed its edge along his lower lip. His dark eyes narrowed.

"I–I think so. They tried to kill me once before, a long time ago. But I got away."

Morgan nodded, his eyes speculative. "And why did they want you dead?"

"I don't know, I'm not sure. It's a long story, Mr. Morgan. Please, you have to help me. They've done something to Ken, my–my husband, he went to town and never came back. That one out there," she gestured at the large front window, through which the clearing and forest were darkly visible, "he was waiting for Ken somewhere on the road. I have to find him. And I have to get the police."

"The police? Well, I guess you've come to the right place, then, since I'm a cop."

"What?" Julie's eyes widened. Morgan took a few paces to his left. Julie turned her head to watch him.

"Of course," he added in a soft drawl, sliding the coin into his shirt pocket, "I don't work around here. I'm from Harrisburg. In Pennsylvania. Do you remember Harrisburg, Julie? Or should I say, Carole?"

"Carole?" Julie frowned and shook her head. The man on the dock had also called her Carole. She felt like she was drowning. "Harrisburg? What are you talking about? I–I don't understand."

"Of course you do. All you have to do is think about it. You remembered those two, didn't you?"

"No," she whispered.

The room suddenly shifted. Julie couldn't breathe. The glass dropped from her numbed fingers. She sat frozen, staring at Morgan who now stood between her and the door. His quiet, menacing voice drove at her like daggers.

"This should have been over years ago. Such a simple thing, killing a helpless unarmed woman. Anyone could do it. But they screwed it up, didn't they? They lost you on that bridge. They let you get away."

"My God!" Julie breathed, rising, her heart thudding. "You're not Morgan, are you? You're part of this. You're with them!"

"Actually," the dark haired man gave a rueful chuckle, "it would be more accurate to say they're with me. Or they were, until you fucked them up. I don't take kindly to someone killing my men, Carole. That's another one I owe you."

"Owe me? For what? Why are you doing this? Who are you? Why do you keep calling me Carole?"

"You really don't remember, do you?" His narrowed eyes studied her trembling body. "That's funny. I thought the amnesia was just a crock. But it is coming back, isn't it, Carole? A little piece at a time. That's what makes you so dangerous. That's why I can't let you live."

He took a step toward her. Julie backed away, shaking her head.

"No. Please."

"We've been looking for you a long time, Carole. Almost three years. By now you should be nothing but a pile of bones at the bottom of Swatara Creek, and here you are standing in front of me. You're a very lucky little bitch, Carole, you know that? Luckier than you deserve to be. Not even the so-called pro I sent after you in Buffalo could manage to kill you. You even outsmarted him, didn't you?" He smiled at her, a grin of pure evil that collapsed to leave his hard face twisted with malice. "But you haven't outsmarted me. You crawled straight to my doorstep, right where I wanted you. Now it's time to close the book on you."

He reached for her. Julie whirled and ran toward the back of the room, where two doors stood ajar, hoping one would lead out the back of the cabin. The dark haired man let her get halfway to them before he spoke.

"Musuko!"

A large, powerful dog slunk through the left-hand door, hackles raised. Gasping, Julie skidded to a stop.

"Back her up, Musuko. Bring her to me."

The dog stalked toward her. A low growl sounded in its throat. The snarling lips exposed long sharp teeth. Julie backed away, whimpering, arms raised to shield her face. The dog pushed her across the floor until she backed into the pine-framed armchair in which she had been sitting.

"Good boy," the man's soft, expressionless voice said. "Break."

The dog's body relaxed, taut muscles loosening as it backed away from where Julie cowered against the chair. It moved five feet, then lowered its rear haunches to the floor, its bright eyes intent on Julie's every movement.

"That's good, Musuko. Guard." His dark gaze shifted from the dog to Julie. "I wouldn't try anything if I were you, Carole. Musuko loves to bring down his quarry. But you already know that, don't you? You're well acquainted with his various... talents."

Julie, bewildered, looked at the lean, hard man standing to her left, his hawk-like face sneering in mockery. He was waiting for her to run, hoping she would try to escape. She could see the anticipation in his eyes, the pleasure that watching the dog attack her would give him. Time shifted. Memories flowed in the empty spaces of the past, triggered by his expression. He'd looked at her like that before, she knew, without knowing when, or how she knew it.

"No. No," she whispered and looked back at the dog. The room dimmed. Bricks appeared where log walls had been. She heard pings echo from the bricks. Something hit her, slammed her onto the ground. Pain ripped through her right calf. Julie screamed and curled her arms over her head.

"What is it, Carole? What are you remembering?"

The amusement in the mocking questions shattered the vision, left her gasping at the knowledge that remained behind. The beating, the murder, the men capturing her, she remembered most of it, even this man's name: Wilkes. A police Captain. Eyes wide, she turned and looked at him.

"It was you. *You* killed that man. It wasn't me, it was *you*. I saw you shoot him."

"That you did. You saw me shoot Cliff Davisson. And now you can watch while I shoot you."

He reached out, grabbed her right arm below the wrist. Pulling her closer, he twisted her arm, forcing her down to her knees. With his right hand he pulled a small revolver from a holster at the small of his back.

"You've caused me a great deal of trouble, my dear," he snarled, wrenching at her arm. Julie screamed. "A whole lot more than you're worth. Now I've got two good men dead and one hell of a mess to clean up, thanks to you. So I'm not going to make this easy for you. Or quick." Jerking her arm up he snugged the barrel against the base of her right hand. "I think I'll start here and work my way down. Nice and slow."

He cocked the gun. Julie shuddered and cried out, terrified.

"No, please, don't! I won't say anything, I swear I won't!"

"You've got that right." He smiled and bent her arm back further.

"It won't matter if you kill me. It won't stop them from finding out what you did."

"Dead women don't talk, Carole."

"They'll still find out. That man, he-he taped your meeting. He hid the recorder, I saw him set it up. Someone will find that tape, and it'll be your voice on it, and your name. It won't matter that I saw. It'll all be on the tape."

"You're lying."

"Then go ahead, kill me. See if it makes any difference."

He stared at her, his dark eyes burning. Julie could see his thoughts racing. He looked at the gun, then pulled it away from her hand and stared at the dog while he thought.

"No, it doesn't matter even if there is a tape," he said finally. "After all this time, it won't be any good. It'll be ruined, just sitting there like that."

"How do you know? How can you be sure?"

He looked at her, his eyes like ice. Julie gasped at the hatred that poured over her. The gun moved, rose until it pointed between her eyes. Terror wrung a mewling protest from her lips.

"There were papers, too!" she cried. "Even if the tape is no good, the papers will be. They'll know whatever it was he had on you. You won't get away with it."

Wilkes froze, his eyes locked on a faraway distance. When they returned to her, they seared her with their intensity.

"We searched that alley, every God-damned inch of it. Why didn't we find them, this tape and papers? Where are they?"

Julie knew he would kill her if she told him. She would only remain alive as long as he didn't know where the incriminating evidence was.

"I–I don't know. I-I-I don't remember."

"Tell me!" He squeezed her arm, sending shooting pains up into her shoulder.

"Oh, God, don't. Please, don't hurt me. I don't know where they are, I swear. I don't remember."

"Then think about it!" he roared.

He smashed the flat of the gun into her left cheekbone. Her face exploded. Agony clawed up into her skull. She slammed onto the floor. Her body curled against the anguish. She couldn't breathe, couldn't move. Warm stickiness flooded over her face, dripped off her nose and chin onto the multicolor braided rug. Waves of nausea washed over her and she fought not to be sick. A moment later, Wilkes grabbed her arm and hauled her up again.

"Tell me!" he shouted, shaking her. Pain flashed in her head like burning red sparks. "Where is it, Carole? Where is the tape? Tell me!"

"No," she gasped. "Don't... know."

"Damn you!"

He raised the gun again, his left hand now fisted in her shirt. A loud crack split the night. The front windowpane shattered, echoed by the crash of a vase exploding on the bookshelf against the rear wall. Another crack. More glass broke. A bullet bored through the cushions on the armchair and buried itself in the thick pine wing, a mere two feet from where Wilkes stood over Julie.

He dropped her and dove onto the floor. Another bullet smashed through the front window, hitting the couch inches from his shoulder. A hoarse shout followed close on its heels.

"Let her go, you bastard! You touch her again and I'll kill you!"

"Ken," Julie cried, her voice a cracked whisper. He wasn't dead. Oh, thank God, he wasn't dead. She tried to move, but pain defeated her.

"Either your boyfriend's about as lucky as you are," Wilkes growled, "or my men fucked up again. Maybe you did me a favor by getting rid of those frigging idiots."

He grabbed her shirttail and yanked her across the floor, away from the window. Julie, fighting the pain exploding in her head, struggling to remain conscious, had no strength left to fight him. His back against the thick log wall, Wilkes reached down and hauled her to her feet. He wrapped his left arm around her body, pinning her arms to her sides. Her knees buckled and she hung limp in his grasp. Through pain-clouded eyes she saw him signal to the dog, who still lay hunched on the floor where Wilkes had put him. The animal rose and disappeared into the back of the cabin. Wilkes opened the front door and stepped into the opening, holding Julie as a shield.

"Put the gun down," he ordered, his voice like flint. "Drop it, or I'll kill her."

He brandished the gun, letting the lamplight streaming from the cabin glint on the shiny metal. Julie dragged her head up, tried to focus on Ken's blurred figure fifteen feet away. Wilkes pressed the gun below her right cheekbone, jamming her head against his chest. Her agonized moan echoed in the dark air.

"Julie! Damn you, let her go. Stop hurting her."

"Drop the gun. Now, or I'll blow her fucking head off."

"No," Julie whispered, knowing her voice would never carry to Ken's ears.

"Drop it," Wilkes shouted again, jabbing the gun barrel into her cheek. Again Julie moaned as more pain surged through her face.

"All right!" Ken yelled. "All right, just don't hurt her."

"Ken, no," Julie sobbed, watching Ken lower the huge gun he held and drop it into the grass. There was nothing to stop Wilkes from killing him now.

"I've changed my mind, Carole," Wilkes said, his soft, menacing voice hot in her ear. "I really don't need you. Now that I know the recorder and papers are there, I can find them on my own. After all, I've got a whole police department to help me, don't I? So, say good-bye, Carole. It's been nice knowing you."

He pulled the gun from her face, gestured with his hand. A dark form streaked out of the night and launched itself at Ken, who stood staring at Julie clasped in Wilkes' arms. Julie screamed as the dog's body left the ground. Ken turned, threw up his arm, and went down beneath a hundred pounds of snarling attack dog.

Wilkes turned and aimed the gun at the oil lamps inside the cabin, three shots in quick succession. The lamps shattered, spewing flaming oil over the couch and floor. Then he spun Julie around, shoved her backward into the room and leveled the gun at her. She slammed into a wooden straight chair and fell just as Wilkes pulled the trigger.

Like molten lava, fire arrowed into her body and exploded in her hip. The chair tipped over, entangling with Julie's legs. She landed on the floor with a heavy thud. Her head struck the leg of the upturned chair and she spun away on a kaleidoscope of whirling color. Pain and darkness fought for possession of her. In mere seconds darkness won. She didn't hear Wilkes slam and lock the thick wooden door, trapping her inside the cabin with the spreading, oil-fueled fire.

CHAPTER THIRTY-TWO
July 19, 1990; 11:30 pm
Bear Lake, New York

Ken twisted as he fell under the dog's ferocious assault, trying to protect his head. The snapping jaws closed on his left arm and the dog shook him like a rag doll. Pain seared into him, shocking him. He'd thought that arm was numb. He punched at the dog's head with his right fist but it didn't seem to even notice his attack. Dimly, Ken heard shots, three in rapid succession, one more a moment later.

Julie! Alarm surged through him. He had to get to her, help her. He couldn't let that bastard hurt her anymore. He renewed his attack on the dog, but it was no use. The animal was unbelievably strong. Ken needed what energy he could muster just to protect his neck and face from the slavering, foaming jaws.

He twisted in the grass, rolling beneath the savage assault, seeking escape. His hip rolled over something hard. The gun he'd dropped, the one he'd found in the grass near their cabin. Ken reached down, pulled it out from under him and scrabbled his fingers around until at last it fit his hand. He tried to raise the weapon but in his weakened condition it felt like a ton. He didn't think he'd be able to aim it, much less pull the trigger.

The dog shifted, moved astride him. Its nails scraped over his belly. Sharp fangs snapped mere inches from his jugular. Ken heard the dark-haired man call out, felt an answering vibration shudder through the animal though it did not loosen its bite. Mustering all his strength, Ken propped his gun hand against his ribs. Twice it flopped back into the grass, knocked askew by the dog's furious lunging before he could force his finger to pull the trigger. In the distance sirens wailed, but Ken, intent on destroying the dog, barely heard.

At last he managed to wedge the gun between his body and the dog's. The huge fangs shifted, plunged into his left shoulder. Screaming from pain so intense it blinded him, Ken pushed the agony down into his hand, used the pain to force his finger to move. The gun exploded, once, twice. The dog jerked. A yelp vibrated in its throat. Then the teeth loosened on his flesh and it fell limp across his battered body.

Ken couldn't move. He lay on his back, his eyes mere slits, only partly aware of the lean dark figure that stood not ten feet away. Slowly, the man stepped closer, his feet pausing as the wailing sirens drew ever nearer. He stopped and turned his head, his striking profile sharp in the flickering light pulsing from the cabin windows. Then he turned and walked quickly to the station wagon parked near the lane.

No. He would not get away. Ken shoved at the dog's heavy body and rolled it off him onto the grass. He could barely move, but he couldn't let this bastard simply drive off. If he did, he would only come after Julie again. Ken had to stop him.

The man was at the car, had the door open, by the time Ken turned onto his side and pulled his right arm around, the gun still clutched tight in his fingers. He blinked his eyes, trying to clear them. The car door shut and the engine fired. Letting anger over-take him and control his movements, Ken pointed the gun and squeezed the trigger. One, two, four, six, seven times, until the clip was empty. Bullets slammed into the car, tore holes in the door, shattered the side window.

The car pulled away and swung toward the lane. Sirens screamed nearby, the rise and fall of their keening wail dizzying in the dark night. The station wagon bounced over the rutted ground, veered across the lane and smashed against a tree. Its horn blared, a rude counterpoint to the throbbing beat of the sirens.

The gun dropped from Ken's fingers. He turned his head to the cabin. Fire licked up the shattered window and spread undulating shadows across the clearing. Julie. She was still in there. He began dragging himself over the grass, tears and sweat streaming down his face. Dark mists blocked his view. Sounds vanished into a vacuum, only to reappear even louder than before. He groaned aloud with the effort to stay conscious, knowing he was losing the battle.

Police cars burst into the clearing. Headlights and flashing red strobes lit the night and men shouted as they exited the cars. Ken pulled himself another foot closer to the burning cabin.

Legs blocked his way. Someone knelt beside him. He lifted his head, tried to focus in the garish light.

"Julie," he managed to croak before he passed out. "In the cabin. Get her out."

CHAPTER THIRTY-THREE
July 19, 1990; 11:32 p.m.
Bear Lake, New York

"Someone's in the cabin!" Sergeant Wayne Ammer shouted, rising. "A woman! Bailey, Sundberg, get in there, fast! Fenton, you and Aldrich break out the fire extinguishers, see if you can contain that blaze. Henley, get on the radio, call out the fire trucks. And we'll need a couple ambulances out here. Better notify Starflight, too, have them standing by. If this guy keeps breathing, he'll need a trauma unit."

Ammer pushed the cap back on his hairless head and stood staring around the clearing. What the hell had happened out here? This was a sleepy little backwater, for pete's sake. The most excitement they ever got was a runaway tractor. He'd laughed aloud when the Buffalo police had called with their tale of murderers tracking a woman and her lover to the McGuire place. Murderers, on Bear Lake? Get real. But the arrival of State Troopers on the heels of the call had squelched his disbelief. Fifteen minutes later Wayne Ammer had found himself, along with his entire six-man department, following the Troopers to Bear Lake, lights flashing and sirens wailing. His ears still hurt from all the noise.

"Sergeant! There's one in the car here," Willy Young called. "Dead. Shot right through the door, by the look of it."

Ammer sighed and watched his deputies, wearing self-contained gas masks, break down the cabin door. Smoke billowed out the opening as they plunged in. Two others carrying portable extinguishers from the squad cars followed close on their heels. He sure hoped they could get the fire out before it spread. If it did, it could take out this whole side of the lake. As it was, this mess was going to take some sorting out. He sure wasn't looking forward to the paperwork. And the overtime would break his budget.

Phil Bailey emerged with a limp figure in his arms. His long legs took him down the steps and over the grass to where Ammer stood in just a few strides.

"She's still alive," he said, laying her beside the unconscious man and removing his mask. "But she's in pretty rough shape. Beat up good, and shot too, it looks like."

"Well, see what you can do. We've got ambulances on the way. The fire?"

"They're working on it," Bailey said. "Looks like the kerosene lamps fueled it."

"Damn," Ammer said, nodding at Henley who was motioning him over to the squad car. "What the hell happened here?"

Ammer glanced at Deputy Sundberg, who had followed Bailey out of the cabin. In his usual methodical manner, the short, stocky man had begun poking through the grass, making his way around the clearing as he searched for evidence. *Finally getting to use his fancy state training*, Ammer thought. Digging pudgy hands into his hip pockets, the sergeant waddled over to the patrol car, leaving Phil Bailey with the injured couple.

"Trooper Gilmore just checked in," Henley reported. His voice sounded awed. He still held the mic in his hand. "They found a wrecked car up on the perimeter road, lots of blood around but no body. But they did find a body in McGuire's boat. I.D. says he was a cop, a detective, from Harrisburg, Pennsylvania. Homicide. The McGuire place was all shot up, and there was a half-skinned raccoon hanging in front of the door. Weird." Henley shook his blond head. "The State boys are heading this way, going through the woods along the lake."

"All right. Go help get that fire under control. All we need is for this forest to go up."

Henley nodded, dropped the mic on the seat, snatched up the extinguisher and mask that all local patrol cars were equipped with, and headed for the cabin. Ammer pinched the bridge of his overgrown nose. His head was beginning to throb.

Why the hell had they turned in here, anyway? They should have followed the troopers all the way to the McGuire place, let them do all the work. But Ammer knew Gus Morgan wasn't at his cabin. He was down in Mexico somewhere, had been for two months now. When he'd seen light flickering where it didn't belong he'd known something was wrong. Fire had been his first thought, it was a perpetual fear in these parts during the summer. So he had turned down Morgan's lane, just to see. Curse him for being such a damned nosey fool.

"Sergeant, I think you'd better see this," Willy Young called from beside the crashed station wagon.

Ammer pursed his lips, more than a little reluctant to move. Then he made his way to the younger man's side. From the tone of Willy's voice, this meant more trouble. He really didn't want to hear it. Moments later, Ammer wished he hadn't.

"This guy's a cop, Sarge. From Pennsylvania."

Young handed Ammer a slim wallet that contained a shield and a police I.D. card. Ammer studied it in the car's headlights. He'd been more than a cop, he was a god-damned assistant police commissioner. From Harrisburg, just like that dead detective at the McGuire place. Ammer flipped the wallet shut, then looked over to where Phil Bailey still administered first aid to the gravely injured couple.

"And I found these," the deputy added, holding out a thin file and a small plastic bag filled with white powder. "They were on the back seat, under a duffel bag."

A cold shiver went down Ammer's spine. He might be just a backwater cop, but backwaters were no more immune to the late twentieth century than any other place. No one had to tell him what this was. He knew cocaine when he saw it.

Ammer shook his head and opened the file. The deputy held a flashlight while the sergeant inspected its contents. Among what looked to be background checks on a small group of men from Buffalo, New York, and two newspaper clippings—one from Harrisburg and one from Buffalo—he found a missing person report, filed in Harrisburg nearly three years before. At the very back he found a five-by-seven photo of a pretty, long-haired young woman. Art Sundberg strode across the clearing and stopped near Ammer, not speaking until the sergeant closed the file.

"We've got another body, Sarge. Just this side of the tree line." He pointed back across the clearing. "Stabbed. Knife's still sticking in him. I know you won't believe this, but—"

"He's a cop, right? From Pennsylvania." Sergeant Ammer looked back at the bloody body sprawled in the car. "Oh, I believe it, Sundberg. At this point, I think I'd even believe in little green men and psychic hoo-doo."

Sundberg handed the sergeant the dead policeman's I.D. Holding it to the light, Ammer opened it. His brows rose. Not homicide, as he'd expected. This one was from narcotics. Of course, given what they'd found in the car, a narcotics officer made more sense than one from homicide. Or an assistant police commissioner. Scratching his ear, he turned to the cabin. It was almost dark inside, fire licking now in only a few places. It seemed his men had averted one potential tragedy, at least. Ammer took the flashlight from Young, walked back across the grass and played the light over the unconscious woman's face. After a moment he opened the file and looked at the photograph again.

"What do you think, Sarge?" Willy Young asked, the excitement in his voice betraying both inexperience and youth.

"It's kinda hard to tell with the blood and all, but I think this here is Wilkes' missing person, Mrs. Carole Remsen. And I think she has a lot of explaining to do. She and her boyfriend both." He looked at the bag of cocaine and at the shield of the Pennsylvania narcotics officer. "One hell of a lot."

CHAPTER THIRTY-FOUR
July 28, 1990
Erie, Pennsylvania

Paul Ebert, Harrisburg's chief of detectives, stood fuming in the corridor of St. Vincent's Hospital in Erie, Pa. The men with him—two seasoned officers from Erie, a sergeant from Alma where the crimes took place, two Buffalo detectives where the suspects came from and a representative from the New York State Police—kept their distance. Though not direct targets of Ebert's frustrated wrath, they had already experienced its fallout. No one, neither officers nor hospital staff, cared to get too close to this walking time bomb.

Ebert's grief and outrage were personal. He had known the dead officers. For more than fifteen years he had worked with one or another of them. He had come up through the ranks with Ogden Wilkes and considered him not just a good friend, but a great man and an even better cop. Joe Sillitto and Bill Traynor were tops in their divisions, trained by Wilkes himself. It was inconceivable that any of them should die like this.

But it was the inconsistencies in the case that really ate at him, not that he was about to admit that even to himself. What had brought the three men on a fishing expedition to Bear Lake, which did not have a fishing lodge? Why were they only half-outfitted for the sporting excursion? Why was Wilkes carrying a gun whose serial number had been filed off? What had he been doing in Gus Morgan's cabin? And why had Dave Atwood, from his hospital bed in Buffalo, New York, identified pictures of Joe Sillitto and Bill Traynor as the men who had beaten him so brutally to find the whereabouts of the Remsen woman?

There were good explanations for all of that, he knew there had to be. And yet the finely tuned instincts that had made him chief of detectives before his late thirties pulled his nerves taut. They refused to allow him to ignore the suspicion that gnawed at him. He wouldn't—couldn't—rest until he had wrung the truth from that little bitch.

Reed, her partner in the murders, had been no help at all. Ebert had already questioned him twice. Both times Reed had become distraught and babbled about amnesia, mysterious attackers and brick walls until the doctor had finally ordered the detective out and put Reed's room off-limits. Then the family had hired a high-powered legal mouthpiece who now stood guard at Reed's door, refusing admittance to all but hospital staff.

Snarling, Ebert glared at the room where Carole Remsen lay. He'd been here more than a week already, he'd left Harrisburg within moments of receiving Trooper Gilmore's call. He hadn't even gone back for yesterday's funerals, a necessary but anguishing decision he knew he'd never get over. That was one more thing he blamed on her. Nine days of spinning his wheels, and he'd only had one look at her so far, the day they'd moved her from the trauma unit to intensive care.

He'd followed her in, right behind her prick of a doctor, Edwin DiMartino. The self-important little Italian hadn't noticed him until after he'd finished checking the numerous monitors they'd wasted on her. As far as Ebert was concerned, they should have let her die.

"Get out of here!" DiMartino had snapped. "This is a restricted area!"

Ebert had ignored him and stepped closer to the bed, raking his glare over the woman's body. She looked barely human. The skin on her face, neck and arms was raw and discolored. Both eyes had swollen shut. Her ragged breathing hurt to listen to, not that Ebert felt any sympathy for her. As far as he was concerned, after what she'd done, nothing could hurt her enough. He picked up her right hand and pulled the cuffs off his belt. DiMartino's beady dark eyes had actually goggled.

"You can't possibly be serious," he'd squawked.

"She killed three cops. I'm not giving her any chance to escape." Ebert pressed the metal band onto her wrist, cinching it as tight as he could over the abused flesh.

"Escape?" DiMartino's voice rose so high it had actually cracked. "She's not going anywhere, she's in a coma, you cretin. She's had massive blood loss, her left arm is broken in two places, her face has been wired back together, she's got a severe concussion, a shattered hip bone and she's in a body cast with her right leg in traction. Just what the hell do you think she's going do? Get up and tap dance out of here?"

"Not with these on, I'll guarantee that," Ebert said, clamping the second bracelet onto the bed's safety bars. "And I advise you not to remove them, or I'll arrest you for interfering with a police officer and abetting a felony suspect. Got it, doc?"

He'd glared down at DiMartino from his six-feet-four-inches until the doctor sputtered angrily, rolled his eyes in disgust and whirled back to the softly beeping machines. Ebert had yanked on the chain linking the metal bracelets, making sure they were securely fastened, then spun on his heel and left the room. But his actions had put him on DiMartino's shit list. The pear-shaped, Cro-Magnon-hairy doctor hadn't bothered to hide his contempt. Sarcasm had dripped from the few sentences he deigned to bestow on Ebert. He used words of six thousand letters to keep Ebert at bay, and hadn't yet allowed him, nor anyone other than hospital staff, back into the ICU.

It hadn't mattered at first. The woman lay in a coma for six days, he couldn't have talked to her anyway. But she'd been awake for three days now, and still DiMartino ran interference for her. The crimes might have been committed in New York State but, thanks to modern technology that created air-ambulances out of helicopters, the suspects lay in a Pennsylvania hospital. That made for enormously entangled legalities, but they'd worked it out. Show-cause orders had gone in, arrest warrants had been issued, extradition papers signed and delivered. The proper personnel were ready to take the killer and her lover into custody, finalize the arraignment and transfer them into a hospital with a prison ward. Yet here they waited. All that work brought to a halt by a piddling little doctor who thought his shit didn't stink.

The door to her room swung open. Edwin DiMartino, his dark eyes weary, full lips turned down in a pout, walked out into the hall. The door snicked shut behind him. Ebert took a giant step toward him, crowding him against the door.

"You let us in there now, DiMartino," he growled, "or I'll get a court order granting us access. *And* I'll have you arrested for interfering with justice."

"Don't you threaten me, *Detective*. I don't give a fuck what you do to me. My primary concern is my patient, and if I had my way you'd never get in her room." DiMartino matched Ebert's glare and crossed his arms. "I've advised her against it, but she insists on seeing you, so I'll let you in—for ten minutes only."

Ebert started forward but the doctor stood his ground, laying a palm flat on the detective's broad chest.

"I mean what I say. Ten minutes, absolute maximum. A lot less if you upset her. Her condition is still critical."

"Is there anything you can tell us about her condition, doctor?" Steve Olkowski, one of the detectives from Buffalo, asked, his mild tone sounding almost humble in contrast to Ebert's bombast. "What can we expect?"

"She's very weak and in a lot of pain, despite the medication," DiMartino said, crossing his arms again and shifting his attention to the men standing behind Ebert. "Her speech is slow and a bit blurred, and it's agony for her to talk, so don't expect lengthy answers. She drifts in and out, but right now her mind is mostly clear. I can't promise how long that will last. Like I said, physically she's still critical, and her mental stability isn't much better. She's hanging on by her nails right now. She remembers some of what happened to cause the amnesia, but still knows almost nothing of who she is or who her family is. That's a terrifying situation to be in, and she's had all the trauma she can stand at this point. I don't want you pushing her to remember something if she says she can't. She simply can't take any more, either physically or mentally."

"Amnesia." Ebert snorted. "How convenient."

"Convenient or not, it's there and it's real." Ebert snorted again. The doctor bared his teeth at him. "And if you don't control your attitude, Detective, I won't let *you* in at all." The dark, alert eyes shifted among the clustered men. "There's only room for two of you. Sorry," he said as the men muttered in rebellion, "but that's the limit. Two. And I'd rather he's not one of them." He indicated Ebert with a jerk of his thumb.

"I *am* one of them," Ebert growled.

"Then let me tell you this, Detective. If you start pushing at her, or upset her in any way, you're both out. Period. Take it slow and easy. Understood?"

Ebert glared at him. Olkowski nodded. DiMartino turned on his heel and disappeared back into the room. Ebert looked at the men behind him, trying to decide who should accompany him. Wayne Ammer, the sergeant from Alma, carried the arrest warrant. Glenna Thomas, an Erie detective, had the extradition papers. Maher and Olkowski had both interrogated the Remsen woman just three weeks ago when she had been attacked in Reed's house in Buffalo. They could possibly have some insight the rest of them lacked. Ebert decided that, since she was still on the critical list, in traction and handcuffed to the bed, formal arrest and extradition could wait. With a curt nod at Maher, Ebert turned, opened the door, and led the way into the dim, antiseptic-smelling room.

Machines beeped softly, banked around the bed like a set from a science fiction movie. She was looking toward the door, waiting for them, gray eyes wary in her battered face. DiMartino had set chairs near the bed for them, to her right and within her easy view.

Ed Maher murmured a low greeting but Ebert didn't bother. He merely glared at her with icy eyes as he took the seat nearest the bed and pulled out a tape recorder. Much of the swelling in her face and neck had gone down, but the livid bruises that covered her skin looked still unbearably painful. Stitches slanted over her shattered left cheekbone, which had been wired back into place. Her left eye still didn't open all the way.

Maher had caught his breath with an audible gasp at his first sight of her, but Ebert refused to allow either the severity of her injuries or her obvious physical and emotional distress to have much effect on him. He kept his face glacial and thought of his three dead colleagues. Nonetheless, questions rose to plague him, dredged up by instincts he could not quite squelch. Why was the Remsen woman's blood and skin on the gun Wilkes had? If he had taken it away from her, why were only his prints on it? The bullet in her hip came from that gun. Had Wilkes really shot her, locked her in a burning cabin and then walked away? It seemed almost as if Wilkes was the perp, not this woman.

What the hell is wrong with me? Ebert shoved the unwelcome thoughts away. Ogden Wilkes was a cop, for God's sake. He'd simply gone on vacation and walked into a drug deal gone bad. Carole Remsen and Ken Reed had killed Wilkes and his two friends. This little bitch deserved all the pain she was suffering. Ebert knew there was nothing she could say that would change that.

"Okay," he barked. "You willing to talk?"

The Remsen woman nodded. Her lips formed the word 'yes', but no sound emerged.

"You want a lawyer here?"

"No," she whispered. Ebert almost winced as her raspy voice grated down his spine.

"Let's get this clear up front," he said, ignoring Maher when he stirred uneasily in his chair. "Did you kill Detective Bill Traynor?"

"Paul," Maher said. Ebert silenced him with a gesture.

"Detective Traynor. Did you kill him?"

"Who?" She shook her head a bit, a look of seemingly genuine puzzlement on her battered face.

"Won't do you any good to lie, Remsen. Or pretend you don't remember." He leaned closer. His voice dropped an octave into steel as he bit off each word with deliberate precision. "The man in the boat. Did you kill him?"

"I didn't mean to," she whispered, her eyes locked on Ebert's face.

"And Joe Sillitto, out in that field. Did you stab him to death?"

She closed her eyes and nodded. "Yes."

"And your boyfriend shot Wilkes. Well. That's that, then. No point sitting here any longer."

Ebert gathered himself to rise. The Remsen woman stirred, her breath catching in her throat. The handcuffs clanked against the bed rail.

"Please... Don't... go. I... have to... tell you," she said, the words blurred, strangled sounding. Her right arm jerked. Her head rolled on the pillow. Alarms sounded on the machines ranged at the head of the bed.

DiMartino stepped to her side and glared at Ebert.

"Sit down, Detective. Down! And shut up."

The doctor bent over the woman and murmured something Ebert could not hear. She shook her head and closed her eyes. After checking her pulse and heartbeat he injected something into her intravenous tube. Within a few seconds her breathing calmed. DiMartino put his hand on her shoulder and spoke some more, his tone soothing, then she nodded and the doctor looked over at Ebert, dark eyes glittering like glass.

"New rules. I've given her a sedative, she'll be conscious for maybe three minutes. You will sit there and listen to what she has to say. You will not interrupt, and you will not ask questions. When she is done, you will not speak, you will simply leave. If you can't do that, then get out. Now."

Ebert threw his hands in the air. "Have it your way," he said. "Go on, Remsen. Talk."

He checked the tape recorder, then leaned back, tightened his lips into a thin line and prepared to wait out her lies.

CHAPTER THIRTY-FIVE
August 4, 1990
Erie, Pa.

Julie twisted her right arm, trying to ease the pressure of the tight handcuff. The worst of the pain in her body had abated now, but itching from the healing wounds was driving her crazy, especially since she couldn't move more than a few inches. The handcuff kept her arm suspended off the mattress, making her right shoulder ache, a nagging discomfort she hadn't been aware of until the deeper pain had eased. She'd hoped to ask the Harrisburg detective if he would move the cuff lower on the bars so she could rest her arm on the bed, but she hadn't seen him for over a week. She caught an occasional glimpse of the police guard in the hall, but no one other than medical personnel entered the room.

The door pushed open. Julie stopped fidgeting and looked up. The Harrisburg detective, she couldn't remember his name, stood poised on the threshold, a massive hulk of a man with beady hazel eyes, silvering hair and loosening jowls. He held a briefcase and stared at her with an odd combination of anger and pity on his face. Her heart began to thud. *Now what?* she wondered, her breath catching in her throat as he paced toward the bed. Silent pneumatics snicked the door shut behind him.

She couldn't bring herself to speak, wasn't sure she could take whatever further doom he had come to pronounce. She lay still, trying to swallow down the gravel that still peppered her abused throat, shamed that she couldn't keep the pleading fear from her eyes.

"I'm Paul Ebert, Mrs. Remsen. Chief of Detectives, from Harrisburg. I'm sure you remember me?"

Julie nodded, not wanting to say anything until she knew what he wanted with her.

"Is it all right if I call you Carole? Would you mind?"

Julie shrugged, knowing somehow she'd have to get used to a name that meant nothing to her.

Ebert studied her a moment, then set the briefcase down, pulled a key from his pocket and reached for her hand. He unlocked the handcuff and eased it from her wrist. She couldn't stop the low moan that bubbled from her throat as she laid her arm on the mattress. Then Ebert pulled a chair up to the bed and sat.

Still Julie didn't speak. The words dammed up in her throat, held in place by the air of unreality that held her in thrall. The detective nodded and spoke, answering the questions she knew crowded her eyes.

"Based on the few pieces you've remembered, we found the stuff Davisson hid, right where you said it would be. In surprisingly good condition, too, even the tape. It's all there, documented every step of the way. And the tape caught the entire thing—Davisson's murder and your abduction." Intense anger flashed in his glittering eyes and Julie flinched. "Those three were dirty, Carole, about as dirty as they come. Operated one of the biggest drug distribution rings we've ever seen, and with complete impunity because of who they were. No one suspected a thing. Not even me." Self-reproach and sorrow frowned across his wide brow. "I came to say I'm sorry, Carole. For what they did, and for what I added to it. We've dropped all charges against you and Reed." He sighed and shook his head. "And I'd like to fill in some of the blanks for you, if I may."

Julie took a shuddering breath. "I don't think I want to know," she whispered.

"You deserve to. Wilkes and his gang took almost everything away from you, Carole, and put you through hell doing it. The very least I can do is give you back whatever pieces I can."

He leaned forward and reached a broad hand through the bed's safety bar. Closing thick, warm fingers around her icy hand, he began to speak.

* * *

October 14, 1987
Harrisburg, Pa.

Carole sheltered behind some rusty metal garbage cans halfway down the alley and leaned against cold bricks. She dabbed at her bloodied knee with shredding Kleenex. Drying tears chilled her face. What had she been thinking, slamming out of the apartment the way she had? That Vic would come running after her to rescue her from the mean streets? That he would fall on his knees at her feet and beg her forgiveness? Fat chance. Not good old Vic, that two-timing bastard. All he cared about was himself and satisfying his overactive libido.

No, she'd let her emotions run away with her—again—and now here she was, stranded in a really ugly part of town at an unconscionable time of night with a purse that held only a few dollars, a couple of tissues—used up now—her spare ID and not much else, not even her house keys. She'd been so furious she'd grabbed the wrong handbag on her way out. Not the smartest move she'd ever made. And to top it all off, she'd tripped, fallen and irreparably torn her new, very expensive silk slacks, to say nothing of her poor knee.

She glanced at her watch, closed her eyes and leaned her head against the brick wall. Vic was long gone by now, probably sipping a martini in the Air Italia VIP room at JFK in New York with his bottle-blond whore, waiting for the flight to Naples. She couldn't get back into the apartment, which had to be a good three miles to the south, and Wendy's house was at least five miles north of where she sat. There wasn't a working phone anywhere in the area and no cabs braved these streets after midnight. Her head throbbed, her eyes burned and her knee was on fire. Her marriage was a shambles and, in her haste to put distance between herself and Vic—before she killed the creep—she hadn't bothered to snatch up a coat, so she was soon to become a human Popsicle.

Can it get any better than this? she wondered. *Maybe I should find a cardboard box and move right in.*

If she weren't so miserable she'd laugh out loud. She'd managed to entangle herself in some pretty stupid situations over the years, but this was by far the most ridiculous. It was only the fact that it was also dangerous because of the area—and her lack of proper clothing—that kept her from rolling over and just sleeping the night away on the cobblestones. Besides, she wasn't about to ruin her cashmere sweater. It had cost close to two hundred dollars. In no way was it street-sleeping apparel.

A low, rough scraping sound echoed on the crisp air. Carole sat up, heart pounding, eyes wide. Fear choked the breath in her throat. Who was out there? A gang ready to rape and savage whomever they saw? A crazy psychopath looking to torture and kill his next victim? Or just a pathetic homeless person, seeking a nighttime niche? Cautiously, she inched her head up until she could see over the top of the nearest can. A grimy streetlight shed a dim glow on the other side of the narrow alleyway. A tall, thin man in a tan raincoat stood with his back to her, prying at one of the bricks in the recessed part of the wall cater-corner across from her. Hoping he was too intent on his act of vandalism to notice her, Carole shifted into a crouch, intending to flee the alley. Her foot scraped on the cobblestones. The sharp scritch rode out into the night. The man stiffened and turned. Carole ducked down, holding her breath for what seemed hours, listening for sounds of approaching footsteps. But after a long silence, only the clunk-scrape of another brick being moved reached her ears.

She risked another peek and saw the man take a sheaf of papers from an inner breast pocket. As she watched, he folded the papers carefully and tucked them into the space created by the two missing bricks. Then he removed a small tape recorder from a coat pocket, checked it carefully, and inserted it into the space. Light glinted off pale blond hair as he bent to pick up the first brick. When he straightened, Carole got a glimpse of his profile and almost gasped aloud.

Cliff Davisson. She couldn't believe it. The fearless TV reporter inhabited dark shadows that scared the bejeezus out of most of his viewing public. Including Carole. She never thought she'd ever see him in person, much less have a spy's-eye view of him working. She watched him fit the bricks back into place, wondering what he was investigating this time —if this really was Davisson —who he was meeting in this deserted alley at the witching hour. Whatever he was up to, Carole knew it was bound to be really dangerous, as all his assignments were. She wanted no part of it. She'd rather wait for the movie.

She gathered herself to stand and flee, then quickly sank back down on her heels. A car turned into the alley entrance closest to them and stopped, its headlights flooding the area, limning dark shadows onto the walls. Three men got out, leaving the sedan doors open and, backlit by the bright light, walked toward Davisson. Carole couldn't make out any of their features though she could tell that all three wore suits and dark overcoats. They stopped a few feet away from the reporter.

"Let me make you an offer, Davisson," the one in the middle said in a quiet, deadly voice. He was a bit shorter than the other two, compact and lean, with broad shoulders. He stood with an air of casual entitlement, almost indifference, in contrast to the tension that stiffened the men with him. Light glinted sparks from his highly polished shoes.

"Don't waste your breath, Wilkes," Davisson said.

Carole shivered as his creamy voice slid down her spine. It really was him. So, these three were the bad guys. A front row view of one of Davisson's investigations. Imagine. She'd have one heck of a water cooler story to tell when she got back to work.

"I know about the drugs," Davisson continued, "your whole operation, in fact. I have complete documentation of every detail. I tape tomorrow and it airs the next day."

"Then what are we doing here?"

"I'm giving you a heads-up. The way I see it, you've got two choices. Do nothing and I break this story as it stands and you all drown in the fallout. Or do the right thing, turn yourselves in before I go on air, and throw yourself on the mercy of the D.A.—and the public. Make the best deal you can, spare your families some of the shame and heartache." Davisson shook his head. "It's up to you."

He shoved his hands into his coat pockets and struck a relaxed pose, though Carole could see that his shoulders remained tense and his eyes flickered as the two men flanking the speaker slowly moved around him, one to each side. The broad-shouldered man he'd called Wilkes chuckled, pulling the reporter's attention back to him.

"And why would you give us this choice, Davisson?" he asked.

Davisson shrugged. "You're cops. I respect your position, the years of service, the good you've done." He glanced at the man's two companions who now stood on each side of him, one solid and hefty, the other tall and whipcord slender. "That deserves some consideration."

"But not enough to bury this?"

Davisson freed his hands from his pockets and took a deep breath. "No. Never. I'm going to stop you."

"Really? Would a high six figure payment in a numbered Swiss account change your mind?"

"Not even close."

"Seven figures?"

Davisson shook his head. "The story airs in two days," the reporter said.

"Come on, be reasonable. What would it take, Davisson? We both know everyone has his price. What's yours?"

"Sorry. I can't be bought, Wilkes."

The man nodded and hunched his shoulders. "Seems like we need a bit of persuasion here, doesn't it?"

The stockier of the man's two companions reached out, grabbed Davisson and twisted his arms behind him. The tall, lean man pounded a fist into the reporter's gut. Davisson doubled over. His pained grunt drowned Carole's shocked gasp. She teetered, then grabbed the rim of the garbage can to steady herself. The rusted metal surface dug into her palms. The man hit Davisson again, this time in the face. His lip split. Blood ran down his chin to stain his shirt collar.

Ohmygod, ohmygod! Carole's mind screamed as the two men stripped off Davisson's trench coat, emptied the pockets into theirs, and tossed it into a corner of the recess. They bound the reporter's hands behind his back before going through his suit pockets. They removed a small, top-hinged notebook and some loose papers. Then they hit him, over and over, taking turns, mangling his beautiful face until his shirt-front was covered with blood. Halfway through the beating, the two men held Davisson upright as the one called Wilkes stepped closer.

"Any price tag now, Davisson?" he asked.

"Fuck you," the reporter gasped.

Wilkes held up a hand and stepped away as the beating resumed. Tears ran down Carole's face as she watched, frozen in horror. At last they let Davisson sink to his knees. Wilkes opened his suit coat, reached inside and took out something that glinted in the bright headlights. A metallic ratcheting echoed from the bricks and Carole flinched. Davisson dragged his head up, looked at the neat little gun in Wilkes' small hand, then turned his head away, his jaw clenched. Carole, barely able to breathe, rose into a half crouch, wanting to run shrieking from the scene, wanting to do something, anything, to stop what couldn't be stopped, wanting to wake up. Now, now, now! Her eyes met Davisson's. His widened in shock and he shook his head, a tiny movement that combined with the pleading in his face to say, *Don't move, stay hidden, don't make a sound.* Carole clapped her left hand over her mouth to keep from screaming aloud. Her right hand tightened on the metal can. The rusty surface again dug into her palm.

The gun cracked. Davisson flew sideways as the bullet slammed into his head above his left eyebrow. Blood and brain tissue sprayed over the brick wall. The men stood studying the body for long seconds. At last, Wilkes gestured at his two companions. Together they turned and walked back to the car. As they moved, Wilkes handed the murder weapon to the skinny man.

Carole stared at the reporter's battered face, the open dead eyes, the widening river of blood snaking across the cobbles. Then she looked at the three men who stood conversing in low voices, their backs to her. Mindless terror engulfed her. She lost control of rational thought. Her body rose of its own accord. She stumbled around the metal cans and began running to her left, heading for the opposite end of the alleyway. She'd taken no more than a dozen steps before Wilkes' voice shouted behind her.

"What the fuck? Get her! Musuko, take her down."

Footsteps pounded after her. An odd clicking echoed off the brick walls. A heavy weight rammed into her and she slammed onto the rough cobbles. Searing pain lanced through her right calf. Screaming, Carole rolled in agony, beating at the huge furred shape clamped to her leg.

"Musuko! Break!" Wilkes' voice ordered, and with a last savage shake of its head, the dog loosed his powerful jaws, backed a few paces away, and sat licking her blood from its muzzle. The stocky man hauled Carole to her feet and held her tight, arms pinned at her sides. His hard hand clamped down on her mouth. Wilkes stepped close and yanked her purse from her shoulder. Then he turned and headed back toward the car. The man holding Carole half-shoved, half-carried her in his wake. The huge dog paced them, its full attention riveted on Carole.

The man pulled her to a stop near the car. She stood in his uncompromising grip, shuddering with fear and pain. *God please, God please, please*, were the only words she could think of. She knew she was about to die. Horribly, painfully, way before her time. Somewhere deep in the subconscious recesses of her mind, she wondered if Vic would cry, or feel the least bit responsible.

Wilkes rummaged in her purse, pulled out her ID and leaned into the car's lights to read it.

"Well, well," he said, straightening up and turning to look at her, "Carole Remsen. You're a bit out of your neighborhood, aren't you?"

He looked into her eyes and she read her death in his. Fear surged upward and thundered into her throat, reverberating into a terrified groan that leaked out from under the hard hand clamped on her mouth.

"What the hell are you doing down here at this time of night?" Wilkes asked, his tone pensive, as though he spoke more to himself than to her. "And where were you hiding that we didn't see you?" He looked around the alley, nodding when he spotted the cluster of metal cans about fifteen feet away. "Ah. I see." He clicked his tongue. "Too bad, my dear. You picked the wrong night for a walk on the wild side. You've become an unfortunate complication." He smiled at her and reached out to run a knuckle down her cheek. "And I don't like complications."

He gestured to the man holding her and the man's hand loosened, fell away from her mouth. Carole shuddered breath into her lungs and opened her mouth to plead, but Wilkes laid a hand on her face and turned her head to the left.

"You know who that is?" he asked, his voice deadly calm.

Carole flinched at the sight of Davisson's bloodied body. She looked at Wilkes, her lips trembling, unable to find words to answer him.

"Of course you do," he answered for her. "Everyone knows who he is. Was. Do you know who I am?"

Carole shook her head, the word *cops* reverberating in her head. "No," she whispered, her voice quavering so badly she could barely form the words. "I don't want to know. Please—"

He placed a finger on her lips, cutting off her plea. "I'm a policeman, Carole. A precinct Captain, actually. And these are my two top detectives, Joe Sillitto," he gestured at the tall, skinny man, who toyed with the gun that had killed Davisson, then nodded at the beefy man who held her, "and Bill Traynor. And you, my dear, are a dead woman."

Panic exploded within her, and Carole gasped.

"No, please." She hated the gibbering fear and pathetic pleading in her tone, but was unable to stop herself. Even though she knew it was hopeless. "Don't kill me. Let me go. Please. I won't say anything. I swear I won't."

Wilkes smiled and looked at Musuko. The dog, bright eyes still fastened on Carole's trembling body, whined deep in its throat as its front paws danced on the cobblestones.

"Oh, I know you won't, Carole," Wilkes purred.

He doubled his fist and hit her jaw. Her head snapped back, smacked into Traynor's hard chest. Fire exploded behind her eyes, then imploded into darkness. Her strength fled and her legs buckled, leaving her hanging in the detective's arms, grasping desperately at the shreds of her consciousness. Wilkes' voice rumbled at her from a far distance.

"Take her to the usual place. And I don't want her found. Not ever."

Carole felt herself being lifted, then thrown forward. She hit a hard surface covered with rough fabric, her arms and legs folded awkwardly beneath her. The force snapped her eyes open and she lifted her head. They'd thrown her on the floor in the back of the car. *Out!* her mind screamed. *Get out. Now!* She twisted and scrabbled to get to her knees, and reached for the door handle in front of her. Something slammed onto her back, crushing her against the floor, driving the air from her lungs. Black spots swam before her eyes.

"You just stay nice and still, doll-baby," a nasal voice said as the pressure on her back increased, "or I'm gonna have to hurt you."

The car jounced as someone got in the front seat. Carole dropped her head onto the carpet and concentrated on trying to pull air into her squashed lungs.

"You won't have much time," Wilkes said as the car's engine fired. "Do what needs doing and get back here fast. You'll need to be on scene when Davisson is found."

"Don't worry. Won't need more than an hour or so," the driver said.

Carole couldn't tell how long they drove. Pinned to the floor by the heavy foot planted on her back, she kept drifting in and out of semi-consciousness. The smooth road coarsened. The bouncing of the car stabbed pain into her body, and she knew they had left the city limits behind. *Wendy*, she cried into the darkness of her despair. *Mama*. Would they ever know what had happened to her? Would anyone?

The car turned onto a rutted surface that jounced the vehicle from side to side. The man moved his foot off her back as the car slowed to a lumbering crawl. Then they stopped. The dome light flashed as the driver got out. Carole heard the front door snick closed. Her captor's hands pulled her upright. He settled her jammed between his knees and the seat in front of her.

They sat motionless a few moments, Carole too frightened to move. Heat radiated into her shoulders from the insides of his thighs. The car swayed and dipped as thuds behind their seat broke the silence. Startled, Carole turned her head. Still silent, the man touched her face. She froze, her heart pounding like a steam hammer in her chest. She felt his silent laugh, felt it thrum through his body and vibrate into hers. It felt more evil than the dark despair that threatened to devour her.

She moaned and tried to bend her head. He stopped her with a cloth he wrapped around her head, over her eyes. He tied it tight. Alarmed, she raised her hands to pull it off. He imprisoned her hands in his, pushed them down and leaned close to breathe in her ear. She shuddered at the contact. Her lungs refused to work.

"Leave it be," he breathed. He shifted his legs until they imprisoned her arms, holding her motionless. Ripples of dread shuddered through her as she realized this wouldn't end easily. They might have need for haste, but they were going to do unspeakable things to her before they killed her. Footsteps crunched near, the driver got in and they began to move again.

"Now the fun begins," the man whispered.

His strong hand fisted in her hair, arched her head back into his lap. His mouth crushed down sideways on hers, smashing her lips against her teeth, drawing blood that he licked away. His hands played with the buttons on her sweater. The car picked up speed as the curving road smoothed out. The man's hands picked up speed to match. She shook her head and cried out. He grabbed her face and squeezed. Pain shot into her, red hot flashes arrowing down her neck. She pressed against his thighs, shrinking from the agony, her shoulders twisting, pinned hands groping for freedom. He laughed and closed a hand on her breast.

Tears wet the blindfold by the time the car slowed again. He'd opened her sweater to expose the top third of her camisole. Her breasts burned from his touch. When the car stopped and the engine died, he shoved her upright. The car door opened and the driver reached in to pull her out into his arms. He crab-walked her a few steps, then the man who'd been in the backseat with her pulled the blindfold down until it hung like a slack noose around her neck.

She blinked her eyes clear. Thick forest hovered close, pines soughing in the raw, restless breeze. Ice-chip stars glittered in the ebony sky above her head, the roadway limned by the silver light of the thick crescent moon. Her breath gusted out in a vaporous cloud. Cold wormed deep into her bones. Carole's body shuddered uncontrollably in the arms clamped around her. They stood behind the car near a low stone parapet in the center of a narrow bridge. She could hear water gurgling somewhere in the darkness below.

The skinny man who'd mauled her in the car — Joe something, Wilkes had said—stood at the open car trunk, cutting a long hank of rope into five-foot pieces with a broad-bladed hunting knife. He looked up and smiled at her.

"Welcome to Swatara State Park, Carole. Real wild country up here in the high foothills of Blue Mountain. That there's Swatara Creek," he nodded his chin at the almost-invisible water below the bridge, "Swattie to those of us who know and love her. She's deep and dark at this point. Real deep. A good twenty feet even at the end of a dry summer. Right, Traynor?"

"Good as bottomless," the man holding her breathed into her ear, settling his arms more comfortably around her body.

"Can you swim, Carole?" Joe asked.

"What are you going to do?" Carol asked, choking on the words. She looked at the water, then at the open trunk. It held three large cement blocks. Joe leaned down and began tying the rope sections to the blocks. Carole looked again at the water and suddenly realized they were going to sink her alive into the creek. Horror beat a frantic tattoo in her chest.

"No. Oh, no. No, please!" She twisted around in Traynor's arms, gaped into his face. Tears streamed down her face. "Please, don't do this to me. I'll do anything, whatever you want. Please."

Traynor blinked at her. "Anything, sweetheart?"

She looked into his eyes and knew he'd take it all from her, debase her in every way humanely possible. But anything was better than frigid water closing over her head, fighting for air that didn't exist, suffocating in cold darkness.

"Yes," she whispered, her body shuddering so from terror and shock her head nodded of its own accord.

Traynor grinned, captured her wrist in a massive hand and tightened his fingers until she cried out. Then he turned and towed her back down the roadway to where the land met the bridge. A small clearing opened atop a steep rise about twenty feet in from the road.

"This won't take long," he called back to Joe as he dragged her along the pavement.

Joe laughed. "Save a piece for me," he said.

Traynor pulled her up the embankment and into the center of the clearing. Dropping her hand, he spun to face her and hooked his fingers in the knotted blindfold that still hung around her neck. A sharp yank jerked her to within a few inches of him.

"You be a good girl, sweetheart," he crooned, sliding a hand to cup the back of her head, "and I'll make it real easy for you. I'll kill you quick, snap your neck before we dump you in the water. You won't feel a thing. I promise."

Carole screamed. Traynor clamped his mouth on hers, swallowing the sound as he bent her back and slammed her down on the ground. Straddling her, he ripped at her sweater. Buttons flew in all directions. Carole pounded at him with her fists and he slapped her hands aside, then smacked her face twice, two fierce blows that left her gasping for air, her lips bloodied.

"You want it the hard way, huh, sweetheart?" he grunted as he yanked on her camisole, tearing it down the center and exposing her chest. "Good. That's just the way I like it."

He closed his hands on her breasts and squeezed. Carole screamed again, her back arching and her hands scrabbling at the deadfall blanketing the forest floor. Traynor lifted his head, evil eyes glittering, and, acting faster than conscious thought could form, Carole grabbed two handfuls of pine needles and flung them in his face. He yelled, raising both hands to his eyes, and lifted into a semi-crouch. Carole jammed her knee into his crotch with all the strength she could muster. Traynor's eyes bugged. His breath gurgled in his throat. He folded down into the dirt and rolled away from her, his hands cupping his testicles.

"Bill! What the hell's going on up there?"

Joe's shout pushed Carole to her hands and knees, then her feet. Barely able to see in the dark, she ran into the trees, away from the sound of Traynor's retching and Joe's voice. Her shoes, designed for city sidewalks, slipped and skidded on the slippery forest mulch when she tried to head uphill. She fell, rolled down the slope into a tree, then regained her feet and ran on. She ignored the pain and yielded to gravity, heading down. Crashing in the forest behind her told her that Traynor had recovered enough to come after her.

"Where the fuck is she?" Traynor roared.

"I can't see her! I can't see her!" came the frantic answer.

She broke out into the open about forty-five feet past the bridge, her momentum carrying her across the macadam and up against the metal rail that guarded the steep embankment.

"There!" The shout spun her to her right. A hundred yards away, Joe danced in the center of the bridge, pointing at her. "At the end of the bridge! Get her, you frigging moron! Kill her!"

Joe pulled a gun from his shoulder holster and began running toward her. Traynor plunged out of the forest where the edge of the embankment met the bridge, staggering as he tried to orient himself. Joe smacked into him and they both went sprawling. Carole swung a leg over the rail. Joe lifted his gun and fired. The bullet hit the rail not three feet from her and ricocheted into the night. Traynor regained his feet and sprinted for her. Joe aimed the gun again. Carole lifted her other leg over the rail. Her pant leg caught on the rusted bolt holding the rail to the upright. Frantic, she twisted to free herself. Her foot slid out from under her, her slacks tore, and with a terrified scream she rolled down the steep embankment, bouncing off tree stumps and rocks until she hit bottom at the water's edge. Her head slammed into a half-buried rock. Sparks burst before her eyes, erupted into a red-hot geyser. Her body shuddered as she fought the darkness that reached up to claim her.

She woke to white-hot pain and words that reverberated through her. *Get up! Get out! Now! Now!* She clawed up to her hands and knees. The movement roused nausea that surged through her and spewed out her mouth. For long minutes she knelt retching until she gagged from the taste of bile. The entire left side of her head pulsated. Her flesh jittered in agony as though she'd been set on fire. Somehow she forced her fingers to unknot the cloth around her neck. She dipped it in the freezing water and held it to her face, gasping at the initial contact, then sighed in relief as the cold penetrated and eased some of the pain.

Where was she? What had happened to her? Why couldn't she remember? She had been—what? Where? She tried to think, but she found nothing, just a lightless void where memories should be. Alarm began a slow build into horror. Who was she? Her heartbeat stumbled. What was her name? She didn't know, couldn't remember anything. Then her eyes lifted and she saw the bridge.

No! Terror screamed within her, shoved her to her feet. She stumbled into the darkness, head reeling and barely conscious, moving along the stream, away from the bridge. She knew no reason for the overwhelming sense of danger but was equally sure that if she did not move and keep moving, if she stood still anywhere for too long, the danger would overtake and destroy her.

* * *

August 4, 1990
Erie, Pa.

"They didn't get you," Ebert told her after relating the events leading up to the debacle on the bridge, "because two park rangers arrived just then. Thirty seconds earlier and the rangers would have seen you fall down the escarpment. Sillitto and Traynor had their hands full. The park had been closed for hours and they had to come up with a plausible reason for being there. I spoke with the rangers myself. The detectives told them some cock-and-bull story about getting lost and then running out of gas. Just to show what good hosts they could be, the rangers offered to take them to the nearest town for gas, and buy them a meal while they swapped stories. The rangers said Sillitto was pretty reluctant to leave the car there, but when they started probing into why, he gave in and went with them. By the time Sillitto and Traynor'd played out the charade and ended up back on the bridge alone, you had already woken up and stumbled off into the night. Then the call came in about Davisson, and they had to hightail it back to Harrisburg. You spent two-and a half years on the run, Carole. It took them that long to find you."

"How did they?" she asked, wondering what she had done wrong. Was it staying put too long that had betrayed her, or had she done something specific that had drawn them to her?

Ebert gave her a rueful grin, and opened his briefcase. He handed her a photocopy of a newspaper roto gravure page. Picture after picture had been superimposed over others like a kaleidoscopic whirlwind. "It was a fluke, that's all. Wilkes spotted your picture in The Patriot-News."

"What?" Julie was astounded. She would never have allowed her picture to be taken by anyone, not even Ken. "How?"

"Look there." Ebert leaned over and pointed to the lower left of the page, at a small, half-buried picture of a clown presenting an origami crane to a bruised and casted Julie.

The paper rattled faintly in Julie's shaking hand. "I didn't know anyone took that picture. I never saw it before."

"It didn't make the Buffalo paper, they chose one with a little kid in it. But a bunch of free-lance photos went out over the wire and a lot of editors liked that one of you, including those at The Patriot-News. It's amazing Wilkes spotted you in that crazy montage."

"But this was in June." Perplexed, Julie looked at the huge detective. "Why did they wait so long?"

"They didn't. They sent someone after you, a guy named," he checked a file, "Keel. Bernard Maximilian Keel. A pro. We think he's the one who attacked you at the house in Buffalo, and maybe was behind the shootings on July fourth. You were in the path of the bullets. When Keel failed, Wilkes decided to get rid of you himself."

Julie closed her eyes as despair washed over her. "Then this is my fault," she murmured. "All of it. It happened because of me." *Because I didn't leave. Because I stayed*, she thought.

"No. This is not your fault, Carole. Not any part of it. You're the victim here, you and Reed both. And Reed's friend, Atwood. It's Wilkes' fault, and those scum partners of his. And our department's too, I suppose, because we didn't see what was right under our noses."

Julie shook her head. "But Ken," she said, her voice choking off into tears.

"I talked to the doctors, he's going to be fine. In fact, he's gone already."

Julie gasped. "Gone?"

"Yeah, his parents had him transferred to a Florida rehab hospital first thing this morning. He'd been upgraded from stable to good condition, and…"

Ebert spoke on but Julie didn't listen. She lay unmoving, her heart breaking. Ken had left and not even said good-bye. Not that she blamed him. He must hate her for the pain and injury she'd caused, first to Dave Atwood and then to him. She would somehow have to learn to live with that. She'd lost his love and almost gotten him killed by being selfish, staying with him when she knew the only safe course was to move on. She'd broken her own rule. She'd fallen in love and stayed, and both Ken and Dave had paid the price. And she was alone once more. She wondered if life would ever again be worth living.

"Listen, you." Ebert's voice pulled her back to the hospital room. She opened her eyes to find him bending over her, a stern, intense look on his long, narrow face. "You are one of the most brave and resourceful people I know. You escaped against all odds and did what you had to do to survive against even greater odds, all on your own, with no memory and no help. And you managed to bust up a major drug ring. You need to own that, Carole. Be proud of yourself. You're one hell of a woman."

Julie blinked tears from her eyes. She moved her lips, lifted them into the beginning of a smile, the most she could manage, because she knew he expected it.

"Thank you," she said, letting him believe his words had gotten through to her. But all she felt was hopeless despair and grinding guilt for all the harm she had caused.

"Well," Ebert said, straightening up. "This should cheer you up. I've got a little surprise for you."

Julie held her breath as she watched him walk to the door, wondering if he was about to spring some sort of trap on her. She still couldn't quite bring herself to trust him fully. He laid his hand on the lever, then turned and winked at her before pulling the door open. He gestured to someone out in the hall and nodded. Stepping back, he swung the door wide.

A woman entered, her steps a bit hesitant, her smile anxious and shy. Dark brown hair hugged her head like a gleaming cap and waved down onto her wide forehead and hollow cheeks. Her sturdy body had a fragile air about it, as though she had been ill for a long time. Her red-rimmed eyes were almost as deep a gray as Julie's.

Behind her stood a tall, narrow man with thinning red hair. His green eyes lit up when he saw Julie, and he reached out a slender, long-fingered hand to squeeze the woman's shoulder. "I can't believe it, Wendy," he murmured. "It really is her."

They moved into the room and a third figure appeared in the doorway. He paused to study Julie. His hair was as fair as the woman's was dark. Overhead lights glinted on strands of pure gold hidden in the sandy locks that fell over his forehead. He stood with an air of competent authority, a man comfortable in his own solidly-filled skin and sure of his abilities. His gray eyes matched the woman's, the only thing they seemed to have in common.

"Don't just stand there, Michael," the woman said from her position to Julie's right. Tears choked her voice, ran down her cheeks. "Get in here."

The blond man smiled and sauntered up to stand at the foot of the bed beside the red haired man.

"Hey, Sis," he said to Julie.

Julie shrank back into her pillows, her mind in turmoil. She had no idea what to do, what to say. Her breath caught in her lungs and she shook her head.

"Who are you?" she whispered.

CHAPTER THIRTY-SIX
April 8, 1991
Harrisburg, Pa.

Julie stood at the window, looking down at the children playing in the backyard. Her niece, Lisa, and nephew, Colton, Wendy had told her. Wendy, who said she was her sister. Wendy, who kept shoving photo albums at her, insisting she memorize every detail in a fruitless search for memories that no longer existed. Julie had to accept that these strangers were her family. The proof lay between the covers of those books, colorful rectangles of glossy paper that chronicled a life she couldn't remember. Pictures of her as a child, alone and with Wendy or Michael, her supposed brother. Halloweens and Christmases, Easters and summer vacations, birthday parties, proms, graduations, weddings and christenings. Pictures of herself that held no meaning, had no basis in the reality of the life left to her.

Familiar strangers. That's what she'd come to think of the people in this house. Their faces, their voices, their habits grew more familiar with each passing day, yet it wasn't a familiarity born of past association, but rather of close proximity. Though she was getting used to them, they still remained unknown quantities to her. People about whom she knew nothing. People who knew her and had expectations of her she could neither understand nor fill.

A flash of pain twinged into her hip and she winced, shifting position to take more weight on her left leg. She wished the shattered bones had healed more fully and the limp didn't embarrass her as much as it did, but that was another reality she had to accept. The doctors said she was lucky to be able to walk at all and she knew she should feel grateful for that, but somehow she couldn't. The emotional wounds were too raw, too close to the surface. She didn't think they would ever heal.

The doctors also said whatever memories she had regained were probably the only ones she would. Brain damage from the first skull fracture had permanently erased most of her life. She'd had a few quick flashes with Wendy and Michael when they were young and she barely out of toddlerhood, but it was almost impossible to associate those small children with the adults who stared at her with expectation, disappointment and anger in their eyes.

She looked down at the book she held, a fourth grade primer—her speed these days—and sighed. She felt like a prisoner here. Not that they locked her in or kept her from leaving. She could come and go as she pleased. But since she had no money, no job and couldn't drive, she was at their mercy, forced to rely on these people for the bare necessities of life. Wendy had told her she'd been a paralegal in what she'd come to think of as the 'before time.' Now even the most menial jobs were beyond her shattered abilities. She couldn't read well enough to stock items on shelves, stand long enough to cash customers out, or count out change correctly even if the register told her the total amount, not with the way she kept mixing up coin denominations even kindergarteners understood. And since she'd made no appreciable progress in her studies in the last two months, she had little hope things would change for the better anytime soon. One more unwelcome legacy from the Harrisburg homicide division.

And Ken. She couldn't even think about him anymore. She could live with the engulfing emptiness, the desolate barren universe of her life—just barely—as long as she didn't let herself remember his voice, his arms, the safe, sheltering solidity of him.

"Carole."

Julie heard Wendy say the name, but absorbed in her thoughts she didn't connect the sound with herself. She glanced out the window again. The children were gone, the backyard deserted once more.

"Carole? I'm talking to you, don't ignore me."

Julie turned and looked at the woman whose gray eyes were just a few shades lighter than hers. Wendy held yet another photo album in her hands. *Not again*, Julie thought, and closed her eyes.

"My name is Julie," she said.

Wendy slammed the album on the desk. "Okay, that's it! This has got to stop."

Julie froze, fear rushing in to fill the empty spaces inside her.

"What has to stop?"

"This." Wendy threw her hands out. Her voice rose an octave. "What you're doing. It's driving me crazy."

"I'm sorry," she whispered, wondering just what it was she was doing, terrified that her fragile world was about to collapse around her again.

"I don't think you are. I think in a way you're enjoying this." Wendy crossed her arms and glared at her. Julie opened her mouth to protest, but Wendy's voice kept hammering at her. "We've bent over backward for you, making allowances because you claim not to remember things—"

"I don't." Another whisper. Julie couldn't seem to get any more volume into her voice.

"And excusing the way you treat us like strangers. Your family. Strangers!"

"You are."

Wendy grimaced and dismissed Julie's assertion with a curt gesture and a shake of her head. "But this, this Julie thing! It's too much. Just too much."

"No," Julie said, her voice shaking almost as violently as her body. "It's who I am."

"No, it's not!" Wendy screamed. Julie bent her head, pressed the heels of her hands to her brow. "You're Carole, not Julie. Carole! Our *mother* gave you that name, for God's sake. It was her mother's name. *Our grandmother's*. And it was good enough for you for more than thirty-two years. You had no right to change it. No right."

Julie stood shuddering beneath the attack. She had known it wouldn't last, that there was no safety anywhere. She couldn't expect anyone, not even family, to understand what had happened to her and what it really meant. No one had, except Ken. Or maybe not. He had left her, after all. Wendy fell silent and Julie let a moment pass before she looked up. She dropped her arms to her sides and curled her hands into fists to try to contain the terror surging inside her. It took all her courage to open her mouth.

"Do you want me to leave?"

"What?" Wendy stared, her eyes wide with shock. "No. Of course not. Why would you think that? What I *want* is my sister. I've waited long enough. I want Carole back."

She spun and dropped onto the small bench at the foot of Julie's bed, tearing eyes closed, one hand pressed tight over her lips. Then she wiped the wetness from her face.

"You're punishing me, aren't you? Because I didn't know what had happened, that you weren't in Italy. Because I couldn't find you, no matter how hard I looked. Punishing me because I finally started to let you go. You're doing this to get back at me."

Julie limped to Wendy, knelt awkwardly at her feet, and took her damp hands in her own.

"No. Oh, no. I'd never do that. I'm so grateful to you. For taking me in, for doing so much for me. I don't know where I'd be if it weren't for you."

"Then why? You're home now. You're safe, with us. Why do you keep pushing us away? Why won't you be who you were? For God's sake, why did you have to change your name?"

Julie pulled her hands from Wendy's and struggled up to sit beside her on the upholstered seat.

"I don't mean to push you away. It's just—I can't be the person you were waiting for. I don't know who that is." Wendy made an angry, impatient sound deep in her throat, and Julie's heart stuttered. "I'm sorry. But I don't know if I can explain it to you so you'll understand."

Wendy crossed her arms and shifted away from Julie. She turned her head, gave her a speculative look laced with accusation and skepticism.

"You could at least try," she said, her clipped tone as cold as the expression on her face.

Julie closed her eyes and bent her head onto her clasped hands, trying to ease the aching emptiness that filled her. When at last her thoughts attained a semblance of calm she looked over at Wendy, the stranger who claimed they'd once been as close as twins, who'd said not a day used to go by without them speaking or getting together.

"Who we are," Julie said, "our sense of self, is rooted in all the things that happen to us in our lives. Everything we learn, say, think and do. Those memories give us connections to people and places. They tell us how we got to be who we are, and what it means to live."

She paused and looked away, twisting her fingers together until they hurt, as though the pain could help her find the words to express the stark truth that now defined her. "When I woke up after those men—" she swallowed and took a deep breath, "after I hit my head, there was nothing inside me, just this consuming emptiness. I was like a vast, barren plain with no landmarks, no trees or bushes, not even a bump in the ground. I had no sense of anything, no connection to life. No sense of *me*, as though I didn't exist... Had never existed. There wasn't even a thought in my head." Her breath shivered in her throat and she blinked tears from her eyes. "If I hadn't felt so much fear, had such a strong need to run, to keep moving, I think I would have gone insane."

Wendy laid a warm hand on Julie's, stilling her fingers. Trembling, Julie licked her lips.

"It was so terrifying. I had to rebuild myself, a little at a time. From the ground up. And I had nothing to work with. And for a long time, I kept losing myself all over again. I kept waking up cut adrift. For all I knew, I was just an empty shell, not a real person. And then finally, there were a few days that didn't vanish. They stayed with me. Whole days that I could remember. Then I met Ken, and became real again. Became Julie."

She turned and looked again at the woman who expected from her things she could not give.

"I don't think you realize how much of who you are is dependent on the past. All the things you know about yourself. Your favorite color, your favorite food, movie, music. Who your first date was with, who gave you your first kiss. How you met your husband. If you did well in school or not, your hobbies, your talents, your failures, your successes—that's what makes you who you are. And all those things you remember about Carole—about me—I don't know any of it. This person you've been waiting for, I can't be her because I have no idea who she is. I'm so sorry. I wish it wasn't true. But she's gone. All I have here," Julie tapped a fist between her breasts, "all that's left, is the last ten months of being Julie. That's how long I've been alive. Only ten months." Julie wrapped her arms around her shivering body and hunched into herself. "And most of that," she whispered as a lone tear trailed down her cheek, "I wish I didn't remember."

Wendy didn't speak. In the silence, Julie could hear wind prying at the window, the clink of dishes in the kitchen downstairs, the muted inanity of a cartoon soundtrack on the family room television. She tried to find words to break the isolation, but she'd used them all up. She had no more to give. At long last she felt Wendy stir at her side.

"I had no idea," her sister murmured, her voice cracking with emotion. "I never stopped to think, to really think, about what all this had to have done to you. I was just thinking of me, of what I wanted— Carole home again, so everything could go back to the way it was, like nothing bad had ever happened." She gave a half laugh, one of the saddest sounds Julie had ever heard. "But that can't be, because it did happen. It happened, and it changed you, changed all of us. Nothing will ever be the way it was again, will it?"

"No." Julie sighed, feeling very small and alone.

"But you know what I just realized?" Wendy reached over and took Julie's hands, forced her to turn and look at her. "That doesn't matter, not any of it. What does matter is that you're here. You're home, you're safe now and you're with us, your family, whether you remember us or not. And I guess if being Julie is what you need to rebuild your life, then that's okay." She grinned. "Ancient history's boring, anyway. So we'll let the past go and spend our time learning about who we are now, you and me. As women. Like sisters who are meeting for the first time. We'll build our own memories, new ones, starting today. All right?"

Julie thought her heart would burst. Smiling through her tears, she embraced Wendy and for the first time felt as though she truly had a home.

"Listen, though," Wendy said when her tears had finally dried. "You gotta give me some slack on the name thing, okay? You've been Carole to me for so long, it's going to take a little time for me to get used to Julie."

"I can do that. Just, please, don't make me memorize any more photo albums."

"Scout's honor," Wendy said, holding up her hand in pledge. Then she frowned. "What I don't understand, though, is how you can remember Mom, but not me or Michael."

"Oh." Julie winced. "No, I don't remember Mom. Not at all."

"But—"

"It's all been just an act. I probably couldn't do it if she lived around here and I saw her all the time, but since she's in Ceredo with Michael and it's mostly phone calls, I've been getting away with it."

"You've been deceiving her?"

"Honest, I hadn't intended to. But I knew from what you and Michael told me that her health wasn't good. And when we went down there and I saw her face, the pain and fear she'd lived with for so long, the sheer joy when she saw me standing there..." Julie shrugged. "I simply couldn't let her know I didn't remember her. Who knows how much time she has left? Why hurt her by telling her I have no idea who she is? I just can't do that to her."

Wendy laughed. "Well, Sis, let me tell you. That's just the kind of thing Carole would have done. You know," Wendy reached out and ruffled Julie's hair, "I think I'm going to really like getting to know Little Miss Julie."

CHAPTER THIRTY-SEVEN
June 3, 1991
Harrisburg, PA

"Aunt Julie."

Julie looked up from the sixth-grade reader and smiled at Wendy's tousle-headed seven-year-old. Both knees were scabbed, scratches criss-crossed his arms, and a streak of dirt arrowed down one cheek. His t-shirt had torn at the shoulder.

"Hey, Colton. Dinner time already?"

"Nuh-uh. There's some guy here to see you."

Fear shivered through her. "Me? Are you sure?" Julie closed the book when Colton nodded. "Who is it?"

Colton shrugged and turned away from the threshold.

"Did he say what he wants?" Julie asked quickly before the child could disappear.

"Nope."

"Uh, is your Dad home yet?"

Colton, standing with his back to her, shook his head. A twig took flight and dropped onto the carpet.

"Where's your mother?"

Colton looked up at the ceiling, giving Julie a view of the top of his debris-coated head and a long-suffering sigh. "Out," he said.

"Where is the man?"

Colton turned around and gave Julie the benefit of his adults-are-weird google eyes. "Downstairs. Waiting. Aunt Julie…"

"Okay. Thanks, Colton. Tell him I'll be right down."

Colton turned and, as though shot from a catapult, leapt forward and thundered down the stairs. It always amazed Julie that one small, fifty-pound boy could sound like the charge of the entire Light Brigade, horses and all.

Julie set her book on the nightstand, then rose and crossed the room. She paused in the doorway where Colton had stood. She didn't want to go down there. She knew who it had to be, another Harrisburg cop come to harass her about the lawsuit her brother-in-law and his high-powered attorney friend had insisted she file. Ever since the department discovered that the estates of the dead cops had also been named as co-defendants, she'd been called and followed by just about every officer in Harrisburg. To reason with her, they said. She understood their concern. She hadn't wanted to sue anyone, least of all those poor families.

"Listen, Julie," the lawyer, Adam Tanski, had said, "you have to do this. Those men took away your life, your health, your ability to earn a living. They owe you a hell of a lot more than just money, but unfortunately that's the only recourse we have."

"Maybe. But those families are suffering, too, maybe even more than I have. I can't imagine how awful this is for them. I don't want to add to their pain."

"A noble sentiment. But we have to include them, for the integrity of the suit if for nothing else. Listen," he added when she shook her head, "this won't ever come to trial. There's no way the department can afford any more publicity over this. They'll settle, and I'll make sure the city bears the brunt of the cost. We'll take only a minimal amount from the estates. I promise. Okay?"

So she'd given in, and gone from being an object of pity and embarrassment for the cops to a figure they'd come to distrust and, in some cases, hate. And their attempts at reasoning with her now often held carefully veiled threats. It was too bad Colton had answered the door. The man would never have gotten inside if Wendy or Jeff had been home.

It never gets any easier, she thought, her hand tight on the rail as she made her way down the narrow staircase one careful step at a time. No one stood awaiting her in the entry foyer. Colton must have let him into the living room. *Which will only make it harder to get rid of him*, she thought. Taking a deep breath for courage, Julie walked around the newel post. And stopped in shock.

Ken.

The name escaped her lips in a soundless rush of air. He stood with his back to her, gazing out the side window. The lowering sun glimmered a halo around his golden brown hair. Broad shoulders strained the fabric of his knit shirt. He'd lost about thirty pounds and his left arm hung with an awkward-looking twist. Julie's heart twisted in response as despair flooded through her. How could she have done this to him? Why hadn't she left his house right away? She had brought danger and death to his doorstep and he would never be the same. How he must hate her.

He started to turn. He must have heard her, though she'd not said a word. Julie clenched her hands, swallowed hard, and prepared herself to endure whatever he'd come to say or do to her. No matter how awful, she knew she deserved it.

He stared at her a long moment, his face remote, unreadable. A thin scar threaded across his brow and curved around his left cheek. Julie's heart clenched. Then Ken nodded. His smile did not reach his eyes.

"Julie." He shook his head. "I'm sorry, I mean Carole."

"No, it's Julie. I had it changed."

"Really?"

Julie bit her lip, unnerved by the watchful quality in his voice. "It just seems to fit better, somehow."

"Well. It's good to see you. I like the haircut."

"I don't." Julie reached up to touch the short locks curling on her neck. After they'd shaved half her head in the hospital, she'd had no choice but to hack off the rest. She'd already vowed never to cut it again.

"Well." He smiled at her, another smile that didn't reach his eyes. "Good thing the stuff keeps growing."

Silence fell. It seemed like centuries passed until Julie finally broke it.

"Why are you here?" He looked away, an odd expression of pain flitting across his broad face and Julie caught her breath. "I mean, shouldn't you be teaching? Isn't school still in session?"

"I took the year off. Once I was on my feet again, I wasn't quite ready to face all those teenage demons and drama queens."

"I'm so sorry."

Julie limped toward him and he reached out his right hand, though he pulled it back before he touched her.

"It's not your fault, Julie."

"But it is. I shouldn't have stayed. I knew it was wrong. I put you in danger, you almost died because of me. And Dave." Julie blinked and pressed a hand to her lips. "Is he really all right? They told me in the hospital that he woke up, but—"

"Dave's fine." Ken grinned, a real one this time. "You can't permanently damage someone with a head as hard as his. He slept for a couple of weeks, then woke up as arrogant and ornery as ever. Claims the only thing he can't remember is my birthday. I think it's just an excuse not to buy me anything."

Julie smiled because she knew he wanted her to. "And you? How are you?"

"Don't worry about me, honey. I'm doing fine. Can't play baseball anymore, but I'm finding it's a lot more fun on the sidelines, drinking root beer and harassing the hell out of the guys instead of losing with them." He touched her then, caressed her face, traced a finger along the scar that slanted down her left cheek. A shiver traversed her spine. "You're still limping," he whispered. Julie could hear the unspoken questions in his tone.

"I'm doing okay. I won't be running any marathons, but then I never did. I still don't remember most of my life. Probably never will. But I'm up to sixth grade reading, now. I used to be a paralegal, you know. If I had some children's level law books, I could make a mint at the middle school." She crossed her arms and fisted her hands in the fabric of her sleeves. "Do you hate me?"

"Oh, honey, no," he said gathering her into his arms. "Of course I don't hate you."

"You should," she said, her voice muffled by his chest and her unshed tears.

"Never." He tilted her head up and gazed into her eyes. "I've missed you so much. I wrote to you, you know. Every day."

"Wrote to me? I never got any letters."

"Yeah, well, I didn't mail any of them."

"Oh. Why?"

"I wanted to give you time, Julie. To heal, to settle back into the life you'd lost. To find out who you are, who you want to be. Then," he shrugged, "time just seemed to go by, too much time, and I figured I had no right to disrupt whatever you had down here." He chuckled. "Everyone tried to talk some sense into me, even Mom and Dad, but I can be pretty damn hard headed myself. Eventually Dave got tired of my maudlin self-pity. He kicked my butt for about the ten thousandth time in our relationship, shoved me into his car and drove us down here."

"Dave's here?" Julie looked around the living room. "Where?"

"I don't know, somewhere back there." Ken waved a hand toward the kitchen. "He's also got a great sense of timing. Do you know what today is, Julie?" She shook her head. "Our anniversary. Exactly one year ago today, a beautiful, wraith-like woman stumbled up to the park bleachers and changed my life forever."

"Forgive me. I never wanted you to be hurt."

"There's nothing to forgive, Julie. I wouldn't have missed this ride for the world. I love you. I always will."

"And I love you. I've been so alone without you. I thought you hated me, that I'd lost you forever."

"You'll never lose me, Julie. What I came down here to find out is, are you ready now to come home?"

Julie blinked, positive her ears were playing tricks on her. Despite his declarations, he couldn't really still want her, could he?

"What?"

"The house is empty without you. Our bed is cold. My life isn't worth living. And I've been making everybody totally insane, as Dave so succinctly put it. So, come home, darling. We'll have a real wedding and a full lifetime together instead of only a few weeks. Please?" He gave her a quizzical, pleading look.

"Actually, I don't think Dave will let me go back without you."

Julie nodded, laughing and crying at the same time. "Yes, oh yes!" she said. Then Ken kissed her, his mouth devouring hers as his hands roved over her back, pulling her closer. She pressed against him, barely able to believe that he held her, kissed her, buried his fingers in her hair and took possession of her, body and soul. He wanted her. He loved her. Her life had finally come full circle, back into love, where it began.

"Euwww."

Startled, Julie and Ken sprang apart. Wiping tears from her face, Julie looked at her five-year-old niece, Lisa, giggling in the archway. Beside her, Colton, an expression of extreme disgust on his face, looked toward the kitchen doorway.

"Mom! It's gross. They're kissing!"

Wendy pushed through the kitchen door and came into the living room, carrying a tray filled with wine glasses. Dave, behind her, held a bottle of champagne, followed by Jeff, her brother-in-law, who brought fancy-looking hors d'oeuvres.

"I take it she said yes?" Dave asked as he began to work the cork out of the bottle.

Speechless, Julie stared at everyone, at the celebratory wine and festive appetizers. Then she turned to Wendy.

"I thought you weren't here. Colton said you were out."

"I was." Wendy handed Julie a bubbly glass of champagne. "Out in the backyard. With Jeff and

Dave." Wendy laughed. "I had to leave the house. I couldn't let Colton lie, could I?"

"A toast!" Jeff called and they all raised their glasses. "To my wonderful, brave sister-in-law, and her safe return. To a terrific soon-to-be brother-in-law, who'd better take really good care of her, or else. And to young, oops, middle aged love." Ken shook a finger at Jeff and they all laughed. "However hard and rocky the road may be, the destination is always well worth the trip."

They drank, and as Dave re-filled the glasses, Ken leaned down to kiss Julie again. She twined her arms around his neck and gave herself up to the bliss of his presence. Colton's repulsed voice blended into the laughter and joy that filled her heart.

"Oh, yuck. Mom, they're at it again!"

BOOKS BY SUSAN TUTTLE

All of Susan's books can be ordered through any bookstore, as well as ordered through Amazon.com.

FICTION BOOKS

Tangled Webs: Teenage Lia Willett, daughter of a serial killer, left town under a cloud of suspicion and animosity, leaving behind a dead classmate and unanswered questions. Seventeen years later, bizarre circumstances bring her back to Mercerville, where the hatred directed toward her in the past slowly escalates into ever-more-lethal vandalism and threats. Wanting only to live a quiet life, Lia finds herself stalked and menaced by the town and plagued by nightmares of a frightening past she only half remembers. As events spiral out of control, to save both her sanity and her life Lia must unearth the terrifying, long-buried memories of what happened before she left Mercerville. And in the process answer the most important question of all: Is Lia Willett, like her father, a murderer?

Available in both print and Kindle format from Amazon.com

Proof of Identity: an indieB.R.A.G. Medallion Honoree. Danae Holloway is arrested for the stabbing murder of a man she's neither heard of nor met. But the police have eyewitnesses who saw her leave the scene, and her fingerprints are on the murder weapon. Legal Aid attorney, Collin Montgomery, gets her released on bail and another murder occurs. Again her fingerprints are found at the scene and she has no alibi. Collin, believing Danae innocent, desperately searches for answers to exonerate her. But will the truth he uncovers only cement her guilt? Is the court-appointed psychiatrist working to help Danae, or does he have his own agenda? Most importantly, what happens when the facts and the truth don't agree? Just what constitutes proof of identity in a digital age?

Available in print and Kindle format from Amazon.com

Sins of the Past: Sabrina Compton's sheltered life is shattered when her beloved husband is brutally slaughtered. And though their home has been ransacked, nothing appears to be missing. Unable to face the memories the house holds, Sabrina flees to her great-grandmother's cottage on Gaffe Island, off the coast of South Carolina. But the peace she tries to recover there is crushed by the revelations of an intrusive FBI agent, and her life is forever altered by the weight of her husband's devastating betrayal. As a hurricane bears down on Gaffe Island, she discovers her husband's killer is now after her. Will Sabrina survive both the storm and the killer's rage? Will the presence of the F.B.I. agent be enough to protect her? Or are the sins of the past destined to destroy her, too?

Available in both print and Kindle format from Amazon.com

A Matter of Identity: (coming late Spring 2015) Marina Weston, just twenty years old, is left orphaned and penniless in London, England. Saddled with her father's debt and tainted by the stigma of his suicide, Marina has only three options open to her in 1866: hire out for service; become a prostitute, or starve. Far from her American home, but with the help of caring friends, Marina is offered another way and begins to build a productive life for herself. But fate intervenes when she runs afoul of some very powerful and unscrupulous men. Marina finds herself at their mercy, thrust unknowingly into a diabolical plot that will put her sanity, and her very life, at risk. She must find the strength to overcome the evil conspiracy, but when her very identity has been undermined, what is left for her to hold onto? Will Marina emerge with her sanity —and her identity—intact? Or will she end as a pawn in someone else's game?

Available soon in both print and Kindle format from Amazon.com.

It Takes Class: (coming fall 2015) An anthology of short pieces written during timed (15 to 20 minutes each) exercises in the writing classes I teach. These pieces run the gamut from character sketches, to intriguing scenes, to mini-stories. Realistic, romantic, mysterious, dark, arcane or fantastic, there's a genre here for everyone, especially those who like their fiction in short bursts. This volume is a fascinating look into a "slightly twisted" subconscious mind at work.

Available soon in both print and Kindle format from Amazon.com.

NONFICTION BOOKS
These books are available from Amazon.com in print format.

Write It Right Workbook #1: Character, Setting Story offers 26 lessons and exercises in the first 3 of the 12 skills needed to craft compelling fiction and creative nonfiction. *Unit 1: Character* contains 9 lessons and timed exercises that help you create characters who are fascinating, flawed and filled with vision and desire, characters that readers will want to know about. *Unit 2: Setting* presents 7 lessons and exercises that show you how to design vibrant settings and landscapes that will capture and enthrall readers, settings that are fascinating and evocative. *Unit 3: Story* offers 10 lessons and exercises designed to help you discover stories that will grip readers and not let them go, stories that will live on in the minds of readers.

Write It Right Workbook #2: Point of View (POV) presents **15 lessons** to help you navigate the murky waters of *Unit #4: Point of View*. You'll learn the difference between straight, emotional omniscient and classic omniscient POV, and understand the strengths and drawbacks of each one. You'll gain experience in first, second and third person POVs, and work through the differences in shifting, close and alternating POVs. You will learn how to identify which character can best tell your story, and how to remain in that character's viewpoint consistently.

Write It Right Workbook #3: Plot, Dialogue contains Unit #5 and Unit #6. *Unit #5: Plot* contains 8 exercises on crafting flawless, intricate plots that sizzle off the page. Discover what constitutes a viable plot, and how to spot an idea that doesn't have enough depth before you start to write. Learn the importance of a through line, how to analyze ideas for viable plots, and where and how to find plots in the world around you. In *Unit #6: Dialogue* you'll find 8 lessons/exercises that show you how to write sparkling dialogue that sounds perfectly natural while still addressing the six necessary ingredients that make dialogue an integral part of the story. Learn how to write for your audience, make your characters' voices unique, use idioms to infuse verisimilitude, tag properly and incorporate subtext into what your characters say as you write realistic dialogue that serves the purpose of your story and leaves readers amazed.

Write It Right Workbook #4: Scenes, Voice/Style offers 20 lessons and exercises. *Unit #7: Scenes* presents 11 lessons/exercises that take you through the 9 different scene structures and into the scene question and transitions between scenes so that your stories truly live in the hearts and minds of hour readers. *Unit 8: Style/Voice* presents 9 strategies to help you develop your own unique writing style, a clear, consistent voice that will stand out among all the others and be readily recognizable as yours alone. Unlock the essence of voice and style that lies deep within you, innate natural storytelling qualities that, once realized, will enable you to tell a story as only you can tell it. A voice that is uniquely yours.

Coming Soon:

Write It Right Workbook #5: Conflict/ Tension, Subplot presents Units #9 and 10 in a series of 17 lessons and exercises. All stories, not just mystery and suspense, need tension to sustain reader interest. *Unit #9: Conflict/Tension* explains in 9 tension-filled exercises the necessity of tension and conflict in stories and explores how to inject the proper amount of tension into any situation to keep readers reading. The 8 strategies contained in the *Unit 10, Subplot,* will show you how to derive organic subplots from situations, characters and the main plot, how to use subplots to reflect, refine and deepen the major themes of the main plot and how to create an effective and compelling series that satisfies readers as it pulls them through one volume to the next.

Write It Right Workbook #6: Brilliant Beginnings/Extraordinary Endings offers 8 lessons/exercises in each of the last two units of the program. In *Unit 11: Brilliant Beginnings* you will learn the 8 different strategies for crafting a dynamite opening line that will hook readers immediately, methods for completing a compelling first paragraph, and techniques to craft an entirely gripping first page and chapter. These techniques will capture readers and make them continue turning pages. ***Unit 12: Extraordinary Endings,*** takes you through 8 lessons/exercises on the second most important part of your story: the ending. Learn the secrets to choosing the proper ending for whatever story you write, 8 types of endings that will so satisfy your readers that they will eagerly pick up your next story.